Get Happy

Patrick M. Egan

Get Happy

1

I just remembered something that I hadn't thought about in a very long time. That may not sound like much to some people, but it's kind of a big deal to me. Mainly because it was something that used to happen on a daily basis, and for whatever reason, just stopped. And apparently, once it stopped, all recollections of it completely disappeared from my mind. Until now. It's kind of strange how certain activities that were so routine, for such a long time, can suddenly come to an end one day for no clear-cut reason. The most frustrating part of it though, is how easily they can be swept aside and forgotten. As if they never existed in the first place.

And I don't have the slightest clue how this memory even came back to me. I wasn't looking for it, but all of a sudden, it was, boom! - *Here I am again, remember me?*

So, here's the thing: it sounds stupid now, and believe me, it seemed stupid back when it was a regular occurrence, even I admit that much, but completely out of the blue, I remembered how I used to wake up smiling every morning. And I honestly don't know how that could have slipped my mind over this past, who-knows-how-long, because I swear it happened every day for as long as I can remember. No matter what the time or where I woke up, alarm or no alarm, it was always the same: I would open my eyes, stare at the ceiling and do my morning inventory – *"Who am I?"*, *"Where am I?"*, *"Okay, good, that was just a dream."*, *"Man, I have to pee"*, and slowly realize that the whole time I was running through my list, I'd been smiling. With no apparent explanation why. It's not like my list included, *"Time to smile now."* Unless you're some beauty pageant contestant, that would be a pretty stupid personal command. Nope, the smile would just be there. On its own. Unannounced and uninvited. After a while, I sorta got used to it, and would even make fun of it – sort of laughing to myself when, after a few minutes of being awake, I'd realize, *"there's the goofy smile again"*, but being stumped again as to why it was there. I mean, what else could I do? I didn't plan it, it just happened. Which seemed like no big deal, until Julie, on the days that she'd be in bed with me, would wake up, see the smile, get pissed, and demand that I tell her what was so funny. When mornings started with that exchange, I knew I probably wouldn't be smiling again for the rest of the day. You'd think I would have learned.

The first thought I had after remembering my old mysterious smiling activity was whether I should tell any of it to Doctor Melvin, because this seemed exactly like the kind of information he said he wanted to know. Except I'm afraid that if I did tell him, he'd make a much bigger deal about it than need be. I know exactly what would happen. He'd get that maniacal look on his face, start sucking on his pen, then shout: "Aha! So you do remember a time when you were happy! What were you happy about?" And I know if I told him that as far as I could tell, there was nothing conscious about it, that it was just some weird reflexive thing that my face did, he wouldn't believe me. He'd press me for the remainder of the hour to find out "*what it really meant.*" Like I said, I used to analyze the hell out of it when it was happening, and I never figured out why I was doing it. Hell, I'm giving it most of my brain right now, and I still can't say why. Yet, he has the idea that sitting in that small, uncomfortable chair of his is going to somehow make me magically remember. I think he gets a little too over-excited about insignificant matters, blowing them up into much bigger deals than they really are.

It's kind of the same way with this dog. I've thought about bringing it up to Melvin, but I'm even more afraid of what he'd turn *that* into. There's this dog, stupid little white fuzzy thing, that lives in the house behind me. Well, I should say, lives *outside* the house behind me. It's in the goddamn backyard every day, all day. Barking. Like mad. And the owners never tell it to shut up. I know, because I'll stare out my bedroom window for a couple hours at a time, just watching the thing bark, and no one will ever so much as stick a head out of that house to stop it. The only time it's quiet is at night when the damn thing's sleeping. But that's when the neighborhood symphony of wind chimes begins, so there's really no quiet around here.

I'm surprised one of the other neighbors hasn't complained about it yet. The dog, not the wind chimes, although, there's reason enough there to complain, too. What I'm really surprised at is that my grandfather never did anything about the dog. As a rule, that old bastard didn't like anything, so I can't see how this would have been allowed to carry on for so long. He's the kind of guy who would have beaten it with a baseball bat after fifteen minutes. And I can't imagine that it only started barking like this after he died. Unless that's what finally killed him. They said he had a massive heart attack while trying to dial the phone. Maybe he popped an artery trying to place an order for an ammunition delivery. Who knows?

If I could drum up any enthusiasm about it, I might say something, but as it is, I honestly don't care. If anything, the dog is a distraction. A sort of audio and visual white noise. Sometimes, I try imagining what the hell it thinks it's doing, and that diverts me away from thinking about what the hell I'm doing. Or not doing. The thing I find odd, though, is that I swear the stupid thing is staring right back at me! Now, I don't make a big show out of watching it – I'll just sit in my chair with the curtain pushed aside a little, but the furry little terror always catches me and starts staring right back, and barking like crazy. Could be that it just doesn't like me for some reason. There's a lot of that going around lately. I got to give it to that dog, though, it seems pretty damn passionate about something. Whatever the hell that could be is beyond me. I guess I could ask it. Never know, might be the only one who gave me a straight answer in the past six months.

Another thing happening is how I tend to lose all track of time. You don't think about how long you're doing something until you're actually reminded about it. Here's what I mean: I'll be doing something, anything, not worried about counting the minutes, but then, after a while, I'll have this moment of, "What the hell time is it?" And I realize three hours have slipped past. Sometimes the shadows are a giveaway. It's too early for shadows today, so it must have just been a Post-It note in my subconscious that told me to glance at my watch and see that I had to be at Dr. Melvin's office in less than an hour. And I still had to shower. He nearly blew a gasket a month or so ago about me not showering. I tried to tell him that it wasn't bothering me, so I didn't see any reason to go on doing it on a regular basis. Then he took the handkerchief from his nose, yep, he was covering his nose with his handkerchief, and he made like he was trying not to gag. He said that if I was to continue seeing him, (which, unfortunately, I have to do), the very least I could do was shower before my appointment. The guy even had all the windows open and the fans running! And believe me, it wasn't that bad. I couldn't smell anything, and the stink was supposedly on me. So, I ended up promising that I'd shower before each appointment. Not because I thought I needed it, but because it seemed so important to him. And, he said that it was the least I could do. I think that was the key phrase that convinced me, because lately, I've been living my life by *the least I could do.*

While I was shampooing, I started thinking about that whole waking up and smiling thing again. When the hell did it start? Was I always like that? I couldn't remember it happening as a child, but then, who the hell over thirty remembers tiny details of their childhood? I mean, I could have been a serial smiler since birth, but never aware of it. The questions of when did it stop, and why, were what really interested me. You think you'd at least sense when something you did everyday suddenly stopped happening. When you accidentally skip one of the steps in your daily routine, you're met with that *did-I-turn-the-coffee-pot-off,* moment of panic. It's some kind of mind trick, or whatever you want to call it. The other side of it is, how could your own mind even play a trick on you? Isn't it your own damn mind? Aren't you supposed to be in control of it? As it is, I hate practical jokes, but for your own brain to pull one on you? How is that even possible? I'm sure Melvin knows. Probably even has a name for it. I just don't know if I feel like sitting through him babbling about it.

I rinsed and turned off the water, and I'm not kidding, I heard the stupid thing in mid bark. Like it never stopped. So after I gave myself a quick towel off, I walked over and peeked out of a slit between the curtains. I swear, that thing was staring right up at me and barking like mad. The thing is, it's head didn't move, which means that it was looking right up at the window before I even looked out! Now I started wondering if it was psychic. I mean, how could it know what window I was going to look out? There's five in the back of the house, so theoretically, it could have been any one. And why wasn't it looking at any other house? Mind you, I don't really care about this one way or another. It's just an idle curiosity to pass the time. I sort of gave up on caring about things a while ago. But still, I did wonder about that dog. So, I pulled open the curtain, pressed my face against the screen and yelled out the window.

"What? What do you want?"

But the dumb thing just kept barking. As I stood there glaring right back at it, a breeze blew in, and I realized that I should probably put some clothes on. Not just for Melvin, but I didn't feel like giving the neighbors a show. I barely knew these people.

2

I finally found a parking space after driving around for something like ten minutes. What the hell is it about parking lots around medical buildings? I don't mean to sound like a bad standup comic, but come on. They've got like a hundred doctor's offices inside, but only fifty parking spots outside. And face it – people don't carpool to the doctor. Maybe it's all part of the plan. To make it as stressful as possible before your appointment, so they can diagnose you with high blood pressure, anxiety, and who-knows-what-else, just so you can pay out the ass for treatments and prescriptions. I'm not a real big conspiracy theorist, but it could be worth looking into.

And the buildings, too. The one Melvin's in is no different than any other medical building I've seen in my entire life. Forty-two years, and I swear I couldn't tell one apart from another. Long, bare hallways with a dark, nondescript carpet that looks like it hadn't been cleaned in decades, (yet I'm told to shower...), and small reception areas with way too much light and far too many patients. How can this many people all have one o'clock appointments? The whole process is a major infringement on your privacy. Mainly because the moment you open the door to that office, everyone turns in their chair and stares at you. Not quite the reception a person wants when they're coming in to see their shrink. Some of the people look like they've been watching the door waiting for you. Just like that dog, I swear. Only they don't bark. Melvin shares his suite with an obstetrician, and I can attest that I have never been barked at by a pregnant woman. Other women, yeah, just not pregnant ones.

Once I'm in the office, and after the initial eye contact, I usually get one of two responses. People either quickly smile at me then go back to their business, be it reading, needlepoint, or whatever. The other I get is the people who give me a disgusted look, like I did something wrong to them, or like they're disappointed that I'm not someone else. Lately, though, I've noticed a new look: sort of a sorry-never-mind-just-ignore-that look. Which is fine with me. In fact, it would be a whole hell of a lot better if they never even looked at me in the first place.

I proceeded on to the counter and started to sign in, but before anything could even be scratched on the paper, one of the receptionists looked up from her computer.

"Name?"

I dropped the pen back on the counter. "Gleason."

"That your first name, or last?"

"Who uses Gleason as a first name?"

"My niece's first name is Gleason."

I could feel my face wrinkling into one big knot. "No, it's not."

The look she gave me in return told me everything I needed to know about her: this was a person who was determined to be as miserable as possible until five o'clock. Well, guess what, lady? You've got competition, and you're staring right at him. Only, I don't work in shifts - I'm miserable the entire day. I win. And I chose to celebrate my victory by ending the stare down. No sense in bragging.

"Last. I have a one o'clock with Doctor Melvin."

She started typing into the computer, then stopped and looked at her watch. "It's one o'clock, now."

This wasn't news to me, but she acted like it should be, so I just shrugged.

"Your appointment's for one," she went on. "You should always arrive at least fifteen minutes early."

"Why?"

"So you're not late."

"But, I'm not late." I looked over at the wall clock, like it really mattered. "That says twelve-fifty-nine. I'm actually a minute early."

She just turned back to her computer screen and sighed. "Have a seat. Doctor Melvin is still with his last patient."

I stood there for a second and took it in. I was on time, and he was late, but I was scolded for not being early, apparently, just so I could wait even longer. The conspiracy idea was looking more real.

"And don't forget to sign in."

Yeah. And I'm crazy. Right.

It was only a few minutes before the nurse called my name and escorted me to Melvin's office. Not only didn't he look up from his desk, I swear he didn't even notice me coming in. He was too damn busy scribbling down something, I presume, about the last person in there. And, I don't know, maybe he can't afford cabinets or something, but it looked like he had the files for a years worth of patients stacked up on each side of his desk. He looked like a soldier barricaded in a foxhole. I immediately decided not to tell him that, because it's one of those remarks that he would have said meant something more than it really should.

I was in the chair for at least two minutes and he still hadn't looked up, he was just absently sneaking bites from a half eaten sub sandwich in between writing. I could smell the bologna the moment I walked in. Didn't seem very professional, and really not the kind of thing you want from the guy who's determining your future. But, I guess you can't really expect too much from a court appointed shrink.

I thought about clearing my throat, to get his attention, but then it occurred to me: what if *this* was his idea of some sort of psychological evaluation? To ignore me and see how I react. Will I cough and make him think I'm needy? Will I sit quietly and prove to be antisocial? Of course, I could argue that sitting quietly is not being antisocial at all, but actually a sign of confidence. Then again, others might see it as arrogance. But, that would be my problem, would it? I mean, who cares what they think?

Will I lash out in a rage because he hasn't taken notice? Or, will his neglect cause me to break down in tears? What if it's not a test? What if this is simply his personal indifference toward me? Or maybe, just maybe, what if this is all proof of how thoughtless and self absorbed he really is? Yeah, maybe this was his problem. The guy sees patients all day. He's probably numb from it all. And if that's the case, screw him. It's not my problem. So, I just sat there and waited for him to say something. That's been working well for me lately.

Then, after another minute or two – I refused the temptation to check the time, thinking the motion might catch his attention, so I didn't really know how long it had been – he looked up from his papers to find his can of soda and finally saw me.

"Mister Gleason! I didn't hear you come in."

"Been here about five minutes," I quickly said.

He smiled and tilted his head a bit to the right. My right. His left. "Why didn't you say anything?"

I see this look every time I come in. It's his *I'm-more-clever-than-you-are* look, and I really hate it. Mainly because it's a constant reminder of how I used to fall into this trap. Before I caught on. It doesn't work on me now, though. I just turn it right back on him. "Why didn't *you* say anything?"

Ball's in your court, doc.

"Because I didn't know you were in the room."

"Oh, really?" I swear, this guy is so transparent.

"Yes. I guess I didn't hear the nurse announce you. Do you really think I'd just ignore you?"

"Unless it was something else."

He now tilted his head in the other direction. "Like what? A test."

"Maybe. You tell me."

He brought his head back to center and sighed. This was the final sequence in the *I'm-more-clever-than-you* look. It always ended with him looking overly concerned like this. I've wondered more than a few times if he's always like this. I could see him at home, setting mouse traps, assuming for the sake of this example that he has a mouse problem at home. And after he hears one snap, he looks at the mouse and tilts his head to the right. "I got you," he'd smirk. "What are you going to do now?" Then he'd tilt his head the other way and watch some more. After a minute, he'd bring it back to center. "Here, let me help you," he'd sigh, then open the trap and begin the healing process. So obvious.

He scratched his chin with his left thumb, but it was just a decoy to keep me from seeing him sneak a grip around his pen with his right hand. It didn't work. What cliché won't this guy try?

"You seem rather agitated."

I snapped right back at him. "Isn't that what you wanted?"

"Why would I want you agitated?"

"To keep me coming back."

"Is that what you think?"

"Well, that's the way this place is set up, isn't it? The parking lot. The architecture. Your staff out front. You." *First name or last?* What a joke.

He didn't immediately respond. Instead, he just started writing. This was now my cue to shut up. I've noticed if I go on about anything after this point, that's when he starts making way too big a deal out of it. Whatever I said was merely noteworthy for future reference. Any further embellishment on the topic made him think I cared more about it than I really did. That was the trap I used to fall into. So now, I pull back, and he moves on. The whole process had become so predictable I could do it in my sleep.

"*First name or last*? What do you mean by that?"

"Nothing." I didn't realize I said it out loud. But, no harm. He just watched me for a minute, which is always a little uncomfortable. Not that I have a problem with people staring at me, but try having someone you barely care about stare directly at you for two minutes, like they're trying to figure out your deepest thoughts. It's not fifty presents under the tree, I'll tell you that. Then he must have thought he found something because he started scribbling like mad. Which really annoyed me. I wasn't doing anything. I wasn't saying anything. Hell, I wasn't even looking at him. Yet, he saw something to write down. I honestly didn't know what it was, but just in case, I thought I'd better throw out a few things to maybe distract him. "I took a shower."

He just nodded and half smiled.

"Today. Right before," I added.

He nodded again, but this time raised his eyebrows. God, I hate that. Then he looked back down into my file and shuffled through the papers.

"I switched you over to Haldol a few weeks ago. Are you taking that every day?"

Now it was my turn, so I nodded and raised my eyebrows right back at him.

"And how's that going for you?" he asked.

"I don't know. You tell me. You're the doctor." He started writing again. Probably a reminder to himself that I was on to his games.

"Have you seen Julie?" he asked.

"Why would I do that?"

"She's your wife."

"Yeah."

"And have you seen her lately?"

"Nope."

"Because she's living in your house with her boyfriend?"

I caught myself drumming my fingers on the wooden armrest, and tried to stop it before he noticed, but I was too late. His eyes darted over toward my hand and he started writing again.

"If it gets you so mad, why don't you sign the divorce papers and be finished with it?"

"Who said it got me mad?"

"You're not mad that she left you for another man?"

"She didn't actually leave me. She moved him in, and I left." Come on, didn't he just admit knowing that? Another point for me. I swear, it's just too easy sometimes.

"Okay. But, she did have her boyfriend move in while you still lived there. That's a pretty strong statement against your marriage."

I really don't like talking about this with outsiders. It's between Julie and me, and not anybody else's business. But, you can't tell that to him.

"So," he slowly continued. "You aren't really married in any way but legally. In a sense, you could say that she did leave you. Were you hoping to reconcile?"

"Haven't we talked about this like a thousand times already?"

"Talked? No. I bring it up, and you shut down. Look. Why don't we talk about what's really going on?"

"And what would that be?"

He took a deep breath, then quickly scanned the room like he was looking for hidden cameras. "I wonder if you've given any serious thought to what she's trying to do? Between you and me, it's not very nice."

"And what is she trying to do?"

Now he leaned back in his chair and sucked on the end of his pen. Here we go again. I don't know why he's so interested in Julie. It's really none of his concern. Why didn't I sign the papers? Well honestly, I don't know why I didn't sign the papers. I've given it some thought, believe me, but I've never come up with a definitive answer. It's a very complicated matter. All I can say is I just don't know why, and anything I say now would only be guessing. I gave Melvin another look, and I saw that his head was tilted to the right again. Something about it reminded me of that stupid dog. Staring at me. Going on and on about the same thing. Well, in all fairness to the dog, I can't be sure if it's been going on and on about the same thing all this time. For all I know, it could be a very eloquent dog who's well versed on many different subjects, and I'm just not understanding what it's trying to say. The whole thing about that dog knowing which window I'd be in...what's that all about? I mean, how is that possible?

"Daryl?"

"Hmm?" I must have been lost in thought again, because when I looked back over at him, his head was cocked again, but already to the other side. Usually I don't miss the movements. It's like watching the changing of the guard at Buckingham Palace. Predictable, routine and stupid, but you find you can't look away until it's over.

"You didn't answer me."

I wasn't too crazy about his tone, since I didn't even hear whatever it was that he supposedly asked me.

"I was thinking about something."

"What?" He sounded a little too interested and started writing again, so that was the end of that for now.

"What did you ask me?"

"I asked what you thought about it."

I really had no idea what the hell this was supposed to mean, but I was guessing he was trying to trap me into something again, so I just stayed quiet.

Melvin now tapped the pen against his chin. "Okay, let's try something else. Tell me your philosophy of life."

My *philosophy of life*? What the hell is that supposed to mean? He makes it sound like I spend all day walking around the square followed by a dozen guys in togas.

"I don't have one."

"Of course you do. Everybody has one, whether they're aware of it or not."

"They do, huh?" Now he knows what *everybody* thinks. Mister Omnipotent.

"Yes. More or less. *What does life mean? Why are we here?*"

"I don't know about you, but I'm here because the court's forcing me."

He slumped down in his chair and sighed. Another point for me.

"Did you bring your journal?" He was starting to lose his enthusiasm. It was right there in his voice.

"No," I told him.

He looked even more aggravated and wrote down something else. A couple more answers like that, and it's all over for the day.

"You really need to bring it with you. It will help you. Help me help you."

"Help you help me with what?"

"Unlocking the reasons why you're depressed. It could be any number of reasons. Phase of life problem. An adjustment disorder. But I can't get you back to normal again if you aren't upfront with me."

I couldn't help it, but I snorted. "Normal? Compared to what?"

"Compared to how you are now. The way you've been, this isn't normal for you, is it? I want to help you to be happy. Get back to your normal."

How does he know what my normal is? Not only that, how does anyone know what *anyone else's* normal is? I mean, if you ask me, normal changes. Not just from person to person, but within each person, too. Nobody has the exact same normal throughout their life. So, what if he gets me back to some old normal that isn't any good for me now? Then what? Am I stuck in a worse normal? Or can he find me a better normal? And how the hell are you supposed to find that? It's not like I've got some Zagat guide in my head that gives star ratings to each normal I've experienced. I swear, this guy just doesn't have a clue sometimes.

I noticed that he wasn't even looking at me anymore, but down at his half-eaten sandwich instead. I haven't really been hungry myself for a while, but I still understood. I mean, if it was intended to be brain food, no one needed it more than this guy.

"Go ahead. I don't care."

"You really don't mind? I'm overscheduled and don't even have time to take a proper lunch."

I shook my head, signaling that I didn't care, and a split second later he shoved the sandwich in his mouth and bit down. As far as I could tell, it was just a standard sub sandwich that you'd get any one of a thousand chain stores, but man, did he dive into it like it was the greatest thing in the world. I noticed he only chewed eight times before swallowing and taking a drink of soda. According to my mother, that was only one quarter of the proper amount to chew. She used to say "Chew your food thirty two times before you swallow." Not that I always hit that mark, but this guy went to medical school, so you figure he'd know better.

Strange. Of all the things I should and could remember about my mother, one of the most vivid things I recall is her chewing advice. Like I've said before, it's weird what sticks with you and what leaves.

Melvin wiped his mouth with a paper napkin, then started up with me again. "Daryl, everybody has the innate ability to change whatever they don't like about their lives. No one is confined to any particular lifestyle. You just have to decide what needs to be changed, and change it."

"It's that easy, huh?"

He started laughing. "Never said it was easy!" And when I say laugh, I don't mean a tiny giggle, but a big, body trembling guffaw. I didn't really think it was all that hilarious, but I suppose if it was a comment made in a roomful of psychiatrists, it would be a real killer. After a minute, he calmed down enough to finish the thought.

"For some people, it's as simple as changing your routine. Doing something out of the ordinary to challenge and stimulate the brain. Do you have any hobbies?"

Hobbies. That's a scream. "No."

"Well, maybe you should consider one. Learn an instrument."

"I already play guitar. Did. Back in high school."

"Start up again. Or learn a new one. Another option would be to find something you're interested in and enroll in night classes at the community college. You'd stimulate the brain, and, meet new people."

Yeah. All twenty years younger than me. Sounds like a plan, doc.

"Or join a gym! A rigorous exercise not only gives you an immediate endorphin rush, but as you see the results in your body, you start feeling better about yourself long term. Sound mind, sound body. Plato."

The way he was talking, I felt like he was trying to hard sell me into signing up for a twelve month contract.

"Don't worry," Melvin said. "He's in there somewhere. You just have to look for the signs. You'll find a way to lure him out."

"Who? Plato?"

"No. Your happiness."

"*Him?*" I asked.

Melvin gave a much smaller laugh this time. Like one of those embarrassed laughs you make when you get caught doing something harmless, yet still stupid. The kind of laugh I'd expect to hear from him on a regular basis, given just how stupid most of his statements are.

"Sometimes a memory, or even an emotion, conjures such a powerful reaction in a person, they spend years trying to detach themselves from it, so it can no longer bother them. To the point that they start to act like it's no longer part of them anymore. Almost like it's an entirely separate being."

"People with multiple personalities. You think I..."

"No, no," he jumped in. "More like repression. Or compartmentalizing. I've just found that if you address it in those terms to some patients, it can be easier for them to visualize it. And accept it. Sometimes, that *separate being* is right there in the open, but they just don't recognize it. Another way to look at it is like this: Have you ever been in a situation where the topic is science or math, and someone will say, *Oh, gosh, I knew all that stuff in high school, but I don't remember it anymore*? That information is rarely forgotten forever. It's still there, tucked away deep in your subconscious. Detached. And he's in there somewhere for you, too. Imagine a *Mister High School Math* wandering around somewhere. A *Mister High School Science*. A..."

"*Mister Happy...?*"

He let out another one of those laughs. This time, I swear he even turned a little red.

"Okay, I suppose that one has another connotation. But, for the sake of our concerns, I mean your actual happiness. Some people are resistant to the idea of change. They'd almost rather stay in a bad situation than try and get out of it because they're frightened by what the change will bring. Or, they could be resistant to even confront it because doing so creates an implied acceptance that they somehow did something wrong by allowing it to happen in the first place. The reasons for that are myriad. Persecution complexes, insecurity, sense of worthlessness, an addiction to victimization..."

I could tell where this was heading. Another one of his long winded speeches. God, I cant stand it when he does this. I wish I could just tell him that I stopped listening to these months ago, but I know it would only make matters worse. Not only would he never shut up, but he'd be even more unbearable. I found out if I stare in his general direction, and focus on something, say his lapel, or tie knot, then I can shut him off, while at the same time giving him the impression I'm really paying attention. Sometimes I'll catch a word or two here and there, but that's it.

"...It's like with your grandfather..."

There was a mustard stain on his shirt collar. Regular yellow mustard, not anything fancy. It's not like I'm some closet detective, or anything, it just that the mustard hadn't absorbed into the fabric yet and was easy to make out. I focused on the stupid stain and tried to stop listening to the individual words. Ever so slowly, his voice transformed into white noise. Like the dog. Then the two connected. Could it be that dog really was trying to tell me something, but I just wasn't listening? If so, how would it know anything about me to realize something was wrong? Not that there was anything wrong. But if there was, how would it know? Was it possible that it's smart enough to just be able to pick up on things? This brought the whole psychic possibility thing up again. Never having a dog, I had no way of really knowing, but it was really bugging me. As reluctant as I was to face the aftermath of asking, here was a guy right in front of me that probably had the answers. So, I figured, what the hell?

"How smart are dogs?"

I must have cut him off in mid sentence. I don't know what he was saying, but he looked somewhat confused, maybe thinking this was some editorial on whatever it was that he was babbling on about.

"What do you mean?"

"Dogs. How smart are they?" *What do I mean*? What an idiot.

"You never mentioned you owned a dog."

"Because I don't."

"Oh," he said, obviously realizing his own stupidity. "Are you thinking of buying one?"

"No. I don't even like dogs."

This guy just can't answer a straight question, can he?

"Did you ever have any pets as a child?"

"Yeah," I snorted. "Sea Monkeys. But they weren't very smart."

He reached for his pen. Oh my god, is he writing down *Sea Monkeys*?

"So, are they? Dogs, I mean. Are they smart?"

He shrugged, then slurped the last of his soda through the bendy straw. "People have trained dogs to do all sorts of things."

"No, I don't mean training. I mean like, natural intelligence. Do they know things?"

"Hmm. Why do you ask?" This time, he gripped that pen tightly and held it over the paper, poised for an attack.

"Just wondering."

Then it got quiet for a few minutes. He was staring right through me again, only now, he wasn't moving a muscle. Not even his writing hand. Could a shrink get writer's block in the middle of a session? I tried not to look at him, because frankly, I felt a little embarrassed for him.

Finally, he peeked at his watch and started moving around some files.

"I'm sorry, but it's time," he sighed. "I'd like to spend a few more minutes on this, but like I said, today's a little more chaotic than usual. Listen, though, that journal's important. I want you to write down any strong feelings that you have throughout the day. Try to remember times when you were happy before and how they felt. What might help is calling some people from your past. Talk to them. Reminisce about happy times you shared. Maybe that will help move things along a little quicker." I thought he was finished, but it seemed he was just gasping for air after yet another long-winded speech. "You can't just sit in the house. When was the last time you actually talked to someone?"

"Just now." This had to be a trap. I doubted he was that stupid.

"Besides me, Daryl. Have you spoken with anyone recently?"

"No. Don't see the point."

"It's not good for you. Get out, take a walk, go for a drive. Meet with people. New and old. Okay?"

"Write. Talk. Walk. Drive. Meet people. Got it."

He shot me this impatient look. I seriously think he wanted to do the whole head-turning pen-chewing thing again, but lucky for me, he realized he didn't have any time left. "I also think we might want to be more aggressive with the medication. I'm going to give you a script for something else. It's called Remeron. There is a possibility of side effects, so call if you start experiencing anything out of the ordinary."

I got out of the chair and reached for the prescription. He had remarkably neat handwriting for a doctor. "Right," I said, walking toward the door. "And could you find out about my question?"

"What was that?"

"If dogs can be psychic."

"Psychic? I thought you wanted to know if they were smart?"

"Well, it's both, really. Something I've been wondering about."

I could hear him scribbling away as I walked out into the stupid, matted carpet of a hallway.

3

Well, that's over. Again. Same old crap. *How does that make you feel? Why don't you feel this way instead of that way?* Honestly don't know what the point to all of it is. He says it's Julie. The reason I'm going through all of this. But it can't be just her. Even if she has anything to do with it at all. It really pisses me off when he tries to put it all on her. I want to get up and smack him in the head when he does that. I know Julie. He doesn't. We've been married for over seventeen years. She must just be going through something, that's all. Whatever the hell it is, she'll figure it out. I'm guessing I probably wasn't the easiest person to live with sometimes. It's just all this intrusion into my personal life. Of course, it's not like there's anything going on in my life that's all that interesting anyway, but that's not really the point. Just the fact that anybody at any time can insist you start seeing a doctor and tell him all about yourself so they can determine whether or not you need to be put away is absolute bullshit. I don't know these people. And they don't know me. How do they know what normal is? I've read about the way some of these people run their lives. Doesn't sound normal to me. Yet they're going to judge me? I don't know why I get so worked up about it, though, because they're not going to find anything wrong with me, so in truth, there's no reason to worry. I've been going to Melvin for a while now, and I'm sure if he thought I was loony, I would have been locked up some time ago. All he wants me to do is take some new pills and talk to old friends. Guess I should just go along with it. If that's what it takes to shut him up.

All of that emptied from my mind, though, and pretty damn fast, too, because out of nowhere I heard the squeal of car tires coming to a quick stop along with the long, loud blare of someone laying on their horn. I looked up, and I was in the middle of the street just in front of the pharmacy. And believe it or not, there were about a dozen people standing on the sidewalk watching me. Why the hell is everyone nosing into my business? I don't get it.

"What the shit's wrong with you?" someone yelled. "What are you, blind?"

I glanced over to my left, from where the voice was coming, and saw a black Ford Mustang stopped in the middle of the street, less than a foot away from where I was currently standing. It was exactly like the kind of car I wanted when I was a kid. I used to go out with this girl named Audrey. What the hell ever happened there? I can't even remember anymore why we broke up, and we together for about three years. I always used to think that she was The One. There was no doubt in my mind back then that the two of us were going to be married. Man, she was a knockout. And pretty wild, too. For back then, at least. Who knows how it would compare to now. Yeah, I used to imagine me and

Audrey riding around town in a black Mustang. Us in the front, maybe a couple kids in back, the top down, feeling the breeze...wait, that's right. The car I wanted was a convertible, this was a hard top. Still nice, though. And it looked to be in pretty good shape still for being so old.

Then I heard that damn car horn again. Only, it wasn't one long blast like before, but a series of short blasts. The driver was hanging halfway out the window and waving his thick, tattooed arms at me. Did I know this guy?

"Get the hell out of the way, you frigging idiot!"

I turned a step and a half to face him full on. He seemed really pissed about something. Then he slid back into the seat, threw the car in park and popped open the door.

"Hey! You want me to get out and kick your ass?"

I just shrugged. Didn't really matter to me one way or the other. Plus, I don't think my giving an answer would have any bearing on his decision, anyhow. He seemed pretty intent on doing whatever he wanted. So, I just stood there and waited. He squeezed the handle and pushed the door open some more, panting harder with each breath. But, rather than get out and beat on me, he slammed shut the door, then threw the car in reverse and drove around me.

He slowed a bit and crunched up his face as he drove past. "You're lucky, asshole!" He hit the accelerator, leaving a little smoke and rubber as he tore away.

I was never a smoke-and-rubber kind of a guy, but it seemed that a lot of people who owned those types of cars were. I didn't want to own a Mustang just because I could peel out and go fast, though. I suppose I wanted one because I thought it would make me seem cooler. Which is essentially the only reason people have for choosing a car that isn't strictly utilitarian. Even then, though, some people feel the need to be extravagant. Have kids? Do a lot of shopping? Instead of just buying a little minivan, you got these people that buy the extended cab SUV's with the gigantic tires that raise the body so high you almost need one of those rolling staircases they use at the airport to get inside the damn thing. So, I really don't have room to talk about wanting a Mustang just to look cool. Everybody wants that certain something that can give them a little more significance.

Suddenly, some old lady grabbed my arm. "Are you okay, young man?"

I was still standing in the street, and now other cars were honking and driving around me. The old woman started gently but forcibly pulling me to the sidewalk and I noticed that the same group of people who were watching me before were still there. I seriously would love to know what everyone's interest is in me lately. Frankly, it's more than a little pathetic that they don't have lives themselves to be concerned about. I heard someone mumbling about being in shock, then one of the people asked if I wanted to see a doctor, and said that he'd be a witness. I wasn't quite sure what the hell he was proposing, but I can tell you this: I wasn't comfortable with it at all. Where's the government now to judge all of these whackos? There's never a sanctimonious bureaucrat around when you need one. So, I just yanked away my arm from the old lady and walked into the pharmacy.

I dropped the prescription off at the counter and took the only available seat to wait. It was right next to one of those machines that tests your blood pressure. Some little kid was playing around with it, sticking his skinny little arm in the cuff and pushing the button to make it expand. The dumb kid was really getting a kick out of the whole thing. I don't think he'd be so happy, though, if he knew how bad the reading of two hundred and ten over one hundred and seventy that he was getting really was. But, you know, it's not my problem. If the kid has a stroke because no one bothered to notice the numbers, it's certainly not my fault. He must have caught me looking at him, because now he wanted to engage me in some lively conversation.

"Hi. Hi. Hey, mister. Why won't you say hi?"

It seemed like he was going on for a day and a half, but I'm guessing it was really only a few minutes. I don't know, because didn't look at my watch. Didn't think it was anything that needed to be timed. Then again, they rarely ever seem like that in the beginning.

Finally, his negligent mother turned around and smacked him in the back of the head.

"Keep quiet, Cody!"

It wasn't a hard slap, I mean, not enough to induce head trauma, but it was enough to get him crying. And probably not a good idea either, considering the kid had such high blood pressure. He started whining and hitting the machine with his tiny balled up fists. The mother just stood there pretending not to care anymore.

"Not sure if you noticed, but hitting him didn't make him any quieter."

Now she was ignoring me. So, I repeated myself. Just in case it really was only because she didn't hear me over her kid's whining.

No. She heard me the first time, alright. That was easy enough to deduce, seeing as how she got all red faced and glared lasers at me. I retaliated by pulling a Doctor Melvin and tilting my head to the right and raising my eyebrows.

"Buying birth control pills, I hope?"

"*That* is none of your business!" She snapped back.

She was right. I don't care – slap around your kid as much as you want. Have even more kids and beat them, too. Not my problem. I sat back in my chair and leaned my head into the wall. A Tom Petty song started to play in the background, and not the elevator version you'd normally hear in a place like this, but the actual recording. I saw Petty in concert once about fifteen or sixteen years ago, but I think it was before this song came out. Maybe not, though. I couldn't be sure, because I didn't know exactly which song this was. So much of his stuff all sounds alike. To be honest, he probably could have played the same song thirty times in a row at the concert and I wouldn't have known the difference.

No, that's not right. Audrey and I went to that show, so it was more than fifteen or sixteen years ago. I went to a lot of concerts back then, literally hundreds, and of course most of them are now a blur, but I remember that one distinctly because Audrey snuck a small bottle of Jack Daniel's in the front of her pants. She downed the whole thing during the show, along with eight sixteen ounce beers, then threw up on the passenger door of my Dodge Dart on the way home, singing, "*Even the losers*", at the top of her voice.

I never drank whiskey for a couple of reasons. One, I just didn't like the smell of it. And I can honestly say from my experiences that night that the smell of it was just as bad going in as it was coming out. Not too much you can do about that, though. I just rolled down my window and drove a little faster. So, that alone probably would have been enough to keep me from it. But the second, and probably even greater, thing that kept me from whiskey was this fear I had that if I ever drank it, even one stupid sip, I'd end up in some spectacular car crash. I didn't have that reaction to any other alcohol, just whiskey. Not sure why, but it's always stuck with me.

"Mister Gleason?"

I looked up at the counter, and the tech was shaking a little white bag at me. I took this to mean that my prescription was filled and got out of the chair and walked over.

"Insurance card?"

"Don't have one."

He suddenly looked very sad, like I just told him my grandfather died. Which he did, but how would this guy know? Psychic? No, couldn't be. That would be too much of a coincidence.

"We can hold it for you while you go get it."

"No. I don't have one." I said it a little slower, since he apparently didn't understand it when I spoke at regular speed the first time. Which didn't help me, because I really wanted to get the hell out of there. The slapping mom, the crying kid, this guy all sad and confused. I started wondering about how far reaching that conspiracy to make people sick might actually go. I reached into my pocket and pulled out a wad of bills. "How much?"

"Oh, you're paying cash?"

It really is astounding sometimes. You have to wonder how some people have made it for so long on this planet.

"Without insurance," he whispered. "It's a hundred and ten dollars."

The whispering seemed a little unnecessary, but I just let it go. I saw that they had bottles of some kind of vitamin water on display by the register, so I grabbed one and put it on the counter. "This, too."

"There's cold ones over there." And he pointed down an aisle halfway across the store. Warm or cold, I didn't really care, and it certainly wasn't worth trekking all the way over there for something I didn't care about. All I wanted was something to wash down the pill. I peeled off two one hundred dollar bills, then opened both bottles. His hand shook when he took the money. Gives you confidence, doesn't it? While I was swallowing, he waved the change at me and cleared his throat.

"Would you like to talk to the pharmacist?" I didn't respond, and after a short pause, he went on some more. "Do you need to know about side effects?"

I choked down one more gulp then slammed the half filled bottle on the counter. "Doctor told me."

I have to say, I cannot recommend vitamin water. There's no way this could ever be confused with water. It tasted more like a clear syrup that someone crushed a handful of aspirin into. I shoved the bottle of pills back in the little white bag, but left the "water" behind.

"It's some pretty strong stuff," he stuttered.

"I wouldn't doubt it. Tastes horrible." I turned away from him rather quickly and without intending it, came face to face with the child beating mother. I don't think she was expecting it anymore than I was, and she flinched, like I was going to attack her now. So, I stopped and stared directly into her eyes for a minute before walking away. I think she understood.

I was about five or six blocks from my grandfather's house when I suddenly had this strange sensation that something was wrong, so I stopped and looked around. I was on the sidewalk, so it wasn't that again. It was weird. Like this little voice was telling me that something wasn't right. But it wasn't a voice, because I wasn't hearing words. It was more like when you're watching a movie, and tra-la-la, everything's fine, then some spooky mood music starts playing in the background and you just know things aren't heading in a good direction. I had that kind of feeling, just without the music. I put my hands in my pants pockets and spun around a few times. Not that I was expecting an axe murderer to lunge out at me or anything, but truth be told, I wasn't all that familiar with this neighborhood anymore, and this could be where they all lived now. I felt something odd pressing against my back pocket, so I moved my hand to check. My car keys. Damn it, I left the car in the parking lot of the medical building. So, it *was* me standing on the sidewalk after all! Huh. Now I had to decide whether or not it was worth going back. If I had to guess, I'd say it was at least two miles back, and I was getting a little tired. Probably from all the walking. I could always call a cab, but that seemed stupid. Now, there was a voice in my head, and it was yelling, "Aw, screw it!", and telling me to just walk back and get the car.

When I turned around to retrace my path, I nearly collided with some fat guy in a baseball cap who was now standing in my way.

"Excuse me?"

I just shrugged and stared back. "Why? What did you do?"

Then he looks at me like I had fingers growing out of my head. "*I* didn't do anything," he says. With heavy emphasis on *I*. This guy must think very highly of himself.

"Then why do you want to be excused?" I seriously didn't get it.

"Whatever, man" And he just shook his head, walked around me and headed away.

4

It was already getting dark by the time I finally parked the car in my grandfather's driveway. It wasn't that late, but for some unknown reason, I could barely keep my eyes open. All I could think about was my head hitting the pillow and falling asleep. Hell, I almost didn't even need the pillow: on the way back, I think I might have dozed off for a second at a red light. I remember stopping, but then the next thing I knew, some guy was driving alongside me a swearing out the side window. All the more reason to get to bed – it seemed like all day I kept running into these pissed off people who wanted to take out their problems on me. I mean, if that's the way someone's going to be, then what can you do about it? I don't really care. It's just that there seemed to be an unusual amount of it.

Then I tripped on something getting out of the car and fell face down on to the driveway. Oddly enough, it felt good to lay down, concrete or not, and for a few minutes, I really didn't want to get up. And I almost didn't, but it wasn't because of a comfort issue. What got me up was that damn dog. Everything was quiet, except for the dog. I'm guessing it was barking the whole day again. In fact, I'd lay odds it was barking when I pulled up, only I didn't notice it until I was on the ground. Why wasn't anybody telling that thing to shut up? Better yet – why didn't any of these stupid neighbors complain about it? I don't know, maybe someone did, and the owners ignored them. Or told them to go to hell. Maybe the owners are axe murderers. There could be a basement full of the bloody corpses of one time irate neighbors. It doesn't seem all that possible, but who knows? And really, who cares? That dog needed to finally shut up. And if no one else is going to do it, I might as well be the one. Don't know how, just yet. But, I have to do something. I should probably kill it. Just get it over with. Something.

What I did know was that I needed to get a good night's sleep. Long, deep, and undisturbed. During the car ride back, I started thinking about Melvin's instructions. So, I figured I might as well start with finding Audrey tomorrow and ask her some questions about me back then. Oh, wait. That's what happened. That's probably why I fell asleep at the light. I closed my eyes and started thinking about Audrey – what she looked like then, what she might look like now. It's been a while. Too tired to do the math, but it's been at least a couple years before I married Julie since I last saw her. She got married, too. Not sure when exactly. We had a mutual friend, back when I still had friends, who told me her new last name and where they were living. I didn't ask for the information, it was turned over voluntarily, so it's not like I was stalking her, or anything. Tell the truth, I wish *He* hadn't even told me. I would have preferred not to have that knowledge sneaking around in the back of my mind. There were more than a few times since He told me that I found myself for one reason or another on her block. She lived over thirty miles away from my house, but the next thing I'd know, there I was, driving up her street. This strong desire to maybe see her again, even if only for a brief moment. I never figured out what I would do if I did run into her, though. Especially if I caught her with her husband. Or her kids, if she even had any. Then I sort of just forgot about her after a while, and never got any more updates. Talk about things slipping from your mind. God, I'm tired.

Next thing I knew, I was ringing the doorbell of the house behind my grandfather's. The house with the dog. And, I don't know if it smelled me, or if it just heard the bell, but there it was at the side gate, staring at me and blabbering once again. Not as loud as before, though. Now it sounded weak and raspy. Maybe it got a sore throat from barking at me so much before. I rang the bell seven or eight times, but nothing. No answer. The house had a six step concrete staircase with a little porch off the door to the right. The sides of the porch were framed by a metal gate, so it made it close to impossible to get a real look into the picture window, unless you wanted to lean way over the left side of the gate and risk falling into the rose bushes. Which I really didn't feel like doing. There probably wouldn't be anything to see anyway, due to the fact that all of the inside lights were off. Maybe the bell wasn't working. I pushed it again and listened this time. Yep. It's working. Either nobody home, or they're just ignoring me. The dog wasn't ignoring me, though. Stupid thing just kept on going. Wheezing and coughing like it just finished its fifth pack of the day. I walked off the porch and went to the fence, thinking that having a good look at it would help me decide what to do. A few things crossed my mind during the walk over. Cutting its head off was one. Or, better yet, cutting the owner's heads off. Now that I was here though, both of those seemed a bit too drastic. And you can't really blame the dog if no one bothered to teach it properly. Stupid thing.

This was the first time I ever saw it up close, so there was no frame of reference to compare it with, but it didn't look all that good to me. For starters, it seemed like it hadn't taken a bath in a long time. It really didn't have any bad odor to it, but I did wonder what Melvin would say about it, nonetheless. Then all of a sudden, it just stopped barking and fell sideways into the fence. Honestly, at first I thought it was a practical joke. The way it fell over was like some ham actor performing the final death scene in a bad community theater play. I wasn't sure though, if dogs could joke or not, so I stepped in for a closer look at the grubby little thing. It seemed so pitiful and weak, and now I wondered how long it had been since it had last eaten.

"You hungry?"

Okay, I swear the dog smiled at me. Could it really know what I was saying? I suppose dogs do have to learn a little human in order to survive. Kind of like people moving to or visiting other countries where they speak a different language. At the very least, you need to know a few of the basic words to get by: *"Bathroom", "Hotel", "Hospital"*, etc.

What always seems a little unfair about it is that the tourists have to learn all those new words, but the locals never bother to learn how to talk to the tourists in the other language. They just expect the visitors to adapt. Same thing applies to dogs. Why don't us humans ever learn to speak Dog? Not to be fluent, but just the major words. *"Food", "Down", "Shut up"*. Stuff like that. Hell, even me. I never moved or traveled out of the country, but I had to learn a little Spanish just so I could talk to some of the people that worked for me. I mean, I couldn't permanently settle in Madrid, or anything, not unless the locals there wouldn't mind me continually telling them to take out the trash, or bus table six, that is.

The side gate didn't have a lock, just a little metal latch to keep it from swinging open, so I flipped it up and walked into the backyard. I wasn't worried about the dog attacking me – it could barely pick itself up off the ground as it was. Getting caught sneaking around someone else's backyard might be a tricky thing to talk yourself out of, though. I mean, I seriously didn't care one way or another what would happen to me, if anything at all. It was more the idea of possibly having to deal with all of the aggravations that might come after. Ah, screw it. I need my sleep.

Now, I'm no lawn guru like most of the people who live around here, but even I could tell that this yard looked like full blown hell. Even worse than it looked from my back window. In retrospect, I guess I always knew it was bad, but seeing how it was never my main focus when I looked back here, it just never sunk in. Even through the gloom, you could see there were dozens of bare spots where the grass either just didn't grow, or that the dog had scratched away. And the weeds. Jesus. Above my knees and all over the place. If it wasn't for all the bare spots, there would be nothing but three foot weeds growing back here. But, as bad as that was, and it was pretty damn bad, the shit was even worse. There were little clumps of turds everywhere. From the driveway this side of the gate, all over the lawn and up to the door. I've heard them called landmines before, but I guess the metaphor never really registered until just now. I swear, I don't think the Nazi's could have mapped it out better. The question was: what the hell was inside this house that needed this much protection? Bare spots, weeds and shit. Not the things that encouraged strangers to wander over and knock. Maybe they *were* axe murderers, and this was their way of making sure people stay out of their business. It was just as good an explanation as any.

It was near impossible to safely navigate your way through. Just when you thought you were okay, you quickly had to readjust your feet in midair to avoid coming down in another secret pile. And the fact that it was almost completely dark now, made it even more treacherous, but nonetheless, I decided to brave it. I stopped all my intricate maneuvering and walked straight to the back door. I mean, what's the worst that could happen? That I repeatedly step in shit, and I have to wash my shoes? Or buy a new pair? Oh, well then. All missions have a cost.

I knocked, but, just like before, there was no answer. The door had no window, and like a lot of the homes around here, this being a raised bungalow meant that the kitchen window was above my head so once again, I couldn't get a decent look inside. I wanted to just turn around and march straight to bed, which is really where I should be right now. I mean, what the hell *am I* doing here, anyway? Then I saw the dog again and remembered my objective. Now, it was laying by my feet, looking up at me with these big wet eyes and quietly whimpering. Can you believe that? Now, I'm feeling sorry for the stupid thing. I pulled open the screen door and grabbed the handle on the main door. It was unlocked. Incredible. Why hadn't the dog ever thought to do this before? I pushed the door open, and even before I took one step inside, I thought I was going to puke all over myself. I've dealt with some pretty disgusting stuff in my life, but I don't know if I ever encountered an odor this bad. It was more than just a smell, though. I swear I could feel it. Like when you walk through fog. What the hell did these people do? Go out of town and not throw away their garbage collection? I could feel it attaching itself to me. No wonder the dog didn't go inside. Maybe it was smarter than I was giving it credit.

"Hello? Hello?" I called out a few times, but still nobody answered. I was really starting to not like these people. I'm not a big dog fan, but it seemed kind of cruel to leave the damn thing unattended like this for so long.

The door opened onto a landing with stairs to the right heading into the basement and stairs to the left going up to the kitchen. I figured my best bet would be up - the idea of finding a bunch of bloody corpses wasn't all that appealing. My objective was to get in and get out as quickly as possible. But, what was I even looking for? I felt around on the wall for a switch, which wasn't where I thought it should be, so I kicked around in the dark for the first stair. Instead of finding the stair, I found something else, tripped and fell on my ass. Actually, I must have fallen on my left kneecap first because it was beginning to throb like mad. It happened so fast, I couldn't tell what was going on. Damn it hurt. I sat there for a second, but then quickly pulled myself up - there was no question in my mind of maybe closing my eyes and falling asleep here. While I was regaining my footing, I kicked the thing again that I tripped over. I silently hoped it wasn't a disembodied limb, or anything. I reached down and swiped at the air. An open bag. Dog food. Bingo! It hurt to put pressure on the knee, but that smell was wrapping itself around me like bandages on a mummy, and I needed to get back outside as quickly as possible, so I grabbed the bag and moved outside as fast as my aching knee would allow. Another thing I didn't notice, though, was that the screen door had closed behind me, and I sort of walked through it on my way out. Now the stupid thing was jammed and wouldn't push closed. I tried yanking on it a few more times, but ultimately decided to just leave it open rather than rip the thing from its hinges. Call it being a good neighbor.

I could only see one bowl, so I poured a mound of food into the grass, and dropped the bag next to it. Then I filled the bowl with water from the spigot. It seemed small, though, like it wouldn't hold enough water. I was thirsty, maybe that was it. Either way, I turned the faucet so there was a small, constant stream dripping out, and put the bowl underneath. The dog seemed pleased. It dug into the pile of food the way Melvin attacked that sandwich. Out of curiosity, I watched for a minute to see if it would stop eating then take notes. It didn't.

It appeared that I had accomplished my goal: the dog was silenced without having to resort to homicide. Or dogocide. Whatever you call it. Maybe now I could finally sleep through the night without being woken up by barking. But, just to be safe, I thought I better make sure the dog knew this, too. So, I bent over and started talking. Why I thought bending over would help, I don't know. Did I suddenly think the dog was deaf? Just conditioning, I suppose. People are always bending down when they address things smaller than them: animals, kids, old people. Well, the old people usually are deaf, so at least there's a purpose for that.

"Hey. Dog." It looked over at me, cocked its head to the right, but continued chewing. Yep. Just like Melvin. I'll be damned. "I don't know what your name is. I'm Daryl. And I'm staying in that house over there. Right over the fence. Listen, I have to get up early and go see someone. So, I really need to sleep tonight. Very important. Okay? Keep quiet."

Now, it tilted its head to the other side. This was getting weird. I decided I better get out of there before it brought its head back to center and sighed. I pointed out the bottomless bowl of water I so kindly provided to the dumb thing, then started my way back through the field of shit.

Well, the shoes were ruined, just like I figured. There was so much shit on them, that I left a trail from the dog all the way back to my grandfather's place. I bet I probably could have walked three more miles and it still wouldn't have all scraped off. But I'm not walking three more miles just to prove a point. So, when I got to the driveway, I tipped my feet sideways and slipped out of each shoe. I then carefully peeled off my socks with the big toe on the opposite foot, and left all of it by the car to air out. I tried to make a mental note to go out and buy a new pair tomorrow, but I couldn't find any room in my brain to leave the note. It was all dark and fuzzy and I couldn't navigate through it. Kind of like the shit in the backyard. Besides, I'd realize I needed new shoes as soon as I found the old pair all covered with shit anyway.

Now that I was back, it hit me. Why in the hell did I walk all the way around the block? I could have just jumped the stupid fence and been in bed ten minutes ago. Oh, well.

I reached into my pants pocket, pulled out the house key and tried to jam it in the lock, but it wasn't working. Why can't they make locks on houses like they do for cars? Just a little button that goes "beep beep", and the door's open? That would make so much sense. And be so much easier than all this. Never mind. It was the wrong key that was the problem. That would never happen with a beep beep remote. You might end up in front of the wrong house, but when you point and beep, the correct door would always open. I was trying to open the door with the key for me and Julie's house. The place with him there. The idea of somebody else using his key to slip into her lock made me sick. I felt like throwing up again. Could also have just been from all the shit and garbage around the block. Who knows? I leaned my whole body against the door frame and took a couple deep breaths. That used to work for me when I thought I might get sick from drinking. Sometimes worked for Audrey, too. It never worked for Julie, though. Nothing helped her. She always threw up. I know I said Audrey did it once at the concert, but for her that was rare. For Julie, it was a regular event. Never quite understood the point of drinking if the nights consistently ended with you throwing it all back up. But, that's what she did. She'd have her fun, make a mess, then pass out while other people cleaned it up. Probably out drinking right now. But, that's her concern, and none of mine. She can do whatever she wants tonight. I'm going to bed.

I locked the door behind me and started to the bedroom. There was no need to turn on any lights, because the lamp was already on. Not by design. I just can't figure out how to turn it off. I've twisted that little knob over and over again, both ways, and the thing won't shut off. Like some eternal flame, or something. I guess I could unplug it, but then I'd have to go through all the trouble of finding the light switch each time I came back when it was dark. No bags of dog food here, but I'm sure I'd fall over something, that's already been proven. And besides, the bedroom's the first door at the top of the stairs, so the lamp throws off just the right amount of light to get me there. It might not be the best thing for the environment, but then again, neither is a hundred pounds of shit in your backyard. I'll make a donation to something to make up for it.

I fumbled around in the dark trying to strip off my clothes: my shirt came off okay, but my pants for some reason were giving me trouble. I fell sideways onto the bed and tried kicking them the rest of the way off with my feet, but it wasn't working. I looked over at the clock and saw that it was eight forty-five. Really? Eight forty-five? That's all? How could I be this tired? God, I could sleep for a month.

Sitting next to the clock was that damned journal. I swear, every time I see it, I can hear Melvin's voice, *"Did you bring it? Have you even written in it?"*

I had a feeling that the voice wasn't going to leave until I wrote something, so I picked up the pen and started to scribble.

You want to know about me? You want to know what happens to me? Fine. I'll tell you. I stepped in some shit a little while ago...

5

I opened my eyes and looked over at the clock. Now it read five fifty two. Must have fallen asleep. How the hell did that happen so fast? I stared up toward the ceiling and did my usual inventory. I had to pee, but it wasn't terribly urgent, which meant that I didn't sleep for a month like I wanted. Plus, I was still incredibly tired, so it was probably only the next morning. I took a deep breath, closed my eyes, and turned my head on the pillow. What the hell? I had a pen in my hand. Oh, yeah. I dropped it between the pages of the book and sunk back into bed.

I felt myself drifting away when I thought I heard someone calling my name. Most likely I had dozed off for a second or two, and some stupid half-asleep dream knocked me back awake. I forced my eyes to stay open and scanned the room. The sun was starting to come up, and even though the curtains were closed, there was enough light to see that there was no one lurking around the bed. Just for the hell of it, I listened as hard as I could for any unexplained movements. I tried to remain as still as possible, which I guess made me a pretty easy target if someone was there, but after a moment of hearing nothing but the beating of my own heart, I closed my eyes again.

"Daryl! Daryl!"

Okay. That was no dream. That voice was coming from outside my head, not inside. Which in itself was a good sign. I sprung up and flipped myself over, but when my feet hit the floor, I flung forward and fell on my face. My pants were twisted around my ankles. Guess I fell asleep before I could take them off. The last twelve or so hours were suddenly like some Three Stooges movie with me. I half expected at any moment to get hit in the head with a pipe wrench by a guy with a bad haircut. It was more than a little aggravating.

"Daryl! Hey! Daryl! You awake?"

Now that it was light out, I managed to slip out of my pants with little problem. Well, other than the fact that my left hip now hurt like hell. And my left knee, for some reason. But I didn't fall on my knee. Why the hell is that hurting? I got to my feet and tried to orient myself, but I was still so goddamn tired it was hard to focus. Hold on. My knee?

"Daryl! Hey, Daryl!"

There it was again. Groggy or not, I could tell it was definitely coming from outside the house. I pulled the curtains apart and peeked out the back window. There was no one in the yard. Or any other yard as far as I could tell. Empty. Nobody in the gangways between the houses, either. I couldn't even see anybody at an open window. The only life, as far as that goes, was that stupid mutt. It was staring right up at me through the chain link fence, and wagging its tail like mad. I had the strangest dream about that dog last night. Images were coming back to me so strong and so fast that I felt like it had really happened. I looked past the dog to the back of the house. The screen door was bent-up and partially half hanging off the frame. Did I dream that? Because I swear I knew it was going to look like that before I even saw it just now. Probably caught a glance at it before, just never made a conscious note of it. Déjà vu, or something.

I closed the curtains but left enough of a gap so I still had a decent angle to the outside, hoping to catch whoever the hell it was yelling my name. I mean, he had to be close by if I was able to hear it that clearly up here in the bedroom. I stood motionless for a few minutes, my eyes scanning left to right, up and down, for any movement. The dog was still sitting there and looking up at me. I tried my best not to get caught in its gaze. Considering how tired I was, I figured if I did, I'd probably lose myself in another three hour stare down marathon with the dumb thing. Well, whoever the hell it was either saw me and left, or didn't feel like carrying on the joke any further, because I swear I stood there for what seemed like five minutes and nothing happened. I yawned and stretched, then let go of the curtains and headed back for bed.

"Daryl! You coming down, or what?"

This was really pissing me off. The whole *watched-pots-don't-boil* of it. I spun back around as quickly as I could and threw open the drapes. Nobody. How the hell could that be? It wasn't even a second ago. Am I being taunted by an Olympic sprinter? As tired as I was, I knew I had to get to the bottom of this or I'd never be able to fall back asleep. I grabbed my pants off the floor and sat back on the bed to put them on.

"Daryl! Hey! Don't go back to sleep!"

I was ninety five percent sure it was coming from out back. What slowed me down a step or two was the five percent possibility that it wasn't happening outside at all.

"Ben! If you're in there, tell Daryl to come down!"

Ben? What the...? I got my pants up to my waist and started out of the room, but when I tried to button them, I felt a big lump of something hard in my right pocket. Two prescription bottles. Oh yeah. I figured I better take them now before I forgot, and tapped one pill each out of both bottles on my way down. I stopped at the kitchen sink and cupped some water from the tap to help me swallow them. They probably could have gone down without the water, but somebody told me a long time ago to always swallow pills with water, so that's what I do.

I shook my head and swallowed a few gulps of saliva to make sure they went all the way down, and headed for the door.

Then I saw that stupid bat.

I couldn't believe it was still there, in the exact same place it had been for as long as I could remember. Knob end up, leaning against the wall under the back window. Funny that I hadn't noticed it before. Maybe I did, but just blocked it out like I used to try to do as a kid. He claimed the reason it was perpetually positioned there was to combat break-ins. *"This is my guard dog"*, he used to say. As far as I know, it was never used it once, but just the idea of it being there used to scare the hell out of me. To me, it was like seeing a rack of life jackets on a cruise ship. How the hell could you have fun when the constant reminder of potential danger was always right in sight?

He didn't fool me for long, though. As I got older and wised up, I realized what its true purpose was. It became clear that whenever I got in trouble, he always insisting on talking to me in the kitchen. I remember times he had to come pick me up from school. He wouldn't say a word – there, or during the entire car ride back. Then once we got back home, it was straight to the kitchen. He'd always stand right in front of it, so I got a real good look. That was no coincidence. He never actually threatened me with it, just it being there was enough to get me to agree with just about anything he wanted.

According to him, if a break-in were to occur, it would surely come from the back of the house. The idea being the front was too well lit and there'd be too many witnesses. Of course, in this neighborhood, you rarely saw anyone out on the street anyway, so I don't know where the hell all those witnesses would come from. Unless the robber rang all the doorbells and introduced himself, he'd probably be able to do whatever he pleased. That's why I knew the whole premise was bullshit.

But now, hearing these voices I couldn't account for, made me wonder about that, too.

I passed right by the bat, having no second thought, or a first thought even, of taking it outside with me. I figured if a burglar is stupid enough to choose this house to rob, let him have whatever he wants. There's no sense in stopping him. I've been in this place for a large portion of my life, and I can attest to the fact that the only thing that's of any value in here is the water pressure. And, like I said before, I usually only shower once a week, so it's not like I'm relying on that for some endless source of comfort. If the guy can figure out how to take the water pressure, let him have it. More power to him. And pressure to him. Whatever.

So, let them come. Besides, anything of value is elsewhere. A detail he even had hidden from me until recently.

I heard another couple *"Daryls"* before I reached the door, but once I stepped outside, nothing. All I heard then was a few birds chirping and my own breathing. And as far as seeing anybody, well, that was a bust, too. The only movement I could see was that stupid dog, still staring at me through the chain link fence. Again, not to sound like some detective, or anything, but it must have rained while I was sleeping because the ground was wet in some areas. I only mention this because I didn't see any footprints. I suppose you could maneuver yourself around the damp spots like you would landmines, but for what purpose?

That's weird. Something about that struck me as familiar. Landmines...must have been in that dream I had.

I stayed on the concrete patio area by the door and gave the place the once over twice, then moved over to my right and looked down the driveway. No one. No neighbors. No burglars. I did wonder what I would have done though, if some robber jumped out at me. Probably nothing. I'd never seen one before, so maybe because of that, I had this stylized image in my head of a cat burglar from some old movie – black pants, black turtleneck, black hat and black shoe polish smeared on his face. I figured if I saw someone like that, I'd probably be too mesmerized by his looks to really do anything. I honestly think I'd be content watching him scale the wall with a rope and grappling hook rather than trying to subdue him. Then I started wondering why they were always guys. I couldn't remember if I ever saw a movie where the burglar was a woman. I mean, I probably have, but nothing stood out. Why was that? I kinda remember reading something once that said women, for the most part, commit crimes out of passion, whereas the majority of crimes committed by men are out of opportunity. Couldn't a woman be passionate about the opportunity to rob someone's house? I don't know. Makes sense to me. I did read that somewhere, right? I really don't think I made that up just now. I mean, I could have. I'm not an idiot. Jesus, I'm feeling really tired again.

"What's wrong with this guy?"

Okay, there is *nobody* out here, and that sounded like it came from right in front of me. Ordinarily, if something like that happened, I'd probably jump about twenty feet, but I must really be tired, or something, because I didn't move much at all. Just my head. And my heart. That's beating like crazy all of a sudden. But nobody could see that. Even if there was someone here to see anything, which there isn't. Unless they're decked out in some incredible camouflage, like an uncut lawn, or an old garage, but I doubt it. Am I imagining this? I really hope not. I can't begin to guess what Melvin would say about this. Or the sheer amount of pens he'd gnaw through trying to figure it out. And I honestly don't think I could deal with that much head shifting, so I should probably just keep this to myself.

What's weird...well, *weirder*, is that I don't recognize the voice. It seems like, well, if I was hearing an imaginary voice in my head, wouldn't it make more sense if it was a familiar one? Like a parent, or a spouse, or even an evil twin? I don't know, maybe it doesn't work that way. Situations like this weren't covered in Melvin's office, so this is all mere speculation on my part. That would be a good question to ask him though, that is, if I felt like dealing with his tedious nonsense of trying to make a big deal out of a simple question.

Are the voices in your head people you know? Or are they strangers?

Maybe there's a pool of disembodied voices somewhere, and when it's your turn to hear one, you just get whichever one is next in line. Like employees working the phone banks at a customer service call center. That would say a lot in explaining why some people can handle hearing them and some people can't. Say you got lucky, and wound up with a nice, soothing voice in your head – like the guys who do voiceovers for headache commercials, for example. That wouldn't be so bad. But, what if you got stuck with some loud, screeching, fingernailson-a-chalkboard voice? Like the kind of voice that probably inspires headache commercials to be made in the first place? I could understand if you snapped pretty quickly from that and did whatever they said. Just to shut them up. Or, if you got some annoying monotone that just went on and on and never let up. I knew a guy like that. Drove me nuts. Name was Phil something. I could come up with it if I gave it some thought, but I'd rather not. He was the kind of guy who thought he had the answer to everything. Whatever decision you made about anything, it was always a distant second or third choice to what he would have done. Worse part about it was having to listen to him drone on for what seemed like a week and a half at a time explaining why his idea was better. Almost always had something to do with some Harvard study he said he read. I don't know how many studies have come out of Harvard, but if they actually did half as many as Phil claimed to have read, they wouldn't have time to graduate anybody.

Anyway, those unbearable voices are the kind of crap I could definitely see driving someone to the top of a tower with a high powered rifle. I mean, even if the calm headache commercial voice told you to do something stupid, it seems to me that it would be a voice you'd be able to reason with.

"I don't know," you'd say. "Setting my wife on fire seems pretty drastic."

"Four out of five doctors surveyed agree that it's the best way to relieve the pain in your head."

"Couldn't I just take a pill and go to sleep?" you'd ask.

"Possibly," he'd calmly say. "But remember, results may vary."

Now, I can't say for sure whether the voice would ultimately agree with you, but at least there would be room for rational discussion. Not like the other voices.

"So, when I woke up this morning," the droner would drone. "It was four-fifty seven. I know because I looked at my alarm clock. I have a pretty nice alarm clock. It glows in the dark. Not enough to keep you awake, but enough so you can read it in the dark if you want to. I bought it nine years ago at a J.C. Penney store at the mall by my house. They had a sale. It was the last one, and it was a floor demonstration model so there was no box, but the salesperson, his name was Kyle, gave me an extra ten percent off..."

Or the other voice.

"Kiiiiiiill! Kiiiiiiill! Glaaaarblvrft!"

Either one, and it's Tower Climbing time. My voice, from what little I've heard, isn't as calm and relaxed as the voiceover guy, but it's definitely not either one of the others. Right now, the only shocking thing about it is the newness of it. But, if it's going to be a regular occurrence, I'm sure I'll get used to it quick enough.

"You know, even for a human, you look like shit."

Well, that settles that argument. I must be crazy. The voice, the one I was hearing and the one that just spoke, was coming from the dog!

As soon as I heard it, I turned towards the sound, and I mean *that second!* I was ready for it. I turned and I saw the dog's jaw moving. And words, actual words, were coming out.

A couple things immediately struck me:

1. I can't believe how articulate it is. Not that it's going to do headache commercials, mind you, but it did speak clearly and have good enunciation. I was somewhat impressed.
2. Where does it get off saying I look like shit? First of all, I just woke up. Secondly, I'm guessing it hasn't gotten near a mirror itself in a while.
3. Dogs can talk?

As much as I wanted to calculate the impressiveness of point One, or defend myself against point Two, the sheer unlikelihood of Number Three being a reality took prominence in my mind over the others. I stepped toward it and bent down a bit. Something about this, too, seemed familiar. Even the dog thinks it's odd. He just gave me a Doctor Melvin head tilt. Great. Well, as ridiculous as it seemed, I needed to get an answer, so I made eye contact and went for it.

"Did you just say something to me?" I asked.

The dog now took a few steps back, and I swear, its eyes got bigger, but it didn't talk back.

"Hey, I'm talking to you," I went on. "Did you just say something to me?"

The dog's mouth opened. "Yeah. You understand what I said?"

I could feel myself starting to get angry. "Yeah, I understand. And I think it was a little uncalled for. If you think you look any better than I do, you've got another thing coming." Why I was suddenly all about Number Two, I couldn't say, but it was really pissing me off. I mean, who's he to judge?

Now the dog ran up to the fence, stood on its back legs and started wagging its tail like mad. "You can really hear me? I mean, you know what I'm saying? It's not just some coincidence?"

I tried to think for a minute about what possible coincidence could make you think you were hearing a dog speak English. Nothing came to me. Then the dog said something really strange.

"Blueberry muffins!"

I looked around, fully expecting to see someone behind me holding a basket of blueberry muffins, but there was no one else was around.

"What about them?" I asked.

"What about what?"

Is this stupid thing purposely screwing with me? "Blueberry muffins. Why did you say that?"

"You can hear me! You really can hear me!"

"I kinda thought that was already established."

"I just wanted to make sure it wasn't a coincidence. It's happened before. A human will say something to me that seems like it could be a reply to something I just said, but it turns out to be a coincidence."

"Yeah, but 'blueberry muffins'?"

"It had nothing to do with what we were talking about. I figured, if you repeated it, then that meant you really did hear me."

"Well, that makes sense," I surmised. "Now I want a blueberry muffin."

"Yeah, me, too. Wanna get some?"

There have been mornings in the past when I've woken up and not immediately known where I was. There were times I've woken up and not immediately known who I was lying next to. I've even woken up a few times not knowing who I was. But in all those cases, the answers came to me just a few seconds later. This was a new one for me – waking up to have a conversation with a dog. I'm not sure when the answer for this will arrive.

"So that was you calling me earlier?"

"Yeah."

"That clears up a few things," I said. "How do you know my name?"

"You told me."

"I told you? When did I tell you?"

"Last night. When you came over and fed me. Don't you remember?"

Holy shit. It wasn't part of a dream: the broken door, landmines, why my knee hurt. Bending down low. It was all coming back to me.

"Yeah, right."

"You said you had to wake up early to do something important."

Thinking about waking up was reminding me how tired I was. "Yeah, I do. But not this damn early."

"How was I supposed to know? You didn't say how early. You just said early."

"But what made you think I needed you to wake me up? I'm perfectly capable of waking up myself on time."

I swear it laughed. "Are you kidding me? You're usually not up until way after sunrise. When you said 'early', I assumed you meant earlier than that."

I could feel myself getting angry again. "How do you know when I get up? Are you psychic?"

"Dude, I know you're up when I start to see activity. Like drapes moving. Hearing the plumbing when you flush the toilet. Stuff like that. There's really not much else to do back here."

It made sense – the dog was observant. Just the same, though, I needed to know something else. "*Can* dogs be psychic?"

"Some say they are. I'm just not so sure if I really buy into it. I think it's nothing more than parlor tricks. Why do you ask?"

"'Cause for a while, I thought you might be psychic."

It sort of seemed stupid, now that I know it's just because the thing paid attention to certain details. Probably the same tricks psychics used.

"Me? Why did you think that?"

"Things you did. The way you were always barking at me."

"Barking?" It suddenly seemed aggravated.

"Yeah. Barking," I said. I didn't know what he thought I was implying. "The sound you make. You know."

"No, I don't," he spit out. "Tell me."

I wasn't sure I liked his attitude, so I sneered and gave him a couple of his own "woof-woofs".

"What the hell was that supposed to be?" he asked.

"You."

"You can't be serious. You think that's how I sound?"

"Maybe not you specifically. Jesus, cut me some slack. I'm not that good at doing dog voices. But, yeah, that's more or less how you all sound. Well, used to sound. Not anymore."

"Wow. You humans really are full of yourselves."

"What the hell did I do?" I threw my arms up and looked around, like I thought someone would suddenly appear and come to my defense, but no one came. As usual, I was all by myself in this.

"Forget it," the dog said. It actually sounded fairly apologetic. At least that was something encouraging. I guess. "So, when did you start hearing me the way you hear me now?"

"This morning." For some reason, I was feeling slightly dizzy, and really needed to sit, so I lowered myself to the ground and leaned back into the fence. I got an assfull of wet grass, but I was too tired to complain.

The dog turned away from me and sighed. At least, that's what it sounded like. I didn't know dogs could sigh. But, really, why couldn't they? I mean, this one's capable of talking, so I don't know why sighing now seemed all that surprising.

"If you couldn't understand me until this morning," it started. "How'd you know I was asking for food last night?"

"I didn't. I just got sick of hearing you yapping all the time. I wasn't initially coming over to feed you. To be honest, I was thinking about killing you."

"You were going to kill me? Dude, that's so not cool."

"I thought about it, but I didn't, did I?"

"Ironic, huh?"

"That I didn't kill you?" I don't see how that's irony. More like luck for him, and whatever you want to call it for me – having to sit here and talk to a dog when I could be sleeping.

"I hadn't eaten in... damn, I don't know how long. But I can tell you this: I was so hungry, I probably would have died of starvation if I didn't eat when I did. You came over thinking about killing me, but didn't, and instead, you wound up saving me. See? If you never thought about killing me, I'd be dead right now. Ironic."

"I could still kill you," I said.

He stared at me for a moment, then shook his head. "Nah, you won't. Let's go get those blueberry muffins."

Damn thing was annoying me. I'm quickly learning you don't have to be a monotone to go on and on and get on someone's nerves. I'll say this much, the thing had a lot of confidence for a dog. Then again, I don't know how much confidence dogs usually have, so it's not like I have anything tangible to measure it against. I'm sure if Phil were here, he'd know of a Harvard study.

"So, why haven't you eaten for so long?" It's not like I cared, or anything, but I wondered if dogs dieted. Not to say that was the reason it hadn't eaten, but you never know. The idea of fasting for religious purposes crossed my mind, too, but I decided to keep that thought to myself for the moment.

"I don't know. I've been wondering the same thing. I haven't seen my human in a while. I think she went somewhere."

"You're human?"

"Gwen. The person who lives in the house."

"Your owner."

He sighed again. I can verify that it was indeed a sigh. "Word to the wise: That's not a good word choice when talking to a dog. It's extremely insulting. We're living things, not pieces of property."

I wasn't about to go into it with him. Something I learned from Melvin is that certain people feel the need to idealize themselves in order to feel good about themselves and/or their place in the world. He told me that's how Julie seemed to be, according to my descriptions of her. I don't think it's true about Julie, but since then, I have noticed it to be true about other people. So, maybe the dog had a complex like that, too. Who knows? You meet all kinds.

"So, whatta you got to do today that's so important?"

"Huh? Oh, I, ah, have to go see my ex-girlfriend."

All of a sudden, his tail started wagging like crazy. "You gonna do her?"

"What? No."

"Why not?"

"Because."

I'm fully aware that's not much of an answer. But I couldn't elaborate any further because the question, no matter how dumb it was, got me thinking. I mean - did I still want to? *Do her*, I mean. All those times in the past when I'd drive by her house. Or when I'd lie in bed next to Julie and secretly wish it was Audrey, and then of course feel this immensely heavy guilt. The thought of having sex with her was always, and I mean always, something I really wanted. For the longest time I kept the memory of how she looked, how she felt, and I swear even how she smelled, locked away in my head. I wanted to be with her again something bad. There were even a few times immediately after I had sex with Julie that I not only wished she was Audrey, but that Audrey would walk in the bedroom, get rid of Julie, and move in with me. Each time after thinking about that, amazingly enough, Julie and I got into a huge fight that wound up with me sleeping on the floor in the other room. Now, if I'm not mistaken, that's a good example of irony right there. But here I am, possibly just minutes away from actually seeing her again, *coming into physical contact with her*, and the notion of sex never entered my mind. Why not? Do I still? I know she's married, last I heard. Then again, a little thing like marriage didn't stop that guy from moving on Julie. Although that's a little different. Audrey and I had a prior relationship. Julie and *Robert* didn't even know each other until last year. God I hate that name. *Robert*. Not Rob. Or Bob. Or, hell, even Bert. I'd be fine with that! But, whenever anybody goes full name like that, instead of using the multitude of available shortened versions, it drives me crazy. Nine times out of ten, you immediately know that person thinks way too highly of himself. How many Michaels, Timothys and Thomases does the average person know? I don't mean on business cards, I mean in everyday conversations. Guys that actually go by their full given names? Probably not many, I'd bet. Now, how many Mikes, Tims and Toms do people know? A hell of a lot more, that's how many. I have to go full name because there is no shortened form of Daryl. That's usually the easiest tip-off to figure out what a guy's all about. I suspected something was wrong the first time I heard his name mentioned. "*Robert* and I are going out for drinks." I knew it when I heard the name that he was going to be trouble.

"You okay?"

"Huh?"

"Your face," the dog said. "It looked kinda weird. I've seen that look before on male dogs coming out of the vet's office."

"Just thinking of something," I told him.

"Thinking about humping her? But, what else there is to think about, right? I know I'd be doing it like crazy if I could get out of here. You know how long it's been? Shit, I'm embarrassed to admit."

"So, you have a wife somewhere?"

The thing laughed. "Get real. Things don't work like that with us. You find someone, bang, and it's over. No commitments. No regrets. Just have some fun, and move on."

"And the females – they're okay with that?"

"Why wouldn't they? I'm telling you, it's not like your world. Dogs don't need a spouse. Our humans take care of everything. Feed us. Bathe us. Protect us. Trust me - nobody wants another dog around full time taking away from their attention. Know what I mean?"

I swear, this constant yammering was really getting on my nerves. It was just as bad as when I only heard the stupid thing barking. Maybe even worse. I got up and started back into the house.

"Where you going?"

"I'm going back to bed."

"What, are you kidding? You slept the whole night. How could you be tired? Besides, it's a beautiful day! Come on, it's time for muffins and bitches!"

"I'm tired. And don't go calling me, okay? I'll wake up when I wake up."

"Whatever," he sighed. "Do what you gotta do, I guess. Hey, thanks for the food, by the way. I'm feeling better than I have in a long time. I owe you."

Great. A horny dog owes me. Just what I need. I'm sure if something bad happens to me, he'll be the first one I turn to for help. Idiot.

I walked back into the house and gave that bat a closer look. Maybe it was finally time to put it to use. But then I'd have to walk around the block again or hop the fence, and I really don't have the energy to do either. Even the stairs seemed too much. I dropped to the floor in the hallway and closed my eyes.

When I woke up again, the sun was still out, but I had no idea if it was the same day. My legs ached, my knee especially, but that was no clear indication. It could just be from sleeping on the floor. Actually, I fell, I think, and that's why my knee hurt. All these weird images were popping into my head, which was creating havoc for my internal fact checker. Why *was* I sleeping on the floor, anyway? I gave myself a quick stretch and hobbled over to the bathroom.

While I was peeing, I started to mentally sort through a few things. Why I always seemed to click off my daily to-do list while I was in the bathroom, I don't know. By now though, it was just an uncontrollable habit and not worth the analysis. Okay, I needed to see Audrey. I needed to take my pills. Wasn't there something else? Then another memory, or wannabe memory, bubbled to the surface. I needed to verify. So, I zipped up, grabbed a pair of shoes and a jacket from the closet, and headed out to the backyard.

"There he is! How 'ya doin', buddy? You up for good this time?"

Yep. There's a talking dog, alright. I dry swallowed a pill from each bottle and walked to the car.

6

I committed to memory the location of the house, but I had no guarantee that she still lived there. It had been a few years since I made my last pass by, and to tell the truth, I had no idea at the time if she was even living there. I couldn't even tell you if I had the correct house. The thing is, I never actually saw her during any of my little trips. I merely drove past a house where I was told she lived. I was working off of information that I got from an old friend of mine Chester Woods. *Woody*. That's what he wanted everybody to call him. I didn't on principle. I could never get past the connotation. The idea of hanging out with a guy named *Hard On* didn't sit well with me. I never told him that, though. I'm sure the thought occurred to him, as well. It had to. The problem was, you couldn't call him Chester either, since he absolutely hated that name. He didn't even like the acceptable shortened version Chet. Parents just don't spend enough time pondering the implications of the names they foist on their kids. So, whenever I needed to get his attention, I'd just call out, "Hey!" I swear he never caught on. And if he did, he didn't seem to care.

He was kind of a maniac, always finding ways to get into trouble. And finding ways to get me into trouble, too. So, it was never like there were these deep meaningful conversations where we needed to call each other by name in order to connect and make a point. When we weren't blabbering on about putting a band together, him on vocals, me on guitar - it was pretty much just the two of us driving around in this crappy old Ford LTD that he forever seemed to be putting new spark plugs into. The two of us getting drunk and looking for women. To clarify, we both got drunk, but he was the only one who ever found women. Okay, I found them, too, it's just that they never wanted to be me who found them. Of course, I was dating Audrey at the time, and not actively looking for women, anyway, but it still kinda bothered me. I don't know what it was that caused that reaction, or rather, lack of reaction, in women, but it sure lingered around long enough. He used to say that it wasn't anything I did, it was merely the fact that his personality was so powerful, women were too interested in him to ever notice anybody else. It was hard to tell if he was saying that because he was trying to make me feel better about the rejection, or if he was really a full blown egotist. At the time, I didn't care one way or the other: he had a fake I.D and a car, so we always got beer and he always drove. Well, not always, but most of the time. I did my fair share of driving, his car or mine, when I had one, but usually his. But for two reasons only - when he was either too plastered to drive, or if he was somewhere with a girl and wanted to be left alone. But regardless of who actually drove, it was a pretty good arrangement, and back then, you couldn't really ask for much more than that. Well, except for girls other than Audrey not liking me. That's something I figured would disappear once we no longer hung out together, like when the witch dies, the curse is lifted, but the damn thing lingered with me for a long time. Even after I went into the Army. And then, it only got worse.

There are a lot of vets who don't talk about their service, each with their own personal reasons, but by and large, I think it's because they would rather pretend that certain things didn't happen. Some are haunted for all their lives by images from the battlefield that can never be erased from their minds. And others, well, there are others like me, who are just plain humiliated by their experience. When I joined the service, I figured it would be a cinch getting women interested in me. I'd have the uniform, be in good shape, and he'd be nowhere around. But, of course, no luck. I was closing in on one year into my hitch, and I still couldn't get a woman to even look at me. Then it really hit rock bottom: believe it or not, I actually had a prostitute turn me down. She propositioned me as I was leaving a bar a couple miles from the base. I had no better offers, so I said okay and followed her back to this scummy little motel. I can't remember what we were talking about, but by the time we got back to her room, she told me to leave because my conversation depressed the hell out of her. After a few minutes of pathetic begging, I realized there was no changing her mind, so I got up to leave. But then she stopped me and told me I had to pay her at least twenty bucks just for wasting her time. When I told her I wouldn't, she started screaming. Probably not my best decision. Some guy came in the room, I guess it was her pimp, and started pushing me around. I didn't do or say anything to the guy. Not even fight back. I remember thinking *if I just go limp, maybe he'll stop hitting me and let me leave*. I was wrong. Not only did he beat the shit out of me, but he took everything I had. My wallet, my dog tags, and my uniform. For some reason, I blamed it all on Woody.

Even though it was a big deal at the time, hell, everyone in the entire base knew about it, it's not a subject I like to talk about. Sometimes people would nose around too much and ask why I left after eleven months, and I always said it was because I got a medical. It's really none of their damn business, is how I feel. The only ones who know are those people who have to read my record, like the government, or Melvin. I didn't even tell Julie the truth. I doubt I would have told Audrey either, even if I had seen her again. Julie eventually found out, though. It's amazing how much personal information you have to divulge just to do something simple like buy a stupid house. Really pisses me off. Sometimes I think I'm just going to live in a camper.

I sat parked in front of what I believed to be Audrey's house for quite a while before I even thought to look down at the dash and see what time it actually was. 3:35. Would have been a smart idea to have looked at the clock *before* I parked, so I knew how long I was sitting there. Stupid. Anyway, however long I was there, I saw no car in the driveway and no activity in the house. I felt like the stupid dog staring at the curtains for movement. I figured I'd wait until four, and if a car didn't pull up by then, I'd take off and come back some other time. Maybe. I don't know. This whole idiotic thing was Melvin's idea. This I can confirm: sitting in a parked car for who knows how long is not making me any happier. Especially with the sun angling the way it is right into my eyes. Apparently though, I'm not the only one being bothered by it, because no sooner than I thought it, the blinds in the front window of the house closed.

Now that I had confirmation someone was home, I shut off the engine and opened the door. Then some car came out of nowhere, squealing it's brakes and laying on the horn. I wondered for a minute if it was Audrey. I looked over and it slowed down just enough so the woman inside could let me see her giving me the finger. It was only a couple seconds, but I'm positive I didn't recognize her, so I don't know what that was all about. Maybe she thought I was someone else. Sometimes I think I have one of those faces. Not good looking or ugly enough to merit instant notice, and just indistinctive enough to blend in with a lot of other people. I would guess that if you really cared enough about it, there's both pros and cons to something like that. For example, say if you're a serial criminal, not being immediately recognizable would be good. You always hear the police searching for some guy who's, "White, medium height, medium build, brown hair." Well, hell, who isn't? Or a character actor even. I imagine it would be easier to play a variety of roles if you didn't have any overly unique qualities about you. I couldn't count the number of times I was watching some movie and didn't realize until later that the costar was in something like a thousand other movies I've seen. It's just that he didn't immediately stand out like the lead, so it doesn't hit you until you read the credits. But not everybody has the fortune or opportunity to exploit their ordinariness like that. Some people, probably the majority of them really, are forced to just live with it. I bet that for those people who have no choice but to live it, that being ordinary, more than anything else, is the single most distressful and overwhelming aspect of their lives. Not deaths in the family, or divorce, or medical problems, because that happens to everybody. But having to deal with the idea that you'll never be different or special. That you're *common*, and no matter what, it's never going to change. Poor bastards. Probably why so many people have hobbies.

It seemed like a nice enough house. Hard to tell though how big it was on the inside. It had a second floor, and probably a basement, too, so even if it wasn't very long front to back, the extra floors maybe gave you enough room. Depending on how many people lived there, of course. Toss in a couple kids, a mother-in-law and a dog, and it could get pretty crowded. Plus, all these houses around here were right on top of each other. Hardly any room at all between your neighbors. These goddamn suburban developers are amazing. All they care about is how much money they can squeeze out of the little land they have to work with.

And as soon as they're done building there, they pull up stakes and move to another plot of land to build on that. They don't give a shit about people as individuals, or what the community will be like. They don't give a second thought to all of the stress these people now have to deal with. The massive debt. The struggle to get by. The arguments. Financing the cost of trying to live your dream by actually living less of a dream than you ever envisioned. Not to mention the worst part: having to make new friends from the perfectly random group of neighbors that have been thrust upon you, all of whom are themselves trying to cope with the same stresses and problems that you are. All castaways themselves from some other place where they couldn't fit in. How is anybody in their right mind expected to ever live like that? There's no flexibility whatsoever. No room to grow. No possibility to try and do something different with your life. You're forced to settle and exist. The only people these developers care about are themselves. But, the truly incredible thing about it is how they cleverly brainwash everyone into thinking that they really *do* care about you. I mean, after all, they built you a house! And that's some long, hard work, right? Sure, it's crap quality-wise, paper thin walls and cheap materials, and more than you could really afford so you'll probably have to sell it in a couple of years anyway and buy something even smaller and crappier, but gosh, they took the time and built it for you! Aren't they just a swell bunch of fellas?

Full blown idiots, if you ask me. Both them and the short sighted people who buy their houses.

I stepped up onto the porch and rang the bell. I was afraid if I knocked, I might accidentally punch a hole through the door. A minute later, I thought I heard mumbling on the other side of the door, but who knows where the real source of it was coming from. I've already communicated with a dog – for all I knew, the door itself could be trying to tell me something. I really doubted it, though. The concept seemed rather illogical. Dogs are already alive, and have the apparatus to talk – mouth, vocal chords, that kind of crap. But a door? No, I ruled that one right out pretty fast. This wasn't some Disney cartoon, I was sure of that.

Yet, when the door opened, I saw this short, skinny man wearing sweat pants and a sleeveless tee shirt, and all I could think of were the Seven Dwarfs. Now, I don't know if that was déjà vu, or psychic powers, or what, but it was a little bewildering whatever it was. To think of one thing, then boom, see something associated with that exact thought a moment later. I noticed that happening a lot to me lately. Whoever this guy was, I was fairly sure he wasn't one of those dwarfs, but I couldn't get the thought out of my head. It's just that he just seemed so tiny. I gave a quick look at the wall behind him, half expecting to see pencil marks showing the progress of his growth over the years.

Now, I'm no hulking monster by any means. At last check, which was years ago, I was just over six foot, but I honestly think I've been shrinking a bit lately. Still, I think six foot would be a safe number to use. This guy couldn't be no more than five-three. I've seen short adults before, mostly women though, and never thought anything of it. And I honestly couldn't care less how tall or short the guy is. It's just that seeing him immediately followed my thinking about Disney cartoons, so the two connected into a whole. Like I said, I highly doubted the possibility, yet, I couldn't help but wonder that if it were true, which one would he be. No glasses, so that narrowed it down to six. He didn't seem old, but he was leaning on a cane. Now I couldn't remember if one of them had a cane or not. Was there a *"Limpy"*?

"What the hell you staring at?" he snapped.

Grumpy. Definitely. Don't know how I missed it. The scowl should have been a dead giveaway.

"You from the state?" he asked.

It seemed like such an odd question. I mean, I just met this guy, and he wants to know if I'm from out of state? It made no sense. You might as well just walk up to a stranger and ask, "Do you have coupons?" I don't know what made me think of that example, but I guess it's as good as any.

"This state?" I asked him back.

"Yeah, *this* state," he said, twisting up his face. "What other state would you be from?"

This idiotic line of questioning was starting to get to me. It was like that ancient Greek philosopher that would keep asking questions until he proved how much smarter he was than you. I remember Julie always telling me how much she admired him. Socrates, I think. I don't know, I always confused them. Well, whoever it was, I'm not sure why this little guy here was acting like him, but I didn't appreciate it.

"Look, buddy," he started, but then stopped awkwardly and grabbed his back with his free hand. He made like he was suddenly in too much pain to continue, but that somehow, he'd try and get through it. Seemed kind of suspicious.

"I don't know what you think you're going to find," he went on. "But I don't like the accusation. Regardless of whatever anybody else might say, this is legit."

Grumpy was quickly becoming Dopey. And even though I only met him a few minutes ago, I thought it was safe to say those were the only two dwarves he had the capacity to turn into. So, rather than just stand there and continue to bore myself silly on a guy with such limited range, I decided to move ahead with my mission.

"I'm looking for Audrey Preston. Does she live here?"

His little face squished together a little tighter. "Audrey *Preston*," he spit out. "There's no Audrey *Preston* here! Who the hell are you?"

If he didn't know who Audrey was, I didn't see how telling him who I was would help matters. And like I said, this guy was getting on my last nerve anyhow. Truth be told, he was really more like an evil troll than anything like a dwarf. Cartoon dwarves were at least somewhat amusing. I tried to imagine this one whistling a happy tune, but the odds seemed ridiculously high.

"What do you want?" he whined.

I leaned down closer to him and yelled. "I'm looking for Audrey Preston!"

I couldn't help myself. It happened before I had a chance to stop it. Like an unknown reflex.

That seemed to throw him. He recoiled and took a quick step back. A little too quick for a guy with a cane, if you ask me. It seemed obvious that I was getting nowhere with this guy, so I straightened up and was ready to walk away when I heard a voice from inside the house.

"Daryl?"

I turned back around and looked over the guy's head, which wasn't really difficult to do. There was Audrey at the opposite end of the room, smiling at me. Other than looking a little older since the last time I last saw her, she seemed pretty much the same. In fact, I was studying her face so much that I didn't even notice she was half naked until I watched her arms reach up over her head and slip on a shirt. Dopey, Grumpy, whichever one he was, didn't see that, though. He was too busy staring at me like a math test he wasn't prepared for.

"Oh my god, it is you," she whispered. She stepped in front of the gremlin and gave me a hug. I could feel her braless breasts rubbing back and forth over my chest. It seemed like a little too much movement for what I expected to be nothing more than a simple *long-time-no-see* hug. Not that I cared on way or the other. It was apparent that he cared, though. A little too much. I could see over Audrey's shoulder his little red face screw up even tighter. I still had no idea who this little creature was. Her boyfriend? The gatekeeper? The whole thing was very odd.

"I missed you," she said, rubbing her lips against my left earlobe and planting a tiny kiss.

This really set him off. He was leaning into that cane so hard, I thought it might snap in half. "What did you say?"

She looked directly into my eyes, but spoke to him. "Archie, go in the other room."

Archie. Another cartoon. This was getting weirder and weirder. On the bright side, at least he wasn't insisting on being called Archibald.

"Don't you tell me what to do. This is my house!"

"And this is my friend."

"What? From those goddamn chat rooms? I knew this would happen. You gave out your address, didn't you?"

"*Chat rooms*!" She stopped squeezing me and let out a loud, sarcastic cackle. I don't ever remember a noise like that coming out of her body before, but it sure sounded well practiced now. "Chat rooms are so fifteen years ago! This is what I'm talking about with you."

Suddenly, it looked like a light bulb turned on inside Archie's head. He broke into a sly grin and started shaking his finger at me.

"*Daryl*. I know who you are. You're the ex-boyfriend."

Then a light bulb went on in my head. "Why did you say she didn't live here?"

"You asked for Audrey *Preston*. She ain't that anymore. She's Audrey Casper now."

I looked down at him. "Like the little ghost?"

What the hell was it with the glut of cartoon references all of a sudden? I guess maybe I could write it down and ask Melvin. Maybe. But probably not. I don't know.

Audrey took hold of my hand and gave a little laugh as she turned to face him. His eyes darted down to our hands for a second, but shot right back up in no time at all.

"Like in *Archie* Casper. Her *current* husband."

"Jesus, Archie, I swear," she sighed. "You can be such a dullard."

"A what?" he snapped.

She didn't respond. Instead, she lifted her hand, the one that was still holding mine, and swiped away some stray hairs that had dropped across her face. On the way up, and on the way back down, too, she made damn sure to ever-so-casually brush the back of my hand against her breasts. It was difficult to tell if he saw anything from the angle he had looking up at us. I figured she was just trying to get a rise out of him. I didn't care for him too much anyway, so I didn't object. Plus, it's not like I was getting turned on by it, or anything. I mean, I'd felt these things before when we were going out, but any excitement I may have felt in the past was now replaced by a matter-of-fact, and not-all-that-meaningful, element that I was hard pressed to explain. I can remember a time when I adored these things, like they were somehow greater than life itself. Seriously. I don't think I could possibly calculate the amount of time I spent pondering her breasts. In retrospect, it was probably time I could have used doing something more important. What though, I haven't a clue, because nothing else I invested my time in ever amounted to anything worthwhile. Subconsciously, I was probably aware of that, which would explain why I spent so much time contemplating her breasts. Hell, I had to look forward to something, didn't I?

Then it hit me: Audrey's breasts. There's something that made me happy! On second thought, no. That was no good. I couldn't walk into Melvin's office telling him the only thing I could think of that ever made me happy was a pair of boobs. Knowing him, he'd probably want to see pictures of them for proof. Besides, I can't say if they actually made me *happy*. More than likely, they made me feel something that just I assumed was happiness. This whole endeavor was really starting to be a full blown pain in the ass.

Speaking of...

"You were in the service," he hissed. "Right?"

There was that damned déjà vu again.

"But, you ahh, had an early discharge," he added.

Early discharge? I wondered if that was his idea of sarcasm. I just shrugged, though. I didn't feel like reliving painful episodes of my past with this guy.

"Why?" he asked.

"Why what?"

"Why'd you leave so early?"

Audrey sighed. "Archie...shut up."

"You going to give me a home loan?" I asked.

Audrey erupted with that brand new sound again, and led me by the hand out the door to the front stoop. She slipped her fingers down to my wedding ring and gave it a few twists. It wasn't like she was trying to steal it, so I said nothing. Archie quickly followed behind us, seeming to rely less and less on the cane.

"I was in the service. Did my BCT at Fort Benning then stationed at Fort Hood. Where were you?"

"Goddamn it!" Audrey bellowed. "Who gives a shit?"

"Just curious, that's all. Having a talk. So, ahh, what was your MOS, Gleason?"

BCT and MOS. Here's yet another example of things that I used to think about a lot, well, maybe not *think* about, but at least be very aware of, that somehow disappeared from my mind. Which really isn't so bad in this case. My little stretch in the army was something I never wanted to begin with. Not that I have anything against the Army, or the Navy, or any the rest, because I don't. Well, I do get seasick, but you can't fault the Navy for that. It's just that the Army just wasn't the place for me. Now, I met a lot of guys who loved being in there. I mean, just loved it. Like it was the first thing in their life that ever made any sense to them. I never once felt like that myself. And not just in the Army, either. Never had that sense of fitting in anywhere.

My Military Occupational Specialty was what's known as 11B. Infantryman. Just about everyone else had a specialty, but not me. Didn't care, I guess. What was the point?

The little cartoon ghost started snorting out a series of sarcastic laughs. "You don't even know what I'm talking about, do you? You probably weren't even in the Army."

"He was in the Army," Audrey snarled. "He got kicked out for fighting, okay? He nearly killed an MP. That was it, right?"

How getting beat up by a pimp turned into me nearly killing an MP, I don't know. But it sounded a hell of a lot better than what really happened, so I stayed quiet.

"How many pushups can you do? I used to do a hundred in sixty seconds. Wanna go? Come on."

He dropped his cane altogether and started down the stairs, presumably to the concrete walkway so he could show off his push up skills. As if that mattered. It's not like we won World War Two because we could do more pushups than Hitler. I hate this shit. Go ahead. Do a *thousand* pushups in sixty seconds. Hell, do five thousand and have a heart attack. If that's what it takes to shut you up.

Audrey gave me a little nudge in my side, then looked down the street. "Did you see a flash?" She stopped then looked around for a second or two. "There it is again. Is someone in that car parked down there?"

Archie spun around towards Audrey, then followed her eyes to the other end of the street. There were at least a half dozen or so parked cars, but as far as I could tell, there were no flashes coming from any of them. Hell, you couldn't even tell if there were any people sitting in any of them. These discrepancies however, did little to quell Archie's paranoia. He took Audrey's words as concrete truth. Pure fear shot across his face, and for a moment he froze. I mean, not a single movement, not a single sound. He was like a statue in the park. And as stupid as he looked, it was the only thing that made him tolerable. Then my cell phone rang, and he snapped out of it, immediately grabbing his lower back with both hands and limping up the stairs and into the house.

"Don't forget your cane!" Audrey laughed. She picked it up and promptly chucked it against the door.

I squinted and took a good look down the street. "I don't think there's anyone down there."

She waved it off with a little laugh. "He's trying to get a settlement saying he was hurt at work. He thinks they got spies everywhere taking picture of him."

"Oh," I said. "And they'd use *flashbulb* cameras?

"Like he'd know any better,"

My cell rang a few more times. I really hate this thing. Number One, I have no use for it. I despise talking on the phone, so I never make any calls. And Two, the few times someone called me, it's never been anything but bad news. I'm not even sure why I bother to carry the thing around. Melvin suggested that if I found a soothing ring tone, or just put it on vibrate, that maybe I wouldn't get so aggravated by it. Well, right now I've got some stupid kid's song blasting out of my wildly vibrating pocket, and I honestly don't feel any less aggravated.

"Do you have to get that?"

"No."

The ringing and shaking eventually stopped. She stared deep into my eyes, then smiled and squeezed my hand again. "I can't believe you're here. It's been so long."

"I want to ask you something."

"Oh, yeah?" she giggled. "Still married, huh?" She gave my ring a few more twists.

"Yeah."

"Happy?"

"Well, that's what I wanted to talk to you about."

She took a deep breath, then looked around, like maybe there were people with cameras. "Not here. Do you know Casey's Bar and Char?"

"No."

"It's here in town. On Commons, right by the mall."

I wasn't hungry, but I thought maybe she was.

"Alright. You want to ride with me, or should I follow you?"

"Not now. Tonight. After eight."

"Why eight?"

"I don't start work until then."

"Oh. You work there."

"Yeah. I work there," she sounded a little snippy, but I let it pass. I figured the combination of having to live with this guy *and* work at a sports bar could put anyone in a mood from time to time.

"Okay."

"Casey's. On Commons. By the mall. And as close to after eight as you can."

She blew me a kiss and sort of skipped back into the house. I stared at the door for a minute. I'm not sure why, it just seemed like the thing to do. I didn't head back to the car until I felt that door was adequately stared at.

There's only one problem in regards to meeting her: I never heard of Commons Road, and had no idea which mall she was talking about. Every one of these suburbs is like a separate world onto itself. And I swear, if you're not familiar with each one, it's like you might as well be visiting from some remote Russian farm town. Even when I first got Audrey's address, I had no idea where it was or how to get there. I had to find the directions off the computer. But I didn't have a computer with me at the moment. My phone could text and take pictures, but I never bothered with the idea of getting one with internet access. Never thought I'd need it. I suppose I could just stop and ask someone. The way she said the name gave me the impression that it was a pretty well-known place. I'm sure all the locals will know where it is. If not, they're probably idiots. Which I'm not ready to rule out.

With that solved, I now found myself with yet another problem. What to do until eight? I couldn't think of one damn thing. I guess I could go to the restaurant now and wait in my car, but that seemed pretty stupid. I could sit here, but that seemed even worse. In the end, which to be honest was all of about two minutes of entirely useless thought, I decided to drive back to the house and wait. It was only about twenty or so miles back, so I could at least grab a few winks until I had to be at...what was the name of the place? Damn it. It'll come to me. I know it's by a mall. Like that helps, though. There's about four malls for every person around here.

God, I'm so tired. I don't get it. It's not like I haven't slept enough. Maybe I should take a multi-vitamin, or something. There was this dishwasher at the restaurant a few years back named Randy. Used to take vitamins a couple times a day. The guy had a ton of energy. Always bouncing around, talking, laughing, and singing. I swear, the guy never seemed to slow down. He drove me a little crazy, but you never saw cleaner dishes. Even his work station shined. And the guy never complained about overtime. Then one day, he was a no show for his shift. Never saw him again. Didn't even came in to pick up his last check. I wonder whatever happened to him? Never found out. Now I wonder if maybe he just crashed. A person can only put out so much until they finally hit their limit. And if that's going to happen, there's probably no amount of vitamins can stop it. Still, though, I have to do something. I know it won't be a bottle of vitamin water. I had a half a bottle of that and almost fell asleep in the driveway. Talk about useless. Maybe a couple cups of coffee. After I wake up from my nap, though.

I didn't check, and I have no idea why I never think to check, I should really try to remember that better, but I'm pretty sure I made decent time back from Audrey's. It was a fairly uneventful drive, seeing as how most of the idiots on the road were heading in the opposite direction - back to the suburbs from their ever-so-rewarding jobs in the city. Some people make me sick. It wasn't until a couple blocks or so from the house when things started to change a bit. I swear I was hearing voices again. People calling out. Not my name this time, but to each other. Like I was hearing the conversations of people who weren't there.

"Here he is!"

"He's here! Pass it on!"

"Are you sure it's him?"

"He's coming up to me now. Yeah, it's him! It's him!"

I wasn't driving fast, and I had my windows rolled down, so the voices were easy enough to hear. Weird thing is, the further I drove, the more I started having this strange sensation that they talking about me.

"He's at the stop sign now!"

Yep. It had to be me. I was at a stop sign, and there were no one other cars behind me, or at any of the three other stops at the intersection. Just me. Not sure why the hell I'm suddenly so interesting that someone would waste their time talking about me at a stop sign. Unless whoever this is, they do it with everyone. Some joke.

I kept my foot on the brake and sat there for a minute, curious to see how they'd react to me not moving. I tried my best to seem nonchalant. Give them the impression that I hadn't noticed them talking. I even put my cell phone to my ear and made like I was having a conversation. This gave me an opportunity to really take a good look at where they could be coming from. I scanned the whole area, but there was no one to be seen. Not on the street, not in cars, not on porches, not peering out windows. I even gave St. Francis' a good look. A church seemed like a likely spot for people to talk about me, but that was empty, too.

Then I started to wonder all over again if it was really happening outside. I mean, is it possible to have a voice in your head that just narrates what you're doing? Because, that would *really* be annoying. Forget about the droner or the nails-on-the-chalkboard guy - to have every trivial detail of your daily life announced back to you as you do it, like the play-by-play of the world's most boring sporting event?

First Announcer: "He's taking a pee."

Second Announcer: "And it's a long one."

First Announcer: "He got some on the seat."

Second Announcer: "And he's walking away without cleaning it. I can't believe it."

First Announcer: "I'm not surprised. This is nothing new for him. Remember back to the midnight pee of last Wednesday. What a mess that was."

If anybody ever worried that their life might be tedious and worthless, just wait until it's verified by a pair of commentators. That right there could be enough to send you over the edge. It's bad enough that you have to live it. I closed my eyes, hoping this wasn't a permanent thing. But the hope was short lived. The stupid voices came back.

"What happened?"

"He isn't moving?"

"What do you mean?"

"I mean, he's not moving. He's just sitting at the stop sign."

"He's sitting at the stop sign? I thought you said he was driving."

"The car! He's *in the car*, which is *sitting at the stop sign*! My god, Cupcake!"

"Don't get snotty! I just didn't understand, is all!"

If someone had asked me, say three months ago, if I could tell the difference between voices in my head, and voices outside my head, well, first, I'd think they were nuts. Who asks a question like that? But, if forced to answer, without a doubt I would have said, *yes, of course!* The difference would be obvious. I can now say with firm conviction that sometimes you can't tell. More importantly though, it can get to a point where it doesn't make a difference where the voices are coming from. If you hear them, you hear them. The source is unimportant. Certain things just push a guy no matter what. And at that moment, I was feeling pushed. There was no tower nearby, and I didn't have a rifle, but I did seriously consider driving the car head on into one of the corner houses. Which, believe it or not, is one of the main reasons I never bought a corner house.

"Daryl! Daryl! Hold up!"

I recognized that voice. It was the dog's. I opened my eyes and sure enough, there it was running through the intersection straight for the car. Maybe they weren't in my head after all. Another car pulled to a stop behind me, but I had to wait for the stupid dog before I drove off again. I wasn't sure how good its reflexes were and didn't want to risk hitting the thing. He ran over to the passenger side, jumped up to the window and pulled himself the rest of the way in with his front paws. Not bad moves for a stupid little dog.

"Glad I caught you," it panted.

"Did you just hear a bunch of people talking?"

"What do you mean? When?"

"Just a second ago. Like, people saying what I was doing. Where I was going."

"That wasn't people. It was some of the other dogs. I asked them to keep a lookout for you."

"So, now I'm hearing other dogs, too?"

"What, did you think you'd only be able to just hear one? That would be kind of weird, don't you think?"

I guess it did make sense.

"We should get out of here," he quickly said.

"Why?" And then it hit me. "What are you doing out of your yard?"

"She's dead."

"Who?"

"Gwen. My human."

"Oh."

That still didn't answer my question, though. How does his owner being dead explain him being out of the yard? I was about to ask him, but I got distracted. For some reason, there was suddenly a giant tangle of cars around me, trying to move in all directions, each driver screaming out their window and laying on the horn. I swear, this right here is one of the reasons the world is so screwed up. Everyone only looking out for themselves, trying to rush past everyone else, not caring about rules, or how they ruin things for others. Maybe the dog had a point. Getting away from this crap was a good idea. I took my foot off the brake and turned right.

When we reached the stop sign at the next corner, I saw flashing lights a couple blocks down to my left.

"What's going on down there?"

The dog looked over. "That's what I'm talking about. It's the police. They're looking for you because of my human."

"Me? Why?"

"Well, for one, there was a footprint trail. You must have stepped in some shit. Leads straight to your house."

That seemed kinda familiar.

The dog took a couple sniffs. "Is that why you're wearing Ben's shoes? And coat?"

I looked down, and I swear it was the first time I noticed what I was wearing. I guess I grabbed them without thinking this morning. That was kind of weird.

"How do you know they were his?"

"Dude, I know what he smells like."

"Why would you know that?

"'Cause the guy's my bud."

"*Was*."

"What do you mean?"

"He died. A few months ago."

"No. Really? That's why I haven't seen him," Then he paused for a minute. I swear, it almost sounded like he was crying.

"How did he die?" he sniffed.

"Heart attack."

"Why didn't you tell me?"

Why didn't I tell him? Is this thing serious? I'll make a mental note to alert the dog community whenever anything like his comes up again. Idiot. I took my foot off the brake and made a left.

"Where are you going?"

"Going back to the house. Didn't you just say the police were looking for me?"

"Right," the dog said. "Which is why you probably want to lay low for awhile. Anywhere. Just away from here."

"Why? I didn't do anything."

"What are you going to tell them when they ask what you were doing there last night? That you got sick of listening to me *bark*, as you put it, and were on your way over to kill me?"

"No..."

"And what about you breaking into the house? How are you going to explain that?"

"I didn't break into the house. The door was open."

"Loud, underfed dog. Unlocked back door. And remember that smell? That was probably her. So, ah, why didn't you report any of it to the police?"

This was really getting me pissed off. "Because you told me this morning that she wasn't home! And I took your word for it!"

He sighed and tilted his head. I can't even begin to tell you the new level of pissiness this brought me to.

"*I* told you? Is that what you're going to tell the cops? A dog told you his human was gone? You don't think that might get them a little suspicious? Of you?"

I pulled the car over in an empty spot on the street about a block and a half away from the police cars. I needed to think about this. I wasn't crazy about driving away and giving anyone the impression I did something wrong, but on the other hand, I certainly didn't want to hang around and get accused of something I'm not guilty of, either.

"Why can't you just tell them?" I asked.

That would be the easiest way to handle it. But, heaven forbid anything easy ever happens to me!

"Hate to break it to 'ya, Bud, but I tried, and no one understood me."

"Well, maybe there's some other cop at the station that could. You know, like a sergeant or a captain. And don't call me '*Bud*'. I hate that."

"Sorry." He stopped for a second, took a deep breath, then went on. "My whole life, I've only met two people who could understand what I was saying. You're number two. You want to take the chance that there's a number three, and it might be a cop working at this precinct?"

I bit my freaking lip I was so mad. I made a three point turn and headed back down the way I came. The dog spun around and watched the scene behind us get smaller and slowly disappear.

"The way I look at it," the stupid thing started. "She probably died a long time ago. It wasn't a murder. You're the first person who's been in the house since she went missing. I would have smelled anyone else getting in there. It'll probably take them a couple days to figure that out themselves. Just lay low for a little while 'til it blows over."

"Where'd you learn to talk like that?"

"She used to watch a lot of cops shows. You pick things up."

"Well, it sounds stupid," I told him. "Especially coming from you."

"What the hell's that mean?"

"You. You're a dog. That's what it means." Geez. I guess dogs really are stupid.

"What's with the attitude? You should be happy this dog watches cop shows, otherwise you'd be in jail right now. All I'm doing is trying to help the guy. Humans..."

'*Humans*'? What the hell is that about? I'd like to know where this stupid thing thinks it has the right to be exasperated with "humans" as a species. It lives in a goddamn backyard! Its experience with irritating humans is incredibly limited at best. Hell, I've come across more annoying humans just today than this stupid mutt has ever dealt with in its lifetime. I really wanted to go off on the dumb thing about it. I really did. But then I thought I should give it the benefit of the doubt for being so stupid. I mean, it's not the dog's fault that it hasn't met as many infuriating people as I have. Lucky him, really. No shit, lucky him. With all of the crap you have to put up with as a human, I think there's something to be said for being a dog. No work. No responsibilities. Just live in a backyard and have someone take care of anything you need. Sex whenever you want it. And apparently, you're even able to get in a few hours of TV a day! Not too bad, if you ask me. Sure as hell beats being a human. Of course, there's always the problem of what happens if your owner just up and dies on you without warning, and you're stuck in that backyard for a month without food. It's not like there's an awful lot of job opportunities for homeless dogs. Of course, there's a parallel here with humans, too – up to a point, everything can seem great, then all of a sudden, it can all fall apart without you even realizing it. And then what?

I gave a quick peek over to my right, wanting to see what he thought about all of it, but the stupid thing was halfway hanging out the window, licking at the breeze with his tongue. I had a feeling it wasn't going to give me it's full attention if I started a conversation right now.

Dogs. How 'bout that? I turned back to the street and saw that I was suddenly closer to the expressway ramp than I thought. I had to force my way past a couple of bastards who wouldn't let me get in front of them and accelerated onto the onramp. Idiots.

7

I don't know what the hell I was thinking, but the next thing I knew, I was parked outside of my house. Not my grandfather's where the cops were, but the one Julie still lives in. Must have been some reflex. I honestly don't ever remember thinking this was where I wanted to go. It was like I was on autopilot, or something. Which is something I do a whole lot more than I'd actually like to admit. And after every occurrence, I get mad at myself for not paying attention and swear to never allow it to happen again. So, I make a promise to myself to focus more in the future. Because that's really the root of it right there. Not focusing. But, here I am again, on the landing strip of yet another stupid autopilot trip. You'd think I'd have learned by now. I don't know, maybe it's a good thing I ended up here anyway. I mean, Melvin wanted me to ask people about being happy, and I'd need to get around to Julie eventually, so why not now? Some reason, though, I couldn't get myself to get out of the car. After a minute or two, the dog finally noticed and spoke up.

"Why are we stopped? This your safe house?"

"No. And stop it with the cops and robbers talk. *Safe house.* Are you serious?"

"Where are we then? I smell a female. That girl you went to see this morning?"

"That was Audrey. This is Julie's."

"Dude! Two in one day! Now you're talking."

"Audrey's my ex-girlfriend. Julie's my wife."

"You wife? If she's your wife, why is she here and you at Ben's?"

Here we go again. First Melvin, now the dog. Everyone prying into the details of my personal life. Maybe I should turn it around and start asking personal questions about them. I really should. Wonder how they'd like that? I got out, slammed the door and marched up the steps. That dog was really starting to piss me off again. I was so mad at the stupid thing that I couldn't even get my key to slide into the lock. I tried wiggling it in, angling it in, and turning it upside down. Nothing. I know it's the right key, so why won't it work?

"Are you sure this is your house?"

I looked down and wouldn't you know it, the dumb thing's head was cocked to the right. Its right, my left. I wanted to kick it down the stairs when I saw that.

"Get back in the car."

I put my hand on the knob and was just about ready to jam the key in good, when it turned and was pulled opened from the inside.

"That her?" the dog asked.

I nodded to the dog then took a long look at Julie.

"Eh," the dog went on. "You could do better."

"What are you doing here, Daryl?" Julie asked. And not too pleasantly, I might add. Not that I really care one way or another how she sounds, but it made me wonder if maybe she had trouble with her key, too. I hoped it wasn't that she understood what the dog said, because that wouldn't end up good. Just in case it was, I shot the dog a nasty look.

"Shut up," I told it. "That's not nice." And to really sell it, I sternly wagged my finger at it. I even jingled the keys a little. I thought it added a little something. Which, I guess, it did.

"I changed the locks," she calmly said, looking over at the key. Now, she was a little too pleasant. "You know, the police called here looking for you. What's going on?"

"Nothing. My neighbor died. Is that why you changed the locks?"

"No. I did that last week."

"Why? What happen?"

"Nothing happened," she said. "I was trying to *prevent* something from happening."

"What?"

"This. You showing up unannounced and trying to come inside."

"*Much* better," the dog mumbled to itself.

I spun my head around and snapped at the stupid thing. "Will you shut up about that?"

"I didn't know you got a dog," Julie said. "What's its name?"

"I don't know. It's not my dog."

"Steve," the dog said. "I thought I told you."

I had to look back down at it. "That's not your name."

"Yeah, it is."

"Who names their dog *Steve*?"

That's just stupid. Yeah, it's better than *Steven*, but that's not the point. Only, I didn't feel like getting into it with him right now. Not when Julie's looking like this. I've known her long enough by now to know she was mad. No matter how much she pretends not to be. She has this habit of forcing herself to keep it together – like a pre-school teacher on her first day of work trying to stop the kids from fighting. Nonetheless, I wanted her to know this fight wasn't my fault.

"I've only known him for a couple of days," I told her. "I think he's a bit of a liar."

"Hey!" Steve snapped. "Where's that coming from? Not cool!"

Now she looked worried. Don't know why – not sure how much trouble a lying dog could cause.

"The dog is a liar?"

"Yeah."

"Oh my god. There is really something wrong with you, isn't there?"

"No. I'm telling you, it's not me. It's him."

"Now you've got the police looking for you. I wish you would listen to me, Daryl. I know what's good for you."

"That's why I'm here."

"Really?" she asked. A sense of calm seemed to spread over her. It's pretty obvious she just wants to make sure I'm okay. Melvin is so far off on his assumptions about her. I really wish he could understand.

"I don't trust her," Steve said to me. "I'm not getting a good hit off her."

Now this thing, too. *Steve...*

"Did you finally decide to give me the account number?" She smiled out a sigh and stroked her fingers across the side of my face. "It really is for the best, sweetie."

"No. That's not why."

The corners of her mouth curled up and she slowly brushed off my jacket with her hand, like it was covered in loose hair. "Daryl, I'm just thinking of you. You need someone responsible watching the money. So you don't do something stupid."

"Money?" Steve yapped. "Daryl, dude. Seriously. This ain't good."

Before I had a chance to set the stupid thing straight, a voice came from inside the house. "Let me handle him, Jewel."

Without having to look, I knew it was *Robert*. Why he was hiding inside was beyond me, but I preferred it to actually having to look at him. Julie didn't miss a beat, though.

"Stay out of this, Robert."

The dog stuck his head inside the doorway and gave a couple of sniffs. Julie didn't miss this opportunity, either. Without even looking down, she placed her foot underneath Steve's belly and firmly nudged him back out on the porch. This is what's great about Julie: in the span of five seconds, she took care of two intruding idiots without even showing one sign of being flustered. I wish Melvin was here to see this.

"She does that again," Steve mumbled to himself. "I'm gonna bite her. Wife or no wife."

"So, why *are* you here then, Daryl?"

"Doctor Melvin asked me to find out something."

She steadied herself against the door frame and pulled herself blank. "Okay. What?"

"Was I ever happy?"

The serene blank slate quickly transformed into an angry scowl. "What the hell is that supposed to mean?"

I shrugged. "I don't know. Do you ever remember me being happy?" I tried to rephrase it, but a question like that seemed pretty simple enough already.

She straighten up and spoke in calm, measured breaths. "I withdrew the divorce papers. Because you needed help. Because I care about you, Daryl."

"Yeah, I know."

Robert's voice oozed from inside the house again. "Jewel, just let me..."

I hate it when he calls her that. *Jewel.* It's so lame. But she cut him right off before he could go any further. "For the last time, Robert."

Damn, Julie's great. I was getting the sense she might be rethinking this whole living arrangement. Buyer's remorse, so to speak.

"Come on, let's get out of here," Steve panted.

"Just wait," I told him. At least, I think I said it out loud. It was hard to tell. I know for sure that I thought it. It's just that I started staring at Julie's face, and I felt like I was slipping into one of those time-loss trances again. I wasn't aware of anything else in the world but her lips: naturally red and thick, and curved right now into a big smile. She looked so happy.

"Let's go somewhere and talk about this. Maybe get a couple drinks? I know: we can go to Marcella's. Order a couple steaks. Bottle of wine. Or two."

I knew where she was going with this. Marcella's was our place. The restaurant we were at when we decided to get married. I always thought there must be something magical about Marcella's, because prior to that night, I had never once thought about marrying Julie. Not that I was against it, or anything. We had been going together for a while, and at that point the sex was pretty good and happening on a regular basis. Looking back on it, I guess you could assume we were happy, but trying to recall how it felt escapes me now. I know at the time I was pretty darn happy about having a lot of sex. Who the hell wouldn't be? But that's the only clear realization I can muster.

The night was originally set up to be a mini celebration for me being asked by her father to become the assistant manager of his restaurant. I thought we should go there that night, to her dad's place, but she said it would be tacky for the new assistant manager, and possibly future co-owner, to be openly celebrating in front of the other workers. I guess that made sense. So, we went to Marcella's and somehow were able to get the best table in the house – a little two-seater right next to the fireplace. I remember we sat next to each other, rather than across from each other, even though the table was rectangular and meant to have people sit across from each other. But Julie said she didn't care, and moved her chair next to mine. I can't even tell you how many bottles of wine we must have gone through. I'm not even sure if the food or the service was any good. All I know is by the end of the night I had a future wife in addition to a future job and it finally felt like my life had some meaning. Doesn't feel that way anymore. I'd sure as hell like to know what happened and when. Not that it would do me any good now, anyway. I mean, it's not like there's going to be some kind of test on it where I'll be required to know dates, or anything. That would only help if you were able to go back into time so you could fix it. And as far as I know, that's not possible. No matter what the TV shows claim.

"What do you think," she whispered. "Wanna go? It's still early, I bet we can get our table."

Then it hit me. "I can't," I told her. "I have to meet Audrey at eight."

She exploded. "Your *ex-girlfriend* Audrey?"

"Yeah."

"What the hell are you doing meeting her? Did you forget you're still married?"

Steve mumbled something, but I didn't catch it over Julie's screaming.

"She said she wanted to talk about me being happy," I said. "And she asked first."

"Cancel it."

I started to tell her I couldn't even if I wanted to, seeing as I don't have her phone number, but before I had the chance to speak up, she grabbed my arm and started trying to pull me inside.

"You're not going anywhere," she scowled. "Now get in here."

Steve was now yelling a stream of obscenities at her, and I don't know if she understood the exact translation, but I was pretty sure she was aware of the intent. She let go of my arm and took a step back.

"Call him off, Daryl."

Robert apparently forgot Julie's instructions to stay out of it. He rushed to the door, pushed aside Julie, and came right at me. Only, he neglected to look down, and stepped directly into a pile of freshly produced shit. Robert's foot went up, while the rest of him went down. It looked like a banana peel gag from a silent movie. Julie's attention quickly turned from me to him. She tried to catch him in mid air, but the doorway was too narrow for her to get into any proper position. As a result, he bounced into her, and they both went down: she hit her back against the door then crashed on her ass, while he went head first onto the hardwood floor.

I remembered back when we originally bought the house, we were given the option of carpeting or wood floors. I wanted carpeting. She wanted wood. So that's what we got. Mahogany. A very hard wood, indeed.

Julie moaned in pain and desperately tried to wiggle free her legs from under a limp, motionless Robert. She screamed out his name, even slapped his face twice, but he offered no response. It struck me as odd how little emotion I felt about this. Here was this Robert, a guy who I really don't like, lying in a heap on the ground, and I couldn't even manage a snicker of delight. I mean, you'd think an event like this would finally register a click or two on the happy scale. But, nothing. I couldn't even get myself to feel sorry for him. Or Julie. It was kind of an awkward moment. It seemed like I should say something, comforting or otherwise, but other than possibly reminding her of her previous flooring decision, I couldn't think of a damn thing.

Steve was taking deep breaths to get himself to stop laughing. "Come on, dude, let's blow. You can thank me later." And he scampered down the stairs.

He was probably right: I really didn't think I was going to get anywhere else with this conversation tonight. So, I followed him down the stairs and headed back to the car.

"I swear to God, Daryl," Julie screamed.

I stopped just before the street and turned back around. That look she was giving me. I couldn't count the number of times in my life that I've been on the receiving end of that stare. Shortly after we were married, we went to a small bed and breakfast for a long weekend. I guess it was okay, I don't really remember the trip itself all that much. My most vivid memory is of the day we came back home and realized that I had never turned off the TV before we left. Which wouldn't be so bad if it wasn't for the fact that some stupid video game was left running, as well. While we were gone, the image of the game menu burned into the TV screen and ruined it. That was the first time I remember seeing that look on Julie's face, and believe me, that image has been burned into my mind just as indelibly as the video game image was burned into the TV. So, when I saw it again, I thought for sure that I was in for it. Only, it didn't happen. This time she just stared at me in silence for a few seconds, then started slapping Robert in the face again. I'm no CPR expert, but if he did happen to come to, with the power and fury that she was whacking him, I bet he'd immediately go unconscious again. I figured I should get out of there before she could get her legs free and do the same to me.

8

Steve and I headed back to meet Audrey. Still with no idea of where that actually was. I turned onto a main street near her neighborhood, but I swear, it felt like I was driving around in circles. According to the clock radio on the dash it was seven thirty two, so I did have a little bit of time to sort through my brain and find the name of the place before she wanted me to be there. Of course, now it was almost dark, and the possibility of stumbling across it seemed rather remote.

Steve took a couple loud sniffs. "Where are we going?" he asked. "We passed this same spot at least four times already."

"I'm supposed to meet Audrey somewhere, but I can't remember where."

"You keep going down the same couple blocks. Do you expect some gang of magical fairies to suddenly make it appear?"

"You know, there's no reason for the attitude."

"Oh no? How about this: I'm hungry and I really have to take a piss. I think those are pretty good reasons."

"Well, it's dark, you know? I'm driving and trying to read street signs."

"Whatever. I have an idea: How about you take a left up here instead of your customary right, and I'll read the signs to you?"

Okay, I admit it: I guess maybe I was lost and going over the same old ground. I just wasn't too crazy about having a dog point it out to me. So, I eased over to the next lane and when I got to the light, I turned left. I tried to read restaurant names to myself while Steve called out the street names and suggested directions.

"Milhorn," Steve said.

I shook my head. I knew a guy a long time ago named Milhorn; if that was the street, I would have remembered it because of that.

"You read pretty good for a dog."

"Gee, thanks," he said back – rather sarcastically, I might add. "Dawkins."

Again, I shook my head. That's weird, I knew someone named Dawkins, too. I guess the more people you know, the greater the chance of something like this happening.

"Kleegman."

I knew a Kleegman, too! Tony Kleegman. Went to high school with him. In fact, I went to high school with Dawkins and Milhorn, too. And the main reason I knew them was because they each dated Audrey right before I did. This was too much of a coincidence. The dog was messing with me, or something. I pulled over to the curb and threw the car into park.

"Why are we stopping," Steve asked. I could tell by his tone that he really had to pee, but I didn't care. I needed to get to the bottom of this.

"What's with you saying those names?"

"I thought that's what you wanted. You said they were hard to read."

"Those weren't the real street names!"

"On the little green signs, right?"

"Don't pretend you don't know what you're doing. Those were all names of guys Audrey dated."

"Dude. That's weird."

"No, it's not. What are you trying to do?"

"I'm not trying to do anything. How would I know the names of the guys she's dated? You think I'm psychic, or something?"

I didn't know what to say. I really didn't. It just seemed like way too many coincidences. It occurred to me, though, that okay, for the sake of argument, let's say he is psychic. What would his motive be for doing all this? I mean, it's true, some people don't need a secret agenda for messing with other people. They just do it out of sheer nastiness. I couldn't tell if Steve had that streak in him, or not. Maybe he's the kind of dog who thinks messing with humans and getting them all worked up and paranoid is fun. I've seen humans do the *pretend-to-throw-the-stick* gag with dogs. Maybe this is some form of revenge. Then again, if I'm one of the only humans who can understand him, why would he risk pissing me off like that? It didn't make any sense. Unless he's really off his nut, which I suppose is possible. I don't know him all that well. Guess I'm just going to have to keep a close eye on him.

I dropped it into drive and pulled back into traffic, even though I still had no clue where I was going. I was starting to wonder if I was ever going to figure it out.

"Audrey ever date a guy named Commons?"

I thought about it a second. The name Commons sounded familiar, but I couldn't place it.

"Why?" I asked him. "You know something?"

"That's the street we just passed. Wanted to see if the boyfriend theme was continuing."

Then it hit me. I slammed on the brakes and made a u-turn over the yellow line. I must not have been the only one who was lost, because I heard a lot of honking and what I think was a crash. Some people drive like morons. It was getting close to eight and I had to get moving, so I made a conscious effort to keep my eyes open for future idiots.

"What the hell you doin'?" Steve asked. "I think I let a little go on the seat."

"Commons is the street she said. Which way you think?"

I stopped the car in the middle of the street just before the intersection, so I didn't have to make anymore last second maneuvers depending on the way he chose. He stuck his nose out the window and took a couple sniffs.

"Hmm. Left."

I accelerated and turned left like he said. And I have to say, I was more than a little surprised at just how busy this street was, and I never even heard of it before. Okay, I know there are millions of places I've never seen or heard that are just as busy, but what struck me as odd is that I felt like I should have known this place. Audrey lives here and it's not all that far from my house, but I knew so little about it that it almost seemed foreign. I half expected to get out of the car and not recognize the language.

Suddenly Steve screamed. "Pull over in that parking lot!" So, without giving it a second thought, I jerked the wheel to the right and stepped on the gas. Only one problem. There was no driveway. The car jumped a curb and we tore through a row of bushes. I thought for a moment about putting on the breaks, but quickly abandoned the idea. I mean, what good was stopping in the middle of a bush? I ricocheted between the steering wheel and the seat, trying my best to keep a grip. It seems odd to think, but I was mildly surprised at just how thick these bushes were. It seemed like we were driving in them for quite some time. There was really no way of telling, but it felt like maybe we were hitting them length-wise, rather than cutting through the middle. Strange.

Once we were finally out, it was just a few feet of short grass before we in the parking lot and were back on asphalt again. There weren't as many cars in there as I would have expected. Maybe that explains why it was so busy on the street. Who knows? I pulled into a spot and turned to see if Steve was okay, but instead of being on the seat, he was spread out on the passenger floor, looking very much like one of those long fuzzy things you lay at the bottom of a door to keep the cold air from coming in.

"Steve?"

It took a few seconds, but he eventually spoke up. "What the hell was that?" is what he finally said.

"You said turn," I told him. "And I turned. I told you I can't really see in the dark. I assumed you were watching for me."

"Open the door, please." His voice was calm, but he sounded a little irritated. I figured maybe he hit his head on the way down to the floor, so I didn't press him on it. He immediately jumped out and ran to the back wheel and lifted up his leg.

"Ooooooh, mama," he mumbled to himself. Although, you could barely hear him over the noise from his stream.

"Do you have to do that on my car?"

"Hey, you're lucky I didn't do it *in* your car."

He had a point, I suppose. I can remember a few times when I was trapped in a car and really had to go. Then again, when I finally did get out and go, it wasn't on the back wheel. Stupid dog.

"That felt good," he said. "Don't you ever have to go?

I just shrugged. I don't know, I go when I have to go. Don't really think about it that much.

"How 'bout you get me something to eat now?"

He was kind of a pushy little thing. I don't see why he couldn't just find something on his own. Dogs have been around for thousands of years. Don't tell me every single one of them down through history needed a human to get it food. Not only that, it's not like I had all this available time to go looking for a pet food store.

"I have to meet Audrey. Can't you wait a bit?"

"Look, there's a place right over there," he motioned his head to the other side of the parking lot. "Run in there and get me a couple a cheeseburgers. It'll take two seconds."

I took a look to where he was pointing, but I couldn't really make it out. Still, though, there was something about the place.

"Says, Casey's Bar and Char," Steve said.

"How 'bout that. That's where I'm supposed to meet Audrey."

"No shit. Well, ain't that a co-inky-dink?"

Co-inky-dink. I hate that crap. I really, really do. Even if it was one.

I peeked at my watch. It was just a little before eight, so I started my way across the ridiculously huge parking lot. I guess it would have made more sense to get back in the car and find a spot closer to the restaurant, but my legs were feeling stiff from sitting for so long, and I figured it was good to give them a stretch. Steve followed alongside of me, sniffing and mumbling something to himself. I couldn't make out what he was saying, but that was fine by me. I had other things on my mind, and really didn't feel like having to deal with him, too.

I started thinking about the questions I wanted to ask Audrey, but for some reason, they all sounded really stupid. I have no idea why I didn't prepare for this. *"Was I ever happy? Were we ever happy?"* I saw how well that line of questioning worked with Julie. The other thing that occurred to me was, how in the hell would she even know? How does anyone really know if someone else is happy? I mean, if I don't even know whether or not I'm happy, how would anyone else? All you can really do is guess, or take their word for it. Here's a great example. Well, not so great, really, from my end of it. A few months ago, Julie told me that she used to fake orgasms when we had sex. And according to her, it wasn't just a few here and there, either. It was an amount somewhere in the mid triple digits. All this time, I thought she was, you know, enjoying things, *happy*, but then I find out she was just pretending. Thinking about it now, I mean, why would she do that? And over such a long period of time? Honestly, why wouldn't she have just said something? Did she think I wouldn't care? Did she think I couldn't be bothered? It's not like I wasn't trying, because I was. Hell, there were some nights when I tried quite a few times. So, the effort was there, but it's not really my fault if they weren't effective. Primarily, because I thought they were. So, I started wondering if maybe this was actually her problem and she was just passing it on to me. But then she started in with how she never had to fake anything with Robert. I didn't know what to say after that. Robert had no problem finding the words, though. He laughed and offered to give me advice on how to get women off. I knew what that was, though. That was just him trying to act cool in front of Julie. Guys like that never say anything unless they have an audience to impress. Besides, I already knew what to do. At least, I thought I did. Then a disturbing realization hit me: I couldn't remember the last time Julie and I had sex. If I had to make a guess, I'd have to say it was well over a year. Maybe even more. Not sure why, either. I sorta remember it started out where I'd come home from work and she was already in bed sleeping. No big deal. But as the months went on, I'd come home and she wouldn't even be there, so then I'd just go to bed alone. Then I started coming home and Robert would be there, and I started sleeping in the other bedroom. I can't believe this whole thing was all about orgasms. I mean, if it was, why didn't she just say something?

I felt something grabbing at my pants leg and I almost fell on my ass. It was that stupid dog. I swear, if he bit through these pants...

"Hey! Stop, will 'ya?"

"You stop. I'm going to get you some food in a minute. Quit eating my clothes."

"I've been yelling at you to stop for the past two minutes."

Two minutes. How the hell would he know? He doesn't have a watch.

"I know," I told him. "Two cheeseburgers."

"No, not that. Come here."

He ran over to the back door of a blue Toyota. A female voice was coming from inside.

"Get your human to reach in the window and unlock the door, would 'ya?"

I looked inside the car, and there was a little white poodle with a big pink bow staring back at me.

"Don't worry," Steve told me. "She won't bite you."

"Look," I said. "If you think I'm going around freeing dogs, you got another thing coming."

Steve smiled. "You ain't letting her out. You're letting me in. In more ways than one, if you know what I mean."

"You want me to break into the car so you can have sex?"

"Damn right," he said. "Now, come on. Snap snap." He was up on his hind legs trying to peer through the window. Believe me, it wasn't a sight you wanted to see.

"Your human can understand you?" the poodle asked him.

"Yeah. And you, too. Pretty wild, huh?"

The poodle turned and glared at me. "Then listen to me, asshole. You open this door and let him in, or I'll hunt you down and gnaw your freaking leg off."

Not that I was worried, because I really didn't think the poodle was capable of following through on her threat. I mean, sure, she seemed pretty aggressive, but it really just came down to size. And the truth of the matter was she was far too small to take off a human leg. I guess if I was incapacitated somehow, and if she had all day, she might be able to bite through, but still, it didn't seem plausible. She was spunky, though. You had to give her that. The window was left slightly open to give her some air, which was just barely enough for me to reach in. Luckily my arm was just long enough. The damn button was like halfway down the door, then I still had to slide it over. I miss the old days when all you had to do was reach as far as the bottom of the window and pull up on a little button.

As soon as it was unlocked, I opened the door then slid out my arm. By that point, Steve was already inside.

"How long you gonna be?"

"No idea," I told him.

"Alright," he said. "I'll find you. Just don't close the door all the way, so I can get back out."

I don't know. I shut the door a little bit then walked back toward the restaurant. What was I supposed to do? At least he wasn't bugging me.

In addition to it having a stupid name, I wasn't all that impressed with Casey's Bar and Char. The first thing I noticed was how it reminded me of Melvin's office building. Not in the layout, but in the sameness. In the fact that it seemed like just about every other goddamn restaurant you walked into nowadays. It had a chain store feel to it, even though I was fairly certain it wasn't even part of a chain. Rows of wooden booths against the walls, tall wooden tables scattered across the floor, oversized bar in the middle of the room with very few customers seated at it. Hell, it even had the requisite sports banners and neon beer signs. And everyone knows how important those are! I'll even bet my inheritance that the menu's full of items like, "The Char-burger" and the "Char-terhouse steak". Probably even a little Mexican dish called "Casey-dillas". I hate that crap. The thing with these places is that they want so desperately to make you feel comfortable, they won't dare risk doing something even slightly different. They want so badly for you to like them that they lose all sense of their own identity. Why in the world would anyone choose to be like that? Unless it wasn't some premeditated decision. I guess it's possible it simply evolved that way over time. Everyone starts with a similar basic structure. But rather than go off and be yourself, you start seeing what customers like in other places, and slowly add that to your décor, in the hope that they will eventually like you just as much. Before you know it, there's no distinguishing you from the next guy. Or, next restaurant. And really, all that can be done at that point is either a total make over, or to be replaced altogether. Only to have the cycle repeated again. Seriously, it has to stop somewhere.

Get Happy

I remember wanting to shake things up and try something a little different with my restaurant. Okay, it wasn't really my restaurant, but that was part of the problem. Business started dropping off a little bit and I thought I'd tweak a few things. Nothing major. One thing I thought it needed was a new paint job. I was sick of looking at the same beige walls every day. So, for a couple of nights after we closed, I stayed until five in the morning painting. I fully expected it to go at least a week, but was surprised at how much I could get done when I was by myself. I thought it looked pretty good. Not good enough, though, I guess. It wasn't long before the regulars started to complain to my father-in-law Chuck, who was the actual owner. On paper only. In reality didn't do anything but complain and pocket all the profits.

It wasn't just that they disapproved of the change in color, which was a very cheerful sage green, and still to this day can't imagine anyone disliking it. Apparently, there was a long list of problems that they were holding their tongues about, and according to them, the new paint job was the last straw. It was the service, (too much turnover, too many young people), the menu, (I switched from serving French onion soup to potato because very few people ever ordered it), the parking, (the spaces were too small, even though the size *never changed* in over forty years), the lighting, (some said too dark; others said too bright. Go figure), the scent of the soap in the ladies room, (it smelled like soap), and about a dozen others. Someone even complained that our cashier gave out too many pennies when making change. This unexpected uprising pushed Chuck off the deep end. He raced from his winter house in Florida and accused me of every offense in the book. His main concern though, the one I heard over and over again, was that I had been doing my best to put him in the poor house.

He cut my salary by twenty percent and stepped in as manager for three months. *To teach me a lesson.* I'm sure he would have stayed on longer than that, but when they found him dead in his car, that sort of ended his tenure. It actually ended a lot more than I ever anticipated. Within days, Julie and I found out that Chuck was way over his head in debt. He somehow finagled six separate loans out on the restaurant for over three million dollars – all of this long before I painted the walls green and purchased soap that smelled like soap. The day after he died we were visited by members of a "neighborhood organization" who let us know that he had outstanding loans with them, as well. The restaurant was quickly boarded up and every last thing Chuck owned was turned over to the various creditors. I remember sitting in the parking lot one day watching as they took away the last few things left inside: the neon beer sign and two sports pennants that he had put up the week before he died.

They never did figure out if he was murdered, or if it was suicide. The bullet in his head didn't do much talking. Even two years later, I'd still get phone calls from detectives asking me if I recognized a name as an acquaintance of his. I never did, mainly because Chuck never told me anything worthwhile when he was alive.

I was next in line, so when the hostess asked *"How many",* I told her I was meeting somebody. Admitting that you're only a party of one is never advisable. I mean, it's bad enough that I'm even in a place like this, but to come here by yourself? The place wasn't my choice, so I don't want to take the blame for it. Besides, *parties of one* always attract a lot of unwanted attention. You walk in with a party of twelve, and no one blinks an eye. You come in alone, and I swear, it has the same effect as when the wait staff gets together to sing "Happy Birthday" to some poor mope. Only, rather than sing "Happy Birthday", it's like they're singing, *"You're alone! You're alone! People must really hate you! Hey everybody, look over here! This guy's alone! This guy's alone!"*.

At least, that's what it feels like.

So Kryssi, that was the hostess' name, as spelled out on her badge, pointed me to the bar and suggested I have a plate of nachos. I honestly don't know what a plate of nachos has to do with waiting for Audrey. Some people just amaze me.

The bar wasn't crowded, but there were enough people scattered around to give the impression of a crowd. Luckily, I was able to grab a stool that at least had no one sitting on either side. My butt wasn't in the seat for more than five seconds before a bartender was in my face. A young guy who looked like he just spent six hours in front of the mirror.

"How 'ya doin', Chief? What can I get you?"

Chief. Like I'm sitting here in goddamn war paint, or something. God, I hate this place.

"Two cheeseburgers to go," I told him. "And a plate of nachos, I guess."

"Two Char-cheeseburgers. How do you want 'em done, Boss?"

Char-cheeseburgers. I knew it. It was almost too easy.

"I don't know. Medium," I told him. I knew I forgot to ask Steve something.

"Wanna try our drink special? The Rumpumpelstiltskin." He pointed behind the bar to a board where the name and the price were handwritten in gold chalk. "It's a mixture of rum and pumpkin liqueur. But we don't shake it. We spin it. Get it?"

"No. I really don't."

He gave me a smile that looked about as fake as his tan, then walked away. Which is what I wished I could do. I really couldn't wait to leave.

"This place is a joke, isn't it?"

I looked down toward the floor, thinking Steve got in somehow, but it wasn't him. It was the guy two stools away from me. I hate it when I pick the wrong spot. Now I'll be stuck in a conversation with some stranger for as long as I'm sitting here.

"I've been trying to get another beer for I don't know how long," he said. "They just keep friggin' ignoring me. Nothing new there."

I admit, that is irritating. I hate being in a place where the size of your chest determines the amount of service you get. But, what did he want me to do about it? I wasn't the manager. And obviously, I had no chest. The situation was out of my control. So, I just nodded and shrugged, figuring that would end it. But he took it as code and slid over one stool next to mine.

"Mind?" he asked.

Well, yeah, I did. But what could I do? Push him off? That'd be even worse than ignoring him. I swear – some people's social skills.

"Maybe if I'm next to you, it'll help," he said. "It sucks when you're alone. Nobody notices you."

Which was a weird thing for him to say. And not just because it was the exact opposite of what I was thinking earlier, but because, well, I just was thinking the exact opposite of that earlier. I don't know, maybe on some level it's not all that strange. I mean, sometimes when you're by yourself, that's really all you let yourself think about: being by yourself. So, both of us being alone, it isn't all that difficult to imagine that we'd have a similar train of thought. At least the wait staff wasn't singing to us.

While I was staring half-heartedly at one of the many dumb drink menus they had scattered all over the bar, I felt a finger graze across the back of my neck. I spun around on my bar stool in time for Audrey to lean in and plant a kiss on my earlobe. The lonely guy next to me nearly fell off his seat when he saw this. Not sure why, but he had this incredible look of surprise, like he just watched me peel off a fake face and reveal myself as the killer.

"Hi, Sexy," she said. "I'm glad you came."

The guy next to me cleared his throat. "Hi, Audrey."

She looked over at me with half a smile. "Friend of yours?"

I shrugged. "Just met him."

She wrinkled her eyebrows and turned back around to him. "Do I know you?"

"Well, know you, no, not really," he stammered. "I've seen you around. I mean, I'm in here a lot. To eat."

"Oh." Then she turned and faced me again. "I just have to get a couple things, then we can get out of here."

"I thought you had to work."

"That's just what I told Archie," she smiled. "I'm off tonight."

"Alright," I said. "I'm just waiting on a couple cheeseburgers."

She laughed and disappeared into a back room. It wasn't that forced cackling laugh that I heard her use earlier – it was the old Audrey laugh that I knew from the past. It was nice hearing that again, although I'm not all that sure why she thought me waiting for two cheeseburgers was all that funny. Unless it had something to do with the cheeseburgers themselves. I sorta wondered if I should warn Steve before he eats them.

The guy next to me tapped his empty beer bottle on the bar a couple times. "You the husband?"

"Which husband?"

"Audrey's. Audrey's husband."

I figured he meant Audrey's and not Julie's, but you never know. It just seemed like something I should clarify before I gave him an answer.

"No," I told him. "Her husband's some little cartoon dwarf, or something."

His laugh sounded slightly familiar, but nothing I could immediately place. At least I knew why he was laughing.

The bartender walked by and the guy next to me waved his empty at him. "Excuse me! Can I get another over here?"

The bartender didn't even blink. Just kept moving like the guy wasn't there. Then I started to wonder, with the weird things that have been going on with me, could it be possible that this guy really wasn't there? I studied him for a minute, then gave him a little shove.

"Hey," he yelled. "What the hell was that for?"

"Just checking." The beer cooler was right in front of us, so I positioned my toes on the lower rung of the barstool, giving myself an additional foot of height, then leaned forward and reached behind the bar. It was so much easier than the car door with the poodle. I slid open the lid, grabbed a couple bottles and handed them to him.

Nobody noticed. Nobody complained.

"Heineken," I said. "That's not what you're drinking, though."

"No. It's better. Can you reach the opener?"

Turned out there was an opener sitting on the ledge, so I really didn't even have to move that much. He snatched it out of my hand and popped open both bottles.

"Thanks. Thanks a lot."

"No problem," I told him. "Wanna glass?"

He smiled, shook his head no, then lifted the bottle to his lips and took a deep swallow. Afterwards, he let out a huge, "Ahh", like he was just saved by an oasis in the Sahara. Then he motioned over to the other bottle on the bar.

"Aren't you?"

"Nah. They're both yours."

"Thanks," he said. Then he tipped his bottle in my direction. "Cheers."

I'm not sure, but I think my response was akin to the phony bartender smile. I really didn't mean it to be, but I had a feeling that's the way it came off. If it was, it certainly didn't seem to bother him too much: that first bottle was nearly gone already, and he was still *ahh*-ing all over the place. I mean, I was happy for the guy that he finally got his beer, but the noises that were coming from him were a little unnecessary.

"Don," he said.

"Huh?"

"My name. It's Don. Don Gerrity."

The first thing that struck me was that we had the same initials. D.G. I was just about ready to let that bit of information pour out of my mouth before I decided to quickly shut the hell up. I got cops looking for me about my dead neighbor, and now I'm in here stealing beers for a guy I just met. Technically, I guess I haven't really stolen anything as of yet. If someone caught us, we could always just pay for it. But still, I didn't want to go passing along my name to this Don guy so quickly. I was trying to come up with a good fake name, but I honestly couldn't think of anything decent. Every name I thought of seemed way too bland, and I don't know, if you're going to change who you are, you might as well make yourself sound exciting, right? Then two names popped into my brain – Otto and Fenton. Only thing was, I couldn't decide which to use. Guess I could use both. Otto Fenton. That sounded cool. Like an international smuggler. Or, like from the old movies, someone who ran an import/export company. It reeked of intrigue.

But then Audrey came back. "I got your cheeseburgers, Daryl. Let's go, huh?"

That ruined that. I could no longer be Otto Fenton, importer/exporter. I was Daryl. Murder suspect and beer thief.

"Daryl," he said with a smile. "That's a good name. Nice to meet you, Daryl."

I was going to shake his hand, or rather, the thought of doing it at least crossed my mind, but before I could follow through, Audrey took me by my right elbow and gently pulled.

"Come on, Honey. We have to go."

"One sec." I freed my arm and reached back into the cooler. Just like before, no one noticed me grabbing two more Heinekens. And who gives a shit if they did? Let them arrest me.

"Thanks," Don said, as he lined them in a neat row.

"Yeah." I slid off the stool and Audrey and I walked away.

"We gotta get out of here quick," she whispered. "But not so fast that it draws attention."

That sounded like a job for Otto Fenton, international smuggler. He knew how to do that. He had to. It made sense now. This is why she called me Daryl: She didn't want Otto identified. We walked one behind the other at a breezy pace, but not too breezy to attract interest, quietly slipping out the front door just as she had hoped, without anyone paying us the slightest bit of notice.

When we got close to my car, she handed me one of the three bags she was holding on to.

"Here's your cheeseburgers," she said.

"What's in the other bags?"

"Let's just get out of here."

"Everything alright?" I asked her.

"Oh yeah," she smiled. "Hopefully for a while."

Out of habit, I checked inside the bag and realized that I never got my nachos. I was sort of tempted to go back inside and complain, but she seemed to be in a hurry, and to tell the truth, I really didn't want the damn nachos anyway.

We were heading down the wrong aisle, so we cut between a couple parked cars to get over. Steve was laying underneath my car and jumped out as soon as he saw us. I was going to warn him that he should always check for cars first before running out like that, but I didn't. Probably because it occurred to me that if he did get hit, I wouldn't have to put up with him anymore.

"Those my cheeseburgers?" he asked.

"Yeah," I told him. "But wait 'til we get to the car."

Audrey stopped for a moment and looked around. "Who are you talking to?"

"The dog," I said.

He ran up to her and gave her legs a couple big sniffs. "Mmm. She smells good. You gonna introduce me?"

I swear. Now I have to start introducing him? "Audrey, this is Steve. Steve, Audrey."

"He's cute. How long have you had him?"

"Yesterday. As soon as I found out my neighbor died."

"Oh, I'm sorry," she said. "Were you two close?"

"Never met her."

I unlocked the passenger door for Audrey, then walked around and opened the driver's door. Steve jumped in first, and sat down next to Audrey. I didn't get in right away though. Instead, I opened the back door and started carefully laying out the food on the back seat.

"You can eat back here," I told him. "Just don't get any on the floor."

Audrey looked slightly concerned. "Should you be feeding the dog those?"

"I don't know. But that's what he asked for."

She let out a little giggle then opened one of the bags she had placed on the floor. By now, the overhead light had turned off, so I couldn't make out for certain what she was holding. She must have noticed me staring because she answered the question before I even asked it.

"Scotch. Thirty year old Macallan, to be exact. Goes down as smooth as goddamn olive oil." She twisted the seal off the cap then smiled from ear to ear and gave a yell. "Let's go have some fun! Just like the old days."

"It's...about...damn...time," Steve mumbled between chews.

"Don't talk with your mouth full," I told him. "It's not polite."

I started the car and drove out of the parking lot.

9

Other than Steve's loud munching, and his lone comment about how much he loved French fries, the car ride was dreadfully quiet. Audrey gave no further instructions. She only seemed interested in sneaking looks out the windows in between slugs off her bottle.

"Let's go have some fun," is the last thing she said. I wasn't quite sure what she had in mind, but I really didn't think it was this. I wasn't even sure where the hell I was driving. Once again. I only made a right out of the parking lot because I didn't feel like crossing traffic. I've been driving in a straight line ever since. I guess I figured if she thought I was driving in a direction opposite of where the fun was, she would tell me.

I thought this might be the perfect time to ask her a few of my *happy* questions, but she seemed like she had something else on her mind, and I kinda wanted her full attention when I asked. So, to kill some time, I took a shot at answering the questions for myself by forcing back some memories. And I swear, every detail I retrieved was filled with noise. Music, laughter, talking, screaming, etc. It always seemed like we were in the middle of a party. As far as I could remember, there were never any long stretches of quiet like this. The problem was, I couldn't find any indications if all that noise or laughter had ever truly made me happy. I just couldn't feel it anymore.

Having no idea how long her self-imposed silence was going to last, I figured I may as well just start asking the questions out loud. I was just about to speak – I mean, I literally had my mouth open – but Steve beat me to it.

"Damn, that was good," he said. "Can we get some more?"

"You're still hungry?"

"Gotta get my energy back, if you know what I mean. Three times, buddy. Three times. Woulda done her four, maybe five times, but her damn human came back."

"Alright." I tried to stop him, but he was intent on sharing his experience with me.

"Never had a poodle before. Not usually my type. I normally like 'em with a little more meat on their bones. But the guys in the neighborhood are always going on about how you have to have a poodle at least once before you die. I have to tell you – it wasn't all that amazing. Now, don't get me wrong, if I come across another poodle in the future, I'm not turning her down. I mean, that would be stupid. But it's not like I'm dedicating my life to nothing but poodle banging. I once had this Rottweiler. Oh baby, you wanna talk about firm..."

"You know, you're disgusting."

Audrey looked at me with these big, sad eyes. "Why? What do you mean?"

"Not you," I told her. "Steve. He's going on about some poodle he just had sex with. Be glad you can't understand him."

I could see her looking at me from the corner of my eye. And what had started out as a rather forlorn stare quickly turned into a smile and a big laugh.

"God, I love you," she panted. "You're the greatest."

"Thanks."

Steve sounded a little pissed. "What did you do?"

I just shrugged. To be honest, I wasn't quite sure what I did either, but it did seem like I now had her attention.

"So, I wanted to ask you something."

"I know," she said. "I wanted to talk to you about something, too."

"Okay."

"No. You go first."

I didn't feel like trying to think of some clever way to slide into asking, so I just dove right in.

"Do you know if I was ever happy?"

She hummed out a little laugh and put her hand on my right thigh. "I can think of quite a few times when you were pretty damn happy."

"I don't mean sex. I mean, in general. You know. The rest of the time. When we weren't having sex."

"You don't remember?"

"No. I guess not."

"Well, I think so. We were always having fun, right? So, yeah. You were happy. Why wouldn't you have been? I don't ever remember..."

Her voice slowly trailed off. It reminded me of listening to the radio in the seventies, when every song faded out, rather than having some big definitive finish. What made me think of that, I don't know.

"What?" I asked her.

"Nothing," she said. "Not now. Oh, here, you haven't even had any yet, have you?" She reached over and balanced the bottle on my lap with her left hand.

I took a sip, trying hard not to smell it, and swallowed as fast as I could. Speed swallowing didn't seem to be the key, though. Thirty-year-old-olive-oil or not, it still burned my throat, and my eyes started to water. I knew there was a reason I never drank this before. I took a couple deep breaths and waited for it to pass. When she reached back for the bottle, I happened to catch sight of something on her left wrist.

"What's that?"

"What?"

"On your wrist. That a tattoo?"

"Mmm hmm. It's my beautiful little heart." She took a minute to gently stroke it with her index finger.

"When did you get that?"

"I um, a few months after...after we weren't together anymore."

"Oh. It's nice. That your only one?"

"I've got three more. But those are hidden."

"Are they really weird, or something?"

"No. It's just that this one means the most to me, and I always want to remember it."

"How come?"

"Because it was my first."

I looked at her up and down, trying to imagine not just where the others were, but what they were. She said they weren't weird, but that's really a matter of personal perspective. I didn't figure her for a butterflies-and-unicorns person. But she certainly wasn't the *"Mom"* or *"Hell Bent For Leather"* type, either. I assumed there was some fair compromise in the middle. But what? Perhaps a bottle of Jack Daniels surrounded by roses. Or nachos! Maybe that's why Kryssi suggested them. I almost got a tattoo when I was in the service, but changed my mind at the last minute. I told the guy it was because I couldn't decide between the eagle clutching the American flag, or the ridiculously muscular devil holding a pitchfork. Truth is, I just chickened out. I didn't even want a tattoo in the first place. I just figured it might help me fit in a little more, and those seemed to be the two most popular tattoos in my platoon. But standing there looking around at everyone, it struck me: do I really want this? I wasn't all that crazy about being in the service in the first place, so do I really want a permanent reminder of a miserable experience drawn on my body? The answer was a lot easier than I thought. I simply walked out. The aftermath wasn't so simple, though. I got caught leaving the place by a couple soldiers I knew. Total assholes, by the way. The kind of people who decide they don't like you before you can even open your mouth and give them any valid reason. So, what started out as a possible way for me to blend in ended up having the complete opposite effect. Next day, everyone in camp was all over me about chickening out. I tried to tell them that it was really because I couldn't decide, but none of them were buying it. Probably not the guy at the tattoo place, either. But I didn't really care what he thought. I don't know, maybe I should have just gotten the stupid thing. I could have put it on my upper arm, or something. No one would have been able to ever see it. Unless I wanted them to. But, I'd always see it. And I'd always remember. I wonder what it was that Audrey wanted to remember?

"Daryl!"

I saw her body tense the second before she screamed, but for some reason, I thought nothing of it. She was pointing out the front window to show me that we were headed straight for the rear end of a car stopped at a red light. It all seemed to be happening in slow motion, but I'm going to take a wild guess and say that it was actually happening pretty damn fast. By this point, I didn't have any time to break and avoid a collision, so I grabbed the wheel with both hands and pulled to the left. The left front tire bounced hard over the concrete median, momentarily throwing all of us out of our seats. It was like driving through the bushes earlier, except worse. Mainly because the bushes didn't have traffic coming straight at you. We hit the intersection and were greeted by headlights racing toward us from both directions. I'd like to be able to give an exact replay of all my stunning maneuvers, but to tell the truth, I don't know what really happened. It was right around here that it became nothing more than a blur of honking, screeching, crashes and screams. The screams were from Steve. Audrey still didn't say a word. All I know for sure is that after about a dozen swerves in a dozen directions, I finally merged with one direction of traffic and just floored it. Only, there wasn't as much traffic headed in that direction anymore. The majority of it was in my rearview mirror - stopped back at the intersection either avoiding an accident, or part of one. Damn whiskey. I had a feeling this would happen if I drank some. I eased off the accelerator and put on my turn signal to change lanes.

"Whoo hoo!" Audrey screamed. "Just like the old days!"

She raised her bottle in the air, toasting no one in particular, then cocked back her head and took a drink.

"Just like the old days?" Steve mumbled. "You mean you couldn't drive back then, either. Holy shit, Daryl, I don't know who's crazier: you or her. Maybe I should drive from now on."

"I think you scared Steve a little," Audrey said.

"Yeah. He was just complaining how he wants to drive from now on."

She let out her nice laugh again, but this time, finished it off with a long relaxed hum.

"Let's hear some music," she loudly announced. Then she dug around in one of her bags, pulled out a CD and slid it into the player.

"Tom Petty!" Steve screamed. "Excellent. I love this guy!"

How the hell the dog knows about Tom Petty is beyond me. Could the guy really be that popular? I mean, I guess it's possible he heard him on the radio, but the only way his human could have been a Petty fan was if she was Petty's grandmother. And, I'm sorry, but that's something I would have known because *that* would have been news. Believe me, the people in the neighborhood would have never stopped talking about a headline like that. I remember when I was a teenager, a guy two blocks away had a cousin in some western suburb who once delivered a pizza to the lead singer of REO Speedwagon. Kevin something. He ordered a large sausage and mushroom, and got a free liter of Pepsi. Not because he was in REO or anything. Everybody who ordered a large pizza got a free liter of Pepsi. The cousin said when he got there, Kevin something was wearing a Zeppelin shirt and was watching the local news. Nice guy, tipped a dollar and a quarter.

That story hung around for years. It was nothing though, compared to Mr. Avello's story. Mr. Avello was the guy next door, and back in the sixties, he once supposedly gave an emergency haircut to Frank Sinatra. The way he told it, Sinatra was playing a concert somewhere in downtown Chicago, I can't remember where exactly, the old Arie Crown I think, and during the show, Frank suddenly feels like his hair's a bit too long. Why in the hell anyone would have that going through their mind while they're on stage singing Cole Porter songs is beyond me. Anyway, once the show's over, he goes backstage and starts yelling at everyone, "Why didn't anybody tell me I look like some kind of goddamn hippie?" Then he looks around and notices some lighting guy who just had a haircut, and comments on how good it looks. Again though, if Sinatra could divine that a complete stranger just recently had a haircut, why couldn't he figure out that he needed one himself before he went out on stage? But, this wasn't my story. So, Frank wants to know where he got it, and this lighting guy tells him he went to Enrico Avello. He says it like Frank's supposed to know who this is. And of course he didn't. But when Frank hears that the guy's name ends in a vowel, he acts like they're long lost relatives. Sinatra then announces that he wants Enrico to cut his hair. Only, it's now after midnight, and the barbershop is something like fifteen miles away. But that doesn't matter. Frank can't wait – he's got two women up in his room and he refuses to go in there all shaggy. Luckily, the lighting guy had been getting his hair cut by Mr. Avello for over twenty years, so he knew his home phone number. Why? Who knows? I lived right next door to Mr. Avello, and I didn't even know his number. Anyway, Sinatra gets on the phone and demands his services. Mr. Avello jumps at the chance. Frank though, makes Mr. Avello promise in advance not to tell a soul. Something about him not wanting to be bothered at one in the morning by a gaggle of middle aged women with their hair in curlers when he had a pair of twenty-two years old back that the hotel. "That, Mr. Sinatra, is no problem!" Avello meets Frank at his shop, and gives him his desperately needed trim. Afterwards, Sinatra tells him it's the best cut he's ever had and insists that whenever he's back in Chicago, Mr. Avello will be the only one to cut his hair. Frank gives him two hundred dollars and leaves, presumably to visit the ladies in waiting.

According to his wife, Mr. Avello scoured the papers everyday for the rest of his life, looking for notices when Sinatra was coming back into town, so he could have the shop ready for him. But he never heard from Frank again. Great story, but just one problem: no witnesses. During the cut, the chauffeur stayed in the car, it was one a.m., so no one else came in the shop. Plus, Mr. Avello forgot his camera and he never asked for an autograph. So, because of all that, no one believed it for a second, even though Mr. Avello constantly swore on the grave of every saint he could name that it was true. I must have overheard that story being told a thousand times when I was a kid. I remember a few times asking my grandfather about it, once I finally grasped the importance of someone actually meeting Frank Sinatra. And every time I brought it up, it was met with sneers, laughter and ridicule. Then again, he never liked Mr. Avello anyway. He seemed to hate all the neighbors.

I could never decide, though. About the story, that is. I'd go back and forth each time I'd hear it told. Sometimes I'd think it was true merely because of how many years he kept telling it. I mean, if he was really telling a lie, and nobody believed him after the first few times he told it, wouldn't he have just dropped it and hoped it was eventually forgotten? Or, maybe no one forgot, and he was just too embarrassed to ever tell the truth. Then again, if you repeat something enough times, you can get yourself to start believing it. So, who knows? I mean, it really doesn't seem all that outlandish to think Sinatra freaked out about his appearance and demanded a haircut before he got laid. I just don't see why he needed to drive so far out of the way to get it. But, that's the artistic temperament for you.

"So," Audrey asked. "What's this all about?"

"All what?"

"You and this, *was I happy* stuff?"

"It's kinda complicated."

"I hate complicated." She brought the bottle to her lips and took another swallow. Man, can this woman hold her liquor. "Tell me about her."

"Who?"

"Your wife."

"Oh. Her name's Julie."

"You love her?"

I was about to answer, but it turned out that she wasn't quite finished with her thought.

"...More than you loved me?"

Damn.

I couldn't begin to guess how many times I thought about this exact question over the years. I just never thought anyone else would ever ask me. Especially Audrey. Julie on the other hand, I could easily imagine hearing Julie ask me. Actually, I'm a little surprised she never did. And like Mr. Avello's Sinatra story, I've gone back and forth over the details of this one, too. Obviously, I was crazy about Audrey when I was young. I used to think she was *The One*. Which at the time meant her and no one else. Ever. Then a few years later I met Julie, and ended up thinking she was *The One*. Thing is though, I still had feelings for Audrey while I was with Julie, which is something I always felt guilty about, even though Julie never knew it. I felt guilty just thinking it. But at the same time, I was crazy for Julie, too. I know it's not supposed to be that way, but it was, and there wasn't much I could do about it. Audrey was wild and fun. Uninhibited and spontaneous. With her it was always something new. You felt like there was no controlling it, but you still never worried. That wasn't Julie at all. Julie was much more restrained. She always seemed to be in total control and knew exactly what she was doing. And after my fiasco in the army, that appealed to me. I started to like the idea of knowing where I was going. Having a goal. Not being surprised. And probably more than anything, I liked being part of something. That was a rare feeling. My parents died when I was a little kid and I got pushed off to my grandfather. It was just the two of us for fifteen years, and never once did it feel like family. What it really felt like was some old man I hardly knew being forced to babysit me when clearly he would rather be alone fishing somewhere. And that was on the good days. Both Audrey and Julie made me feel good, and both gave me something that hadn't previously been there in my life.

So, I didn't know what to tell her. It was like having to choose between pizza and lobster: I love them both, but there's a big difference between the two. Not that I thought she was setting me up for it, but this really felt like one of those traps where either answer was wrong, so no matter what you were screwed. And I certainly didn't think this long hesitation before answering her was helping me any. A new song started and Steve sang along, but he was really mangling the lyrics, which is a major pet peeve of mine.

"Shut up, would you?" I told him. I hate that. If you're going to sing, at least know the damn words, otherwise hum.

Audrey took a deep breath and turned her head toward her side window.

"You have kids?" she asked.

"No. You?"

"Well, not officially."

"What does that mean?" I asked her. "Like your pets, or something?

"It…was just a joke. Forget it."

If it was a joke, I didn't get it, and that made me feel uncomfortable for some reason. Maybe she did mean a pet, and I made her feel stupid. I really hoped not, though. I let out some corny nervous laugh and thought it best if I keep talking.

"Always wanted kids."

I'm not sure why I said that because it's not entirely true. *Always* isn't the right word. *Used to* is more like it. After Julie and I got married, that seemed like the natural progression to me. Had the job, the car, the house, all that was missing were the kids. I brought it up a couple of times, but after talking it out we agreed that kids would just get in the way of me focusing on my career. Guess I should have stopped for a moment and realized the career we were talking about at the time was as an assistant manager in a restaurant owned by my father-in-law. Which as I understood it, meant that whenever he was ready to leave, I'd step in as manager, no questions asked. He even talked about co-ownership when he retired. Not much to be motivated about. Don't get me wrong, I met an awful lot of people who loved it, and were very successful, too. It just wasn't for me. There were just too many days when I felt like I was a temp filling in for the regular guy. Only, I was the regular guy. I never said anything about it to Julie, because I knew where that would lead. Early on, there'd be times when I was discouraged or frustrated, and I'd broach the subject, looking for a sympathetic ear. Instead of sympathy though, she'd try and set me straight. She'd tell me life wasn't easy, that we weren't born into privilege, and how foolish it was to think that I, or anyone else like me, was special enough to not go through these things. All perfectly valid points that succinctly put everything into perspective. Too bad none of it ever made me feel any better about the situation. And that's when the fighting would start. My stubbornness, or inability to recognize the obvious, she'd say. Those faults alone probably would have made me a failure as a father.

Audrey sighed loudly and gently flicked at my wrist with her finger. "Do you have any regrets?"

"In general?"

"Nothing like, 'I wish I didn't get that haircut back in the eighties'. A really big one. Something that you can't stop thinking about, no matter how hard you try."

"Yeah. Getting in this car," Steve muttered. I shot him a nasty look in the rear view mirror and he put his head down.

"Are you mad at me about something?" I really wasn't sure where she was headed with all this.

"I was afraid you'd be mad at me," she said.

"About what?"

Then she switched gears and acted like we weren't even having that conversation anymore. Or ever.

"Still talk to Woody?" she asked.

"Him? No. Not for a hundred years, or so. He just kinda dropped off the face of the earth."

"No kidding. So, where are you going?"

"No idea. Just driving."

"Can we go back to your place?"

I was about to say yes, but then remembered about the police wanting to talk to me and told her no.

"Yeah," she whispered. "We can't really go to my house, either."

Steve's head shot up. "Did you tell her about the cops?"

"No."

"Let's just go somewhere then," she said

"Okay," I said. "Where?"

"I don't know. Anywhere. Just you and me, my sweet darling."

"Hey!" Steve shot.

"Let's just *go*!" she shouted. "Get the hell away from here."

Then I remembered. "Oh. You said you wanted to tell me something."

"Huh? I don't know. Never mind." She tipped the bottle back into her mouth and took another huge swallow.

This had to be something about whether I loved her more than Julie. I still didn't really have a definitive answer, but I also didn't want to not say anything and make her feel bad, either. So I slowed down until I found a spot, then pulled over.

"I don't want you getting the wrong idea. For what it's worth, you were the first girl I ever loved. I mean, you might have had a lot of guys love you before me, but you were my first. I know I'm asking about being happy and all that, but back then, all I wanted was to get married and have kids with you. Only thing is, I can't for the life of me remember why we broke up. I swear, I don't know what happened. It was like one minute we were together, then the next, we weren't. Then the next minute I was in the Army, then I wasn't. And then there was Julie. And then...time went by so damn fast. I hope I didn't do something that screwed us up. Can't really say I blame you if you were mad. I know that doesn't help much now, but I wanted you to know."

"Daryl...!" She looked like she was about to burst into tears.

"What?" We were parked, so it wasn't like we was going to crash, or something. She turned her head again and gave a look at the building we were parked in front of. *The Cozy Nest Motel.*

"I...let's get a room," she said, taking a breath before continuing. "Here. Probably better if you go in by yourself."

"Now we're talking," Steve laughed. "And you better let me go in with you two! I never saw humans do it before."

Stupid thing. I shut off the ignition and got out of the car. I was only a yard or two away when I could have swore I heard Audrey say, "I love you, Daryl". But when I looked back around, she was staring straight ahead, and not at me.

Stupid voices.

I walked through the short parking lot to the grimy little office, wondering what the hell she wanted to tell me. I don't ever remember her being this upset about anything in the past. I had a feeling that somehow, it all had to do with that cartoon dwarf of a husband. It was nothing more than a hunch, but just the idea of it was getting me pissed. I wanted to jump in the car, drive back and beat the crap out of him. I've never been much of a fighter, I was only in maybe seven or eight my whole life and lost each one, but I figured Archie wouldn't be too tough. He was like a foot shorter than me, and supposedly had a bad back. But really, what good would that do? He'd only recover and be a dick all over again. Plus, Audrey made it sound like he was kind of lawsuit crazy. Who needs that? No, beating him up wasn't good. If it's true that he hurt Audrey, the most efficient move would be to kill him. I mean, in the grand scheme of things, what would it matter? Would anybody even miss him? I'd probably get an award. Not that I wanted one.

Ever since the restaurant, I have this thing about noticing bad paint jobs. And the walls around the front desk of this motel were beyond bad. I'm going to take a wild guess and say that the original color was white – which in itself isn't any major stroke of creativity to begin with. But now, after decades of neglect, it resembled a dirty tie-dye tee shirt, with various shades of brown swirling randomly about the room. Years ago, I took a photography class at a local community college. I had one off day a week from the restaurant, and Julie said I should use that time as an opportunity to go out and do something rather than sitting around all day and complaining. So, that's what I did. I had it in my head that taking a couple night school classes would elevate me a little closer to Julie's level. She graduated from college with a Master's in Philosophy. I didn't even apply to a college. And just in case either of those facts ever slipped my mind, she was more than happy to take the time and remind me.

Anyway, I remember the instructor, this guy named Ian, telling us there is no such thing as *ugly*. That if any of us were to see something we immediately thought of as ugly, we should try instead to look at it as a piece of art. His thinking was if you do that, try to look at the ugly object as a work of art, you'll be able to see beyond your preconceived ideas and discover the it's inner beauty. Something like that. What I remember precisely is feeling like an idiot watching everybody else in the class nodding their heads, acting like they all understood, and me sitting there not being able to make sense out of it. If something is ugly, how can it be beautiful, too? It seemed like some concept you could only grasp if you had gone away to college for four years. And I didn't. In fact, I never went back to that community college again after that night, either.

The idea intrigued me though, and I promised myself to do as Ian suggested, hoping maybe to one day understand. I always tried to keep a look out for any examples of ugly so I could see for myself if there was any truth to it. Well, I found probably the most perfect example of it right here, and no disrespect to Ian, but I have to say this wall smashes that theory of his to pieces. If there was an inner beauty here, it was covered in far too many layers of disgust to be noticed. Too bad the classroom of nodding jackasses couldn't be here to see how wrong he was, too.

Behind the desk was an old man, sitting in a beat up chair and watching a rerun of *Match Game* on a tiny black and white TV. I was going to say something, but I thought I'd wait a minute, because Gene was just starting to get the answers from the celebrities. *Match Game* always held a certain appeal to me. My grandfather was adamant about not letting me watch this show when I was a kid because he thought it was filthy, which of course made it the only show I ever wanted to watch. I was maybe eight or nine the last time I ever watched it with him, which in fact, was the last time I watched it until I finally caught it in reruns years later, and I don't recall the question, but Brett turned over her card to show the word *"bazooms"*. My grandfather loudly exhaled his disgust, stood up and shut off the TV. When I asked him why, he refused to talk about it. He only said I couldn't watch it ever again, then stomped off into the garage and started working on one of his cars. Alone.

As soon as he left, I yanked the dictionary off the shelf and nearly ripped out the pages looking for the word, but I couldn't find the damn thing, no matter how many different spellings I tried. So, I had no idea what the hell was going on. Believe it or not, I didn't even know the true meaning of *bazooms* until high school. And I distinctly remember the day when the definition became clear: I was in gym and Danny Morgan started talking about *WKRP in Cincinnati*. "That Loni Anderson's got a nice pair a bazooms, huh?" Everybody started laughing, and of course, since laughing in school was strictly forbidden, Mr. Calhoun had us run three extra laps. But I didn't care, because a light bulb went off in my head and I finally knew. It was hearing it alongside the word *"pair"* that cleared everything up for me. I swear, if I hadn't heard it phrased like that, I'd probably still not know what it meant. Context is everything, I guess.

Sure enough, five out of the six answers I saw on the little black and white behind the desk were some variation of the word *"boobs"*. And believe it or not, Brett actually said *"bazooms"*. The only different answer was from the last celebrity, who said *"carpeting"*. Since I didn't hear the question I had no idea if that made any sense. All I know is if I had heard that as a kid, it probably would have confused the living hell out of me for more years than *bazooms* did.

After the last answer was revealed, the old man weakly clapped his hands and let out a tiny wheeze. I don't know how I didn't notice sooner, but he was hooked up to a portable oxygen tank. You'd think the long rubber tubes sticking out of his nose would have given it away. When he caught me standing there, he jumped about a foot, and I got concerned for a minute that he might die before I got a room.

"Why didn't 'ya say sumpin'?" he rasped.

"I was waiting for the answers to be finished." I found myself having to scream because of how loud he had the TV.

"I guessed ta-tas, too. That's five for me." He bent over and scribbled the number five on a piece of scrap paper.

Ta-tas. There's one you don't hear too often. Especially from an old guy with tubes in his face. He leaned over and turned down the volume a little, which meant that I could now hear if an airplane landed in the parking lot.

"Shoulda been six for me," he grunted. "*Carpeting*. What the hell kinda answer is that? I don't know why they let her on the show. Dummy. Now, whatta 'ya need? A room?"

I nodded. I mean, what else would I be in here for? The entertainment?

"One hour, three, or for the night?"

"I don't know."

He didn't seem to care for my response. It was almost like I said *"carpeting"* and stole a point from him. He turned away, untangling his tubes to get more slack, and browsed through a group of keys dangling on hooks in the corner.

"Hmm. How many of there are 'ya?"

"Three. What do you need? A credit card, or something?"

He slowly twisted around and gave me a tired stare. “Cash only. What’s that in yer pocket?”

I grabbed hold of one of the bottles from the outside of my pants and gave it a rattle. “Pills,” I said.

“Well, that makes sense. There is three of ‘ya. Better get it for the whole night then. Forty bucks.”

I peeled off two twenties, took the key for room one eleven and moved to the door. By then, the volume had been turned back up to full blast, and the theme music coming out of the commercial was just starting up again.

Carpeting. What the hell could the question have been?

I rounded the half wall that blocked off the view of the parking lot from the street and headed back toward the car. There was Steve, pawing at the back window and screaming something or other at me, but I couldn’t see Audrey. I figured she was probably bent over, fiddling with her bottle of scotch, or looking for another CD. Then I half wondered if she was passed out. She was sucking down the booze pretty good. That would be just my luck: right when she’s finally ready to talk, she’s out cold. She used to be able to out drink anyone. I got close enough to see inside the passenger window, only, she wasn’t there. I didn’t think much of it at first. I figured maybe she ran out of scotch, and ducked into a liquor store. I looked down the street to see what was open, but Steve started yelling even louder and ruined my concentration.

“Open the door, Bro! Unless you want it all over your seats!”

I let him out and as usual, he instantly let loose, without any concern to where he was aiming. Must be nice. I can’t imagine what kind of trouble I’d get into if I did that.

“Why can’t you be like other dogs and go on a fire hydrant or a tree?”

“I’m not into that whole territorial thing. It’s kind of juvenile, don’t you think?”

“Where’s Audrey?” I asked it.

“How should I know? I thought she was with you.”

“You saw me get out by myself.”

“She went in after.”

“No she didn’t.”

He finished and lowered his leg. Right into one of his puddles. I honestly can’t see how this stupid dog can live with himself.

“I thought that’s where she was going,” he said. “She started crying, said ‘*I’m sorry*’, and got out.”

“What the hell did you say to her?”

“Nothing, dude. Besides, she doesn’t understand me, anyway, remember? And I have to tell you, I’m getting a little tired of you thinking everything’s always my fault.”

“Then why did she say *‘I’m sorry’* to you?”

“I don’t think it was meant for me.”

"*Sorry*? For what? Audrey!"

My voice filled the street, but then disappeared as quickly as she did. I took off down the block, hoping I'd stumbled upon something, but I couldn't find a trace of her anywhere. Or anyone else, for that matter. All the stores were closed and there wasn't another person to be seen. Where the hell could she have gone? She didn't get that much of a head start. I mean, how long was I in the hotel lobby? Just a little longer than a commercial break, right?

Steve caught up with me, although he didn't seem to be in that much of a hurry. I swear, this dog's priorities.

"I lost her back there," he said.

"What? You saw her?"

"Her scent. Goes from the car to that newspaper box back there then just stops."

Alright, maybe I was a little too quick to question his priorities. I doubled back to the newspaper box. Not sure why, I mean, it was obvious she wasn't there anymore, but something about knowing it was the last place she was drew me there.

"There's no bus stop, so I'm thinking she got into another car," Steve went on. "Probably an accomplice. Could be a set up."

"There was no accomplice, okay? Don't do the stupid cop show stuff."

"Alright," he sneered. "What do you think happened?"

"I don't know. Maybe something to do with that idiot husband of hers."

"You mean, like her kidnapped her?"

"I don't know. I have to find her. She was going to tell me something. Maybe something important."

I wanted to run again, look a little harder, but a powerful wave of exhaustion swept over me, and at that moment all I wanted to do was lay down and close my eyes. It felt like someone was holding a pillow over my face, and I finally realized it was pointless to fight anymore.

"You okay?" Steve asked.

"I'm not sure."

"Did you get a room?"

I nodded. At least I tried to, but I was afraid if I moved my head too much, I'd throw up. This is why I don't drink whiskey of any kind.

"Come on," Steve calmly said. "We'll look for her later. What room are we in?"

"One eleven."

I followed him for what seemed like forever back down the empty street and across the parking lot to the room. I fell against the door with all my weight and worked the key into the lock. It opened a little quicker than I wanted, and the next thing I knew, I was on my hands and knees. What the hell was happening? I've never in my life been this tired before.

"Daryl? You okay?"

I opened my mouth to speak, but rather than words, vomit came pouring out. I was surprised by how much, considering I hadn't really eaten a thing all day. Once the initial burst was over, I spent a few minutes spitting and coughing up stray pieces from my mouth, but I felt a little better. As far as that goes. I took a couple breaths, then maneuvered myself around the puddle, found the corner of the bed and somehow managed to pull myself up. It was much more of a struggle than I suspected. The little amount of strength I was able to muster didn't last long, and I fell directly onto the bed.

"Turn on the light, would 'ya?" Steve asked.

Luckily, the nightstand lamp was close, so I groped around without having to turn my head to see. Not that I thought I might ralph again, but I didn't feel like risking it.

"Oh, dude," Steve cringed once I clicked the light on. "They are not going to be happy with you."

"I'll get it in the morning. I need to sleep."

"Whatever. Reach me the remote before you drop."

I had felt it on the table when fumbling for the lamp switch, so I lobbed it at him on the bed. He carefully nosed it around so it pointed at the set, then pressed his paw down on the power button. I closed my eyes and drifted off listening to Steve flicking through the channels.

"Shit...Shit...Shit...Come on, show me something good."

10

The very moment I reopened my eyes, I already had three questions in my head: *Where am I? Who are those people talking? And what is that god-awful smell?* I looked down and saw Steve camped out at the foot of the bed watching what looked to be a soap opera. That answered two of the three: motel room and television. I figured the smell was from Steve, and I was all geared up to yell at him for going on the floor, when I remembered that the foul odor was from me. I looked to my left and saw the pile I created on the floor. A small squadron of flies hovered above it, and I'm not certain because everything was still a little blurry, but it looked like something was crawling in it, too. Not a pretty sight, but not anything I wouldn't expect to see in a joint like this, anyway.

I repositioned myself and stared up at the ceiling for a minute, slowly retrieving as much information as I could from last night. But the memory of Audrey disappearing quickly overpowered anything else waiting to be uncovered. Why would she have gone to all the trouble of asking me to meet her if she was just going to sneak off in the end? And unless I completely missed it, without really saying anything relevant either?

I wanted to spend more time pondering all of that, but the combination of barf smell, and having to listen to the tearful announcement that someone named Lance was found murdered in the bedroom of his identical triplet's ex-wife was all too distracting. Rather than thinking of Audrey, I found myself wondering about identical triplets, and how anybody could actually confirm which one was dead. Only on a soap opera, I guess. Some people will fall for anything.

"Turn that off."

"Hey, you're finally awake," Steve cheerfully said. "Give me a minute. I just wanna see what happens next."

I pulled myself up, and quickly opened both windows and the door to relieve the room of the smell. The sunlight was a little harsh, but the cool morning air was more than welcome.

"Why don't you..."

"Shhh!" Steve hissed. "Just a sec. Just a sec."

I can't believe I'm getting shushed by a dog. *This* dog, especially. All the times I yelled from my window for this thing to shut up and it wouldn't? Now this? I swear.

I left the door open and headed toward the bathroom. And unless I wanted to walk over the bed, the only way to get there was to cross in front of the TV. So, I made sure to take my steps as slow as possible.

"Hey, come on! I can't see!"

I decided to use my time in the bathroom to go over a possible to-do list for the day, but Steve butted in before I could even get started. With the list, that is.

"Okay, commercial," he yelled from the other room. "What did you want to tell me?"

Something I'd love to know: why is it that I can't interrupt him, but it's perfectly fine for him to do it to me? It's plain to see that nobody bothered to teach this thing manners. I, on the other hand, purposely waited to zip back up and flush before responding. I hate talking to people while I'm going to the bathroom, whether it's some chatty stranger at a public urinal, or Julie walking in on me at home. I don't know, it just seems so uncouth. And a little unsanitary. I wonder if that's something I should tell Melvin?

"Commercial's not that long," he impatiently shot.

"I was just going to say, door's open, so run out and go."

"Oh. Thanks but, I already went. Couple times, in fact. Watch where you step." Then he started giggling.

I looked down and saw three huge wet spots each with a steaming little turd in the middle.

"What the hell is wrong with you?"

"For one, you were sleeping. And two, what difference does it make? You already ruined the carpet last night."

"Fine. Whatever. We have to go."

"The show's not over!"

"Too bad."

I dug into my pockets looking for my keys, but found my pills first. I didn't want to forget to take them, or I'd never hear the end of it from Melvin, so I went back into the bathroom, picked out one from each bottle and bent over to grab a handful of water from the sink.

"Oh, Daryl...I think you better come out here!"

"What, in the name of the Holy Mother," someone shrieked. "What did you do to this room?"

I didn't recognize the voice, but I had a feeling it wasn't coming from a friendly visitor. I forced down the pills, then stuck my head back into the other room. An old man was standing in the doorway, a different old man than from last night, at least I think he was different. This one was tube-less. He was bracing himself against the door frame with one hand, and clutching his heart with the other.

"You are so screwed," Steve laughed.

"Hey," I told him. "You did some of this, too!"

"I most certainly did not!" the old man gasped.

"I was talking to him," I said, and pointed to Steve.

The old man turned as white as a cloud, probably even whiter than the original shade on the front desk walls, and took a couple awkward steps back toward the parking lot.

"Don't you go anywhere. I calling police." And he wobbled away in the direction of the office.

"You're right. Maybe we better get outta here, buddy boy," Steve said.

"Don't call me that. I'm not your buddy."

"Man, you're really a downer sometimes."

"If you don't like it, leave," I told him as I walked out of the room.

"Seriously, why don't you loosen up a bit? You're so tense. It's kind of a drag."

Thing was, I wasn't tense in the least bit. I couldn't care less about the carpeting, or even what the old man thought about it. I'll just pay for the cleaning and be done with it. But the cops were a different matter. Not that I thought they'd lock me up for a little puke and dog shit. It was more the timing of it. I wanted to find Audrey, and I knew that if I got dragged in by the cops, they'd eventually find out about the other police wanting to question me about my dead neighbor. And again, not that I worried they'd lock me up for that, either, but I'm guessing the questioning wouldn't be some quick little meeting. Even if I did have the time to waste, that wasn't how I'd choose to waste it.

I wasn't sure how much a thorough cleaning cost, so I peeled off two one hundred dollar bills and dropped them on the bed. Hell, maybe they could buy some paint with that, too.

We had almost reached the street when I started getting yelled at again.

"You don't go anywhere!" the old man yelled from just inside the office door. "I have police coming now!"

"I gotta go. I left money for you on the bed."

"I am no whore!"

I tried to get that image out of my head as fast as I could, but it wasn't easy. I was suddenly haunted by the picture of him tugging off his moth-eaten green sweater, while attempting to do some seductive dance for my pleasure. I know I was putting way too much thought into it, but it was out of my control. I hoped the traffic would distract me from thoughts of old male whores.

"Where we off to now, acquaintance-boy?"

"What?"

"Hey, you made it clear you're not my buddy," he went on. "I gotta call you something. So, where to?

"I'm gonna find Audrey."

"Seriously? Dude, she cut out on you mid date. I'm no expert on all-things-human, but even I know that's pretty cold."

"Mind your own business. Besides, I don't know what really happened last night. That's what I need to find out."

"I don't get why," Steve said.

"It may sound stupid to you, like I care what you think anyway, but I need to find out something, okay?"

"If you were ever happy," he said. "I know. I know all about it. What I don't get is, what more do you want to know? I thought you already had your answer."

"How do you figure?" I asked him. "Because she disappeared?"

"Not just that. What you said last night about always wanting kids. That true?"

"I suppose. I don't know. Why?"

"Well, you couldn't have been too happy with her when she got the abortion, right?"

"What are you talking about?"

"Dude, it's cool. I know the whole story. Ben told me. And I wasn't prying. He's the one who brought it up. Unless there was another Audrey from high school, and I got it mixed up. Did you knock up somebody else back then?"

I yanked the wheel to the right and pulled into an empty space.

"My *grandfather*?" I really had to laugh. "How could my grandfather tell you anything?"

"Dude, I told you," Steve said. "'Til I met you, there was only other human who ever understood me. Ben. We talked all the time. The stories that guy used to tell. I'm gonna miss him."

"He understood you?"

"Yeah. I just said. Pay attention, huh?"

"He *talked* to you? You two had *conversations*?

"I really don't know how much more I need to spell this out. Yes. We talked. All the time."

"Figures. He just barely ever said anything to me. Usually nothing more than one syllable words and grunts."

"I think he always felt bad about that."

"So, let me get this straight: My grandfather told *you* that Audrey had an abortion, but he didn't tell *me*. No way. That's exactly the kind of information he couldn't wait to tell me. He'd get to show me how stupid and useless I was, and put me in my place."

"You didn't know? I can't believe that. How could you not...? Damn, doesn't anybody ever tell you anything?"

"No. No way. For one, how would he even know? I mean, even if it were true, and I'm not saying it is, how would he know, and not me?"

"From Audrey's mom, he said."

"Okay. That makes no sense. He didn't even know her parents. Never wanted to. Never even tried!"

I don't know why he was doing this to me, but it was really pissing me off. I think Steve knew, too, because he got quiet for a minute, then looked up at me, tilted his head to the right, and started to calmly explain.

"Look, I'm not trying to upset you. This is what Ben told me: One day, the summer you were nineteen, Audrey's old lady called him and said that she was pregnant. Audrey was. From you. And she wasn't happy. The mother. She said Audrey was going to stay with some relative out of state, and put the baby up for adoption."

I wanted nothing more than to laugh the whole thing off as some stupid dog just making stuff up, which wouldn't have been too difficult considering what I already knew about the little liar. But damn it, this voice in the back of my head started up. Not a Droner, and not a Screamer. It was more of a Whisperer. Sorta like being at a party and overhearing a private conversation from another part of the room. I don't particularly like eavesdroppers, but it was happening inside my head. How can you not listen to that?

"The dog may be right," the voice was faintly telling me. "Think about it. You thought something was wrong back then, too."

I was trying my damnedest to force out any memory that might have been locked away deep inside my brain, but I swear, if anything was there, it refused to reveal itself. I tried to picture that year. Slowly, I remembered that summer. We both had jobs – me at a record store, and Julie a waitress at Vic's Pizza. It started coming back to me how right about that time she all of a sudden stopped going out with me during the week, saying she needed to work some extra hours. I didn't think much of it. In fact, I was trying to work as many shifts as I could to make extra money to buy a car. My old one had just died. It was bad enough that we had to walk everywhere we went by ourselves, but on the nights we'd go out with Him, *Chester*, he'd pick her up and drive her home.

Then I remembered how even on the weekends, she was different. Not only did she hardly say a word to me, but a couple times she turned down the Jack Daniel's I bought her. I remember thinking she must have been sick to say no to whiskey. That wasn't like her.

"There's more," the voice whispered. "A lot more."

Then another sliver of information reappeared. A few days later she called and asked me to meet her at the mall. I figured she'd be alone, but when I got there, she was with a group of her friends. None of them ever liked me all that much anyway, but this time they all acted like I had some disease. Her included. And I remember worrying then that something might be wrong, like was she mad at me about something? If so, what? What did I do now? And I remember standing there, feeling like the enemy, and looking uncomfortably at Audrey hoping for some kind of sign, when it hit me that three weeks had passed since the last time we had sex.

What the hell? *That's* what I focused on? Here she was, pregnant and scared, and all I could think about was, *"something must be wrong because I haven't gotten laid in a while."*

"Why didn't she just tell me?" I asked.

"He said the mother threatened her," Steve replied. "She made her promise not to tell you. Or else."

"Why? What did she think I'd do? Run? I would have married her. That day."

"Um...There's no other way to say this, Dude, but *that's* the reason. I don't know if the mother didn't like you specifically, didn't like the idea of Audrey marrying young, or what. Ben didn't go into details. Just that the old broad didn't want it happening."

"She hated her mother. I can't believe...wait a second. *Adoption?* Not ahn abortion? So, what are you saying?"

"She ran off one day, didn't tell anybody where she was going. Just disappeared. Seems to be her thing, huh? Doesn't any of this ring a bell? Her taking off like that?"

I closed my eyes and tried to sort through what was coming back to me, but the answer wasn't there. I knew a piece or two was still missing.

"Anyway," Steve continued. "Ben said the mother went nuts calling your house every day, blaming you, saying you had to be hiding her somewhere and not telling anyone. That kinda shit. Then about a month later, Audrey finally called her, said she had an abortion, and wouldn't be coming back home ever again. You really didn't know anything about this?"

"No. I don't know."

"So, she just disappeared. Your girlfriend. The one you claimed to love. Didn't say a word, and you didn't go looking for her? I wouldn't care myself, but that's what humans are always doing on TV. Seems weird."

I must have been forcing for the release of that memory something fierce, because it came roaring in from nowhere and hit me like one of those giant fake tidal waves you see in a bad movie. Powerful, fast, and destroying everything in its path. My grandfather did tell me something. To be accurate, he didn't *tell me* anything. What he did do was give me a piece of paper with a message, in his handwriting, saying that Audrey called. It would have been right around that time. The note said she was staying with relatives for the summer, then going straight to college in the fall. That's it. No number. No mention of which college or even which state. I remember feeling numb, like I had been quick-frozen and unable to move anymore. All I could do was stare at that note. I had no idea what it meant. She never talked about college, now out of the blue, she was going? And so quickly? I couldn't believe it was over, and this was how it ended. With a phone message. And who knows if she even called? That could have just been him for all I know, trying to screw up my life again.

"Why didn't you?" Steve asked.

"Why didn't I what?"

"Go after her?"

"Why? She said she was going to school."

"And you believed that?"

This stupid dog doesn't have the slightest idea. Just doesn't get it. His life is nothing more than jumping from one female to another without any worry. I'm sick of him thinking he has all the answers.

Exactly like Melvin. Alright, even if I had wanted to do something, tried finding Audrey, what could I have done? Nothing, that's what. She made it pretty damn clear she didn't want to involve me in the decision anyway, or else she would have told me. She did what she wanted to do. And if there's one thing I've learned in life, it's that if somebody has their mind made up, I mean truly made it up, there's no getting them to change it. It's pointless to even try. It would have just been another fight that I ended up losing, and what good would that have been?

Still, there's no real proof it's true. I'm probably reading way too much into this.

I mean, she would have told me if we were going to have a kid, right?

11

All I did for the next, I don't know how long, was drive. I needed to do something that didn't take a lot of thought, and to me, driving was the obvious choice. The only brain power required is the knowledge of a few simple rules of the road, and you're on your way. And even if you can't recall every written rule, there's an unspoken understanding between drivers that keeps everyone safe and moves them smoothly along: I'll work with you if you work with me, that way no one gets hurt. You stay in your lane, I'll stay in mine. And if you do need to get in front of me, give me a little warning and I'll let you in. Plain everyday considerations. Don't be a jerk. Millions of people, everyday, abide by these simple rules.

Unfortunately, not everyone chooses to follow along. Some people have an entirely different idea of what the rules should be and how each rule applies to them personally. They'll drive like idiots with little or no regard at all to the other guy. These drivers are generally easy to spot, and when you do cross paths with them, the best thing to do is back off and let them pass. Of course sometimes you could be humming along for hours, thinking everything in your lane is just fine, when you realize you've been suckered into keeping pace with an inconsiderate driver, and inevitably, you're the one being pulled over instead of them. It's not fair that your life gets upset and they escape without blame. I don't know, maybe those people eventually get caught too, but it always seems they're the type who can somehow sense where the speed traps are, and slow down just in time without getting caught. Or, if they are stopped, they're able to smooth talk themselves out of a ticket. Either way, they're right back on the road within minutes and doing it all over again. It's not right, but really, what can you do?

Somewhere in the middle of my trip, I decided to head back to Casey's. I had no idea if Audrey was scheduled to work a shift today or not, but at the very least, I could find out when she was on next and come back then.

I pulled into the parking lot, and was able to find a spot up close on the first pass. That rarely ever happens to me. I tried to think of it as a good omen.

I held the door open for Steve, and he immediately leapt out and began squirting all over the front wheel of a Range Rover. They're built to drive through some pretty nasty terrain, so I couldn't really say anything about him peeing on the tires. Plus, I never really cared for Range Rovers all that much, anyhow.

After he finished up, he took a few suspicious sniffs at the air and stepped out into the aisle.

"What are we doing back here?" he asked.

"I told you. Looking for Audrey."

"I don't know about you, dude."

"Yeah, well, I do," I told him.

"You do, what?"

"Know about myself."

"Really? Tell me all about it then."

"Shut up."

He started laughing himself silly. I really didn't see what the hell was so funny and just left him there by the car.

The door of the restaurant was propped open and there was Kryssi, standing alone by the hostess station.

"Hi, Kryssi," I said.

She turned and giggled. "I'm not Kryssi. I'm Myssi," She came to attention and puffed out her chest. I'm guessing she intended this as a gesture to help me better read her nametag. It had to be read on a slight angle, but it said Myssi, alright.

"Don't worry," she went on. "*Everybody* makes that mistake. We're twins. Are you a friend of hers?"

"She suggested I have nachos."

"Oh, wow!" she sang, stretching out the vowel sound for a good seven seconds. Judging from her expression, you would have thought I said she pulled me out of a well.

"I'm really looking for Audrey. Is she here?"

"I don't know."

In the silence that followed, I counted to ten.

"Okay," I said, trying not to overcomplicate things for her. "I'll ask at the bar."

The place seemed unusually empty, as far as restaurants go, and out of reflex, I glanced up at the clock. Three-eleven. Figures. I hated this time of day. That painful lull between the lunch rush and the dinner rush. For the wait staff, it was about two and a half hours of filling napkin holders, salt and pepper shakers, condiment bottles, and wiping down tables. In effect, doing whatever you can to look busy until the next customer comes in. As a manager, it was two and a half hours of watching your employees trying to look busy while hoping that someone would come in and order enough food to justify keeping them on the clock. It was a stretch of time that felt twice as long as it actually lasted. There was only so much busywork that you could do to keep yourself occupied before you found your mind wandering all over the place. And that's what I really hated about it, because in order to kill time, you started wondering and worrying about things that are better left alone. It was right around three-eleven that I decided to paint the walls sage green.

Mid-afternoons can lead a person to make rash decisions.

Mid-afternoons are nothing but trouble.

I peeked into a back hallway that led to the kitchen. A couple busboys were off in the corner laughing about something in Spanish – I was able to make out a few words here and there, but nothing about Audrey. On the wall opposite to them was a time clock, and if this place was like any other restaurant I knew, that meant there was a schedule posted somewhere near it. Nobody seemed to care about me sticking my head in, so I thought I'd take the chance that maybe nobody would care if I took a walk in, too.

"Daryl?" I heard someone call. "That you?"

It wasn't Audrey, so I quickly spun around, wondering who the hell else in here knew me by name. It turned out to be Don, that guy I met yesterday. He was at the bar, sitting in the pretty much the same spot as he was before.

"It is you!" he said. Then he silently mouthed *"Come here! Come here!"*, and waved me over to him with both hands for added emphasis.

"Just like old times, huh?" he laughed. "Sit down. Sit down. You hungry? Miguel! Come here, *s'il vous plaît!*"

"Isn't that French?"

As I sat down next to him, Miguel, one of the busboys from the back, came running up to us.

Don pointed at me and gave a little smirk, like he was up on stage and guessing which playing card I had tucked away in my pocket. "Cheeseburger, right?" Then he turned back to Miguel. "Can you get a cheeseburger and fries for my friend?"

"Actually," I told him. "I could use two."

"Can you do two, Miguel?" Don asked.

"Okay!" Miguel smiled.

There was something weird going on. This Miguel was just a little too eager about taking on the task of fetching me a cheeseburger. It reminded me of the look I used to see on the faces of the people who would ring my doorbell and ask me to read their pamphlets. I planned on asking Don as soon as Miguel left the room, but it turned out I didn't have to wait that long to be shown the reason for his odd enthusiasm. Copying my move from yesterday, Don leaned unnoticed over the bar, reached into the cooler, and removed three beers. He handed two bottles to Miguel, who promptly shoved them in his pants pocket and ran out of the room. The last one Don popped open and placed on a coaster in front of me.

"I gotta tell 'ya," he beamed. "You are a genius. A frigging genius!"

"How do you figure?"

"This!" he announced, wildly waving his arms in front of him. "*This* is how I figure. After you left last night, I sat here and had at least ten more beers. For free! I just did what you did: reach out and take it. I kept waiting to get caught, but I never did. It's eye-opening, Daryl! Freakin' eye-opening! And I owe it all to you."

He slapped me on the back and clinked his bottle into mine. I wanted to tell him it was no big deal, but he was so excited about it that it seemed a shame to disappoint, so I clinked his bottle back and had a swallow.

"How'd Miguel get involved?" I asked him.

"Later on, I got hungry. Problem is, the cooler only holds beer, not food. Duh, right? So, Miguel, Miguel comes by to bus a table over here. I slip him a beer and ask him, *'Can you get me some chicken strips'?* And you know what? He brought me chicken strips! I had a steak for lunch today! And eight beers. For free, Daryl! *Free*!"

"Maybe you shouldn't be so loud about it."

"You wanna know something? My entire life, people have always acted like I wasn't there. I'd walk into a room, and it was never, *'Hey, Donny-boy's here! How 'ya doin', buddy?'*. It was always like, *'That's weird. There's something different about the room, but I can't put my finger on it. Did you move that table?'*. I can't tell you how many times I've sat at this bar and watched people come in for *their very first time*, and after ordering three drinks, the bartender knows their name. Knows their kid's names, for chrissakes. I have been coming in here for eight years. Eight years, Daryl. And nobody knows who the hell I am. Or cares."

"Why do you keep coming in then?"

"Because it doesn't matter where I go," he said. "It's the same all over. Always has been. They might notice me initially, but in time, I become invisible. Then yesterday you, *you*, showed me the answer to the whole problem."

"By stealing bottles of beer?"

"Yes! All I've ever done is feel sorry for myself. And get angrier and more resentful. To the point where...but then this...it's so simple. I'm mad at myself for never thinking of it before. You showed me it doesn't matter what other people think by turning it around and aiming it right back at them. No, I probably won't ever get anyone to really notice me, but who cares? Because now, I use their petty indifference to my advantage. Today it's beer and food, but tomorrow, it can be anything. I've never been happier in my life. Thank you. Really. Thank you."

Then it happened. He hugged me. I've seen this a lot, guys hugging each other in public. Not the hugs that come after the team scored a touchdown, but real bonding-moment hugs. And whenever I saw those, they made me uncomfortable. It's not a homophobia thing either. That doesn't bother me. Whatever two other guys want to do together is none of my concern. I've just never had another guy hug me before. Ever. Always felt a little weird. And now those feelings are officially confirmed.

"Alright, alright," he said, finally loosening his hold on me. "Enough about me." Then he scooted his stool an inch or two closer to mine. Why does he need to be so close? *There's nobody else in the bar*. I swear, I'm never showing anybody how to get free beer again.

"So, how'd that go with Audrey last night?" he asked. He tapped me a couple times with his elbow and let out a little laugh. "What'd you guys do?"

"Nothing," I told him.

"Come on. Who am I gonna tell? No one knows I'm here."

"Really. Nothing."

"I told you my secret."

"We drove around for a while. She said she wanted to tell me something."

"And?"

"I don't know, she never did."

"Why? You guys get in a fight?" He actually sounded like he felt sorry for me.

"No. I don't think so. Something happened."

"That's what I'm asking. What happened?"

Usually by this point, I already would have told whoever was bugging me that it's personal, and none of his damn business. But there was something about the way he was acting that kept me talking. His constant stream of questions didn't have the same feel as that persistent nagging I'd get from Dr. Melvin. Or Steve. Listening to Don, I got the impression that, for whatever reason, the whole thing between Audrey and me was very important to him. Plus I figured, what's the harm? I don't know him, he doesn't know me. And who knows? Maybe he'd have a better angle at the story than I did.

"She disappeared," I told him.

He gently shook his head and sighed. "Ran away, you mean?"

"What? You know something?"

"I got to know quite a bit about the people around here. You know, overheard conversations and such. Another benefit of being invisible, I suppose. And I've heard enough stories to figure out that she when she gets scared, she runs away."

"Scared of what? I didn't do anything to her."

"Maybe that wasn't the case. I could be wrong. What happened? Details, details."

It took me an entire two and a half beers, but I told him everything I knew about Audrey. And I mean, everything. From what Steve told me to what I remembered on my own. I couldn't believe the words that were pouring out of my mouth. The interesting thing was that he didn't ask one question, or interrupt me for any kind of clarification. He quietly listened, and then when I was finished, sat back and took it all in. I imagined it was a lot like talking to a judge. Not in court and under oath, but informally. Sitting in his living room and telling him your problems.

He must have reached a decision about the whole mess, because his expression jumped from calm contemplation to *"By George, I think I've got it!"*, in less than a second. If there was ever a better example of a light-bulb-over-the-head moment, I don't think I've ever seen it.

"Yours is the little heart!"

"What?"

"On her wrist," he said. "The tattoo of the little heart?"

"Yeah, I saw it. But, what about it?"

"That was her first. That's yours."

"Her first what?"

"Abortion," he whispered. "I knew your name sounded familiar. I don't know why I didn't make the connection before."

"What do you know about it?"

My stomach gave a twist, and I felt like I was going to throw up again. I had to press my palms down hard on the bar to keep from spinning off the stool. Jesus, was it was true?

"I told you, you wouldn't believe the stuff I've heard. But don't worry, I won't say anything. Promise."

"Tell me what you heard."

"Okay, about a year ago, Audrey and the husband got into some big fight. What else is new? Only this night was different. She didn't want to go home, so she hung around here after work and got smashed, I mean, blood-transfusion-in-the-morning *smashed*, and I heard her spilling her guts to Vicky, this other waitress."

"And Audrey told her she had an abortion?" I asked him. "Mine? My baby?"

"Yeah. *Daryl's*. For what it's worth, she said it was the biggest regret of her life." His voice trailed off as he finished the thought. I swear, you'd almost think this had happened to him instead of me. "She kept saying she was in love with you and wanted to get married and have the baby. But, as she put it, her batshit crazy mother screwed it all up. She said her mother was ranting how, *'No baby of a whore would ever be her grandchild'*. She threatened to kill all three of you in your sleep if Audrey married you and kept the baby. Can you imagine that? Threatening to kill your own daughter and grandkid? The old bag demanded Audrey give the baby up for adoption, but Audrey said she couldn't just *give away* a baby, so she ran away and had an abortion. She told Vicky she never wanted to forget what she went through losing it, or you. And that's, that's what that tattoo's for."

"She has other tattoos. Hidden..."

"Yeah, I heard. I don't know where those ones are. She didn't say. I'm guessing none of those guys meant anything special to her. Mistakes that she wanted to learn from? Who knows? But yours, yours is right there on her wrist. You can't run away from that. She said, *Daryl was my only love*. That musta been horrible for you."

I finished off the last half of my beer in one long swallow just as Miguel reappeared and cheerfully deposited three greasy bags next to me on the bar.

"My grandfather knew, but he never told me."

"Maybe he knew how much it would hurt you."

"She was trying to tell me last night, but I wasn't listening. Or just didn't want to hear. I need to find her. Miguel, go see when Audrey's next shift is."

"I dohn think she work here again," Miguel said.

"What do you mean?" I asked.

"She supposed to be work here now, but she no never show up. No call up sick. Nothing. Her husband call to find her, too. He say he no see her since yesterday."

"Somebody has to know. Maybe your manager? Can you ask him?"

"He busy with police."

I looked at Don, but if he was concerned at all, he certainly didn't show it.

"Why are the police here?" I asked.

"Someone break in safe last night. Steal lots of money and very s'pensive scotch whiskey." He turned around and headed back toward the hallway.

Don reached for two more beers. "Can't blame me for that. I hate whiskey. Never acquired the taste for it."

"Audrey."

"It doesn't sound like you'll be seeing her anytime soon," Don said.

"I, I don't know who else to ask."

"Ask what?"

"That's why I went to her. I had to ask her."

"Ask her what, Daryl?"

"I have to find out if I was ever happy."

Don looked very concerned again. "You don't know if you were ever happy?"

"It's a long story."

"I'm not in any hurry," he said.

So, I told him.

I don't know what got into me today, but I'm Mister Blabbermouth, all of a sudden. I will say though, I didn't get into every specific detail. I just gave him a general idea. And like before, he sat there listening thoughtfully and not saying a word.

"I'm sorry to hear that," he said after I was finally through. "There isn't anyone else you can ask?"

"No."

"No friends or relatives?"

"I better get going."

I grabbed the bags of food from off the bar and stepped down off the stool, but Don took hold of my arm to stop me before I could get far enough away.

"Hey, I'm sorry," he said. "I didn't mean to hurt your feelings."

"You didn't," I told him. And I meant it. So what? It isn't my fault I don't have any friends.

"Listen," he said, putting his arm around me again. I prepared myself for another hug, but luckily, it didn't happen. "I think I might be able to help you. You want to be happy, right? This is, wow, this is proof we were meant to meet each other. Sit.

Please. Okay, so, every year, a group of people go on vacation together. A bunch of miserable, unhappy wretches who feel like life has pissed all over them. I think you should join them."

"A vacation with a group of unhappy people? I hope you're not a travel agent, because you're bad at it."

He let out a laugh. "Don't you see? That's the point of it. People who have rotten lives fifty weeks of the year get together for two weeks and let loose!"

"How is that different from any other vacation?"

"Most people, Daryl, go on vacation to relax. This is going on vacation to live! To be wild! To be a pirate!"

I wasn't sure if I heard him right. He was talking pretty loud, and the room had a definite echo.

"Did you say, *'Be a pirate'*?" I asked.

"They call themselves The Secret Pirate Foundation. The way I heard it is, years ago, a couple guys were complaining about how they were fed up with their lives – their jobs, their wives, their family and friends. Same old shit. What it came down to is they hated who they were and what they became. They wished they could completely reinvent themselves, but they realized that was impossible. You can't just become a brand new person when everyone else knows your history. The other people will refuse to accept your changes. But they couldn't let go of the idea. So, they decided to test the theory out and go somewhere where nobody knew them. New York. The moment they pulled into town, they dropped their past lives, all their inhibitions, and became two entirely new people, with fake names and careers, never once speaking about home, their real families, or anything else.

"After two weeks of living like invading pirates, doing anything they wanted at any time without question, they ran out of money. They decided it had to be cash only you see, so their real identities weren't revealed. But, on their way to the ATM, they started confessing to each other that, yeah, it was fun, but they couldn't live like that every day of the year. They decided two weeks was all they needed. And they've been doing it ever since. Think about it: Shed your crummy life and live out your dreams – even if only for a couple weeks. This year's gathering is less than a month away. You should meet me there, Daryl. Maybe you can find your happiness."

"And that works?"

"Everyone swears by it."

"You?"

"Well," he sighed. "I chickened out. Don't get me wrong! The desire and need are there but, I don't know what to do. I mean, I know *what* to do. It's just that I'm not much of a doer. I'm so used to watching other people live their lives, I get kinda lost when it's my turn. You know what I mean?"

"Maybe."

"Plus, going by yourself puts you at a disadvantage. I wasn't invited, so I didn't know any of the other people personally. It seems lonely being a pirate by yourself. Everyone else had friends to share the experience with. It's not the same telling a stranger about your exploits. There's no personal reaction. Come with me, huh?"

"To New York?"

"Actually, no. It's always in a place different. The new location gets passed along through code and word of mouth. It's all very, very hush-hush. Hence the *Secret* in the name. This year, all I know is it's in Nevada, but I don't know which city yet. What I can tell you is there's clues placed all along the way. Some subtle, some not so. Signs, random strangers. Tell me you're going."

"Going where?" a voice asked.

I looked down and saw Steve walking toward the two of us. Don yanked around his head and stared curiously at him.

"How did a dog get in here?" Don asked.

"Yeah," I said. "How'd you get in here?"

"Door was open," Steve said. "Didn't see a sign."

"Is that your dog?" Don asked me.

"I guess so," I told him. "This is Steve."

"And you say he talks, huh?" Don added. "Woof! Woof!"

"Are you kidding me?" Steve snapped. "Typical human."

"Ha ha. He's cute," Don said. "What breed is he?"

"I don't know. What breed are you?"

"English wolfhound," Steve said.

"No, you're not," I shot back. "Why do you have to lie so much?"

"Fine," Steve said. "I'm a mix of whoever was in a yard with an open gate. Someone at my vet's once said I may have some English Wolfhound blood in me, so technically, it's not a lie."

All I could do was look up at Don and shake my head.

"Mixed," I told him.

Don put his hand on my arm. "I'm telling you, this could help you. If nothing else, you'll go to a new place and meet new people. Go with me. Be my crewmate"

"Yo, Daryl! Go where?" Steve asked impatiently.

"To be a pirate in Nevada," I told him.

"So, is that a yes?" Don asked.

"Don't pirates need water?" Steve asked. "For their boats?

"Can't go home," I said to Don, purposely ignoring Steve.

"Then you'll come? You have to come!"

"Okay."

"Excellent!" he shouted. Then he hugged me again. Guess I should have expected that, but I didn't.

"Am I missing something?" Steve asked.

"So, all I know is, drive to Nevada. And pay attention. Clues will be hidden all over. Festivities officially begin last weekend of the month. See you there, Buddy."

"Why does he get to call you Buddy?" Steve asked.

I didn't feel like getting into it with him again, so I didn't even bother to respond. I scooped the bags of food off the bar and started walking out.

"And remember," Don called out. "I won't be Don!"

"What the hell does that mean," Steve asked. "*He won't be Don*? Is that our lunch? Good, I'm starved."

Flanking the door now were both Myssi and Kryssi. Myssi puffed out her nametag like before while excitedly pointing me out to Kryssi. First she gave Myssi a confused stare, but then Kryssi looked over at me, and I saw the light bulb turn on over her head. A much dimmer wattage than Don's, but a light bulb nonetheless. Kryssi smiled big and stepped into my path.

"Nachos!" she happily announced.

"Right," I said.

Myssi and Kryssi loudly cheered each other as I stepped outside into the bright afternoon sun.

"Nachos?" Steve complained. "Why didn't you get cheeseburgers?"

I swear, this dog's priorities.

12

I stopped short of the aisle where my car was parked and gave the strip mall a long look. It was jammed with the sort of businesses you'd expect – tax preparation, dry cleaner, sub sandwich place, a Starbucks, go figure, a copy shop, etc. Long time ago, I used to think copy shops were the biggest scam around. And yet probably the most profitable. Imagine someone saying to himself, "People shouldn't have to go to the library just to make copies. The quality is crap, and they're closed on Sundays. What if I opened a place that was more convenient? With wall-to-wall copy machines and paper products as far as the eye could see? Would people come?" I mean, seriously, who thinks of that? A frigging genius, is who. You charge five cents a copy, *and have the customers do all the work themselves*, and you're recouping your investment by the end of your first year. After that, it's all profit. Well, for a while it seemed that way. Now that everybody has a personal computer, people do of their copying at home, and those shops aren't nearly as busy.

You think it would be that way across the board – as soon as customers have the ability to create a product in their home, the businesses that once offered those services would disappear. But, not so.

What I really kick myself for not getting in on the ground floor of is the coffee shop craze. Independently owned or a franchise, it wouldn't matter. These places are, and always will be, guaranteed money makers. First of all, you've got ridiculously low overhead. I mean, look at the way they're put together: the furnishings are nothing more than an assortment of mismatched furniture somebody found at a flea market. Then you've got a dozen or so coffee and tea pots behind the counter, and maybe an oven in the back to bake muffins and pastry. But I know for a fact that a lot of these places don't even bake on premises – they have a fresh delivery once or twice a day. That way you not only save money on a stove, but on the cost of the insurance for having a stove. That's a huge chunk of change for a business owner. Throw in all the supplies, the condiments, a couple boring light jazz CD's, and a few struggling art students to smile and pour, and you're ready to rake in the cash.

Now, location is usually a big factor for how well a business will do, but with these places, location doesn't even play into it. Shops like these giant customer magnets no matter where they sit.

I guess I don't get it, and probably never will. How much easier and cheaper is it to make your own coffee at home? But I swear, a Starbuck's could pop up in the basement of funeral home, I mean, they could be embalming corpses right next to the cappuccino machine, and there'd still be a line out the door. But, boy oh boy, if you're lucky enough to have a place in a strip mall, one right off a major intersection with an abundance of parking spots and walking traffic, you are set for life. You, your kids, and their kids. I see places like that and it really pisses me off. How lucky some people can be. All it takes is one decision, just one stupid decision, *"I'm going to open a coffee shop",* and your entire life is turned around for the better. No more struggle. No more worry. Coffee never goes out of style. It's forever, for chrissakes.

You'd figure, considering the way things turned out, that my attitude about them would have changed, but I'm staring directly at one right now and the anger is bubbling straight to the top. I doubt I could even get myself to just step inside one. I'm afraid of what I might do.

The only positive about seeing this place was that it served as a reminder that I needed cash. There was a Bank of America branch on the other side of the parking lot, so after we finished up our burgers in the car, we took a walk over. Since I was a kid, I always liked banks. Not just because they held your money, which is a very convenient thing for me, considering recent developments, but also, because of how they feel on the inside. Clean, orderly, secure and quiet. You always know what to expect when you enter a bank. No surprises. No arguments. No drama. No unnecessary negotiations. You go in with a plan, you leave with that plan successfully executed. And sometimes, they'll even give you a sucker on the way out. I imagine it's what some would describe as a Zen-like experience. Never having one myself, I can't say firsthand whether that's accurate or not, but I've heard it thrown around enough to get the general idea.

So, I wasn't surprised in the least bit when a security guard stopped me only moments after walking in.

"Sorry, sir," he said. "No pets allowed inside."

I looked down and glared at Steve. "What's wrong with you? You should know better. Wait outside."

"It's not like I'm going to blow up."

"You better watch what you say, or they'll toss you in jail. Outside."

"This sucks," Steve grumbled.

"They probably heard what you did in the motel room."

The security guard smiled and I walked in, slid a withdrawal slip from a tray on the desk, and proceeded on to the first available teller. He was a skinny kid, easily no more than twenty-three, and wearing a suit about four sizes too big for him. Presumably his dad's or an older brother's. He looked like a poster for one of those movies where the adult magically becomes a kid again, but the clothes stay the same size.

"Good afternoon," he sang. "How can I help you?"

It wasn't until I heard him ask that question that I realized I had entered the bank without bothering to formulate a plan. How did that happen? Sort of goes against the whole Zen-like experience thing.

"I'm going on a road trip for about three weeks, and I want to make sure I have enough cash with me."

"We have branches all over the country, sir."

"Yeah," I told him. "I'd rather have the cash on me."

"True," he said, looking like he meant it. "How much would you like to take out today?"

"I don't know."

"Um," he stammered. "Take as much time as you need to think about it. If, um, if you need help with something..."

"That makes sense. You work with money. What do you think?"

"Well, um, that's hard to say. Where are you headed?"

"Nevada," I told him. No need to get into the whole uncertain-about-the-city stuff.

"Okay. Illinois to Nevada. Three weeks, huh?"

"That's what he said."

"Driving or flying? If you're flying, are the tickets already purchased? What about the hotels? Are they paid for? Will you be gambling?"

"One week of driving. Two weeks at the destination. Haven't paid for anything in advance. How much would you bring?"

"If it were me..." He grinned like he was making a Christmas wish. "Geez. I'd want to have, what? Maybe fifteen thousand? But, I don't..."

"Okay. If that's what you think. Fifteen thousand. Not all large bills."

I filled out the slip and handed him all the essential identification. But, rather than punching the information into his computer, he got all jittery.

"I'll be right back, sir. Please, stay right there."

I'm actually glad he walked away, because I was beginning to have doubts about the dollar amount he suggested was enough. He was right: I had no idea how much it was going to cost for gas, hotels and food each day, not to mention the extra costs of having a dog travel with me. Cheeseburgers alone could easily run a hundred dollars a day. And what if he needs shots? Or a flea bath? How much are those? I suppose I could always use my debit card for gas and hotels, but still, it's good to always have cash on hand. My father-in-law had a saying, *"It's a plastic card you slide into an electric machine. But plastic melts and electricity fails! Then what? You're screwed, is what. Always carry cash. You'll never go wrong"*. Of course, Chuck never turned down a valid credit card in his life, but cash was his true passion. A passion of his that inevitably cost me the restaurant. I guess you could say it cost him plenty, too, but while he was alive, he sure enjoyed himself.

"Mr. Gleason?"

The security guard and a serious looking man in a more properly fitting suit were heading toward me.

"Yeah?"

"Could you come with us, please?" the man in the suit asked. I shrugged and followed behind them.

We walked a short distance down a brightly lit hallway and stopped just long enough for Mr. Suit to unlock an office door and wave us inside. Mr. Suit gave a nod, and Mr. Security walked back out of the office, closing the door behind him. Mr. Suit now flashed me a mouthful of crooked teeth and reached out his hand, which I instinctively shook. Afterwards, I made a mental note to always check the hand being offered to me in advance of grasping it. His was so small, and oozing with warm, sticky sweat, that I was sure I'd have nightmares.

"Mr. Gleason," he said. "I'm Gary Skinner, branch manager. I hope you don't mind: we, heh, prefer to handle large withdrawals in a more private setting, rather than out under the prying eyes of the public. Heh, heh."

We stood there gawking stupidly at each other for a minute before he clumsily motioned to our respective chairs. It was clear he didn't have a set routine down for this sort of thing and was fumbling for any way he could to fill the time. *Elevator speech*, is the way I've heard it described.

"Going on..." His voice fell apart in the middle of the delivery, so he cleared his throat two or three times and tried again. "Going on an excursion, I hear, hmm?"

The guy should be glad this building doesn't have an elevator.

"I guess," I told him.

"You guess?" his heavy lisp provided every *'S'* with its own mini water show. "Do you not have plans?"

"Yes. I'm seeing some sights."

"Seeing some sights?"

"Seeing the sights of six southwestern states."

He was about to repeat it back to me, you could see the preparation, but at the last second, he caught himself, and drew his lips into a tight pucker.

"Have fun."

That officially stopped the interrogation. We sat for the next few minutes in silence – unless you want to count the hissing noises that were emanating from who-knows-where on him.

The security guard reentered and handed Skinner a zippered pouch. This time the guard stayed in the room, watching as the two of us counted the stack of money. Skinner whistling a high C every time he hit a hundred. We were already somewhere past twelve thousand when I remembered that I never told them I wanted to increase the amount. I was going to say something but, Skinner was creeping me out too much. I mean, it wasn't just the noise. Each bill he touched was now covered in sweat. I counted as fast as I could, and when we reached fifteen thousand, I quickly stuffed my pockets and left.

The guard kindly escorted me to the front door – even held it open for me. Another reason why I like banks. The respect everyone shows you. As I stepped outside, I happened to glance down: the entire sidewalk area in front of the door was wet. And there was Steve, sitting in a dry spot by the curb, laughing.

"Woulda taken a shit, too," he howled. "But I already went outside the restaurant."

"Sucker?"

I turned. The guard was still standing in the doorway, but now extending a basket of lollipops in my direction. I picked through it until I found one that looked like grape, then carefully stepped away.

"Have a nice day, sir."

I slid that sucker in my mouth, and started marching my way back to the car when it hit me – how, exactly, do I get to Nevada?

I should find a bookstore.

13

There's something about U.S. street maps that I don't understand. Why do so many different companies publish them when they're all basically the same damn thing? It's like aspirins. If they all have the *same stupid ingredient*, why are there a million different brands? Yeah, with maps there's the size issue – small, medium and large. And then there's the question of personal preference - folded paper, book form, or even in a spiral notebook. But that's it, right? They all contain the same information. It's not like one company offers a map that reveals a secret fifty-first state. Because if one of them did, there's no doubt they'd all be doing it soon enough. It's always the same roads, same cities, same distance calculations. Nevertheless, it took me about ten minutes of standing in an aisle filled with dozens of the same damn maps, doing nothing more than staring and comparing, before I finally snapped out of it. What a waste of time.

I bought the biggest damn one they had and left.

When I got back outside, Steve was bitching again about being left behind. I don't know what he expects me to do. I didn't write the law against dogs being allowed in places of business. In his head, I'm probably expected to stage a coup against the government, or something.

"Why don't you buy sunglasses and a cane?"

He actually asked me this. Who the hell is going to believe this twenty pound mess of fuzz is a seeing-eye dog? I mean, if that's what he wants, I'll do it, just to show him it won't work and how stupid his ideas are, but I'm sure even that won't be enough to shut him up. He'd probably say I wasn't acting blind enough. I know he would.

The strip where Casey's and the bank are located was actually a smaller section of a much larger mall, and I had to walk what seemed like blocks out of the way to find the bookstore. Now, I was all turned around, and had no idea where we were. I tried retracing my steps, but it wasn't working. And the parking lot was just a sea of cars, none of which looked the slightest bit familiar, so that was no help, either. These stupid places are like mazes. You have to plant flags along the way in order to get back to where you started.

An older woman wearing some crazy multi-colored robe and scarf outfit was sitting quietly by herself on a folding chair up ahead. The way she was staring out at the parking lot, you'd think she was looking for her car, too. There was one big giveaway, though: I've ever seen anybody bring a folding chair with them to the mall.

Without saying a word, she pointed her arm toward me and ever-so-slowly raised it above her head, as if the air all around her was forcing it back down, and fighting against it like this was some supreme display of her own strength.

"You are going on a journey," she whispered.

Well, that's not too hard to figure out. I'm holding a map. Okay, yeah, it's inside a bag, but what the hell else this size would be inside a bag from a bookstore? A *big print* book? Maybe if I had the cane and sunglasses, but I don't.

"You are looking for something lost many years ago," she said. "But it is not an item, like a watch. Is that correct?"

She rose to her feet and started tinkling. Not Steve-type tinkling, I would have gotten the hell out of there fast if she did that. Dozens of necklaces and bracelets draped her wrists, waist, and shoulders - glass beads, medallions, etc., - all jangling into each other at different pitches. She had the costume and music, all she needed was a light show and she'd be a self-contained concert.

"You will come inside with me," she calmly insisted.

On cue, Steve started complaining. "I'm not waiting out here again."

"You may bring your dog." And she jingled herself inside the building.

Steve looked up at me. "Do you think?"

I shrugged, and waved him on inside.

The first thing I saw, after waving clear the mushroom cloud of incense that filled the room, was a large placard on the front counter listing the prices for her various services.

Palm Reading $25
Temple Reading $25
Foot Reading $35
Tarot Card Reading $40
Crystal Ball Reading $40
Tea Leaves Reading $40
Miss Lucinda is a Certified Gypsy Fortune Teller

At first glance, it made some sense. I imagine there's a greater level of difficulty in getting an accurate reading from an inanimate object than from a human. Assuming you even believe in any of this stuff. That aside though, I wondered why the foot reading was ten dollars more than the temple and palm reading. Was it harder to read a foot, or was it merely a hygiene issue? You couldn't get me to read a foot for less than two hundred dollars, so maybe that was it.

"What's a *Certified Gypsy*?" Steve asked.

I wasn't sure myself, so I gave the walls a quick scan to look for an answer. To the left was an ornate zodiac chart, to the right, an obnoxiously large painting of a single eyeball. Nothing resembling a diploma was to be seen. I don't know if there was such a thing as a Gypsy college, but what business nowadays doesn't have something framed and notarized on their wall? Kinda of thing like that makes you wonder about the legitimacy of such a claim.

She led us around the counter and into a back room. We passed through a beaded curtain that sounded very much like Miss Lucinda's wardrobe, only louder and lasting a lot longer. I never realized how effective beaded curtains were at blocking light. This room was much darker than I expected it to be. She lit a couple candles, which really didn't help, then sat down at a small table. The only other chair was positioned across from her on the other side of the table. I had a hunch that was meant for me, so I plopped myself into it.

Something about it reminded me of The Spinnin' Room - the record store I worked at as a teenager. Jerry, the owner, petitioned off a portion of the back room in order to create a secret area he called *The Hutch.* The Hutch was where Jerry sold illegal smoking devices: pipes, bongs, power hitters, etc. Obviously, it wasn't advertised, so the only way people knew of the inventory was through word of mouth. Every once in a while, someone would walk in and casually ask if we had any records by *The Hutch.* If Jerry didn't personally know them, or know who sent them, he'd smile and say he never heard of the band. But if he okayed you, you were escorted into the tiny back area and shown some of the most exotic smoking paraphernalia you'd ever seen.

Occasionally, the potential customer would request to *"test drive"* the merchandise, and for reasons such as this, Jerry rigged a ventilation fan that blew directly out to the alley. It was an amazing set-up. Every bowl in The Hutch could have been burning, but as long as that fan was on, there was never a trace of it to be sniffed inside the store. If you were in the alley, however, it was a completely different story. And had it not been for the unfortunate coincidence of an off-duty cop getting head just behind the store I'm completely confident that Jerry would still be in business today.

So, the first thing I did when I sat down in Miss Lucinda's backroom was search the walls for a ventilation fan, but it was too dark, and I called off the search. Seeing as how there was nothing else to do, I killed time by listening to the sound of the curtain. Perhaps it was the idea of the record store still in my head, but I was fairly certain it was tinkling out a Beatles song. At least I think it was the Beatles. I could have figured it out if I heard a few more bars, but the curtain had come to rest and the song was over. The momentary silence ended as Miss Lucinda reached across the table and her music began again. Not the full band, just a couple sections. She clenched my hands and shut her eyes.

I had no idea what I should be doing. Here I was, lured into some mysterious backroom by a strange gypsy woman who was now squeezing the hell out of my hands without providing any instructions, explanation, or advance warning. The thing that bothered me the most was, whatever the hell she's doing was not listed on the board out front. I wondered if she was involved in some sort of Gypsy product research, and that's why I didn't see a diploma.

Her breathing became heavier, and she slowly loosened her grip and reopened her eyes.

"Dark and dismal," she said.

"Boy, she's got you down," Steve quickly shot.

I would have given him a kick, but he was too far away.

Now she was staring directly into my eyes with this wild glare that was maniacally enhanced by the flickering candles. I'm pretty sure I was supposed to stare back - I even tried for a second or two - but it was just too uncomfortable having to watch that crazy face she was making. I decided it best to look down at the table instead. She made no comment about it, like yell at me, or squeeze harder, so I took it for granted it was okay. Just to make sure though, I gave a quick peek up at her. She was still staring holes through me. I couldn't tell one way or the other what this look was supposed to mean. Was it a good crazy stare, or a bad crazy stare? I had no hint whatsoever.

"Negativity," she said, relaxing both her grip and her face. "Saturates your life essence."

"Tell me about it," Steve said.

"Black, corrupted molecules," she continued. "This holds you back from what you seek."

Hate to break it to her, but *my* molecules have nothing to do with it. If anything, it was Audrey's molecules. All of them banding together and running away. That's what's holding me back.

"It is not a girl you seek. It is happiness."

"Whoa. That's spooky," Steve shuddered.

"What you seek is much deeper," she said. "Happiness is not found in a person, and it is not found a place. You cannot get in your car and visit it. Many seek it for years and still never find it. Happiness finds you, Daryl. When it arrives, you must recognize and welcome it, or it may leave, and never return."

Too bad I didn't think to tell that Dr. Melvin. I could have saved myself a lot of time by just putting an ad in the paper and waiting for happiness to find me. This is stupid.

"Did she just say your name?" Steve asked.

"I wasn't listening," I told him.

"This is true," she said. "And from now on, you must listen closer. And watch, and feel, and smell, and taste closer. Awareness must be part of your consciousness."

She stood up and moved to the other side of the room, jingling all the way. An entirely different song this time. She stopped at another table off to the side that I previously hadn't noticed. Her back was to me, so I couldn't make out what she was doing, but whatever it was, she kept herself busy with it while she spoke.

"Experiments were conducted testing the reactions of water molecules to intangible stimuli, such as human emotions and ideas. Glasses of water were spaced apart on a table. Positioned in front of each glass was a card. On each card was written a different message. *Love. Tenderness. Hate. War*. One card with one message next to each glass. In time, molecules from each glass were examined under a microscope. The molecules from the glasses by the positive messages were beautiful. The molecules next to the negative messages were dark and ugly. Your molecules."

I didn't ask to come in here. She hijacked me. And now she's ridiculing my molecules? This woman's got a lot of nerve.

"If positive ideas, simply written out on a card, are powerful enough to cause a reaction from water molecules in a glass, imagine how the water molecules in a breathing, thinking, human would respond."

The increase of her jangling signaled that she was on the move. I know I've heard these songs before, but I was only remembering a line or two at a time. I wasn't sure if that would that be enough to help me recognize them, though.

She walked back toward the table, arms bent at her sides and palms facing up. I couldn't see what she was holding, but her movements gave the impression that she was involved in some ceremony. She elegantly strode past her chair and glided towards me. Now I could see what she had - some sort of rectangular object with a string connected to it. She bent over and carefully hung it around my neck.

"Happiness will never find you," she said. "If you have not opened yourself up to it first."

I tilted my head and saw that attached to the string, hanging just beneath my chest, was a card. And on the card was written a single word:

Happy

"You must wear this always," she said. "Day and night. Outside of your clothes where you can see it. Every morning after you wake, look into the mirror and tell yourself, *I will be happy*. Over time, your molecules, as well as your mind, will absorb the idea. It will become part of your consciousness. You will undergo a transformation. Do you understand?"

"I guess," I answered. "So, how much do I owe you?"

I was ready for this the minute we sat down. There was probably some sign in here I didn't see in the dark. My guess, she was going to hit me up for a hundred and fifty bucks. Maybe two. I told myself I wouldn't go any higher than two fifty, but really, there wasn't much I could do if that was the listed price. It's my own damn fault if I didn't look for it.

Her lips widened into a big, fat, curvy smile. Here it comes. Low prices generally don't follow a smile that size.

"Go," she said, patting the back of my hand. "Go on your journey."

"Okay."

I got up and walked through the beaded curtain. It clinked out a new song, and this time I almost had it - Seals and Crofts? - but then Steve passed though, and the melody changed. Damn it.

"Do not forget to keep your sign on!" she called out. "Perception becomes reality!"

When we stepped out on the sidewalk, I realized she never did tell me how to find Casey's. Going back inside and asking for directions seemed like a weird thing to do after all that. And really, the mall's not that big of a place. I'd find my car eventually. Right?

"Hey," Steve said. "You really gonna wear that thing all the time?"

"That's what she told me to do."

He started laughing.

I can only imagine what his molecules look like.

It was close to dark when we happened to turn a corner and see the sign for Casey's. I pointed it out to Steve and quickened our pace. The faster we're to the car, the faster we're on the road. Seemed like a plan.

"Finally," Steve panted. "Now we can eat."

"We're not eating 'til we stop," I told him.

"We're going all the way to Nevada tonight? How far is that?"

Dogs are so stupid. Luckily, my cell phone started to ring, which gave me an excuse to cut this conversation short. The number was blocked, and I usually don't answer when that happens, but the thought crossed my mind that it could be Audrey at a payphone or something, so I took it.

"Audrey?" I asked.

The response was shrill and loud. "*Audrey*? No, Daryl, it's not *Audrey*."

I was all too familiar with that voice.

"What, Julie?"

"Did you take fifteen thousand dollars out of the bank?"

"Yeah. I just…hold on. How do you know what I did?"

"The manager called. He wanted to make sure you had a pleasant banking experience. Why did you take out so much money?"

"I'm going on a trip."

"Does this have anything to do with your dead neighbor?"

"What? No."

"So, where's this trip you're going on?" she asked.

"Nevada."

"Nevada?" She squeaked. "You mean, like Vegas?"

"I don't know yet."

"Where are you now?"

"Walking to my car."

I could see it about four aisles ahead.

"Drive over here," she told me. "Now. We need to talk about this."

"I don't have time," I told her.

"Daryl, I'm a little concerned about the way this looks. Your neighbor dies, then you withdraw fifteen thousand dollars and take off to Nevada. It's the type of behavior that'll seem very suspicious to the police. What will they think?"

"How will they know I took money out of the bank?"

"If I found out, it won't be too hard for them to. Come over, Daryl. Let's sort this out."

"I have to go."

"Wait. What about Dr. Melvin? You have appointments. Are you just not going to show up?"

"I doubt if he'll notice. He's overbooked as it is."

"Daryl...!"

Then I heard screaming in the background. *Robert.*

"Give me the phone," he yelled. "Now!"

"I will handle this!" she demanded. She tried covering the mouthpiece so I couldn't hear, but it obviously wasn't working out as well as she wanted.

"You tell him these little games are over," Robert shouted. "Or, he's going to end up like his neighbor."

"Robert! What did we agree on?"

"If he blows everything in Vegas, I promise you...!"

She must have wrapped the phone in a towel, or something, because now I wasn't able to hear anything but a few inaudible outbursts. I hung on for a few minutes longer, but she never removed the towel to talk to me again, so I disconnect the call and shoved the phone in my pocket.

"What was that about?" Steve asked.

I shrugged, then opened the passenger door to let him in. Julie was like that. She had a habit of starting off on one topic, then jumping to another without telling you what the first one was about. If you don't question it, and my god, *don't interrupt*, she'll eventually get back around to it and there'll be no fight. Only goes to prove Robert doesn't know a thing about her. She'll come to her senses sooner or later.

There was a gas station a couple blocks away, so after filling the tank, I opened the map to the pages displaying the interstate system for the entire country and tried to work out the best route.

According to my estimation, there were only two viable options. I could either hop on I-80 and take it all the way, or I could take 55 to 70, to 15. The first way brings me to northern Nevada, the second brings me south. Problem is, what if I take the wrong way? I leafed to the Nevada page, and saw there weren't a whole lot of secondary highways. If I go south, but I'm supposed to be north, or vice versa, it could take me forever to get where I need to be. I know Don told me there'd be clues to guide me, but what if I go so far out of the way, I never see the clues?

There was a pounding on the roof of the car, so I looked up. As I was doing it, I knew it was stupid. It's not like I have a glass roof, or anything. It was just a natural reflex, but even so, I hate when I do idiotic stuff like that.

"You can't sit here."

Get Happy

A pair of thick, oily hands were gripping the bottom of my window frame. The face that belonged to the hands was just as thick and oily, and looked like it wanted to grip something, too.

"You gotta get moving," the thick face told me.

I really didn't want to hit the road again without making a decision, so, even though I knew it wasn't the smartest thing to do, I quickly turned to Steve for a suggestion.

"North or south," I asked him.

"North or south *what*?" Steve asked back.

"Just pick one."

"I don't know what I'm picking."

"Yeah you do," I told him. "North, or south. It's not that difficult."

"What are you mumbling about?" the oily guy grunted.

"Which way?" I asked Steve again.

"Which way what?" Steve shot back.

"Oh, I didn't see the map." The thick face said. "You need directions somewhere?"

He straightened up and tried wiping his hands on his t-shirt, but it was a lost cause. The shirt was just as greasy as he was. Then I noticed a symbol on his chest. Unfortunately, the darkness, and the layers of muck, made it barely distinguishable.

"What's your shirt say?" I asked.

"Oh," he said offhandedly. "Ah...*Pittsburgh Pirates*. Somebody gave this to me. I only wear this when I need to."

"When you need to give out directions?" I asked.

I was surprised it was happening already. Whoever organized this was incredibly meticulous.

"I was told to go to Nevada." I gave him a look to let him know I was in on it.

"Yeah, well, I'll get you started," he said, pointing to the street. "Take a left. About a mile you hit 355 south. Take that to 55 south, then 80 west."

I dropped the map on the seat, nodded to the guy, and pulled away.

"Looks like we're going north." I said, hanging a left out of the station. "Good thing you didn't make a suggestion. Who knows where the hell we would have ended up?"

"I was going to say north anyway," Steve grunted. "*Happy*?"

"No," I told him. "*Remember*?"

I'm wondering if I should bring him to a dog psychiatrist. His attention span seems to be getting worse.

14

We were on the road for about four hours when we hit Iowa City. Steve was complaining about having to pee, and we both had to eat, so Iowa City seemed as good a place as any to furnish all our needs. Plus, it was getting late, and I figured we should probably find a room soon. I pulled off at the first exit that looked to be more commercial than community, and kept my eyes open for a motel.

That was probably my only choice on this trip - to stay at motels with outdoor access to the rooms. I couldn't think of a way to sneak Steve into the carpeted lobby of a Hilton. I got angry when that first occurred to me, but then I figured, "So what?". It's *a room*. That's all. A bed, a bathroom and a TV. I fall asleep, wake up, and leave. What's the big deal? I mean, if I was on my honeymoon and planned on actually spending a large amount of time *in the room*, then I'd splurge. But that's not the case. It's not like I'm looking to cut expenses, or anything, but why should I go out of my way to spend extra money on accommodations I don't need? Or care about?

I didn't have to drive far off the expressway before I spotted a glowing sign. The lights for the name were out, leaving *"Motel"* as the only word lit. A generic business with no identity. Perfect. I pulled into the lot.

"Can I pee now?" Steve asked.

I nodded, and we both got out. He ran to the back and positioned himself like he was going to start spraying the wheels, but I gave him a little kick.

"Whoa, dude," he said, moving toward the trunk. "Watch where you're putting your foot, huh?"

"Stay here," I told him. "I'll be right back."

Behind the registration desk was a heavyset woman - not bad looking, I guess, and maybe slightly younger than me. She was wearing a slinky little top, which seemed even smaller in comparison to how big she was. Not that she was huge, don't get me wrong. It's not like she was one sandwich away from being a carnival attraction. But it does make you wonder sometimes, what goes through a person's mind when they dress themselves? Is she not cognizant of the fact that her breasts look like loaded weapons, ready to shoot at any moment and possibly harm someone?

There was no way she wasn't aware of it. I know I certainly was. It wasn't intentional, but I realized that I must have been staring at her chest like it was an aisle full of maps. I lost track of time again, and most likely would have stood there all night looking like a fool if she didn't start laughing. I took the sudden movements as my cue to shift my eyes upward.

"Hi," she said in a soft, low voice. "Welcome back."

"I've never been here before."

She hummed out another laugh and leaned forward on her elbows. "What can I do for you?"

"I need a room."

"Nice necklace. That your rap name?"

I had forgotten all about the sign. Which was completely contrary to the entire reason I was wearing it, wasn't it?

"So, Happy, you looking for a little companionship?"

I shook my head. "I've got a dog in the car."

"Sorry to hear that."

She started to laugh again, but this time she was joined by a small chorus. I peeked to my left and saw three men standing near an open door in the back. When they saw I was looking at them, they all shot me threatening looks. Here they are laughing at me, yet I'm the one who's done something wrong.

"Room seven," she said. "Fifty dollars."

I was about to pay cash, but I realized I never separated the bills, and didn't think it was a good idea to whip out a stack of hundreds with the bank wrap still on it. They might call the cops thinking I just robbed a bank. So instead, I handed over my debit card.

"Let me know is she's not enough for you," she said.

"Who?"

"The *dog* you brought."

"The dog's a he. And he's more than enough."

"Oh."

She bit her bottom lip and smiled, but the other clowns by the back doorway were yucking it up even harder than before. I grabbed my receipt and the key then went back outside.

I have to remember to tell him about this group the next time Melvin suggests I should get out more. Maybe he can make a house call here.

We opened up room seven, and it was every bit as charming as the people in the lobby. But, like I said before, decor doesn't really matter that much to me. I decided to treat this room like I did those idiots – ignore them, and it's over soon enough.

"We gonna eat now?" Steve impatiently asked.

"Yeah. What do you want?"

"I'm cool with a couple cheeseburgers and fries from Casey's again."

"There isn't a Casey's here," I told him.

Jesus, this dog.

"Are you sure?" he asked. "I'm pretty sure I smell one."

"Yes, I'm sure. You're probably smelling yourself. Now, what do you want?"

"Dude, you don't have to be so snotty. Cheeseburgers and fries from anywhere will suffice."

Will suffice? Seriously, what dog talks like that?

"Hey," Steve yelled.

"What now?"

"Help me find the remote before you split."

I scanned the room a few times, which took an entire three seconds, but assumed someone had stolen it because it was nowhere to be found. Then I got a good look at the TV. A dial and an antennae. Oh, he wasn't going to like this.

"How am I gonna change the stations?" he ask whined.

"You're going to have to pick one and stick with it."

This set was so old, it didn't even have a power button. It had a knob that not only turned it on, but also controlled the volume. I hadn't seen one of those in a long time. I wondered if it was even color. It was taking forever to warm up and show a picture, so that didn't bode well.

I figured the least I could do was hold off on getting dinner until a picture came on the screen, so I could find him a station and mess with the antennae if need be. While we were sitting there waiting, and waiting, and waiting, I swear I heard a woman's voice:

"Hey! Anybody around? Anybody out?"

I leaned my ear toward the tiny speaker and gave the set a couple slaps. It wasn't coming from there. I was slightly worried that it was another voice in my head. But why the hell would a voice in your head ask if anybody was around? That seemed like an odd question to ask. You'd think a voice in your head would know better. But then that begged another question: Did it know better? Maybe it wasn't it even talking to me. I mean, is it possible it was trying to reach out to another voice in someone else's head?

This was unexplored territory.

"Helloooo!" the voice called out.

It was definitely a woman's voice. What did that mean?

"You hear that?" Steve asked.

"A woman screaming *Hello*?"

"Yeah."

"Good, I thought it was just me."

"Open the door," Steve insisted. "Come on!"

"Why? Is somebody in trouble?"

"I'm not Lassie, for chrissakes. It's a bitch in heat."

"You've really got a problem," I told him.

"Yeah. You not opening the door fast enough."

"Seriously, you're a degenerate. You should join a group."

"I'm not into that shit. I like my action one-on-one. Now, let's move, buddy boy! I got a lady requesting my presence. Come on, come on, come on, come on!"

There really was no talking to this thing. I snatched the room key off the bed and opened the door. He zoomed past me and was halfway across the parking lot before I even had one foot out on the concrete.

"Hello," the female dog yelled. "Anybody?"

"I'm on my way, baby!" Steve shouted back. "Steve to the rescue!"

Steve to the rescue. Give me a break. He wouldn't know how to rescue someone if his life depended on it. It's simply remarkable - the scope of unfilled promises people and dogs make to each other.

I locked the door behind me and made my way across the street to the Burger King. Not my first choice, but he said he wanted cheeseburgers again, so what are you going to do?

The TV had finally warmed up while I was gone, but the picture was fuzzy and jumping like mad. Here's yet another example of how certain things in your life that used to be a common occurrence can be so easily forgotten over the years. The amount of time I spent as a kid trying to move the rabbit ears to some unknown, yet extremely precise position, in order to fix the picture. A quarter inch here, an eighth of an inch there – no, damn, that's too much! It was enough to make you put your head through the wall. But because you never have to worry about going through all those contortions in order to get picture quality now, these memories got tucked away over time. It was almost nostalgic, flicking around that dial, looking for that one station with the strongest signal. Almost. When people talk about the old days being better, here are the aspects that are casually ignored. After four minutes of clicking, twisting and bending, the only program that came in fairly clear, with the definition of *fairly clear* seriously up for debate, was some nighttime drama on Channel Three. At least I think that's what it was. There were a couple people talking about some woman who cheated on her husband. Whatever it was, it sounded like just the type of program that would hook Steve and shut him up for a little while. And that's what I needed – something to shut him up, because I knew what I'd have to listen to when he got back.

I sat in the room's only chair, with my back to the TV, deciding to watch for any activity outside instead. The room had a full view of the alley that separated the parking lot from the restaurant next door. It wasn't really much in the way of entertainment – every once in a while a busboy would walk out and toss a bag of garbage in one of the dumpsters. I did happen to catch a glimpse of some guy skulking in the shadows that I swear, reminded me of Robert. I'm sure Melvin would have a field day with that bit of knowledge.

Other than that, the scene in the alley was very boring. So, I played a game. *"Which Can Will He Throw The Garbage Bag In?"* Lame, yes, but at least the picture was clear, which was more than I could say for the TV. Maybe if I tried a little harder, it would get a little clearer, but really, why bother struggling with something when you're not even sure if the struggle will pay off? Who knows? I could have spent a half hour fighting for good reception, only to find out that it never gets any better. Doesn't seem worth it.

I was quietly debating with myself over which dumpster to pick the next time the busboy appeared, when I heard Steve outside the window screaming at me.

"Daryl! Daryl!" he was shouting. "Snap out of it!"

I shifted my eyes from the alley down to the ground just outside my window, as I slurped out the last few drops of my soda.

"Why do you have to be so rude?" I asked him.

I pulled myself out of the chair and opened the door.

"What d'ya say?" he asked. "I couldn't hear you."

"I said you're rude. That's all."

"How?"

"Screaming at me, for one. It was uncalled for."

"Dude, it was totally called for," he said. "You didn't hear me the other ten times when I wasn't screaming. You were all zombied-out again."

I was staring directly out the window. There's no way I couldn't have seen him come up, so he had to be messing with me. What is it with this dog and all the lies and exaggerations? I'm so sick of this. But, I knew arguing with him would get me nowhere, so I dropped it, and sat back in the chair.

"Dinner's on the floor." While he was gone, I spread out the wrappers and placed the burgers and fries on top.

"What's with this?" he asked.

"Don't start. There is no Casey's here."

"No, food's fine," he said, still chewing. "I mean the TV. There's no color, and it looks weird."

"It's just old."

"Looks real weird...Whoa! Human's doing it!"

Sure enough, the station I found, the one with the clearest signal, was showing porn. Steve dispensed with the idea of eating and stared intently at the screen. Suddenly, picture quality was no longer an issue for him.

"So, humans do it the same way dogs do?"

"Only the lucky ones."

I walked over and turned off the set.

"What d'ya do that for?" he yelled.

"You shouldn't be watching that stuff."

"Why?"

Why? What a stupid question. I sat back in the chair just in time to catch a busboy make another trip to the alley. Dumpster Two. Damn, I picked One.

"Come on," Steve pled. "Turn it back on."

"Nothing else comes in. I checked already."

"What was wrong with that show?"

"You're such a..." There were probably a hundred words to chose from. The problem was, they were all so appropriate, it was too difficult to decide which one to use.

"Fine," he said, between chomps. "At least tell me what comes next."

"Do I look like a TV guide?"

"No. With those humans on TV. What happens after they're done having sex?"

"How the hell should I know?"

"'Cause you're human, and you've had sex. You have had sex, right?"

"That's none of your business. Besides, real people sex is different from that."

"Those weren't real people?" Steve asked. "You mean, they're robots?"

"What? That's just...who the hell would want to see robots having sex?"

"Might be kinda cool."

"They're *actors*. The whole thing is fake. Real people don't behave like that."

"Like what?

"Look, there's no point in talking to about this. You've never even been in a relationship. You don't get it."

"Get what?" he asked.

"Everything it takes to make one work."

"*I* don't get it? Look at *you*. You've been in what, two big relationships? One left you for another guy, and the other just left. What makes you the expert?"

"Julie didn't leave me," I told him. "And neither of us knows what happened to Audrey."

"But Julie's not with you, either. Sorry, I don't see what's so great about having a relationship. They don't last, so why put yourself through all the emotional pain?"

I knew he wouldn't get it. I closed the curtains, shut off the light and got in bed.

"Now go to sleep," I said.

"I have to pee."

I can't believe this. It's like being with a child. I turned on the light and threw open the door.

"Not here," I demanded. "Go by the alley."

"Whatever."

The woman from the front desk was now making her way up to the door, looking back and forth between me and Steve with each step.

"You have a *real dog* with you?" she asked.

"Yeah," I said. "I told you."

"That's sick."

She made a loud clicking noise with her tongue and headed back to the office.

I stood in the doorway and waited for him to finish. I bet he has no idea how damn lucky he is that I'm the one taking care of him.

15

I woke up with Steve on my chest, licking my face.

"For chrissakes!" I yelled. "Stop it! What the hell you doing?"

"I thought you were dead," Steve panted.

"Get off me."

He stepped off my chest and sat next to me on the bed. "I'm serious. Someone's been banging at the door all morning."

"All morning?" I paused and listened. "I don't hear anything."

"Alright, maybe not *all* morning. But a long time. I don't know how you could sleep through that shit."

"Well, there's nothing now. Maybe they had the wrong room. I'm going back to sleep."

I closed my eyes, and it didn't take long at all before I could feel myself drifting off again. But then Steve pulled me back.

"I'm bored."

"Damn it! Go back to sleep."

"I'm not tired. And I have to pee."

"There never was any knocking, was there?"

"I swear!"

I lifted my wrist to check the time, but my watch wasn't there. Now I'm thinking I never brought it.

"What time is it?"

"I don't know. There's no clock in here. Sun hasn't been up for long."

I opened my eyes for good this time and tried to focus. He was sitting on the other pillow staring back at me with this stupid grin.

"I could go for some food, too. You hungry, Daryl?"

If I wanted, I could reach out and choke him, but I was too tired to make the effort. Instead, I stared at the ceiling and waited for my brain to send the wake up call to the rest of my body. Eventually it got the signal, and ordered that I stretch out the stiffness that had set in overnight. Arms, legs, back, neck, everything that could twisted and extended. Like I was a pair of rabbit ears someone was desperately trying to tune in to the right station. After all the pops, cracks and yawns finally subsided, I stood up and walked to the bathroom.

As I passed the mirror, I remembered the instructions Miss Lucinda demanded I follow. The only problem was, the mirror was covered with so much graffiti, there wasn't a clean space to even see your reflection. It made you wonder why they even bothered to have one at all. The surface was littered with a variety of half smudged phone numbers and women's names, followed by the acts they allegedly perform – I'm not sure what "wicking" is, but apparently, someone named Angie is quite good at it. I mean, why do people do this? Do they actually believe future guests are going to walk out of this room and tell everyone they know that Angie is a good wicker, or that Ray is a gay? What is the point to it, other than a shot of instantly forgotten gratification for the vandal, and extra work for the employee? We had problems with this at the restaurant. Once I paid a busboy twenty dollars to sit in a stall for a few hours on a Saturday night with the hopes of catching one of those lunkheads in the act. By midnight he hadn't caught anybody, so I sent him home. Later on, when nature called, I visited the stall where he had been perched and was introduced to half a wall of brand new graffiti. I fired him the next day. But then he threatened to tell people I paid him to sit on a toilet for five hours, so I had to hire him back.

This is why I hate graffiti.

I turned on the spigot and splashed a couple handfuls of water around the basin to wash away any dirt, then closed the drain and let the sink fill up. Steve stood on the toilet seat and with my help, braced himself against the sink with his front paws. When the water level got high enough, he dipped in his face and drank. I took a pill from each bottle and downed them with a handful of water.

"Ahh!" Steve said, smacking his wet lips. "Tasty. Help me down, would you?"

I grabbed him by the middle and dropped him on the floor. I was about to drain the sink, when I caught my faint reflection.

"You will be happy," I said to it, then pushed down the plunger and released the water. I wasn't sure if Miss Lucinda would approve, but it was the best I could do under the circumstances.

"We going now?"

"Yeah. How's my sign look? Straight?"

Steve gave it a long, considered look, tilting his head to both sides.

"A little to the left," he said.

I gave it a tiny pull, and he nodded his approval. Then we walked out to the car to search down some breakfast.

We sat in the motel driveway with the engine running for a good five minutes, debating over which way to turn. Steve didn't want to turn at all – he wanted me to drive straight across the street and into the Burger King lot. Apparently, he approved of last night's dinner. But the notion of shoveling down another fast food burger, or in this case, breakfast sandwich, made me shiver. I had a flash of winding up like the guy in that documentary who ate nothing but Big Macs for a month. It was so bad for his health that in the end, they had to remove his liver, or something. I don't know for sure, I didn't see the movie. I heard some customers talking about it one day. And dealing with food on a daily basis like I did, it sounded like an interesting movie. I, too, had customers come in and order the same meals every day. Sometimes I wondered if that affected their health.

Emotionally, not physically.

Mr. and Mrs. Partchky, for example, sat in Booth Four at twelve noon, seven days a week, no exceptions, for as long as I worked there, and as I was told, many years before. He would begin with coffee and a bowl of French onion soup. She would have hot tea and a bowl of chicken noodle. For the entrée, Mr. Partchky always had a turkey club on white with fries, while Mrs. Partchky ordered our home style Meatloaf with mashed potatoes and green beans. And at approximately one-thirty, they would place twenty dollars on the table – the bill was seventeen-fifty fifty, the remainder was the tip. Everyone would smile and say goodbye, until the next day when it would happen all over again.

That routine never changed. It was such a given that the servers didn't bother to offer them menus, and we always made sure, no matter how crowded we were, that Booth Four stayed reserved after eleven-thirty. Even on Christmas when we knew there could be a wait for tables, Booth Four was off limits. Sure enough, like clockwork, they would come in with presents for everybody, eat lunch, then go off to be with their family. Chuck always used to say, "*The Silver Platter wouldn't be the Silver Platter without the Partchky's*."

The only alteration ever made to the ritual occurred shortly after I took over as manager. Previously, we had always waited until they sat down before their order was sent to the kitchen. So, I thought it would be a nice way to show how much we appreciated their loyalty if we started cooking their food earlier, before they arrived, to cut down on their wait time. I remember being so proud of myself, finally having *my own regular customers*, and getting the chance to provide them with the type of service I would like to receive myself.

About two weeks after the launch of my new instructions, Charlotte, their regular waitress, confided to me that she was worried something might be wrong. She noticed the Partchky's hadn't been finishing their meals, which was a bit strange in itself, because they normally never left so much as a crumb on those plates. She also said they were acting *"surly"* – that was her exact word for it. Not only had their usual small talk with the other employees all but vanished, but they didn't even appear to speak with each other. No one had any clue what was wrong. Then Charlotte remembered that one of their grandchildren had been sick with pneumonia a month before, and now she was worried that maybe something bad had happened to provoke their odd behavior. Only, she couldn't muster the courage to ask them herself, so she recruited me to do the dirty work.

I stood by their table and tried every approach I could think of, "How's the soup?", "What about this weather?", "Is that a new tie?", but their lips were sealed. They did however, exchange indignant looks with each other following each of my questions. A small crowd of unseated customers had gathered by the register, and since the conversation with the Partchky's was rapidly heading nowhere, I excused myself and started up front. Then I heard a loud noise: Mr. Partchky had banged his fist on the table.

"Why don't you like us no more?" Mr. Partchky's voice creaked.

"We can go other places, you know?" Mrs. Partchky added.

Well, it was clear they wanted to talk now, so both Charlotte and I sat down with them. We found out the whole episode was sparked because of my brilliant new arrangement of preparing their meals in advance. Turns out they liked having to wait for their food. In fact, it was the one thing they actually looked forward to, because the extra time gave them the opportunity to talk with everyone. And now, after all these years, they felt like we didn't want them around anymore and were rushing them out the door just so we could get in the next customer. Mr. Partchky said it hurt them to think that we possibly didn't want them in our family anymore. That remark started Mrs. Partchky crying.

I didn't know what to say. To be frank, I was speechless. Charlotte took Mrs. Partchky by the hand, calmed her down, and explained what happened. In the end, they said they understood, but I really don't think they meant it. In an attempt to prove how important they were to us, Charlotte offered them free lunches for a week. Within minutes, their appetites and their usual dispositions magically reappeared, and the subject was never mentioned again. But I always felt a little uneasy about the whole thing. I mean, here I was trying to do something nice and it was completely misinterpreted. And, it cost me well over a hundred dollars. Of course, nobody considered my perspective. The emphasis was completely on the Partchky's.

After that day, the atmosphere in the restaurant noticeably changed. Even Charlotte acted differently. For a while it was like everyone was on guard, careful not to do or say anything that might cause another incident. Then it hit me – it wasn't any future problems that worried them, it was the past. They were all so embarrassed over the way they reacted, primarily, not taking into account how it affected me. As a result, none of them were ever able to get over their self-consciousness. Which is understandable. Awkward moments of that magnitude have a way of lingering in your head forever. For some, it can shape their lives. And, as I can attest, when people get to that point, there's just no convincing them to believe otherwise.

I wonder what happened to the Partchky's after the restaurant closed?

For some reason, the car was chugging like mad and only getting madder. This I don't understand. It drove all the way out here with no problem, yet now it's sputtering and belching with only the slightest amount of pressure being applied to the accelerator. It even sounded sick when simply idling. Sure, in the past couple years it's gotten fussier first thing in the morning, but that's during the winter. This is August. I wish I knew more about cars. My grandfather could take one apart and put it back together blindfolded. One of his hobbies, some might call them distractions, was to buy and restore old cars. Me, I'm lucky if I can manage to get the gas hose in. Guess some people are just born to do certain things. That would be nice, though – to be able to fix anything by myself. Then again, even if I could, there are so many things broken, I wouldn't know where to start.

I figured maybe a little rest would help. It works for humans, so why not a car engine? We stuttered by a restaurant called *Grandma's Back Porch*, and I pulled to the curb and shut it off.

"I'm getting a whiff of something," Steve said.

"I told you, there is no Casey's here. Get it through your head."

"No, not that. Something else. I know I smelled it before. Just can't place it."

"Must not be that important then," I told him. "Come on."

"What's this?"

"Where we're eating."

"They'll let me in here?"

"We'll sit out at the back porch."

One problem: there was no back porch. All of the seating was inside. Why name yourself *Back Porch* if you don't have one? Granted, my restaurant didn't serve food on silver platters, but no one came in expecting that, though. Which is a little weird if you think about it. Not one person in all those years ever thought to make that joke. Huh. Guess that says something about the level of humor our customers had.

There was no one standing by the door to greet us when we walked in, which is something I couldn't tolerate as a manager. It confuses people. If no one is there to guide them, they either stand there until they get fed up and leave, or they wind up wandering all over the place and go where they shouldn't. If I had to list the *Rules of Running a Restaurant*, that would be in the Top Five for sure.

It was pretty damn obvious no one was coming, so I grabbed two menus off the counter and sat in the nearest free booth. To hell with them if they didn't like it.

Steve sat on his hind legs across from me and leaned on the table.

"Can I get anything I want?"

"I suppose," I told him. "But I don't want you getting sick in the car."

"I won't. What are you getting?"

"I don't know. Some kind of breakfast."

"Ooh!" he shrieked. "Do they have blueberry muffins?"

I'd never seen anyone so excited over something so simple as a breakfast menu before.

A waitress was refilling coffees at the table next to ours, and when she finished with them, she turned our way. I lifted my cup so it would be easier for her to pour. Something I learned from my own wait staff.

"Get out!" she screamed. "Get out now!"

Steve looked at me and shook his head. I knew what he was thinking: *I told you. You should have bought a cane and sunglasses.* Maybe he's right.

"Okay, you win," I said. "Tell me what you want, then wait for me outside."

"I'm not goin' outside," she growled. "Don't you go tryin' to pull any a that."

"I was talking to my dog. Just let him tell me what he wants, and then he'll leave."

"The dog can stay. You're the one's that gotta go!"

Steve was quite amused. "Now, there's a switch."

"And I don't like you comin' in here 'n wearin' that, either," she said, jabbing her finger at my sign. "I don't find it amusing."

A man sitting by himself a few tables away stood up, politely dabbed his mouth with a napkin, and calmly made his way over to us. That in itself drew my attention to him. Just how cool and composed he seemed in contrast to this clenched fist of a scene in front of me. What kept my attention on the man though, was how he was dressed: a shiny blue sharkskin suit with a patterned tie and matching pocket square. He looked like he stepped straight out of a *Rat Pack* movie. I can't remember the last time I saw anyone dressed this sharp. Especially given the fact that it was mid morning inside *Grandma's Back Porch.*

"What seems to be the problem, Gail?" he nonchalantly asked.

"You stay out of this, Aaron. I can handle it."

"Handle what?"

"I'm just eighty-sixin' a bum, is all, and I don't need any of what you think is help."

"I'm not a bum," I snapped.

"Have you taken a look at yourself recently?" Steve asked.

I was guessing none of them were aware of condition the motel's mirror was in.

"Comin' in here, smellin' up the place..." She was set to continue, but Aaron cut her off.

"If smelling bad is your definition of being a bum," he said, pointing across the room. "Then the customers at that table should be told to leave, as well."

Since Aaron and Gail were not engaged in any discreetly hushed conversation, every comment was easily heard by the rest of the room. Including the people who Aaron implicated as malodorous. One man from that group was obviously not pleased with the remark. A fairly big guy, wearing a pair of dirty, baggy overalls and a baseball cap, he pushed back his chair and slowly stood.

"Whad' jew say?" the man sneered.

"I simply said," Aaron calmly explained. "That this man here smells no less pleasant than you do. In fact, an argument could be made that while your aroma is distinctly different, it is considerably worse."

The entire restaurant now turned and stared at the man in the overalls. I thought for sure this would be the last time I saw Aaron. Instead, the man mumbled something incoherent, and everyone at his table quickly filed out of the restaurant, their heads aimed at the floor.

"There's no reason to be embarrassed," Aaron told them as they passed him by. "It was a secret to no one."

"Goddamn it, Aaron," the waitress screamed. "What did I tell you?"

"And what did I tell you?" Aaron coolly and quickly responded. "You need to control these knee-jerk reactions. Empty your luggage, Gail."

"Shut up, Aaron!" she shouted over him. "You can get out, too! I am so sick a you 'n your luggage shit!"

I motioned to Steve, and we both quietly slid out of our seats.

"Okay," Aaron said, pulling his starched white cuffs out from his coat sleeves. "Just realize, my leaving will not help change who you are."

"I'm not lookin' to change myself, Aaron!" she screamed. "I told you that! I'm fine how I am!"

"And that's the problem," he gently replied. "No one looks to change themselves until it's already too late. And Gail, I'm afraid it may already be too late."

"I mean it." Her face was so clenched that her lips barely moved.

"You can't expect to have a stable relationship again until you find a way to..."

"Damn it, Aaron!" she screeched. "Shut the hell up! I hate you!"

She slammed the coffee pot into the table with considerable force, smashing it instantaneously and rocketing shards of glass against the booth where Steve and I had just been sitting. She reflexively jumped back to avoid the hot liquid as it waterfalled off the edge of the table. More than just her face was tense now, her entire body was in on the act. Red, tight and compact. You had the feeling bullets could bounce off this woman's stomach. With the eyes of the restaurant upon her, she began a series of deep, loud, breaths that made her sound like a patient wheezing for the nurse to restart her iron lung. If this little episode was any indication of what her coping mechanisms were usually like, well, you just had to feel sorry for her. And her therapist. And probably, any other member of society that came in contact with her.

She was able to restrain herself for six or seven breaths before the pot handle, and several choice swear words, went flying across the room. The handle landing like a javelin in a short stack of pancakes five tables away. The words landing everywhere else.

She stormed out of the room, right past Aaron. This time, he did not say a word about her behavior. Instead, he produced a money clip from his pocket, extracted a twenty from the thick fold of bills, and dropped it in a dry spot on the table.

"Don't let what she said bother you," he calmly told me. "She's going through a difficult period in her life, and takes out her anger and frustrations on whoever happens to be close to her." Then he motioned with his head to the front door. "Shall we?"

"Shall we *what*?" Steve asked.

Aaron pulled the door open and held it for us. I shrugged and walked outside.

There were a number of restaurants up and down the block, but I didn't want to take the chance of reliving an ordeal like that again, so I resigned myself to fast food. Only, I was pretty sure it was too late to get breakfast at any of those places, and that pissed me off, because I really wanted breakfast. More to the point, I really wanted coffee, and coffee with a burger never worked for me.

"My car's this way," Aaron announced.

He was standing in the middle of the parking lot, pointing to a shiny blue Cadillac, at least fifty years old and in mint condition. I don't think I ever met anyone whose car matched their suit.

"My car's right here."

I poked my thumb over my shoulder at the mess parked behind me. A brown Olds Cutlass that probably wasn't even mint condition when I bought it new fifteen years ago.

"So," he said. "You'll follow me, then."

Steve looked up at me again. "Do you know this guy?"

I squinted to focus on him a little better, but I was getting nothing in return.

"Everything okay?" Aaron asked.

Okay in reference to what? It was one of those questions vague enough to infer almost anything. I assumed though, that he meant getting kicked out by the waitress, so I gave him a steady nod and walked to my car. I'm very aware of the whole *"we reserve the right to refuse anyone"* motto. Of course, I've never personally seen it demonstrated before, let alone have it actually happen to me. But if someone chooses to implement it, there's not much room for argument. The language is fairly straightforward. So, if that's what he meant, then yeah, I was okay.

"Gail was right," Aaron said. "Out here in the light, you do look a mess. Regardless, there was no excuse for her to handle it in such a manner."

I guess I now know what that question was actually in reference to. Is it really too much to ask for everyone else to start paying attention to themselves, instead of harping on how other people look?

Steve and I climbed into my car, and I locked the doors and buckled my seatbelt, careful not to bend my Happy sign.

"So, what now?" I asked him. "Burger King?"

"You mean, my first choice?"

"Don't."

I slipped the key in the ignition and turned. Apparently the rest didn't help the car one bit. I was immediately greeted with a symphony of clunks, whistles and grinding. First the waitress, now this. Can maybe one thing go right for me?

I floored it four, five, six times, to try and blow out whatever was clogging it up, but nothing helped. Pain in the ass. I need to get back on the road.

Steve sniffed at the air. "What's that?"

If he was going to say something about Casey's again, I was going to lose it. But that wasn't it. What he smelled was smoke. Seeping through the vents in the dash and the gaps between the hood and the panels.

Great. Just great. I swear, I don't even know why I bother.

I was amazed at how quickly it was filling up the inside of the car. It only took a matter of seconds before Steve disappeared in the haze. The front window was next to vanish, followed directly by the steering wheel. The last element to fade away was the noise. It was suddenly so very peaceful, like I was flying alone inside a cloud.

My calm was momentarily disturbed by a succession of loud bangs. Thunder, more than likely. These were, after all, dark clouds I was floating through.

But it wasn't thunder. It was yelling, accompanied by the unwelcome reminder that I wasn't flying at all.

"Get out!"

The voice belonged to Aaron.

It sounds stupid to admit, but I had trouble locating the door handle. You'd think finding something as simple as a handle should be instinctive, but when I reached for the spot where I thought it should be, it just wasn't there. Trying to locate it any other way wouldn't be possible, my eyes were already burning and it hurt like hell to keep them open. Even breathing was becoming a bit of a challenge. There was nothing else to suck in our lungs but smoke.

Steve's disembodied voice struggled to call out. "Daryl? What the...?"

I closed my eyes and held my breath, while making another attempt to locate the handle, but I soon realized I was only moving my hand along my left leg. I couldn't even find the door now. How stupid is that?

Now that my eyes were closed, the sting began to dissipate, and I could feel myself drifting off. I was so tired. One of the voices in my head promised that sleeping would make all the pain disappear. At the moment, I was inclined to agree, considering that the other option wasn't very pleasant. I figured I could catch a little sleep, and by the time I woke back up, the smoke would be gone. Maybe then I could finally accomplish everything I've wanted without all these impediments.

Find Audrey. Find the pirates.

Find my happiness.

Then a voice screamed at me. So loud, that it hurt.

"Unlock the door!"

This one wasn't in my head. It was Aaron. Again. This guy, I tell you.

"Hey!" he yelled. "Un-lock-the-door!"

Surprisingly, I found the button on my first try this time and the door immediately flew open, evacuating much of the smoke inside. Steve climbed over my lap and fell into the street. A pair of hands wrestled me loose from my seatbelt and yanked me from the car. I dropped to my hands and knees and coughed up puffs of dark smoke. I'm pretty sure I'd seen something like this in a cartoon. Damn Acme cars.

Aaron lifted me by the sides and helped me to the parking lot.

"Steve..."

I grabbed him by the collar and dragged him along with me.

We managed to get about fifty feet away when I heard another bang. This time it wasn't Aaron pounding on the roof. It was the car exploding. I've never seen that happen in real life, only in movies and television, and it was nothing like you'd expect. Nobody was thrown through the air like Hollywood wants you to believe. There was one quick, extremely loud *boom!*, and it was over. A giant cloud of smoke appeared, then vanished, like the end of a magic trick. *Voila! Your car is destroyed! Thank you!* The hood blew open, very nearly flying off its hinges, and every window shattered.

And of course, each and every one of the nosey little gawkers that streamed from the restaurant were now cowered like babies, fearfully covering their precious heads and ducking for safety. Not one of those idiots realized that their actions had no consequence. Waiting until you see the blast before you protect yourself will always be one second too late. Lucky for them it wasn't anything massive, or they'd all be casualties. I bet they'd all go home and brag to their families about how they flirted with death, saved only by their instincts and incredible reflexes. Idiots.

Wouldn't you know it, as soon as they felt they were out of danger and they pulled themselves out of their crouches, not one of them made the slightest damn move to help, or even see if I was okay. This is what I always talk about: some people are so damn quick to criticize and gossip, but not one person is willing to offer any advice or assistance. Drives me crazy.

I looked down at Steve, who was alternating between shaking off the soot, and coughing up little blobs of ugly.

"You okay?" I asked him.

"I guess," he said. "What the hell happened?"

"Car blew up," I told him.

"Gee, thanks," he snipped. "Me being just a stupid dog, and all, I didn't realize."

And don't think I didn't pick up on his snotty tone, either. What did I do to deserve that? Seriously?

Aaron slipped his hands into his pockets, took a deep breath then exhaled with a frown. The guy's suit wasn't even wrinkled. How did he manage that? Was it the material?

"As one goes out, another comes in," Aaron remarked, to no one in particular.

Steve and I just looked at each other.

"What the shit does that mean?" Steve asked. "Is he a car salesman?"

I just shook my head.

Aaron quietly opened his trunk and pulled out two blankets, which seemed odd since I wasn't cold or on fire. I suppose the gesture was meant to be nice, though, so I didn't correct him.

"I'll drive you to the hospital first," he said.

He opened the back doors of the Caddy and carefully laid the blankets over the passenger and back seats. An entirely different gesture altogether.

"I don't have to go to the hospital," I told him.

"You don't want to see a doctor? After all that?"

"No. I'm okay" Then I looked down at Steve. "What about you?"

He gave a nervous shake. "No way. I hate vets."

"He doesn't want to go either," I translated.

"Fine," Aaron shrugged. "Then we'll just carry on."

"Where are we going?" I asked.

"We're going home, of course. After you're cleaned up, I'll feed you some breakfast."

"Going home?" Steve asked.

There was a tone again in Steve's voice, only this time it was an all-too-obvious hint of distrust. Not sure what the basis of his suspicion was, though. I mean, the guy pulled us out of my car right before it exploded. Yeah, he seemed to care just as much about his car as he did us, but is that supposed to be part of some evil agenda? I don't think so. What it could be though, is another clue. Needless to say, I'm not too keen on the idea of my car having to blow up just so I can get directions, but what are you going to do now?

I swear, being around a paranoid dog is a little off putting at times.

16

We were on the road for a good long time before anyone spoke, which lent a certain familiarity to the trip.

"Was there a lock on your gas cap?" Aaron finally asked.

"No. Why?"

"I've been trying to place it. I'm certain I smelled kerosene. You get enough of that in your engine, and you've got trouble."

"Is that what you smelled?" I asked Steve.

"No," Steve said. "I don't even know what kerosene smells like."

"Did you ask that question to your dog?"

I didn't feel like getting into it. Just my luck, I'd tell him the whole story about Steve's sniffing and wind up finding out that there actually is a Casey's around here. I'd never hear the end of it.

"Hmm," Aaron hummed. "Just a while longer."

I was surprised by the amount of sub-divisions around here. Being Iowa, I fully expected to see a farmhouse with a hundred acres of corn, drive for ten minutes, and then pass another farmhouse with the same setup. I'm sure that's all out here somewhere, but it wasn't where Aaron was taking me. Other than a few slight variations in design, the homes I was seeing could be smack dab in the middle of any neighborhood in the country. Proof of that was, the further he drove, the larger the houses and the land that surrounded them became. It's that way no matter what city you're in. Almost like some kind of law, or something. The closer you are to the center of town, the smaller the house and the land will be. I'm not sure how far we out we were, but I'm guessing it was as far out as you could go from one town before you found yourself starting toward the center of the next town. Everything was enormous.

He pulled into a driveway that was at least as long as the street I lived on. Not kidding. We actually passed through a pair of iron gates that he opened with the push of a button on his dash. Iron gates? In Iowa? Are there problems with gangs of delinquent cows?

The house itself was so big, I figured it could easily hold six of my houses with room to spare. It was the kind of place you'd expect a Senator to live in. No, I take that back. It looked like the kind of place where a group of Senators would *gather*, along with a couple dozen foreign diplomats. To sign a treaty, or adopt new laws.

There was smaller building off to the side. Smaller in comparison to the house, but not in comparison to much else. It sat directly next to the main building, but didn't seem to be part of it. Maybe this, too, was an Iowa thing. It looked like a barn, but I always assumed barns had windows, so the animals could get air. Perhaps it's some kind of detention center for all the bad cows. Solitary confinement, or something. Teach them all a lesson.

Aaron pushed another button on his dashboard, and a door on the extra building started rolling up. It was a damn garage! With ten doors. Side-by-side, but separate of one another. Ten!

As we drove inside the lone open stall, the question being asked by all the voices in my head was answered: Yes, all of the other compartments were filled. Unbelievable. Nine other cars were parked inside – each as old, if not older, and looking just as cherry - as the one he was driving.

I swear, these cars were living more comfortably than a lot of people I knew.

"Ten cars?" Steve asked.

Yep. This is the kind of crap that really gets me. Like he was rubbing our noses in it. *Look at all the cars I have.* Unfortunately, that feeling didn't stop at the garage. It was even worse when we walked inside. I'd never seen décor like this. It was like stepping out of a time machine and onto the set of an early 1960's *swinging bachelor pad* movie. The place reeked of ascots, Henry Mancini and gin rickies. Now the sharkskin suit made sense.

I could feel myself getting angrier and angrier with each step. At first I wasn't sure why, but then it finally hit me: this was one of my big fights with Julie. When we bought our house, it was new construction, so the basement was unfinished. Nothing more than your standard concrete floors and walls, with exposed beams and pipes in the ceiling. She was fine with it staying that way. For a while it served only as a place to keep all the boxes we hadn't emptied from the move. My plan, though, was to fix it up. I didn't want to be one of those people who had an entire space that was never used. But I didn't want to just toss a couch and a couple of rugs down there, either. I wanted to do something different. So, I hit upon the idea of turning it into a lounge. More than just a bar, a couple stools and a TV - nothing special there - everyone does that. I wanted to have something eye catching. Something with an air of glamour and mystery, but was also a fun place to hang out.

Something like this.

Julie of course, was firmly against it. First, she said it sounded too trendy, which I didn't get, because we didn't know anyone else with a basement styled like that. She said it didn't matter if I never saw any examples of it, *people did it*, and she knew it. She also insisted that after a while we'd grow to resent the whole thing because it wasn't *us*.

Which led directly to what she claimed was her real argument: that we had yet to create an identity as a couple, and so we shouldn't rush into anything like this.

Identity as a couple? That comment made even less sense to me. We had been married about five years at that point. If we were ever going to have some special *identity as a couple*, wouldn't it already have been formed by then? She said not necessarily, and that we should wait and see what ours developed into.

I told her that I had never really given it much thought before, but if I had to guess, I'd say that a couple's identity was a mixture of both their individual identities. Things like, how they acted as a couple, what they believed, and what they liked and disliked. And I liked this idea of a lounge. I liked it lot. Which to me, meant that it was part of our identity, right? So, didn't this mean that our identity as a couple was already shaped?

Apparently not.

So, I asked her how people in a relationship went about achieving that identity. She looked deep into my eyes, smiled, and said, "Well, Daryl, they don't achieve it by decorating their basement like a whorehouse."

It was one of the few times I was prepared to fight. I really wanted this lounge, and it was not going to look like a whorehouse. I had never built anything from scratch before, and here was my chance to finally make something on my own. Money was always a big thing with her, so I played up the angle of how it wouldn't cost us that much because I was going to do everything myself. I had the basic design in my head, all that needed to be done beyond that were things like hunt down the furniture, and get a couple books on home improvement. I told her I was going to teach myself how to hang drywall, rewire the electric, things like that. Sure, it might take a little extra time, but it would be done *our way*, which to me, supplied us with that identity she thought we were lacking. It seemed like an easy sell.

Unfortunately for me, there was never such a time in our relationship as a seller's market when it came to things like Julie changing her mind.

"Even if I did let you do this," she said to me. "And you were somehow able to cobble a room together without the whole thing falling apart, there's still one major drawback to this plan of yours: who would ever use it? You have no friends to invite over. Which means it would be just you, sitting alone in your own private Xanadu, like Charles Foster Kane. Any way you look at it, the whole endeavor would be a colossal waste of our money, not to mention the time that you could be spending doing something productive. You do see that, don't you, Daryl?"

She was right. I didn't really have very many friends at that point, probably because I worked so much. To me though, it would have been like *Field Of Dreams*: if I build it, the friends would come. But I never had the opportunity to find out. In the end, she convinced me that our money could be better spent in other ways.

Of course, I was never privy to what any of those other ways were. All those boxes sat in that unfinished basement until the day I moved out. Probably still down there. I highly doubt *Robert*'s done anything with them.

Too bad I couldn't have shown her this room. If she had seen this as a model at Pier 1, or something, I'm positive it would have changed her mind. Nearly everything I had in mind was here on display: hand carved tikis, metal starburst clock, bamboo paneling, you name it. He even had bongos. The depth of detail was amazing. The closer you looked, the more you saw. But, there was a subtly to it, as well. As far as I was concerned, it was perfect. Just enough to make it real, but not so much that it dripped into overkill.

"You like the room?" Aaron asked. "Designed and built it myself."

I swear, I wanted to punch him.

"Down the hall, first door on the left," Aaron said. "It's by far the largest guest bedroom. It's equipped with an on-suite. And please, brush your teeth. Your breath is horrible. You'll find clean clothes in the closet."

He then turned and walked out of the room.

Steve gave me a look. "And you don't know this guy at all?"

"Nope."

"For what it's worth," Steve said. "I don't think you smell *that* bad."

"Thanks."

"You want me to pee on something?"

"Not really."

"We could break something?"

"Let's just wash up."

This Aaron is probably a lottery winner. That would explain a lot.

For some reason, I didn't feel like taking the first shower, and since we really couldn't do rock-paper-scissors, or any of those other reliable old stand-bys that determined the order, I used the only method available to me: I'm bigger and human, so the dog goes first.

While we waited for the water to reach the right temperature, we set a couple ground rules. He promised not to shake off until I gave the okay that I was out of the spray path, and he also promised not to complain. All I had to do in return was promise not to get any in his eyes. Easy enough. So, I got him good and wet, lathered him up with some shampoo, and gave him a good scrubbing. After I covered his eyes and rinsed, I turned off the water and closed the shower curtain so he could shake it off. But then the little dummy stepped right out afterwards. And when I tried to push him back inside and he got all testy with me.

"What are you doing?" he asked.

"Shoving you back in."

"Why?"

"Rinse and repeat. It says so on every bottle."

"Come on."

"Hey. No arguing, remember?"

"Fine."

I assume dogs don't think it necessary to read labels. He'll catch on, though. He seems fairly bright.

Now, I've never been one of those people you see in soap commercials who act like they had some life changing experience just because they took a stupid shower, but I have to admit, I did feel different. Refreshed. Not like I was going to break into song, or anything, because I've always found that to be somewhat disturbing. To this day, musicals freak me out. How is it that strangers are all supposed to know the words and choreography to some song? I could never buy into it. Just too much of a coincidence.

It turned out Aaron was indeed correct: the closet was filled with clothes, but due to the fact that he has about three inches and maybe thirty pounds on me, nothing was going to fit. I found a robe and a pair of pajamas, one-size-fits-all, thankfully, and I slipped into those. They were comfortable enough but, what's the deal with offering someone a shower and clean clothes if you can't make good on the offer? I felt a little stupid walking around some strange guy's house in the middle of the day dressed like a little kid at a sleepover.

"Dude. Can I have a hat?"

Steve was parked in front of the closet and staring up at a row of fedoras and bowlers on the top shelf. Bowlers? I haven't seen a bowler since the last time I watched a Laurel and Hardy movie.

"He won't have your size," I told him.

"How about you have a look, anyway?"

As we rummaged through, we found that every hat was a different size, which meant we were each able to find ones that fit. Why the hell were the clothes all one size, but the hats different sizes? Wouldn't it usually be the other way around? Does the guy's head expand? I remember hearing something about Alfred Hitchcock having a variety of clothing sizes in his closet. Apparently, he'd jump on and off a litany of diets and go through drastic weight changes on a regular basis. Maybe this Aaron is like that. But seriously though, his head? I never heard that one before.

I gave Steve's hat a little tilt to the left, and he trotted over to the full length mirror to give himself an examination.

"Not bad. Not bad at all," he said. "Aren't you gonna wear one?"

"I don't feel like a hat."

"Suit yourself. Don't forget your sign."

I grabbed the Happy sign from under of my pile of dirty clothes on the bed, and the two of us went in search for the kitchen. Good thing he remembered about the sign, because it slipped my mind. A couple more days, and I'll have the routine down.

Considering how hungry he said he was only an hour ago, I expected Steve to run full steam and start eating straight out of the pan.

Instead, he slowly strolled through the hallway, nose up in the air and taking in the smells with every sniff.

I'm not sure, but I think it had something to do with the hat.

"Bacon," he said with a long inhale.

A few steps later he sniffed again. "And breakfast sausage."

"Is that French Toast?" he asked, this time almost panting.

"I don't know," I replied. "Maybe. All I smell is bacon and coffee."

"Which one's the coffee?"

"How am I supposed to tell you that? It's the one that smells like coffee."

"Never had it. Guess I don't know what it smells like."

"Really? You never had coffee?"

"You ever see a dog drinking coffee before?"

"No, but I never heard a dog talk before, either."

"My human drank tea. Besides, coffee's not one of those things humans tend to share with dogs."

"You should try a cup," I told him. "I bet you'd like it."

"Really? Awesome."

We entered a kitchen that was at least twice as large as any I'd ever seen. It's gotten to where I'm pretty damn sick of everything around here being so damn big and expensive. As far as I could tell, this Aaron guy lived alone - then again, a family of five could be living their entire life in another part of the house and you'd never hear them. But if I'm right, and he does live alone, why does one person need this much space? Or this much stuff?

"Sit," Aaron said, pointing at a table filled side to side with food.

The table sat six, (Aaron and that family of five?), but held enough food for triple that. Steve's nose proved to be pretty accurate - there were serving trays loaded with bacon, breakfast sausage, sliced ham, scrambled eggs, hash browns, pancakes, waffles, toast, and bagels.

Two questions popped into my head: Where did all this food come from? And, how the hell long were we in the shower?

"Are the customs different out here in Iowa?" Steve asked. "'Cause, my human back home always ate off plates."

I looked around, and he was right. The only plates I could see had food on them.

"Can I just dive in?" Steve asked.

"No," I told him. "Aaron? Umm, where do we find plates?"

"Underneath the napkin," he replied.

I scanned the table and saw a large cloth napkin with the phrase, *Never Be Afraid To Ask For Help*, written on it in big block letters. I wasn't sure what that was in reference to. Was it supposed to mean in the kitchen, or in general? Not only that, was it meant for other people, or was it a reminder for him? It didn't appear that he needed any help, though, so I was a little stumped.

"Does he eat wet, or dry?" Aaron asked.

"How's that?" I asked.

"Your dog," Aaron explained. "The food he eats. Is it from a can or bag?"

"I'm not eating no damn dog food," Steve insisted. "I want this!"

"He's fine with this," I told him.

"Not a good idea," Aaron said. "I have top of the line all natural dry dog food. Developed by a veterinarian. I'll pour a bowl of that."

"I don't want that shit," Steve protested.

"Really," I told him. "This is all I've ever seen him eat."

"I'm sure if he could talk, he'd tell you," Aaron said. "I know my dogs prefer their food to mine."

"Do your dogs talk to you?" I asked him.

"In fact, they do. Through extensive study, I've been able to discern a distinct tonal variance in their barking, which allows me to comprehend exactly what they are trying to communicate."

"What a load of crap," Steve said, munching on a sausage. "Hey, ask him if any of his dogs are females?"

"Are your dogs males or females?" I asked.

"Two males."

Steve tilted his head to the side. "Hmm..."

I had an idea what he was implying, and I didn't think it was right. He shouldn't be questioning Aaron's sexuality right in front of him like that, or even worse, if he preferred the company of a completely different species, so I simply ignored Steve's comment and continued loading our plates. He sat up on his hind legs and leaned on the table with his front ones, watching my every move.

"What are those?" he asked, pointing his nose toward a basket.

"Blueberry muffins," I said.

"Yes," Aaron said. "With fresh blueberries. I have several bushes in back."

"Hot damn!" Steve screamed. "Snag me a couple!"

I made sure both of our plates had a little bit of everything, which pleased Steve to no end.

"Coffee, too! Don't forget you want me to try some!"

Now I was having second thoughts. Did I really want to introduce Steve to caffeine? What can I do, though? I offered, and now he was looking forward to it.

"Can I have another mug?" I asked Aaron.

"Something wrong with that one?"

"No," I said. "It's for Steve."

"Your dog? He drinks coffee?"

"Not really, but he wants to try some."

"You know, with that hat on, it looks like he should be drinking tea." Aaron offered a little laugh at his joke, but no one else joined in.

He quietly eyed me for a minute, then walked over to a cabinet and came back with a mug. I figured plain black probably isn't the best way to get acquainted with coffee for the first time, so I mixed in a little cream and sugar. Not too much, just about equal to what I put in myself. I waited for Steve to have a taste before I sat down, just in case I had to make any adjustments. He leaned forward and gave it a sniff.

"Careful" I cautioned him. "Might be a little hot."

He tested it with the tip of his tongue, then gave it a big slurp.

"Hmm. Not bad. How 'bout just a touch more sugar?"

I stirred in another half spoon of sugar, then sat down to eat. It wasn't until that first forkful of pancakes hit my mouth that I realized just how damn hungry I was. I must have looked like some idiot in one of those stupid eating competitions they show on TV when there aren't any legitimate sporting events going on. I couldn't get the food off the plate and into my mouth fast enough. I caught Aaron staring at me a couple times, but I didn't care. Not unless there was a prize involved, and probably not even then.

It didn't take me long to wipe that first plate clean. I was prepared to get seconds, but I swear, I hadn't even completely swallowed my last piece of food before Aaron started in on me.

"Let's talk," he said.

For the record, I was on Chew Seventeen. You'd think the guy could wait until my jaw wasn't active.

Steve shot me a suspicious glance. "Damn it, I knew it! If he tries anything, I'm biting him! Good and deep."

"Something wrong with Steve?" Aaron asked. "It's the food, isn't it? Unable to digest properly, is my guess."

I shook my head, and put up my hand to hold back Steve.

"Alright," Steve said. "But I'm keeping an eye on him."

"He's fine," I said. "It's just the way he is."

"Tell me about the sign."

I happened to notice that both Steve and I were out of coffee, so I grabbed the carafe and filled us up.

"Thanks, Buddy," Steve grinned. "I like this stuff. It's really good. Really, really good."

Yeah. This caffeine thing with him might be a mistake.

"So," Aaron blurted. "You're not going to talk?"

"Talk about what?" I asked.

"The sign?"

He pointed at me and drew what I assumed to be a smiley in the air.

I added our sugar and stirred.

"Just have to wear it. That's all."

"Hmm," Aaron hummed to himself, seemingly not too pleased with my answer. That didn't stop him from continuing with his line of questioning, though.

"And another thing, why are you wearing my pajamas?"

"None of the other clothes fit me."

"So," he said, drawing out the 'o' sound. "You tried on everything, then?"

"No," I shot back. "You're bigger than me. I didn't see the point."

"The point would have been to look at the tags. That closet contains my collection of vintage clothing. And as a collector, you buy what's available, not what fits *you* specifically. There are many different sized garments in there. Had you not given up so quickly, you would have noticed as much."

"Can I bite him yet?" Steve snarled.

I shook my head no – it was meant for Steve, but it also served as an overall response to Aaron.

"I'll wear this until my clothes are clean," I told him.

Aaron sat back in his chair and actually looked like he was deciding about whether or not it was okay if I stayed in pajamas. It came off as rather arrogant, and if I cared the least bit, I'd probably be offended. I mean, if he doesn't like seeing me in his pajamas, I'll just go sit in another room while my clothes are in the wash. But the thing is, if you have a problem about people wearing your pajamas, then don't keep them in a room that's filled with clothes you're offering them to wear.

Some people are so oblivious. And that's no kidding.

"I suppose that's all right," Aaron said, rising from his chair. "Not every step is equal. Sometimes the path is smooth and even, other times you step cautiously to avoid what lies ahead. But, as long as we keep moving forward, and allow this to only be a temporary stop, we'll be fine."

"What the hell is he talking about now?" Steve asked incredulously.

I gave Steve a little shrug while taking another sip of my coffee. When I turned back to look at Aaron, he was gone.

"Where did he go?" I asked Steve.

"Damned if I know, dude. But, I say, let's get out of here."

"In pajamas and a robe?"

"Maybe if I keep the hat on, no one will notice you."

"Where are we going to go? We don't even have a car."

"Oh, yeah," Steve said. "What about that?"

"Need to get it fixed."

"Fixed? How long will that take? The damn thing exploded!"

I hadn't really thought about it like that. It was still on fire when we left. I imagine it's out by now, though. The interior of the car I don't care about, I can always drive with the windows open to air out the smell, so that will save some repair time. It's the rest of the car that worries me. Probably just needs a tune up and an oil change. And a real good wash. That doesn't take long at all.

"We're not gonna stay here, are we?" Steve asked.

"When?"

"While the car's being fixed."

"No. We don't have to." I said. "We can always sit in the waiting room. They usually have TVs and coffee."

"Cool."

So, that's the plan. Call for a tow. Wash my clothes. Get a ride to the mechanic. Tune up and oil change. Car wash. Whole thing shouldn't take more than a couple hours. I didn't see a problem. Maybe it's him, but I'm getting the sense that dogs are either big worriers, or really paranoid.

"Hey," Steve whispered. "He's back."

Aaron made a beeline for the table. He looked different though, like something was bothering him. I noticed that he had clothes draped over his arms. My clothes. Was he going to wash them? Maybe Steve was right and there is something wrong with this guy. He didn't have my socks and underwear on display, so I guess I could be thankful for that.

"Okay," Aaron sternly announced. "Explain this."

I wasn't sure what he meant. Again. This guy asks some really vague questions, but expects succinct answers.

"Your pockets are full of cash and drugs, and your phone won't stop ringing."

"Did you see who's calling?" I asked him.

I'm guessing though, that wasn't the response he wanted to hear, because he scowled and released a long, woe-is-me sigh. Sorry, but if Audrey was calling, I wanted to know.

He took a couple steps closer, and was about to say something else, when bells started to ring. The loud, deeply resonating type a hunchback would be generating up in tower. Did he have a tower? I guess anything's possible with this guy.

Steve jumped about three feet.

"What the shit is that?" he yelped.

Aaron lifted a remote control off the counter and pointed it at the wall to my left.

"Someone's at the front gate," he said.

Hidden panels in the wall slowly slid open behind me, revealing a flat screen TV monitor. He pushed another button and the TV turned on, showing a wide shot of the front gate from above, but all that could really be viewed from that shot was a man standing outside his car. Aaron must have pressed another button because the angle changed to a camera trained directly at the front gate, where a policeman could clearly be seen standing next to the open door of his idling squad car.

"Aaron, it's Jake," came the voice through the TV. "Open the gate. I have to talk to your friend."

I assumed he meant me, but he was really jumping to conclusions by suggesting I was his friend. Of course, when the guy sees me in Aaron's pajamas...

"He called the frigging cops on you!" Steve shrieked. He leapt over the table and landed at Aaron's feet, staring up at him menacingly and poised for attack.

"Just say the word, Daryl!" he announced through gritted teeth. "I'll bite his damn leg off! Tell me. Now? Now?"

Aaron didn't flinch. He calmly reached into his right pocket, removed what looked to be a small piece of pipe and put it to his mouth.

"Ahh! Jesus!" Steve screamed, instinctively covering his ears with his paws.

Within seconds, two of the largest, most muscular dogs I've ever seen in my life came galloping into the kitchen. I honestly didn't think I'd be alive long enough to even worry about talking to the sheriff. One dog was locked in and headed straight for me, the other had an angle on Steve. Various suggestions on how to handle this were shouted by the voices in my head:

"Throw a plate!"

"Grab a knife!"

"Grab your chair!"

"Get under the table!"

"Get *on* the table!"

"*Push over* the table!"

"Run, you idiot! Run!"

"Yeah, maybe he's right. Run!"

But, I did nothing they instructed. Instead, I just sat there. I didn't even clench up. It was strange how serene I felt, how positively devoid of concern I was, at facing the inevitability of being eaten alive. The scene was unfolding so fast, this giant killer dog bearing down on me, and the dozens of warnings echoing in my head, that I neglected to think how Steve would fare. At least I could fight back if I wanted to. But, one appropriately placed snap of that dog's jaw, and Steve would be history. Little shredded pieces of history. So, I grabbed the arms of my chair, and readied myself to jump up and lunge in Steve's direction when the monster made his move. If nothing else, maybe I could stop it long enough for Steve to make a run for it.

They were only inches away from the two of us, drooling at the prospect of an early lunch, when they both slammed on the brakes and skidded to a stop. And just as coolly as Aaron, they stood at attention, not making a sound, just staring us down and grinning, daring us to make a move.

I shifted my glance toward Steve. He was still on his belly, covering his head with his front paws, but now there was a large puddle of urine underneath him. Luckily, the kitchen had tile floors, so I didn't think it was a big problem.

Aaron looked surprised. Almost like he had fully expected the dogs to eat us, and was now wondering what happened to change their minds. Maybe these dogs had never actually eaten anybody before, and the real possibility of doing so repulsed them. Not likely, but at the moment, I couldn't think of what else would make Aaron looked so astonished.

"Tell me about these," he said, holding out both his arms. "Green light..."

Green light? I had no idea what the hell he was talking about.

"I won't tolerate this under my roof. Yellow light..."

Now at least I knew what he was doing. But I still didn't know what he wanted to hear from me.

"The sheriff will be here any second, Daryl."

His tone had changed. It sounded cautious, like he was trying to protect me from some imminent danger.

"Why did you come here?"

Why did I come here? I swear, this guy's like Melvin with the stupid questions.

"Why?" he me asked again, a little more insistent this time.

"Because you drove me here. Remember?"

He looked down at his hands, gently bouncing each one in the air, like he was trying to balance out their weight. First my clothes and all the money, then the pill bottles, and back again. I wasn't sure exactly what was going through his mind, but it seemed like there was an awful lot of it. And that it was mildly painful.

"I don't know what you want me to tell you," I said.

"Did I bring a drug dealer to my house?"

"No. My name's right there on the bottle. And there's probably a receipt in one of the pockets from the withdrawal."

He closed his eyes for a moment, then exhaled and shook his head.

"Hans. Boris," he called in short puffs of air. "Out."

The dogs dutifully spun around – the one on the right clockwise, the one on the left counterclockwise, like the Fred and Ginger of attack dogs – and disappeared from the kitchen just as promptly as they arrived.

The bells rang again. Only not hunchback bells, this time around the sound was more reminiscent of competing Santas outside a department store in winter.

"He's at the front door," Aaron said. "Stay here."

Aaron set everything down with a tiny sigh, then whisked himself off to the front door. Once he was gone from the room, I turned my attention back to Steve. He hadn't moved from the last time I checked on him. I could see his body rising and falling with each breath, so I know he didn't die of fright.

"Steve?" I called out. "Hey, they're gone."

"I know," he said in a miserable whisper. "I'm not an idiot."

"Didn't say you were. You okay?"

"This sheriff," he finally muttered. "He's probably here because they want to talk to you about my human."

"Yeah."

He slowly pulled himself up off the floor, gave his fur a good shake, then cleared his throat.

"Don't say *anything*," Steve instructed. "You hear me? This one ain't going to question you. He's only here to hold you until the cops from back home show up. Anything you say to this hick can only screw you deeper. Play your zombie act with him. Or tell him you want to lawyer up."

"What cop show was that from?"

"Dude, it's not from a cop show. It's common sense."

Something about hearing that phrase *"common sense"*, set off an internal alarm. I've never heard of sending one sheriff, by himself, to retrieve a murder suspect. Granted, I don't watch as many police shows as Steve, but those I did see had dozens of cops decked out in riot gear, battering rams, and more guns than they'd ever need, just to bring in that one suspect. And I would imagine that same theory in TV exists in real life, too. But, while I understand how they want to protect themselves at all costs, what happened to the concept of *innocent until proven guilty*? I didn't kill the woman. She was already dead when I got there. Is it my fault I didn't jump straight to the conclusion that an awful smell meant a dead neighbor and immediately called the cops? I had a sinking feeling nobody was going to believe any of my story. I don't even know if I would.

The most unsettling idea of having the cops after me was the prospect of dying. And not just the whole right-there-and-then aspect of it. Primarily, it was the realization that I never gave my own death much thought before. If anything, I'd have to admit that I've spent way more time in my life thinking about other people's deaths than mine. Not that I was ever hoping for people to die. Well, not everyone. There were a few, but that's not my point.

I suppose if pressed for an answer, somewhere deep down I've always had the vision, like I bet most people do, of being an old, old man and dying in my sleep. I'll even confess that at one time earlier in my life, I told my friend Woods that if I had to go, I wanted it to be after a wild orgy with four women, each with a different hair color. But even when I envisioned it in that setting, it only happened after I became a very old man, and I had fallen asleep on top of the blonde. I'm not even sure if sex was involved.

Like I said, I never really gave it too much thought, but if I had, it would probably be something like that, I guess.

So, the thought of dying in a gun battle with the police in the middle of who-knows-where Iowa didn't seem as appealing as my previous option. Plus, you couldn't really even call this a battle, seeing how I was unarmed. It was shaping up to be more like human target practice than anything else. I considered asking Aaron for a gun, but with my luck, he'd probably only have ancient powder muskets. And unless I was ambushed in a medieval theme restaurant, that wasn't the type of firepower I needed. Especially if I was expected to take on a SWAT team.

The whole concept of *going out in a blaze of glory* is rather stupid if you put any real thought into it. You're going to wind up dead, right? In only a manner of minutes. The odds of your survival are somewhere in the area of a billion-to-one. So, in the end, what difference does it make if you brought down fifty people with you, or went out alone? Both scenarios reach the same conclusion. You. Dead. It's not like you'll be able to do a victory dance in front of your killers at the morgue. You're all dead, which sort of negates the whole vengeance angle. It would make more sense to put five bucks down on yourself and hope you live to collect the five billion dollar winnings.

Vengeance is strictly for the living. It honestly does dead people no good whatsoever.

I glanced up at the clock. Two-twenty. That figures. Middle of the afternoon.

After a few minutes, Aaron came strolling back into the kitchen. Alone, and in a much better mood. Then it occurred to me. If that one sheriff knew him well enough to call him by his first name, then maybe all of them did. And if that were the case, I'm sure none of them wanted to be responsible for busting up their friend's fancy decorations. My guess was that they were busy setting up sharpshooters around the perimeter of the house, leaving Aaron with the job of luring me outside, so the massacre could happen on the lawn where it would be nice and neat. Unnecessarily overdramatic, but efficient, I suppose.

I poured myself another cup of coffee.

"I know what this is about," I told him. "How long are they giving me?"

Aaron pulled a chair away from the table and sat. "He didn't say exactly. I assume they want to see you before the end of the night."

Patient group. The type that insists on getting it done right. Got to give them that. I stood up and walked to the window to get a look at my death squad. Steve came running over to join me, jumping onto the window seat and pressing his nose against the glass.

I focused in on the tall grass about a hundred yards out, but I couldn't see sharpshooters positioned anywhere.

These guys were good.

"You think there's more cops out there, don't you?" Steve nervously asked.

I nodded, then reexamined the horizon with a good strong squint, double checking for any possible movement.

"Me, too," he added. "I just didn't want to say it out loud."

I don't know why. Saying it out loud wouldn't have changed anything.

"We gotta split, dude" Steve added. "Wait until dark's what I'm thinking. Make a run for it."

Running. That, to me, is a close relative to the *blaze of glory* shootout. You're only delaying the inevitable, so why bother? I suppose there's some who believe there is a difference, though. They would argue that you might be able to get away by escaping and hiding. After all, they'd mumble through their fake moustache, it's far easier to hide, or get lost in a crowd, than it is for one guy to take on twenty armed cops. The odds are much more in your favor.

But again, for what purpose? To stay alive, yeah, maybe, but you have to consider what kind of life you'd be living. Never being able to stay in one location for too long. Always looking over your shoulder. Living in constant suspicion of everyone you meet, wondering if their "friendship" is really just that, or if there's a secret agenda.

Not much of a life, but, believe it or not, there are people who live it. Actually, I guess I'm living it right now. Never thought of that.

Neither of those routes led to an agreeable end result, which meant I was really only left with one choice. Give up. Sure, I'd get sent to prison, probably death row, but at least then I'd have the opportunity to plead my innocence for a while.

It's not glamorous, and there's no guarantees you'll ever win, but it does keep you alive.

"Don't be upset," Aaron chimed in from the table. "That's why you're here. For me to help you."

It was kind of creepy how it seemed like he knew what I was thinking.

"You're going to help me?" I asked. "How?"

"First off, you need to take care of this little business with the sheriff."

Little business? Is that how he's going to help me? To shoot it out with them?

"He said it's a lost cause," he said.

"Yeah. I figured."

"I was right. Kerosene. Jake thinks you were pranked by one of the frats. This time of year, no car with license plates from another Big Ten state is safe."

That's what they wanted to talk about? The car?

"I took the liberty of telling Jake you didn't want to file a report. Doing so would merely be an exercise in futility. Even if they did find the culprit, it would only culminate in you spending more money, and time, in court than your car is actually worth. Still, we need to move it, or the county will haul it to their yard in the morning. And you don't want that. They will kill you with fees. I know you have money, but that's just nonsense. I'll call Andy – he owns a junkyard outside of town. There might be something salvageable. He'll give you a decent price. Then tomorrow, we'll see about finding you another one."

"Another what?"

"Car. Aren't you listening to me? Think of it this way: you needed a better car anyway, am I right? Now, I'm not condoning the behavior of these miscreants, but, even before the fire, it was obvious you were way past due for an upgrade. Why not look at this as an opportunity?"

Steve tilted his head up at me with a look of disgust. "This clown *is* a car salesman, isn't he? You don't think he did all this just to get you to buy off his lot, do you?"

I shrugged and headed back to the table. Who knew what the hell all this was about. I thought for a while that he was the next signpost, but I guess I was mistaken.

Aaron sat back down and stared into his half-finished plate of food. "Believe me, I'll be having a conversation with both the faculty and the student governing board. Not only is this conduct dangerous, but it affects the town's economy. People will stop visiting if they anticipate being victimized. Perhaps that will get them thinking."

He must not have like the way the bacon looked, or something, because he pushed the plate aside, then took a deep breath and exhaled with a delicate laugh. "I don't know why I doubted it. I knew you were the one when I saw you in the restaurant. Funny how it works sometimes."

Steve snuck me a look. "What's he talking about now?"

I downed my coffee and set the cup back on its saucer. I was eager to hear about this myself.

"I never know when it's going to happen." He looked up to the ceiling, like he was expecting a spotlight to shine down on him that very second. "Having to help someone. I just get this sense. Before I even meet them. Almost like a premonition. There have been situations when I could swear I was meant to work with someone, but it ends up not being right. And why? No premonition. This morning, though, while I was driving into town, I got it right here." He patted down his stomach twice with his right hand. "It's funny. I thought the only reason I stopped at that restaurant was because I was hungry. Then when you walked in, I knew. You, Daryl, are my latest project. Finding that money threw me at first. I've never questioned a premonition before. Now, *now* I'm thinking, maybe the money has something to do with your problem. It's more than you just being marooned here and needing help to get traveling again, isn't it?"

"Marooned?" I said. Now I was feeling like I was having a premonition.

"Mm hmm. Stranded."

"Like a pirate."

Aaron just smiled.

Steve shook his head in disbelief. "I'll be a son of a bitch."

17

"So, tell me about the money," Aaron continued. "I knew it wasn't obtained illegally the moment you didn't panic and run when the sheriff was at the door."

Another one of his premonitions, no doubt.

"I just sensed it," he added.

Score one for me.

"So, I've been brainstorming," he continued. "Is it everything he owns in the world, and he's now heading to a new destination, with the intent of carving out a new life for himself? But I quickly discarded that theory. If it was all that you owned, you'd take better care not to leave it laying around where someone else could find it. And then when you saw me with it, you didn't fight to get it back. No, this isn't everything. This is a portion. My guess is, merely a small portion. I'm right, aren't I?"

He unfurled this big grin, like he was some panelist on a game show, and was real close to guessing my secret. No sense in stopping him now. Like I could if I wanted to.

"Okay. Helping you. Helping you...Right off the top of my head, I can see a few things that could be changed for the better: in addition to the new car, you're obviously going to need new clothes, *toiletries*, and of course, luggage. And a more secure way to transport your cash on hand. Perhaps a mini safe. Clearly, that's not the crux of your problems, not why we were drawn together, but they are needs that must be attended to."

I picked up the carafe and tipped it into my cup, but only a few drops trickled out.

"Is there anymore?" I asked.

"Oh, yes. Of course there is."

He gave his hands a quick wipe on a napkin, then took the carafe back into the kitchen.

"So, back to how you acquired the money. I wondered if it was in any way similar to how I made my money..."

A small island was the only thing physically separating the dining room from the kitchen, so I was positioned to see and hear everything without having to strain. Yet for some reason, he felt the need to not only talk *louder*, but to also *over articulate each word*. Like I was some deaf relative he was trying to communicate with. It was rather annoying. I wanted to tell him that I could hear him, and that I wasn't a lip reader anyway, so there was no reason for him to going through all this, but like I said, I didn't think it would do any good.

"Now, I made the bulk of my money back in the nineties. *Investments*. *Stocks*. During the Dot-Com craze. Were you in on that? Madness. *Get big fast!* That was the mantra. I was obsessed. Every cent I made was used to buy more stock. And I tell you, *I couldn't lose*. I made *more money* than I ever thought I'd see in my life. Or ten lives. It was like I had a printing press. *I never saw anything like that before*."

Luckily for me, my cell phone started to ring, and that's what finally got him to shut up. He fished the phone from the pile of my clothes he left on the counter, and brought it over to me, along with a fresh pot of coffee, gracefully sidestepping the puddle Steve left on the floor.

"Here you go," he said, handing me the phone. "What happened there?"

"I think your dogs scared him a little."

"Does he need to go outside?"

"I'm not going outside," Steve said. "Not with them out there."

"He's fine."

I looked at phone screen. Julie. Great. Between her and Aaron, it was like having to decide which was better: death by knives or the rack.

I stabbed the answer button and brought it to my ear.

"Hello," I spoke.

"Daryl?"

"Yeah."

"It's Julie."

"I know."

"I've, I've been trying to call you all day and you never answered. I have no idea where you are. I'm still your wife, you know? You can't just disappear like this."

"I'm in Iowa."

"Iowa?"

"Why did you say it like that?"

Something about it struck me as strange. It wasn't like, *Iowa? What the hell are you doing in Iowa?* It was more like, *Iowa? Oh, no. Didn't you hear?* Like this was the state that was currently under alien invasion.

"Are you, um...Is everything okay?"

"My car blew up."

She didn't immediately respond, which was normal for her. Whenever she was angry, she'd pause an extra second or two in order to find the exact word or phrase to attack me. But the silence was so uncharacteristically long, that I wondered if I was in a bad cell area and I had lost her. It just wasn't like her to go this long without pointing out how something like this would never happen to her. So, I pulled the phone away and had a quick peek.

Four bars. But still no criticism.

"Julie? You there?"

"Daryl, come back."

I could have sworn that I was actually hearing worry in her voice. Something about it didn't seem right.

"I just said the car blew up. Didn't you hear me?"

"I heard. You don't need the stupid car. You can take a train. Or fly. Just get back here."

"I can't," I told her. "I've got somewhere to go."

"Daryl, this is ridiculous. What's in Nevada?"

"Pirates."

"*Pirates!* You're making no sense. Are you in the hospital?"

"No, I'm in a millionaire's mansion."

"There's no reason to be a smartass. I'm just concerned. I've always tried to steer you in the right direction, but you never listen."

"Julie, I have to go."

"I don't like this."

I disconnected the call and dropped the phone on the table. It figured she didn't understand.

The moment the call was over, Aaron immediately snapped right back into his game show persona, not making any mention whatsoever about the strange new scene playing out directly behind him: a middle aged woman in a French maid outfit mopping up Steve's puddle of piss.

"I'll be out of your way in a second," she said.

"You're not in the way at all," Aaron warmly responded.

"Daryl?" she asked. "You need anything, dear?"

I just shook my head no, and she went on mopping.

"Alright," Aaron said, with a huge grin and a single clap of his hands. "It looks like we're getting somewhere. Who was that? Wife? Girlfriend? Let me see. You've got a ring on, so again…wife, or girlfriend?"

He let out a self-amused laugh and stared at me, waiting for an answer. Turned out that he didn't have to wait too long, because after a moment, he provided himself with one. Just like the little laugh he provided to his even littler joke.

"I want to say wife, because it didn't seem like you wanted to talk. I am right, aren't I? Of course I am. That type of behavior is tolerable towards a wife, but not a girlfriend. You said *pirates*. You mentioned pirates to me just a minute ago, too..."

Oh, my god, could this guy talk. He was even worse than Melvin. At least Melvin's excuse is someone's paying him to ask stupid questions. This guy's doing it in his spare time.

"Daryl?"

Aaron had both palms flat on the table and was stretching forward toward me as far as he could. He looked like he was about to lift himself out of his chair and hop on the table.

"*Pirates?*"

"What about them?" I asked.

"I think you know."

I swear, for a guy who claims he wants to help, he's kinda hard to understand. He should come with footnotes. Really couldn't hurt.

"I'm getting another sense, Daryl. That rather than outwardly expressing yourself, there's an inner monologue constantly running through your head. I'm right again, aren't I? Of course I am. You don't need to be gifted with premonitions like I am to see it, either. All a person has to do is spend a little time watching you. And that I have done. Daryl, you need to tell people what is on your mind. *Communication.* It's foremost to human survival. How do you think we could have evolved as a species if none of our ancestors shared their thoughts or feelings with each other? Well, I'll tell you. If no one said, *"This is my cave"*, or *"I don't like it when you do this"*, and instead, packed those feelings away in their emotional luggage, eventually, all that repressed anger would have exploded, and they would killed each other off. We wouldn't be here right now. It would have ended long ago. Nothing, Daryl, will ever move forward or change if you don't speak up. You need to share your insights and opinions. I can't help you unless you help me."

"You want me to tell you what I think?"

"Yes. But not just me, Daryl. Everyone. All the time. And we should start right now."

"Right now?"

"Yes, right now. Tell me what you are thinking. Your every thought is imperative. Do you understand that?"

"Okay. You are really fucking annoying. Do you understand *that?*"

The maid gasped. "Language!"

Steve fell off his chair laughing.

"It's a step in the right direction," Aaron said. "But she's right. I don't appreciate being spoken to that way. Show some respect."

Show some respect. That struck me as a little odd. Although, not quite as odd, I must admit, as a woman in a French maid costume who appears out of nowhere to mop up piss. I know I was on the phone, but how could I have missed that entrance? It made me think of that line I've heard people say countless times to others who made some kind of mess: *"Are you going to clean that up? Or do you think some pixie is going to magically appear in the middle of the night and clean it for you?"*

Who would have guessed that the pixies not only existed, but also wore maid outfits?

"What are you thinking right now?"

He waited for me to respond, but the whole pixie thing didn't seem that important to rehash.

"Daryl, I'm serious. Stop censoring yourself from the public. You should always let out your thoughts, whether someone else asks to hear them or not. So, come on, now that you started, let's keep it going. What are you thinking? Right now? Let it out."

"Well, right now I'm still thinking that you're annoying. And also that you're a little nuts."

"Okay. What else. I know there's more."

"Frankly, I've been wondering how any of this is supposed to help me."

"Trust me. Opening yourself up and letting people know what's inside will help you immeasurably. It's one of the main principles I stressed when I was a Life Coach."

"Life Coach? What's that?"

After a short, self-satisfying laugh, he explained. "A Life Coach is a personal instructor. A qualified motivator. Life Coaches guide people towards a particular goal. You become Teacher. Confidant. Warden. It was a career with its share of fulfilling moments, but..."

"But what," I demanded. "No one liked it because it's like having your father follow you around, constantly criticizing you, and telling you what to do? Come on, say what you're thinking."

Ha-ha. Got him.

"My approach was simple," he continued, without hesitation, or acknowledgement of what I said. "Yet effective. I dedicated myself completely to my subject. I observed them, deduced the problems they couldn't see themselves, then formulated a strategy which would ultimately attain the radical life changes they required. Regrettably, the level of help most of them are willing to accept rarely rose above that of babysitter. You cannot expect success if you defy every instruction given to you. If I were performing this solely as a source of income, then perhaps I could learn to tolerate their infantile behavior. But, I am far too serious about my intentions, and their noncompliance made it impossible. So now, I only help those who I feel truly need my help. Free of charge."

Then he stopped and stared at me again.

My turn, I guess.

"So, you've been waiting for me to show up, so you could point me in the right direction?"

"Hmm..."

He tipped back his head, making sure not to break eye contact. It was like I had made some deeply penetrating point he'd never previously considered. For a moment, I...

"Speak, Daryl" he insisted.

"What?"

"What you're thinking. I thought we had an agreement."

"Fine. What's with that look? You making fun of me?"

"No. I just never heard my work described that way before."

"So, what do you do then?"

"I help people," he smiled. "With...directions."

"Now you are making fun of me."

"No, I'm really not. I just like the sound of it."

"Come on, Steve."

I stood up, intending to leave, but in the time it took me to straighten my legs, I realized there was nowhere else to go. Having no clothes and no car put me at a slight disadvantage.

"Is something wrong?" he asked.

"I don't know. Okay, yeah. Everything. Random women in maid costumes cleaning your floor, for one..."

I motioned over to where she was, but she was already gone.

Aaron cut me off. "That wasn't some *random woman,* Daryl. You should know that."

"Fine. She's not random. To you. But to me, you're both pretty random. It's all really goddamn random!"

"How so?"

"Well, you say you're supposed to help me, but, you don't have a clue about what's going on with me."

"I know exactly what's going on with you."

"You do?"

"Yes, even if I don't know all the details yet. Trust me, I've been there."

"I doubt that."

"Sit down," he said, motioning me back to the chair.

Steve looked up at me and sighed. "We're not leaving yet, are we?"

I shook my head and sat back down.

"I know exactly what you are going through," he started. "You lack direction. You're not sure where you're going, how you're going to get there, or if you'll even know when you've arrived. The path that leads to your destination is littered with distractions and misinformation. It's easy to get lost, and even harder to stay on track. Which is my job. To make sure you follow the correct path."

"What if it's not the right path, though?" I shot. "What if you're wrong?"

He drew in a deep breath and leaned a little closer to me. It felt like he was preparing to tell me a relative just died, or something.

"Because, Daryl, I know what's best for you."

"I don't see how. You don't know me."

"I know you more than you think. Let me tell you a story."

"I thought that's what you were just doing."

I didn't even realize I had said it out loud until I saw the look on his face.

"There was a time when I had none of this. I was like you, looking everywhere for direction with no one to guide me. I wandered through a series of unsatisfying jobs, but I needed something more. I needed leverage. And what better leverage, than money? At the time, the dot-com craze was just starting, and investors were making a killing. I took everything I owned, and bought stock. In what seemed like no time at all, I was richer than I had ever dreamed. I was finally in a *position* to do exactly what I wanted, but the truth was, money by itself wasn't enough. It didn't feel right. I was richer than I had ever dreamed, but I was still unfulfilled. So, I sold my stocks, and put it all in safe mutual funds. Two months later, the market crashed. People lost everything. But not me. I was saved. And then, like a lightning bolt, it struck me. *The truth.* I knew the truth before anyone else did. I may not have realized it consciously, but I felt it here in my gut. I decided from that moment to tell people the truth.

"Speak what you see. Truth is an incredibly versatile tool. It can be a weapon, but it can also be therapeutic. What other apparatus can both wound and heal? It not only shows others what they refuse to acknowledge, but it also sets you free. And the best aspect about the truth is that everyone has access to it. Young, old, rich, and poor. It shows no prejudice to race or gender. It's there for all to use! Unfortunately, too few are willing to employ it. So much of our lives is spent biting our tongues, not saying what really needs to be said for fear of hurting someone's feelings or getting them mad at you. And for what? In the end, keeping silent helps no one. Why? Because over time, people become so entrenched in their own bad habits and toxic behaviors that any hopes of correction by self realization is close to impossible. But by speaking up and telling the truth, you remove any and all burdens from yourself. No longer must you lie and hide. No more having to put up with situations that you despise. Telling people how you feel, and what you see, relieves you of having to deal with the guilt caused by any future outcome your silence may have created. Of course, some people are not equipped to hear the truth at first. You must think of it as a process. Initially they may seem receptive, but after a while, they become angry..."

I cut him off. "Probably because you talk so goddamn much."

"Excuse me?"

"You tell me you're going to help me, but I've hardly said a word. All you've done so far is talk about yourself and make *guesses* at what could be wrong with me."

"Does the farmer yell at the thunderstorm for being too loud, when the accompanying rain will help his crops?"

He had me there. What I mean to say is, if his goal was to shut me up, he succeeded.

"Some people may think I talk too much," he *continued.* "But, that is a miniscule price to pay for having someone fix your life, isn't it? Look at lawyers: if you need to sue someone, a lawyer will charge up to one third of the future settlement to take your case. What about doctors? They demand payment up front, before they've even tried to heal you. And if they never do, your money will not be refunded. Those are steep prices to pay, don't you agree?"

There had to be a way to get him to shut up.

"So, are you going to help me, or what?"

"Well, let's see: How about you start with the pirates? What's that mean?"

He told me to talk, so whether he liked it or not, talk is what I did. I started with the Doctor Melvin saga, moving into what Don told me at Casey's about the pirate convention. From there I filled him in about the guy at the gas station, meeting Miss Lucinda, and pretty much anything else I could recall.

So essentially, he heard everything.

I have no idea how long I was talking. All I know is I would have been done a hell of lot sooner had Steve not kept interrupting me to complain about either being hungry or having to pee. And each time I finished dealing with him, I could never remember where I left off in the story. I know there were more than a few instances where I wound up repeating myself. Eventually, I asked Aaron if I could just shove Steve in front of a TV somewhere. Once that was accomplished, wouldn't you know it, I wasn't bothered again.

The story stopped when I got as far as the restaurant, figuring he could fill in the rest, since he had been part of it. By the time I finally finished, Aaron was sitting cross-armed and cross-legged, leaning back into a dining room chair, and presumably, processing the story.

"This is fascinating," he said with smile. "Especially the part where I'm supposed to be involved."

"What do you mean, *supposed to be involved?*"

"Before we even met. The way you gathered that I was involved. The two of us, our premonitions, are so similar, don't you think? Truly fascinating."

"You didn't know?"

"I told you I only knew on the drive over. But, if you mean *specifically*, like why, no, I didn't. Not then."

I suddenly had this sick feeling in my stomach, like for a second, maybe I might throw up. I took a couple deep breaths and steadied myself.

"So, you're not involved?" I asked him.

"I never said that. Haven't you been listening?"

"Well, are you the next one who's going to give me directions, or not?"

"Daryl, not all directions come from a map."

"What's that mean? You're just gonna point?"

"Look. I never came out and *told you* I was a signpost, did I?"

"No, but you said you were going to help me."

"And I am. But, you assumed that the two were the same. While they're not exactly the same, I do believe they are somehow connected. You were convinced I was your next link, correct? Why? Because you were guided by something other than a map. Something that could not be confirmed or denied *until after* I helped you understand the importance of speaking your mind. You see what I'm saying? I didn't give you *directions*. I gave you *direction*. Now...?"

"Now, what?"

His face snapped into a tight wrinkle, like his mind drove too fast over a mental pothole. "*Pirates?*"

"What about them?"

"That's what I'm asking you," he said. "What exactly does that mean? *Pirates*. Who are they? What are they? Is it a nickname? A metaphor? Or, are they actual pirates?"

"I doubt they're *actual* pirates. Just regular people, who act like pirates for two weeks a year. Weren't you listening to anything *I said*?"

This guy needs to take his own advice.

"Perfectly. I'm attempting to clarify. I don't understand how running away from your problems for two weeks a year fixes your problems."

"I'm not running away."

"I meant them. You say these people are unhappy with their lives. Pretending to be someone else for two weeks doesn't change anything in the other fifty weeks."

"Then that's their problem, not mine."

"I really want to meet these pirate people. It sounds like quite a few of them could really use my help."

"And when you're helping them, are you going to stop in the middle and think about helping someone else?"

"Right," he said. "Let's focus on you. So, are you trying to get happy *again*, or find out if you were ever happy in the first place?"

"Both."

"And these pirates, they're supposed to provide you with the answer."

"That's what Don said."

"And what did Julie say?"

"What do you mean?"

"Was she able to offer any insight into whether or not you were ever happy?"

"She thinks withdrawing the divorce papers should be enough to make me happy."

"Oh, I see. She wanted a divorce? When was that?"

"I don't know. A while ago. She filed the papers, then a few months back, she changed her mind."

"Why do you think she did that?"

"She's just going through some phase, is all. It'll pass."

He dropped his head and stopped talking, staying frozen like that for about a half a minute. It was like someone unplugged him. Eventually, the plug was reinserted, and he started pacing the room.

"I feel it's all about this stack of money. And I'll tell you why: I thought this was a simple job until we came back here. Everything was proceeding along quite smoothly, then I come across your money and *bang!* I felt it right here." He patted down his stomach again, just in case I wasn't paying attention the first hundred times he explained where his premonitions develop.

"So, yes, I'm certain, my mission to help you concerns your money."

"Like an infomercial? You going to offer me investment advice?"

He loudly sighed as he collected the money and neatly stacked it in front of me on the table.

"So, this is what then? Traveling expenses?"

"Yeah."

"How long did you think you'd be able to live off this?"

"No idea. Course, I didn't expect to have to buy a new car, though."

"Is that going to be a problem?"

"Not from a money standpoint. I'm just not crazy about how it will set me back time-wise. Going to the dealer, picking out the car, all of it. You could be talking days."

"So, money's not a problem?"

"No."

I think he sensed I wasn't telling him everything.

"What is it?" he demanded. "I was right, wasn't I? This isn't everything you have in the world, is it, Daryl?"

I don't see why this is any of his business...okay, fine.

"No."

"Care to explain?"

"Not really, but I don't think there's any way around it, is there. It's an inheritance. My grandfather died, and he left me some money."

"A lot?"

"A little over a million cash."

"Hmm. That's quite a sum to fall into."

"I guess."

"How long ago?"

"I don't know. About six months."

"Have you indulged? Boat? New house? Anything like that?"

"I did get a new house. His. I moved into it a few months ago."

"What about your other house?"

"What about it?"

"Did you sell it?"

"No. Julie's still living there."

"Oh."

I yawned, probably bigger than I should have, but considering the line of questioning being thrown at me, I really wasn't too concerned with hurting Aaron's feelings.

"So, what did he do, your grandfather?"

"Do we really have to do this?"

"Yes, Daryl. We do."

"Fine. Construction, remodeling, repair. He built the house himself. The one he left me."

Aaron had that game show grin again. I just looked away.

"He fixed things?"

"Basically. Yeah."

"Fascinating. You know, there's nothing quite like the satisfaction that comes from fixing something with your own hands. Absolutely fascinating."

"Will you stop saying that? It's really annoying."

"Tell me more about your grandfather."

"I don't know. He could fix anything. Plumbing, electrical, cars. You name it. But unless he was fixing bank vaults, I don't see how he made that much money. I mean, the entire time I was growing up, he made it seem like we were always flat broke."

"That generation, growing up during the Depression, they were pretty good at stashing away large sums while living meagerly. There was always a fear that it could happen again."

"Yeah. That's what he did all right."

"You should be thankful that he did. Look at what you have now as a result."

"Why wouldn't he tell me?"

"I'm sure he had his reasons."

"You know how many times in my life I could have used this? Why would he allow me to struggle so much when it would have been so easy to help?"

"Maybe he didn't want to see the whole thing disappear."

"Half then. That would have been good. Not with him, though. The guy kept everything stashed away. Everything."

"So, you saw him a lot when you were growing up?"

"Well, yeah. I lived with him."

"For how long?"

"Until I was nineteen."

"Your parents, too?"

"Both died when I was little. That's when I moved in."

"No brothers or sisters?"

"Nope. Just me and him. My grandmother died too, when I was six, or so."

"That's why you got everything."

"Yeah. Lucky me."

"Did he die before Julie filed for divorce?"

"After. I'd love to know where it all came from. That's the unsolved Agatha Christie."

"It's really not that big of a mystery. Neither is the reason why Julie withdrew the divorce papers."

I didn't know where he was going with this, but I had a feeling I wouldn't like it.

"What do you mean?" I asked.

"It's simple, right? An inheritance isn't considered marital property. So, in a divorce settlement, she wouldn't see a penny of it. But, if she's still married to you..."

"No. No, that's not it at all."

"Did you ever change your will?"

"No. Why would I do that?"

"It is something to consider. What if...well, imagine if that explosion was bad enough to kill you. You two are still married, right? She'd get everything."

"What are you saying? That Julie blew up my car?"

"What I'm suggesting is that she has more to gain as your wife than she does as your ex-wife."

"That's not what it's about. She's just confused about a few things. Robert doesn't help matters, either."

"Who's Robert?"

"Her friend."

"Her *friend?*"

"Yeah. He lives...he's living with..."

I was so tired, I could barely keep my eyes open. It's weird how quickly it hit me, this sense of powerlessness.

Aaron walked over and took hold of my shoulder. I wasn't all that crazy about it, but I also wasn't in the mood to fight.

"Daryl? You okay?"

"I'm really sleepy all of a sudden. Right after that damn yawn."

"You had a pretty big day, Mister. Looks like it's time for bed."

"No. No. I don't want to go to bed."

I tried to stand, but my legs wobbled and I fell back into the chair. Probably good Aaron was there.

"I know," he said. "But it's late, and you need your rest."

"I have so much to do.

"I know. Come on."

He helped me to my feet and led me through what seemed like an endless series of hallways. How big was this damn house? I swear, it felt like we were walking for a half an hour. I started to wonder if he was screwing with me and just taking me down the same couple path six or seven times. I had to orient myself. Find a landmark. The walls on both sides were lined with paintings, so all I needed to do was pick one out and pay attention. If I saw it more than once, I'd know something wasn't right.

Great idea, but it posed a bit of a problem. I was too damn tired to even focus, and I swear, each painting we passed looked the same as every other: a dark wooden frame surrounding a pitch black canvas. And, as tired as I was, I knew that couldn't be right. I mean, who the hell has a hallway of nothing but black paintings? Unless...What if it intended be like some kind of Rorschach test? I really wouldn't put it past him. I dug in my heels, forcing us to stop for a moment, and fell shoulder first into the right wall.

Ow.

"These pictures..."

"Yeah. Classics, huh? Here we go, we're almost there."

Finally, we reached the door to my room. Before I went in, I squirmed my way over to get a good look at the painting to the left.

"Is that...?" I asked, poking at it more than pointing.

"Elvis. You have good taste. That's my favorite of the black velvets, too. Deliciously tacky, isn't it?"

"Yeah. *Fasc*inating."

I think I was asleep before I hit the bed.

18

The next thing I knew, someone was jabbing me in the ribs with a giant heart-shaped pillow covered in rhinestones. It took me a moment before I realized it wasn't a pillow at all – it was Steve, nudging me with his nose.

"Daryl," he kept saying, over and over. "You awake?"

And over. And over.

"I am now."

I must have been having a dream, but what it was about, I can't remember. The only possible hint was that the chorus to "*Love Me Tender*" was playing in my head. It didn't seem worth investigating, so I let it go.

"I'm sorry," Steve said.

"That's okay. I'm not crazy about that song anyway."

"What are you talking about?"

"*Love Me Tender*."

"Dude, you sure you're awake?"

I opened my eyes big and looked around the room rummaging through my personal inventory: Dark, probably middle of the night. Faint glow of streetlights sneaking in between the curtains. This room...Aaron's house, right? Yeah, that's right, I was tired, and he put me to bed.

I was really awake this time. And not all that happy about it, either.

"Why the hell did you wake me up?" I creaked.

"To tell you I was sorry."

"You woke me up to tell me you're sorry for waking me up?"

"Are you really sure you're awake?"

"Damn it, Steve! Yes, I'm awake! Now, let me go back to sleep."

"Are you going to let me explain?" he asked, in a rather snotty tone.

This stupid dog, I swear.

"I thought you did? You said you were sorry."

"But, you don't know about what, do you?"

"Fine," I snapped. "What? Tell me."

"For not protecting you today. I'm sorry."

"When," I asked. "Back in the hallway?"

The Elvis painting. Okay, now I remember. That must be why I had that song in my head. And Elvis wore rhinestones. That solves that.

"The hallway? What happened in the hallway? No, for one, in the car. I jumped right over you. Didn't even try to pull you out. Then with Hans and Boris. The thing is, I've never been much of a fighter."

"Don't worry about it. Just, go back to sleep."

"I'm serious. Don't act like it was nothing."

"Well, it kinda was nothing."

"Thanks. Here I am, trying to connect..."

"Look," I told him, trying not to sound as aggravated as I really was. "With the car, after Aaron opened the door, I'm pretty sure I just fell right out. So, it wasn't like I needed your help anyway. But, with those dogs, they were ten times your size. They would have killed you if you tried anything."

"But that's the point, dude. I *didn't* try *any*thing. I've never really had to protect anybody before. And, the first time I'm supposed to be protecting you, I freeze."

"You're supposed to be protecting me? I didn't know that."

"Well, yeah. It's like, rule number one of the Code."

"The Code?"

"*Man's Best Friend?* I know you never had a dog before, but come on, you had to have heard about it. Seriously."

"Can we please talk about this later? I really need to get back to sleep."

"Yeah. Whatever. So, what was this hallway thing? Something else happen I didn't do anything about? I don't know if I can handle anymore of this negative shit."

"It was nothing. A dream, I think."

"Okay. Well, that's all I wanted to say. That I'm sorry, and I promise to always protect you from here on."

"Alright."

I closed my eyes and drifted off watching Elvis sing *"Hound Dog"*, while Steve stood off to the side keeping an eye on everything.

They both wore matching capes.

I wondered if that was Elvis' idea, or Steve's.

I woke up again, and on my own, at ten fifteen. I only know this because of the enormous clock on the wall directly facing the headboard. Once that came into focus, so did the dozen or so large over-stuffed pillows, a pair of standing lamps with red fringe shades, the tan shag carpeting and the shiny green and gold vertical striped wallpaper. As kitschy as it looked, something about it all felt very familiar. Déjà vu, maybe? No, I don't think so. More like I woke up in a Doris Day movie. I'm sure Julie would have said "*whorehouse*". I have no doubt about that.

I wondered how the Silver Platter regulars would have reacted to a redecoration like this. I suppose I could have just said, "to hell with it", and changed the name to the *Groovy Bachelor Pad Restaurant.* But with a name like that, I'm guessing the graffiti in the bathroom would only get worse. There's always a certain amount of bad with the good, isn't there?

Steve was still passed out on the other side of the bed, so I moved as slowly as I could not to disturb him. The memory of our middle-of-the-night conversation had just came back to me, and I figured if he really was planning on protecting me, he should probably be well rested.

I gave a stretch while stifling a yawn on my way over to the window. Somebody was gunning their car engine like they were waiting for the green flag at a speedway, and I thought I'd take a look at who the clown was, and if I could, get their attention and wave for them to stop. But all I could see were Hans and Boris off in the distance, mauling and eating a small animal about the size of Steve.

I took another look back at the bed. This little guy is going to protect me?

On the nightstand next to the bed I found my pills, my *Happy* sign, and all my money. Aaron must have brought everything in after a fell asleep. The thought was mildly disturbing, but in a sense it's better than having to work my way through the maze of this house trying to locate everything by myself. If he only had a map. I gathered up the bottles and the sign, and brought them into the adjoining bathroom.

Today was going to be a pain in the ass. I knew that much already. My top priorities were to find a dry cleaner and a new car. In that order. I sincerely doubted whether any car dealership would welcome me in pajamas.

Then again, I am paying cash, so you never know.

I dug out a pill from each bottle and cupped my hand under the faucet, deciding not to use the plastic drinking cup with the cartoon bunnies that was stationed at the side of the sink. Weird, I had a cup just like this when I was a kid. What the hell was with this guy? Doesn't he ever throw anything away?

After swallowing, I splashed a little cold water on my face, then draped the sign around my neck and looked in the mirror.

"You will be happy," I told the fellow staring back at me. He seemed different from what I remembered. Older, and slightly worn out. It crossed my mind how looking at something like that could ever make me feel any happier. But, Miss Lucinda seemed pretty sure of herself, so I complied.

And now all day with Aaron, too. Yet another experience not conducive to finding happiness. Oh well, it's not like it's the first time I ever had to deal with someone who gets on my nerves. I should be used to this by now. All I need is to get these two things accomplished, then I'm out of here. If he really starts bugging me, I can test his own advice and tell him how I feel. Maybe he'll get pissed and shut up for a while.

I twisted off the water and turned back toward the bedroom, but I must have swung my elbow too wide, because I smacked one of the bottles off the sink. Dozens of little brownish pills scattered all over the floor.

"Shit!"

I got down to both knees and started picking them up, but then the next thing I knew, Steve was on my back. Literally.

"Daryl?" he shrieked. "You okay?"

"Yeah, I'm fine. Now get down, would 'ya?"

He pushed off my back and settled down behind me.

"I heard you scream. What happened? Were you shot?"

"No, I wasn't shot. Jesus, Steve. I dropped my pills. Don't step on any of them. *Shot?* Where'd you get that?"

"Okay. Okay. Just checking." He took a couple sniffs at the air and his tail shot straight up. "Smell that? Blueberry muffins and coffee! Let's go, buddy! I need you to pour!"

Stupid dog.

There was a note on the kitchen table telling me to go ahead and help myself to coffee, muffins, or anything else I wanted to make, if I felt so inclined. I was half surprised to see it was written on paper. With this guy, I sort of expected it to be scrawled an original Etch-A-Sketch. Or on the back of an autographed photo of Cesar Romero.

Steve jumped into the same seat he occupied yesterday, he's such a creature of habit, and threw his front paws up on the table.

"Come on, buddy-boy," he sang. "Let's go! Load me up!"

The energy this goofball has is truly amazing. I'm sure got less sleep than me, but he's bouncing all over the place while I can barely keep my eyes open.

"Aren't you tired?" I asked him.

"No. Should I be?"

"How late were you up last night?"

"Pretty late. I watched a *Hogan's Heroes* marathon."

"You were up watching *Hogan's Heroes*? Seriously?"

"Dude, dogs love *Hogan's Heroes*! Especially that Schultz. Guy's a riot. 'I know *nuh*-thing!' Hey, did shit like that really happen in World War Two? Prisoners sneaking into town posing like German soldiers, and all that? Where's my coffee?"

"I'm thinking you don't you need any."

"Dude! You're killing me! Coffee! Coffee! Coffee!"

I figured it wasn't worth the fight. So, I grabbed two cups from the cabinet and poured, while Steve whistled the theme song to *Hogan's Heroes*.

"I didn't know dogs could whistle."

"That's probably 'cause you only heard the ones who can't, but think they can. Very disturbing."

I measured out the cream and sugar like he told me yesterday, and peeled the wrappers off of two muffins.

"Hot!" he shrieked after his first sip. "Damn."

"Blow on it."

He leered at me and giggled.

"You're a pig."

Car salesmen, Aaron, and Steve. This day was really shaping up into something special.

I was about to settle in and start on my coffee and muffin when I heard that engine revving again. It was louder than before, probably because the bedroom was a two mile hike from the kitchen. I moved to the window, but there was still nothing to show for all the noise.

"I'll be right back," I told Steve.

"Where you going?"

"Just want to take a look at something."

"Alright. Hey! Before you split, hows about you turning on the TV for me. Maybe the marathon's still going on."

I walked into the other room, switched on the set, and headed out the door.

The sun was angled right in my face, and there wasn't anything I could do about it but squint. Maybe Steve put the idea in my head, but with the pajamas, the coffee and the squinting, I felt like the nosey neighbor in a sitcom.

Maybe I'll have a few cameos in an upcoming marathon.

I followed the sound of the engine around the corner to my left, which was good because the sun was now at my back and I could relax my face.

Aaron's garage. A couple bay doors were open, but only one with streams of exhaust pouring out of it, so that's where I headed. The hood was up on a gorgeous, mint condition black Mustang convertible. I'm not the kind of guy who can tell the year of a car by looking at it, but I'm pretty sure it was mid-sixties. There wasn't a scratch on it, the damn thing looked like it should be on a rotating platform at the auto show. The only anomaly was a bumper sticker:

HELP Is Not A Four Letter Word.

Aaron was in the front seat, stepping on and off the accelerator, nodding his head with approval. I was so caught up in studying the car that I didn't notice how close I had gotten to the tailpipe, and as a result sucked in a face full of fumes. My gagging is what finally got Aaron's attention.

"Daryl," he said, turning toward me. "Morning. You okay?"

I offered a series of pathetic nods, while waving my free hand in front of my face. By now, the smoke had dissipated and there was no reason for any further gestures, but somehow I just couldn't stop myself.

"You shouldn't stand so close to the exhaust."

"Thanks," I said.

Lot of help, this guy.

He was wearing an old fashioned gas station attendant's uniform. Dark gray work pants, with cuffs, and a matching jacket with two patches on the chest – one that read *Texaco*, and the other that read *Vic*. Christ, he even had the pressed white shirt and tiny black bow tie!

I just shook my head and sipped my coffee. I know I promised to do like he said, but I figured it was still a little too early in the morning for me to be doling out the truth. I'm sure with practice, I'll be able to do it around the clock.

A wave of disgust swelled up inside, and the coffee I just swallowed flowed back out of my mouth. Luckily, that's all that came out.

"Something wrong with the coffee?" Aaron asked.

"Smoke," is all I could manage to say. My tongue was too occupied with scraping the sides of my mouth to finish verbalizing the thought.

"Yeah," he announced. "That's no good. So, what do you think of her?"

He smiled proudly and motioned his arm across the car.

I spit off to the side, then gave it another look.

"Sixty-eight," he proudly announced. "Three-oh-two four barrel V-eight. Drives like a dream. Everything but the audio system is original. Six Infinity speakers. Kenwood amplifier and CD changer. You have an MP3 player?"

"No."

"I can give you mine. Over ten thousand songs, and not one of them bad. So, you like it then?"

I shrugged and gave half a nod.

"I knew it. Something about you screamed *Mustang Lover*. Convertible, though. Not hard top. Felt it right here. Keep it for as long as you need it."

"What?"

"You made it abundantly clear last night that you weren't looking forward to wasting any valuable time car shopping today. This will get you back on the road."

"I can't take your car, Aaron."

"Why not?"

"Because, I don't know. It's too much. Let me give you some money, at least."

"I'm not taking money from you, Daryl. I want you to have it. You need it more than I do."

"Are you sure?"

"Very sure. Besides, taking it helps me. I came across a Packard, Forty-nine, and I could use the space."

"Why do you collect all this stuff? The cars, the furniture?"

"Everybody collects something."

"I don't."

"Sure you do."

"No," I shot back. "I don't."

"Nothing? Ever?"

"Nope."

"Not baseball cards, or shiny rocks?"

"I just said, no."

"Fascinating."

"That word again..."

"Well, it is fascinating. It may explain a few things about you."

"I asked why *you* collected, not me."

"I collect things that appeal to my sense of beauty. My idea of art. But, there are a variety of reasons why people collect. Some do it in order to connect with the past. To have reminders. Some to fill a void. Whatever the rationale, being surrounded by certain objects or ideas gives a person a sense of comfort, even security. Whether it's Picassos or turtle figurines."

"Or paintings on black velvet?"

He leaned his head back and smiled. "Some things in life don't require any explanation."

"And you don't mind me driving your art cross country?"

"Not at all. Art is meant to be seen and appreciated."

"All right."

I ran my knuckles across the smooth metallic shell. You didn't need the car turned on to feel its inherent power. I tried to imagine Audrey in the front seat, laughing, and screaming out the lyrics to some song.

Then I saw it, and everything came to a halt.

"It's a stick?"

"Don't tell me you've never driven a stick before? I'm surprised. A man who worked with his hands like your grandfather surely would have driven a stick."

"He did," I said. "He just never showed me."

"He never showed you? Or, you never asked him?"

"Even if I did ask him, he'd woulda just said no. That's all he ever said when he bothered to talk to me."

"A stick's much easier than you think. Get in."

I slid into the driver's seat, while Aaron darted over to the passenger side. I already felt more comfortable than I ever did in my old exploded car. Not like the seat was padded in any special way, there was just something about the car itself that felt right. Almost like it exuded a sense of security. Maybe I should collect these?

Then the weirdest thought popped into my head. When I was really young, maybe three or four, I had this pair of pajamas that I was crazy about. They were white with green and gold pinstripes, long pants and a long sleeved top with buttons down the front. Looking back, they were really nothing special, and I have no idea why I liked them so much. Maybe because of how soft they were. It was this thick cotton, almost like a terry cloth. Who knows why kids obsess over the things they do? A good example of that was this kid who lived down the block, Paul Lipinski.

Why I was suddenly thinking of pajamas and Paul was beyond me.

When we were about eight, Paul was adamant about this dog collar and leash. He carried it with him wherever he went. Goofy thing was, he didn't own a dog, and as far as I knew, never did. He just insisted on having that collar and leash with him at all times. Where an eight-year-old, non-dog-owning kid got his hands on a collar and leash in the first place was always a bit of a mystery to the folks in the neighborhood. Rumor was, that it originally belonged to the parents, and that Walter happened upon them *"using it"* one day, and for whatever reason, he later appropriated it for his own inclinations.

Kinda creepy, but that's how rumors are.

Paul himself never offered up anything in the way of an explanation. In fact, when anybody asked, he'd stare at them like they were speaking some foreign language that he didn't understand. After a while, people stopped asking and just kinda got used to it, figuring it was just some phase that would fade away in time. It wasn't really until after he was in high school, and still carrying the collar and leash around, that people began to seriously wonder about Paul.

Although my fixation on those pajamas wasn't as bizarre as Paul's, there was one common detail about our obsessions: no one knew why. In fact, I have a memory of me wearing those pajamas, and my mother tucking me in for bed. She'd playfully poke my nose and say, "Why must you *always* wear those pajamas? Are you silly like your mommy?"

Even after I grew way too big to fit in them anymore, I still wanted to keep them around. And like I said, to this day, I don't know why, I just really *needed* them for some reason. Then one day, they were gone. I went into a panic, and practically tore apart the house searching for them. My grandfather hit the roof when he found out what I was doing, yelling at me to grow up and let go of all that childish crap. He told me I was being selfish, that I already had everything I ever needed. I didn't understand the logic, but with him, you never did.

They stayed missing, and after a while, I just forgot about them. Until now. I can't believe I let that happen. Yet another thing to add to the list, I suppose.

I wonder if Paul still has his collar and leash? Last I heard of him was about fifteen or twenty years ago. He was working for some independent production company in Los Angeles making direct-to-video movies. Sounded like his childhood peccadilloes didn't affect him too badly.

"So, you think you want to give it a try, Daryl?"

"Give what a try?"

Aaron sighed and adjusted his skinny bowtie.

"You weren't paying attention to a thing I said, were you? What were you thinking about?" He just sounded so disgusted with me.

So, I told him. "Pajamas."

"Oh," he said, perking up a bit. "That's perfectly understandable. We weren't going into public, per se. I was just going to take you down this dirt road. No one's ever on it. But, if you'd like to change first. If that would make you more comfortable."

I completely forgot that I was still wearing these stupid pajamas. Maybe that's why I was thinking about that old pair. Who knows? I wouldn't mind changing first, but since there was nothing clean for me to wear, it really wasn't an option. Besides, even if someone did see me, it would only be from the chest up, so all they'd catch is a pale blue shirt with white ribbing. Nothing all that strange about that. Especially around here. Some of the cowboy shirts I've seen in just the past two days are more embarrassing than any pajamas I've ever come across.

"No," I told him. "I'm here. Let's just do this."

Aaron nodded and flashed that big stupid grin, like we'd just come back from the commercial break and it was time to start the Second Round.

"Adjust your mirrors."

It sounded no different than, "*Hands on your buzzers...*"

"They're fine," I said. "Now what?"

"How do you know they're fine? You didn't touch them."

"I didn't need to touch them. I looked, and they're fine."

"That's impossible. They're set for me, and I'm taller than you, so they can't be *fine*."

I shifted each mirror about a sixteenth of an inch just to get him to shut up. Even though the alterations did absolutely nothing, he smiled and shook his head again.

"Buckle up."

"That's what I planned."

Which I really was in the process of doing.

"Good, good. Now, the seat."

"Aaron!"

"Don't *Aaron* me. Just check the seat."

"I like it like this. It's fine."

"No need to get testy. We are now ready to drive. Push down on the clutch with your left foot, and make sure the shift's in neutral."

I found the clutch and stepped down, but before I even had a damn chance to shift, he reached over and did it himself.

"I thought you wanted me to do it?"

"I had to show you where neutral was," he explained.

"You could have just told me."

"This was easier."

Oh, yeah. This was *so much* easier.

"Now," Aaron continued. "Turn the key."

"I figured that much."

Don't know where I'd be without this invaluable help.

I kept my foot pressed down on the clutch and turned the key. Why I knew to do that was because it suddenly came back to me about the old, crappy VW Bug *He* had. He called it his "Three Bug": he bought it for three hundred dollars, had sex with three different women in it, and wound up totaling it three months later. What I remembered was how he always complained about forgetting to push in the clutch before he started it up.

I hadn't thought about that in years.

"Daryl," Aaron called out, punctuating it with a slap to the back of my shoulder. "Talk to me."

"What?" I exclaimed. "I already know to push in the clutch when you start it."

"Then why aren't you doing it?"

I looked down, and saw that I was turning the ignition over and over again, but with my left foot firmly planted on the floor. It must have slipped off the clutch. I'm not just new to this car, but I'm new to a stick, too. I don't know why he's making such a big deal out of this.

Probably these stupid slippers he has me wearing.

I kicked my left foot hard on the pedal and turned the key again. This time, it started up no problem.

It's just one of those things that needs time to get used to, that's all.

"Now, push in the brake," he said.

"Okay."

"Don't take your foot off the clutch! I didn't tell you to do that."

"You said, *push in the brake*."

"Right. But I didn't say, *foot off the clutch*. Keep your feet pressed on both."

"You coulda said that."

"Then I would have been repeating myself."

It was like that the entire time we were out. *Ease up on the clutch. I said EASE up. That's not easing, that's jumping. Watch the tachometer. Watch the speedometer. What are you doing? Watch the road!*

I seriously thought about driving to a car dealership and getting a trade in, but I didn't think they'd give me much in return for Aaron.

After who-knows-how-long we were out, much longer than I wanted, I know that much, I think I finally got the hang of it. Once I realized that it was simply about patterns, it was a cinch. Follow the established pattern precisely, or something's going to go wrong. And since I'm not very good at fixing things, it's much easier to get with the program, as my grandfather used to say. This way, if something screws up, it won't be because of me.

Once it was parked safely back in the stall, Aaron gave me a big, fatherly pat on the same shoulder that he whacked not too long ago.

"You did good," he proudly announced. "Go change, and I think you're ready to go."

"Change into what?" I asked. "I still haven't gone to a dry cleaner yet."

"Don't worry," he said. "Just wash up. Go on, now."

Maybe there was one of those One-Hour dry cleaners nearby. Even so, if you factored in travel time, I'd be finished with my shower long before he got back. I mean, for one, I wasn't even dirty, so I wouldn't be in there very long as it was. I just didn't understand the rush. I don't know, maybe he owned one of those joints and he could get them to do it in half the time. Would have been nice if he mentioned that yesterday.

Not to sound like Aaron, or anything, but when I walked back into the house, I had this strange feeling that something wasn't right. I stood by the table and tried to figure out what it could be. Was something broken? Moved out of place? Maybe a burner was left on and a pan was smoking. Nope, it was none of that. What was it?

Then I heard mumbling coming from the other room.

"Daryl? That you?"

It was Steve, and to be honest, it sounded like he was in the middle of a panic attack. Maybe the *Hogan's Heroes* marathon was over, and he was anxious to get going. But that wasn't it at all. He was in the chair where I left him, but rather than watching TV, he was face to face with Boris and Hans, who were licking their lips and poised for attack.

"I say we eat him," one of them hissed.

"Sounds like a plan," the other one whispered back. "He'll make a nice little snack."

"We just need to get him outside."

"No kidding. One tiny stain, and that psycho human of ours will throw a fit."

"What's going on?" I asked. I knew very well, so I'm not even sure why I bothered.

"Hey, Daryl," Steve trembled. "Time to go, yet?"

"Make like you want to play," one said to the other. I had no idea which one was which. "Maybe this one will think we're buddies and tell us all to go outside."

"If you think I'm going to let you outside just so you can eat Steve," I told them. "You're stupider than you look."

"How the hell did he know?" one of them asked.

"Just a good guess."

"I bet you weren't playful looking enough," the other shot back.

"Why is this my fault?" the other complained.

"Will you both shut up," I told them. "You sound like you're married."

They stopped bickering and shared confused looks with each other. "How's he doing that?"

Steve straightened up and smiled. "My human can understand dogs."

"Bullshit!" they called in tandem.

"Don't believe me?" Steve smirked. "Watch this: Schultz! What's going on here?"

I came to attention and gave Steve a nervous salute. "I know nuh-thing, Commandant. Nuh-thing!"

"*Hogan's Heroes*," the both said, in stunned unison.

"That's not the only power he has," Steve bragged. "He can make you burst into flames just by pointing at you. Show them, Daryl."

"Not inside," I told him. "You heard what they said. Aaron would throw a fit. Come on."

I plucked Steve off the chair and dropped him on the floor. Not a far drop. He was fine.

"*That* was awesome," Steve panted.

"Yeah. You do a pretty good Colonel Klink."

"Thanks. Your Schultz could use some work, though."

Like it's going to be part of our national comedy tour, or something. I swear.

I took a quick shower, just in case Hans and Boris decided to attack while I was unavailable. After toweling off, I pulled on the robe and walked back into the bedroom. But it was like I had stepped into a different room. Any and all signs that I had spent the night were removed. The bed was made, complete with tightly tucked hospital corners that would warm the heart of any drill sergeant. The pillows were fluffed and symmetrically arranged, and I swear, the end tables had been dusted and waxed.

Then I saw the suitcases, along with the matching garment and tote bags. Next to them was a man's suit, laid out on the bed without a single wrinkle. None of these were mine, yet, resting on top of the suit coat were my cell phone, my *Happy* sign, and a handwritten note, neatly folded over once.

Daryl,

Aaron selected some clothing for you from his personal collection. He is confident that he not only matched your size, but your style, as well. (Don't tell him, but I switched a couple things I thought would look better on you).

I hope you don't mind, but I took the liberty of visiting the store today and purchasing a few "personal" items for you. The importance of clean underwear cannot be overstated. You will find them inside the suitcase, along with the rest of the wardrobe.

Good luck on your journey. We'll miss you. I hope you know there will always be a room waiting for you here.

Margaret

I wasn't all that crazy about other people picking out clothes for me. It's one thing to say, *"Take some stuff from the closet"*, but for them to make the decision *for* me was a little irritating. It did, however, save me some time, so I couldn't complain too much.

However, there was that other matter. Who the hell was Margaret?

The clothes looked like they all fit, but I don't know if I'd go as far to say it's my *style*. In fact, the suit this Margaret character put out for me was unlike anything I had ever worn before. An olive colored two-button wool blazer, with pants the same material, only in a dark gray, with narrow cuffs. The shoes were two-toned black and white oxfords, the kind that look like you're wearing spats. I was also provided with a plain white shirt, and a skinny black tie.

I mean, it looked nice, and it was pretty damn comfortable, but I really wouldn't say it was my style.

I kinda wished they had found me a hat to go with it.

Speaking of hats, where the hell was Steve? The door was open, but I didn't see any signs of a struggle, which would be very obvious in this room.

I hung my *Happy* sign around my neck, gripped the suitcase and headed for the door, but I was stopped by one of those stupid feelings again. Maybe Aaron was rubbing off on me. Man, I hope not.

I threw the suitcase back on the bed and opened it up. Nope. So, I grabbed the tote bag and took a look inside. My money, and both pill bottles. Good. I headed again for the door, but that nagging feeling would not leave.

Did I take my pills this morning? I'm pretty sure I did.

Or, did I? Damn, I hate when I can't remember.

As I made my way toward the garage, bags in hand, I could feel the churning in my stomach getting worse. What the hell was it? Damn Aaron for passing this on to me. I thought for a moment that I was going to vomit. I had to find Steve.

I went outside and ran the length of the house, only to find him once again locked in a face to face stare down with Boris and Hans. They didn't see me, so I slowed my run to a creep, trying to make as little noise as possible, so I could grab Steve before the lunch bell rang.

Only Steve wasn't cowering in fear this time. Boris and Hans were. He had both of them squatted deep on their hind legs, and backed against the wall. I wanted to keep my distance to see what happened next, but Steve caught me, and called for me to join them.

"Here he comes now," Steve vigorously announced. "Go ahead. Ask him yourself, if you don't believe me."

"And he'll really know what we're saying?" one of them asked.

Steve gave his head a quick shake of disbelief.

"Dude, you just don't get it, do you? Test it out. Prove me wrong."

Boris and Hans shifted nervous glances between the two of them, each tacitly urging the other to speak. Finally, one of them, I still had no idea who was who, broke the repetition and turned his head toward me, careful not to make direct eye contact.

"Did you blow up a car the other day?" he meekly asked.

I stole a quick look at Steve. Had either one of the two giant idiots bothered to look up, they would have seen Steve violently nodding his head in a series of short quakes in order to influence my answer.

Not very subtle, this dog.

"Yeah," I told my questioner. "I blew it up."

He gave a little cough and pawed at the ground.

"Why?"

"I don't know. Maybe because I wanted a new one."

They both gasped, and recoiled from Steve as far as they could, until stopped by the wall of the house.

"Told you," Steve bragged. "He's not like any human you've ever seen. He's awesome. He's even teaching his powers to me. Wanna see me blow one of you up?"

"Hey, come one!" one of them protested.

"That's not cool," the other added.

"Then stop acting like dicks, and maybe I'll let you live. Got it?" Steve then looked at me. "Ready to go?"

"Only if you are," I told him.

"Oh, I'm ready, bro. We got time to stop at Burger King?"

"Sure."

Steve inched in a little closer to the two of them.

"Mine treats me like a human, too. I eat fast food."

Oddly enough, that comment affected them more than the possibility of spontaneous combustion. Their envy of Steve gnawing daily on Whoppers nearly unhinged their jaws.

Steve smirked, and strutted slowly toward the garage.

"That felt good. Thanks."

"For what?" I asked. "I didn't do anything."

"Oh, yes you did," he insisted. "Yes you did. We should celebrate. I could go for a couple cheeseburgers and an Irish setter. What about you?"

I know I wasn't supposed to hold back and say everything that was on my mind, but I didn't want to ruin his buzz, so I just kept quiet.

Irish setter. Well, at least he has taste. I've always had a thing for redheads myself.

Julie is a brunette.

The moment Aaron saw us, his smile stretched out almost as wide as his arms.

"Look at you," he beamed. "I hardly recognize you. Did she lay out that suit out?"

"Yeah."

"She did a good job. It looks like you were born to wear it. You have to look good to be good."

"Uh huh."

He tugged at his chin and nodded, like he was in full agreement with a private thought.

"Although, a hat...yes, a hat would have really topped it off. No pun intended. She never was one for hats, though. Hates when I wear them. Anyway, we're going to hate to see you go."

"Where is she?"

He put his arm around my shoulders and gave me a little squeeze.

"It was a little too much for her," he said, lowering his voice to a serious whisper. "Don't take it personally. She just has trouble saying goodbye."

"That's kinda rude," Steve mumbled.

I wasn't all that far off from agreeing with him.

Aaron tipped up his head, and angled down his eyes.

"What? Tell me. I thought we had a deal?"

"I really don't think you want to hear it."

"I do."

"Fine," the words just fell out of my mouth. "It's just that I never understood people who can't say goodbye. Properly. Makes you feel like you don't mean anything to them."

"That's one way of looking at it. Of course, it would be the wrong way."

That really ticked me off. I was about to lay into him good, but then Steve started laughing, and it distracted me for a second. And Aaron being Aaron, that slight pause was all he needed to jump in and take over.

"Did you ever consider that some people are incapable of saying goodbye because they care *too* much? And maybe it scares them thinking that this goodbye, or any other, might be the last one they ever give?"

"If that's true, then wouldn't it give you all the more reason to say goodbye? In person?"

Aaron stared blankly and slowly shook his head. I felt like I just chose the wrong answer to the very first, and easiest, question on his game show.

"So, let's see where we are. You've removed two answers. You phoned a friend, and you asked the audience. What are you going with Daryl? We need an answer?"

But before I had the chance, he answered for me.

"Some people are simply unable," he finally said, after a way too long stretch of head shaking. You would have thought he was trying to screw it back into his shoulders.

No one likes an overly judgmental host. Especially the contestants. There's already enough pressure.

"Not everyone says goodbye. It's too difficult to accept the terms of finality."

"Then don't say *goodbye*," I told him. "Say, *so long*. *See 'ya later*. Something like that."

"It's not the words, Daryl. It's the act itself. They begin to imagine all the inevitabilities in life and it frightens them. Deep down, they know the truth, but they'd rather not think about it."

"I thought you were all about telling the truth. Get her to speak her mind."

"She did. That is her truth."

"Well, it might be good for her, but it's not that good for other people."

"What's more important, Daryl? Hello or goodbye? You should focus more on what lies ahead, then what's been left behind. Speaking of, she wanted to make sure you had this."

He reached into the backseat and pulled out a small cooler.

"A care package for the road. There's bottled water, six turkey sandwiches, and bags of sliced carrots."

"So what, does this mean no Burger King?" Steve grumbled.

"Thanks," I told him. "But, we were going to stop at Burger King."

"Why in the world would you want to go there?" Aaron insisted. "When you've got plenty of fresh food already waiting for you? This is much better for you."

"I kinda promised."

"Promised who?"

I bobbed my head downward.

Aaron scoffed. "Steve? He's a dog. Dogs do what you tell them. Besides, he shouldn't eat human food anyway."

Steve turned his head and gave a sideways look at Boris and Hans.

"Schultz!" Steve commanded. "I want you to blow him up! And those two mongrels, as well!"

I could hear their gulps and whimpers from where I stood. Aaron's expression changed, and he diverted his eyes to my right.

"Boris! Hans! Now, what gotten into them?"

By the time I turned around, they were both gone. Steve thought this was a real side splitter.

"Close the gate!" he screamed. "Call the guards!"

He could barely get the words out, he was laughing so hard. He also lost the German accent halfway through, but that's nitpicking.

"Him, too," Aaron spoke over Steve. "Maybe they smell a squirrel. Anyway, here's this."

He leaned into the car and set the cooler in the backseat.

"There's a lock on it. Make sure it's in place, or else everything could spill out."

"Right. Well, we should get going."

"Okay. Now, you have everything? I see you have your sign. Be careful driving with the top down. That sign of yours can fly right up in your face. All it takes is a second."

"I'll keep that in mind."

"What about your money, and your medicine?"

"It's all in here."

I raised the suitcase, then tossed it on the backseat next to the cooler. And he had a fit about it, too. What else is new?

"You can't just leave that on the backseat!"

"Why?"

"Because," he incredulously announced. "Everything you have is in there! Your money. Your clothes. Put it in the trunk."

"But, what if I need something from it?"

"Then you pull over and open the trunk. It's not that big of an ordeal, son."

"I don't want to have to keep pulling over whenever I need something..."

"What will you need in there that's so important?"

"Well, money, for one."

"You don't have cash *on you*? Jesus, Daryl. Here, take this."

He dug out a wad of bills from his own pocket and forced it into my hand.

"I have my own money in the bag."

I tried to give it back, but he clenched his hands into fists and hid them behind his back. The two gestures preformed together were ultimately redundant, but I didn't make point of it. Maybe he couldn't decide which to choose.

"I know. I know," he said. "Just do me the favor. Take the money. I'll your bags in the trunk."

He pulled the keys from the ignition, then yanked the bags from the backseat.

"I know how to put things in a trunk," I told him.

"Then why didn't you do that in the first place?"

He popped open the trunk, and made a grand display of putting the suitcase inside. I couldn't see what he was doing from where I stood, but it was obvious he was trying to prove some point. Now those redundant hand gestures didn't seem like such an innocent mistake.

"Driving around with the top open," he mumbled to nobody in particular. "Leaving a suitcase full of valuables where anybody can grab it. Lucky I'm here with you. There."

He slammed it closed and moved over to me. Only this time, he wasn't staring directly at me like he usually did. His eyes were glued to the ground and he was taking his sweet time in between steps. When he finally did make it over to me, I swear, it was a good two minutes just to walk fifteen feet, he turned over the keys and shook my hand.

"We're going to miss you. Take care of yourself. I hope you find what you're looking for."

"Thanks."

"I still don't know about these pirates, though. I really hope you're not getting in with the wrong crowd."

Five different voices simultaneously screamed responses at me, but choosing any one of them probably would have kept me there longer. So, I merely sighed. A nice loud one, accompanied by a little head shaking.

I think he got the message.

"Now," he announced, clearing his throat. "What you want to do is take Eighty west."

"Right."

"Don't get on Thirty-five. There's no reason to take that. You'll just go out of your way."

"Okay. Okay. Steve, get in."

I held the driver's door open and Steve jumped in and settled himself in the passenger seat.

Now Aaron let out a disgusted sigh.

"What?" I asked.

I sure as hell didn't want to ask, but I figured I had to. The reason for my sigh was obvious. His, not so much.

"You're going to let the dog ride up front?"

"Yeah. His name is *Steve*. And *Steve* can ride anywhere he wants."

Steve sat up and raised a paw. "My man! High four!"

High four. Is he kidding?

"Do you know how dangerous that is?" Aaron panted. "What if he grabs the wheel, or shifts gears?"

"Until an hour ago, I didn't know how to shift gears, so I doubt he can. It'll be fine. Seriously."

He leaned against the car and picked some imaginary lint from his uniform.

"Look," he said quietly. "I don't want to fight."

"Well, neither do I."

"Promise me you'll do what I taught you: always speak your mind. Tell people the truth."

"Okay."

"Promise you'll remind yourself every morning."

"Okay. I promise."

I bent down into the driver's seat and closed the door.

"Seat belt," he sang out.

"Give me a chance," I sang just a little louder.

"And stay on eighty the entire way."

"I don't know if I can," I said.

"Of course you can. It's a straight shot."

"No, I mean, I have to follow whatever directions I get along the way."

"If you take the Seventy-Six through Denver, the city traffic is going to slow you down. I know what I'm talking about."

"I'm sure you do," I said. "You always do."

"What's that supposed to mean? I'm just trying to help. Isn't that what you want?"

I expected, as usual, to be yelled advice by any number of voices: *Just ignore it. Don't say a word. It's not worth it, he won't listen anyway. You want a bigger fight? Walk away.* I gave them time, but none of those recommendations were offered. What I heard surprised me.

Go on, tell him.

It was virtually unanimous. Except for…

Cut down on your red meats.

There's always one.

I released my grip from the steering wheel before my hands fused to it and stretched out the cramps.

"You want me to tell the truth, Aaron? Fine. But, there's something I need to say that you probably won't want to hear."

"Let's hear it," he dared me.

No hemming and hawing. No deep breaths. No sighs and no contemplation. I jumped right into it.

"You're a very smart guy," I calmly stated. "And you want to help people by sharing all the things you know. That's great. But the thing is, your people skills suck."

I waited for a response, but he didn't immediately provide one. And that moment of hesitation was all I needed to continue.

"Don't get me wrong," I insisted. "You're a nice guy with good intentions, but, one-on-one, you can drive a person crazy. It might explain why so many people stopped accepting your help. You expect everyone to do things *your* way, and you're overly critical when they make mistakes. That doesn't help. It causes resentment. You have a lot to offer people. You really do. If you could only find a way to do it without having personal contact. Like, write a book."

"You finished?" he dryly asked.

"I'm just doing what you told me to do. That says something, doesn't it?"

"You better get going. You're wasting valuable time."

I started it up, pressing in the clutch this time, shifted into reverse, and rolled out of the garage. I offered one last goodbye to Aaron, then headed down the long driveway, finally shooting out through the narrow opening of the gates. As I slid out onto the street, the sun broke through a gap in the clouds and filled the sky with light. I had nothing to shield me anymore, and it was a hell of a lot more light than I expected. My eyes refused to open beyond the thinnest of squints, which as anyone can imagine, makes it pretty damn difficult to drive. The compulsion to turn around and go back to sleep was more than tempting. Even if only for a few more hours. Sealed up in a dark room, nestled warmly in bed, my head sinking deeper and deeper into the pillow.

That's all I wanted.

So, there was only one thing to do.

I slapped myself in the face. So hard, that it provoked tears. I was wide awake now. My eyes adjusted to the brightness, and I focused back on the road.

With all of the warnings and advice Aaron threw at me about the trip, he neglected to mention how to get back to eighty. He had to have known I wasn't paying attention on the way out here. I don't know. When I got to the corner, I figured I had to make some decision on which way to go, so I came to a complete stop and tried out my navigational skills. Unfortunately, the only available tool I knew how to use was the sun, but it was straight above me, and burned to look at. Figures.

"Go left," Steve instructed.

"Are you sure?"

"Sure as shit."

There's a phrase I've heard all my life, but never quite grasped the inference. Obviously, when you see shit, you're instantly sure of what it is. But, wouldn't the same be true of everything you encounter? If you see a bird, you're sure it's a bird. The same goes for cows. Or cars. Or rain. There's no mistaking any of them. So, why not, *Sure as birds*, or *Sure as rain*. Why does it always have to be something disgusting?

Speaking of rain, he never showed me how to put the hood up.

I sure hope it doesn't rain. Shit.

19

As it turned out, we made it back to eighty fairly easily. Steve remembered the entire route. Either that, or he's a real lucky guesser. I noticed we weren't alone in trying to find our way through unfamiliar territory. There was a car with Illinois plates following behind me who looked to be even more tentative about directions than I was. It's not like I was watching the other car the whole time, but they'd stop, then start, then slow down, then hit the gas again. They never got close enough for me to get a good look and confirm it, but I'm guessing it was some sort of improperly folded map problem.

Which reminds me. I need a new map.

Geez, you need a lot of stuff for a simple car ride.

Speaking of car rides, I was a little worried at first that maybe I wouldn't like the convertible experience. Testing it out with Aaron on side roads wasn't a problem, but I assumed being on the expressway with the top down would be equivalent to driving through a tornado. Turned out, I was wrong. I was steady at seventy, open road, open hood, and it wasn't that bad. Felt about the same as having all the windows rolled down. The only troublesome thing about it was Steve. He was leaning against the passenger door and hanging his head and front paws out the window. I thought at any minute he was going to get lifted by a gust of wind and blown out to the street. He hung out the window in the other car, too, but at least then, there was a good chance he'd bounce off the inside of the roof first, and I'd have a chance to collect him on the rebound. I found my eyes switching from the highway to the passenger seat, expecting at any minute for him to be sucked out and turned into instant road kill.

Sounds like something they'd sell at a truck stop: Instant Road Kill. Just add water.

It didn't seem like the safest way to drive. For either of us. Plus, I got a headache from all the movement. Maybe next stop, I could buy a rope and tie him to the door handle. Save us both a little pain.

We found a Burger King a few exits ahead. Steve claims he smelled it a mile before we saw the sign, but I'm not buying it. I'm starting to think he has some complex. Like he needs people to be impressed with him, or something.

There were quite a few cars in the drive-thru, but I pulled in anyway, rather than going inside. I don't know, maybe it's just me, but it never fails that I get stuck whenever I go inside. And not just in a long line. It's the other inescapable nightmare that happens to you while you're waiting.

Small talk.

God, how I hate small talk. Strangers standing around thinking their *only* option for that particular moment is to ensure that everybody else's time waiting is even more miserable and uncomfortable than it has to be.

I come here all the time. It's usually not like this.

I come here all the time. It's always like this.

I remember when this whole area used to be nothing but swampland.

Who cares? Not me. Honestly. I don't care if you've done a complete mathematical study on the ratio of wait times. I don't care how you feel about the weather. And your hypothesis on the ever-changing flavor of ketchup is none of my concern.

I just want my food, and I want to leave.

So, if a drive-thru is available, I'll always choose that over going inside. It's just not worth taking the chance. Because if you risk it, more than likely you'll get caught in that type of situation where you're forced to hear about someone's granddaughter's tuba lessons, or them wondering what dinosaur meat must have tasted like. And I swear, you'll just wind up wanting to stab yourself. That's probably why these places give out plastic utensils.

We called out our order and then drove around to the window as we were told. We hadn't even come to a complete stop before a pimple-faced teenage boy stuck out his head and shared with us his total lack of interest for his job.

"Eightee...," his muttering was so apathetic, the words themselves didn't even care where they traveled.

"How much?"

"Eigh...senben."

I wasn't even sure if he was speaking actual words. It sounded like someone talking in their sleep. Or casting a secret spell. His eyes were half closed, so either was possible. And I hadn't turned into a frog, so he was either half asleep, or just really bad at magic.

"Something wrong with this guy?" Steve asked.

The sound of Steve's voice, for some reason, shook the mope out of his coma, and for the first time, he focused on us.

Barely.

"Hey," he sluggishly squeaked. "Cool car."

"Thanks," I told him.

"Izzit a spy car?"

"What did that idiot say?" Steve asked.

"A spy car," the kid answered. "One that talks. You know, like the movie."

Steve gave me a look. "Can he hear me?"

"I don't know." I looked back at the kid. "Can you understand him?"

"Who?"

"My dog."

"Your dog? What? Like the movie?"

"I don't know what movie you mean. How much is it?"

"Depends on where you go. Usually like seven or eight bucks, but the matinees are cheaper."

"Slap him," Steve suggested.

I sort of wanted to, but I didn't. I non-violently handed him a twenty, instead.

"Hey," I remembered. "You wouldn't happen to have any rope in there, would you?"

His voice trebled slightly. "You are a spy, aren't you?"

"Yeah. I'm a spy. Just don't tell anybody, huh?"

"Right."

He took a deep breath, then poked at a few buttons on the register, and counted out my change.

"Make sure you count that," Steve advised.

"Hey," the kid proudly noticed. "You got a dog."

"You got to be kidding," Steve said.

"Is he a spy dog?"

"Yep. He's my partner."

"No way."

He handed over our bags, and I quickly pulled away toward a parking space.

"Spies?" Steve asked. "I thought we were supposed to be pirates?"

"Well, we're not yet."

"I can't believe someone trusts that guy to work with money."

"Forget about work. How would you like someone like that to be your human?"

"No thanks. But like they say, *you can't pick your human*."

"Ours is, *you can't pick your parents*."

"Six of one, half a dozen of the other," he mused. "There's no room up here. Lay it out in back, will 'ya?"

He hopped between the seats and into the back, while I retrieved the bag from the floor and stepped out of the car.

"We are gonna be pirates, though, right?"

"That's what Don said."

"Shit. There's no cup holders in this thing. We have to sit here until I finish my coffee."

It would be so much easier for me if dogs had functional paws. I mean, if they're able to talk, why can't they hold their own coffee?

After we finished eating, I shoved as much of the garbage as I could into one bag and walked it all over to a can in the parking lot. Steve, of course, followed along, even though he was unable to carry anything. It's not like I couldn't handle a bag and two empty cups on my own, it's just that I wonder if his inability to hold anything is becoming a convenient excuse not to offer any help.

"Geez, sorry," Steve spit out.

"Sorry about what?"

"Hold on a sec."

He lifted his nose high in the air and sniffed deeply.

"Do you smell that?" he dreamily inquired.

I took a couple whiffs.

"Grease?"

"You humans amaze me. You think you're so superior to us stupid animals. All the things you can do, yet you have the worst sense of smell. It's a female, Bud-o! She's around here somewhere."

He slunk toward a row of high wooden fences that bordered the far edge of the parking lot, sniffing and calling out along the way.

"Hello? Where are you, you naughty little creature? I know you're out there somewhere. Would someone like to have a nooner with little old Steve?"

Within seconds, we heard scratching from the other side of one of the fences.

"Hey! I'm over here! The brown fence toward the end!"

She sounded a tad overexcited, like they were old friends, or something.

"Hang on, baby! Lover-boy is on his way! Daryl, I need a hand!"

"Do you know her?" I asked.

"Yeah, we met online, at a dog dating site. Come on!"

"There's no reason to be snotty," I told him.

"How the hell would I know a dog in Iowa? Now, get over here. You're wasting valuable time."

"How are you going to get over?" There was a tone of desperation in her voice. In all my years, I was never able to elicit any sense of anguish like that from a woman. What in the hell was so special about Steve?

"My human will do it," he announced. "If he ever drags his ass over here."

Sometimes I really dislike this dog.

"And what am I supposed to do?" I asked him. "Tear down the fence?"

"Lift me up, and drop me over."

"You'll kill yourself."

"What's a little bruise or two?"

"You don't even know what she looks like. Don't you maybe want to find out a little about her first? See if the fall is worth it?"

"You crack me up. Now, let's go."

I set down the garbage and picked up the runt with both hands. The fence was easily seven feet high, and with no gaps between the boards, so I couldn't see the landing area on the other side. For all I knew, he could fall directly on barbed wire or polished metal spikes. It was doubtful, but there's always that possibility.

"Hello," he cooed. "Move over, darling. I don't want to break anything important. Alright Daryl, drop me."

I extended my arms as far as I could, then let go. A second later, I heard a tiny thud.

"You okay?"

"Fine," Steve called out. "I'll call you when I'm done."

The one thing you couldn't accuse him of was a lack of confidence when it came to females. I'm a little surprised they put up with it, actually. I can't imagine any woman I've ever known having sex with a stranger just because he was helped over a fence.

I grabbed the garbage off the ground and walked to the trash can. Damn it! Now I had that stuck in my head: *did I* know any women who were like that? Granted, you can never really know everything about a person. There's always going to be a certain measure of secrets, omissions, and outright lies with anyone. But I think for the most part, it's easy to fill in the blanks about a person the better you know them. It could just take a awhile.

Unfortunately, that time quickly arrived, because suddenly, I was finding it far too easy to fill in the blanks of every woman I ever knew. I pictured all of them, each in their own little scenario, having sex with random fence-hoppers. And not just Audrey and Julie. It was waitresses, customers, librarians, classmates, you name it. Geez, there were even old women from the neighborhood when I was growing up. It was nuts. I mean, Mrs. Delveccio from down the street? There's no way in hell she would have ever done anything like that. I'm fairly confident about that. The woman looked ninety-five and smelled even older. People would have gladly jumped a fence to *avoid* having sex with her. Even so, I couldn't stop myself from thinking it. There she was, in her crummy old housecoat and slippers, smoking a Lucky Strike and having sex with a strange guy, just because he jumped her fence.

What's worse, the Delveccio's didn't even have a high fence. Very little effort would be required to jump it.

I rammed the bag and the two cups into the overstuffed garbage can, hoping if I pressed hard enough, I could cram these stupid visions in there as well. But it was obvious they wouldn't leave without a bigger fight. In fact, I went straight from women I knew directly to women I only knew indirectly. So, I added my second hand, really leaning into it and grunting like mad. Just as I was struggling to force out the image of Margaret Thatcher and a man with a tall ladder, I felt someone tap me on my shoulder.

It was that odd guy from the take out window.

"I know yer busy," he slurred. "But here ya go."

He reached out to show me a long piece of rope.

"Oh, thanks."

"Is that some kinda code?" he asked.

"What?"

He pointed to my *Happy* sign.

"Oh. Something like that. It's the, uh, name of my secret mission."

I tucked the sign inside my jacket.

"Majestic."

Before the conversation could get any deeper, Steve called. "Daryl! Finished!"

I motioned for the kid to leave, and headed back to the fence.

"You have to go," he female anxiously demanded. "My human will be back out here any minute."

"Seems getting out's going to be a bigger problem than getting in. Daryl? You there?"

"Right here," I told him.

"How we gonna work this one, partner?"

I wrapped the rope twice around my hand, then dropped the other end over the fence.

"Can you reach it?" I asked him.

"Yeah."

"Then bite down on it, but not hard enough to bite through."

"Oday," Steve mumbled. "Now whad?"

"Just hold on, and start walking up."

I pulled as evenly as possible, trying my best not to tug the rope from his mouth. I figured he was about halfway up when I heard a loud gasp.

"Oh, no," Steve's female groaned.

"What in the world!" shrieked a different female voice. "Is that dog levitatin'?"

"Geb me outta heh!"

Three more pulls, and Steve was at the top of the fence. As I reached up to grab him, the thought flashed in my mind: *What if I hopped the fence? Would this woman...?*

"Arnie," the human female growled. "Call the police! And getcher rifle!"

Not only did that answer my question, but it effectively got rid of the visions, too. I guess not everyone would be so welcome to a fence hopper.

I reached up and took Steve around the belly, then lowered him safely to the ground.

The drive-thru kid watched in stunned amazement. There was even drool leaking from the corners of his mouth, but I didn't think too much of it since I had no way of knowing whether that was anything unusual for him.

"That's why you needed the rope," he murmured. "You're doin a job."

"Remember. Don't tell anybody."

"No way."

My cell phone rang, and I thought the kid was going to jump out of his skin.

"Who's that?" He panted.

"Who do you think?"

"No way..."

I pressed the button and brought the phone to my ear.

"Yeah?"

"Daryl?" A male voice on the other end asked.

"Code name," I demanded.

"Excuse me?"

I gave a shrewd wink to the kid.

"Code name," I repeated into the phone.

"It's Doctor Melvin."

"Good. Now, what is my mission?"

"Your *mission*?"

I kept my gaze fixed on the kid while waiting for Melvin's answer.

"To be happy?"

I disconnected the call and looked at the kid.

"It all checks out. We have to hit the road. Thanks for your help."

"Yeah. Later."

Steve and I started back toward the car and the cell rang again.

"What?" I asked into the phone.

"Daryl? It's Doctor Melvin again. You hung up on me."

"Bad connection."

"Listen, Daryl, how are you feeling? Is anything wrong?"

"Should there be?"

"I was contacted by Julie. She said she was worried about you. That you might be in some danger."

"There's always a little danger in the spy game, Doc."

"I don't understand."

Sirens began to wail in the distance.

"That's the police. I have to go back to my mission now."

"Daryl...!"

I ended the call and slid the phone into my inside jacket pocket, then reeled the rope around my hand as we moved back to the car.

I dropped Steve onto the passenger seat, and tried to fashion a noose out of the rope, but the stupid knot kept unraveling.

"What the hell?" Steve protested.

"Shut up. It's is so you don't fly out the car."

The sirens were getting closer, so I dumped the rope on the ground and drove away.

"Don't fly out of the car," I instructed him.

20

"I'm hungry."

"Are you serious?" I yelled over to Steve. "We just ate an hour ago!"

Okay, there was one of the big drawbacks of driving a convertible. It's loud. There's nothing shielding you from the outside noises. In fact, there's no such thing as *outside* noises anymore. Just noises. So, if you want your dog to hear you, you have to be just as loud.

"Dude, sorry, but I don't have control over it, you know? Hungry's hungry."

"I didn't want to stop until we really needed to."

"Then don't."

"What?"

"I said, *then don't*!" Steve shouted. "Just gimme a sandwich from the cooler!"

"I still have to pull over to do that!"

Sometimes I really wonder about this stupid thing.

"Do you mind?" he yelled.

"Fine!"

There was an exit coming up ahead anyway, so I flicked on my blinker and started to drift into the right lane. Almost immediately I heard the quick squealing of tires and someone really laying out on the horn. I gave a check in the rear view mirror, but there was no one that close behind me, so I have no idea what all the commotion was about. Then I saw a car swerving hard from the left lane, cutting it a little too close for the other drivers.

More Illinois plates. I wonder why I keep seeing those so much. Maybe because they're so familiar to me, they're just easier to recognize. I bet if I started paying attention, I'd probably Rhode Island plates over and over again, too.

I veered onto the exit ramp, followed a couple car lengths behind by the other car from Illinois. If they stop where we do, I'll have to ask if they've noticed a lot of Illinois drivers, too, or if it's just me.

"Smell that?"

I shook my head. "We don't have time for you to go have sex again."

"Coffee, Daryl. I smell coffee. And you're kind of a prude, aren't you."

"I am not."

"You should listen to yourself sometime. If you did, you'd hear a prude. And a pretty damn big one."

"Oh yeah? What about you?"

"I'm having fun. You should give it a whirl."

"I'm married."

"Exactly."

"What the hell does that mean?"

"Nothing. There's the coffee shop."

I pulled into the lot and threw it in park, but I was so mad, I forgot for a minute that I was driving a stick, and sailed my hand upward alongside the steering wheel.

"Tell me," I insisted.

"Okay," Steve said with a sigh. "You go on all the time about wanting to be happy, but you never do anything about it."

"What do you think this trip is about?"

"I talking about Julie. Why don't you just sign the papers? You're miserable with her. How can it be any worse without her?"

"This thing isn't going to last forever."

"What thing?"

"Forget it," I told him.

"That *other guy*, you mean? *Robert? That thing?* Dude, she left you for someone else. Face it."

"You don't know. You don't, 'cause it's not what you think. It'll work itself out. It always does."

"It does?"

"Yeah."

I stepped out of the car and slammed the door. This stupid dog doesn't have the slightest idea what it means to be married. He doesn't even know what it's like to be in a relationship, for that matter. Life must be pretty damn easy when all you do is jump from female to female, never having to worrying about the things the rest of us have to deal with. So far, the only details he's been concerned with is how to get back over a fence. And I had to help him.

"I know enough about it to know it's stupid," he said.

"Enough about what?"

"Marriage."

"Your human wasn't married. What could you know?"

"I watch TV. I see what it's like. Wives think men are stupid. The husband works hard all day at some stupid job, then comes home and gets henpecked. *We need this, we need that. Why don't you tell your boss you want a raise?* What gets me, most of these women don't do anything all day other than sit on the phone and bitch to other women, but it's the husband who's an idiot. And some of these guys are doctors and lawyers. They can't be that stupid. You keep waiting for them to stand up for themselves and fight back, but all they do is hide in the garage and work on their cars. It's like they stopped being men as soon as they got married. Who needs it?"

"I told you before. That's TV, Steve, not real life. Big difference."

"Art imitates life. I've heard that before. In a couple places, so it must be true."

"Just because...hey, wait a second. How did you know what I was thinking?"

"About what?"

"This. You not knowing anything about relationships."

"Thinking it? Dude, you were talking it. Out loud."

"No, I wasn't."

"Then how did I know? I'm not psychic. We went through all that already."

That was weird. I could swear I was only thinking it.

"Well, you weren't," Steve said. "You were talking."

It happened again!

"What happened again?" Steve asked.

"Stop it!"

"Stop what? Listening to you? Believe me, there's times I wish I could. Behind you."

"*Behind me?* What the hell's that mean?"

"Talking to your dog?" a strange voice asked.

Oh. That, *behind me*. I turned and saw some bum of a guy, dirty clothes, looking like he hadn't showered or shaved in weeks. He was so filthy, it was nearly impossible to zero in on an age range. He could be eighteen, or he could be eighty. Well, maybe not eighty, but at least sixty.

"I'm thirty," the bum said.

What?

"You're doing it again," Steve commented. "Talking out loud when you think you're not. You need to focus, buddy."

"You should listen to your dog," the guy advised. "They know."

"You heard what my dog said?"

"Sure did. Now, give me five dollars."

"What? Why?"

"Five more dollars, and I can get a new flash drive."

"You want a new flash drive?"

"Yes. Now come on, it's only five dollars. Were you using it for something else more important than my flash drive?"

"How do you even know I have five dollars on me?"

"Oh, you have five dollars on you," he confidently stated.

"You don't have five dollars on you?" Steve suspiciously asked. "I thought you were loaded?"

"See," the bum went on. "Your dog said you have five dollars."

"You really know what my dog said?"

"Ah ha!" the bum shouted. "So, you do have five dollars!"

"I know this trick," I told him.

"Oh, yeah? How's it done?"

"I don't know."

"Well, I'll tell you for ten dollars."

"I thought you wanted five."

I do," he said. "But it's five extra if you want to know the trick."

"What's the second five for?"

"I wouldn't mind eating."

"Oh."

I looked him up and down. If this was just some con game, he was really throwing himself into it.

I turned back to the car for a quick check with Steve. Just to make sure I wasn't doing it again.

"Did you hear that?" I whispered.

"Yeah, he's hungry," Steve whispered back.

"Nothing else?" I whispered again.

"And he wants a flash drive. Why are we whispering? It's not some big secret. Give the guy some money. By the way, what's a flash drive?"

I pulled the money out of my pocket and fanned through it. All I had were hundreds. I must have used the only small bills I had back at Burger King. Great. Most places don't even take hundreds anymore. Thanks, Aaron.

I peeled off one of the useless bills and handed it to the guy.

"A hundred?" he muttered. "Are you serious?"

I didn't like where this was headed.

"Look. You can't fool me," I told him. "I've seen this scam before. You keep having me switch out bills until you have the whole stack. It's an old Abbott and Costello routine, or something. But, I'm in kind of a hurry, so, to save some time, here's three more. That enough?"

I carefully laid the extra hundreds in his hand, then safely shoved the remainder back in my pocket.

"Yeah," he weakly replied. "That's enough."

"Good. Come on."

I motioned toward the coffee shop, and Steve eagerly leapt out of the car and dashed through the parking lot full steam. As I opened the door for the two of us, I took a look back. The bum was standing where I left him, still staring down at his hand.

If he loses that money, he's not getting any more from me. I can't be responsible for everything lost by the wind.

There were a couple people in line ahead of us, which gave me some time to contemplate the menu: Indonesian, Costa Rican, Kenyan, Panamanian...Jesus, all I want is coffee, not a frigging geography lesson.

"Four hundred dollars is a lot of money, isn't it?" Steve asked.

I just shrugged. "I don't think it's a lot of money. Not anymore, at least."

The man immediately in front of me turned around and aimed a nod in my direction.

"It sure seems that way, doesn't it?" he smirked. "Standing here now, it's easy to say, twenty years ago, who would have thought anyone would ever pay close to four dollars for a cup of coffee, right? But I guarantee you, if you could go back in time, things wouldn't be everything you remember them to be."

Goddamn it. I'm standing in a line, aren't I?

"What are you babbling about?" I shot back.

"Their prices," he answered. "You said it wasn't a lot of money nowadays. But, I'm saying, someday in the future, we'll all be looking back on this saying, *remember when?*"

"I wasn't talking to you."

He gave a look behind me, then twisted his head to his left and right.

"Oh. Who were you talking to?"

"Not you."

The barista caught my eye and flashed me a slightly-above-minimum-wage grin.

"Who's next?" he called out.

My time-traveler acquaintance spun around and stepped to the counter.

"I am," he said, then mechanically reeled out what I assumed was the same order he placed every day.

I, on the other hand, had no idea what I wanted. And Steve, well was just positively mesmerized by the choices.

"Damn," he finally said. "This is hard. Okay, umm, I think I'll have the Guatemalan."

"How'd you figure that one out?" I asked.

"I don't know. It says it's flavorful."

"What a stupid thing to say."

The time-traveler peered over his shoulder as he pocketed his change.

"You don't have to be so rude," he told me.

"Excuse me," I said. "I didn't know being rude was a privilege only granted to you."

I was pretty sure he mumbled *"asshole"* under his breath as he stepped aside, but it was hard to tell because his voice blended so seamlessly with the whiny Kenny G. sax solo squeaking from the speakers. I think they were both the same key.

The barista eyed me again.

"Hello. What would you like?"

"So, do you have any coffees that are un-flavorful?"

He dropped the grin and peeked up at the menu.

"I don't understand."

"It says the Guatemalan is *flavorful.* That's sort of redundant, isn't it? I mean, all coffee is supposed to have some amount of flavor, right?"

"Yeah," he stammered. "I guess so. I didn't write it."

"Hmm. Good thing, 'cause it's really dumb. Gimme two Guatemalans, I guess. Flavor sounds good."

"What size?"

I looked down at Steve.

"Since you're Mister Big Spender today," he said. "I'll take the Grande. And a blueberry muffin."

The barista leaned over the counter, then wagged his finger at Steve.

"You can't bring animals in here," he chided.

"I have to," I told him. "I'm blind."

"Then how did you know about the Guatemalan being described as flavorful?"

"He read it to me."

"Your dog did?"

"Yeah. He's a seeing-eye dog."

Steve started laughing it up. "That's pretty funny."

"Sorry, sir. But, it has to go outside."

"Look," I insisted. "There won't be any problems. We'll sit in the back. Out of the way. We just want to have our coffees and go."

"*We*?"

"Yeah. Me and him."

The grin snuck back. Even bigger than before. "Your dog reads, and drinks coffee?"

"Why else would we be here? Think about it."

Three new employees now meandered toward us and stared down at Steve. It's kind of sad really to see how empty other people's lives are.

The barista pushed his tongue against the inside of his bottom lip, then spun around and met in silent conference with his fellow workers.

"I tell you what," he said, rubbing his hands together like some cliché evil genius. "He can stay, *if* he actually drinks the coffee. I want to see this."

"Alright. Two Grandes, and two blueberry muffins."

I took out my roll and handed him a hundred. And once again, his grin disappeared.

"We don't take bills over twenty."

I looked down at Steve.

"Guess we have to go somewhere else."

He jerked his index finger in the air to stop me. I swear, you could see the idea formulating in his head. If he were a photo, the caption would read:

The plot thickens.

"Hold on. How 'bout this? If your dog drinks an entire Grande, it's on the house. If not, I keep the hundred. Deal?"

"Whatever."

I was tempted to leave. I really was. Not because I didn't think Steve was up to the task. Hell, I would have bet another hundred he'd ask for a refill. I was just sick of playing these stupid games. Why does everything have to be such a ridiculous challenge sometimes?

"Here you go..."

And then there was his tone. Like he doubted us. More than doubted us, actually. It was a certainty that was magnified by the smug look on his miserable little face. He was telling me that I was a liar and he knew it. This was his trap. And he was going to catch me.

I truly hate people like this.

I took the order and walked it over to the condiment station, being watched every step by anyone who wasn't busy with a customer.

"Too bad we didn't know this in advance," Steve lamented. "We could have gotten a couple travel mugs thrown in."

I had a sip from each cup for taste, then motioned Steve toward a table in back.

"There. In the corner," I said.

My grinning barista popped up behind me and without any advanced warning, and grabbed my shoulders. I almost dropped the damn coffees. Idiot. True, they didn't cost me anything, but still.

"No, you don't," he sneered. "Take this table here. I want to watch."

"I don't get it," Steve said. "What the hell is the big deal?"

"I don't know. Just, some people..."

We took our seats and, well, as uninteresting as it sounds, began to drink our coffees. With half the restaurant watching us in breathless anticipation.

It was more than a little silly. It was plain dumb.

I reached across the table to grab hold of Steve's cup, but was instantly scolded by the barista.

"What are you doing?"

"Holding the cup so it doesn't spill."

"No you don't," he warned me. "When you touch it, you're gonna do some kind of magic, or something, aren't you? No. He has to drink it on his own, or the whole thing's off."

"Can you squeeze the bottom with your paws?" I asked Steve.

"I guess. Guy's a little paranoid, isn't he?"

Steve steadied the cup with his front paws and sunk his tongue into the coffee.

"Good job," I said.

"Thanks. You know what? This is flavorful."

My turn to drink. It was okay. Not great, like I was going to run out and buy a plane ticket to Guatemala, or anything.

After we finished, the barista seized Steve's cup and gave it, and Steve, a thorough examination.

"You're telling me," he announced with utter astonishment. "This dog drank that coffee?"

"You stood right there and watched."

He took hold of Steve's collar and pinched it.

"Where's the hose?"

"Up your ass," Steve said, jerking himself away.

"That's not nice," I told Steve.

"What?" the barista demanded.

"He said the hose was up your ass."

Everyone within earshot laughed. The barista hunched over and scanned out the windows with a look of pained confusion.

"I know what this is," he finally decided. "You guys are some comedy show. Okay, you got me. You got me!"

The laughter in the room doubled, and he proudly displayed his embarrassed smile to the crowd.

"People would watch a TV show about a dog drinking coffee?" Steve asked incredulously. "Dude, we could be so famous!"

I sighed to myself and pushed my chair away from the table.

"Let's get out of here."

We worked our way to the door, supported by the loud cheers and vigorous applause of everyone in the room.

What the hell is wrong with these people? All I wanted was coffee.

As soon as we hit the parking lot, Steve came to a stop.

"Who are they?"

There were five guys at the far end of the parking lot hanging around my car. Two of them were leaning up against it, two sitting on the on the trunk, and one pacing back and forth next to it, punching the air like he was waiting to get into the ring. It was like watching actors getting into character before auditions for *West Side Story*.

"You know them?" Steve asked.

"Nope. But they better not scratch the thing up, 'cause I don't feel like listening to Aaron's complaining."

I walked to the car feeling completely indifferent about these idiots. Steve though, insisted I stay a couple feet behind him. About halfway there, the guy leaning on the back fender noticed us approaching and said something to the rest of them. I couldn't make out the words, but I had a pretty good idea, because just like that, they were all off the car and slowly advancing toward us.

Whatever the hell this is, I hope it doesn't take long. I really don't have the time.

Eventually, they stopped and formed a line, side-by-side, blocking a direct route to the car. It was like I traveled from one universe and into another. These fellows were the exact opposite of the cheering/back-slapping crowd I left inside the coffee shop. My initial assessment of the situation was that I had two options: either walk through them, or walk around them.

Blaze Of Glory Shootout or *Making A Run For It*. It really pissed me off that those were my two immediate default options.

I decided right there to develop an Option Three. Everyone, I figured, needs a Number Three.

I came to a stop, and stared right back at them.

The true purpose of stopping was to merely give me a minute to focus on all the possible alternatives, but there was something about performing this simple act that seemed to throw them off guard, so I gave up trying to come up with other choices and stuck with this.

I mean, why not? It worked. They weren't doing anything more than staring back, and exchanging odd looks with each other. It reminded me of being at the zoo, and making eye contact with some stupid, caged animals.

I had no idea how long I could hold them like this, but judging from the dopey looks on their faces, I guessed it could be quite a while. So, after a few seconds, I started counting in my head. I wasn't sure how much time had passed before I thought to do it, so I just started from seven. Seemed about right.

Seven...Eight...Nine...

"I'll take the short one," Steve grunted. "Only 'cause I know I can jump as high as his balls. After I bite them off, I'll take a chunk outta whoever's left."

Fourteen...Fifteen...Sixteen...

It was amazing. They continued to stand there gaping at me like a bunch of clueless rubes. More than likely, the exact demographic that had to be informed about coffee being flavorful. Dolts.

Twenty-one...Twenty-two...Twenty-three...

Then the guy closest to me stepped forward and gave me a quick shove.

"What are you doing?"

Twenty-three. Longer than I would have guessed.

"Nothing," I told him.

The Shover was the same guy that was punching the air. I don't know, maybe he's training for something. Or, maybe he has some problem with involuntary muscle spasms. Who knows with people like this?

"Yeah, you were," another one added. This one was some skinny guy, about half my age, who had both his arms from wrists to elbows covered in band-aids. I'd love to know what that was about, but I didn't think this was the time to ask.

"You called us names," he slowly continued.

"And you was counting," another one added.

Shit.

"Why'd you start with seven?" Band-aid Arms asked.

"'Cause he thinks we're stupid," The Shover announced, punctuating the word *stupid* with increased volume and another shove. "You're the stupid one, 'cause now, it's not just for the money."

"Is that it?" chimed in one of the previously silent members of the group. "You think we're *stoo-pid?*"

If pressed, I'd have to say *yes*. Significantly stupid. *Noticeably* stupid. I mean, the guy in my face right now was sporting this leather fringe vest, like he was a castoff from the Village People. Talk about stupid. Buy a mirror.

The Village Person stepped in a little closer.

"What did you say?"

"You're doing it again, aren't you?" Steve snapped. "Here I thought you were going all *Gunfight At The OK Corral* on them, but it's really *One Flew Over The Cuckoo's Nest*, isn't it?"

"Quiet."

As I shot a quick glance down at Steve, The Shover drew back and released a big, wild swing that was headed directly for my right cheekbone. I heard one of them shout, *grab the dog*, then everything went black.

When I came to, I was on my back looking up at them. None of them had traveled too far from where they were before the punch, so I'm guessing I wasn't out too long. Maybe a second or two. So quick, you probably couldn't even say I was ever out, but I had to be at some point, because I don't remember falling. And my head hurt like hell. The back of my head, and not my face. So, either I whacked it on the pavement, or this guy has some weird mystery punch that radiated pain to other untouched parts of the body. I tried to get my bearings to stand, even though I had no idea what the hell that would achieve, other than maybe providing these jerks with an easier target to sucker punch.

Mister Village Person crouched down and reached for Steve. Probably not the smartest thing he ever did. I swear, it was like Steve was waiting for this moment, because as soon as that arm came close enough, his jaw snapped like a mousetrap. The next thing I heard was teeth sinking deep into muscle, immediately followed by high-pitched squeals of agony. The guy wildly shook his arm, trying desperately to free himself, but Steve only clenched tighter, refusing to let go. The rest of them formed a circle around him, frantically swiping at the air, and making otherwise futile attempts to pull Steve off their buddy's forearm.

They were far too distracted at this point to bother with me anymore. So, I managed to scoot a few feet away from the fracas and as I did, Band Aid arms reached into his pocket.

"Cut him off!" the Pusher screamed. "Do it!"

Band Aids flicked his wrist and popped open a switchblade. His eyes ballooned to twice their normal size as he held the dirty metal blade high above Steve, focusing on the best time, and place, to bring down his arm.

My mind went blank. I wanted to scream, but the words refused to form in my mouth.

Another voice spoke up instead. Not in my head, but from somewhere behind me. The words did not match the cheerful manner in which they were loudly sung to us all.

"The cops are coming! The cops are coming! Run for the hills! Oh, the humanity!"

The other four cast fearful looks around the parking lot, and without discussion or debate, ran off in four separate directions. Steve relaxed his jaw and dropped harmlessly to the ground. Mister Village

Person delicately cradled his bloodied arm against his chest and stumbled toward the street, howling and crying every step of the way.

Steve shook himself off, then began spitting out chunks of flesh. It was going to be a long time before that guy could do the *YMCA* dance in any proper fashion again.

"You okay?" he panted.

"Yeah, I think so. His shrieking probably hurt more than the punch did."

"You heard that, too?" Steve laughed. "Damn, that was so high, I thought only I could hear it."

"What are you doing!" came the voice from behind me again. "Waiting for them to come back?"

I peeked around and there was the bum again, a few yards behind me, manically hopping up and down in place like an sugar buzzed kid on a trampoline.

"That was you?" I asked. "You called the cops?"

"How could I call the cops? No one could break a hundred! Ha ha!"

"So...?"

"So, I lied!" he shouted. "There's no cops coming. Yet another compelling reason to leave, don't you think?"

He bounded over and pulled me to my feet. I had barely regained my balance when he abruptly let go and made a mad dash for the car.

"Shotgun!"

He stretched out his arms, and without breaking stride, planted his hands on the top of the driver's side door and lifted his feet off the ground. In one smooth, continuous movement, he straightened into a handstand, then pushed straight up off the door. His momentum gracefully arced him backward and high in the air, like a diver so sure of his target that he wasn't afraid to go in feet first. At the last second, he bent his knees ever-so-slightly and twisted forward, landing perfectly in the passenger seat, with only the gentlest of *thwumps* rising from the leather upholstery.

"Ta da! And he avoided the gearshift, ladies and gentlemen!"

"What the hell is that?" Steve asked.

"Well, he did call *shotgun*," I told him.

21

I kept a close eye on the sidewalks while I drove to see if there was any sign of those idiots. Not that I was worried about running into them again. I was just a little curious to know what the hell it was all about. They didn't want money. They didn't want the car. So, what then? Were they just out looking for kicks?

Holy crap. I can't believe I just said that. *Looking for kicks?* That's something my grandfather would have said.

I also found myself sneaking looks at the guy in the seat next to me, wondering what the hell he's all about, too. All he's been doing is bouncing up and down in his seat like he's on one of those old quarter-a-ride wooden horses outside a department store.

Okay, I have to admit, it was a pretty complicated way to enter the car, so maybe he's just proud of himself and this is his little private celebration. Then again, he could have punctured something valuable on the landing and was squirming in pain. Some people can be so hard to read.

We passed a sign notifying us that the expressway entrance was just up ahead. Was this guy coming with me? He didn't seem like anyone who knew the location of a Pirate Convention, but you never know. He could be another guidepost, or he could just be another nut. I figured I better find out before I got too far along.

"So, what are you?" I asked him.

Without pause, he shouted back. "Yes!"

Maybe he didn't hear me right.

"No," I said, "I asked, '*What* are you'?"

"I heard you. And I answered, 'Yes'!"

"Well, what kind of answer is that?"

"A single-syllable one."

"But it doesn't answer anything."

"It doesn't, huh? What if I added an extra syllable? Yes, *sir*. Is that better? Or, is it that particular one syllable word you object to? I could say *couch*, if that makes you feel any better."

"What the shit?" Steve said from the backseat.

The guy turned around and looked right at Steve. "Couch!"

"Dude," Steve said. "Pull over. This guy's freaking me out."

Steve was right. The last thing I wanted to do was drive aimlessly with some loon who can flip in and out of cars. Okay, I never say him flip *out* from one, but if you could flip in that easily, the reverse couldn't be much different.

There was a little strip mall to the right, which was really no surprise, seeing how those damn things are everywhere. I pulled into the parking lot.

"This as far as you're going?" he asked.

"No," I told him. "Who only goes as far as a strip mall?"

"You'd be surprised. How far are you going, then?"

"Nevada."

"Nevada," he said it dreamily, like it was some exotic island that he'd only read about before. "Where in Nevada?"

"Don't know."

"Never heard of it. That by Vegas?"

"It's not the name of a town. I just don't know where."

"But, you want to know, don't you?"

"Yes."

"How do you intend to find out?"

"I don't know."

He laughed. "Traveling to Don't Know, Nevada, using the *I Don't Know Trip Guide*. Good plan! Bravo!"

"You have a better one?" I asked.

"Maybe," he hissed. "Maybe not."

"Come on," I told him. "Either you do, or you don't. I don't have time for games."

"Oh, everyone should have time for games! Life's a game. Not *Life* the board game, I don't mean that, although, they are pretty similar, aren't they? You pick your car, put yourself in it, then spin the wheel, and move around the board to discover your fate. Pretty much the same concept here. Except for the wheel spinning. There should really be more wheel spinning in life, don't you think?"

"Look," I sneered. "I don't have time for this."

"Time," he sang. "Time won't give you time. Who needs that?"

"I do! I have to get to Nevada by a certain time, so I need as much as I can get."

"Time is a man made concept."

"No, it's not," I quickly countered. "Time has *always* been there."

"Not in the sense it is thought of today. Time is a triviality that humans could very easily live without. Unfortunately, they've conditioned themselves into thinking it's a requirement essential for their very existence. Tests have been conducted where people are placed in windowless rooms with no clocks, televisions, radios, computers, phones, anything that can give them an indication of time or date, and after a while, the people get loopy. Not over the lack of contact with the outside world. They go crazy because they don't know what time it is. Silly when you think about it, isn't it? Why would these people need to know what time it is? They've already conceded to be part of an experiment. Knowing in advance they can't leave their area of confinement. So, they have nowhere they need to go. No one to see. No job. No responsibilities. Just them in a room, getting back in touch with the natural rhythms of their own internal clock. Eating, sleeping and waking when the body says so. But they can't allow themselves to do it.

The lack of an external means of time measurement is eventually too much to bear.

"And why? Because, just like that expensive house in the suburbs, or that dog they bought only to later ignore, people convince themselves that it's a *need*, so as a result, everybody wants it. *Excuse me, do you have the time? Is that the right time? If I only had a little more time.* People rushing around like idiots, cutting drivers off on the highway, completely ignoring anyone and everyone around them in their pursuit to save a few seconds, or to get there first. And for what purpose? Contrary to popular belief, *time* is not *money*. You cannot save time for a rainy day. When it's your time to go, you can't look at the doctor and say, 'Over there, in my top drawer, I have a big bag full of time I saved over the years. I'd like to use some of it now.' People shouldn't try to save time, they should try to *use* time.

"In our very early days, man only comprehended time in large blocks. They knew when it was morning and noon because of the angle of the sun, and night when it was dark. They knew seasons because of the weather. No one complained. Life was fine. But then some Brainiac happened upon the idea of splitting that time into smaller slices, and all hell broke loose. Evil things like schedules began to appear, and the idea of time took over their lives. Yet, no one of importance thought to ask why. Had they, it would have been realized that man created it for the sole purpose of controlling lesser men. They want you to believe that every single minute matters. But, does it? Do you honestly think every single minute matters?"

I was about to answer, but I quickly realized I had no idea what to say, so my jaw hung open. He filled in the words my mouth could not produce.

"What then, about every single second? Every half second? Every millisecond? Billisecond, if that's even a word. And what of words? Their story is similar. Does every word you say matter? Every sentence you speak? Must they all mean something infinitely important in the big picture? No, not really. Don't people waste words, just like they waste time? And so what if they do? Should they drive themselves crazy thinking of the least amount of appropriate words to use? What a waste of time that would be! Spending extra time trying to not to spend extra time! Can you think of anything crazier?"

He stopped to catch his breath, which was long enough for me to finally ask a question.

"Is there something wrong with you?"

"Oh, I don't have time to get into that! Hahahaha!"

He slapped his hands together and continued laughing.

"What are you?" I insisted. "*Who* are you? And don't say *yes*, or *couch*, or some other stupid one syllable word that leads into another rambling rant. Give me real answers."

"*Real* answers? Hmm. Real answers. Now, there can be real *questions*, but can there ever any real *answers*? For example: Start with *what are you?* Ever see *The Breakfast Club?* They found out that each one of them were a combination of things: A brain, an athlete, a basket case, a princess and a criminal. Ever see it?"

"A long time ago, but..."

"There you go again with your obsession of time. Okay, skip the movie. Let's take something I'm sure you're much more familiar with: Water. What is *that*? There's an easy one, huh? The most common response would be that it's a liquid. But what happens if you boil it? Why, it becomes a vapor. Gas. Ooh, what about when it's cold? Look what's happened to our water! It's ice! A solid. You see? If you desire anything close to resembling a *real* answer, you'll have to be specifically real in your question."

With what seemed like very little effort to me, he somehow went from sitting down to standing on top of the seat in one quick move. He then grabbed onto the windshield and swung himself out of the car.

Just like I figured. He can flip out, too.

"Are you a gymnast?"

"What if I said yes? What if I said no? What does it mean to be a *gymnast*? Regular competition? Being a member of the team? What if you suck, but you're on the team and still have regular competitions? Or, what if you possessed the agility of a cat and the strength of a bear, but aren't on a team and never compete? Are you still considered a gymnast? The question I pose is this: Must a person be in constant routine to declare themselves a particular type, or is innate ability and preference enough?"

Steve and I responded in unison. "We have to go."

Then Steve gave a little laugh. "That was weird."

"Us, or him?" I asked.

"Talking to your dog again?"

"Maybe," I said. "Maybe not." I figured I'd turn his nonsense right back on him. He must have thought it funny, because he started laughing, too.

Why the hell do so many people find such meaningless shit amusing?

Steve climbed over into the front seat. "Hey, fix your sign."

The string was still around my neck, but the sign was behind me, wedged between my back and the seat. It must have gotten spun out of place during the to-do in the parking lot. I pulled it to the front and untwisted it so it was facing the right direction.

"Better," Steve said.

"What it that?" my crazy ex-passenger asked.

"My sign" I said, then angled it so he could see it better.

His mood and tone both changed very quickly.

"*Happy,*" he said. "Who are you?"

"You're asking me?" That was all I planned to say, but then I remembered. "That's kind of a vague question. You need to be more specific. Ever see *The Breakfast Club*?"

"Yeah," he shot. "I'm the one who first brought it up, remember?"

Okay, so maybe I went one step too far with using his own words against him. Big deal.

"Did Waverley send you? Are you his spy?"

"Whoa," Steve gasped. "Now, *that's* weird!"

"Waverley? I don't know anybody named Waverley."

"Uh huh." He shot. "This is all one big coincidence."

"What's one big coincidence?"

"Every piece of data I collected belongs solely to me! No one else!"

His voice became loud and rough. The voice I imagined he used whenever he found another bum sleeping in his box.

"That makes sense, I suppose. But honestly, I don't know what you're talking about."

"Then why do you look so surprised?"

"Well, for one, your mood swing sort of threw me."

"And...?"

"And," I continued. "You're the second person today who asked me if I was a spy. Kinda odd, is all."

"Odd, indeed. So, are you?"

"A spy? No. Well, I mean, not that I know. If I am, somebody forgot to tell me about it."

"Okay," he said. "Then what's with the sign?"

"What about it?"

"Why so evasive?" he asked.

"I'm not evasive," I told him. "I'm confused. What does my sign have to do with anything?"

"Why are you wearing it? What does it mean?"

Here we go again...

"Why is it any of your business?" I asked. Aaron said to speak my mind. I figured it couldn't hurt.

"Exactly the response one would expect from a spy."

"Look, I'm not a spy!"

"Prove it."

"Fine. I'm being forced to see a psychiatrist. He seems to think my only *problem* is that I need to find a way to get happy again. After he told me that, I met this guy at a restaurant. Don. And he invited me to a secret Pirate Convention in Nevada where he swears I'll find it. Happiness, that is. And that's where I'm headed."

"What does that have to do with the sign?"

"I'm getting to it. A couple days ago, I met a psychic who told me wearing this sign will help. Gets rid of negative molecules and helps my mind, or something."

He relaxed his body and smiled. "And how's that going for you?"

"I don't know. Haven't check my molecules lately."

"You don't know much, do you?"

"I'm starting to wonder."

"Wondering is good!"

"Not the kind of wondering I'm having."

"Not true. Wondering leads to investigation. And you know what investigation leads to? Answers. Some of which may turn out to be real."

"The hard part is trying to decipher between what's real and what's not."

"Very good. Okay, I believe you."

"You believe what?"

"That you're not here to spy on me."

"Okay. Why, though?"

"Pirates in Nevada? Psychics? Who would make up a stupid story like that? You have to be telling the truth."

He crouched like he was going to jump back into the car, which caused Steve to show off some gymnastic abilities of his own - he sprung straight up into the air and flipped over into the backseat.

"Not bad," the guy said. Then he opened the door and climbed into the passenger seat just like any other normal person would do.

"Name's Russell." He stretched out his arm to shake hands.

"First, or last?" I asked.

"First."

"I'm Daryl. That's Steve."

"First or last?" Russell asked.

"First," I said. "I don't know his last name."

"Dude," Steve exclaimed. "It's Gleason!"

"That's right. His last name's Gleason. I sorta adopted him."

"Daryl and Steve Gleason. Pleasure to meet you both. Now, if you'll drive me to the park, I can get my stuff and we can go."

"Go where?"

"Back to your hotel. After I shower and a shave, we can discuss all of this."

Discuss all of what?

I wasn't even planning on stopping in this town, and now it looks like I'll be staying the night. I didn't have the slightest idea where we were. All I really knew was, if I wanted to, I could still get in five or six good hours of driving before calling it a night. A person could get pretty damn far in that time. But, that's not what I did. Instead, I followed Russell's directions to some park so he could pick up his things.

I don't know why. A feeling in my gut, I guess.

Damn Aaron. This has to be his fault.

I half expected his *park* to really be some abandoned lot. So, when I drove up to a big, open area loaded with thick, well-groomed bushes and trees, you know, an actual park, I was a bit surprised. It even had a big playground area for the kids. Nice, I guess, if that's the kind of thing you're into.

I sat in the car and watched Russell casually pass by the families, the joggers, and the few others who were out enjoying their own brand of idleness, and walk down to a remote corner, where he stopped and reached in to some bushes. He was pretty far away, so I couldn't immediately make out what it was, but as his return gradually brought him closer to the car, it became clear that he was carrying a small suitcase.

So, if he keeps his stuff here, does he sleep here, too? If so, where? In those same bushes? It couldn't just be out in the open like that. Not only would you need shelter, but you'd be easily noticed, which would make you a vulnerable target when asleep.

"Are you crazy?" Russell said. "Bushes hurt like hell. I sleep at the top of the slide over there. Under the covered fort. The park's closed at night, so no one bothers me, and I'm always up before they come in the morning. Pretty sweet, eh? Ha ha!"

"I was doing it again."

"What?" Russell asked.

"Nothing."

Steve started laughing. He didn't say it, but I knew it was directed at me.

"It *was* directed at you," Steve smirked.

Again! Damn it.

It was obvious by now that I was spending the night here, so I should probably remember at some point to ask where "here" is. No matter what the answer though, it still meant that I needed to get another room.

I am not sleeping on top of a slide with this guy. I know that much.

Maybe it was because I had usually waited until it was dark before I chose a place to stay, I don't know, but there was something about seeing these motels in the light of day that was downright depressing.

How could I have not noticed any of this before? The signs out front should have been a major tip off. Forty-dollar-a-night rooms. Vibrating beds. Two and three person Jacuzzis. Cable? Who advertises *cable*? It's like advertising a floor. The dumbest was the place that offered *"Free Morning Wake Up Call"*. Do other places charge for that?

It only took me seeing four or five of them like this before I realized I had no desire to ever stay at any of these flea traps again. The thought occurred to me that they were probably the same dumps those lowlifes from the parking lot frequent, and once that revelation came to me, I couldn't imagine myself stepping inside one again.

To be honest, I don't even know why I thought that I had to stay in crappy places like these. Money certainly wasn't the question. I think it was primarily the convenience. They were all over, so I didn't have to worry about hunting one down, and when I wanted a room, all I had to do was reach into my pocket. I didn't have to waste time filling out a bunch of paperwork, showing ID, waiting for elevators, etc. In and out, no questions asked. Very easy.

It wasn't until now that I realized what *no questions asked* actually got you in return.

Russell told me there was a Holiday Inn about five miles away, and a Hilton about ten. It was rare for us to ever go anywhere when I was growing up, but the few times we did, Holiday Inn was the only place my grandfather would stay. "Maybe not the fanciest," he'd say. "But dependable. And reasonably priced. You can't go wrong with a Holiday Inn."

I drove to the Hilton.

Since I didn't know this Russell too well, or at all, when it came down to it, I decided it best to get two rooms. I kept having this vision of being stabbed to death in my sleep, and that made me a little uneasy.

The desk clerk couldn't have been nicer to me, but was giving Russell strange looks. I told him we were in town on business, and the airlines had lost Russell's bags, all he had was his carry-on, and there wasn't much in that to get by. This bit of info caused the clerk to quickly change his tune.

"Isn't that a shame?" he announced, in a tone that delivered exactly the proper amount of outrage and empathy that anyone ever hoped to hear in a customer service agent.

"Here are your keys," he continued, this time in a much more old fashioned, whatever-I-can-do-to-serve-you voice. "I will make sure housekeeping brings up a toothbrush, toothpaste, comb, razor, the works. And if you like, we can call the airline for you. See what we can do about getting those bags to you a little quicker."

Russell started laughing. "Yeah. See what you can do about getting me some extra flier miles, too, huh?"

"Wouldn't that be nice?" the clerk smiled, then went back to entering my information in the computer.

Russell rapped his knuckles on the desk. "Aren't you going to say anything about his sign?"

The clerk looked back up, his eyes moving directly to my chest.

"Mmm," he cheerfully hummed. "Very nice."

"It's a black magic talisman," Russell announced. "Wards off vengeful spirits, controls the weather, and makes your goats fertile. Very ancient."

"No it doesn't," I explained. "I don't even own goats."

The clerk pretended not to listen.

"Excuse me," I said, clearing my throat to get his attention. "Do you allow pets?"

"I thought you just said you didn't own any goats?" he said with a sly smile.

"Not goats. Dogs."

"No sir, we do not."

"Good. Good," I haughtily replied. "Last place I stayed did. Couldn't get a decent night's sleep. One last question. Is there a door by the elevator? I have a couple heavy bags that I'd rather not lug all over the place."

"Yes, at the end of the hall," he said. "But, I can call the bellman..."

"No. I can handle it. Thanks."

I gave Russell the key to his room, then I walked back outside.

Steve was still in the backseat, half his body hanging out over the side.

"Can I come in now?" he asked impatiently.

I started up the car and drove around to the side of the building.

"They don't allow pets," I told him.

"No shit," Steve shot back. "None of them do. Didn't stop us before."

"This one's different."

"You're not leaving me out here all night!"

"Of course not." After finding an out of the way spot to park, I discreetly slipped my luggage out of the trunk, and unzipped the tote bag. "Get inside."

"You're screwing with me, right?"

I didn't want to open the bag until I knew for sure that we safe in the room. All it would take is for one employee, or another guest, catching so much as a glimpse of hair, and we'd be goners. Steve was none too pleased with this mode of transport, I could tell. Not that he made any noise about it – he knew better than that. What he was doing though, was thrashing around, which made it look like the bag was a prop in some tacky magic show. So, every time he shifted position, I gave the suitcase in my other hand a little shake, as well, to give the impression it was intentional. Although I'm pretty sure if anybody was watching they'd have thought I was having some mild convulsive fit.

Once inside the room, I double locked the door, put the bag on the bed and unzipped. Steve's head shot up and he immediately started in with this ridiculous series of big, wheezing gasps for air.

"Jesus, Steve. A little over dramatic, you think?"

"Yeah? You try it."

"I couldn't fit inside."

"And I couldn't *breathe* inside, smart ass!"

"It's a zipper, not a vacuum seal. You could breath."

"Maybe I don't like small spaces, okay?"

"You should have said something. Sorry."

"Guess I didn't know 'til now."

I opened the mini fridge, but to my disappointment, it wasn't an honor bar, just an empty refrigerator, and I really wanted a drink.

"Daryl?"

"What?"

"I have to pee."

"You should have said something before!"

"And again! I didn't know 'til know!"

Unbelievable, this dog.

"Then you'll have to get back in the bag." I said.

"No way! Come on, dude, I really have to go!"

"I'm telling you right now - do not go on the carpet! This place has my name. You're not even supposed to be allowed in here. They'll think I did it."

"Don't make me laugh," he said, clearly straining to hold back more than just a laugh.

"You know what? Go in the tub. Aim for the drain and don't get your feet wet."

"Good idea."

He said it like it was the first damn one I've ever had in my life.

When he came back in the room, his mood was much improved, and he asked to watch some TV. So, we flicked through the channels looking for anything even vaguely interesting. If you ask me, the search wasn't even worth it, but the fact that the picture quality far surpassed any place we'd previously stayed seemed to make up for the lack of content. After a short deliberation, we settled on a *Love Boat* repeat.

I tried watching for a few minutes, but it was an episode I'd already seen, with Charo, and oddly enough, Gene Rayburn from *Match Game*. I didn't feel like putting in the effort, and sitting through this show took a considerable amount of effort. I decided instead to head downstairs.

"Here's the remote," I told Steve, laying it on the bed face up for him. "If Russell comes by, tell him I went to the bar for a drink."

"And just how the hell am I going to do that?"

"He said he understood you."

"I'm not sure I believe that."

"Fine. I'll write a note. If he comes by, slip the note under the door..."

"Shhh!" Steve spit. "Can't you see I'm trying to watch? Just try his room now."

I swear. Probably best if I just leave, before we get into some stupid fight.

Russell didn't answer after I banged on his door four or five times, so I leaned in to give a listen. I thought maybe I'd hear the shower, or the TV, but I didn't pick up anything. Either these doors are incredibly soundproofed, or he wasn't inside.

I should have asked for an extra key.

Get Happy

As I was making my way down the hall toward the elevator, something strange caught my eye: a guy in a white robe, pressing his ear to a door for a few seconds, then moving on to the next door in line.

Russell.

"What are you doing?" I called to him.

"Listening."

"For what?"

"I don't know. Something, I suppose."

He moved to yet another door and repeated the maneuver. I figured he must have heard something, because he lingered a longer than he did at the others.

"Why?" I asked.

"Why not? You were doing it."

"I was looking for you."

"It must have worked! Here I am!"

The door abruptly opened, catching Russell off guard. He jumped back a step just as a middle aged man in plaid boxers stuck his head out of the room.

"Can I help you?" the man grunted.

"I don't know," Russell said. "What's your specialty?"

"What are you talking about?"

Russell straightened up and adjusted his robe. "May I ask you sir, what makes you happy?"

"Look, I don't know who you are, but..."

The man stopped mid-sentence when a woman began whispering behind him.

"Joe? Joe. Who is it?"

Russell tugged his terry cloth lapels and smiled. "I withdraw the question. Good day, sir."

The man disappeared back into the room and slammed the door. Russell giggled to himself and walked toward me.

"Why did you ask him that?"

"Research."

He put his hands on his hips, which caused the front of his robe to separate. It was only then that I realized he was naked underneath. I wish I'd known sooner.

"Where are your clothes?"

"Some strange lady came into my room and took them."

"What? Why did you let...?"

"Daryl. Housekeeping. They're being laundered."

"Oh. Okay. I was coming to see if you wanted to go down to the bar."

"Sounds great. Let's go."

"Not like that. *No shirt. No shoes. No service.*"

"That about covers everything."

"Not quite."

Russell laughed again. "You do make a valid point. The blame can only fall to them for not being more specific."

I almost told him that I wasn't intending to make a joke, but I just kept quiet about it and let him think it.

"Come on. You can wear something of mine. We're about the same size, more or less."

"Talk about not being specific. A comment so ambiguous that it could be employed in nearly any situation. *Why, of course darling, I feel the same way about marriage as you do, more or less. Actually less.* Or, *this is more or less the same job as you had before, (more), with more or less the same pay, (less), and more or less the same hours, (much more).*"

"Do you want the clothes, or not?" I asked him.

"More or less."

"More," I told him.

He laughed again, and followed me down the hall.

Since he was only borrowing them for a short time, I didn't bother asking him what he liked best. I simply removed the top suit from the garment bag, and grabbed the first underwear and socks I found. It was obvious he didn't like what I chose for him, but really, it was just too damn bad. This is what I gave him, and he's just going to have to deal with it.

"You can change in the bathroom."

Steve was still on the bed, mesmerized by the stupid television show. And I'm pretty sure he turned the volume up since I left. I can't imagine what he's going to be like when he gets older.

"What are you watching?" Russell called from the bathroom.

"I'm not," I told him. "Steve is. *The Love Boat.*"

"Your dog likes *Love Boat*?"

"Are you kidding, Bro?" Steve said. "*The Love Boat*'s awesome! Watching humans with all your dumb relationship problems is hysterical."

I looked at Steve. "Why didn't you tell him to shush?"

"Commercial."

Russell looked completely different all cleaned up and dressed in a suit and tie. Almost like two separate people. Even the way he carried himself – his posture was more pronounced and he appeared taller than before. I half wondered if the shorts fit him right.

We circled the main floor looking for a bar, but only found a restaurant, so rather than wandering around like idiots, we stepped inside.

The maitre d' seemed outright annoyed at Russell's request for a table by the window. Out of the thirty or so tables in the place, only two were occupied, so it made no sense for the guy to get so testy. It certainly wasn't due to a coverage problem, and I didn't see any *reserved* signs. If this were my restaurant, I would have sent that clown home.

From a purely subjective stance, I have to admit, I was taken aback by Russell desire to sit by a window, but not for the same senseless reasons the maitre d' had. You'd just assume that a guy who lived on the streets wouldn't want to stare at them through a window while he ate. If I was in his situation, I'd want to face a wall. But that's just me.

We hadn't even touched the menus before our waiter appeared at the table.

"Start you off with drinks?"

If there were awards for Worst Attitude, Restaurant Division, this place had to be a lock for an annual nomination. First the sighing, disgusted little maitre d', now a waiter who acts likes his shift was over five minutes ago and was just stuck with another table. I was going to ask him if he had his car running, but then I was worried he'd spit in my drink, or something.

"Vodka martini," I said

"Do you have a wine list?" Russell asked.

The waiter reached into his back pocket, produced a foot long laminated card, and handed it over to Russell. Why the hell he was hiding it in his back pocket, I don't know.

Russell studied it like he actually knew what he was doing. "I'll take Number Seven."

"The Close Doo-Boys."

"*Cloh dew bwah,*" Russell corrected.

"A vodka martini," he repeated, not writing it down. I hate when waiters do that. "And a glass of cloh..."

"No, no," Russell interrupted. "I want a bottle. *A glass*? What good is that?"

"Yes, sir. And what convention are you with?"

"We're not with any convention," I told him.

"You're not?"

"No. Should we be?"

"No. It's just..."

"Your sign," Russell interrupted. "He thinks it's an ID badge."

"Well, it's not," I shot back.

"Okay," he shrugged. Then he spun around and walked away.

"Uncorked!" Russell called out as an afterthought. "I wish to see the wrapper removed at the table." Then he turned back to me. "Not that I distrust them, but at those prices, you want to ensure that you're receiving a freshly opened bottle."

Not having read the list myself, I had no idea what that particular bottle was going for, but I didn't want to embarrass him, so I just let it slide. I kind of felt bad for this Russell, him being homeless and everything, but really, there's only so much you can do. Particularly with my schedule being what it is. So, I thought we better have a little talk. Tell him what's on my mind, like Aaron said.

"How much do you need?" I asked him.

"It's not a matter of need. No one truly *needs* wine. This is pure craving."

"Not wine. Money."

He gave a little laugh. "I don't know. How much does anyone need? How much do *you* need?"

"I don't need any. But that's not the point."

"Lucky you."

"I mean, any *more*."

"Rich?"

"More or less."

He laughed a little harder. "So, all this money, and you're not happy?"

"It only came to me a couple months ago."

"Were you happy before?"

I was getting sick of this question.

"And you think these pirates will help?" he asked.

"I don't know. Maybe. Couldn't hurt."

"Pirates, traditionally, were a group of murderers, thieves and rapists who fled to the sea in order to avoid prison or execution. Aren't you afraid they'll take your money and kill you?"

"I really doubt they're *that* kind of pirates."

"So, *pretending* you're a murderer, thief and rapist, just without all the messy details? What's the point?"

"He said it's people who are unhappy with the routine of regular life. They get together for two weeks to forget their problems and live in the spirit of pirates. Free of cares and worries."

"Interesting. And you have no inkling where it is that they meet?"

"I get the clues as I'm being led there. I thought maybe you were another one."

"You thought I was a clue? I only know what you've told me. I would love to go, though. Will you let me know where it is when you find out?"

"Why? Are you unhappy?"

That seemed like a stupid question for a homeless person.

"Is being unhappy a requirement for attendance?"

"Beats me. I just don't know if anybody off the street can get in."

Again, probably not the best way to phrase that.

"What is it?" he asked. "Some special by-invitation-only secret pirate club?"

"Actually..."

I started to tell him, but he wasn't listening to me anymore. Something outside the window was pulling at his attention.

"Do you think trees have feelings?"

"What?"

I looked out, and saw two landscapers cutting away the dead branches from a large tree across the street.

"You're asking me if that tree has feelings?"

"You talk to your dog," he said.

"Not quite the same thing."

"Those old, withered branches being removed were affecting the health of the tree. If they waited much longer, it could have been too late, and the whole plant would have rotted and died. So, I ask you: do you think the tree felt any that? The sickness, or the surgery?"

"I have no idea."

"Not even a guess?"

"Okay. Maybe," I conceded. "To some degree."

"But how? A tree doesn't have a central nervous system. No brain to process information."

"That's what I was trying to say before."

"Yet," he continued. "Flowers know when to open and when to close. They know to bend toward the sun if they're stuck in the shade. To dig their roots through the dry soil in search for water. So, even though it seems highly illogical, do you think it's possible this tree was aware of its affliction? If so, does it feel better now? Let's take it a step further: if I asked it, would it have an opinion on the subject? Are the other nearby trees who are happy for it? Will they have a get well party?"

Then he jumped up from his chair and sprinted to a large potted fern across the room.

"What about this plant? Does it have feelings? It has no dead limbs, but what if I do this?"

He grabbed a frond and ripped off a sizable chunk.

"Do you think this plant is in pain now?"

"I really don't know," I said. "But, I wouldn't like it if you did that to me."

"Ahh, yes! *Physical* pain. What about emotional pain?" He stuck his face in the center of the fern and began scolding. "You're a bad, bad plant! None of the other plants in here likes you! I heard them talking. They'd rather have a philodendron move in!"

The waiter came back and set my drink on the table, then walked toward the fern and extended the bottle of wine for Russell's inspection. Once he saw the wrapper was still intact, he nodded, then redirected his focus back to me.

"You don't care, do you?" Russell sneered.

"About whether a tree can feel?" I asked. "I guess not."

I peeked over at the waiter to see if he had any feelings on the matter, but he was too busy wrestling with the cork to notice.

Russell broke eye contact with me, and hurried his way back to the table.

"What is your name?" he asked the waiter.

"Jason," he replied with a grin.

"Jason. How appropriate. You're hacking away at that cork like it's a horror movie. Allow me."

The waiter looked more confused than embarrassed and handed the bottle over to Russell, who deftly popped it open with very little effort.

"Jason," Russell continued. "How do you know if a plant is happy?"

"A plant?" Jason repeated, obviously trying to connect this line of questioning to the uncorking of a bottle of wine. "Like grapes, you mean?"

"Grapes *are* plants, yes!" Russell boldly confirmed. "But I'm not referring to the wine. Any plant. A tree. A weed. One of those ugly things over there. Doesn't matter."

"I didn't know they could be happy."

"That's awfully prejudiced of you. Are you one of those types of people who wish to deny plants happiness?"

"No."

"Fine. Then how can one ascertain if a plant is happy? Think, Jason. Think hard."

Jason's eyes slowly glazed over. He peered around the room for help, but there were no other servers in sight, and no other tables to wait on, so he all he could do was to look back at Russell and smile weakly.

"If it's healthy?"

Russell gave Jason a hearty back-handed slap to the chest.

"Health!" Russell joyfully proclaimed. "Good answer! Not the correct answer, but as logical a starting place as any. What the eye can see. The eye of an outside observer. Is it then your deduction that all healthy people are happy people? What about you? You seem fit."

Jason took a small step backwards.

"I have to check on another order!"

And with that, he vanished.

Russell didn't seem bothered at all by Jason's quick departure. He calmly straddled his chair, grabbed the bottle of wine, and lifted it six inches or so above his target. Tipping the bottle ever-so-slightly, he created a thin, unbroken crimson stream that slowly filled the glass.

"In order to reach a logically valid conclusion," he said, staring at his pour. "You must compile as much data on the study subject as possible. Sample size is a key element. Consequently, observation is not enough, because it does not tell the whole story. You have to ask more questions, accumulate more data, to get as close to the true story as possible."

"But," I jumped in. "You can't ask a plant a question, can you?"

"You can, Daryl. But as you witnessed, they can be most uncooperative."

He then fell silent as he set down the bottle and began to swirl the wine in the glass.

I wondered if during this moment of quiet I was supposed to contemplate all that nonsense about the plants. I gave it a shot, but couldn't help wondering what exactly there was to consider. So instead, I did the next best thing: I sat back in my chair and sipped at my martini. And with this suit on, I'm sure it gave the impression of my being a learned man engaged in very profound thought. Thoughts about the emotional state of plants.

But my mind didn't linger on the plants. It focused on the martini, which surprised me considerably. It tasted like top shelf vodka, had just the right amount of vermouth, and was nice and cold. It was, quite possibly, one of the best I've had in some time. Made by someone other than myself, of course. I really don't think it's much of a stretch to expect a bartender to make a martini correctly. I mean, come on, it's only two ingredients and garnish. How difficult is that? Apparently, very. I had to stop ordering martinis whenever I went out, which wasn't all that often anyway, because I wasn't able to find a bartender capable of fixing a decent one. Which is why I became a bottled beer man at bars and restaurants. By default. Hard to screw that up. Not impossible, though.

So, it wasn't until just now, when I was reflecting on how unexpectedly good this one tasted, that I realized how strange it was for me to even order a martini in the first place. It's been years since I've done that. I mean, I'm glad I did, because it's very tasty. But it's still odd, nonetheless. I'd blame it on some old voice still lingering in my head, but I don't recall hearing anything other than my own voice when giving my drink order.

"What are you thinking about?" Russell asked.

I was right. I did look profound.

"My martini."

"Really? That's all?"

He had this smirk on his face, like he knew exactly what I was going to say, and was just waiting for me to say it. Now there was another voice in my head. Aaron's.

Always speak your mind.

So I did.

"Why are you homeless?"

He snorted a short laugh, then brought the glass to his nose and sniffed.

"Blackberry," he said, to seemingly no one in particular. "Licorice. And oddly enough, my Aunt Carol's living room drapes. Did you know that the rule to analyzing a wine's nose is, whatever the drinker smells, they're correct?"

"No, I didn't know that."

"One of the few instances in life where whatever you think or feel, you cannot be wrong. Isn't that wonderful."

He wasn't crazy. A little goofy, yeah, but not a certifiable nut job like most people you see sleeping in the park. And he was pretty clear headed. Probably more so than me at times. Maybe his downfall was just too embarrassing to share with strangers, so that's why he goes off on these weird little tangents. To distract. That would be understandable.

But still, I wanted to know.

"I don't mean to pry, but what happened?"

"Happen? What do you mean?"

"To make you homeless."

"Oh. I'm not homeless," he said with a smile.

"What then?"

"You really don't know?" He appeared genuinely amazed by the fact that I didn't know the circumstances.

"How would I?"

He gave me a long look, like he was mentally trying to work out a puzzle. "I've spent the past ten years compiling data for my research."

"Data on what?" I asked.

"Happiness."

22

So, that pissed me off.

Here I was feeling sorry for the guy, to the point of giving him a couple hundred dollars cash, then paying for a separate hotel room, and what I'm guessing to be a fairly expensive bottle of wine. And what does he do in return? Make fun of me. Spin wine in his damn glass and tell me it smells like window coverings in his relative's house.

A person can only take so much. I figured if I collected Steve and got right back on the road, I could still get in that driving time I missed by stopping here.

"Something wrong?" Russell asked.

"I had a feeling about you," I muttered, and walked away from the table.

"Yeah? And?"

There really didn't seem to be any reason going into it with this misfit, so I just kept moving.

"*That* is one of society's biggest problems, you know."

Okay. This one stopped me in my tracks. I was curious to see how I was personally affecting society in such a negative way.

"What is?" I asked.

"*Feelings*. Don't have a feeling. Have a *fact*! A feeling is nothing more than unsubstantiated conjecture. Far too many people draw conclusions before all the evidence is in. As they say, it's not over until the fat lady has collected all the data. That's how plants and animal survive. The need for food and water is a fact. If it were a feeling, we'd have sunflowers going on diets because they felt they were too fat."

I said I didn't want to get into it, but this guy was pushing my buttons.

"Look," I shot back. "I don't like being mocked."

"How did I mock you?"

"You think this whole thing I'm doing is stupid, don't you? Meeting the pirates, trying to find out if I was ever happy."

"On the contrary. I find it interesting for a variety of reasons. I do. Didn't I say I wanted to join you?"

"You could have been making fun of me then, too."

"I wasn't, Daryl. Then, or now. I truly am collecting data on happiness. Strange coincidence us running into each other like this, wouldn't you say?"

"Who are you? What do you do? Work for an ad agency?"

"Please! Don't accuse me of such an odious activity."

"What then?"

His lips curled into a smile and he tapped his fingers on the stem of his glass. I immediately got the impression he'd been dying to talk about this, but was waiting for the appropriate time.

"I was a PhD candidate in philosophy," he started. "And for my doctoral thesis I chose *happiness*. On the surface, it may appear simple enough. *What makes people happy?* But, once you begin to study that question, a multitude of parallel and ancillary questions arise. What is happiness? Is it the same for everyone? What keeps people happy? Is it easier for certain people to obtain happiness than others? If so, why?"

"That's a good question," I muttered to myself.

"Which one?" he asked.

"All of them," I said.

"You'll be happy to know you're not alone in your thinking. Or, maybe you won't be happy to know. That is the interesting dichotomy of happiness. The ideas and manifestations of happiness are as individual to each person as their own fingerprints. But unlike fingerprints, the patterns can change over time, and occasionally without any warning. Just when you think you've settled in on things being a certain way, suddenly it's different, and now you have to find a way to readjust yourself to the new pattern. It can be quite disconcerting."

"Sounds about right."

"People may claim to like change, but when the facts are in, what they like even more is being able to personally control what gets changed and what doesn't. Unfortunately though, happiness cannot be controlled. Like the weather, it quite often can't even be accurately forecasted. How many times in your life has it rained when the weatherman insisted it wouldn't?"

"Is that a metaphor?"

"If that makes you happy," he smiled.

"You really like that joke, don't you?"

"Never get tired of it."

Jason the waiter returned to our table, but not quite all the way to our table. He came to a stop a good six or seven feet further away than he did the last time he visited. He may as well have been on the other side of the window.

"Can I get you gentlemen anything else?" He had the tone of a stage performer testing the post hypnotic suggestion he had just implanted on us.

"Before I forget, let me have two cheeseburgers and a six pack of Bud. I'm going to bring them back to my room."

"Great idea," Russell happily announced. "Off to our rooms! We can continue with this tomorrow."

"I didn't mean we had to leave right now."

"This works out well for me. It's been a long time since I laid on a clean bed in a room all by myself and stared mindlessly at television. Believe it or not, I'm actually looking forward to it." Then he looked up at Jason. "Let me have another bottle of this, and a cork screw. I'll order room service later when I'm hungry."

I couldn't wait to see this bill.

Steve was still lying on the bed watching TV when I returned.

"Hey," he said, refusing to turn away from the set, even though whatever he was watching was at commercial break. "I thought you'd be out all night with that guy."

"We're going back out tomorrow."

"Tomorrow? We're staying another day?"

"Yeah. I don't know. I guess. What are you watching?"

"Back on," he hissed. "Shh."

I walked over to the desk and removed the empty ice bucket the hotel so graciously provided to me for the length of my stay.

It actually said something that in the pamphlet.

"Can you fit your face in this?" I asked.

"What the hell?"

"Just, can you, or can't you? Simple question."

I tossed it on the bed a few feet away from him. He gave me this look, like he didn't trust me, then cautiously sized up the bucket.

"You're not sneaking me out in this."

"Why do you have to be so damn suspicious? I brought you something from the restaurant, okay? You don't have a bowl, so I thought this would work instead."

I pointed to the desk behind me.

"You got me beer? Dude!"

"And a couple cheeseburgers. The beer's for both of us, though."

"Awesome!"

I opened two beers, sticking the rest in the empty refrigerator, then lifted the bucket off the bed.

"How 'bout I keep this on the floor. I don't want it tipping over."

I slowly poured in one bottle, careful not to create too much foam. And as expected, he dove right into that before I even had a chance to unwrap the burgers.

"Fries, too," I noted as I removed them from the bag.

I was about to put everything straight on the bed, but then I thought better of it, and unfolded a bath towel as a makeshift placemat.

"Ahh!" he sighed. "Damn, that was good. Let me have another."

"You finished that already?"

"I was thirsty. So, what happened with Mister Crazy Pants?"

"You want some water instead?"

"Get real."

I grabbed another beer and poured it into the bucket while he jumped up and attacked the first cheeseburger.

"Turns out he's a doctor in philosophy," I told him. "Or wants to be, at least. He's studying happiness."

"That's weird."

"Yeah."

"That why we're staying longer? Is he one of your road signs?"

"Maybe. He says he isn't, though. And don't talk with food in your mouth. I told you about that before."

The first cheeseburger disappeared so quickly, you'd have guessed it was vaporized rather than eaten. He paused momentarily, craning his neck in what I'm guessing was some attempt to swallow whatever stray bits of food were still hanging around in his throat, then leapt fully stretched toward the beer bucket.

"Slow down, huh?" I advised. "This isn't a race. You'll get sick."

He didn't respond, not because he didn't hear me, but because his mouth was too busy lapping up Budweiser.

"Hit me!" he finally belched.

"Seriously. Pace yourself. We only have a six pack, and I'm not going back downstairs."

"Don't they have room service here?"

"Yeah, probably..."

"Then, jus do thatthen!"

I couldn't believe it. He was slurring.

"You're already drunk."

"No. No," he insisted. "That's wha room service does! You call and say *I wan beer*. Then they come to your room and knock on your door..."

Right on cue, like a scene in a sitcom, there was a knock at our door.

"Whoa!" Steve declared with drunken awe. "Izzat room service?"

"No. It's not room service."

"How do you know? Can you see through doors?"

"I know it's not them because I didn't call them."

"But wouldn't it be freaky if it was? I mean, wouldn't that be *freaky*?"

The knocking repeated. This time louder.

"Mister Gleason?" came a voice from the hall. "Mister Gleason? Are you in there? This is the manager. If you don't answer, I will have to use my pass key."

I turned to Steve and put my finger over my lips to quiet him.

"Right, right," he said, which negated my whole directive of him staying quiet.

"Just a minute!" I called. "Here I come."

I motioned for Steve to hide in the bathroom, and once he was safely out of view, I opened the door. Four people stood outside. Three in hotel uniforms, and one in a terry cloth bathrobe. People seemed to like those. I made a mental note to try mine out later in the night.

"Mister Gleason?" The man in the center asked. I assumed he was the manager.

"Yes?"

"Do you have a dog in your room?"

"No. Why do you ask?"

"We received a complaint that there was barking."

"Barking?" I repeated, acting like it was the most absurd notion in the world. "Oh! The TV. There was a dog on the program I'm watching. Sorry if it was too loud."

The manager took a half step inside and took a cursory look around.

"A dog? On that?"

I glanced back at the set. *Gilligan's Island* was on. Damn it.

"I've seen every episode at least ten times," the manager informed me. "I don't remember there ever being a dog. A gorilla and a lion, but never a dog."

Ten times? You'd think the manager of a big hotel like this would have better things to do.

"I was flipping. The dog was on another program."

"It wasn't on TV," insisted the woman in the robe.

"What makes you so sure?" I asked.

"Because I heard you, too," she confidently added.

"So what? I talk to the TV. I was telling it to find me a good program."

"That is certainly *not* what you were saying!"

"How do you know what I was saying? Were you spying on me?" Now I eyed the manager. "Is this something that happens often at your hotel? Guests spying on other guests? And you condone this behavior? I think I'd like to talk to your boss."

The manager looked genuinely terrified. "No sir, it does not," he declared. Then he turned his shoulders in the direction of the woman in the robe. "You must have been mistaken, ma'am. There's obviously no dog here."

"Then what's that?" she defiantly asked. "That sound?"

We all fell silent, and listened.

There was a brief moment between the dialogue, laugh track and inane music when we could distinctly hear something that sounded like a stream of water hitting porcelain with great force. Only I knew it wasn't water. And neither did the folks on the island, because the laugh track kicked in halfway through.

All eyes turned to me. I shrugged, and decided to stick the same game plan.

"Sounds like someone has their faucet turned on. I take it back, I guess you can hear everything through these walls. How much am I paying for this room?"

"Nothing, Mister Gleason," the manger quivered. "There will be no charge. To compensate for your inconvenience."

"What?" the woman in the robe crowed.

"But, I paid cash in advance," I said.

"If go to the front desk, you will be reimbursed."

"I will. Tomorrow. Goodnight."

I released the handle and the door swung shut on its own. As I started for the bed, I could still hear unhappy mutterings coming from the hallway, so I reopened the door and dramatically placed the *Do Not Disturb* sign over the outside knob. The manager nodded emphatically, subtly nudging his two underlings to move on. My red faced neighbor glared at me, then marched back to her room.

"This is why I shove you in tote bags," I announced.

Steve bounded from the bathroom, swaying side to side and laughing raucously.

"That was *so cool*!" he gleefully squealed.

"Shh! You want them to come back?" I patted the air with my left hand for added emphasis. He sluggishly bobbed his head and brought his volume down a few notches.

"Right. Right," he whispered. Or rather, tried to whisper. "*Shh.* I heard the whole thing. Man, did you tell her off. Blammo! In your face, woman! Very smooth. You got that from Ben. I could tell."

"What?"

"That's how your grandfather was. Dint take shit from no one. Dint let nobody get in his business and tell him what to do. Nope. Not 'ole Ben."

"Where you getting this from?" I took a swig of beer and reached for the remote.

"What do you mean?" Steve asked. "Hey, buddy, I could use another cold one over here."

Without putting any thought into it, I dutifully retrieved another beer for him. "I mean, what makes you think he was ever like that?"

"From stories he told me."

"What stories?"

"I don't know. *Stories!* You know better than I do." He watched the bottle empty into the bucket and didn't make his move until the last drop fell. "Thank you," he sang out, then ambled over and slurped away.

"As far as I know, the only person he wouldn't take any shit from was me."

Steve pulled his snout from the bucket, and greedily lapped up the foam that clung to the fur around his lips. "Why don't you like talkin' 'bout him?"

"Why don't you talk about your grandfather?"

"I dint have one."

"That's stupid. Everybody has a grandfather."

He squinted his bleary eyes and thought about it for a moment. "Yeah. I guess you're right. I dint know him. How's that? Better?"

"What happened?" I asked. "Did he die?"

"Never met the dude. Never met my grandmother, either. Or my mother, or my father. My human bought me a week after I was born."

"Wow. Sorry."

"What's there to be sorry for? That's the way it is. Most dogs don't know their families, and the one's that do wish they didn't. Way too much responsibility and worry. That's not the way dogs are wired, you know? All that crap just gets in the way."

"In the way of what?"

"Life!" he shouted. "Fun! I've seen it before. These stupid little arranged marriages. One boy dog and one girl dog. It never works! Never! A dog can get laid anytime he wants. He doesn't need some wife hanging around all the time telling him where he can and can't go. Where to take a dump. Where to leave the chew toys. It's just pathetic."

We were interrupted by someone pounding on the door again.

"Shit," Steve whispered to himself. Quietly this time.

I just shook my head and pointed the remote at the TV, hoping if I ignored them, that they would give up and leave. But I hadn't clicked through four or five channels before it started up again.

Was it going to be like this the whole damn night? I threw the remote on the floor and flung open the door.

"What?" I growled.

This time, the only person standing in the hallway was my immediate neighbor. No hotel staff. Just her and her robe.

"There's no way you can get out of it now," she snarled.

I was this far from telling her off, when suddenly, her eyes lit up. And I knew why without having to turn around. She saw Steve. That had to be it. I could see her silently crafting her next five moves. Three and four were going to be big trouble. But then her eyes darted to a different part of the room, and her expression quickly changed.

"Oh, um," she stammered. "I, ah, never mind." And she disappeared back into her room.

What the hell did he do?

I turned around to see a dog on television, in the middle of delivering a Shakespearean monologue. I can honestly say I had never seen this show before.

"Into this breathing world," the dog crisply articulated. "Scarce half made up..."

The door swung closed and Steve wandered out from the other side of the bed.

"Talk about luck, huh? I just started pushing buttons and this popped on."

"Luck? It's a talking dog. How are we going to explain that?"

"Dude," Steve slurred. "She didn't hear a *talking* dog. She just heard *a dog*. Like any other stupid human would hear it. You're the only freak who hears us talk."

"So, now she thinks that's the barking she heard."

"Prob'em solved, my man. I think that calls for another brewski."

"But that's it, okay?"

"Okay. Okay. He's pretty good, isn't he?" Steve nodded toward the dog on the screen.

"You know him?"

"You kidding? That's Sir Barkley. An English wolfhound."

"Hmm. Never heard of him."

"Very famous in our circles."

I took out the last two beers, poured one in his bowl, then brought the other back to the bed and settled in for the rest of the show.

"By drunk prophesies, libels and dreams..."

I'd always known there were dogs in the business, but I never knew any of them were this good.

23

When I opened my eyes, I found myself staring directly at the ceiling. And as I silently took personal inventory, I had a sense that I wasn't alone.

I swear, if it's that woman in the robe again...

"Morning!"

It was Steve, lying horizontal to me, with his nose inches from my ear.

"What are you doing?"

"Nothing," he said. "Watching you while you were sleeping, is all."

"That's kind of creepy."

He paused for a moment. "You're right. Didn't seem weird 'til I said it out loud."

"What happened?"

"You fell asleep during the movie last night."

"No, I mean, did anything happen?"

"What? In the movie?"

"Like a minute ago."

"While you were sleeping?"

"Right when I woke up."

"No," he said with a suspicious tone. "What shoulda happened?"

"Was I smiling?"

"No. You were still as can be. That's kinda why I was staring at you. You never move. It's weird."

"You don't have to move to smile," I told him. Dogs, I think, sometimes don't know these things.

"Yeah, but you weren't doing that, either."

"Figures."

I yawned, then went back to checking off my inventory list.

Does every ceiling look the same? I don't think I've seen one different this whole trip.

"I have to pee," I said to no one in particular, then rocked myself over to the left and pushed down into the bed until I was sitting.

"You ahh, you might want to rinse out the bath tub."

"What did you do?"

"Everything," he smirked. "But at least I got it all in the tub this time, right? You gotta give me that?"

I stepped into the bathroom and looked into the tub.

"I think I'm going to be sick."

"Come on, you were asleep. What was I supposed to do? Besides, isn't this what buddies do for each other? Clean up the drunken mess from the night before? There's a scene like that in every college movie ever made."

I spun the faucet dial to the left until it stopped, then pulled it forward to activate the shower.

"From now on, I don't want to hear any more complaints about the tote bag."

"We could just get rooms on the first floor. Ever think a that? I could jump in and out a window."

I took a deep breath through my mouth and held it as long as I could while I took care of my original objective for entering the bathroom.

"Looks like I won't be taking a shower today," I said as I walked back into the bedroom area.

"Don't they have maids here?"

"You're disgusting."

"Now what I say? Damn, you're cranky in the morning."

"I am not."

I'm really not. It's this whole not smiling thing. It must make me look grumpy.

I fingered out two pills and swallowed them with a couple big gulps from my complimentary bottle of water. Maybe enough of these will get me smiling again. The pills, not the water. Suddenly, I had this strange feeling, like I was forgetting something. Which obviously I was, and accounted for the strange feeling. But why, I hadn't a clue.

There was a knock at the door. This couldn't be because of Steve. He wasn't talking all that loud. Unless someone caught a whiff from the hallway, but they'd have no idea it came from a dog, so that would be really rude to knock on a door and blame a person for smelling up a bathroom he's paying for.

Aha! Talk to the desk clerk about a refund! That's what I was forgetting. Was that it, though? It's something I have to do, but I'm not sure if it's exactly the cause of my strange feeling.

I opened the door, and there was Russell standing in the hallway, showered, dressed and looking far too chipper.

"Good!" he exclaimed. "You're ready."

"Ready for what?" I asked.

"To go out! Talk. Eat. Drink. See if we can answer any of your questions."

"Yeah. I guess so."

I opened the tote bag and dropped it on the bed.

"Inside."

"Aww, come on!" Steve complained.

"I won't zipper it all the way." Then I looked over to Russell. "He's claustrophobic."

"I see." Judging by the sound of his voice, I didn't really think he did see.

Steve was taking his sweet time climbing into the bag. He was still a good three feet away, staring at it like it was a time capsule, and he was the artifact I intended bury inside it.

"You wanna eat, don't you?" I asked him. "I'm going to be out for a long time, and you're not authorized to order room service."

Bingo. That did the trick. He hung his head, loped over to the bag and squeezed inside.

"Not all the way. You promised."

"Don't worry."

I left a good measure unzipped, then picked him up and headed for the door. Then it hit me.

"Here, hold this."

I passed off the bag to Russell then marched back into the bathroom.

I looked in the mirror and straightened my sign.

"You will be happy," I instructed my reflection. "Always speak your mind, and always tell the truth."

That was it.

On my way out, I reached into the shower and shut the water off. Yet another thing I had forgotten about. Not sure what was suddenly up with me.

"What was that?" Russell asked.

"What?"

"That thing you muttered to yourself."

"Just something I have to do every morning. Supposed to help."

"Like wearing the sign."

"Yeah."

"Hmph," is all he said. Noises like that can hold a lot of meaning. I wasn't sure what this particular utterance was meant to convey, but I wasn't going to ask. If he had something to say, he'd say it. Hasn't stopped him so far.

We stepped into the elevator and rode down to the lobby in silence.

"Mister Gleason!"

The clerk who checked us in yesterday was waving me over to the front desk.

"What's this about?" Russell asked.

The clerk stood motionless, smiling directly at us our entire trip to the desk. Like a lighthouse guiding in a ship. It was kind of disturbing, to be honest.

"Our night manager left instructions that you are to be reimbursed for your stay with us," he finally said.

"Right," I told him. "And we're staying one more night."

"Oh. Hmm. He didn't say anything about additional nights."

"Are you sold out?"

"No."

"Then what's the problem?"

"Nothing, Mister Gleason. Wait here, I'll be right back."

The clerk snatched a few papers and promptly moved into the back room.

Russell checked in all directions for eavesdroppers before leaning into my ear and speaking.

"What am I missing here?"

"Nothing, really. Some woman on my floor accused me of having a dog in the room, and the manager wanted to compensate me for the inconvenience."

As I lifted the bag and set it on the counter, I could hear Steve's barely muffled giggling.

"Here is a perfect example of the importance of data," Russell remarked. "Had they asked more questions, and not jumped to a hasty conclusion, they would have uncovered the truth."

"But had they uncovered the truth," I muttered in a low whisper. "They would have kicked us out."

"Huh," Russell exhaled. He turned away, but the smart ass smirk was evident.

"What?" I asked.

"Didn't you just look in the mirror and vow to tell the truth?"

He was right. That is what Aaron told me. I assumed he meant to be honest with myself and not lie about my feelings, not that I could *never* lie in general. He didn't make that clear. Never lying seemed like it could get you into even more trouble, though.

"I'm not sure if that's exactly what he meant."

"You could call him and ask for clarification," Russell said. "Or, you could find out on your own."

The clerk emerged from the backroom with slow, determined steps and a look of profound seriousness on his face.

"Mister Gleason, I'm sorry, but..."

I put up the stop sign then pointed to the bag. "I want you to know, there's a dog in this bag."

His eyes bounced wildly from the bag to the papers in his hand, then he abruptly excused himself again.

"Great," I shot to Russell. "Let's go get our stuff."

As we turned back toward the elevators, we were momentarily stopped by four uniformed landscapers, walking backwards, single file. Each one was pulling a dolly with a large potted plant.

"More plants?" I sneered, a bit louder than I imagined. "Doesn't this place have enough already?"

"Not *more*," the first landscaper smiled. "*Replace*. Whole buncha ferns in restaurant die overnight. Crazy."

Russell cleared his throat. "Isn't that something?"

Steve giggled again.

He wasn't even there, so I don't know what the hell he was laughing at.

"Mister Gleason?"

It was the clerk again, only this time he wasn't waving me to the counter. He was running across the lobby to meet me.

"Mister Gleason," he panted. "I just spoke with our day manager, and you and your, *friend*, have complimentary rooms for the length of your stay. You said, *one more* night, correct?"

"Mmm hmm," I hummed.

"Very good. If you need anything else, please let us know." And he darted back to the front desk.

"I told him the truth."

"That you did," Russell beamed.

Then my arm began to randomly jerk at my side.

"Can I *please* get out of this bag now?"

A single eyeball could be seen peeking out through the gap in the zipper.

"We should go," I announced.

"Good," Russell said. "I'm hungry."

"Shotgun!" Steve shouted.

Russell looked concerned. "Is he okay?"

"Oh, he's fine. He just called *shotgun*."

Lunch was at Wendy's. In the parking lot, of course. Steve refused to get into the bag again until we were back at the hotel, which meant we had to eat in the car, and not inside at a table. And since nobody had a preference, I pulled into the first fast food franchise we came upon.

We finished rather quickly, and for a long time after, no one said a word. Each of us stretched out in our seats, like we'd all just awoken from comas, staring blankly at nothing in particular. The lethargy was so thick, you could cut it with a chainsaw. That is, if any of us could summon the energy to do so. Or, if any of us had a chainsaw.

Even the voices in my head were out of it. I swear I heard a couple of them yawning.

Finally, the silence was broken.

"This is the life, huh?" Steve lazily announced. "Food. Fresh air. Relaxation. All I need is to find myself a little tail, know what I'm sayin', bro? Am I right?"

He raised his paw in the air. I'm not high-fouring a dog because he wants to have sex again.

"You know," he continued. "I can't for the life of me figure out why you can't be happy. This is it, right here. *Happiness*. What's the problem? I gotta whiz."

He leapt out of the car and headed for a row of bushes.

"He's talkative today, isn't he?" Russell asked.

"Little *too* talkative, if you ask me."

"So, you would say this is unusual for him?"

"No, not really. Damn thing's always talking. He's just happy today. And whenever he's happy, he likes to yak it up."

"You sound annoyed."

"I hadn't thought about it before," I admitted. "But it's a little like he's rubbing it in my face."

"Do you think it's unfair that your dog is happy, and you're not?"

"I don't know. It's just a hell of a lot easier for a dog to be happy, isn't it?"

Russell sat up and leaned over the front seat. "Why do you say that?"

"There's nothing complicated about his life. Food and sex. That's it."

"There you go jumping to conclusions again."

"How is that jumping to conclusions? He's a dog and I'm a human. There's a big difference."

"And you think humans, with our highly evolved brain functions, are above such primordial impulses?"

"Yeah," I shot back. "I do."

"You don't think sex makes people happy?"

"That's not what I said."

He was pissing me off with this know-it-all crap.

"Okay. Let's try a little experiment. Watch the people as they walk in and out of the restaurant. Study their facial expressions. Their body language. You do that, and I'll be right back."

He vaulted out of the car, with much more grace than Steve, by the way, and ran across the street into a hardware store, leaving me to sit by myself and watch the expressions of people as they entered or exited a Wendy's.

Really, there must be something better I could be doing with my time.

I forgot my watch again, but I knew it wasn't quite lunch yet, because they were just switching over from the breakfast menu when we pulled up, which meant it was that time of day again. Only the morning version. That dangerous stretch of time between crowds when it stopped being busy, but you had to find a way to stay busy just to keep out of trouble.

I still hate it.

Steve jumped back in the passenger seat and made himself comfortable.

"What are you doing, D?"

"Watching people," I told him.

"Why?"

"Not sure."

"Then why you doing it?"

"Russell said to."

He sighed, then sat up on his back legs. "Alright. I'll watch with you."

The restaurant's side door was directly in front of us just across the lot, and we kept our eyes focused on it. For what seemed like maybe five minutes, the door did not move. Made me wonder what was wrong with the place. It could be that the door was locked, but it had me worried that there was some massive food poisoning incident recently, and people were staying away for a reason. I ran a quick vital signs check of myself. No pains. No nausea. One voice did complain of dizziness, but that voice is always going on about being dizzy. I stopped listening to it a while ago.

A car pulled in and parked four spaces from us. With saying a word, both Steve and I responded to the new activity by turning our heads in its direction. The restaurant door was still in my peripheral vision, so I wasn't really worried about missing anything.

A man, probably early twenties, stepped out of the car and walked without hesitation toward the restaurant door. A good ten seconds later, a woman about the same age stepped out of the passenger seat and slammed shut her door. It didn't take much detective work to know this was obviously intended to get his attention. She was glaring his way when she let the door fly. It was of no concern to him, though. The noise didn't even break his stride. He moved straight to the side door and walked in. She waited for a moment, grunted to herself, and stomped her way across the lot.

"What are we looking for?" Steve mumbled out of the corner of his mouth.

"Don't know exactly. He said watch their faces and their body language."

"Russell said?"

"Yeah."

"Where the hell is he, anyway?"

"Ran into the hardware store across the street."

"Probably needs something to tighten his loose screws."

"Maybe," I said. "So, what do you see from these two?"

"They were fighting about something. She's pissed. And he ain't getting none later."

"You got that right."

"Okay, that's done. Now what?"

"Here comes two more."

Another couple were now heading toward the door. A man and a woman, probably mid thirties, walking near each other, but still about five feet apart.

"Are they together?" Steve asked.

"Don't know. Possibly."

The man opened the door and held it for the woman, who gave a half-hearted nod and walked in.

"What the hell, man," Steve grumbled. "Shoot me now."

"What?"

"*That* is exactly why I'm glad I'm a dog. Frigging relationships."

"What now?"

"Come on. It's like a death sentence. The first couple's fighting, and the next were like zombies. Could two people look more bored and apathetic? How the hell can anyone live their life like that?"

"Maybe they're just going through a rough patch."

"Please. If the only reason to get into a relationship is love, then why hang around once the love is gone? I don't get it."

"Because they hope it will come back."

"Is that what you're hoping happens with Julie?"

"Julie still loves me."

"Really?"

I know he was never going to get it, and I didn't feel like arguing.

"Looking at their faces and body language, I saw two people who were once in love. Probably married very young."

"Who?" Steve asked.

"That second couple. But marriage was more than they expected and they were forced to give up their dreams. Now, they're secretly resentful of each other."

"Then leave!" he exclaimed. "Start over! Damn."

"It's not that easy."

"Ah, yeah it is. *See 'ya*!"

"You have no idea. And stop hissing at me."

"I'm not hissing." He quickly scanned the area. "What the shit? Daryl, look."

Russell was now standing by the wall of the building directly behind us. The sound was coming from the can of spray paint in his right hand.

"What are you doing?" I called out.

"I bought bright yellow," he screamed. "I thought it would stand out the best against the red brick!"

Steve couldn't take his eyes off him. "*Who*," he read. "Okay, what's that next letter? I've seen it before. Is it Greek, or something?"

"No. It's a heart," I told him. "A symbol, you know, another way to write *love*."

"*Love*. No shit? Dude, that's confused me for years. I never understood what the hell that was. Thank you. Goofy humans." He went back to reading the wall. "*Who loves...tits*?" He let out a little laugh. "That is what that says, right?"

"Yep."

"Are you sure this guy said he's a doctor, and not that he *needs* one?"

Russell added a question mark as an afterthought, then sprinted back to the car.

"Now," he contentedly declared. "We sit back and wait."

"For what," Steve asked. "The cops?"

I looked Russell straight on. "What was that about?"

"Like I told you. We're conducting a little experiment. Watch."

The message on the wall was the first thing anyone with a set of working eyes would see when leaving the restaurant. So, we settled back and waited patiently for exiting customers.

The door slowly pushed open and an elderly lady made her way out. Her head was angled downward, in order to watch the path ahead of her, which made any examination of her face impossible. But after a moment, she straightened up enough for the three of us to get a good look.

Since Russell's public inquiry was such a quick read, two short words, a symbol, and punctuation, it didn't take long for her already dour expression to turn even more unpleasant. Her thin, pale lips rainbowed into a scowl, forcing the loose skin on her cheeks to mimic the same pattern. It was like a series of horseshoes had been molded into her face, each one just a bit smaller and tighter than the next. She let out a quick *Harrumph*, then tugged closed the lapels of her coat, as if she was worried the message was written specifically about her, or something.

Russell lifted himself off the seat and waved at her.

"Excuse me, ma'am, can I ask you a few questions?"

I figured she'd just turn her head and walk away in embarrassment, but instead, she flung herself around and stomped with purpose back into the restaurant.

"I'll get her when she comes back out." Russell said. Then he poked me in the shoulder. "So, happy?"

"Because you embarrassed an old woman? Why would that make me happy?"

"Not you," Russell clarified. "Her. Do you think she's happy?"

"After that? I wouldn't think so. She's probably telling the manager, or calling the cops."

"So?"

"*So?* I don't want to go to jail because of your naughty graffiti."

"First of all. We're not going to jail. Sure, investigators could question the clerk at the hardware store and possibly draw a line back to us, but no one is going to those lengths over this. Secondly, *naughty?*"

He had me there. It was another in a series of stupid word choices lately. I took the keys out of my pocket, but Russell grabbed my hand before it reached the ignition.

He had a remarkably strong grip.

"What about before that incident?" He asked. "Was she happy then?"

"I don't know. She didn't seem all that happy."

"Because...?

"How would I know, Russell? If you want me to make a guess, I'd say..."

"That's just it!" he exclaimed, jumping into a crouch on the seat. "I do *not* want you to *guess*! I want you to *know*. Know the facts, not the fiction. I'll give you an example: Remember our waiter yesterday? Jason? Remember when he guessed that maybe healthy made happy? Coincidentally, that was an early theory of mine, too. I had noticed that athletes usually appeared happier than other people. I wondered, why? Was there a connection between happy mind and happy body? If so, what was the cause? The endorphin rush from exercise? The adrenal rush from competition? The confidence and power that comes from strength and muscle control? A stronger immune system? What if it wasn't physical, but instead mental? Could it be the camaraderie? What about the knowledge that you are so much stronger and fit than most other people you encounter?"

"Or richer," I interjected.

"Right. There's that prospect, too. So, rather than just interview them, I decided to test the theory myself, and I started working out with a group of gymnasts from the university. Olympic hopefuls. Some of the best in the country. They taught me floor exercises, rings, bars, the horse, the vault. I threw myself into it completely. After a year of rigorous, daily training, I was in the best shape of my life. And do you know what I learned?"

"No idea."

"Don't you want to guess?"

"I thought you didn't like me to guess?"

"Ha ha! Very good! I will tell you what I learned. I learned that Jack was only doing it to please his father the ex-football player. I learned that Marcus desperately wanted to find a soul mate, but was selfish with his time and could never commit to any long-term relationship. I learned Ted fought off his secret sexual desires for other men by overcompensating and bedding every woman who came his way. And I learned that Larry, who was the best pure athlete of the bunch, was also the most neurotic, and refused to accept how good he was. He spent most of his time subconsciously sabotaging himself in order to create a plausible justification for his neuroses."

"That's...interesting, but, what's your point?"

"My point is, I was personally happy because of the great shape I was in. But the others, who were in far, far better shape, weren't even close to being as happy as I was. So, athletics wasn't it, and I was once again brought back to *why?* In order to find real answers, you have to dig deep. Question everything, and by every means available. And if it means causing other people to feel uncomfortable doing so, like that old lady, understand that it's just one of the sacrifices you make in the search of truth."

"You really shouldn't have done that to the wall."

"Why?"

"Asking who likes tits isn't an answer you need to dig deep for, Russell. Plus, there are rules..."

"You can't always follow other people's rules, Daryl! Not even your own. Because they're sometimes wrong! Every major discovery in the world has occurred because a previously held rule was broken. And before that rule was broken, most people believed it to be correct. *Guessing* didn't prove that the world was round. Darwin didn't *assume* evolution. They had to be investigated. Tested. And in order to do that, they had to question and break rules."

"And what, you're out to prove that graffiti laws are wrong?"

"No, Daryl," he said with a trace of disgust. "That's not what I was trying to prove. Although, I do think the law is obtuse. It's only aim is to control the underclass, not to keep the city clean and sparkly. Why are billboards twice the size acceptable, but graffiti is not? Revenue. Taxes. The only difference between a well lit cigarette advertisement and the hand painted phone number of a woman who gives good head is that one generates revenue. Well, they could both generate revenue, but that's an entirely different story. Ha ha ha!"

He clapped his hands and stood on the seat.

"I told you this guy's nuts," Steve mumbled. "I'm getting out of here. You know, hardware stores don't just sell spray paint. They sell axes and shit, too. Who knows what the hell else he bought there?"

"Stay in the car," I told him.

"Don't worry," Russell smirked. "I'm not going anywhere."

"I wasn't," I started to explain, but then decided against it. The old woman had just walked back outside, and I could tell Russell wasn't paying any attention to me anyhow.

"Excuse me!" he shouted. "Ma'am!"

She turned and flashed Russell her horseshoes.

"Can I ask you a few questions?"

I caught her sneak a quick peek up at his message out the corner of her eyes. She was old, but she was no dummy. She connected the two.

Russell flipped backwards out of the car in one fluid movement, perfectly sticking the landing, and finishing by smiling and throwing both hands in the air. Like that would give him a better score. However, the judge from Little Old Ladyville was horrified by this maneuver, and ran toward the street as fast as her legs could move her. Which, surprisingly, was much quicker than I would have bet.

"Wait!" Russell made a move to follow, but I laid on the car horn.

"Russell! Haven't you done enough to her already?"

He looked directly at me, and as serious as could be.

"No. I did not collect all the information I needed."

"Information for what?" I realized I was screaming, so I took a breath and tried to bring it down a notch. "What does any of this have to do with happiness?"

He smiled. Not that phony *look-what-I-did* gymnast smile, but like he was the Genius Hermit of the Mountain, and one of us stupid mortals finally asked him the right question.

"Why, it has everything to do with it. And nothing! That's the amazing aspect of happiness: its flexibility. Its ever changing properties. It's emptiness and it's fullness. It's yin and it's yang. It's pork and it's beans. It's Captain and it's Tennille!"

Steve stuck his snout over the front seat. "Do you have any idea what he's yammering about?"

I shook my head. "I don't understand any of it."

Russell's excitement meter hit the red.

"That's just it! Nobody understands! But that doesn't stop any of us from reaching for it. That old adage, *insanity is when you try the same thing over and over again, but expect a different result*, gets a free pass here. Insanity is defined by abnormal behavior. And abnormal behavior is when you do something out of the ordinary. But, can it be considered abnormal and out of the ordinary if everybody is constantly doing the same insane and abnormal activities?

"How to achieve, and keep, happiness is one of mankind's biggest, and most frustratingly unanswered questions. Just when someone thinks they may have the answer, they realize they no longer do. Or that the answer itself was incorrect. Or inconclusive. Happiness: the search for it, the fleeting ownership of it, and it's inevitable loss, have been an endless well of inspiration for literature, film, art and music. Let's just look at music. The sheer volume of songs written about happiness is staggering. *I want to be happy, but I won't be happy, until I make you happy too!* Well, what if you can't make me happy? What if it's impossible? Does that mean neither one of us will ever be happy? It's explored in every genre imaginable. Ever hear of The Jesus and Mary Chain? They have a song called '*Happy When It Rains*'. Very understandable. Rain is soothing, right? Well, what about the Carpenters? *Rainy days and Mondays?* They always got her down. Karen Carpenter would not have been a good match for those guys. Then there's the electric violinist Jean-Luc Ponty. He has a song called, *'The Art Of Happiness'*. It's a fine song, if that's your thing, but it's an instrumental. What exactly does that tell you about happiness? You can argue that happiness is within the melody, or the structure, but the reality is, you can name a song with no lyrics anything you want, can't you? The song could have been called '*The Art of Dog Shit*'. The music is still the same, but because the title's changed, does it offer at the true meaning of dog shit? Now, jump from songs to band names. Then there was a Canadian band in the 90's called The Pursuit of Happiness. Know what happened to them? They got screwed over by their record label and were ultimately forced to break up. So much for that pursuit. Is that what true happiness is? A pursuit that will never cease? The bigger question is, do songs really tell us anything? Are they meaningful to anyone other than the artist?"

"I think music is extremely meaningful," I told him. "You just have to listen to the right songs."

"I keep looking, but there's so many to cover. I could go on for a week just listing examples, and I still wouldn't be finished."

"Then, maybe you shouldn't start," I told him.

"From the beginning of life to the end of existence..."

So much for listening me. And I wasn't too crazy about this time frame he presented, either.

"...From the cavemen who chiseled it on their walls, to the teenager right now who's scribbling in a diary about her recent breakup with the love of her life. Everybody aches for it, everybody gets it, and everybody loses it. The cycle never stops. Seems so senseless, doesn't it? Especially when you consider how simple the answer really is."

"What do you mean?"

The young couple who looked to be in a fight now walked out of the restaurant. Russell hopped on the hood of the car and watched them like they were his favorite TV show. I'm fairly certain if Aaron were here, he'd have a fit about Russell's choice of seating.

The guy saw the message first. He smiled, then pointed it out to the woman.

"I love hers," he smiled.

"David!" she shrieked.

"They taste like lemons!"

The woman broke down in a quick fit of red-faced giggling. "Shut up!" She gave him a meaningless slap on the arm, followed by a big hug.

"Sorry," he quietly said.

"Me, too," she replied.

They walked back to their car. I could tell Russell was mentally noting the whole encounter.

Then the other couple walked out. The apathetic couple, as Steve called them. In their case, the woman saw the graffiti first. She looked terrified, and mumbled something inaudible to her husband. He gave the immediate area a quick glance, looking almost as scared as she was, and when he caught a glimpse of us, he hooked arms with her, and moved double-time to their car. Heads hung low the whole trip.

"What do you think of that?" Russell asked.

I got out of the car and walked up front to face him.

"Are you serious?"

"About what in particular?"

"You said you know the answer. To happiness."

"Don't you have any reaction to those two couples?"

"No. I don't care about them. Do you know the answer?"

"What if I told you I did? What if I told you I discovered a simple mathematical formula that could guarantee you, or anyone, happiness forever? Would that make you happy?"

"Very much?" I told him.

I began to hear a faint ringing coming from somewhere.

"Would it really?" he asked.

"Of course it would. It worked for you, didn't it?"

He turned his head toward the back wall.

"What is it?" I asked.

"It's your phone."

"My phone?"

"Yes. Your phone. It's ringing."

"Are you going to answer?" I asked.

"I think you should answer it."

"What? No. I want you to answer it."

"I can't answer it. Only you can."

I reached into my pocket and pulled out my phone.

"Doctor Melvin?" I said, reading the screen.

"Who's that?"

"My psychiatrist."

"There is research which suggests psychotherapy is a scam. That all the answers people need are already inside of them."

"Research doesn't always give the right answers."

I put the phone to my ear. "Hello?"

"Daryl? This is Doctor Melvin?"

"What do you want?"

"Were you sleeping?"

"Sleeping? What? No. I'm standing in the middle of some parking lot." I swear, I don't know how this guy got his medical license.

"Daryl," Melvin calmly said. "You've missed your appointments. You need to come in and see me."

"I told you, I can't! I'm far away!"

"And you know this, how?" Russell blurted, rudely interrupting my conversation.

I told Melvin to hold on a sec, then gave Russell a look. "How do I know what?"

"That research doesn't always give the right answers? I would think in order to reach a conclusion such as that, you'd have to amass a significant amount of research. It sounds to me like you're guessing again."

Then he laughed. A little snicker, like he knew exactly how wrong I was. The guy could be such an ass.

"So what if I am guessing?" I spit back. "You know, what the hell are you, anyway? You're a philosopher, but you refuse to guess at anything. Isn't that what philosophers are supposed to do? Guess? Form an opinion? 'Cause if it was all nothing but fact, it would be *philosophy*, right? It would be science. And another thing, aren't philosophers supposed to do a little more to explain the mysteries of life than just compile information? I mean, you sound more like one of those annoying people at the mall who stop you to ask stupid questions about toothpaste. That's all you have, are questions. I haven't heard one answer yet. I mean, it's one thing to compile the research, but eventually you have to employ it, right? Explain how you think your toothpaste will make everyone's life better. You tell me to not follow rules, but you know what? You can't even stop yourself from following rules. *Get all the information in before you come to a conclusion.* That must get very tiresome. I know it's worn me out just listening to it."

"Daryl? Daryl?" It was Melvin, yelling into the phone.

I turned away from Russell and pressed the phone to my ear. "What?"

"Are you okay?" Melvin asked. "What's going on?"

"I told you: I'm in a parking lot with a guy who said he knows the answer to happiness."

"And what did he tell you, Daryl?"

"Nothing. You called before he could explain."

"If you want to ask, I can wait."

When I turned back around, Russell was gone.

"Where did he go?"

Steve motioned toward the other end of the lot. "He took off down there."

"He's gone," I told Melvin.

"Daryl..."

"I could have gotten the goddamn answer," I screamed. "But you ruined it!"

I turned the phone off and shoved it back in my pocket.

"We gonna try and find him?" Steve asked.

"We have to."

I climbed back in the Mustang and pulled away, taking direction from Steve as he sniffed the air trying to pick up Russell's trail. We drove around the rear of the building and back up to the street, but when it was time to pick left or right, Steve didn't say anything.

"Which way?"

He took a couple sniffs, then dropped his head.

"Which way?" I asked again, a little louder this time.

"I'm not sure," he sighed. "The guy musta been all over the place. I'm picking up his stupid scent everywhere."

"Shit."

"Sorry, bud. Now what?"

"I don't know. I don't know where he went. And I don't know where to go next."

"Do you think he was supposed to help you find the pirates?"

"He said he had the answer! If he had the answer, Steve, I wouldn't need to find the damn pirates!"

"Okay. What the hell. Calm down. How 'bout we try the park?"

"Yeah. Good."

It wasn't far from where we were, so I figured, if that's where he went, we should beat him there.

We made every light, which never happens to me, and found a spot that seemed in an open enough of an area that we couldn't be missed, just in case he was looking for us, too. Steve went in one direction, and I in another, scanning as much ground as we could. But, after way too long a time, the two of us met back up by the swing set where Russell said he slept.

"He's not here," Steve said.

"You looked everywhere?"

"Yeah. Checked the bushes, looked up in the trees, hell, I even went inside the bathrooms. Men's and Women's. Damn, those broads leave a mess."

"The bushes!" I yelled.

"I checked 'em. I said that."

"No," I said over him. "That's where he kept his suitcase. He didn't have his suitcase when he left the Wendy's parking lot."

Steve smiled. "Because it's at the hotel!"

We ran back to the car and sped back to the Hilton. That should have been the first place I thought of. He's probably there trying to finagle another couple free days from the manager.

Steve stayed in the car this time. I didn't really need him for this, so there was no reason to go through the whole ordeal of talking him into the bag, then carrying him around.

That same clerk was standing at the counter, which made me feel a little uneasy. And not just because of that weirdly hypnotic grin of his, either. I already had too many interactions with this guy, and it was only a matter of time before he became suspicious. I had to play it cool.

"Mister Gleason," he called out. "I believe housekeeping is in your room right now, sir."

"That's fine," I said. Very suave. Very Cary Grant. "I'll just wait with my friend in his room until they're finished."

I gave my jacket lapels a downward tug, and pivoted on my heels toward the elevator. I may have even looked like Cary Grant, too. Who knows.

"He's not in his room, sir."

I spun back around, quite sure that any trace of Cary Grant I may have acquired had just drained away. "What did you say?"

"He's not in his room," the clerk repeated. "He left a short while ago. He had his suitcase with him."

I felt lightheaded, like I might pass out, or at the very least, just fall down and make a fool of myself.

"Did he say where he was going?"

"No, sir."

"Did he say anything? Leave a message for me?"

"He didn't say anything. I just happened to see him walk out. Will you not be needing that room tonight?"

I stumbled into the elevator and pushed the button for my floor. The maid's cart was outside my door. I pushed it aside and walked in.

"Hello," the maid stammered in broken English. "I clean some more for you still."

I grabbed my suitcase and left the room.

With Russell gone, it made no sense hanging around here any longer. I had no idea what I was supposed to do, or where I was supposed to go next. So, I just pulled out onto the street and a few minutes later, found the highway again and headed west.

24

When we were teenagers, Chester Woody and I, when there was nothing better to do, would get in the car and drive. No set destination, no plan. We'd gas up, both the car and us, and drive in some new direction. I guess it could be argued that was in fact an actual plan, even though there was no goal beyond that. And picking up a twelve pack to keep us company during the journey.

Now that I think of it, I always paid for the beer. Always. And half the gas! What the hell was I thinking? Maybe because he always drove, he felt he was owed some livery fee. Who knows.

Another thing I always supplied was the music, which I was always aware of. It used to piss me off because he always had a problem with anything I brought. Didn't matter. It was always *the wrong one*. It was either a band he heard too much, or someone he knew too little about. Frigging Goldilocks. I'd say, "Fine. You pick something next time." And he'd go, "You're damn right I will." But he never did. Sometimes, just to make a point, I wouldn't bring anything, and we'd drive for hours in silence, not even saying a word to each other. Gave you a lot of time to think.

I nearly forgot about all those times. The idea of driving aimlessly right now, without direction, must have brought it all back. The weird thing about back then was, it never seemed pointless. Truth be told, it was quite the opposite: in those days, having a destination was what seemed pointless. It was the journey itself that mattered. I wish I could remember when that sensation ended. Lately, it seems like I won't even get into the car unless I know exactly where I'm going. Or, at the very least, have a basic idea of where I'm heading, along with the knowledge I'll be given more specific directions when I'm on the road. It would be easy to blame some of it on gas prices, but that wouldn't make sense with all the money I have now.

There was a specific Chester trip that came back to me. Damn, I hate saying that name. I could kick myself for not giving him a nickname back then, because repeating that hideous name almost makes me not want to think about him anymore. Chester Woody. Who does that to a kid?

There are two major streets, a mile apart from each other, that run north and south through the western section of Chicago: Pulaski Road and Cicero Avenue. If you drive south, out of Chicago and beyond its immediate suburbs, Pulaski changes names a few times. For a while it becomes Crawford, then back to Pulaski, then back to Crawford, and finally Governor's Highway. Cicero, stays Cicero. That is, until Governor's Highway bends west and merges into Cicero. The two then combine to become Route Fifty.

Neither one of us were aware of all these twists and changes that were ahead of us. And why would we have been? The two streets run parallel to each other for something like a hundred miles. Why would anyone expect all that to suddenly change? It surprised the hell out of me. Him too, probably. But, I can't be sure. He didn't say much.

The other surprise about that trip was stumbling onto Manteno.

Growing up, the word Manteno was both a joke and a threat. When you said someone was *"Going to Manteno"*, they didn't simply mean the town. They meant the mental hospital located in the town. Adults were constantly throwing it around in order to make fun of one another. If someone was acting stupid, you'd hear *"You want a room in Manteno?"* Any outlandish statement by one was followed by the retort from another: *"He's on the first bus to Manteno tomorrow."* Over time, that was abbreviated to merely, *"He's on the bus"*. That's all anyone needed to hear. The point was made.

It's been closed up for years, but it must have been a horrible place when it was open. I only say that because adults were pretty hush-hush about it around us kids. The few times an adult would slip up and say it around me, they'd instantly get weirded out. Sometimes going as far as apologizing. Like they just outed Santa, or something. Maybe they just assumed the idea of a crazy house might scare kids too much. Or, sound a little too interesting, and that if I ever tried to find out more, the information would damage me emotionally, or something. I swear, the reaction of the adults to their stupid slips of the tongue did more harm than any actual description probably would have, because after that, whenever I heard the word *Manteno*, I imagined the absolute worst. Wild-eyed patients in straightjackets, chained to walls and whipped by sadistic interns. Babbling. Screaming. Crying. Bugs. Rats. Shit. Manteno wasn't a punch line for me. It really did scare me half to death.

It was dark by the time we saw the first street signs on the highway: *Do Not Pick Up Hitchhikers*. We still had no idea where we were, but we did agree that wherever it was, it was potentially dangerous. And to a stupid teenager, dangerous translated into fun.

I was the first to see a sign mentioning Manteno. There may have been others before, but if so, they were either lost in the darkness of an unlit street, or just general inattentiveness on my part. Probably because of this other thing I used to do: when the music wasn't on in the car, I would "play" whole albums in my head. I was almost to the end of side one of the Buzzcocks *Singles Going Steady* when I noticed one, so I lifted the needle and spoke.

"You see that?" I asked him. "Manteno. We're in Manteno."

"Kick ass!"

"That's why we were seeing all the *Do Not Pick Up Hitchhikers* signs."

"Why?"

He wasn't very bright.

"In case there's a breakout," I told him. "They want the escapees to stay close enough so it's easier to find them. It's the same thing by prisons."

"That the kinda shit they teach you in high honors?"

"You mean you didn't make those signs in woodshop?"

"Fuck you."

Like it was my fault I had high honors classes. I didn't ask for them, that's just where they put me.

It was quiet for a while after that. Until, that is, our headlights caught a couple women standing on the side of the road. That's when he got excited and pulled over.

"What are you doing?" I asked.

"Maybe they're hookers!"

"Hookers. In the pitch dark, in the middle of nowhere."

"It's so the cops don't see them, dumb ass."

"They could be from the crazy house, too."

"Even better. And cheaper."

Of course. He had no money. So, even if they were hookers, he wouldn't be paying anyway.

We came to a stop, and he jumped out of the car and hollered back at them.

"Need a ride, ladies?"

"What are you doing?" I asked him. "You saw the signs."

"I didn't see their thumbs out, did you?"

"Come on. Let's get out of here."

"I wanna have some fun. Don't ruin this."

"Christ. Audrey's gonna flip. She's already pissed I didn't go out with her tonight."

"Shut up about Audrey for once, will you?"

It was so dark, I couldn't get a real good look at them until they were practically in front of me. They had okay bodies, I guess, slim and not too short or too tall. But it was obvious they were at least twice our age, and I remember that unnerved me for some reason. It's not like I had anything against older women, because I didn't. The whole trip had some ominous feeling to it as it was, and seeing their faces caused some *straw-that-broke-the-camel's-back* reaction. So much so that I had to squeeze the car door to keep myself from shaking.

"You're just a couple of boys," the one closest to me smiled. "How old are you two?"

"Twenty four," he announced. And if I remember it correctly, his voice cracked in the middle.

"Even if that were true," the closest one said. "You'd still be babies." She gently traced the outline of my left ear with her fingers.

I was squeezing the damn door so tight, I thought my hand would go numb.

"Seventeen," I mumbled. Something about her fingers stroking my head triggered a bizarre confessional sensation in me. I suddenly wanted to tell her about shoplifting Doritos the day before, but luckily I managed to fight the urge and keep it to myself.

One quick look at him and I knew he wished I had kept our ages to myself.

"So," he shot. "Do you want a ride, or what?"

The women must have known this sudden spurt of hostility was directed more at me than them because they gave each other a quick look and laughed.

"I'll ride in back with you," the ear stroker said to me.

There was nothing I could do about it at that point, so when she opened the door and climbed in, I followed right behind her. Sure, I could have refused, but I didn't know how the hell I'd get home if I did. I couldn't afford the cost of a taxi, and I certainly wasn't the type of person other people would ignore warning signs to pick up.

"What's your name?" mine asked. I started to answer, but stopped when I noticed him glaring at me in the rear view mirror.

"He's Joe," he said. "I'm Tom."

"Joe and Tom, huh?" mine hummed. "Okay then. I'm Princess Wilma, and she's Princess Betty."

"That's not really your names," he said.

"Shall we exchange ID's?"

"Princess Wilma it is," *Tom* said, then he slipped the car into drive and pulled away.

Princess Betty broke her silence. "Do you drive with Jesus?" she asked.

"There wouldn't be any room," he laughed. He was the only one, too.

"There's always room for Jesus," Princess Betty solemnly stated.

"Okay, but he's gonna have to sit in back with them two. So, ahh, how far do you two go?"

Wilma shook her head. "You are so obvious."

"What the hell's that mean? Hey, uh, uh..."

"Joe," I reminded him.

"Joe. I know. Is there any left?"

I reached down and counted the beers by touch. "A few."

"Well, whatta 'ya waiting for, stupid? Pass 'em out! We'll stop for more after."

I handed one to everybody. "There's four."

There was really five. I don't know why I said there were only four. Maybe because I paid for them.

"Stroh's," Princess Wilma whispered.

"It was on sale." I swear, it was like her fingers were still on my head. It was goofy. What was next? Another minute or so around this woman and I'd be putting myself as the second shooter on the grassy knoll?

"I like Stroh's."

She held the can close to her face for a minute, and I thought maybe she was trying to read the ingredients in the dark, or something. Then she popped it open and went into some heavy breathing routine, like she just broke into a safe without the alarm going off. At the time, I remember thinking, *maybe she's just really thirsty*, but looking back on it now, it was a pretty odd gesture no matter what the reason.

"So, you have girlfriends?"

Again, he jumped in immediately.

"Nope, nope, nope. We're both bachelors, out looking for a little fun. You wouldn't happen to know where we could find some, would you?"

Princess Betty started giggling and pinched her nose to keep from leaking beer on herself.

"Oh, Sweetie," Princess Wilma purred. "You don't know what fun is." She took a couple quick sips then turned my chin toward her.

"You look familiar. Do I know you?"

"I don't know. Where you from?"

She slid closer to me and poked my nose with her finger.

"I asked first."

She really didn't, but I wasn't going to argue because I was definitely not comfortable with this whole situation. I mean, if Audrey did find out, that was it. Luckily, I saw a 7-11 out in the distance and demanded that we stop. I gave the excuse that it was for more beer, but really I was looking for a chance to talk to him alone. To remind him that he was a major idiot.

"Come on, *Tom*," I said as I opened the door. "We'll be back in a sec."

"Why don't I just go," Princess Wilma asked.

"No, it's cool," I insisted. "He never gets carded."

"But if he does," Wilma explained. "And I go in right after him, it'll look suspicious. Small towns don't like suspicious."

"Good point," Princess Betty nervously added. "Let's not raise suspicions."

"Fine."

"Give me some money," Princess Wilma said.

I waited a moment to see who responded.

"You deaf?" Tom shot. "Give the lady some money."

I didn't have anything smaller than a ten, so that's what I gave her.

"Mind if I buy some peach schnapps, too?"

There goes my change, I thought.

As she slid out of the backseat, Tom opened his door.

"I'm going in with her. You two stay here."

"No," I shot. "Let Betty go in with her."

"I'm gonna make sure she gets the right stuff."

We were seventeen. Anything cold and cheap was the right stuff. We didn't even care about the cold part half the time.

I rolled the window all the way down and leaned sideways so my head could halfway hang outside. I remember thinking how damn dark it was. No moon. No stars. There weren't even lights on in the parking lot. And quiet. It really gave you the feeling you were in the middle of nowhere. The only real noise to be heard was Princess Betty's inelegant slurping. She must have married into royalty, because that was definitely a behavior that would have been corrected by attending the proper schools.

It seemed like they were in there forever. I had my watch on, but it was too dark to read it. And I couldn't see them because we were parked off to the side, so there was no window to look through. What was taking so long? It was like fifteen or twenty minutes. Were there that many choices?

Then Princess Betty spoke. "What do you believe in?" That was out of frigging nowhere. She wasn't even looking at me, so I wondered if saying it out loud was just an accident. I know I have the tendency to accidentally blurt things out, so I said nothing. But then the longer the question remained unanswered, the more self-conscious I became of it. Like the quiet was suddenly somehow all my fault, and only I could correct it.

"Me?" I asked.

"Who else? What do you believe in?"

She still wasn't looking at me. I mean, it wouldn't take that much effort. She was in the front passenger seat, and I was in back behind the driver's seat, so all she had to do was turn her head. Maybe this proved she was royalty after all.

"Like, a god, you mean?"

"Like, whatever you believe in. God. Love. Respect. Sliced bread. The Beatles. Do you believe in anything?"

"I never really gave it much thought."

"It doesn't take a lot of brain power." She sounded aggravated. "It's what you *believe in.* Happiness. Power. Dreams. Absolutes. Do you believe tomorrow is another day? Do you believe the Cubs will ever do it next year? What?"

"I don't know."

I really didn't have an answer, but I was thinking about it.

"You have to believe in something. Didn't your parents teach you anything?"

"My parents died when I was little."

"So, you're an orphan?"

"Might as well have been. I live with my grandfather."

"My friend knows someone like you. She has a…so, your grandfather, didn't he teach you anything?"

"Yeah. How to avoid talking to people who annoy you."

I meant that as a slam against my grandfather's parenting style, but she must have taken it personally. She reached her left arm over the front seat and poured the remainder of her beer on my leg. I remember being somewhat impressed that she was able to hit her target without looking at it.

"What the hell?" I wasn't much, but it was just enough to drench my right thigh.

"Now, give me that last beer you're hiding."

"What? No."

I had no idea how she knew about that anyway. Maybe she had eyes in the back of her head. That would explain a lot.

I was trying to figure out what to do about my pants when I saw Princess Wilma running around the corner of the store. She stopped by the front fender and motioned with her head for Betty to get out. Betty let out a sigh that only I could hear, and then gave the handle a quick tug.

"What's this?" I asked.

"Looks like traveling time again," Betty mumbled to herself. Then she turned around and looked straight at me for the first time. "You have to believe in something. Your life will be nothing without it."

She stepped over to Wilma for a short inaudible conversation, then Betty walked away. I suppose I should have gotten out and asked a few questions, I mean, I had no idea where he was, and they were acting kind of squirrelly, but it was like I was attached to the seat. I couldn't move. Wilma peeked in at me through the windshield, then hurried over and opened the back door. I frankly did not know what to expect, but her leaning inside and kissing my forehead was very far down on the list of possibilities.

"I'm glad I got the chance to see you, Daryl," she whispered. And then, just like that, she was gone.

A minute or two later, he came walking back, and in no particular hurry, either.

"What the hell just happened?" I asked. "You told her my name?"

"Drop it."

"What did you do? Why did they take off?"

"I don't know. Who cares? Let's just go."

"Where's the beer?"

"Didn't get any." He fumbled with the keys, then finally started up the car.

"You have my money?"

"She does," he mumbled.

"What? Why?"

"Just shut up, alright? You said enough already."

"What the hell did I do?"

"Everything was going so cool, then you had to go open your big stupid mouth, you know?"

"No, I didn't. I was in the car!"

He was doing eighty, which wasn't smart, because we were still in town.

"Everything was going so cool," he repeated through his teeth. "I coulda had her, man. But then she starts asking questions, about you, and she pulls back and takes off. It had to be you sayin' we're seventeen, or something. You fucking blew it for me."

"You sure it was me? You weren't being too pushy? Maybe trying something she didn't like?"

"No. It was you! You wanna walk back? Now, shut up!"

I thought about what Princess Betty said. If I did believe in anything, that story of his wasn't it.

25

I had no idea where we were. Steve and I had been driving all afternoon, and neither one of us had seen anything we could call a sign. Well, a sign for us. For all I knew, we could have veered hundreds of miles off course. I really needed to get back on track. And soon.

"This sucks," Steve yelled.

"Yeah, I know," I yelled back. "I got the point. You don't have to keep saying it."

"I'm just saying, is all," he screamed.

This had to be the twentieth time he's said it already.

"What's that?" He pointed his paw at a sign up ahead for a restaurant.

And about the fiftieth time he reminded me he was hungry.

"We'll eat later."

"Not that!"

I felt a drop on my face. Then another. I gave Steve a quick look then turned back front to the road.

"Not funny," I yelled. "Stop it!"

"Dude, that's what I'm talking about!" He gave the air a couple sniffs. "Uh, oh!"

"What?"

I didn't have to wait for his answer. Within seconds, there was a deafening clap of thunder and sky opened up. All over us.

"Put the damn roof up!"

"I told you! I don't know how!"

It was like standing under a waterfall. I learned something, too: it doesn't make a difference how fast or slow you move through the rain. If it's coming down this hard, you're going to get soaked. And if the roof is down, so is the inside of your car.

"How far away was that restaurant?" I screamed.

"Said ten miles, but that was a while ago!"

I could barely see twenty feet in front of me, so the exit ramp came up on us as a surprise. I cut hard to the right, and made the ramp, but I must have pulled it too sharply because we started to hydroplane. I lifted my foot off the accelerator, correcting the spin by turning to the left. Good thing I paid attention in driver's ed. We skidded back and forth all the way down the ramp, eventually straightening out at the stop light.

"Dude, don't do that again."

"Kept us from going off the road, didn't I?"

Sometimes, I don't think this dog sees the bigger picture.

The restaurant was to the right. It looked more like an old two story farmhouse than a traditional restaurant, but if it got me out of this weather, I wasn't going to be nitpicky. The parking lot was huge, like a strip mall with only one building. But there were no other cars to be seen.

Just one lone motorcycle. With my luck, the place was probably closed. Who knew when the next stop was.

I drove close to the door and tried to read the sign through the never ending blanket of raindrops.

"It says it's supposed to be open!" I yelled to Steve.

"I'm not waiting out here!" he declared.

"No, you're not!"

Just then, the door pushed open from the inside and a woman stuck her head out. A waitress, I assumed. She was wearing an apron.

"What are you doing?" she called out to us.

"Getting drenched!"

"Well, close your top, silly, and get inside!"

"I don't know how!"

"Oh, my god! Are you serious?" She was laughing.

"I am *very* serious!"

"Okay," she giggled. "I believe you."

I hate rain.

She disappeared back inside, and I turned off the ignition. Steve and I bolted from the car and made our way inside as fast as we could. The waitress reappeared, now wearing an orange rain slicker, and pushed moved past us through the narrow vestibule.

"Be right back."

"Me, too!" Steve announced.

He walked four paces to the left, while the woman darted to the car. And without any difficulty, she closed the roof.

I felt like an idiot. I had no idea it was that simple. Steve pretended not to watch her as he did his business, but I could tell he was. When she opened the door and he came scampering in, I was ready to catch holy hell from him, but he didn't say a word. He just shook himself dry in complete silence. So, I figured it was only good manners if I returned the favor by not saying anything to him about spraying all his water onto me. Not like it made any difference. I was already saturated.

She came back inside, pulled off her hood and smiled. "You poor things. Let's get inside."

"My dog's coming in, too!" I demanded.

She jerked her head back. "Of course he is."

I realized I was still yelling.

"It's loud out there."

"I bet."

She held open the interior door for us, and as I walked past, I caught her sucking in her lips and holding back a laugh.

"What's so funny?" I asked.

"Sorry," she smirked. "It's that sign around your neck. I was just wondering if you had one that said *Wet*."

I glared at her, but all that did was make her release the laugh she was trying to stifle. Good thing I arrived just in time to make this woman's day.

Steve and I headed toward the nearest booth. He was already dry, but I was dripping a river behind me. Someone should make clothes for humans that were like dog hair. Clothes you could just shake dry after a rain. Why can't smart people come up with ideas that actually help us?

"My god, all that water!" the waitress exclaimed. "You must be freezing." She ran into the back and retrieved a stack of towels and what looked like a dishwasher's uniform: white pants and a white pullover top. One size fits all.

"Take these and go change in the bathroom."

"I have clothes in my trunk."

"Oh honey," she said. "You open that trunk and everything in there'll get soaked, too. You can do that once the rain's done. Go on, now. I'll get you some hot coffee and food."

"I like her," Steve said.

I grabbed the towels and the clothes and puddled my way to the men's room.

I stopped at the mirror and took a good look. She was partially right. I should be wearing a different sign. One that said *Disaster*. It made me think of the last time I was fully clothed and soaking wet. My honeymoon. I got drunk and fell off the dinner cruise boat. It was one of those big deal dinners that you had to dress for, so there I was, jacket, tie, leather shoes, the whole works. Drenched. I guess it was a hell of a big deal, my falling off the boat. I'm told a woman at a nearby table screamed, and that set off some chain reaction. By the time my head bobbed back over water, there were sirens and horns, spotlights waving all over, and people playing ring toss with life preservers. Finally, someone from the crew jumped in the water and swam me back to the boat, where I was yanked up by anyone and everyone who could get a hand on me. It actually took me a while to comprehend what had happened, because at the time, it seemed like some bad dream. That feeling didn't last long, though. Having a stranger sit on your stomach and pump your chest brings you back to reality pretty damn fast. The moment I started coughing up water, everyone started to cheer and applaud. I felt a lot better, hell, I even felt sobered up, but they still insisted I go to the hospital. So, Julie and I were placed in a smaller boat that hurried us to the dock, and from there we were transported by ambulance to the hospital.

Julie didn't say a word the entire ride. I thought maybe she was too scared, too freaked out, to speak. To make matters worse, when they asked for an insurance card at the hospital, I realized I had lost my wallet. There was something like a thousand dollars inside. Mostly traveler's checks, but that wasn't the point.

They put me on a gurney and shoved me in a room, and for a moment, the two of us were alone while we waited for a doctor. And I'll always remember this: Julie first looked around to make sure no one was watching, then she leaned over and punched me in the arm! Pretty damn hard, too.

"Thanks for ruining my honeymoon! Do you have any idea how embarrassing that was for me?"

We left the hotel the very next day. A week earlier than scheduled. She told me in the cab that she would be handling all our money from that day on. That was the last thing she said to me until we were back home. Fun trip.

While I was in the stall peeling off my clothes, there was a soft knock on the outer bathroom door.

I'm leaving some hangars on the sink for you," she said. "They'll dry easier that way."

So, after I slipped on my whites, I squeezed out the excess water from my other clothes and draped them on the hangars. I dried my sign with a paper towel, and rehung it around my neck. The shoes I didn't know what to do with, they were still dripping wet, so I just carried them back with me to the table.

Theoretically, I'm not breaking the service rule: I have shoes. They're just not on my feet. I never realized that loophole until now. Those signs never say you must be *wearing* shoes and a shirt, just to be in *possession* of them. Interesting.

I scooped up my wallet, money, keys and cell phone, all as soaked as my shoes, and left the bathroom. Steve was sitting at a four top in the middle of the room, with a bib tied around his neck.

"Check me out, bro! Do I look classy, or what?"

A steaming pot of coffee sat on the table, so I poured us each a cup and stirred in the cream and sugar.

"What should we get?" Steve drooled. Good thing he had the bib on.

"I don't know. Let's see what they have."

But there were no menus to be found. I tried looking for the waitress, but she was missing, too. The kitchen was on the other side of the counter to my right, and from the angle we had, it was impossible to see inside. But of course, that didn't stop me from craning my neck in every conceivable direction in the hopes of breaking the Laws of Physics. I honestly don't know why I do the things I do sometimes.

"You notice we're the only people in here?" Steve nervously asked. It was a line you'd expect to hear in a horror movie, delivered by the guy you know you won't be seeing at the end.

"The rain is pretty bad," I assured him. Even though that only explained why nobody would be coming in now, not why no one is left.

Were there any slasher movies that took place in an out-of-the-way diner? I couldn't think of any off the top of my head. And I couldn't decide whether that was good or bad. Good, because there was no frame of reference for any wannabes to follow, bad, because there's always going to be some lunkhead who wants to try something new.

Finally, the waitress reappeared, but it wasn't to deliver menus. She was delivering plates. I looked around to make double sure. Yep, we were the only customers.

"Did you order already?" I asked Steve.

"Just think about that for a minute," he replied.

"Nice, thick rib-eyes," she said. "Medium for you, and rare for your cute little dog."

She then set down a third plate at an empty chair.

"And this is...?" I started.

"Well done. I know. It ruins the flavor. But, that's the way my mom cooked it for me, and I just got used to it. Old habits, huh? Double baked potatoes and spinach. And, there's a special surprise for dessert, but I'm not telling you what it is just yet."

She let out a tiny laugh, then produced a lighter from her apron, and lit the candle in the middle of the table.

"I'm Marcy."

"D-Daryl," I stammered. "He's Steve."

"Hi."

She inhaled deeply and smiled, then went right into cutting her steak. Steve and I, on the other hand, forgot we even had a steak in front of us. We just kind of sat there, moving our eyes from the plates, to Marcy, then back to each other. He was trying to tell me something, but it was a little difficult to know exactly without actually hearing the words. I was momentarily relieved when a couple of the voices in my head broke the silence.

"Run! Get out, now!" warned one.

"Don't listen to him," insisted another. "She's kinda hot. And she made you a steak!"

"A steak," the first one yelled back. "Which means steak *knives*! I'm getting out of here!"

"I thought of one," a third blurted out. "*Blood Diner*. Couldn't tell you the plot, but we saw it at the drive-in. Late eighties. Remember? You took Audrey. It was pretty stupid."

"Cut back on your red meat," yet another one added.

I wish just once that one had something new to say.

"Did I forget something?"

Outside voice. Outside my head, I mean.

"Yikes," Marcy continued. "Are you a *say Grace* person, and I just ate before? What's wrong with me sometimes? I'm not like that, you see, a Grace-before-meals gal. Really, I'm not a Grace before *anything* kind of gal, ha ha ha! So I'm not used to people who are. But, if that's who you are, well, that's okay, that's okay. We can start again. Are do overs allowed? I'm not sure what the rules are about this kinda thing."

"No, no," I said.

"Really? No do overs?" she sadly mused. "That's harsh."

"No, I mean, I don't know what the rules are, either. I'm not a *say Grace* person."

"Oh!" she exhaled a nervous laugh. "Because you weren't eating, so I thought...*did I forget something?* 'Cause I can fix whatever..."

She pushed her chair away from the table and rose to a crouch above her chair.

"No, no," I said, picking up my knife and fork. "It looks great."

"Really? You're not just saying that, are you?"

"No, seriously. It's great."

"Thank you."

Steve smiled. "I'm just gonna eat now."

"Yeah," I said. "Let's eat."

The rain never did let up. If anything, it came down even harder, which probably explained why nobody else turned up to the restaurant. The combination of pouring rain, thunder, lightning, and hail acted like a giant *Do Not Disturb* sign for the rest of the world. Whatever temptation there may be to bother other people is subdued by the prospect of turning into a loaded sponge. Or getting zapped by a million volts.

Rain isn't half bad if you look at it that way.

It took me a while to eat the steak. Not because there was anything wrong with it, but because my mouth found itself busy saying things like, *I don't know*, *what?*, and *how many*, in between bites. I swear, I never realized there were so many variations to the joke about screwing in a light bulb. Lawyers. Mathematicians. Union workers. Russians. Italians. Californians. New Yorkers. Oregonians. *Oregonians?* That's the one that got me: I don't think I'd ever heard a joke about people from Oregon in my whole life, but evidently, they don't like nuclear power plants, or talkative Californians.

"Is everything okay?" Marcy quietly asked.

"Huh? Oh, yeah. Just great."

"Really? 'Cause, well...forget it. Never mind."

"What?"

"Well, okay. It's just that, well, you didn't laugh at any of my jokes. Is it because you heard them all before? If you did, you should have said something. I could have told other ones. I know a whole lot."

"No. No. I mean, I heard a few before, but most of them, I think they were new ones to me."

"Just not a joke person then?"

She wasn't looking at me. Instead, she was watching the empty baked potato shell skip around on her plate as she poked it with a fork.

"No," I said. "I like a good joke."

The fork dropped from her hand and clanked loudly against the porcelain plate.

"So, were my jokes not good," she choked back. "Or was it the way I tell them?"

"No. No. It's not you. Honest. It's me."

She took hold of my wrist and gently squeezed. Her hand was very soft for a waitress.

"What's wrong?" she asked. I thought she was going to start crying.

Steve looked up at me and smiled.

"Don't mind me, bro," he said. "Hey, you gonna finish your potato?"

I shook my head and put what was left of my potato on his plate with my free hand.

"You can tell me," she softly said.

The conversation was cut short by a bright flash of light, followed immediately by a crack of thunder so loud that it sounded like it was directly on top of us. Which it probably was, since it knocked out all the electricity. She squeezed my wrist a little harder, but once it was evident that darkness was all we were in for, she loosened her grip and stood up.

"I'll go lock up," she whispered. "Why don't you grab some more candles from the other tables?"

She guided herself to the front door with the single flame of her lighter, both locking the door and flipping over the *Open* sign. When I saw this, I became self-conscious of the fact that my sign only had one side. It seemed like there should be something written on the other side, but what? *Open* and *Closed* made sense because they're opposites. But, do I really need a sign that says *Sad*? Not only would it be unnecessary, it's kind of against the whole point of why I'm wearing the stupid thing in the first place. Plus, I didn't need a sign to be reminded of that.

Still, it seemed like it needed a side two.

The candles weren't anything more than highball glasses with a votive inside, so I was able to easily pinch two together in each hand. I could have done three in each, possibly even four, but we really didn't need that much light. It's not like Miss Lucinda was showing up.

When she came back, she reached across the table to light each one. Her arm brushed against me on and I caught a whiff of her perfume. I know I smelled it before, but couldn't place it. It was flowery, and reminded me of being young. It suited her well.

Now that it was darker, I figured I could sneak a good peek at her without it seeming so rude. Or making her think I was some leering pervert.

She was a little older than I first thought. My age, maybe a little younger, but not much. Blond. Natural, too, not a dye job. I'd never dated a blond. Well, in reality, I only "dated" two women my whole life, Audrey and Julie, and they both had dark hair. I think that's why I always had this thing for blondes and redheads. Especially blondes with big green eyes, which, coincidentally, is what she had. And when they caught me staring back at her, I got nervous and fumbled for something to say.

"So, are you, ahh, sure you can just lock up?" I asked. "You won't get into trouble, or anything?"

She gave the back of her left hand a teasing slap. "I'm such a bad girl."

Crappy weather, electrical outages, it didn't matter, there was no way I could ever get away with closing the Silver Platter early. And I ran the damn place! We'd get hit with a foot of snow, and people would still show up expecting to eat. Once, just like this, lightening hit a transformer and killed the power in the entire area. Over five thousand homes and businesses were out from around nine at night until four in the morning. And guess what happened? Customers came in. At first, everyone who was there when it went dark hung around, waiting it out, hoping it wouldn't last too long. But eventually, I'd say about an hour, all of the customers and most of the staff left, so for security purposes I locked the front door. But wouldn't you know it, a couple minutes later, someone was banging on the glass. At first, I thought it was looters, but Karen, a waitress, put a flashlight on them, and we saw it was just the Kendalls. After that, her flashlight found the Browns, the Tulleys, and a few more families. I tried to explain the situation, but it did no good. Everyone insisted on coming inside. We had to cook by candlelight while they sang songs in the dining room. It was a real pain in the ass. And of course, they all hung around until the lights turned back on. More than half of them fell asleep in their booths. Nice that they got to do that, but I had to stay awake to run everything. Next time they came in, I gave each of them a bill for their food that night. Not one person paid. In fact, they all act like they were horribly offended. Some left immediately, others never even came back in again. I'd love to know where people get off sometimes.

As if suddenly remembering, Marcy stepped over to the counter, and returned with a bottle of wine and two glasses.

"Will you do the honors?" she asked, handing me the bottle and a corkscrew.

"Only two glasses?" Steve complained. "That's a little rude."

"It's wine," I told him. "Not beer."

Marcy giggled. "Steve likes beer? Seriously?"

"Yeah."

"Well, I have beer, if he really wants some."

"Yeah, of course I do! Tell her yes!"

I shook my head, and she laughed again.

"Be right back. Don't you go nowhere!"

She snatched a candle from the table and walked to a stand up cooler behind the counter.

"Does it matter what brand?" she asked.

"No. Anything's fine."

"Heineken," he chanted. "Heineken!"

"Shut up," I quietly warned him.

She set two bottle of Coors on the table, slid away his dinner plate and replaced it with a soup bowl. While I opened the wine, she poured his beer it in the bowl. I didn't even have to tell her.

"Dude, I like her," Steve said. "A lot!"

He shoved his snout in the bowl and greedily lapped it up.

"This is so funny," she said with yet another laugh. "I used to know this guy, a long time ago, who liked to get high, and he'd blow marijuana smoke up his dog's nose. I used to think that was real mean, 'cause like, well, the dog didn't have a choice, you know? This guy, right? He'd hold the dog's nose while he exhaled the smoke in it, so you never knew if the dog liked it or not, 'cause he was forcing it on him. But Steve, you can see he likes it. That is so funny! A dog that likes beer."

"He likes it a little too much," I said.

I happened to look across the room and out the front window, and caught a pair of headlights in the parking lot.

"A car just pulled up," I told her.

"Oh, well."

"What if it's a customer?"

"Too bad," she whispered. "I already have one."

Again, I couldn't decide if that was good or bad. Good, because mass murdering waitresses would welcome the extra people. The more the merrier. For the killer, at least. Bad, I suppose, because she could just be a simple one-at-a-time serial killer.

"But, what if it's the owner?"

"I wouldn't worry about that."

"I don't want you to get into trouble because of me."

She leaned in a little closer and hovered over a candle. Her face glowed, almost like the light was casting itself on nothing else in the room but her. Then I noticed her hair was dangling just a bit too close to the flame, so I pushed the candle aside. Why I'm saving possible murderers from catching fire, is beyond me.

"I own the place," she said, clicking her tongue. "Now, stop worrying and pour the wine, silly."

I actually thought of Russell as I grabbed the bottle. I didn't get a good look at the label, and wondered if it was anything he would approve of. I succeeded in filling the glasses without spilling, so that was a plus in my column. When I finished, I set down the bottle and we clinked glasses.

"To the serendipity of a stormy night." She had a very soothing voice. The idea of her being some maniacal killer was starting to seem a little unlikely. But you never know. I heard this is how the good ones are.

"Cheers," I offered back.

For no particular reason, I thought about what my stupid grandfather used to say before downing a shot of gin: *Here's mud in your eye*. I never did understand just what the hell that meant. And since there was never anybody to ever toast him back – I'd usually hear him by himself in the kitchen, raising his glass to the empty room – I never knew if there was supposed to be a response to that. It seemed like a real stupid thing to say, but that was my grandfather. He was something of a King in that field.

"Mmm," she hummed, swallowing her sip of wine. "This is nice."

"I haven't tried it yet. I'm still swirling."

"Oh, not the wine. Well, yes, the wine is good, but all of this, I mean. It's nice, isn't it?"

"I'm liking it so far," Steve chimed in.

"So, what brings you out this way? I'm guessing you're not from around here, or I would have seen you before."

"We're from Chicago."

"Oh, my god!" she squealed. "Are you really? I'm from Chicago! What part?"

"I grew up on the southwest side, then moved to the suburbs when I got married. I've been living back on the southwest side for the past few months, though."

"I'm just the opposite. I grew up in the suburbs. Des Plaines. You know where that is, right? Then I lived in the city, north side, before I came out here. Oh, how wild! I haven't been back there in years. Has it changed much? That's a silly question, right? How would you know what changed for me? Oh, my god. How funny. So, down south, huh? Did you live near that store with the crazy giant Indian statue?"

"Not far. That was the old Capital Cigar Store. Now, it's a doctor's office, or something."

"Yeah! Right. You never forget something like that. What suburb? You know, did you live in later?"

"Mokena."

"Oh, wow." she gasped. "That's where the mental hospital was, right?"

"No, that was Manteno."

"Manteno!" she said, nodding her head. "That's right!"

"I was just thinking about Manteno not that long ago. *On the bus*. Did you ever hear that one?"

"*On the bus!* Oh, my god, I remember that! That's what they'd say about anyone who acted crazy, right? *They're on the bus*."

"To the loony bin."

The door started rattling, and we both turned our heads. We saw the shadow of someone standing outside, trying to yank open the door.

Steve didn't turn to look. He stared straight at me.

"Dude, how can you be like that?"

"What?" I asked.

"Shh," Marcy quietly instructed, and then blew out the candles.

"Do you know who it is?" I asked.

"No."

Whoever it was started pounding. So hard, I thought for a moment that the glass would break.

"Hey! Open the goddamn door!"

It was a guy, and I thought the voice sounded vaguely familiar, but I didn't see how that could even be possible. I suppose Aaron could have tracked me down, or even Russell, but this guy wasn't calling out my name. He was just banging and swearing.

"I know you're in there! Open the fucking door!"

Marcy's breathing became louder and faster, and she began swatting her hands down on the table.

"What are you doing?" I asked.

"Where's your cell?"

I reached over to my pile of stuff, found my cell phone and handed it to her. She fumbled with it for a few seconds, then smacked me in the shoulder with it.

"How do you turn it on?"

I took it back and pressed the button, but nothing. The damn thing wouldn't even light up.

"It's dead. Probably the battery's wet. Don't you have a phone in here?"

"It's a plug in, so it's gonna be out, too. My cell's upstairs."

"Open the door!" His voice was getting even louder.

"Want me to check?"

"No. Something's not right," Marcy anxiously declared. "He's not saying that he wants anything. If a person needs help, they say so, right?"

"I wouldn't know."

She took me by the hand and tugged me from my chair. "Come with me?"

"Okay."

"Grab the wine," she said.

"My beer, too," Steve announced.

We felt our way behind the counter, down a short hallway and up some stairs, with a bottle of wine, two glasses, and a bowl of beer. Not easy in the dark.

I bounced off the frame of an open door and into to a room. A chair was to my left, so I set the bowl on the floor and plopped myself down. Marcy carefully stepped to the window and peeked outside.

"Where are you?" Steve asked. "I can't see a thing."

"I'm right here."

"Where's my beer?"

I gave the bowl a little kick so he could hear it sloshing. It must have worked because I heard that tongue of his going to work. Dog has no manners.

The pounding and shouting had stopped, and all I could hear now was the rain against the building. And Steve, but what else is new? I figured since we hadn't heard any glass breaking, quiet had to be a good sign. Unless this guy was some kind of ninja, which seemed highly unlikely. Then again, we could be in the heart of ninja country for all I knew. Which wouldn't be good.

"The car's still there," Marcy said.

"Is he inside?"

"I can't tell. Yes! The brake lights just flicked on and off. He has to be."

"It was nothing then. Just wanted to get out of the rain, probably."

"Maybe." She backed away from the window, removed the lighter from her pocket, and brought the flame to various candles throughout the room.

Steve stood on his hind legs and leaned into my knees. "Dude," he panted. "You see where she brought us?"

I gave a quick look, trying not to seem so obvious about it. Even with my sneaky sideways glances, it didn't take long to figure out that we were in her bedroom.

"It's about damn time you got in on some of the action," Steve snickered. "I was starting to wonder about you."

"Quiet," I said, pushing him off me.

"I thought some music might be nice," she said. "There's batteries in this old boom box, but all I have is a Nat King Cole cassette. Is that okay?"

"Yeah. There was a dishwasher at my restaurant for a couple months who played a lot of Nat King Cole. Even made me a tape. That was a long time ago."

"You own a restaurant, too? What a coincidence. How funny!"

"Didn't quite own it. It was my father-in-law's. I was supposed to get it eventually, but he had some money problems, and the place folded. Long story."

"Speaking of stories," she said. "We were talking about something just before the lights went off, weren't we? What was it? What was it?"

"I don't remember."

"Sorry, by the way."

"About what?"

"Me," she sighed. "The thunder. The lights going out. The guy at the door. Stuff like that flips me out. I don't like it. I'm glad you were here with me."

She placed a hand on each side of my face, then leaned in and kissed me. For a moment, she was really getting into it, moving her head side to side, and trying over and over to slide her tongue into my mouth. The fact that I wasn't opening my lips must have snapped her out of the mood. She pulled away and sat in the chair next to me, careful not to break eye contact.

"What is it?" she whispered. "Now I remember. This is what we were talking about. I asked you what was wrong."

"Nothing."

"Really? I just kissed you, and you didn't kiss back."

"I'm married."

"So, you're married, and you're from Chicago, but you're here all by yourself."

"Hey!" Steve yelled. "What am I? Invisible?"

"Why isn't she with you? You can tell me."

"Because she's back home. My home. With her boyfriend, okay?"

"Oh. I'm sorry."

"Well, don't be. Things like this happen to people who've been married for as long as I have."

"They do?"

"Yeah. This won't last. She'll get over it."

"And then everything will be back to normal again?"

"Here we go again with *normal*. What's normal?"

I picked up my glass and sloshed the wine around the sides.

"Daryl," she said, ever so gently, "What happened?"

"The short version is, I haven't been very happy lately. At least, that's what my shrink thinks. It got me wondering if I've *ever* been happy."

"You know, I have time for the long version. If you feel like telling it, I feel like listening."

I picked up my glass and brought it to my lips. "Here's mud in your eye."

"What does that mean?"

"I was hoping you knew.

It turned out to be a two-bottle story. She excused herself halfway through to retrieve a second, which I dutifully uncorked and poured before continuing. There were moments when it felt like I was yapping way too much, but she didn't exhibit any of the fidgety gestures I usually see from people who are bored to tears with your story, so I plowed through it. Once again.

If you count my visits with Melvin, I've told this story, or large portions of it, well over two dozen times already. And every time I do, I find myself feeling less connected to it. It's like I'm trying to remember the plot to some stupid movie I saw a long time ago, rather than relate a series of events that actually happened to me. Oddly enough, that's what bothers me more than any element of the story. The whole feeling of detachment when I'm telling it. That, and the idea that other people care so much about it. I mean, if I don't care, why the hell should they? It's none of their business. Yet, I always end up having to tell someone the whole stupid thing. Busybodies.

The bright side is, at least I wasn't being charged a co-pay when I told it to her. Not that it really mattered.

I finished with, *and then I pulled up to your front door and met you.* As with the others, I didn't think I needed to tell the rest. Hopefully she remembered the parts that included her. When it was clear that I was finished, she sat back in her chair and covered her mouth with one hand.

"That's horrible," she gasped.

"Yeah," I said. "And what's worse is, I'd bet anything that he fools around on her. He's just the type."

"Not that!"

"What then?"

"Your wife. If you can call her that. How could anybody do that to a guy as sweet as you?"

"She said the problem's me."

"Oh, my god! No, it's not. Even if it was, and it's not, but, even if it was, you don't do that!"

"The guy can't even handle his liquor. She told me, three drinks, and he's useless."

"What does that have to do with anything?"

"I don't know." I swear, it made sense to me before. Just one of those pieces of information that's good to know. "Seemed worth mentioning."

"Daryl, listen. You are not the problem. She is."

"It just happens with people sometimes."

"But, it doesn't *have to*. And if it does, that doesn't mean it's right. What about the other one? What happened to her? Did you ever find her again?"

"Audrey? No."

"Are you looking?"

"Wouldn't know where to start even if I wanted to."

"You poor thing. No one should have to go through that kind of mess. You need a friend, don't you?"

She reached out her hand, and gently ran her fingers down my jaw line.

"You have a nice face. Thin, but nice." She paused without breaking eye contact. "Don't you ever smile?"

"I guess I used to."

"*You used to?*" She giggle. "What does that mean?"

"Means, I think I did. At some point in my life. I just don't remember why."

"You're funny."

"I don't remember that, either. Could have been, but I doubt it. Nothing seems much fun anymore to me."

She stood up and took off her apron. As soon as that was discarded, she slipped out of her shirt and shook her hair.

"What are you doing?" I asked her.

"I'd like to try and make you happy again," she cooed. "Come to bed with me."

"Dude!" Steve gulped. "See if she has a dog!"

Don't get me wrong, she was very attractive, and possessed just about everything a guy could ask for, in all the right places, and with no defects or deformities. I was sure of that, because I had a pretty good view. There was just that one little thing I couldn't get past.

"I told you," I said. "I'm married."

"You're as close to being divorced as you could be."

"I can't."

She rose from the bed and moved over to me. Close enough that I could feel the heat of her chest spread across my face. And that smell! What was it? So close, so sweet, I could taste it on my tongue.

"Are you sure?" she asked.

So close, yet...

"Yes," I said.

"No!" Steve whined. "Seriously, what is your deal? This chick is so hot, *I* want to do her! You really disappoint me, bro. I can't be in the same room with you right now." And he disappeared into the hallway.

"Don't I excite you?"

I thought she was trying one more time, but instead, she was waiting for my answer. When she realized one wasn't imminent, she picked up her clothes one-by-one and slowly worked her way back into them.

"So, you felt nothing?"

"No. Not really."

"Why?" she asked. There was no trace of anger, bitterness, or resentment in her voice. Only curiosity. "She's with another guy, right? What difference would it make to her?"

"She'd never know," I explained. "So, probably none. It wouldn't feel right to me, though. I never thought about it until just now. If I was with you, or anyone else for that matter, it would mean I didn't want to get back with her."

"And you honestly want to? Get back together?"

"She is my wife."

"Even though she's with this Robert?"

"She doesn't have feelings for him. He means nothing to her."

"You're sure about that?"

"She's not pressing the divorce anymore. That's a good sign, right?"

"No. She tried to have you committed, Daryl."

"She wasn't trying to commit me. She said she was just trying to help me."

"Okay, I admit, I don't know her. But, I think I know you, and you deserve better. Better than her. Better than what you're going through."

It was quiet again. The Nat King Cole tape ended long ago, so I focused in on the rain. I couldn't believe it was still falling so hard and steady after all this time. How long was this damn thing going to last?

By now, she was once again fully clothed, with the lone exception of her apron. That remained on the floor. She even stepped on it as she reached for her wine glass.

"I'm sorry," she added. "I can't agree with you about this, but I didn't mean to make you feel uncomfortable."

"Don't worry about it. Women are always throwing themselves at me."

She laughed, and pressed her fingers against her lips in order to keep the sip of wine in her mouth.

"It wasn't that funny."

"Sorry," she said. "How about something really funny instead? Ever hear the one about the three nuns and the dirty priest?"

"Yeah."

It sounded vaguely familiar, like all those jokes do, but I wasn't in the mood to hear another one.

"Thank you," she said.

"For what?"

"For staying. Helping me."

"I didn't do anything," I told her. "Never have."

"Daryl, you're a great guy. You are. You can't let other people define who you are. Just because some people might, I don't know, *hate lifeguards*, doesn't mean there's something wrong with the people who are lifeguards."

"Lifeguards? Why would anybody hate lifeguards? They save people. That makes no sense."

"Okay. I don't know why I said lifeguards. Maybe all this water. Car mechanics. How's that? Cops. Mimes. Some people hate blondes. Some people hate brunettes. Some people think size matters, others don't. Cities, suburbs. North, South. You could go on forever. The point is, don't ever let anybody make you feel bad about yourself or what you like. Don't let other people define who or what you are. Be true to yourself. Okay?"

"Okay."

And just like that, the lights turned back on. It's strange how that happens. You spend hours in darkness, then *bam*! - you can suddenly see. Luckily, there weren't any switches flicked on in her room, so I didn't go blind from the sudden change. The bedroom door was partially open, which allowed just enough light from the hallway to sneak in so we could slowly readjust.

"Yay," she smiled, then jumped up and headed toward the door. Guess her readjustment period is a little quicker than mine.

"You gonna open back up?"

"No way," she laughed. "That's it. I'm closed for the night. Just give me a minute to shut it all down."

She wasn't out of the room for more than a few seconds before Steve wandered back in.

"Did you screw her?" he sneered.

"No. I did not."

"Dude! Are you gay?"

"How could I be gay? I'm married."

"Come on, I'm not stupid. My human used to watch the Lifetime Channel. That shit happens. Julie left you for Robert. Maybe because you weren't giving her any."

"She didn't *leave me*, okay? And, for the record, I'm good in bed. Show a little respect for the person who takes care of you, huh?"

"Me? What about you?"

"What did I do?

"Earlier. Talking about *the loonies in Manteno*," he said. "And *on the bus*."

"Yeah, what about it?"

"I'm just saying. You don't set a real good example about showing respect for the people who took care of you."

"How is talking about Manteno disrespectful to my grandfather?"

"Not Ben."

"Who then?"

"Your mother."

26

"My mother?" I shot. "What are you talking about?"

Steve tilted his head to the right. "I know the whole story. Don't be embarrassed."

"What story?"

"About your mom. Pregnant at sixteen. She wanted an abortion, but your grandmother won't allow it. So, she had you, and a week later the bum that got her pregnant disappeared. Standard stuff if you're a dog, but to you humans, it's a big deal. She couldn't take that he ditched her, so she tried to kill herself. That put her in Manteno for a while. As soon as she was released, she tried again. By then, your grandmother was dead, but Ben couldn't deal with her and you on his own, so when she was twenty or so, she went in for good. Your mom was so upset, she refused to see him again. Wouldn't even talk to him on the phone. Every once in a while he'd get a call saying she escaped, but they'd always catch her after doing something stupid in town. Did I miss anything?"

"Where did you all hear that?"

"Ben told me."

"He told me they died in a car crash..."

"No," Steve firmly stated. "That's not what he said."

"...But this is the story he tells a dog?"

"Dude, he told you the truth. He told me so. When she was in for good. He said five years went by, and you didn't say a word about it. Then one day, out of the blue, you started talking about how they died in a car crash. *You*, not him. He assumed it was just your way of dealing with it, so he left it alone."

"I don't believe it."

"Why Ben would lie to me?"

"Because he knew you'd tell me his version one day."

"That's a stretch, don't 'ya think?"

"Then where is she now? We'll go find her."

"I can't remember the name of it. *Saint* Something. He said he tried to get in touch about the arrangements, but you never called back."

"She's dead?" I had that sick feeling in my stomach again.

"You thought she was dead anyway, right? What's the problem?"

"When?"

"Four years ago, I think."

"She was alive that whole time? And I never knew it?"

"Don't get pissed at me. I didn't do anything."

I got up, walked to the window and looked outside, but it was too damn dark to see anything. That car was still there, though.

"Why didn't he tell me?"

"He did," Steve insisted.

"When I was what? Four or five? Would it have killed him to mention it again, you know, maybe when I was older, and knew just what the hell he was talking about?"

"You had that whole car crash story going. He probably figured bringing up the truth would upset you. Maybe you should have called him back."

"What an asshole."

"Who?"

It was Marcy. She was back into the room, with another bottle of wine and two more beers.

"Check it out," Steve cheerfully announced. "She brought me more beer. What a honey, huh?"

"Who's an asshole?" she repeated.

I didn't feel like getting into it, so I tried to change the subject.

"That car's still out there."

"I saw," she said, apparently unfazed that I didn't answer her original question. "You're not leaving, are you? I mean, it's still raining pretty hard."

"I don't want to, but I guess I have to."

"Why?"

"To find a hotel."

"Stay here."

"I told you..."

"I have a second room," she blurted. "And more wine and beer. Please? I'd like the company. Besides, your clothes and your car need to dry out, right?" She laughed, then flashed a wishful smile and waited for my reply.

"Okay," I said.

"Yay!" she playfully sang. "I'm so happy!" Then she handed me the new bottle, along with the corkscrew. "Would you mind? I can never do it right."

"How did you drink wine before I showed up? Do you just ask random customers to open bottles for you?"

"Something like that," she said, humming out a little laugh at the tail end.

When I finally worked the cork out of the bottle, it popped much louder than usual. Marcy was pouring beer into Steve's bowl and not watching me, so the unexpected noise startled her.

"Oh! My god!" she said, catching her breath, once she realized what it was. "That was just the cork. Okay. Wow. That was loud. So, ah, what were we talking about? Your wife, and..."

"I don't want to talk about me anymore. Let's talk about something different."

"You have any suggestions?"

"I don't know. What about you?"

"Really? You don't mind if I talk about myself?"

It was strange the way she said it. Like she had been previously forbidden to talk about herself, and had just now been granted approval for the very first time by me, the Grand Duke of Tell-Me-About-Yourself. What makes me feel bad is, that's not exactly what I was suggesting. I meant, *what about you...? Do you have any suggestions for our next topic*? But she was so damn excited over thinking I wanted to hear her life story that I just ran with it. I felt kind of stupid getting Nice Guy credits, but at least I didn't have to talk about my lousy life for a while.

She rearranged the other chair so it faced mine, then squirmed around until she found a good comfortable position.

"What do you want to know?" She asked with a big smile.

I had the sinking feeling that at any second, she was going to pull out a pie chart.

"I don't know. Whatever you want to tell me."

"Honestly?"

"Sure."

"Oh, my god, really? I don't know where to start. There's so much to talk about. I usually hear about everybody else's life, you know? *Could I have some more coffee, and tell you about all my troubles?* I don't really get to talk about myself with a lot of people. I knew there was something special about you when I first saw you. I knew you were different. So many men I've known, and I don't mean this in a bad way, I don't, because, it is what it is, but, they're just not people you can count on. You know what I mean? They're nice enough, up to a point, but then it's clear that they're really just in it for themselves. Which is fine, right? People have to put themselves first. And it's not like I'm planning on changing anyone to fit into my idea of the perfect mate, or anything. We are who we are. Nothing wrong with that. But so many, and I really mean that, *so many*. Like, *most. Ninety-nine percent!* It was an article a long time ago in *Cosmo*, or something. For the overwhelming majority of men, the focus is so much on themselves that all they have to offer to women is this surface level appeal, and even that's only for a limited amount of time. Like a warehouse sale, right? *For a limited time only. While supplies last!* Ha ha ha! Mmm... don't get me wrong, they can be incredible, absolutely wonderful darlings, but only for a couple, maybe three, dates. Which is simple, because for that time, their only objective is the woman. Do whatever you can to get her. They have to make a good impression, right? So they focus on nothing but her. And for that short time, she's the most important thing in their universe. Which means, they're on their best behavior, and all of their bad habits and shortcomings are temporarily shelved. But after that, once they think they've bagged you, forget it. The mask falls off. Sometimes, it explodes! Trust me, I've had my share of exploding masks. Those are the absolute worst, because you're still picking up little pieces of them for a long time after. Know what I mean?"

I was still taking it in, and not quite ready to admit whether I understood or not. But, that didn't matter. She started up right where she left off.

"Soooooooo," she said in one long exhale. "Once I read that, once it was confirmed, I decided that it wasn't worth it anymore."

"You gave up on men?"

She burst into laughter. "Oh, god no! If I gave up men, you might as well put me on the bus! I couldn't do that. Wow. Yeah, men are out for themselves, but you can't really blame them for that. Because *all* people are out for themselves, right? You have to take care of yourself. Even friends and family, they may act like they care deeply about you, and they really might, but when it comes down to it, when it's time for the choice to be made, right?, they only find time for themselves. So, I decided to take care of myself, and not hang around until the mask disappears."

"How do you do that?"

"I'm never with a guy more than once or twice. Usually just once."

"What do you get out of that?" I asked.

"Sex!" she howled. "Ha ha! Okay, I'll admit, it's not always the greatest, but I experience none of the problems brought on by a relationship. No jealousies. No resentments. Nothing in the back of your mind about the fight you two had yesterday, how he left the seat up, or how he gave the checkout girl a suspicious smile. None of that junk that clutters your mind. It's just two people who want to have a good time. And if you go into it knowing that, it's great, right? Then, you know, I meet someone like you. You don't have a mask. That's one of my weaknesses. Guys without masks. And instant gratification. Ha ha ha! My god, I can't believe how easy it is to talk to you."

"Yeah."

I filled my glass up to the rim, and drank half of it in one swallow.

Steve nudged his nose against my shin. "Ask her if she believes in reincarnation. I'll bet you anything she was a dog in a past life."

Marcy bent down toward Steve. "More beer, boy?"

"Dude, take her with us?" Steve begged.

"Is it okay?" she asked, motioning to Steve's bowl.

"Sure."

"I just realized," she said with a wink. "I never checked his ID. He is old enough, right? I don't want my license pulled."

"How old are you, Steve?" I asked.

"I turned six a few months ago," he said. "Big party. You shoulda been there."

"He's in his early forties, in human years."

"I would have never guessed," she cooed. "You look so young for your age."

She twisted open another beer and poured it into his bowl.

"So," I asked. "Does this happen a lot?"

"Me getting dogs drunk?" she laughed.

"No. One night stands."

"Depends on what you mean by a lot. What's a lot to you? Do you have a number?"

"Not off the top of my head."

"Well, how many women have you been with?"

"Two and a half."

"*A half*?" she giggled. "You mean, like a midget?"

"No, she was fully grown. Half because we were going to, but we didn't."

"You mean, like what just happened with me?"

"Not really. I planned on having sex with her from the beginning."

"And she changed her mind?"

"Something like that."

"If nothing happened, why do you even count it?"

"Because of the intention. And, I already added her to the list before we were going to do it."

"You have a list, too? My god! You and me, I tell you, it's really weird. So, this one, she was two and a half?"

"She was one and a half. Julie was the next whole number."

"I can't say I ever had a half. Unless I count you, then you'd be my first. My god. *Two and a half*? You're pulling my leg, right?"

"No. Besides, if I was pulling your leg, I'm pretty sure that would move me up from half to three quarters."

"If that's the way it works," she laughed. "My number's a lot higher than I thought."

She stood up, walked over to her dresser, and removed a thick book from the top drawer.

"What's that?" I asked.

"*My* list. Every man I slept with. I wrote down all of their names, along with the dates, and as much information about them that I knew."

As she sat back down, she quickly fanned through the pages for me. It wasn't as thick as *War and Peace*, but it was certainly wasn't *Fun with Dick and Jane*, either.

"Are you a blackmailer?"

"Oh, my god!" she laughed. "I could be, couldn't I? No. This is just for me. My little memory book. Okay, not so little, right?" She laughed again, but this time it was more of a raspy howl.

I heard a mini thud, and saw Steve leaning into the wall, mumbling to himself. This dog cannot hold his liquor.

"A long time ago," Marcy continued. "I had this girlfriend, and we were talking about the men we'd been with. *Complaining*, about the men we'd been with, is more like it. Well, anyway, she was going on about a couple of them, about how they'd been lousy boyfriends, and such. But, she couldn't remember their names! She said that was proof of how bad they were. But I thought, *how horrible is that?* To forget the name of someone you had sex with! And the one guy, she was with the one guy for six months! It was so cold. And what about the guy's feelings, you know? Yeah, okay, they might have been royal pieces of shit, and the relationship was long over, but how would you like to find out your ex-girlfriend thought so little of you that she couldn't even remember your name? So, that night, I went home and wrote down the names, birthdays, descriptions, so on, of each guy I'd been with. And from then on, every time I was with someone new, they'd go in the book, too. I like to think everyone I've been with remembers me, so it only seems fair that I do the same.

"Let me show you. I'll pick an early one at random. Okay, here: Neal Cosgrove. January tenth, nineteen-ninety-eight. Insurance salesman. He was seventy three."

"You had sex with a seventy three year old guy?" I asked.

"God, no. *Number* seventy three. He was only forty four years old."

"In nineteen-ninety-eight?"

She thought about it for a moment. "Yeah. He'd be pushing sixty now. Weird to think, huh? He was blond. Slightly balding. Bet he's all the way there, now. Five foot six. I'm five-five, so he must have been just a smidge taller. He lived in Arizona, and he was...oh, my god!"

"What?" I asked. Her eyes were open as wide as her mouth.

"He was a pirate!" she squealed.

"What do you mean? Like the ones I'm looking for?"

"You know, I knew something about your story rang a bell, but I couldn't put my finger on it. Yes! He was going to a pirate convention. I wrote it down! *Two weeks of wild, drunken debauchery.* God, now I remember. He wasn't all that great looking, but when I heard *pirate*, blam! It was like an aphrodisiac! Do you know how much that turned me on, to be a wench taken by a pirate? Anyway, it says it was somewhere in Minnesota, but he didn't know exactly where. He had to follow the signs! Oh, Daryl, this is good, isn't it? See? I might have forgotten all about this if I didn't write it down!"

"Yeah. Lucky for me you recorded the names of the thousands of guys you had sex with."

"It isn't *thousands*," she giggled. "I don't think."

"Does this make you happy?"

"What do you mean?"

"All these guys."

"I told you. I like being with men, but I don't like being in a relationship."

"It sounds like a cop out. I don't buy it."

Her smile fell. "Why not?"

"You say you don't want a long term relationship. I don't believe you."

"It's true. Long term relationships don't work."

"As soon as you write down someone's name in that book, you've committed to a long-time relationship with them. And that whole speech about making sure you take care of yourself. Look what you did for me tonight. Your life is taking care of other people."

"As a waitress! Which just proves my point. Short term relationships work the best. With customers and men."

"I think you're being selfish."

"How is that selfish? I only go out with a guy a couple times. It ends before anyone can get serious. How is that hurting anybody?"

"You're hurting yourself. You told me to be true to myself, and not deny myself fun, but you're not living up to either one yourself."

"How?"

"Just look at tonight. We didn't have sex. We talked. We found out about each other. And you enjoyed it. That's what happens when you get involved with someone. But, you're not giving any relationship a chance. You're not giving any guy a chance. All because of one stupid magazine article? All men are not alike. If they were, you wouldn't need that book."

Marcy gripped the armrests of her chair and bent forward. "This is what happens when you trust someone and open yourself up. You get shit on."

"How did I do that?" I asked her. "I was only saying what was on my mind. That's important."

"I feel sick."

"Marcy...?"

"I have to open up in a few hours."

"I wish you'd just listen for a second."

"Please get out. Go!"

She actually did look like she was going to puke. Her skin was about as white as the uniform I was wearing. More than likely, it was from all the wine. I grabbed Steve by the collar, hit the lights, and stumbled over to the spare bedroom.

Man, was Steve out. You'd think being lifted by the throat would wake someone up, but not him. His snoring was the only thing keeping me from wondering if he was dead. I set him gently on one side of the bed, then slipped myself between the covers on the other side.

I listened for the rain between Steve's periodic blasts, but heard nothing. Hopefully, it was all cleared up, and tomorrow would be much smoother.

27

Someone should really do a study on bedroom ceilings. Specifically, on how so many of them look the same. Maybe a topic as dull as that wouldn't appeal to many people, but it's one thing I found to be very interesting about this journey. Every morning when I wake up, it takes me a minute or two to remember where I am, because all the damn ceilings look alike. People don't really give much thought to ceilings, and I think that's where the problem lies. In the past, they were treated as something special. Artists were even hired to paint murals on them, but who notices a ceiling anymore? The light fixture attached to it might get a look or two, but rarely the ceiling itself. It's deemed as merely *functional*. The thing that keeps rain off your head. And because of that, because the ceiling does its job, no one bothers to look up at it enough to reflect on the importance, and the need for individuality, that's given to walls.

Walls get paint. Walls get paneling, sometimes floor to ceiling, sometimes just a wainscoting. Walls get art. Often times, the wall becomes art. A wall can be a backdrop or a focal point. Walls are alive. But a ceiling? Nothing. They're invisible. Insignificant. Until, that is, there's a problem, like a crack, or a leak. Then everyone notices, and not in a positive way, either. It's always accompanied by negativity - anger and swearing and threats - like it's somehow the ceiling's fault that it's cracked. No one blames the wall when they see something bad hanging on it. Like the tacky overabundance of diplomas, or Elvis on black velvet. Or even the photos of your wife with another man. The feeling is, the wall has no control over that. It's just doing what it's told.

Ceilings should be given the same consideration. For one, they should stop getting the blame whenever things go wrong. And even more importantly, they should be celebrated for what they are and what they've quietly done over the years. This is the ceiling that's keeping rain off *me*! This one is special, and deserves better treatment. I'm not suggesting every one be transformed into a mini Sistine Chapel, but it really is time to end the injustice.

I continued to stare at the highly unremarkable ceiling while I went through my checklist. I had to pee, I estimated that it was about nine in the morning, and I was pretty sure I hadn't smiled.

That was about it. Another day. More repetitiveness.

I stretched out my arms and legs, gave a good loud yawn, then sat up and examined the wall next to my side of the bed. There was nothing so special about it. If anything, it was disgustingly bland. This wall had nothing to brag about. Yet, it was an easy bet the stupid thing would get unwarranted credit for something before the week was through.

Out of the corner of my eye, I noticed the nightstand. Two pill bottles, along with a stack of money, and a pile of other things. I picked up a bottle to have a look. Daryl Gleason. That was weird, because I didn't remember putting them there. Nevertheless, it saved me from having to search for them. They both accompanied me to the bathroom.

I realized that Steve wasn't anywhere in the room. That didn't really mean much, though. If I learned anything about him, it was that he pretty much went wherever he wanted, whenever he wanted. Maybe Marcy did have a female dog. I never asked.

I pushed open the bathroom door, but it came to a stop well before the wall. And, it said *ouch*. I squeezed in and found Steve lying on the other side. He sort of looked like Marcy did last night.

"Dude," he muttered. "What's with slamming a door into me?"

"I didn't know you were there," I told him. "What are you doing?"

"I threw up last night?"

"Great. Where?"

"Don't worry, I got it all in the toilet. Just couldn't flush it down."

I gave a cautious peek. He was right. It was all in the bowl. Not even a drop on the seat.

"Good job," I said.

"Thanks. Now, how's about rewarding me with some coffee?"

"Give me a minute."

I flushed first before I peed, because, well, who wants to see that? When I was finished, I flushed again, and stepped over to the sink. Two pills and a handful of water later, I focused in on my reflection.

"You will be happy," I said to the scraggly guy who was mouthing the words back to me. "Always speak your mind, always tell the truth, and always be true to yourself. Don't let others define you."

"You're not hung over in the least bit?" Steve rasped.

I gave myself a quick check. "No."

"Maybe I should drink wine from now on. Hurry up with that coffee, would you?"

When I stepped back in the bedroom, I found my clothes hanging from a hook on the back of the door. They were in terrible shape, not close to being wearable by any stretch of the imagination. So, I took my keys off the nightstand, I still don't remember putting them there, and headed downstairs for my suitcase.

I came out of the hallway and was surprised to find the place packed with customers. Surprised, only because I hadn't picked up on any of the obvious clues: the smell of coffee, the banging of plates, the separate conversations at each table that melded into one indistinguishable drone.

This had been my personal soundtrack, twenty four hours a day, every day, for the past fifteen years. Even when I was away from the restaurant, whether it was in my car, or on the couch in front of the TV, this music played inside my head as loud and clear as any other sound swirling around me. I heard orders being called out to the cooks, and the cooks calling back to the waitresses when the order was ready. I heard the sizzle of the hot oil as it received a basket of frozen fries. There was the clatter of dishes being piled into a bus tray, the ring of the register, the hostess's *hellos* and *goodbyes* to each and every customer, and knowing in an instant whether she meant it or not. The phone, the *check please?*, and a thousand others that weaved in and out.

And, I would wake up in the middle of the night humming the elevator versions of *"Tie A Yellow Ribbon"* and *"I'll Be There"*, because that was the order those two songs played, every day, on the piped-in station we subscribed to. I knew that play list by heart, but those two always stuck out because of their coupling. The main character in the first song wondered if the love of his life would still be waiting for him after so many years of being gone. And even though his anxiety is relieved in the last few lines of the same song, it's the second song that really provided the much needed confirmation. Life can be like that. Sometimes a yellow ribbon tied around a tree is merely a symbolic gesture, not meant to infer lasting devotion, but intended more as a token to commemorate that singular moment of finally seeing each other again. It can contain as much sentiment as a Christmas card from your dentist. It's the reminder that follows, whether it arrives a day, week, or one song later, that cements it. *I'll be there*. That's not just a one shot deal from somebody only trying to make a good impression. That's from a person who really cares.

There's even a verse at the end, where the guy tells the woman that if she finds someone new, and if that new guy turns out to be a jerk, not to worry - the first guy will still be there for her. I used to like that guy. The first one. To me, he was proof true love existed. Now I'm wondering if he isn't just as much of a jerk as the second guy.

Come to think of it, the guy from the first song was *on the bus*, wasn't he? That explains a lot.

I walked out into the dining area and looked around for Marcy. I thought I found her, but it turned out to be another waitress. That surprised me, too. For some reason, I had it in my head that she not only owned the place, but did everything herself, which is a pretty stupid notion coming from a guy who ran a restaurant himself. Granted, there weren't as many tables here as there were at the Silver Platter, but even if only half those tables were filled, I couldn't have worked it alone.

The kitchen seemed to be the most likely place, so I zigzagged my way there between tables. At least three people asked for refills of their coffee, and one asked me what kind of pie we had. Since the coffee station was on the way to the kitchen, I soon found myself carrying both pots, regular and decaf, and moving from table to table. I don't know what compelled me to do it. Especially since I had no idea what flavor pie she had.

"Daryl?"

I looked behind me and saw Marcy, rounding the counter with an armful of plates.

"What kind of pie do we have?" I asked.

"Apple, cherry, blueberry, pecan...What are you doing?"

"You looked busy."

"I can handle it. You should go."

She breezed past me and delivered the food to a nearby table. I waited at the counter until she was finished.

"What do you want?" she snapped.

"I just want to talk about last night."

"There's nothing to talk about. I was wrong, that's all. Now look, I'm busy."

"I thought you said you could handle it."

"I can."

"I wasn't trying to upset you."

"You didn't upset me," she coolly responded. "I had too much to drink, and needed to get to sleep."

"You said so yourself: I don't have a mask. I was told to speak my mind and tell the truth. I have no hidden agenda. Hate me if you want. It doesn't really matter. We'll never see each other again, just like you want. But remember, you told me I deserve better than Julie. I was essentially saying the same thing to you. You deserve better than you're allowing yourself to have. Don't let your past define you. You might think you're happy, but I'm starting to realize that what looks like happy isn't always real."

She turned away and stared out the front window. That did very little to advance the conversation.

"I just have to get my suitcase," I continued. "Then I'll be out of your hair. After I grab a couple coffees for me and Steve. And maybe some of that blueberry pie. He likes blueberries. That's it. Other than table four wanting their check, that is."

That last part wasn't too difficult to figure out. The guy was standing up and waving at us like we were planes trying to land in a heavy fog. How Marcy could have missed him, since he was directly in her flight path, was beyond me. Luckily I saw, and warned her before she crashed. She acknowledged the guy, wiped here eyes, and descended to his table.

The Mustang's front and back seats were fairly dry, but there were still puddles on the floors. And there was already a pretty heavy mildew smell. I figured it only needed some air, so I rolled down the windows. That alone wasn't going to do the job, I knew that. The winds from speeding on the open road were what it needed. Now, if I only knew how to open the stupid roof.

I grabbed my suitcase and went back inside.

A tray was now sitting on the counter. On it were two plates, each with a healthy slice of blueberry pie, and two coffees. One in a to-go cup, and the other in a soup bowl. Since I didn't see any other customers who would require a soup bowl of coffee, I assumed it was for us. I tossed on the needed condiments and balanced it my free hand upstairs.

"Arrgh!"

Steve was still in the bathroom, moaning up a storm.

"Getting ready for the pirates?" I asked.

"Dude, don't make me think of waves."

"Here. Got you some coffee and a slice of blueberry pie."

"You're the best."

I set the suitcase on the floor and brought the tray into the bathroom.

"It's that bad?" I asked.

"You have no idea."

"Oh, I think I have a pretty good idea."

I opened the medicine cabinet, found a bottle of aspirin, and took out two tablets.

"You, too, huh?" Steve groaned.

"This is for you."

I placed them on the countertop, and crushed them as much as I could with the tip of my thumb, then scooped up the pieces and added them to his coffee.

"Fix you right up," I told him.

"Mmmm. Oh, you might want to rinse out the shower."

I twisted on the dial and stepped into the other room.

The next suit on the pile was a solid dark gray jacket, narrow lapels and two buttons, matched with light gray cuffed pants. The shirt was white, nothing special there. The tie was a thin, and silver colored with four green diamonds arranged themselves in a diamond pattern. Once again, a perfect fit. I folded the old suit into the front zipper pouch and made a mental note to find a dry cleaner.

I walked back into the bathroom and found Steve on all fours, the coffee and pie completely gone. Both slices.

"Believe it or not," he said. "I think I'm feeling a little better."

"Good, 'cause I don't want you getting car sick."

"Are we leaving?"

"Yeah."

I turned off the shower and gathered all the dishes on the tray.

"Why? I like it here."

"She told us to leave."

"What did you do?"

"You got me. Some people are like that. Just looking out for themselves."

"You think she's like that?"

"That's what she says. I really run into all the winners, don't I? Aaron, who thinks his ways are the best. Russell, who has a thousand questions, but no real answers...let's just get out of here."

I grabbed the suitcase and the tray and headed back down.

"Damn, this place smells good," Steve said. "Could we snag a little something for the road?"

"You just ate. We'll stop later."

Out of courtesy, I thought we should wait to say goodbye, but Marcy was nowhere to be found, so I set the tray on the counter and walked out to the parking lot.

The roof of the Mustang was down. And attached to the dashboard was a sticky note.

There's a switch under the dash. But just in case, I left something else on the seat.

XOXO

On the front seat was an umbrella.

I put Marcy's note in my pocket and quietly headed back toward the highway.

28

All I can say is the combination of coffee, food, aspirin, and fresh air must be extremely powerful, because Steve went from monster hangover to just *monster* moments after we hit the road. It started when he apologized for falling asleep on us, and asked what he missed. After repeating to him for like the thousandth time that *no, I didn't have sex with her*, I made the mistake of mentioning what Marcy told me about her sex life. So, of course, that meant that Steve felt he needed to share with me every dog he could recall having sex with.

"Miss Bubbles. Miss Cutie Pie. Miss Sophie. Queenie. Princess. Lady. Lady Bubbles. Rosie. Daffodil. Pansy. Another Lady. Make that three Lady's. Lucky..."

And then, after rattling off more names than I could count, or wanted to count, for some unknown reason, the conversation transformed into a non-stop interrogation. Of me. Like it was my fault what Marcy did with her life.

"I don't see why you're so bothered by it," he yelled.

"I'm not," I yelled back. I kept the top down, hoping all the yelling would make him hoarse. No such luck.

"Then why do you keep mentioning it?"

"I'm not the one talking about it. You are."

"Yeah, blame me."

"Okay."

"If she were a dude," he asked. "Would you care about how many women he slept with?"

"For one, you're a guy. I know about your sex life, and I already said you were a pig. And two, I don't care. Listen closely to two. Two's the big one."

"Yes, you do."

"You're driving me crazy, Steve."

"That's a short drive. The exit was way back there."

"How many men did Audrey and Julie sleep with?"

"I wouldn't know."

"There's a big difference between not knowing and not caring."

"I didn't say I didn't care. I just don't know."

"Weren't you ever interested?"

I paused for a moment. "No."

"You were about to talk to yourself again, weren't you?"

"Look, this isn't about me."

"Yes, it is."

"No, it's not," I insisted. "And I'm done talking about it."

"How can you be done talking when you haven't said anything? Why weren't you ever interested? In how many, or who? I find it interesting."

"You're a pain in the ass. You know that?"

"Yeah, that's right. I'm a Pain-In-The-Ass Dog because I don't care who screws who. Or how many times. And you're the Perfectly-Wonderful Human Being because you think there should be some boring ceiling on the number of times."

"Why did you say *boring ceiling*?"

"Because it means *limit*, right? And a limit in this case would be boring. Did I say something wrong?"

"It's just...never mind."

"So, you do think there should be a ceiling, or not? Tell me, how many people does it take to screw someone else?"

"Is this a joke?"

"Why? Have you heard it before?"

"Okay, you really want to know? Personally, yes, I think she's been with too many guys. And no, I don't know what the cutoff point should be."

He paused and sighed. "Why?"

"What do you care?"

"Call me curious."

"I don't know. Nobody wants to be with someone who's been with that many guys."

"Apparently they do," he laughed. "Or the number wouldn't be that high."

"I doubt any of them knew the number in advance. And when I said *be with*, I meant in a long-term relationship."

"Why does it matter?"

"I don't know. It just does."

"So, you think a woman should save herself for a real relationship."

"Yeah, I guess."

"But Marcy said flat out that she didn't want to be in a long-term relationship with anyone."

"I don't think she was being honest with herself. I think it was a diversion from the truth."

"So, you know better than she does? Now you sound like Aaron."

"That's not fair."

"What's not fair is you, bro. So, what's the number? What's the limit? I'll take an estimate. Doesn't matter."

"Depends on the circumstances, I guess."

"Alright, let me ask you this: what happens when a gal *thinks* she's in a real relationship, and sleeps with the guy, but then finds out later that the guy's not so good?"

"They work on it, or break up."

"Like you and Julie, huh?"

"That's different! Don't twist this around!"

"Well, what if the same thing happens to her over and over again? Five dudes. Ten dudes. Twenty dudes. All starting out with the best intentions, but ending in the crapper? Is that wrong?"

"That's not what Marcy was doing."

"So you think a woman should keep getting involved, just to continue getting her heart broken? You think that's okay, but sleeping with the same amount of men just for fun isn't?"

"I don't know."

"And what about the opposite? What if a woman can't ever find a guy who she wants to be in a relationship with? Or, can't find a guy who wants to be with her? Should she be a nun her entire life, just hoping that maybe, someday, the right dude will finally pop into her life?"

"I said I don't know."

"Look, D, I'm not a human, but I don't think you can expect a woman, or a guy, to keep themselves pure, waiting for the perfect partner to magically appear one day. Am I right, or am I wrong?"

"I'm trying to drive, okay?"

"I'll take that as you saying I'm right. Because I am. That's the end of your lesson for the day. Now find a goddamn restaurant. I'm hungry."

"I didn't want to be compared, okay? It's bad enough to be on someone's list and find out you're not Number One. I don't want to find out I'm not even in the Top Five. Or the Top Twenty!"

"How do you know that would even happen?"

"Because I made the mistake of asking Julie once. And she refused to tell me. Then she laughed. So, I don't want to know, okay? Case closed."

Finding a restaurant was now seemed the most important thing we needed to do. Yeah, I was also a little hungry, but mostly it was to ensure that the subject stayed closed. I was sick of talking about everyone else's sex lives. To me, it's similar to telling jokes: the first couple are an interesting diversion, but if you don't have any to share yourself, it starts to get annoying very fast. Especially when the other person does nothing but throw one one-liner after another at you. Enough already.

I had no idea where we were, but it didn't really make a difference. The area we were driving through was relatively built up, so I was sure we'd find something.

And, I was right. They had a Burger King, which on this journey, is a sure sign of civilization. We placed our order and pulled up to pay, but, when I reached into my pocket, all my money was missing.

"What do you mean, missing?" Steve asked.

"Missing," I repeated. "Gone. Not there."

"Put it on plastic," he said. "What's the big deal? You're rich. We'll worry about it later."

"I have to debit this," I told the cashier.

"Sorry," she said. "Our machine's out."

It wouldn't have mattered, because when I reached back for my wallet, that was gone, too.

"What the hell?" Steve whined. "What'd 'ya do with them?"

"The suit! They're in my suitcase. Gotta be."

I pulled out of line, but didn't see a spot in the lot, so I parked on the street and popped the trunk. Sure enough, my wallet was still stuck in a pocket, but my money was nowhere to be found.

"Dude, did she rip you off? That's cold. Maybe you were right about her. Not everything, but some."

I stuffed my wallet in the back pocket of the pants I was wearing, and ran inside the Burger King.

"Do you have an ATM?" I called out to no one in particular.

There were two employees behind the counter and a few customers in front of it. They all exchanged silent glances with each other, but none of them made any move to answer me. Finally, the girl from the drive through window stuck her head into the restaurant and greeted me with a smile.

"No," she said.

Why that would have been such a difficult thing for the rest of them to do, is beyond me.

"Do you know where I could find one?" I asked.

"Somewhere nearby," she smiled. Then she added, "And dogs aren't allowed."

"Racists!" Steve yelled.

Again, not one of them said a word.

I gave the door a shove and we walked outside.

I scanned up and down both sides of the block, looking for a machine, but couldn't see one. No bank, either. There were quite a few businesses, though. One of them had to have a machine.

I walked inside a bakery, a drugstore, a sandwich shop, and a laundromat, and not only did none of them have an ATM, but each person I asked thought I meant something entirely different. The lady at the bakery thought I was looking for a special pastry, the druggist thought I was looking for under the counter drugs, the lady at the sandwich shop said she didn't have a grill, and the woman at the laundromat told me I had to wash everything on my own.

I swear, if my goal was to just get as annoyed as possible, I was really hitting my stride in this town.

I asked Steve. "Do you understand me?"

He laughed. "Dude, don't get me started."

The fact that he could make a joke out of it told me that he was at least able to comprehend what I was saying. Tell the truth, I started worrying that maybe the words coming out of my mouth were different from the words I was trying to say. I saw a TV show like that once. This guy's brain wanted to say "table", but it came out of his mouth as "Ottoman Empire", or something like that. What's even worse, even though his mouth was saying Ottoman Empire, his brain thought he was saying table. It's some disease, I can't remember what it's called. Which probably isn't very good, either. Par for the course.

Steve and I wandered back and forth down a couple blocks, peeking in windows and looking for signs.

"Do you know what money smells like?" I asked him.

He thought about it for a moment. "Yeah, I think so."

"Well, try to smell money. Lots of it. That might help."

Then I heard a voice singing *Can't Buy Me Love.* I knew immediately that it wasn't coming from inside my head. None of them had this kind of vocal range. Or an acoustic guitar. I turned around and saw a guy sitting on the sidewalk just behind me, picking out the notes on his guitar and sounding nothing like Paul McCartney. Circling the ground around him were a variety of drawings, photographs, a couple CD's, and his guitar case, which was flipped open and served as an oversized tip jar. There was both green and silver inside, not much, but certainly enough to pay for lunch.

"Why are you playing that song?" I asked.

"I can play another one if you like," he replied. "I know quite a few."

He placed his fingers on the neck without looking and began to strum another song. I could never do that. I always had to look where my fingers were. I listened to the new song for a moment. I'm not sure, but it sounded a little like Mozart.

Steve wandered over and laid down outside his perimeter.

"This is pretty good," Steve said, pointing his nose at one of the drawings.

"I don't need a song," I snapped. "Or artwork. I need money."

"Can't buy you love," he said. "And it can't buy you happiness."

"What the hell made you say that?"

He pointed at me with his pick. "Your sign. Pretty bold."

"What is?"

"Your statement. I get it. *You* are the art. A sort of interactive Post-Realism."

"I'm trying to find money."

I stared directly at him and tried to be as firm and as clear as possible.

"We misplaced our money," I shouted. "About ten thousand dollars. And we just need a machine."

But he just sat there, smiling and slowly nodding his head.

"Steve, tell him."

"Avocados," Steve yelled.

The musician briefly looked down at Steve, then back to me.

"Why did you say, *Avocados*?" I asked him. "That made no sense."

The musician laughed, then strummed a G chord.

"It doesn't matter what I say," Steve said. "This guy ain't gonna understand me."

He strummed another chord.

"The Great Irish Potato Famine!" Steve exclaimed.

Another chord was played. F sharp, I believe.

"I can lick my balls!" Steve yelled. "Can you?"

The guy laughed and strummed again.

"Do you understand him?" I asked.

He smiled and hit another chord.

"What's the deal with airline food?" Steve sang.

I looked down at him. "Airline food? What do you know about airline food? You've never been on a plane?"

The guy laughed harder, and this time, he played more than just a single chord. He was pretty damn good, but it wasn't helping me any.

"Do you understand me?" I asked.

"Very much," he said. And just kept on playing.

"Then what are you doing?"

"I didn't think you'd mind integrating our work. One street performer to another."

"I need money!" I yelled. I really didn't know how much clearer I could be.

"That's cool," he softly sang. "You can take, whatever we make. There's much more at stake."

"Like burgers on a plate!" Steve crooned.

"That doesn't rhyme," I told him.

"You're such a tight ass," Steve complained.

I shook my head and started walking toward the end of the block. I wasn't more than four or five steps away when the musician started clapping and laughing even harder.

"That really works!" he shouted at me.

I kept walking.

"Wait up," Steve moaned.

When I turned the corner, not even five feet away, was the elusive ATM. I swear, it's like one ordeal after another anymore. Why do people find this sort of thing amusing?

I withdrew three hundred dollars and started to head back to the Burger King, but Steve stopped me.

"Dude, look! A Mickey D's."

It didn't matter to me. One's the same as the other. So, we made our way across the street.

I remembered seeing a dry cleaner earlier. It didn't have an ATM, but it did have one hour service, so I figured, what the hell? After lunch, we walked back to the car so I could bring in my suit.

The guy didn't seem all that pleased when I told him I wanted it back in an hour.

"I try," is what he said.

"What do you mean, *try*?" I asked.

"Very busy."

"Then you shouldn't offer it."

"We offer!"

"So, it'll be ready in an hour?"

He franticly scribbled something on the receipt.

"Try. Very busy. Close at five."

"Then your sign should say that," I insisted.

This got him very upset. His voice turned into a tight squeal.

"Sign say that! Sign say close at five!"

"Not that. You should change your sign to, *Maybe an hour, maybe not*."

He grabbed the suit in one hand, and stormed off to the back of the shop without saying another word.

"Now what?" Steve asked.

"I guess we got an hour to kill."

"Maybe," he laughed. "Maybe not."

Once again, we were back on the street with no idea where to go. We already ate, so hanging out in a restaurant wasn't the answer. Neither was a coffee shop, because I just had three cups at McDonald's and really couldn't stomach any more. There was a bookstore. I could waste a few minutes in there, but I knew Steve wouldn't be welcome. I didn't dare say that out loud, though. The slightest mention of *No Dogs Allowed* always set him off. I can't really say I blame him, but I just didn't feel like listening to it.

We walked to the opposite end of the block and turned the corner. Sitting there on the ground in front of me was that same musician. Another corner, another surprise discovery. Lucky me. I thought about doubling back, but it was too late, he caught us.

"Hey, Happy," he said. "I've been thinking about you ever since you disappeared."

"Have you now?"

"Never trust a hippy!" Steve announced.

"He's not a hippy," I told Steve. "Hippies have longer hair."

This guy's hair was just below his ears, but it looked like he hadn't done anything with it since he rolled out of bed. Then again, who knows, it could have taken him an hour to get it that way. It's not like I cared one way or another. Why would I? The only thing I was curious about though, was why he kept looking down at Steve and laughing.

Steve wondered, too. "Do you understand me?"

The musician immediately looked up at me with a big grin.

"Do you?" I asked. "Understand, I mean."

He nodded. "I get it."

Steve was in awe. "Whoa...!"

"But, I wanted to talk to you about it. To make sure I'm not missing any of it."

"There's nothing to miss," I told him. "Just listen."

He tipped his head back in deep contemplation and nodded. "Yeah. Right. I see. It's all there. Right in front of me. But not just me. In front of everyone. What you're saying is each of us has to make the conscious decision, for ourselves, on how we perceive it. You aren't a performer, but not the only one. I am, too. We're *all* performers! Including your dog. And at the same time, we are also all the audience. Subject observer, observer subject. If there's no line to cross, no wall to break down, you're free to be anything at any time. That's genius."

I felt this weird, unsure look growing on my face. The kind that emerges the moment you realize that the damp five dollar bill Grandma just gave you came from inside her bra.

"Do you have any idea what he's talking about?" Steve asked me.

"I'm not too sure," I told him.

The musician laughed again.

"Good," Steve said. "I thought it was just me."

"I love it," he said, motioning to me and Steve. "I'm Gavin, by the way."

"Daryl. He's Steve."

"Steve," Gavin hummed. "Great name. It's perfect."

"I had nothing to do with it. His last human named him. He's second hand."

"She didn't name me Steve. I did. And what's with the *second hand* shit? You make me sound like an old pair of pants."

"You named yourself Steve?"

"Hell ya. Much cooler than the stupid name she gave me?"

"What name was that?"

"If I wanted everyone to know my real name, I wouldn't have changed it."

I just shook my head, which caused Gavin to break into a fit of giggles. He pulled a small digital camera out of his pocket and aimed it at Steve.

"You mind?" he asked, then started clicking away before he was given an answer. "I love the vaudevillian element. The modern twist on classic ventriloquism. Highlighting the hierarchy of relationships. Showing how the domineering partner speaks for both by giving the impression they're listening to the submissive partner, when in reality, they aren't *listening* at all. You are showing the audience, which is both you and I, and I love that, that you, as the domineering partner, are imposing not only your *will* on the weaker companion, but your *words*, as well. In the end, you show us that in a human relationship, the submissive partner has as little power or influence over the dominant partner as a dog does in his relationship with its owner. It's just brilliant."

I didn't think I was trying to say that, but he seemed so excited about it that I didn't say anything more than just *thanks*.

"Hey, if you're not doing anything right now," he continued. "It's cool if you maybe wanna hang out. I'd love to share with you. Maybe...give a little help?"

"Do you think this guy's supposed to give you direction?" Steve asked.

"I don't know," I said.

"You don't know if you want to hang out?" Gavin glumly asked.

"No, I was answering Steve."

Gavin smiled. "Oh, I didn't hear him."

"He wants to know if you're my next signpost."

He thought about it for a moment. "That's awesome. Yeah. Yeah, I suppose so. You could be mine, too. That's the way it works, isn't it?"

"So far," I told him.

He raised his guitar toward me. "You play?"

"I used to. Quite some time ago."

"Wait here!"

He removed the guitar strap from his shoulders, then pushed himself off the ground, and jogged toward a van parked a few spots down the street. I couldn't determine the exact make and model, but it was older, and had definitely seen better days. He opened the back, pulled out a second guitar case, and made his way back to us.

Steve, in the meantime, was marveling at the drawings Gavin had spread out on the ground.

"He drew these?" he gasped. "Himself?"

"I imagine. Be kind odd if he didn't."

"How do you humans do that? They look so real."

"Just takes talent is all. Well, talent and practice."

"Could he show me how?"

"How to draw?" I asked. "I don't think dogs can draw."

"Racist."

"Okay, first off, you need to stop saying that. Dogs aren't a race. They're a species. So, I'd be a speciesist. If that were even a word. Secondly, it's not just because you're a dog. It's because you don't have a thumb. That's sorta key to drawing."

"Once I saw a show about a human who painted with her feet. You have thumbs on your feet?"

"Why do you make everything so challenging?"

"You guys okay?" Gavin asked, huffing and puffing as he handed me the second guitar case. I figured it was due to him being a bit overweight, and nothing else.

"Yeah," I reassured him. "Steve's just being goofy."

"No, I'm not," Steve insisted. "Ask him! Go ahead!"

"He wants to know if you could teach him how to draw."

And again, Gavin did not answer immediately. He leaned back and contemplated it, like it was some deep philosophical question that needed to be poured over before reaching a decision.

"Yeah," he finally nodded. "I can. If it worked, wow, that would be seriously badass."

"See?" Steve disdainfully shot.

I quietly opened the case he handed me and removed the guitar.

"It should be ready," Gavin said. "I just tuned it this morning."

"Good," I said. "It's been a while."

"Let me hear."

I strummed twice. It sounded good to me.

"Tighten your A," he said.

I gave it a quarter turn, then plucked the string.

"That's it. We can go back to my place later. I can give him a few lessons, and we can hang out and talk."

I heard laughter coming from behind us. Before I could turn around to investigate, the color drained from Gavin's face.

"*Tighten your A*," one of them repeated, in a rather insultingly affected gay voice.

"Yeah," said the other, in what I'm guessing was his normal voice. Which sounded pretty stupid on its own. "Gay-vin likes his A's tight. Ain't that right, Gay-vin?"

"You'll find that out later on at his 'partment," the first one said to me. "When the two a you *hang out*."

He waved his index finger like a pendulum in front of his crotch.

Their laughter was cruel and sarcastic. I could feel the muscles in my throat clench, and I didn't even know these fools.

Gavin froze, staring straight ahead out to the street, seemingly focused on nothing in particular. Like he was trying to ignore the entire episode until it was over.

I'm guessing that's what he was doing, because I do the same thing whenever I have blood drawn. If I didn't, I'd probably pass out.

"I don't like this," Steve muttered.

I patted my palm in the air, telling him to wait and see.

"I don't recognize you," the first one said to me.

"Maybe he's in one a these," the other slurred, and grabbed one of Gavin's pictures from the ground. "This you?"

"Hard to tell," the first one said. "He's wearin' clothes."

"Nah," the second laughed. "It's not him." And he ripped the picture in half.

Gavin remained motionless.

"You want me to bite him?" Steve asked.

I shook my head.

"I got it," I said.

The second guy reached down for another picture, but I quickly stomped my foot on it, missing his grimy fingers by less than an inch. He snapped back his hand and straightened up.

"Ten bucks," I demanded.

"For what?" the second one asked.

"You know for what, Tom," the first one laughed, as he blew kisses in the air.

"For the picture you tore. Ten bucks. Or I call the cops, and the price goes up. Way up."

"How you like this, Carl? Gay-vin's new butt buddy's a threatnin me."

"It's no threat," I calmly said.

"And what you gonna 'rest me for? I din rip no picture. Yer foot was on it. It ripped when I grabbed it. Ain't that right, Carl?"

"Yeah, that's right," Carl innocently grinned. "We did nothing wrong here."

"Destruction of property. Harassment. Threat of violence. Stealing. Ten bucks."

"Fuck you," Tom spit.

"*Fuck you* is fifty. But I don't see why you'd want to pay for that when you've got each other to do it for free."

"Did you just call me gay," Tom sneered. "I'll shove the neck a that guitar right up yer pansy ass."

"Good job, Slick. Shoving a wooden stick up my ass would really prove your heterosexuality. Twenty bucks."

"Twenty!" Tom roared. "Well then I better rip me up another one!"

As he bent down, I looked behind them and waved.

"Officer!"

"Yer full a shit," Tom said.

"No, he ain't," Carl nervously informed him. "It's Larsen."

Frankly, I was somewhat surprised when I heard the siren turn on. I didn't think I yelled that loudly.

I heard Gavin's camera clicking behind me.

"Thirty bucks," I coolly announced.

"You said ten," Tom complained.

"Sold. Cash only. Our machine is down."

"Good one," Steve snickered.

Tom squeezed a ten dollar bill from his pocket and promptly crumbled it into a ball and threw it at my chest, just as the squad car was pulling up alongside us.

"There a problem?" the policeman asked through his open window.

"Nope," Carl said, starting straight at me.

"These boys giving you a hard time?"

"They were just buying some art," I said. "Weren't you?"

They both squinted and bared their teeth, but quickly turned and walked away.

"And you," the cop said to Gavin. "I told you before: you can't sit in one place for more than an hour."

"He hasn't been here more than ten minutes," I told him.

"And I'm saying, move. Got it?"

He paused a second or two. Not for an answer, I don't think, but more for dramatic effect. Gavin started gathering up his things, and the cop drove off.

"Sorry about that," Gavin whispered.

"You didn't do anything."

"Yeah. That's the problem. I never do."

29

Woody was a bully.

I still hate saying that name, but that's beside the point.

I think I even knew it back then. The bully part, I mean. I didn't use the word at the time, but that's what he was. Not the blatant lunch-money-stealing or, I'll-kick-your-ass-for-no-reason, kind of guy. If he was, I wouldn't have hung around with him. His thing was ridicule. I never understood why, but it was like he got off on berating people. And most of the time, it was people he didn't even know. He'd just walk up to someone and unmercifully tease them for no reason. Boys and girls alike. In that case, he was very impartial. He even attacked friends - I got the treatment more than a few times myself. The only person he didn't launch into was Audrey. Why she was spared, I never knew. Not everyone was so lucky, though.

I remember the job he did on this girl named Olivia. We were juniors, she was a freshman. Quiet, unassuming, kept to herself. Invisible. Like most people in high school, actually. Unfortunately for her, she was also rather heavy. Not horribly, but just enough for Him to paste a target on her.

This particular episode happened in May. Our high school had a swimming pool, which meant everyone was forced to take coed swim as a gym credit, and that year, Olivia was in our class. Seven months into the class, and he didn't say a word to her. Maybe he hadn't noticed her before because we cut so often. Or, maybe he just figured it was her time. Anyway, it was the beginning of class this day, and everyone's standing around waiting for the teacher, Mister Poole, seriously, our swim teacher was named Mister Poole, when suddenly, He, Woody, catches sight of Olivia standing by herself in the corner. Alone, and stuffed into an orange one-piece.

"Holy shit," He called out. "Anita Bryant would die if she had to squeeze an orange as big as you!"

The room was primarily ceramic tile and water, so the slightest sound echoed like you were inside a mineshaft. His words were still bouncing off the walls when everyone turned and looked at Him, and then at his target. Poor Olivia, she had no idea what was about to happen. He taunted that girl for five minutes straight. That might not seem long, but when you have to stand there by yourself, in a bright orange one-piece with a little rip in the left seam, it's murder.

I've sat by myself and timed it on my watch, years later, trying to replay in my head each insult and every horrendous second of laughter.

You're the only beach ball that could drain a lake. Pause for ten seconds of laughter. *You're as big as the sun. Hey, when you take your pants off, does your moon cause an eclipse?* About fifteen seconds of laughter. *When you stand on the side of a street in your bathing suit, do drivers slow down, thinking there's road construction?* Not as much laughter, but a good five seconds anyway. *What's your name? Olivia? It should be All-Livia.*

Some of the comments didn't make sense, but it wasn't the words themselves as much as it was the pure disgust with the way they were delivered. But, some of the words were brutal. The worst was probably the two minutes or so he spent talking about her sex life. Well, the lack of it. Things like, *the reason no one ever dates you is you're so fat, they don't know which fold to stick it in.* And nobody made any move to stop him. Not even Olivia, who just stood there and took it, until she cried so hard that she puked. That's when Mister Poole finally walked in. He saw the puddle of vomit, and yelled at her some more.

She ran out of the room, and incredulously, everyone acted as if nothing happened. We just jumped in the pool and began class.

The thing that bothers me the most was the laughing. Not theirs, mine. I hated myself for it. I hated being part of it. And I hated not having the courage to stop it.

Olivia didn't come back to school after that. Nobody saw her again until the following fall. She grew two inches and was as thin as a rail. I didn't even recognize her until someone else pointed her out to me.

Of course, He took full credit for her transformation, telling everyone who'd listen that if he hadn't said anything to her before, she'd never look the way she did now. Believe it or not, he even took it one step further, and actually hit on her. He claimed a week or so later that he screwed her a couple times and then dumped her, but I don't know about that. There was never any proof. Yet, that didn't stop half the school from believing it.

I was firmly ensconced in the half that thought it was bullshit. It just didn't make any sense to me otherwise. Still doesn't. I wish I would have said something about that, too.

I followed Gavin's van for about a mile or so before he pulled into the short paved driveway of a one story house in yet another one of those bland, cookie cutter neighborhoods that I've been finding all over the damn place. Well kept lawn and landscaping, nothing out of place or falling apart. Made you sick to look at it. Made you curious, too, because from the little I knew of Gavin, this didn't seem like his kind of place.

A two car garage connected to the house, and I intended to pull alongside of him, but he parked smack dab in the middle, so my only options were to get right behind him or park on the street. As unfriendly as it seemed, I picked the street.

Steve and I hopped out and helped him unload. He still wasn't talking much, other than a few *thanks* sprinkled here and there, and a nod or two at what needed to be brought inside. I hoped this was only a phase, because I couldn't see how he was going to help me by keeping quiet. I needed more than just pointing and grunting.

His living room was not what I expected. Normally when you walk into a house, it's customary to see a couch, couple chairs, tables, a picture or two on the wall, and maybe a TV. Some people do choose to have a separate room for TV viewing, but other than that, that's the basic layout, with minor alterations from house to house. Boring, predictable, and ultimately, the same.

That wasn't Gavin's place at all. To start off, other than two folding chairs, there was no furniture. Floor to ceiling shelving units, jammed with albums and CDs, lined two full walls. There were thousands of them - organized alphabetically, and chronologically within each artist or group. He even had it broken down by genre. This guy had to have worked at a record store. Another wall was lined with stereo equipment, amplifiers, and guitars. It felt more like an attic than a front room. The last wall was the picture window, and in front of it was an easel, supplies, and a stack of canvases. On the window itself was painted a mural of a road that stretched out beyond the horizon.

It was quite impressive, yet strangely, that wasn't the first thing that crossed my mind. My first thought was, *he's not married.* Even if I wanted a room like this, Julie would never allow it.

He set his case down by the other guitars, and without a word, wandered off into another room. That's when I began thumbing through his library like an overeager teenager. I couldn't believe the array of music. It was like my collection. I immediately moved to the Punk section. That was my music. What I listened to the most. Until Julie, that is. She claimed punk was nothing but noise, with no redeeming value. To her, there was no difference between the Dead Kennedys and the Dead Milkmen. British punk or American punk. I don't know what it was with her. Maybe sound waves distorted as they moved through her ear canals, who knows, but she insisted it sounded all the same, and she wouldn't listen to any of it. Or let *me* listen to any of it. In fact, she wouldn't even let me bring my collection over from my grandfather's house. In the beginning, I actually had to sneak albums over one-by-one and hide them in our basement. Even then, I could only listen when she was sleeping. Sitting in the dark at three a.m. and blasting NOFX in a pair of headphones, but having to suppress the urge to scream out the lyrics, wasn't nearly as fun as it should have been. All the sneaking around made me feel like I was cheating on her, and I didn't care for it a bit.

I was reading the back of an album when Gavin walked back into the room.

"What's that?" he asked.

"Nine-Nine-Nine," I said, scrambling to find it's proper place back on the shelf. "*High Energy Plan.* Love this album. Haven't listened to it in forever."

"I didn't take you for a punk," he continued. "I would have thought Jazz. Or classical, even. Something like Schoenberg."

"I like all kinds of music," I told him. "But, this was my favorite when I was younger."

He carefully removed the record from the sleeve and placed it on the turntable. The first notes to *Homicide* played, and all the years since I last heard it were erased. I remembered every lick and every snarl, like I just listened to it yesterday.

"But not anymore?" he asked.

"Huh? Oh, I still love it. Just don't listen to it as much as I used to."

"What do you listen to now?"

"Whatever anyone else is playing."

He smiled and nodded. "Exactly! I get it."

"This dude's freaking me out," Steve said. "Let me out, huh? I'm gonna see if I can get laid, or something."

"Alright," I said, walking toward the door.

"That's something you should seriously consider," he mumbled. "Before you explode."

"Be quiet," I told him. "And don't get lost."

"No worries. I'll take a squirt in the driveway."

I looked back at Gavin. "You mind?"

"What? Let him out? No. Be my guest."

Steve scampered out, and I closed the door. When I turned back around, Gavin was standing in the middle of the room, looking slightly nervous.

"Do you smoke?" he asked.

"Not anymore. I did for a few years when I was a teenager. Almost two packs a day."

"I didn't mean cigarettes."

I can't remember the last time I even smelled pot. Or whatever it's called these days. I swear, it was everywhere I went back then. If I wasn't getting high myself, there would always be a cloud hanging nearby: the back room of the record store, alleys, cars, concerts, etc. In fact, that was the code Jerry, my boss at the record store, used for getting high. *It's supposed to be cloudy tomorrow*, meant he was going to score some weed the next day. Sometimes he'd get real slick and tell you where the clouds were coming in from. *Clouds are coming in from Mexico.* Or Hawaii, Colombia, whatever. Not only was it stupid, it was ridiculously transparent. I mean, if anyone listening had even the slightest knowledge of weather forecasting, they would have caught on immediately. I could be wrong, but I don't think there's ever been a cloud system that moved from Colombia straight north to Chicago.

Gavin closed the drapes and turned on a row of track lights just above the wall of instruments. He dimmed it to where he liked it, but still had the consideration to ask my opinion.

"Are you okay with this?"

I nodded, and sat cross legged on the floor.

He made a beeline to the CD rack, slipping out an oversized Bill Monroe box set.

"You listen to bluegrass?" I asked.

"Listen?" he smiled. "No."

At first, it struck me as odd that he walked right past the stereo and sat down without putting on the disc, but sometimes, I'm a bit slow on the uptake. The reason was simple. There was no disc inside to play. The box was his vault. I got the joke, but personally, I would have picked a different artist as a hiding spot. I'd be afraid that getting high would forever be associated with banjo music, and it would ruin the fun. Especially if I ever had the misfortune of experiencing a bad reaction, which did occur from time to time. You'd be in a weird mood from the beginning, or maybe you had something troublesome lurking in the back of your mind, and rather than it mellowing you, the pot would have the opposite effect. You'd freak out and couldn't calm down.

That sensation mixed with banjoes...I don't know. Seems like the perfect combination to drive you over the edge.

"You good with a joint," he asked. "Or should I get the bong?"

"Whatever's easier."

Rolling must be easier than having to get up and walk, because that's what he started doing.

"So, who were those guys?" I asked him.

He didn't look up, or exhibit any other indication that he had even heard the question. His eyes remained focused on the rolling.

"No one," he finally sighed, continuing uninterrupted with his work. "Just the Moron Brothers."

"Does it happen a lot?"

I waited, but he didn't respond.

"Why do you let them do it?"

I waited, but he said nothing, so I leaned my head back, closed my eyes and listened to the music.

Let's face it/the boy can't make it with girls...

The music caused me to become aware of time. At least two minutes of the song had played, and Gavin had neither spoken, nor lit up, and I knew rolling didn't take that long. I reopened my eyes and saw that he was now staring straight back at me with a look of utter confusion.

"I don't know," he whispered.

"You don't know what?"

"Why I let them do it. Why I let any of them do it. Honestly, I wish I was stronger. Like you."

"I'm not so strong."

"You stood up to them. Immediately. And I froze. Just like always."

"Yeah, well, it's not like I have a lot to lose. Who knows? If that cop wasn't there, they might have killed me."

"I doubt that."

He lit the joint and took a long toke.

"The way you just swept in," he said, desperately trying to keep any smoke from escaping his mouth. "It was like being rescued by Errol Flynn."

He exhaled and passed it to me.

"Did you say, Errol Flynn?" I asked. It was hard to tell exactly with his voice being so pinched at the time.

"Yeah. Like, *Captain Blood.*"

"A pirate." I said, inhaling deeply. I didn't gag, and nothing oozed out. Just like riding a bike.

"Yeah. How he swung onto the ship, and freed all those prisoners from the galley, remember? What did he say? Something like, *You're free men now. You can leave, or you can join me.*"

"Yea, but you're not a prisoner."

"Who says I'm not!" he blurted out. But then he caught himself and quickly unclenched. "Sorry. I didn't mean to yell at you, but I am a damn prisoner, Daryl. In this town, like George Bailey. Sorry to mix my movie metaphors."

"You married?" I asked. "Have kids?"

"No."

"Well, that's what kept him in Bedford Falls. What's holding you back?"

He fell silent again and took another hit. Once more, I waited for him to speak, but he remained silent.

"Believe it or not," I continued. "That's what I'm doing. Trying to find pirates."

He had that look on his face again, like I just revealed some deep mystery of life that he didn't quite understand. The look people have after unsuccessfully twisting a Rubik's Cube for anything more than a minute.

"What do you mean? Someone stole your material?"

"No. Actual pirates. Not *actual* pirates. There's this group of people who get together in secret. For two weeks every year, they live with no restrictions, like pirates."

"Seriously? Where?"

"Not sure exactly. Somewhere in Nevada."

"But, how do you find out *exactly* where?" He suddenly became very excited.

"It's a secret. I was just told to follow the signs."

"What signs? Like street signs? Billboards?"

"There's all kinds. They're very discreet."

"So, it's not legal?"

"Everyone uses fake names, so, probably not."

He took another hit and passed it to me again.

"You have a fake name?"

"Only an international smuggler-slash-spy name. I don't have a pirate one yet."

"I'd *love* to be a pirate. That would be perfect."

"Well, why don't you?"

"Yeah, right," he smirked. "You saw how I was back there. I mean, I have it in me. I really do. Inside, I'm like, I'm like this mad man. A pirate. I am a pirate! There's so much I want to say. So much I want to do."

"Then go say it and do it."

"If it was only that easy, Daryl."

"Why isn't it?"

He sighed. "Promise you won't laugh?"

"No danger there."

He reached over, lifted a guitar from its stand, and rested it on his lap.

"I…I don't know what to do!" He nervously drummed his fingers on the body. "I know. Sounds stupid, right? It's just...where to start? Well, that's just it right there! What to do, and where to start! There's so much I like, so much I can do, I don't know what to aspect of my art to focus on. But at the same time, I don't want to give up any of it for the sake of focusing on just one."

"So, why can't you just do it all, then?"

"My tastes are all over the place. People would think I'm a schizo. It wouldn't make sense."

"Who cares what people think? Always be true to yourself. Don't let others define you. I say that to myself in the morning."

"Okay, okay. Punk, for example. I love screaming *fuck you* to conformity. Not being like the rest of society. The problem is, I like too many other things that are considered acceptable to society. It feels hypocritical."

"Like what?"

"Well," he shrugged, and gave a short pause. "Okay. Sometimes I like to listen to the Grateful Dead. But punks *hate* the Dead. You see the problem?"

"Who cares? It isn't about them, it's about you."

"Do you like them?"

"I have a couple albums somewhere, because of an old boss, but that doesn't matter. Look, didn't you just say punk was about nonconformity? What could be more nonconformist than a punk listening to the Dead?"

"I don't know," he said, trailing off into thought.

"Now I'll give you an example. Did you ever wonder about the punks who claim they don't want to be like the rest of society, but all dress the same? Same ripped jeans and t-shirt, same haircut, same Misfits patch on their jacket. How the hell is that different? The movement was created so they could separate themselves from everyone else, yet if you really are different, you can't be one of them? That's stupid. Punk shouldn't tell you how to act. You're supposed to do whatever you want. Is there some authority on what's punk and what's not? Fuck authority! You do what you want."

His eyes popped wide open, and he lifted himself off the floor. "You're right! Goddamn it, you're right! I'm putting on the fucking Dead."

He lifted the Nine-Nine-Nine album off the turntable and slipped it back into the inner sleeve, then picked out a CD and dropped it into the player.

"You know what else?" he declared. "I like show tunes!"

"You're not going to put any on any of those, are you?"

"Not now."

The music started and he sat back down in front of me.

"*Eyes Of The World.* Listen to Jerry's guitar on this song."

His head slowly bobbed up and down to the music while he rolled the next one.

"Were you ever in a band?" he asked.

"Yeah. A couple in high school. I was lead guitar and vocals for The New and Improved Quartet."

"Who came up with that name?"

"Not me. Anyway this friend of mine convinced the rest of the band that we needed a better singer."

"Better than you?"

"Yeah."

"This was your friend who said that?"

"Yeah."

"Who was this?"

"Chester Woody."

"That's worse than the band's name."

"Yeah. I didn't like that, either. Anyway, he talks his way into the band..."

"Wait, hold on," he interrupted. "This Chester guy said they needed a better singer, and he was talking about himself?"

"Yeah."

"Didn't that piss you off?"

"He was my friend. I didn't think about it because, you know, now he was in the band with me. But looking back on it, yeah, it kinda does piss me off."

"So, that's why you were called the New and Improved Quartet?

"No, that was our old name. Once he joined, he convinced them into changing it to the New and Improved Quartet Plus One."

"That's even worse. Was he any good?

"No. He didn't sing as much as he tried to take over. Every show, every rehearsal, all he did was tell everyone else what to do. The other three didn't like it, so he talked me into quitting with him and forming a new band."

"How'd that work out?"

"That fell through. He never wanted to practice, or audition anybody. Most times we just ended up sitting around getting drunk."

I looked around the room and saw another stack of paintings leaning against a wall.

"I really like your work," I said. "You know, I wanted to be an artist for a while."

"No kidding?"

"Yeah. Really got into it, too. But, I started getting interested in music, and that sucked away my time. Which do you like to do more? Do you have a preference?"

"I don't know. That's part of the problem."

"What came first? Art or music?"

"Hmm. You know how a little boys can turn anything into a pretend gun? I was always one of those kids who could turn anything into pretend drums. Drove my parents crazy. They liked it better when I drew. I remember once I...whoa!"

It was like he suddenly remembered that he left the stove on, or something. I really hoped we didn't have to clear out quickly, because I wasn't in any shape to drive.

"What's the matter?" I asked.

"My first clear memory of drawing!"

"What about it?"

"An ad for an art school in the back of magazines. *Can You Draw This?* You remember? They had you draw a turtle or..." He smiled and waved, urging me to release the memory.

Then it hit me.

"A pirate."

"A pirate!" he gasped. "That's what I drew! Isn't that fucking weird? How it all connects sometimes?"

"Yeah. You know, speaking of that, I was in the Army."

He instantly exploded with laughter.

"What's so funny?" I asked.

"We weren't talking about the Army."

"No. I know. But, *things connecting*. Something from earlier made me think of it. I was in the Army..."

"That's what you were saying," he giggled.

"Wasn't my choice. My grandfather forced me to join. But I couldn't fit in. Anywhere. I had no friends. I hated it. Fucking hated it! And I don't know why, but this rumor started up about me."

"What kind of rumor?"

"That I was gay."

"Really?"

"I'm not. Wasn't. Then or now. But everyone believed it, so it was enough to get me discharged. Just before *Don't Ask, Don't Tell.* I wish I would have stood up for myself a little more."

"Why? Did you want to stay in the Army?"

"No. I wanted out. Any way I could. So, I didn't deny it because I knew they'd kick me out. But, it still bothered me that I didn't stand up for myself. That's the connection. I see the same thing with you. You didn't deny it because it would have antagonized them more, and kept the fight going. You need to stand up for yourself."

"But, Daryl," he calmly spoke. "There's nothing to deny. I am gay."

"Come on, be serious. I'm trying to make a point."

"I am being serious. I'm gay. Does that bother you?"

I answered without having to even mull it over. "No. It doesn't. It's just kinda surprising."

"You're right about the other point, though. I didn't stand up for myself. Not that they deserve any kind of explanation. It just pisses me off. So fucking much! I mean, I know what I want to say. I have all the words. But, I can't get myself to say them."

"Are you afraid of getting beat up, or something?"

"Maybe I was before, but now, now I don't care. I almost wish someone would kick my ass. Maybe I could use it as motivation. I don't know what I'm afraid of. Okay, that's a lie. I know exactly what I'm afraid of."

"What?"

"People not liking me."

"No offense, but they already don't like you."

"Getting laughed at, Daryl."

"They were doing that, too."

"Not them exclusively. In general. It's like this song." He pointed back at the stereo. "What if you woke up and found out that you really were the eyes of the world. If you, and you alone, were able to show everyone else what's right and good. But no one believed you, and they laughed in your face?"

"Like you were a god?" I asked.

"Yeah, I suppose."

"That's impossible. No one god can convince everyone in the world what's right and good. People have tried for centuries, and it's never worked."

"Thanks," he glumly shot. "You just ruined the song for me."

"What if the line means *your* world? What if it's saying, one day you'll wake up to find out that *you* are the eyes of *your* world? You are now in control, and no one else? You are the one and only god of your life."

"Holy shit, Daryl! Holy fucking shit!"

His arms began to shake. I knew it. I had a feeling about this stuff being stored with banjo music.

"That's it! All these years, I've been looking at it from the wrong perspective! Inside out, instead of outside in. It's so simple. I get it! That story about Chester Woody wasn't real, it was an allegory. You had me going for a minute. Thinking that you'd let somebody control you like that. I can't believe it's that simple! You did it. You woke me up!"

He jumped to his feet and began walking in circles and punching short jabs in the air.

"It all connects!" he shouted. "It's all connected!"

There were times in the past when I'd get high and think I had stumbled upon an answer to one of the secrets of the universe. I'd get excited and scribble my illuminating discovery on anything I could find before the thought slipped away. Then I'd spend the next day trying my best to decipher it. None of it ever made sense sober. It was a little awkward sitting there watching someone else go through the same process, because it made me wonder just what the hell I must have looked like back then.

I heard scratching at the door. "Daryl! I'm back! Open up!"

Making it to the door on foot didn't seem all that important, so I just crawled. Sure, I had to reach up a bit for the doorknob, but it wasn't that big a deal.

"What the hell's going on?" Steve asked.

"With what?"

"You walking around like me, and him screaming. You two in a fight?"

"No. I just woke him up, is all."

"And he hit you?"

"Nobody hit anyone. I said something that made him happy."

"Did it work on you, too?"

I considered the question. "No."

Gavin spun around and faced us.

"Steve!" he joyfully exclaimed. "I am my own eyes! Isn't Daryl amazing?"

"That's what you told him?"

"Yeah."

"What are you? High?"

"Yeah."

Gavin laughed. "You guys are great. I love you guys!"

He dropped down to his knees and gave us both a hug.

"Is this guy gay, or something?" Steve asked.

"Yeah." I replied.

"I can't leave you anymore. I miss too much."

Gavin leaned his face up to mine. "I'll do it if you do it."

"What?" I asked. He had me a little worried.

"Be the god of your own life. Be your own eyes."

"Okay."

He nosed in even closer. "Promise me."

"I promise."

"Thank you, Daryl." He smiled and bent toward me, then at the last second, changed course and planted a big wet kiss on Steve's mouth.

"Dude!" Steve shouted. "Boundaries!"

"I have so much to do," he mumbled to himself.

"Then go do it," I told him. "Nobody's stopping you but you."

He fumbled to his feet and ran out of the room.

"What got into him?" Steve asked.

"Reefer."

"Is that what that smell is?"

"Yeah. We had a little."

"A little my ass. You're wasted."

"No, I'm not."

"You gonna have more?"

"Maybe. Why?"

"'Cause I want some."

"You want to get high?"

"Why not? We're out of beer."

"True."

I couldn't really say no. I was smoking it myself. That's a pet peeve of mine. People who say no to other people about things they do themselves.

Steve giggled. "You're talking out loud to yourself again."

"Was I?"

"Yes. Now, gimme some of that. What do I do?"

"I'll blow it into your nose. Just inhale and hold it in as long as you can. Got it?"

"Yeah. Simple enough."

"Ready?"

He nodded, so I lit up, took a deep drag, and exhaled slowly toward his nose.

"Hold it in!" I croaked.

He nodded again. Then coughed. And it all leaked out.

"That's not how you do it."

"Come on, bro, it's my first time. Gimme a break here."

He held it in a little longer the second time, and got a little better with each consecutive attempt. By about the tenth or eleventh hit, you would have thought he'd been doing this for years.

When the second joint was gone, Steve rolled over on his back and stared up at the ceiling. I leaned against the wall and quietly listened to whatever Grateful Dead song this was. They were in the middle of some really long instrumental, and I kinda forgot what it started out as.

"Dude," Steve said. "Am I really seeing stars, or am I hallucinating?"

I lifted my head to the ceiling and took a look.

"He painted the ceiling."

"That is awesome!"

Steve started coughing in a series of short, controlled bursts. I knew what that was immediately.

"Dry mouth?" I asked.

"Yeah. What the hell?"

"It happens. I'll get you something to drink."

I must have stood up too fast, because I lost my balance and fell sideways into the wall. It's easy to forget these things when you've been out of practice for so long.

I staggered into the kitchen and went straight to the refrigerator. Suddenly, I was very hungry. There wasn't much inside, but I grabbed anything that looked edible, then scavenged through the cabinets.

Luckily, I found a serving tray, and loaded all my discoveries onto it: plastic wrapped slices of American cheese, a half jar of pickles, a box of saltines, lunchmeat that was at least a week past it's sell-by date, but smelled fine, celery, an open bag of Doritos, an unopened bag of Oreos, and a box of Chardonnay.

It was a very big serving tray.

I turn on the faucet and splashed some cold water on my face before filling up Steve's bowl.

The water felt good.

I grabbed hold of the tray and ever-so-carefully walked the tightrope back toward the living room. But, before I made the pivot, something caught my eye. There, leaning next to the back door, was something oddly familiar. And not quite right.

"Gavin!"

The word sounded strange. Not just the word itself, but the actual sound of it after it left my mouth, like it wasn't my voice that said it.

I tried it again.

"Gavin!"

Nope. It was my voice. Garbled. And rubbery. And definitely a different color than usual. A light gray smeared with rust.

I didn't like it.

My arms began to ache. I looked down, and somehow completely forgot I was holding the tray. How in the hell could I forget that? How weird.

What was I doing? Oh, yeah.

Can't believe how tired I am.

Steve was still laying on his back, staring at the ceiling and wildly licking his lips.

"Dude, I can't get my tongue wet!"

"Here."

I set the tray down on the floor, and moved the bowl in front of him. He flopped over on his stomach and dove right in. I didn't count or anything, but I'm guessing he licked it dry in less than twenty seconds.

"Ahh!" he exclaimed, loudly smacking his newly dampened lips together. "You know what? You are awesome. Seriously. You're seriously awesome."

"And you're stoned."

"No, I mean it. You saved my life. You bring me on your trip. You take care of me. You're just, really awesome. I love you, bro."

"Okay."

"Okay," he repeated. "Your voice sounds goofy."

"That's what I was thinking. Hungry?"

"Nike lever before. Like never before. Like. Never."

I opened all the bags and jars, and spread it all out on the floor like a buffet table.

"Spears!" he yelled.

"What?"

"Pickle spears. Love them." He greedily gobbled one down.

"Oh yeah," I said. "That reminds me. You'll never guess what I found in the kitchen."

"Pickle spears."

"No."

"Yeah, you did. I just ate one."

"I didn't mean them. I meant something else."

"What?"

"A baseball bat! By the back door, exactly like my idiot grandfather had it. Does he intimidate little kids, too? Maybe I was wrong about him."

"Who?"

"Gavin. I mean, what's with the bat?"

"Maybe he has it to protect himself. Like Ben did."

"What?"

"I mean, look at him. He's kinda like Ben, wouldn't you say? He obviously doesn't fit into this neighborhood, either. I'll bet there's probably a lot of people around here that want him to move out, too."

"What are you talking about? *Move out*?"

"Ben had that bat in the kitchen because people were threatening him, right? Trying to force you guys to move."

"No. He had that bat there to scare me into listening to him."

"*No*. He had the bat to *protect* you. From the asshole neighbors. They weren't real thrilled when they heard about your mom being pregnant. It was even worse when they found out she was committed to Manteno. At first, people just stopped talking to him. Then things got a whole lot worse."

A fragment of a memory came back to me. "Someone threw a brick through the front window."

"Yeah. That's what he said."

"There was a note attached, but..."

"The note said it would be best for all of you to move. He thought the stress is what killed your grandmother. Losing her friends devastated her. Her and Ben used to go out a lot, with those very same neighbors. But after everything with your mom, the interactions stopped being friendly. That's why he got the bat."

"He told me it was there just in case. I thought he meant just in case he needed to beat me with it."

"Seriously? What old man would beat his grandson with a baseball bat? Dude, that's rough. Even for you."

"Again. I wish he would have told me."

"He didn't want to upset you. What good would it have been to get you worried that someone might break in? I'm tired."

"Me, too."

"Do we have to find a hotel right now? Can't we just take a little nap? This carpeting is soft. Like grass. And the breeze feels so good."

"Yeah, I s'pose. Gavin! Hey, Gavin! Oh, well. He can wake us up when he wants us to leave. You wanna go outside first? Take a pee? Steve...?"

He didn't answer. Dog can't handle his weed.

30

Somebody was poking me in the arm with a whole salami. It was still cold from storage, and slightly damp from who knows what. It was Olivia Putnam, the girl from swim class. Only, it wasn't skinny Olivia like I last saw her. It was fat Olivia, and she was wearing an apron with the name of my restaurant on it. Which is weird, because we never had custom made aprons. I always wanted to get some, but my father-in-law thought it was an unnecessary expense. An indulgence, is actually what he said.

Screw him. The apron looked good. I just needed to know where she got it, because I wanted to order more.

I don't know what the hell she's doing with the salami, though. We don't sell salami.

"Daryl! Come on!"

"No. I'm not putting salami on the menu."

"What salami?"

The laughter that followed wasn't from Olivia. It was Steve. Come to think of it, I don't think I ever heard Olivia laugh, so I wouldn't know what hers sounded like anyway.

"Hey, wake up," he giggled. He jabbed his nose into my arm. It was cold, and slightly damp. "Dreaming of salami? That's kinda different."

I opened my eyes and struggled to focus. Sunlight was pouring through the drapes, and my neck and back were stiff as hell. Guess that's what I get for sleeping on the floor.

"Something wrong?" I asked.

"Nope," Steve replied. "Just bored. Been up for a little while. Wouldn't mind going out for a bit."

"Why didn't you ask Gavin to let you out?"

"He's not here."

"Where'd he go?"

"How should I know?"

"Didn't he say anything?"

"He was gone when I woke up."

I pushed myself up and stretched. I hate it when I have to stand up before I can do my inventory.

"Does it seem like there's something missing?"

"Like what?"

"I don't know. But, I swear there was more stuff here before."

"I couldn't say. Maybe." Steve patrolled the room and gave a couple sniffs here and there.

"Why would he just leave? Without saying anything?"

"Hey, check your phone. Maybe he left you a message."

I reached inside my pocket, but the phone wasn't there. It wasn't anywhere else, either.

"That's gone, too."

"He took your phone? Shit! The car better still be here!" Steve darted off to the window and peeked behind the curtains.

"Why did he leave?" I mumbled to myself. "I thought I helped him."

"Car's still there. Man, oh, man, Aaron woulda been pissed! Speaking of that, open the door, huh?"

"Yeah, me, too. Then let's get out of here."

I pulled open the door for Steve, then doubled back toward the bathroom. I tried to avoid looking in the mirror, but the damn thing was so big, it was impossible not to notice.

I stared at the face looking back at me. It was getting to where he was barely recognizable anymore.

The voices inside my head were getting louder.

"Who is that guy?"

"Who *was* that guy?"

"Whoever he is, does he have a future?"

"Have you been eating enough roughage?"

I choked back two pills, and gargled a slug of mouthwash from a bottle I found on the counter.

"You will be happy. Always speak your mind. Always tell the truth. Be true to yourself. Don't let others define you. And be the god of your own life."

I turned out the light, and walked to the car.

Come to think of it, it has been a while since I had a salad.

We gassed up and got back on the road, heading west to who knows where. Steve sat up front next to me and didn't say a word for most of the trip. He even stayed buckled in without the slightest complaint.

Which, of course, made me very suspicious.

But that wasn't the subject on the top of my mind. Gavin was. Why did he just cut out like that? Of his own house, even? It made no sense.

At first, I wondered if something happened in the middle of the night while we were sleeping. Maybe those bullies from the street came by and he ran. Except, if that were the case, I'd think they would have roughed me up a bit. Unless they kidnapped him, which I guess is possible. It would make sense then that I was untouched, because they wouldn't want any witnesses to their crime, so they just left us to sleep.

Then again, he was pretty excited last night. What if he came back in the room, but saw we were asleep, so instead, went outside to burn off some of the extra energy? Then at some point, passed out on someone's lawn? He could have been picked up as a vagrant. What if he's sitting in jail right now, waiting for me to bail him out? What if I was his only phone call, and I'm nowhere to be found?

But that wouldn't matter anyway, since I don't have my cell phone. What if that was it? What if he wanted to make a call, so he lifted it from my pocket? But there was no signal inside, so he went out to the street? And that's when those guys found him and kidnapped him?

I remembered the last moments we were together. He leaned in a little too close saying thank you, then turned and kissed Steve. Did I react in a weird way? Did I give him the impression that I was worried he might kiss me? Okay, I was kinda worried, but in truth, I'd be worried if a straight guy did the same thing. But he doesn't know that.

Did I embarrass him? Did he leave because of me? After all my *helping*, did I make him feel like there was something wrong with him?

Shit. I'm such an idiot.

We passed a sign notifying us of a Starbucks just five miles ahead.

"Coffee?" I asked Steve.

"Dude, it's like you read my mind. Hey, that was fun last night. We shoulda taken some of that pot with us."

"That would have been stealing."

"He took your phone."

"We don't know that. I could have left it somewhere."

"Maybe. We coulda left some money for it. The pot, I mean."

"Yeah. We could have done that."

"Anyway, we should stop at a store and pick some up."

"You can't buy pot at a store."

"What?" he moaned. "Why not?"

"It's illegal."

"Are you serious? Beer, too?"

"No, beer's legal."

"Really? We should stock up on beer then."

"Okay."

I caught a whiff of the coffee, so I gave the wheel a short tug to the right and drove down the exit ramp.

One of the benefits of chain restaurants like Starbucks is, you always know what to expect. Which is good because I really needed this cup of coffee. And when you feel a need that strongly, you don't want to endure an inferior, or unfamiliar, product. While it might not be the best coffee around, it certainly isn't the worst, and that's what makes people partial to it in cases like this. You want what you know without worry of failed experimentation.

No surprises.

"I just want a house blend," Steve said. "The largest size. Whatever they call it."

"Venti," I told him.

"I'll be happy to take your order, sir" the man behind the counter said. "But first, I have to ask you to put your dog outside."

"Species-ist!" Steve muttered. "Did I say that right?"

I looked down at him and winked.

"That's not my dog."

"But," the counter guy insisted. "He came in with you."

"So, if I held the door open for your mother, would that make her my wife?"

Steve thought that was hysterical. The guy didn't.

"Your dog has to leave."

"And I'm telling you, it's not my dog."

"Fine."

He stepped around from the counter, and reached out his arms in what I'm guessing was an attempt to shoo Steve toward the door. It didn't work. Instead, Steve dropped into a crouch and gritted his teeth.

"You touch me," Steve warned. "And you'll never pour coffee again, bud."

The guy carefully inched backwards until he was safely behind the counter again.

"You say he came in with me?" I asked.

The guy nodded.

I turned and faced the rest of the room. There were only a couple customers inside, none doing anything that looked to be too important, so I walked around from table to table, with Steve following closely behind.

"Does this dog belong to anyone?"

They all looked aggravated that I even asked. The only one who didn't act like I was begging for change was some teenage girl sitting by herself. She just looked up long enough to weakly shake her head "no", and then went back to absently stirring what looked to be iced coffee.

"That's not your dog?" The guy asked once more. "Then why's he's following you?"

Steve laughed again.

"Look," I plainly stated. "How about you just give me my order, and I'll get out of here. If he came in with me, maybe he'll leave with me, too."

"What if he doesn't?"

"Call the cops, I guess," I said, and then pointed toward the parking lot. "Look, I have to drive another four hundred miles or so today, and I need to wake up."

The guy looked out the front window.

"That your Mustang? The convertible?"

"Yeah."

"That's an awesome old car."

"And getting older by the second. Two venti house blends, please?"

He paused for a moment, weighing his options, I suppose, then begrudgingly rung me up and poured the two cups. After I added the appropriate amounts of cream and sugar, I bent down and spoke to Steve in the same exaggerated manner adults sometimes talk to babies.

"Hey, doggie! Hey, boy!" I said. "Would you like to come outside? Would you? Huh?"

"You sound like an idiot," Steve giggled.

"Would you like some coffee?" I continued. "Some house blend with cream and sugar?"

"Please stop talking like that."

"You shouldn't give dogs coffee," the guy shouted to me as we were stepping outside.

"You couldn't even chase him out of your store," I shot back. "And I'm supposed to take advice from you?"

I took a couple steps toward the car, but Steve came to a stop.

"Hey," he said. "You mind if we drink it here first? It's not that easy for me to drink coffee while we're moving."

There was a little courtyard off to the side, no surprise, so we grabbed a table and sat down. Steve propped his front legs on either side of the cup, and cautiously flicked his tongue inside.

"Mmm," he hummed. "I needed that."

"Not feeling well?"

"Physically, I'm fine. No hangover, or anything."

"What then?"

"Feeling a little weird, I guess."

"How so?"

He took a swallow of coffee, then plopped back into the chair and sighed. "I got a couple things on my mind that I need to work out."

"Okay."

I took another sip then stretched out my arms. While in mid-yawn, I happened to catch the guy inside the store staring out the window at us.

So, I directed the rest of the yawn at him and waved.

I couldn't hear what he said, but I'm pretty sure it wasn't "*Thank* you."

"Ready?" Steve asked.

"You're finished? I still have half a cup."

"Yeah, well," Steve stammered. "I don't know. Let's just go, huh?"

"Okay."

After I made sure he was safely buckled in next to me, we found our way back to the highway.

We were about ten miles down the road when Steve started sniffing the air.

"I smell something," he announced.

"What now?" I asked.

"A female. Definitely a female"

"You want me to stop?"

"No, not a dog. A human."

"Someone from the coffee shop?"

"Maybe," he said. "I don't know."

He sounded strange. Not quite himself.

"What happened?" I asked.

"When?"

"Maybe something go bad for you last night?"

"I'm not sure."

"If you want to talk about it..."

"Okay, maybe," he sighed. "Four different females, *four*, but, I don't know, I..."

"Just tell me."

"Alright. Believe it or not, I wasn't interested. Not with sex in general, but sex with them. Three of them were dumb as cats, and the other one was *just so annoying*, I thought I was going to put my head through a wall. My whole life Daryl, I never cared one way or another about who they were, or what they were like. But now, I suddenly wanted it all to mean something. And you *really* wanna hear something sick? I started thinking how nice it would be to have one female. *Forever.* Someone I could talk to. Someone who liked what I liked. Someone I could grow old with. What the hell is happening to me? It's like I'm turning into one of you."

"You want me to help you?"

"That's why I got in the car."

That was a new voice, and it wasn't from inside my head. It was from the back seat. And I swear, if Steve didn't react the way he did, I would have been fine.

"It's a girl!"

He jumped out of his seat belt, and landed in my lap, directly on top of a rather sensitive area. Instantly, my eyes began to water, and for a moment I could only see stars. What's weird is I didn't even notice that the car was in a spin.

Not until the girl screamed.

"Ahhhhhhhhhh!"

I gripped Steve tightly by his collar, and tried to redirect the car into the proper flow of traffic. Truth be told, there was probably a good ten seconds though, when I had no idea which the correct direction was.

The answer came when I saw the cars pointing straight at us.

That, was the wrong way.

We were spinning to my right, so I when we spun back around and put the cars in the rearview mirror, I straightened it out and applied slow pressure to the brakes. As soon as we hit the gravel of the shoulder, I pressed a bit firmer and came to a complete stop.

It took me a while before my heart slowed down, though.

"How are you doing?" I asked, clearing my throat.

"What the hell is wrong with you?" The girl screamed. "Why did you do that?"

"You scared me."

"I scared you because I was telling you why I got into your car? That makes sense."

She was being sarcastic. That was easy enough to deduce. The scowl was the big tip-off.

She pushed her thick, black, Buddy Holly glasses back up the bridge of her nose, and tugged the red knit ski cap down below her ears. The scowl, apparently, needed no adjustment.

"No," I said. "I got scared because I didn't know you were in the car."

"You were talking to me."

"No I wasn't."

"*What's wrong?*" She said, poorly attempting to imitate my voice by comically lowering hers. *"Something bad go down for you last night? You want me to help you?*"

"I was talking to my dog."

"Ha ha. Real funny. Is this thing okay to drive, or what?"

I shifted into neutral and tapped the accelerator.

"Everything's okay. Take a deep breath."

"I'm breathing fine," she snapped. "Just shut up and drive, okay?"

I shifted into gear and pulled into the right lane.

"Why did you get in the car?" I asked.

"Let me out then," she said.

"All I did was ask you a question. You're in my car, after all."

"Oh, I get it. You car, your rules. No kidding, was it mandatory for every adult to go to Asshole Camp, or do you all just become that way?"

Geez, this girl is snotty.

"Did I say anything wrong? No. I just asked why you were in my car. I don't think that's all that horrible or intrusive."

"Fine. At the Starbucks, you said you were driving far away from there."

"So are a lot of cars that stop there."

"You have a convertible. It was easy to get in."

"That's it?"

She sighed loudly and kicked the back of my seat.

"Because of your bumper sticker, alright? *Help is not a four letter word.*"

"Oh," I said to myself. But, she heard.

"What?"

"This isn't my car."

"Don't try to pull the same crap on me that you pulled on that idiot selling you coffee, okay?"

"I'm serious this time. It's not my car. I'm borrowing it."

"And here I thought maybe it was a sign. Lucky me."

Steve gave me a look. "You hear that?"

"You're looking for signs, too?" I asked.

"Look for them, yeah," she muttered. "Just never find them."

"You need help?"

"I need a ride. Can you help?"

"I meant more like, why do you need help?"

"Will you drive me, or not?"

"Where are you going?"

"*Anywhere!* Just as long as it's far away from here. Look, if you won't, I'll find someone else who will. Maybe some big muscly truck driver with tattoos in strange places, or some drooling little perv in a panel van."

I watched her in the mirror. She said it all straight faced. No sign of a smile or a smirk. In fact, judging by the tone of her voice, it was almost like she was daring me to stop and let her get picked up by some psychopath.

"I'll take you. At least I know you'll be safe with me."

We drove past a small cluster of businesses, one of which boasted a large digital sign displaying the time and temperature.

2:56. That figures.

It was a rather peaceful drive. Traffic was nonexistent. There were long stretches were it seemed as if we were the only car on the road, which was welcome. That, and Steve nodding off. Not that he really bugs me, or anything, it's just that sometimes I enjoy the quiet, and when he's awake, there's less chance for quiet to happen.

And as odd as it sounds, until she finally spoke up again, I had forgotten there was a girl in my backseat.

"This is so incredible *boring*!" she moaned.

"Sorry," I replied. "Didn't you bring anything with you? A book?"

"I can't read in the car. I get nauseous."

"A radio?"

"A radio?" she scoffed. "What is this? Nineteen seventy? Yeah, I brought my Walkman, too! I just can't decide what eight-track to pop in there. Pat Boone, maybe?"

"I'll put the car radio on."

"You won't pick up any stations out here."

I turned the dial just to prove her wrong, but for some reason, nothing was coming in clearly. Could be an antennae problem.

"Told you."

"Do you have any CDs?" I asked. "This has a player."

"No. All I have is my iPod, but I can't even listen to it. It's too damn loud with the top down."

"You want me to stop and put it up? Maybe then you won't be so cold, either?"

"I'm not cold," she snarled. "What makes you think I'm cold? Oh my god, what are you looking at?"

She pinched the material of her thin, spaghetti strap top and pulled it away from her chest so she could give herself a quick, yet somewhat private, examination.

Not to be mean, but even if that is what she thought I was looking at, I'd have to have telescope eyes to notice any activity in that area on her.

"Your hat!" I shouted.

"What about it?" she asked.

"You're wearing it because you're cold, right?"

She shook her head in disgust and flopped back into the seat.

"What about earplugs?" I asked. "Don't you have any?"

"*Buds!* Ear *buds*. Oh, my god. And, yeah, how the hell else do you think I tried listening to it? On my magic invisible speakers?"

"I'm pretty sure this has an iPod hookup, but I don't know where."

"Are you serious?"

She dove over the front seat and examined the stereo, waking up Steve in the process.

"What the...?" he grunted.

"It's right there. Why didn't you say anything before? Jesus, I was ready to shoot myself in the head back there."

"Be careful," I said.

"I'm not going to break it," she snapped back.

"I didn't mean the stereo. I meant you. You should have your seat belt on."

"Okay, grandpa."

"I'm forty two," I told her.

"Oh, god," she mumbled to herself.

She removed a chord from her bag, plugged in, and within seconds we had music.

Very loud music. But rather catchy just the same.

"I can't believe this old beater has an mp3 player. It's so steam punk!"

She slid back into her seat, and immediately started singing along and playing air drums.

"Who is this?" I asked.

She must not have heard me, because she just kept on singing, so I asked louder.

"Who is this?"

"You never heard of them," she quickly answered during an instrumental break.

"Try me."

She shook her head and sighed.

"All Time Low."

"I've heard of them," I said. "They sound good."

"Please don't say that. You'll just ruin them for me."

Steve let out a little laugh. "She's cute."

"Yeah," I said. "Thanks."

"Are we gonna stop soon?" Steve asked. "I'm hungry. And I gotta take a whiz."

I tilted my chin up. I don't know why, seeing as how I wanted to talk to someone in the backseat, but I did it anyway.

"You hungry?" I asked her.

"Yeah," she nodded. "I don't have much money, though."

"Don't worry about it. How's a burger sound?"

"I guess," she shrugged.

"If you have a preference."

"Maybe some place a little healthier than a greasy fast food joint. They're so gross."

"Like what? A sub, or something?"

"Better than burgers," she said.

"Kid's nuts," Steve said. "Ain't nothing better than a burger."

I was about to tell her what he said, but it was time to sing along with the lyrics again, and I lost her.

We drove a couple more miles until I found a sign for a place called *The Sub Standard*. I understood that it was play on words, but it seemed like a misplay. Why would anybody want people to think their restaurant was substandard? You may as well call it, *Stay the Hell Away, This Place Sucks*. But, since there were no other sub shops in the area, we had no choice. I turned off at the appropriate exit and pulled into the lot.

"Keep quiet when we go inside, okay?" I said.

"Keep quiet about what?" the girl asked.

"Not you," I said. "I was talking to him."

I pointed down to Steve.

"You think he understands you?"

"More than you think."

"How do you know?"

"I...it's, it's complicated. I just do."

"Must be nice."

"Can we cut the chatter and go inside?" Steve said. "I'm starving."

"Not always," I told her.

My order took all of five seconds: two foot long roast beefs on whatever bread and condiments it came with.

The girl's order was slightly different.

"I want a foot long turkey. But, I want it on multigrain bread. Toasted twice. With no sauce and no cheese. Just the turkey and the veggies. Lettuce, onion, pickle, green pepper, jalapenos, and tomato. Extra all that." Then she looked at me. "Is that okay?"

"Sure," I told her. "Just as long as I don't have to eat it."

"It's so much healthier this way. The rest of that junk will kill you."

"What to drink?" the clerk asked her.

"Large Coke."

"How is that healthy?" I asked.

She sighed rather loudly. "You're not going to start with me now, are you?"

The clerk smiled and waited for me to flash one in return. Instead, I handed him my debit card.

"Where do you want to sit?" I asked her.

"I don't care," she said. "Just not by a window."

I carried the tray to a table that was far enough away from both a window, and other people. It kind of felt like I was a freshman in high school again.

"So, what's your name?" I asked her, as I unwrapped Steve's sandwich.

"Why?" she muttered.

"Y?"

"Yeah. Why?"

"Okay. Don't get testy. What's the *Y* short for? Yvette?"

She sighed again. Loudly. "Really? Not the letter *Y*, the question *why*. As in, *why do you want to know? Why do you care? Why does it matter?*"

"*Why are you being such a pain in the ass?*" Steve shot back.

She didn't answer that one. Not that I expected her to.

"It would just be nice if I knew your name, is all."

"Because it's your car, your rules," she spat.

"No. I never said that. If you don't want to tell me your name, that's fine."

"And what then? You'll just leave me here?"

"I didn't say that, either. If you don't want me to know your name, don't tell me. Whatever you want. Trust me, I've felt like that before. There's a lot of people I wish never knew my name."

And with that, we all began eating. Steve even showed some manners by taking the time to quietly chew each piece and completely swallowing before taking another bite.

"How is it?" I asked to no one in particular.

"Not bad," Steve said. "Not bad at all."

I looked over at the girl, and instead of repeating the question, I just raised my eyebrows. I always thought it was interesting how such a simple facial movement like that was considered a universal signal for inquisitiveness.

I wonder how that started. Maybe it went all the way back to caveman days. Since they couldn't really communicate with each other verbally, anything new they saw, which was pretty much everything back then, they'd just raise their eyebrows out of curiosity. Makes you also wonder if any of them ever got a decent answer. I mean, if they couldn't speak, and didn't know yet what raised eyebrows meant, they probably thought the person trying to ask them something was having a stroke. It must have been tough not being able to communicate with people.

"It's Sinatra," she said.

I immediately turned my head and looked around the room.

"Where?" I asked. Then it hit me. "Wait. He's dead."

"This again?" she said. "My name. It's Sinatra."

"Really?"

"Yeah."

"No, it isn't," I said.

"Okay, fine. It's not."

"What is it really?"

"*Sin-ah-tra*," she sharply pronounced.

"You're serious."

"Yes."

"No kidding. Are you related?"

"Only to idiots."

"So, what's your first name?"

"I just told you."

"No, you didn't."

She tensed her face and puffed a cloud of air out her nose. Well, not an actual cloud, but close enough.

"Oh. My. God. This is a joke, right?"

"Really? Sinatra's your first name?"

"Yes. And to answer your next question, no, they don't call me Sin. Nobody does."

"That's not what I was going to say, but, really? Nobody does? That's kind of a cool nickname."

She looked at me, dead serious, with no hint at all of a smile, and spoke calmly and slowly.

"Um, no it's not. It's pathetically stupid."

"Okay."

"What's your name?

"Daryl."

"Do people care you Dare?"

"No. Nobody ever did. But that's kinda cool. Why didn't I ever think of that?"

"Because it's not cool," she whispered. "Please don't call yourself that. Especially around me."

I looked over at Steve, who was apparently waiting for me to notice him. I could tell because he raised his eyebrows.

"Oh. And this is Steve."

"Steve? Really?"

"Better than *Sinatra*," Steve shot back.

"Both your names are just fine," I told him. "So, Sinatra, where you headed?"

"I don't know."

"Really? You just hit the road?"

"Yep. Where are you going?"

"I don't know, either."

"You making fun of me?"

"No. It's..."

I stopped short of finishing, and sipped at my Coke.

"You were going to say, *it's complicated*, weren't you? But you stopped yourself because you didn't want to risk making it seem like you were blowing me off again."

"Yeah. How'd you know?"

"Because you're trying to *relate* to me."

"You don't have to say the word like you're describing your weird aunt's Christmas sweater."

She laughed a little. I think.

"Hey," Steve said. "You think she's going where we are?"

"Maybe," I said.

"Maybe what?" Sinatra asked.

"No. I, I was talking to Steve again."

"You said *maybe* to your dog."

"Yeah."

"Why?"

"Because he asked me a question."

"Your dog."

"Yeah. He wondered if you were heading where we are."

"Okay. You're weird."

"To think that we'd both be going to the same place?"

"Yeah. Right. That's the weird part."

"All right," I started. "If I tell you something. No, forget it. You won't believe me."

"You don't know that."

"I know it seems strange, but, we understand each other. Steve and I. For some reason, when he talks, I hear it as actual words. Everyone else hears it as barking."

"Do you mind," Steve said. "I told you, I hate that word."

"You're right," she said. "I don't believe you."

"It's true."

"Okay. Prove you're not just crazy. Or a liar."

"Well, I don't know how to do that if you can't hear him, too."

"I know," she proudly announced. "You go outside, and I'll whisper something to him while you're gone. And when you come back, have him tell you what it was."

"Okay."

"And don't look back and try to read my lips. Go out. Don't turn around. Count to ten, then come back in."

"Fine."

I got up and did as she instructed. I walked outside, stood by the curb with my back to the door, and counted. When I hit ten, I walked back in, and sat down.

"What did she tell you?" I asked Steve.

"It makes no sense," he said.

"I don't care. Just tell me."

He took a moment to remember the exact order, then let it out.

"Seven jack snowmen. Limber lumber dig a hole in the brain pocket of fancy that. I hear my elbow."

"What does that mean?"

"Hell if I know."

I must have had an odd look on my face, because when Sinatra saw it, she began a desperate attempt to fight back an attack of the giggles.

"I don't know if I'll remember it all," I told her.

"Give it a try."

"Seven jack snowmen limber lumber," I said. "Limber lumber..."

"Dig a hole..." Steve prodded.

"Right, I got it. Dig a hole in the brain pocket of fancy that, I hear my elbow."

The invasion of the giggles was instantly repelled by an unexpected counterattack of shock.

"How did you do that?" she asked. Her mouth was open so wide, that when she spoke, her lips didn't touch each other.

"He told me."

"It's some kind of trick."

"It's no trick."

"Okay. Okay. Come here," she commanded Steve. "Get behind me. And you look the other way."

I turned my chair away from her as she requested.

"Can he count?" she asked.

"Does she think I'm an idiot?" Steve snarled.

"Yes," I told her. "He can count."

"How many fingers am I holding up behind me?"

"How many, Steve?"

"Three," he said.

"Three," I echoed.

"Now five," Steve said.

"Now five," I relayed.

"Now six. Four on one, and two on the other."

"Now six. Four on one, and two on the other."

"Now it's two," he said. "Each middle finger."

"Now, you're flipping off Steve with both hands," I told her. "Or me."

As I shifted my seat back around, she quickly rummaged through her backpack until she found a pen and some paper.

"Can he read?" she asked.

"Yeah," I responded. "Quite well, actually."

She opened the notebook to a random page and held it in front of Steve's face.

"Tell him what that says," she demanded.

"*I can't take this*," Steve read. "*I thought Jordan loved me, but he won't stand up to my parents. I can't live with their toe-tali-tarian rules. But I also can't be with someone who doesn't want to fight for me. I don't mind fighting for what I want, but I refuse to be the only one who does the fighting.*" He stopped reading then looked over to me. "And she has a lot of those heart symbols, but they're ripped in half."

"You're running away?" I asked her.

"What?"

"Your parents don't like you going out with Jordan, but Jordan won't stand up to them, so you're running away from home."

The color drained from her face, and her head swiveled back and forth between Steve and me.

"How did you...? I had it in my bag the whole time. You couldn't have read it."

"If I can help you," I started to tell her, but she interrupted.

"I feel sick."

She grabbed her bag and ran off to the ladies room.

"So," Steve said. "Does that mean she believed you?"

"Seems like."

"Poor kid."

I was sipping my soda, and had to stop myself from spitting it out on the table.

"What did you say?" I asked him.

"*Poor kid*. What did you think I said?"

"*That*. Just not the type of thing I ever expected to hear from you, is all."

"I don't know, bro. The more I'm around you, watching, and listening to your stories, the more I start to understand a bit what it's like to be a human. It must suck losing someone you've gotten attached to."

"Why didn't you understand any of this before? You've had lots of contact with other humans."

"My human wasn't really like other humans. For one thing, she was real old."

"So? What does being old have to do with it?"

"She had no family. The whole time I was with her, the only relationship she ever had was with Ben."

"What do you mean, *they had a relationship*?"

"That's what it's called, right? When you spend a lot of time together? Go places? Do things?"

"You got the word right. I just find it hard believe. Did they spend a lot of time together?"

"Shit, yeah. All the time. He'd sleep there, even though he lived right behind us."

"He spent the night? Did they ever...?"

I couldn't say the word, so I just raised my eyebrows. I'm really not sure why I'm doing that so much lately.

Steve nodded. "I think so. Sure sounded like it."

"Oh, gross!"

"I guess they must have loved each other. Now that I think about it, she spent a lot of time crying right around the time you said Ben woulda died. She never talked about it, so that's why I never knew. But she used to watch so many movies where women cry when guys don't come around anymore, I just figured they broke up. She was a wreck. Wish I woulda known, 'cuz I woulda been nicer to her."

"Could she understand you?"

"No. Only me and Ben."

"Yeah, see? I don't know what you could have done."

"I still feel like shit about it. Damn, this sucks."

"I didn't know you liked her that much."

"I'm not talking about that. Feeling emotions. *That* sucks."

The bathroom door creaked open and Sinatra headed toward us, clutching her bag with both hands. For a moment, I thought she might break into a sprint and run for the door, but she didn't. She kept moving at that ridiculously slow pace back to the table, like she was performing a drunk test for a cop, and then sat down.

"What are you going to do?" she quietly asked.

"About what?"

"Are you going to tell anybody? Call the cops?"

"Why?"

"Because, I'm legal age! I am!"

"Okay."

"And I'm not doing any crime."

"I never said you were."

"So, what n-now?" she asked. It wasn't cold inside the restaurant by any stretch, but she was shivering. Good thing she had the hat.

"You mean, *right now*?"

"Yeah."

"I'm finished eating, so I was going to leave."

"Oh," she quietly whispered.

"You don't want to go with anymore?"

"I do."

"Okay. Let's go."

"Wait. Why do you want to help me? Do you mean it, or are you really some kind of creep?"

Steve laughed. I shot him a look to shut up, but it didn't work.

"Why is he laughing?" Sinatra asked.

"How do you know he laughing?"

"It's pretty obvious, isn't it?"

"He thinks he's being funny," I told her.

Steve laughed even harder. "You should see your face, bro!"

"But, he's not," I finished.

I put all the trash on the tray, and walked in the direction of the garbage can. Halfway there, Sinatra stopped me and grabbed what was left of her sandwich.

"I might get hungry later," she said.

When we got to the car, Sinatra climbed into the front seat. No questions, no hesitation. It was like she belonged there. I could tell Steve wasn't too thrilled with having to sit in the back, but amazingly, he didn't say a word about it. Simply hopped in and kept quiet.

Then, as if it were the next step in our daily routine, she plugged in her iPod and pressed play. I had no idea who the band was, but they seemed to make her happy. I slipped into reverse, but before tapping the accelerator, I turned the volume a little louder.

"Do you mind?" I asked.

She smiled. "No. Are you kidding?"

She ripped off her hat and deeply inhaled into the wind. Her hair was bleach blonde with streaks of green running through it. It was cropped shorter than on any woman I've ever seen, but it seemed to fit her.

So did the smile. It fit her nicely.

"You didn't ask me about the volume," Steve sulked.

Him, not so much.

I don't know exactly how long it was that we were driving, other than the fact that we listened to five albums all the way through. She made a point of telling me that she wasn't like the other kids her age who would sometimes only buy a song or two by a band – she bought the entire album. Even if she didn't really care for any of the other songs. She needed to have it, she said.

And I could relate. I was always an album collector. Never singles. Unless, of course, there was a song I liked that wasn't released on an album, then I'd buy it. For one, they were difficult to manage because of their size. And they scratched a lot easier, because the sleeves were usually cheap, and no matter how careful you were, they always ripped, so the records rubbed up against each other. I didn't like singles.

I know things are different now – you can fit an entire musical library in a piece of plastic and metal no bigger than your hand – but it was nice to hear that there were other people out there who needed the whole album.

I was familiar with the names of all the groups she played, either from people at the restaurant, reading about them, or simply seeing them on TV. Most of what I heard was pretty good. She laughed and called me old when I told her I never heard of a movie called *Motion City*, therefore, I wasn't aware of its soundtrack.

Nice kid.

"*A total calamity the choices I have made!*"

Being laughed at and getting called old isn't particularly enjoyable. Which is probably why I didn't say anything about the rest of her music. Not even about some band she described as being *screamo.* Obviously not my first choice, but she seemed to like it.

Steve, on the other hand, had no problem complaining. "D, I can't handle this shit much longer!"

Finally, after what seemed like hours, that album ended and her next selection began. Hearing the opening notes to this one was almost as jarring as the last one.

"REO Speedwagon?" I shouted.

She let loose with a raucous laugh. "Oh, my god! I *love* this album! It's *sooo* cheesy!"

Being that it was their greatest hits, I knew every song, but chose not to sing along with her.

"Is this what you listened to when you were my age?" she asked.

"Me personally? No."

"So, you only know it because you heard it from a friend who, heard it from a friend who..." She laughed again.

"I mean, I know the songs, it's just that I usually listened to other stuff."

"I was making a joke."

"Yeah, I know."

I've heard variations of that stupid joke every time someone mentions REO. I know kids can be sensitive about stuff like that, so I didn't say anything about that, either.

She continued singing along with every song. Not as enthusiastically as before, though. I thought maybe something was wrong, so I peeked over at her. The sudden relaxation was due to a change in focus. She was now drawing the name of a band on her forearm with a black pen.

"That's wrong, you know," I told her.

She tossed her head back and clicked her tongue. "Let me guess? I'll get ink poisoning? Cancer? Boys will think less of me?"

"No. There's no *E* in Nirvana."

She threw the pen on the floor and quietly watched the scenery as it passed by on her right. With no singing.

Somewhere around the sixth song, I started to get really tired. I guess I hadn't been paying attention to the fact that the sun went down quite some time before.

"We have to find a room," I blurted.

"What do you mean?" she nervously asked.

"I'm really tired. It just hit me all of a sudden."

"I," she stammered. "I don't want to."

"We have to."

"Can't we just keep going?"

"Can you drive a stick?"

"No."

"Well, if we wait any longer, I won't be able to either, 'cause I'll be asleep."

"I don't want to stop."

"Sinatra, come on. You'd have your own room, if that's what you're worried about."

"No. I just don't want to."

"I'm tired. You're tired. We have to sleep somewhere. How about the car? We can pull into a parking lot somewhere. Put up the roof. It will be like we never stopped. Would that be okay?"

She thought about it for a moment.

"Okay."

There was an exit up ahead, with a twenty four hour diner just down the street, and I pulled into a space toward the back so we'd be out of the way.

Steve jumped out and ran toward the bushes while I put up the hood. Then I went to the trunk and grabbed a couple sport coats from my suitcase.

"What were you doing?" she faintly asked.

I showed her my supply of jackets.

"I don't have any blankets, and it might get cold."

"*Get* cold," Steve complained. I'm freezing already."

He stretched out in the back, and I threw one of the coats over him.

"Will you roll up the windows?" he asked.

"Yeah, I will."

"You will, what?" Sinatra asked.

"Roll up the windows," I told her.

"How did you know that's what I was going to ask?"

"Intuition, I guess," I said.

She obviously still doesn't have the whole, *I can talk to dogs* thing down yet. Oh, well.

I rolled up the windows and wrapped her up with the rest of the coats.

"So, you never told me," she said.

"Told you what?"

"Why you want to help me."

"I didn't?"

"No. Tell me why you want to help me."

"For a few reasons, I suppose."

"Like..."

"For one, you need help."

"Do you help *everyone* that needs help?"

"No, but you came to me. That made me somewhat obligated."

"You could have just said no. Or, brought me to the police."

"I had a feeling the police couldn't give you the kind of help you need."

She yawned. "Do you have any kids?"

"No. Well, not really. Almost."

"What do you mean?"

"I probably shouldn't talk about it."

"Tell me."

"I'm not sure if that's such a good thing to do."

"Figures that you'd turn out to be one of those adults."

"What kind of adult is that?"

"The one's who don't tell kids the truth. The *because-I-said-so* crowd."

"That's not what I was doing. It's just kind of private, that's all."

"Forget it then." She turned her head away and pouted.

"All right. You have a point. Just recently, I found out that an old girlfriend of mine had an abortion."

"Really? And you never knew before?"

"No."

"How'd you find out? What happened?"

"How about if I tell you tomorrow? It's a long story, and it's kinda late..."

"Please! I want to hear it now. Tell me!"

"Okay. A long time ago, I went out with this girl named Audrey. I loved her very much, and I thought she loved me, too. I even thought we'd get married. Then one day, she started acting strange around me. I didn't think much of it at the time, but the next thing I knew, she broke up with me and disappeared."

"What do you mean, *disappeared*?"

"Vanished. She was never heard from again. I had no idea what happened. Then, a few years passed, and I ran into an old friend who told me where she lived."

"Did you find her and talk to her?"

"No."

"How come?" she asked.

"Well, I didn't really know what to say. Besides, I was married to another woman at that time, and it just didn't seem right. I was curious, though. I drove past her house a couple times, but never saw her. Then one day, I decided I wanted to see her. We talked, and she told me what she did."

"Did she tell you why she disappeared?"

"No. I assumed it was because she was pregnant. Which is why she was acting weird, too."

"How was she acting weird?"

"She used to be this incredibly affectionate woman. I mean, always, and anywhere."

"Skip the pictures, okay?"

"I don't mean that. I mean, holding me, hugging me, touching me, kissing me. Stuff like that. When we were together, there was no mistaking that she was my girlfriend. Now I wonder if she was acting like that just because she was drunk a lot."

"Did she act like that with other guys?"

"The only other guy we were ever really around was Chester Woods. I mean, she'd be silly with him sometimes."

"Who's that?" she grimaced.

"He was my friend. The guy who later on told me where she lived."

"What a horrible name. How'd he know where she lived? Were they still friends?"

"They were never really *friends*. Not to say they were enemies, or anything. I mean, they were comfortable being around each other, you know? For example, he'd give her rides places when I was working. Back and forth from her house. Stuff like that. Even when she started acting strange towards me, he'd drive over and talk to her for me."

Steve interrupted. "So, this douche bag was spending time with her when you weren't around? *Before* all that started happening?"

I looked over my shoulder. "Yeah. So?"

"What did Steve say?" Sinatra asked.

"He was asked if Audrey was spending time with Him before she starting acting weird."

"And," Steve added. "Before she got pregnant."

"What's he saying?" Sinatra breathlessly asked.

"*Before she got pregnant*," I repeated. "He's saying she spent time with him before she got pregnant. Yes," I answered. "Right before."

Something didn't feel right.

"Did you ever think, maybe," Steve continued. "That's why she started acting flaky? Maybe it wasn't your baby. Human guilt is pretty powerful shit. Those damn *Lifetime* movies are always saying so."

"What?" Sinatra pleaded.

"Steve says the baby wasn't mine. That it was Chester's, and that's why Audrey was acting that way."

Sinatra clicked her tongue. "Oh. My. God."

"You think so, too?" I asked.

She rolled her eyes and sighed loudly. "It's always the same story with you men."

"What do you mean?

"It's always the women's fault, isn't it? We're such bitches."

"That's not what I said. I didn't say it's always their fault. Not all the time."

"Just most of the time, then?"

"Well..."

"Poor Daryl. So manipulated and controlled by women. Well, what if it was true? What did you do to stop it from happening? Why did you let them get away with it? I bet I can guess. Because you *couldn't*.

Because you were so detached from your emotions, it didn't make a difference how they acted. Their behavior gave you the perfect excuse to play the victim, instead of taking charge. The truth is, you *let* them do what they did, didn't you? You refuse to take the responsibility of making any decisions yourself, that way, you can't ever hold yourself accountable for making the *wrong* decision. Plus, that would be too much work for you, wouldn't it? You want an easy life. So easy, you expect us to do all the work. So, we accept it. We do all the work, make all the decisions, but then when it's a decision you don't like, you start crying about it. *This isn't what I want*! Well, you want something better? Then you better work for it! Life isn't a restaurant. You can't send back a meal you don't like. Sometimes the food sucks. Deal with it like a man! I can't do all the fighting by myself!"

She took one quick breath to try and collect herself, but all the pent-up anger and frustration exploded into an ear shattering wail. Her glasses fogged up and the tears streamed down her face.

I followed my first instinct by putting my right arm around her shoulder, and squeezing her left hand with the other. I thought for sure that she'd throw me off, push away, yell some more. But she didn't. It calmed her. She squeezed my hand back and buried her face into my chest.

Steve put his front paws on the back of the seat.

"We shoulda brought some pot," he said.

"Shh!"

I shook my head and motioned for him to lay back down.

"Hey," I whispered to Sinatra. "It'll be okay."

"No, it won't," she sobbed. "I loved him."

"*Did?*" I asked. "Or still do?"

Her only response was to continue whimpering into my chest.

"Running away doesn't help or solve your problems. That's what Audrey did to me. It only made things worse."

She lifted her head and stared directly into my eyes. She looked like a scared baby. I wanted to hold her even tighter.

"I'm not the one running away!" she insisted. "He left me!"

"He did? I don't remember hearing that part."

"We used to be one. Together. But, as soon as my parents started pushing for us to break up, he backed away. It's as good as leaving me. If he loved me, he would have fought for us."

"Why were your parents against you? What did they do?"

"What didn't they do? I'm the fifth of ten kids. It takes too much time for them to deal with each of us on a personal level, so they make these ridiculously strict rules that they expect everyone to follow, To the letter. There's no negotiating. What they say goes. They don't care about me as a person. They just want order. I can't live like that."

A clump of hair was sticking out sideways, so I gently pressed it down and draped it behind her ear.

"Look," I told her. "I don't know this Jordan, but, before all this happened, was he nice to you?"

She swallowed a mouthful of air before answering. "Yes."

"Was he ever mean to you?"

"No."

"Did he ever make you feel like you were unimportant to him? Like your parents make you feel?"

"No."

"So, you loved him, and he loved you. Very much, I'm guessing. Then this happened, and he didn't react the way you hoped. Do I have it right so far?"

"Yeah."

"Okay. Maybe all this caught him by surprise, too. Maybe he didn't know what to do, or how to do it. Maybe right now he's mad at himself for the way he reacted. Maybe he thought you overreacted, and was freaked out. Sometimes people move at a slower pace than others. It doesn't mean they've done anything wrong. It could just mean they haven't come up with an answer yet."

"Then why hasn't he come for me yet?"

"Does he know where you are?"

She swallowed. "No."

"Then he could be looking everywhere but the right place. Don't give up on him, okay? Go back home and talk to him."

"Would you come with me?"

"Oh, honey, I can't."

"I thought you said you wanted to help me?"

"I have to find some people of my own."

"Can I come with you then? Please?"

I thought about it for a moment, and the answer spit out a lot quicker than I expected it would.

"Sure."

I could feel the smile on her face without even looking.

"Thank you, Daryl."

"Let's get some sleep."

The back of her head slowly slid down my stomach and came to rest on my right thigh. The last thing I remember was putting my hand on her shoulder, and pressing deep into the seatback. It was a little cramped, but I needed to close my eyes as soon as possible, so I wasn't going to argue.

31

The next sensation I felt was my heart - racing at what seemed to be ten times its normal speed. To say I was startled awake by Sinatra's screaming would be something of an understatement.

"Daryl! Help! Stop! Ahhh! Daryl!"

Steve's voice mixed in. "Daryl, dude! Wake up!"

It took me a moment or two to process where we were, what was happening, and that it was all real, and not just some nightmare I was having. Finally, when I "came to", so to speak, Sinatra was sitting on my lap and crying just as hard as she was before we fell asleep.

And Steve was perched in her lap.

Brave companion I've got.

"What the hell's going on?" My voice was raspy, like I hadn't spoken in over a week.

"Some guy, I don't know who...!"

"There was this guy, I swear I know who, but I can't...!"

Their loud, shrill voices were bombarding my ears far too rapidly to properly make sense of what they were saying.

"Stop!" I demanded. "Just, please, one at a time."

Sinatra gulped for air, then started again. Much slower, and in a register closer to her normal voice.

"I was sleeping, and the noise musta woke me up. Some guy, some guy was trying to break into the car!"

"What?"

"She's not shitting you, D!" Steve added. "There was. I know him from somewhere, too. I just can't place it."

"What was he doing?"

"Breaking in!" she yelped. "He had a coat hanger. He was trying to jimmy the lock on my side."

"I got it!" Steve gasped. "It was the guy from Marcy's restaurant! Remember? He was trying to break in there, too!"

"Are you sure?"

They answered simultaneously. "Yes!"

"What did he look like?"

"I don't know. He had a ski mask on," she said. "The kind with the eyes cut out."

"He ran over that way," Steve pointed his nose toward the right side of the parking lot. "Let me out. I'll find the bastard."

"No, you stay here," I told him. "Watch Sinatra. I'll find him."

As usual, I didn't have my watch, but judging from the sky, I'd have to say it wasn't too long after daybreak. Even so, the parking lot was more than half full.

I gave one last look back at the car before starting my search. "Lock up," I screamed. "And start honking if you see him!"

I walked slowly and deliberately through the lot, looking between the cars, as well as inside of them. What I didn't ask Sinatra and Steve was how long ago he ran away. By now, whoever it was could have already cleared out. But since there was no way of knowing for sure, I continued to look for anyone who seemed suspicious to me.

For a while, I saw no one. Not just anyone that might be suspicious, but no one at all. Then, I spotted someone. A man zigzagging a path about twenty yards to my left.

"Hey!" I screamed. "You! Stop!"

He looked over at me, and paused for a moment, but then continued on toward the buildings.

"What do you want?" I shouted. "Why are you doing this?"

He broke into a sprint. I thought about chasing him, but he was too far ahead. I would have never caught him. Then I saw someone else inside of a car. And the car wasn't running. That was odd. Maybe that first one wasn't my guy, after all.

I ran up to the car and pounded on the hood with both fists.

"Is it you?" I called out. "What do you want?"

He was about fifty, maybe fifty-five, in a dark brown suit and a yellow and green striped tie. I peered in the windows for a ski cap, but I didn't see one. Which meant nothing at all, really. He could have shoved it under a seat, or in the trunk. He could have just ditched it altogether.

"Hey!" I shouted. "Answer me!"

By now, he had jammed the keys in the ignition. He seemed a little too nervous, and even tossed me a shifty glance before he sped away. That had to have been him. I mean, why else would he have looked at me like that?

"You don't think I know?" I screamed to the sky. "I might have been sleeping before, but I know now!"

Then I heard a car honking, over and over again, from somewhere in the parking lot. Sinatra and Steve! I told them to honk if they saw him. I spun around, briefly losing my balance, but catching myself before I fell.

I'm not sure how it happened, but just like that, the parking lot was now full. I turned in slow circles, looking as far off as I could, but I had no idea where they were. Or where I was in relation to them. I could still hear the honking, faintly, but it was impossible to narrow down precisely where it was coming from. There was no movement anywhere. No markers. No signs. Just me surrounded by a sea of cars.

"Where are you?" I waved my head to the left and right as I yelled, hoping to broadcast my voice to the widest possible area.

The honking continued, yet seemed to grow quieter by the second.

"I can't see you! I'm afraid I'm lost! Help me!"

Just then, someone grabbed my right arm from behind.

"Sir?" the voice sternly said. "What's the problem?"

I jerked around and saw two policemen. The one who had my arm let go, and they both reflexively put their hands on their gun butts.

"I'm going to have to ask you to calm down and tell me what's the matter."

"I can't find my car," I told them. "Isn't that pretty evident?"

"So, you're yelling at it?" the first one asked. The second one smirked, and I swear, I wanted to slap that little smile off his face.

"Sinatra and Steve are inside. I'm yelling for them."

"Frank Sinatra and Steve Lawrence are in your car? Lucky you. Can we meet them?"

Now they were both smiling. Assholes.

"Where are you?" I screamed again.

"Sir!" the first cop loudly demanded. "You need to stop yelling."

"But they're in trouble! Someone tried to break into our car and hurt them. I think he might be back. Can't you hear the honking? I told them to honk if they saw him."

We all listened.

"I don't hear any honking," the second one said.

"They were honking just a minute ago. I hope they're okay."

"Are you sure it wasn't in your head?" the first asked.

"I'm parked here somewhere. It's a sixty-eight Mustang convertible."

I wanted to continue looking, but the first one grabbed my arm again and prevented me from turning around.

"What's that around your neck?" he asked.

"It's a sign."

"*Happy?* What's that mean? Are you a party clown?"

"Figures you wouldn't know. Fucking idiots."

"What did you say?" the second one shot.

"Sir," the first one began. "Can you tell me your name?"

"Daryl Gleason," I snarled.

"And, can you tell me where you are right now?"

"Yes!" I shot back. "I'm in a parking lot!"

He pressed further. "Can you tell me a parking lot *where*?"

I thought for a second. I really didn't know where.

"Do you know what state I'm in?" I asked.

"Idaho," the second one said, shaking his head.

"Idaho? How the hell did I get in Idaho? I'm supposed to be heading for Nevada."

They both took a short step back and exchanged looks.

"Have you been using meth today?" the first one calmly asked.

"Meth? No! Look, I have to go!"

"You're not going anywhere, sir."

"What's that in his pockets?" the second one anxiously asked.

"That's my medicine. I need to take a couple by the way. But first, I have to find my car. The girl could be in trouble!"

"What girl?"

Now they both looked concerned. Finally. I swear, some people you have to hit over the head. The first one took my arm again, gripping it much lighter this time, and led me to his partner.

"Larry, take him back to the car. Sixty-eight Mustang, you say? What else can you tell me about it?"

"Convertible. Keys are in the ignition. There's a bumper sticker. *Help is not a four letter word.*"

Officer Larry escorted me back to their police car, which was parked in the first row outside of the restaurant. It always amazes me how cops manage to get the best parking spots. He opened the back door, and gave me a quick pat down. The only thing he was interested in were my bottles of medicine, which he took and put in the front seat with him.

"I told you," I said. "I need to take those."

"Later."

Now that he had all that annoying procedure out of the way, he helped me in the backseat. He even did that thing you see on TV where the cop puts his hand on the person's head so they don't smash it into the roof. I never understood that. I've been getting into cars all my life, and never once did I bang my head against the roof. Never knew anyone else who did it, either.

These cops must really think we're stupid.

I settled in and looked out the back window, hoping to see if the other cop found my car yet, but I couldn't even see him anymore.

People were starting to come out of the restaurant now. I watched them as they made their way back to their cars. They all thought they were so clever, trying not to be noticed as they sneaked their little peeks at me in the backseat. Going to their stupid jobs. Working their asses off just so other people can get rich. It's so pathetic.

"I don't have to work anymore!" I screamed at a pair of women in ugly Tuesday dresses and saggy pantyhose. "I'm a millionaire!"

I wanted to roll down the window, but there was no handle or switch, so I slapped my hand against the hard glass.

"When will you learn?" I shouted.

"Hey," Larry the cop sneered. "Knock it off."

The women turned their heads and scampered off to their sad little car, their high heels clicking on the asphalt like a confused metronome.

High heels. On those women?

"I.D.?" Officer Larry indifferently asked.

"It's in the car," I told him. "My wallet's in the trunk."

He removed the microphone from the squad's radio and spoke into it.

"Zeke," he slowly spoke. "Mister Gleason here says his wallet's in the trunk, and that it's okay for you to find it."

"Will do," Zeke replied.

"Zeke," I mused to myself. "Who the hell name's their kid Zeke?"

"Someone who's named Zeke. That's his father's name."

"Don't you think someone named Zeke would know better than anyone not to name someone else Zeke?"

"That didn't stop your dad from naming you Daryl."

He pressed a couple buttons on some dashboard computer.

"My father's name wasn't Daryl," I informed him. "It was Steven. Hey, I never thought of that before."

"Where do you live?" he interrupted.

"In the car!" I yelled. I just got done telling him. "My dog's name is Steve."

"So, your dad named the dog after him, but named you Daryl? That's screwed up."

A loud blast of static filled the car.

"Larry?" Zeke said over the radio.

"Yeah, Zeke?"

"Found it. Meet me back at the station."

"Roger."

Larry reattached the microphone to the radio, then flicked on the mars lights, but not the siren.

"Are they safe?" I asked

"Guess we'll find out when we get to the station house."

"So, was *your* dad's name Larry?"

He shook his head no.

"Your mom's?" I asked.

"Keep quiet."

Neither one of us said another word until the car stopped at the station. Which wasn't really any big deal. The backseat was actually comfortable, and there was a lot of legroom.

32

All my life, I've never been inside a jail cell. Which is pretty remarkable for a guy my age. Especially coming from the neighborhood where I grew up. I knew a lot of guys, and women, too, to be fair, who spent time behind bars. Some, in holding cells like now, but others who were sentenced and spent actual time in prison. Jerry, the guy who owned The Spinning Room, did three years in Joliet for possession with intent to sell.

As far as I knew, he wasn't what you would call a *dealer*. Yeah, he'd sell to friends, but that was it. Mostly, he bought for himself, sometimes in large volume if he happened to like the particular product. Unfortunately for him, he happened to really like a new shipment on the worst day possible.

And that's all it takes for everything to completely fall apart. One stupid day.

According to Jerry, his guy in Cicero just acquired some primo shit, his phrase, not mine, so he bought a pound. It sat in four equal sized bags on a table in the Hutch, right out in the open, as he blissfully puffed away.

At that exact same moment, an off duty cop was in the alley getting a blowjob from this pathetic barfly that inhabited a tavern a couple doors down. Apparently, the cop caught a whiff of Jerry's exhale as it floated through the vents, and decided to investigate. Maybe to cover his ass. Who knows?

That part was left tout of the trial, however. The cleaned up version was that the cop was on his way to his car. But word got around, and everyone in the neighborhood knew the real story soon enough. Not that it changed anything.

I was actually scheduled to work that shift, but switched with this other guy named Will because I had band practice.

Will was sentenced to nine months at Decatur as an accessory.

For working my shift.

I never heard from Will again. I did, however, get a couple letters from Jerry, asking me to visit. But I just couldn't do it. For one, I was scared. I had already been questioned by the police after the arrest. I told them I had no idea if Jerry smoked pot, possessed pot, or sold pot. All of it, of course, was a flat out lie. When the guy was low on cash, that's what he used to cover the shortage of my salary. Not that I was protecting him, or anything. I was afraid they'd arrest me as an accessory for never saying anything in the past. So, I worried that if I kept up any kind relationship with him, be it through the mail, or in person, as soon as I turned eighteen they'd throw me in prison, too.

I always felt bad about not responding to his letters. Like I abandoned him. There was really nothing wrong with him. He was a nice guy. Funny. Knew a whole hell of a lot about music. And, he was always very cool to me. I had free reign to order any album I wanted. I filled that hippy shop up with as much punk as I could. And he was cool with it. He never acted like I was just some stupid employee of his. He talked with me, and more importantly, he listened. We'd sit in the Hutch for hours after he closed, checking out new bands, getting high, and talking. No one else ever did that for me. No one. He once told me if he was ever going to have a kid, he hoped it would turn out like me.

And I left him to rot alone in a jail cell without ever visiting and saying thank you.

I am such an asshole.

Nobody looked in on me for what seemed like hours, which I thought was a little heartless. And possible illegal. It was like the treatment they'd give a guy in solitary, hoping to break him.

The last person I saw was the cop who brought me in here. There were no other prisoners, because there were no other cells. I was placed in a narrow paneled room with a single cell at the far end. Three sides of iron bars and concrete wall in back. Outside my little room was a table and four folding chairs. It had the feel of a small *time out* area for mischievous office employees. Except, this was no office. There were no clocks. No windows. No phones. Nothing.

I tried calling out a couple times early on. First, a steady chorus of *hello*, and *officer*, but when those didn't work, I shouted random nonsense, hoping someone would get curious and check.

"John Wayne was a Nazi!"

"Help! I'm being repressed!"

I even sang *Memory*, well, as much of it as I could remember. Why I even knew the lyrics was a little jarring. After going through the whole thing eight times, including a dance mix of my own creation, I realized either no one could hear me, or no one cared enough to visit. Then again, maybe it wasn't visiting hours. I wouldn't know though, since I was going in and out of sleep, I had no idea of the time, or even whether it was day or night.

I started to wonder if Jerry ever felt like this.

With nothing else to do, I laid down on the bench in disgust and stared at the ceiling. I swear, same damn ceiling. Everywhere.

I must have fallen asleep for a minute, because I didn't notice the cop walk up. Not until I heard the key fit into the lock and the door squeak open.

"Alright," he growled. "Come on. Let's go."

"Where?" I asked.

"Wherever you want," he said. "You're released."

"Who paid my bail?"

Sinatra barely knew me, and I doubted Steve had that kind of money.

"There was no bail," he shot. "Come on, let's go!"

He leaned on the open door with one hand, visibly annoyed about something. Did he hear me before? Maybe he doesn't like Broadway musicals. Who knows what, with these people?

Really, it didn't matter, I just wanted to get the hell out of there. I followed him out the door and down a long hallway until we came to another room where Officer Zeke was sitting behind a desk. All my possessions were sitting on top, including both my pill bottles.

I immediately removed one pill from each and dry swallowed.

"You can go." It sounded more like he was trying to guilt me into staying. Kinda like a guy who could tell that no one was having fun at his party and says it's okay if you leave, but doesn't really mean it.

"Just like that?" I asked. "Why?"

"Your doctor wants to see you," he calmly said, shuffling through some papers that he never took the time to read.

"Doctor Melvin's *here*? In *Idaho*?"

He straightened the edges of the stack with the forefingers of both hands, and quietly sighed.

"No," he said. "Not in *Idaho*. I spoke with him a little while ago. He feels it's important for you to see him right away."

"I can't," I told him. "I'm busy."

"Mister Gleason, you need to see him."

"Is it mandatory? I mean, what if I don't? Do I have to stay here in prison, or something?"

"You're free to go wherever you please. But, the court says you have to see him, so eventually, you could be in a place like this if you don't."

"First, I have to find the pirates. Where's Sinatra?"

He sighed again! Was this guy oxygen depleted, or something?

"There's no one here."

"What do you mean? Where is she?"

"Maybe someone picked her up. I wouldn't worry about it if I were you."

"Did she say anything? Leave a message for me? A forwarding address or number? Anything?"

This time he just shook his head.

I couldn't believe it. Another one. All the same.

"What about Steve?" I asked.

"Who?"

"Steve. My dog."

"You have to sign these papers, and then you're free to go. Your car's in the lot."

"What about Steve?"

Suddenly, none of this was making sense.

"What just happened?" I asked. "Why was I brought in?"

"Mister Gleason, as I said, you're free to go. And you should do that. Now."

There was just the one door, so after signing whatever it was that he insisted be signed, I walked through it and followed the long dark hallway that eventually led to the front of the station house. There wasn't much activity in the room – most of the people were on the police side of the desk. I was sure someone would stop me on my way out, or at least ask what I was doing, but no one did. I could feel them looking at me, but other than some inaudible mumbling, no one said a damn thing.

I reached into my pocket for my keys, and pushed open the front door. As soon as the sunlight hit my face, I folded in half like I was punched in the stomach, and puked. A little hit my sign, but mostly it splattered on the sidewalk.

Again, no one said a word.

I straightened up and noticed an arrow on a wall directing people to the parking lot. So, I cleaned off my sign with my sleeve and started walking in that direction.

The car was easy to find. First row center. Cops and their premiere parking spots. It's mind boggling.

The first thing I did was open the roof. While it was taking it's sweet time retracting, I twisted the rear view mirror so I was looking directly back at myself.

"You will be happy. Always speak your mind. Always tell the truth. Be true to yourself. Don't let others define you. Be the god of your own life."

Then it hit me. Sinatra hadn't said anything. She left before we could make a promise to each other. It wasn't right. I just couldn't let her go like that.

So, I looked back in the mirror.

"And always remember her."

My eyes were stinging. Something in the air, I guess. I rubbed them and readjusted the mirror, catching the unwelcome stink of vomit in the process. If there's one thing worse than throwing up, it's smelling your previous offering moments later.

Just as I was shifting into reverse, I heard a familiar voice calling out.

"Wait up, D!"

Steve! Running full steam toward the car from behind. He jumped on top of the trunk just as I hit the brakes, and slid headfirst into the backseat.

"Safe!" he laughed.

I reached back with my free hand, grabbed him by the collar, and lifted him into the front.

He started to gag. "What smells like puke?"

"Puke."

"Dude! We're you gonna take off without me?"

"I thought you left *me*," I told him. "The cop said no one saw you. Where'd you go?"

“I was watching her, like you said. But when I saw it was a cop coming up to the car, I hid on the back floor. Under the jackets. I figured that way I could hear everything that was going on, and if it turned out to be a trick or something, I had the element of surprise, ‘cause he didn’t know I was there.”

“That makes sense,” I said. I backed out the spot and pulled into the street.

“Where is she?”

“I don’t know. Gone. I thought you’d know.”

“Know what?” He sounded as confused by it as I was.

“They said someone came for her.”

“Who?”

“They wouldn’t tell me.”

“Son of a bitch. It better not have been those fucked up parents. I’d like to turn them into chew toys. Assholes!”

“What did you hear?” I asked. “When you were in the backseat.”

“That cop thought you kidnapped her.”

“What?”

“Yeah. It was like he *wanted* you to be a kidnapper. He was asking her all kinds of things. Like, Did you do anything to her? Did you force yourself on her?”

“What the hell? Are you serious?”

“Serious as shit, bro.”

“And what did she say?”

“She told him the truth. You know, that she snuck into the car, and you were trying to help her. But, I tell ‘ya, he wasn’t buying it. Not at all. He kept pressing her. Dude was pissed off you weren’t some psycho rapist. She stuck up for you, though.”

I made a left out of the lot and followed the signs back to the freeway.

“You okay?” Steve asked. “You’re kinda quiet.”

“I’m glad I don’t have kids,” I told him.

“What does that have to do with anything?”

“Because I couldn’t deal with this.”

“With what?”

“This. You try to help them, and they don’t give a damn. They leave without saying a word.”

“Come on. It wasn’t you, buddy! It was those frigging parents. They probably grabbed her and wouldn’t let her see you. I hate those people! I’m tellin’ ‘ya.”

He was getting really worked up about it, so I reached over and rubbed his head.

“Eww! Dude! Major puke smell. Change your jacket.”

“It’ll air out.”

We were back on the freeway, but this time, we were heading out of Idaho and toward Nevada.

"Keep your eyes open," I told Steve.

"You got it, bro!" Steve shot back. "By the way, you did do good, you know."

"About what?"

"Sinatra. You didn't treat her like she was just some stupid kid. You listened to her. You could tell that meant a lot to her. I hope I can be like that with my kids someday. Listen to me, will you? Christ, I need to get laid, and shake some of this human off of me."

There was a sign for a McDonald's in a few miles, so I figured I could kill a few birds with one stone. I put on my right blinker and faded over to the right lane.

"What are you doin'?" Steve asked.

"McDonald's, right?" I said. "I'm hungry. You're *always* hungry. While we're there, I could wash up and change the jacket, and you can do whatever it is you do."

"You know what?" he contemplated. "Don't."

I checked my mirror for clearance, and slid back into the middle lane.

"Okay," I sighed. "Any reason?"

"Let's go somewhere nice. Some place where we can relax. Have a beer. You had a shitty night, buddy. You deserve something better than a Quarter-Pounder. Whatta 'ya say? You and me, just chillin' and talkin'."

"Sure. Got some place in mind?"

"No. But something will pop up. They always do, don't they? And, uh, put your arm in your lap, okay? It's disgusting."

It really doesn't smell that bad. I don't see what the big deal is.

"You know I can hear you," he announced.

"Yeah," I mumble back. "I know."

33

For the next sixty miles or so, I drove with my arm at a ninety degree angle, biceps horizontal to the seat top, forearm flagpoled straight in the air. I was hoping my sleeve would catch more wind this way and air out the smell.

It didn't, of course. If anything, the odor grew stronger. I could understand a smell being resistant to the airing out process, but for it to gain momentum and become more potent struck me as a bit of an anomaly.

I took this as a warning that the jacket needed to be changed quickly, before the stench overtook me. Comic books are full of stories about average people whose lives are changed forever because they were infected by some strange chemical reaction. Just my luck, the smell of my own vomit is some form of mutation, and this will become my superpower.

I tried to be positive about it, but I couldn't imagine how turning into *PukeMan* would make my life any better.

The Ralph?

No. Not even close.

We were nearing a town, so I moved over to the right lane.

"Damn, dude!" Steve yelled. "I was just gonna say! We are so much alike!"

I missed the name of the town, but that didn't really matter. This was just going to be a short stop. It wasn't like we were going to spend the night.

Wherever this place was called, it had a calm, small-town vibe to it. Kind of like Mayberry, expect with taverns. If I remember correctly, Mayberry was dry. Yeah. That's why Otis went to jail every time he was drunk.

What a stupid law.

I didn't feel like driving around at a crawl, trying to decide where to eat from behind the steering wheel, so I pulled into the first open space on the street I found.

It seemed like a safe area, so I left the roof open. Far from the urban sprawl. And, I just wanted to get out of the car. Closing the roof would have delayed that.

Steve leapt out onto the sidewalk as soon as his buckle was undone. It reminded me of the way Russell exited the car. Another person who disappeared that I'll never see again. I opened the door, the more conventional route, and stepped out to the street.

Then I remembered that I didn't grab the keys. It wasn't until I leaned back over the driver's door that I heard another car's engine revving and tires squealing.

A split second later, I heard Steve scream.

"Daryl!"

The car was about fifty feet away, and too far over to my side of the road for the speed it was driving. I watched it for a moment, fully expecting the driver to realize his mistake and abruptly change course. But that wasn't going to happen, so I grabbed the steering wheel and jumped.

I angled myself head first into the dashboard, the rest of my body collapsing hard onto the seats. My face hurt, but it could have been a whole hell of a lot worse.

When I finally collected myself and sat up, Steve was next to me on the seat.

"Dude, you okay?"

"Yeah. I think so."

"What the hell was that?"

"Hell if I know."

The car was gone. Down some side street probably. I gave a quick look around the rest of the area, but of course, not one witness besides the two of us.

"Maybe some idiot texting," I said.

"Looked more like some idiot trying to kill you."

"Don't be so dramatic, Steve."

"Someone almost runs you over, and I'm the one being dramatic?"

I pulled the keys from the ignition, then checked in both directions before making my way to the trunk.

I emptied the coat pockets, then removed my *Happy* sign, followed by my coat and shirt.

"You're changing here?" Steve snapped. "Aren't you gonna wash that crap off of you?"

"Yeah, when we get to the restaurant."

"That's disgusting. You're just putting clean clothes over a dirty body."

"This, from an animal who'd rather use his tongue than soap."

"Hey, at least I do something. And don't knock it. It's an effective stop gap."

"You want to lick my arm? Will that make you happy?"

"Dude, I'm not licking your puke. We're tight and everything, but there are limits. Yo, check it out."

Steve's attention promptly shifted from me, to some dog walking down the sidewalk in the other direction.

"She's hot, right?" he asked, tipping his head to one side.

I thought that was an odd remark for him to make. For one, any human who sees an animal as "hot" should be locked up. That's just wrong. What was even odder than that though, was that the look of the other dog. She was rather small, some type of terrier would be my guess, with thick white fur and a sprinkling of randomly placed black spots.

It was like seeing Steve standing in front of a mirror. And he wasn't too happy when I informed him of this.

"What's wrong with you?" he snapped. "She looks nothing like me! You're just showing your ignorance about the canine anatomy."

"Sorry, but she looks *exactly* like you. Are you sure it's even a girl?"

"Now you're just pissing me off. I don't have time for this now." He turned toward her. If it was indeed a *her*.

"Hey, cutie. What cha doin'?"

The other dog continued walking without the slightest indication that it heard him.

Okay, I was wrong. It was a female.

"Hey, hot stuff!" he yelled slightly louder, probably hoping she was partially deaf, and not just ignoring him. "I'm talking to you!"

This prompted her to stop. She turned back toward Steve and groaned. "You call any of that conversation material?"

"Where 'ya headed?" he confidently asked.

"Away from you," she smiled, then resumed her walk down the block.

"Hey," Steve laughed. "Hold up. I'm not finished."

"You might not be, but I am."

"Come on…I'm just looking for a little help?"

"*Help?*" she scoffed. "I know what you're looking for, Casanova, and it's not help. So, you might as well go back to your master, because I don't have sex with every Tom, Dick and Fido that passes me by. I'm not that kind of girl."

"Whoa. You've got it all wrong. I'm new in town, and I just want to ask you a few questions. What's wrong with that?"

She looked up at an arbitrary spot in the sky and shook her head.

"Then what do you want?"

He took a couple steps closer before he answered.

"Name's Steve. Steve Gleason. What's yours?"

"Keep."

"Keep?" Steve asked. "Keep what"

"Keep walking."

I expected him to get angry and say something rude. What I didn't expect was for him to break into a fit of nervous laughter. It was a little unsettling. And, it was pissing me off. The whole purpose of this trip was for me to find happiness. Not him.

"What are you laughing at?" she asked.

"What you said. It was funny. So, you gonna tell me your name, or are you gonna make me read your collar?"

"That would be a hell of a trick. I don't wear a collar."

"Ooh. Unattached, huh?"

"Yeah. And it's going to stay that way."

Once again, she began to walk away, but this time, Steve ran at full speed to catch up with her.

"Hang on!"

By now, they were out of my audio range, so I had no idea what was going on. Based on what I had heard, I could probably guess, but I didn't really care, though. All the stinky clothes were off, and I had my new jacket on, a tasteful hound's-tooth. I just had to finish up the knot on my shiny maroon tie, and I was all set.

I couldn't see Steve and his female doppelganger anymore, so I assumed the mumbling I heard coming from behind me was just them having made their way back around the block already.

When I turned to talk to him, I instead found some guy in a wheelchair attempting to push himself forward past a stubborn bulge in the concrete.

"Come on, Walter," he repeated to himself, in what I felt to be horribly misguided self-encouragement. "Show off that upper body strength!"

With every failed attempt, he'd laugh to himself, then roll back a few feet, and try it all over again.

"Can I...?" I carefully began.

"Yeah," he said, slightly panting. "I'm pretty sure you could. Problem is, I can't."

"I mean," I tried to clarify. "Do you need a hand?"

"No," he matter-of-factly stated, while wiping his palms with a towel. "Got hands. What I need is a leg. Wouldn't happen to have one in your trunk, would you?"

I don't know why, but out of reflex, my head turned toward the open trunk. I caught myself, but not soon enough.

"Nothing?"

"Not in your size," I said.

He gave a little laugh. "Isn't that always the case?"

As he squared up for another launch, I closed the trunk and moved toward him.

"Don't sweat it," he reassured me. "This is all part of my daily routine. I've been fighting with this damn patch of ground for so long, it's gotten to where I'm used to it. Besides, I get to use it as a convenient excuse: all this work builds up a powerful thirst, don't you know."

He lifted his hand from the wheel and pointed down the block. I squinted in the general direction.

"*The Joint*," he continued, rolling his eyes. "Now, I ask you: can you think of a worse name for a business? I do everything in my power to never actually say the name myself. Lucky for them they have the best beer, women, and corned beef sandwiches in town, or I'd find another place."

He smiled, then directed his attention back on his main objective. Getting over that stupid little hump.

He angled his torso forward, arms bent behind him and firmly grasping the tops of both wheels. He stared down that uneven slab of concrete like a defensive lineman trying to psyche out an offensive tackle. I could see his arms stiffen as his hands pushed forward and down. The chair hit the protrusion with such force that it bounced the front wheels a good foot in the air, more than enough to clear the obstacle on the ground. For a moment, I was sure he was going to tip backwards and smash his head open, but he quickly threw his upper body toward his legs and somehow managed to keep his balance.

As soon as the front of the chair slammed back on the ground, he spun the back wheels again, rolling them over the chunk of concrete with very little effort.

He then pivoted toward me, lifting up his arms in mock celebration. Like a wheelchair version of "Rocky".

"Ta da!" he exclaimed. "What do think? At least an eight, eight-and-a-half, right?"

"What?" I asked. "Feet?"

It certainly didn't look that long, but I wasn't about to criticize a guy in a wheelchair.

"No. Eight-and-a-half *points*. My score."

"Your score?" The realization hit me before I was even finished asking the question. "Oh," I stammered. "Yeah, sure. I guess. Eight-and-a-half."

"You okay, kid?"

I hadn't been called kid in such a long time that it took me off guard. I actually didn't know how to respond.

"Why don't you let me buy you a drink?" he asked.

"Shouldn't I be buying you a drink?" I quickly asked in return.

"Why?"

"Because you're in a wheelchair."

"Is that how it works?" he smiled. "Damn. All these years. You know how many free drinks I must have coming?"

He laughed to himself for a second or two, then began pushing himself toward *The Joint.*

"Do they allow dogs?"

"If you're with me, they'll allow anything."

"I don't know. I kinda had another plan." I looked down, expecting Steve to be there drooling for a cheeseburger, but he wasn't there. Where the hell was he? "Damn it!"

"Something wrong?" the man asked me.

"When isn't there? Story of my stupid fucking life." I started walking back toward the car, but then stopped and turned around. "Do you have a pen and a piece of paper?"

"Sure don't. What do you need it for?"

"For the note."

"The note?"

"Yeah."

"What note?"

"That's how it usually works, isn't it? You leave a note, so people know."

Get Happy

"What's your name, son?"
"Daryl."
"I'm Walter. Come on with me. Let's talk."

34

From the outside, *The Joint* looked like any other dive bar in the world. Blacked out front windows. Old wooden door covered with at least ten coats of paint, the most recent, a shade of evergreen, was chipped off in a few spots so you could see the previous colors of navy, white, and fire hydrant red. A small sign hanging above the door was the only indication of what may be waiting inside:

The Joint

Food – Music – Live Dancing

Live dancing? What other kind is there? That must have been somebody's attempt at a joke. If it was a mistake, surely it would have been noticed and fixed it by now. Right?

Walter entered first, pushing through the door backwards. I reached over him to hold it open, but he smiled and waved me off.

"I got it Daryl. Part of the routine."

The sudden burst of sunlight must have shocked everyone inside because within an instant, hands covered eyes, and heads spun back into the shadows.

"Close the door already!" someone grunted from the back.

"Don't they know...?" I started, but again, Walter waved me off. This time with a calming *shh*.

"Well, if the door wasn't so damn heavy," he smilingly shouted out to no one in particular. "I'd be inside already."

A collective laugh filled the room.

"Walter!" a few of them happily shouted.

"Afternoon! Afternoon! I brought a friend with me."

A small chorus sang out. "Hello, Walter's friend!"

"His name's Daryl," Walter announced.

A couple *Hey, Daryl*'s were offered from the shadows. I raised my hand and waved generically toward the voices. Walter hadn't moved toward a table yet, and I felt kind of stupid just standing there behind him, so I pretended like that was my plan the whole time. Not to look stupid, but to stand still. I gave a quick glance around the room. Seemed okay. About what you'd expect from the outside. Maybe held a hundred twenty-five, hundred fifty people max, although I doubt this room's ever been that full.

A large mahogany bar sat centered along the left wall, containing what appeared to be a large variety of vodkas. That was a good sign, as far as bars go. And a good sign for me, I suppose. I could use a couple drinks. Then again, whether it was a good *sign* or not was highly questionable. If all I wanted was good vodka, I could go to a liquor store and buy it anytime I wanted. So, it really wasn't much of a good sign at all. I could feel myself getting more and more pissed off with each passing moment.

We started moving, finally, toward a table in the center of the room that was missing a chair on one side. He headed straight for it without looking anywhere else, so maybe it was reserved for him. All the years I went to bars, no one ever set aside a table just for me.

It looked to me that he had the angle wrong on his approach to the empty side, so I took hold of the right handle and pushed him slightly to the left. This time, without even so much as cheating back to me, he shook me off.

"I have it, Daryl."

I released a loud, agitated sigh, and yanked back one of the chairs.

"What is it?" he asked.

I shook my head and sat.

The bartender, an attractive redhead maybe a little younger than me, definitely a lot younger than him, walked over and set down a bottle of Miller Lite and a glass in front of Walter. Once that was out of the way, she wrapped her arms around his shoulders and kissed his cheek.

"It's good to see you, Sweetie," she gleefully announced.

"It's good to see you, too, Jess. Hell, when it comes down to it, it's good to see anyone, isn't it?"

They both gave a laugh. Probably more out of an unspoken obligation to their friendship since it wasn't all that funny.

She combed Walter's hair with the fingers of her right hand as she spoke to him.

"Want your sandwich order in now?"

"You like corned beef?" he asked me.

I shrugged and looked away.

"You want to see a menu?" she asked.

"They have other things, Daryl. You don't have to get that if you don't want it."

"I don't care. Whatever."

It was quiet for a moment. I can only imagine the looks the two of them were exchanging, but frankly, I didn't really care.

"Two corned beefs," he quietly told her. "What are you drinking?"

"I make a killer martini," Jess said. "You sorta look like a martini man to me."

I nodded and said *okay*.

They had a dartboard and two pool tables in back. You wouldn't see that at Casey's Bar and Char.

"If you want to talk about it," Walter started.

"Talk about what?"

"Or not," he said with a truncated laugh.

He tilted his bottle and slowly poured the beer until the glass was half full. It felt exactly like a test.

"I'm sick of talking," I sternly announced.

"Okay," he smiled. "Then let's not do that. Here's mud in your eye."

He lifted the glass in the air then took a drink.

"What?"

He swallowed, then repeated himself. "I said, *here's mud in your eye*."

"What does that mean?"

"Good luck."

"How the hell is that good luck?"

"Means, *Here's to cure whatever ails 'ya*."

"Why not just say that and be done with it?"

"I suppose you could. Wouldn't be nearly as poetic, though."

"What good is poetry if you can't understand it? What good are *any* words, really? No one listens anyway. No one cares."

"I'm listening, kid," he whispered.

"I'm sick of talking. Sick of it all. What's the use? You spend time getting to know someone, maybe open up to them a little. And for what? They just disappear. I mean, what's the point? Honestly. What's the fucking point?"

"Daryl, everything can't be that bad."

"Oh no? Everything sucks!"

Jess was stepping up to the table with my martini.

"Something the matter?" she asked.

I caught Walter shaking his head as I snatched the martini downed it in one gulp.

"Want another?" she smirked.

I nodded.

"What's that?" she asked. "You in a line-up?"

She was looking down at my chest. The sign had flipped over, so all that could be seen was the blank white back.

"Every day of my life," I shot back. "Only no one ever picks me."

She looked over at Walter. "I don't know if I get that joke. You want to be picked out of a line-up?"

I didn't answer. I mean, what was the point? She obviously wasn't going to get it anyway. I flipped the sign back over and showed it to her. She smiled, and walked back to the bar with my empty glass.

Another ridiculously beautiful young woman, this one a blond, came bouncing over and literally jumped into Walter's lap. The guy has to be paralyzed from the waist down, because otherwise, that had to have hurt like hell.

"Walter!" she shrieked. It was like watching a four-year-old visit a mall Santa for the first time.

"Pammy!" he roared. "Hello, you gorgeous little creature!"

"Oh, I missed you!"

"Well, I'm here now," he laughed.

She grabbed his face with both hands and planted a long lingering kiss on his lips, then threw her arms around him and squeezed tight.

"Jess?" Walter called out behind him. "A daiquiri for Pammy, if you please."

"Already making it," she shouted back.

"Who's your friend?" Pammy asked.

"Pammy," Walter began. "This is Daryl."

"Hi, Daryl. You want me to bring the girls over?"

I could see the question was directed at Walter, but I answered for him.

"No."

"Maybe later," Walter diplomatically added.

Jess came back with the drinks, but this time, didn't hang around to chit chat. I wanted to tell her that the martini was nowhere near being *killer*. It was okay, better than most, but not killer. Maybe she sensed what I planned to tell her, and that's why she left so suddenly.

"I need a couple minutes," Walter told Pammy. "Why don't you order a round for the girls on me, and we can hang out in a bit."

"Sure. Nice to meet you, Daryl."

She made a big production out of wrapping her thick lips around the straw and sucking up a mouthful before leaving. Everything appeared to be a huge production with this woman. Even when as she walked away – her ass cheeks slowly seesawed up and down with each overly dramatic step. It was a little too much.

"Is this a whorehouse?" I asked.

Walter grimaced unapprovingly. "Jesus, Daryl. She's just young and having a little fun."

"Have you been gone then? Like, out to sea for a long time?"

"Out to sea?" he laughed. "No. What in the world makes you ask that?"

"Don't laugh at me."

"I wasn't laughing at you. It's just an odd question."

"No it's not. Since we came in here, everyone's acting like they're seeing for the first time in twenty years."

"I was in here yesterday. Until close."

"Then what's with all the fanfare?"

"We're friends, Daryl. That's how we act with each other. Nothing strange about that. Isn't that how you and your friends act together?"

"No."

"How do you act?"

"I don't."

"What do you mean?"

"I don't have any friends."

"Oh, come on. Everybody has friends."

"Believe it. Don't believe it. I really don't care, but I'm telling you the truth."

"You don't even have one friend?"

"I had one, but not anymore."

"What do you mean?"

"It was supposed to be just the two of us, then he went and ran off with a girl."

"Think of it this way," he laughed. "He left you, then you met me. His loss, because you and me, we're gonna have some fun!"

He raised his glass again in a toast, then took a sip.

"What the hell's that mean? You think it's okay for him to ditch me?"

"You had a need, right? A need for a friend. A companion. Your friend had a need, too. But it turned out, for something entirely different. It sounds like he took care of his need, but that you relied on him taking care of yours. Nothing you can do about it now, except let it go and have some fun."

I threw back the rest of my martini.

"Nice meeting you. I have something to do."

"No, wait. Come on. Sit. Please."

I saw Jess heading our way with the sandwiches, so I sat back down. Reluctantly at first, but then it struck me that I couldn't remember the last time I ate. As soon as I got a whiff it, I knew I was hanging around. Just long enough to eat it, though, and that's all.

"Look at those babies," Walter panted. "I'm talking about the sandwiches, Jess."

She put down the plates then playfully jiggled herself a few inches from his face.

"Sorry," he forlornly admitted. "My vote still goes with the sandwiches."

"You ass." She laughed and gave the back of his head a light smack.

"You forgot the mustard."

She shook her head and walked away.

"You're gonna like this. They make their own corned beef. The entire process take a couple weeks, but it is worth every second of the wait. Mmm. Melted Swiss cheese, but no sauerkraut or dressing like a Reuben. Rye bread toasted so it's not too crunchy, not too soft."

I took a bite out of it.

"Don't want to wait for the mustard?" he asked.

"Not really," I mumbled. I could have just shook my head rather than answering with a mouthful of food, but too bad. Maybe he shouldn't have asked me a question while I was eating.

I'm not sure if she was slow, or I was eating fast, but half my sandwich was already gone by the time Jess returned with the mustard.

"You okay?" she asked, looking back and forth between Walter and me.

"I think so," he said.

He took his time spreading the mustard so it covered every inch of the bread, then placed it back on top of the sandwich.

"Here it is if you want to try some," he said.

"I don't want any," I said, for what felt like the fifth time.

"Fine by me."

He smiled, then shoved a corner into his mouth. The look of joy and calm that spread across his face the second the food hit his tongue reminded me of watching Steve eat a cheeseburger for the first time.

Everything I did for that dog.

"So, where you headed?" Walter asked, but then almost immediately, he corrected himself. "Oh, that's right. You don't want to talk."

I swallowed another mouthful of corned beef. I figured it wouldn't kill me to tell him that much.

"Nevada."

"No kidding? Whereabouts? Reno? Tahoe?"

"Don't know."

"Did you forget, or are you gonna flip a coin?"

He laughed to himself and polished off his beer.

"Two more, Jess darling?" he called out.

"On the way," she shouted back.

"It's not like that," I told him. "I'm supposed meet these people for a convention in Nevada, but it's secret."

He leaned over the table toward me. "I won't tell anyone," he whispered.

"No, I mean, it's a secret. Even to me. I'm supposed to follow signs along the way that lead me to it."

"Sounds interesting. What kinda convention? If you don't mind me asking."

"Pirates."

I took another bite. This was a good sandwich.

"Pirates?" he asked. "Like swashbucklers?"

I nodded and finished chewing.

"Really?"

"What? You think I'm lying to you?"

"No. Why would I think you're lying? You tell me a group of sea-faring marauders are meeting in a secret, undisclosed location in the desert state of Nevada. Why would anyone doubt that story?"

He let out a warm, relaxed laugh, then raised both his eyebrows.

"It's true," I quietly insisted.

"Okay."

One of the girls Pammy was drinking with in the back shouted over to Walter from across the room.

"Hey, Walter! I'm gonna play some songs. Wanna hear anything?"

"Yeah! How about some Adam and the Ants!"

"Okay..." she skeptically replied.

"Adam and the Ants?" I shot.

"It was the first pirate music I could think of off the top of my head. So, what do they do, all these pirates, once they get together? I hope you don't mind. I'm a little curious."

"Anything they want. They're all running away from the things in life that control them. Keep them down. And for two weeks, they try to reclaim their happiness. They let loose and go wild."

"You do this often?"

"Be my first time."

"I see. That what your sign means? It's like an invitation you show to get in?"

"It's," I sighed. "If I wear it, it's supposed to make my cells happy."

"Well now, that's a new one on me."

"Yeah. It was a new one on me, too."

Jess strolled by with the next round.

"Feeling better?" she asked. I don't know if I'd ever seen a smile so big. I swear it had about four feet of extra lip in it.

"It's hitting the spot," Walter said. Then he took her hand before she could walk away. "You have time to sit with us for a while?"

"Not right now," she said, stretching those lips even further. "But I will later. Don't worry."

"Oh, I never worry. You know me."

She ran a couple fingers over his shoulder and moved back to the bar.

For a moment, Walter stared down his bottle of beer like it was another pile of broken pavement, then took a deep breath and filled his glass halfway again.

"You know, Daryl, I don't know what happened to you today. What got you so upset? But, I can tell you from my experience that it probably isn't worth it. Shake it off and let it go. There's always a new day rising."

"It's not just today, Walter. It's every day. Every single goddamn day of my life."

"Well, you said it right there."

"What?"

"*Life*. It could be worse. You could be dead."

"Would it be worse?"

"Holy hell, man, are you serious? Yes, it would. Death is one of the few things guaranteed to put a damper on life. Now, of course, I can't speak from experience, don't know anyone who can, but I feel pretty safe saying so."

"Sometimes I don't know."

Get Happy

"Do you mind if I tell you a little story?"

"What's the difference?"

"Nothing I love more than a captivated audience."

He gulped down the half a glass of beer, then released a loud *ahh.* "Okay, I'm in a wheelchair, right? Want to hear how it happened?"

"Isn't that what I just agreed to?"

He laughed a sincere laugh, not an *I-wish-I-could-reach-you-so-I could-smack-you* laugh. Just the same, I scooted a little further away from him.

"I was in the Army," he started, then interrupted himself, like some knee-jerk reaction. "Ever been in the service?

"Yeah. Army, too."

"No kidding. Where were you stationed?"

"Fort Sill."

"No shit. So was I!"

"Were you really?"

"Yes, I was. Small world, huh? A few years before you, I'd say. Was there a fella name of Blansky still there?"

"Major Blansky?"

"Jumpin' Jesus, they promoted that putz to a major?"

"What was he when you knew him?"

"Lieutenant. Tell me, did you ever have the opportunity to spend any quality time with Major Asswipe?"

"He's the guy who threw me out," I said, sipping my martini.

"Threw you out of what?"

"The Army."

"What the hell did you do?"

"Doesn't matter."

"No, I suppose it doesn't. Whatever it was, be glad you got out in one piece."

"Yeah."

"I only ask because he's the reason I'm in this chair. Ran me over with a jeep. Tried to kill me."

"Blansky? Why?"

"Because he was nuts. I was a sergeant, and my squad was in his platoon. Trouble was, he couldn't command any respect from the troops. No one thought very much of him. Drove him crazy. He had it in his head that my men respected me more than they respected him."

"Did they?"

"Of course they did! The guy was a moron! But, we put up with his nonsense because, well, what else are you going to do? The world is filled with people like that. You can't let them get to you. For a while, we all muddled through it best we could, which probably made matters even worse, because the more he got down on me and my men, the more they bonded with me. And against him.

"Well, one night, on leave, I'm in this bar off base," he paused, leaned toward me, and lowered his voice to a whisper. "And I meet the most gorgeous woman you've ever seen in your life, or anybody else's. I thought I should whisper so I didn't hurt anyone's feelings." He motioned to the group of women in back, who didn't seem to notice that he was even talking. Now that the explanation was complete, he switched back to his normal volume. "Well, we had ourselves a night, Daryl, I tell 'ya. Dancing, singing, drinking, and a few other verbs that end in I-N-G!" He gave a laugh, took a swallow of beer, and continued. "What I didn't know was, this girl apparently was the apple of my Lieutenant Blansky's eye. Turns out she didn't know it, either, but that's oddly not relevant to the story. Anyway, he found out, and ordered me to stop seeing her. Ordered me. Can you believe that? Well, I was a brash son-of-a-bitch, so I had a talk with the captain about it, and the captain saw it my way. Three nights later, after I walked Sarah Lynne home, *Sarah Lynn*, that was her name. Isn't that the cutest damn thing ever? After I leave her place, he was waiting for me in a jeep and ran me over."

"Jesus," I mumbled. I happened to see that Jess was trying to catch my eye, so I quietly signaled for two more drinks, trying not to interrupt Walter's story.

"What he wasn't counting on," he continued without pause. "Were witnesses. Guess he figured it was dark enough that no one would see. Lucky for me, Sarah Lynne was a horny little thing. Apparently, every night after I walked her home, she'd run back out and hit the bars until sunup. So, there she was, watching me from around the corner, like she did every night apparently, making sure I wasn't turning back around for her, and she saw the whole thing."

"Was it reported?"

"Damn right it was reported."

"Then how the hell did he get promoted to major?"

"Ever hear of *General* Blansky? *Major* General Blansky? He's the little shit puppet's daddy. You see, two star generals who really want to be three star generals don't like having negative press about their offspring floating around. Especially when that offspring is in the same branch of the service. So, they made me a deal. If I promised to be quiet, they promised a prompt discharge, along with an extremely generous compensation package to be paid out for the rest of my life."

"But, you're talking about it now!" I whispered, probably a little too alarmist and shrill than needed, because Jess had a very concerned look on her face when she delivered the next round.

"If the Army can hear me in here," Walter smiled. "More power to them."

"Oh, you poor guy," Jess said in a pout directed to me. "Is he telling you his Army stories?"

"Yes, I am," Walter beamed. "If you've got time now to pull up a chair..."

"Ah, *darn!*" Jess said, really overstating the phoniness of it. "I'm just *so* busy!"

Walter laughed to himself as she hurried away.

"Anyway," he went on. "While I was in the hospital, there were moments when the pain was so bad, that I thought I'd rather die. I didn't think there was any point to going on."

"Yeah? So, what did you do?"

"What do you think?" he laughed. "I clearly didn't kill myself. I thought about it. Quite a lot. But after a while, the thought hit me. *You're not going to beat me!*"

"Who? Blansky?"

"Him, and anybody else who didn't like me for whatever stupid reasons they had. I had an epiphany, Daryl. And once the realization sunk in, my entire life changed."

"What?" I asked.

"There are about seven billion people on this planet, right?"

"Yeah."

"Seven billion! So, why the hell should I kill myself because one little pissant doesn't like me? One measly little rat dick that means nothing to my life? And besides, I figured there had to be way more people that liked me than hated me."

"But, what if you know that's not the case?"

"What is so bad in your life? Will you tell me?"

"I'm forty-two, okay? Forty-two! And I don't know if I've ever truly been happy. Even once, in my whole fucking life."

"And that's why you're meeting up with the pirates? That'll fix everything, will it?"

"I don't know anymore. I don't. But I have to do something, Walter. I need to know what it feels like. To see if it brings back a memory. Before it's too late."

"Too late for what, Daryl?"

Why does this always end up happening with me? People just don't get it. I took a sip of my martini and stared at the back of the room.

"I never wear a watch," Walter began. "You know why? Having that information right there on your wrist is like a death sentence. It's a constant reminder of what's gone by and what remains. What are you supposed to do with that information? Worry about a past that you can't change? Fret about a future that hasn't happened? Or might not ever happen?"

For a split second, I thought he was about to stand. Instead, he readjusted himself in the chair, and raised his beer glass high in the air.

"What is the most important time in your life?" he loudly asked.

The rest of the bar raised their drinks. The response was forceful, and unanimous.

"Now!" they chanted.

I could feel my chair vibrate.

"What is our mantra?" Walter demanded.

"Enjoy life! Live in the moment! Fun, fun, fun!"

Suddenly, the only noises heard were the gulping down of drinks, and the mumblings of two people at the end of he bar.

Walter let out a satisfying *ahh*, then set down his glass.

"You're s'posed to raise yer glass, idiot!" shrieked the voice of an old lady.

"Shut up woman," demanded the man next to her in a low, rumbling growl. "Or I'll shut you up."

Everyone else laughed and went back to what they were previously doing. I figured I might as well do the same.

"You have fun," I asked him. "In a wheelchair?"

"I have more fun now than I ever had when I was able to walk on two working legs. I'm surrounded by good friends, good food, good music, and more beautiful women than you can shake a stick. Of course," he laughed. "My stick doesn't shake anymore since the accident."

"So, all these women, you're not...?"

"Haha! I wish."

"You're not going out with any of them?"

"Only in my mind, Daryl. But trust me, up there, I'm getting action on a regular basis. Mentally, I have the stamina of a teenager."

"So, you're not with anybody?"

"Sure I am. I'm with an entire room full of people!"

"That's not what I mean."

"Look. I know the reality without having to test it. Women don't want to be involved like that with an old, broken guy in a wheelchair."

"How do you know for sure, if you've never tried?"

"I haven't met the right woman."

"But, how would you ever know when you met the right one?"

"Simple," he said, wheeling up a little closer to me. "If she answered my test question."

"Which is...?" I asked.

"I'll show you. Pick out any woman in the place."

I looked around the room and pointed to a table by the opposite wall.

"The blond," I said.

Walter pushed down on his right wheel and spun to his left.

"Which blond? Bleach, ash, yellow, or strawberry?"

"Oh, hell, I don't know. Blue jeans and green top."

I don't know why, but he burst into a fit of laughter. Before it completely subsided, he called out.

"Monica!" The yellow blond turned her head. "Come here a second, would you?"

Monica immediately halted her conversation and came bounding over to Walter like she was picked out of the audience to win a prize. When she arrived at his side, she scooted herself on his lap and kissed the side of his face.

"What can I do for you, handsome?" She seductively asked.

"Do you love me?" Walter inquired flatly.

"You know I do."

"Why?"

"Why? That's a silly question. I don't know. A lot of reasons. You're fun. You're honest. And, you're nice to me."

She finished her statement with a nervous giggle.

"Would you do anything for me?"

"Whatta 'ya got in mind, stud?"

"Let's you and me runaway."

"Where to?"

"Toledo."

She quickly pulled her chin into her chest and leaned backwards.

"Toledo? Isn't that in Ohio?"

"Yep. Toledo, *Ohio*. What do you say?"

She studied him for a minute, then unleashed a relieved giggle.

"You're fooling with me, aren't you?"

"If I could I would."

"Toledo," she laughed. "That's *really* why I love you. You're a riot."

She kissed him again, then made her way back to her table of friends.

I was really starting to question this guy's sanity.

"I don't get it. What's in Toledo?"

"Not much. Therefore, if you ever meet a woman who says she'll run away to Toledo with you, hang on to her, because she must really love you. Get it now?"

"What happens if you're already with a woman, but she doesn't want to go to Toledo with you?"

"Then you're in trouble."

"Like them two?"

I nodded toward the angry murmurs coming from over his right shoulder. That old woman was still quietly bitching at the old man.

"Why don't you do something interesting for a change?" she grumbled. "Like blinking, maybe."

I assumed that they were a couple, because people who aren't a couple don't complain like that. They'd either just walk away, or start punching.

"That's old Boog and Hista," Walter whispered. "They've been coming in here since Moses was in short pants."

"Boog and Hista? Who's who?"

"He's Boog. Separately, they're nice enough folks, but together, keep your distance. All she does is nag the guy. And all he does is sit and sip his beer. I call them *Ossified and Harridan*." He paused for a moment. "Get it?"

"Yeah," I told him.

"You're sure about that?"

"Ossified and Harridan. He doesn't move. And she's a nag."

"Damn," he sighed. "Tough crowd."

"Think she ever wanted to go to Toledo with him?"

"When they got together, Toledo wasn't even discovered yet." He paused again, and stared me down with a very judgmental squint. "Nothing, huh? You know, a little sense of humor might help you there, Daryl. They say the first step is acceptance. The second step is the punch line. You can't take life so seriously. Okay? Will you try?"

"Fine."

"Laughter, Daryl. It's life's express lane."

"What the hell does that mean? *Here's mud in your eye. Life's express lane*. Why can't people...?"

Before I could finish, all hell broke loose. Breaking glass, pounding, and screaming, all coming from the general direction of Boog and Hista.

"Can't I have *ONE LOUSY BEER* in peace? Just once?"

"How 'bout I bury you with a six-pack?"

Hista grabbed a half-empty bottle from the bar and flung it at Boog. It bounced off his arm and shattered on the floor.

"You wouldn't even leave me alone in death, you miserable hag!"

She pounded her flattened palms on the bar. "How 'bout I leave you alone now?"

"I'll believe it when I see it."

Walter spun around his chair and watched the scene, not daring to get any closer. "Guys, guys, come on! Hista. Let me buy you a drink."

Neither one of them were listening to Walter, or anyone else who half-heartedly attempted to intervene.

"They go at each other like this every day?" I asked.

"Not like this."

"You want it?" Hista screeched. "I'll go!"

"I wanted it for fifty years!"

"You couldn't live a day without me! You're already half a zombie as it is!"

"I promise you, you leave, I'm taking dance lessons, so I can celebrate in style!"

"You rotten good-for-nothing son-of-a-bitch!"

Hista jerked to her left, and fell off her barstool. Her eyes were glazed, seemingly not focusing on any one thing in particular. The room fell eerily silent. The only sounds to be heard were Hista's heavy panting, and her shoes scraping the floor.

The crowd parted as she stumbled quickly toward the door. She gave the handle a quick tug, then staggered out into the dark street.

How the hell did it get so dark outside so quickly? Was I in here that long?

Now everyone in the bar looked to the person immediately next to them, then slowly they each surveyed the rest of the room. Lastly, all eyes turned to Boog, who looked back at no one.

The elapsed time from the front door closing to the synchronized scrutiny of Boog couldn't have been more than ten seconds.

The length of time it took for all eyes to shift from Boog back to the front door was a millisecond.

It only required a horn honk, squealing tires, and a scream.

A woman standing near the door pushed opened it and looked outside.

"Hista!"

Everyone ran for the door, frantically squeezing three or four at a time onto the sidewalk.

I pulled Walter's chair back a few feet, out of the way from the oncoming crush of people who seemed more concerned with Hista than they did about anyone inside the bar.

Boog stayed on his stool for a moment. It was easy to guess what was flooding his mind, *is this my fault? Did I do this?*

He sprang from the stool with a surprising burst of energy, even considering the circumstances, and hobbled straight-legged toward the door.

I pushed Walter outside, and this time, he didn't refuse.

Hista was crumpled on her back in the street, the crowd having already formed the compulsory gawkers circle around her.

"Did anybody call?" someone asked.

"I just did," answered another. "They're on their way."

"What happened?" came another voice.

"I just saw a car flying down the street."

"It didn't stop?"

Boog worked his way through to the center, pulling arms and pushing bodies that blocked his path.

"Hista?" he whispered. "Hista?"

When he reached her, he carefully lowered his creaky old body to the asphalt and held her gently in his arms.

"Back the hell up!" he bellowed at the crowd. "Give her some goddamn room to breathe!"

I must not have been the only one who feared she was dead, because after she let out the weakest of coughs, one loud, collective sigh was instantly released by the crowd.

"You're right," Boog confessed. "I couldn't live a day without you. Hang on, now. The ambulance is on the way."

Jess raised herself up on her toes and addressed the gathering.

"Did anyone see the car? The make or model? Color? Partial plate? What part of the car hit her?"

A man who I did not recognize from being in the bar spoke up.

"She wasn't hit."

All heads, of course, turned his way.

"What do you mean?" Jess asked.

"There was a car, had to be going at least sixty or seventy, the idiot, but he didn't hit her. He swerved out of the way just in time. She tripped and fell on the street when he honked at her."

Boog's face tightened. "Are you frigging kidding me?" he shot down at Hista. "You weren't hit?"

She curled her lips into a tiny smile. "I'm still hurt, you bastard. I fell on my hip."

"You rotten..."

"I knew you couldn't live a day without me."

She tried to laugh, but it came out sounding like a needle skipping on a scratchy record.

Most everyone shook their heads, *"Those two"*, and slowly filed back into the bar. I was about to do the same, but froze when I heard Steve calling my name.

"Daryl! Daryl! Help!"

He was already by my side before I could make a move.

"She got hit by a car!" he panted. "I think she's dying!"

35

There was no life-confirming cough like Hista's. I couldn't even hear breathing. She was lying lifelessly on the front passenger seat, bleeding like crazy from her head.

I steered with my left hand, trying to apply pressure to the wound with my right, which is what I've always heard you should do. But she was so tiny that I didn't know how much pressure could be too much. I certainly didn't want to cave in her skull while trying to stop her bleeding.

Steve stood on his hind legs in the backseat, leaning over the top of the front seat and staring down at her.

"It was the same car," he said, shaking.

"What *same car*," I asked. "What are you talking about?"

"That tried to hit you when we stopped here earlier."

"That was an accident, Steve."

"Trust me. I got a real good look. The guy drove past us like normal, then made a u-turn and hit the gas. There's no way either one was an accident."

"Why would someone do that?"

"I don't know," he said, starting to weep. "Don't let her die."

We found a sign for a hospital and drove straight there, but it was a waste of time, because they refused treat her.

"There's an animal hospital about fifty miles away," an ER nurse told me.

"Do you think she'll make it that far?"

She took a look down at the dog. "Give me a minute," and she ran inside.

I reached into the car and patted Steve's neck. I could feel his whole body vibrating.

"She'll be okay," I assured him. "I promise."

The nurse came back much sooner than I thought, and handed me a piece of paper with handwritten directions.

"My neighbor is a vet," she told me. "I called him. He'll meet you at his office in ten minutes."

"Thanks."

"Good luck."

I grabbed the directions and drove off.

When we pulled up, the lights were on and an older man in a white lab coat was holding open the front door.

I jumped out of the car and carried her inside as quickly as I could, with Steve following behind.

"What happened?" the doctor asked.

"She was hit by a car. About twenty minutes ago."

"Is she yours?"

"No. I don't know who she belongs to. If anyone. She had no tags."

"And the driver?"

"Drove off. She was with my dog when it happened. I was at a bar. He came back and told me."

"Are we just going to stand here talking?" Steve yelled. "Or is he going to do something?"

"Where should I take her?" I asked.

He held another door open for me, and I laid her on an examination table inside the room.

"Mister...?" he started.

"Gleason."

"Mister Gleason. Wait out there, please."

I walked out to the waiting room and gave it a quick scan. The few magazines they had spread on the tables were all at least a year old, and were pretty useless anyway. *Carnival Magazine?* Was there really a big demand for that here? The TV was off, it being after hours, so rather than scrounge around for the remote, I plopped myself into a chair by the window and stared out into the parking lot.

Everything but a restaurant at the far end of the strip mall was closed, and none of the businesses gave any indication whatsoever of what town we were in. Coffee shop. Shoe shop. A chain hair salon. Tax offices. A copy place. And so on. I could be anywhere, but I'm here. Wherever the hell that was.

"How can you be so damn calm?" Steve asked.

"About what?"

"What do you mean, *about what*?" he spit back. "Valerie's in there, barely alive, and you're staring out a window."

"Valerie? That's her name?"

"Yeah."

"What do you want me to do, Steve? I'm not a doctor. I can't go in there and help. Besides that, she's just..."

"Don't you dare say, *she's just a dog!*" he snapped.

"I wasn't going to say that." Then suddenly, this memory hit me from out of nowhere. "Valerie was my mother's name."

"And Steve was your dad's name. I know."

"How do you know?"

"Ben told me. Why do you think I picked them?"

"What do you mean, *you picked them?*"

"We were talking about how much we hated our given names. *Crazycakes*. Can you believe that? The stupid shit humans name us, I swear. Anyway, when I told her you let me use a human name, she said she wanted one, too, but she didn't really know too many. I said *Valerie*, and... she really liked it."

He started to choke up and quickly turned toward the window.

"Why my parents names, though?"

"That first night. You took care of me. I thought maybe I could take care of you. Make up for what your dad didn't do. It only made sense that her name be Valerie."

"Why would that make sense?"

"Because she lost her family, too. And, because I love her."

"You what?"

"I know. I know. But, I can't stop thinking about her. When she got hit, I thought I was going to die, too. She's all I can think about anymore. That's love, right?"

"I think so."

He hopped into the chair next to me and sat on his back legs.

"You ever feel like that?"

"I don't think I know anyone who's ever felt like that."

He nudged a little closer and rested his chin on my right leg.

"So, what was yours?" I asked.

"My what?"

"Your dog name."

He sighed heavily, and pondered it for a moment "If I tell you, do you promise never to speak it again?"

"It's that bad?"

"Promise?"

"Yeah, sure."

He shook his head in disgust. "Tinkles."

"Tinkles?"

"Before I was housebroken, okay? I was a little excitable, and had a few accidents."

"Wow. I kinda wish you didn't tell me now."

"You promised!"

"Okay. *Steve*. From now on."

We sat there for a while, who knows how long, not saying a word. I think I even dozed off for a minute. Hard to tell.

Then the door to the street pushed open and I saw the back of a wheelchair working its way inside. I jumped up and pulled the door wider.

"Walter. What are you doing here?"

"I heard about your dog. Any word?"

"She's not..."

I was about to tell him that she wasn't my dog, but the pitiful expression on Steve's face suggested otherwise.

"I don't know," I continued. "The vet's working on her now. How did you know where I was?"

"Word got around. A couple people saw what happened. It sounds like it was the same car that almost ran over Hista. The police are out looking now."

"What does it matter? You can't undo what's done."

I sat back down in the same chair and stared back out the same window. I don't know why, nothing had changed.

"I also wanted to check in on you," Walter said. "See how you're doing?"

"Why?"

"Because I'm a little worried about you. And I don't usually worry."

"You shouldn't be worried about me," I told him. "You should worry about yourself."

He laughed to himself. "Oh, I've got nothing to worry about."

"That's your problem right there. You've got yourself believing that nothing's ever wrong, so you can't even recognize what's staring you right in the face."

"Is that so?" he said, slurping in a gulp of air. "What's staring me in the face that I don't see?"

"Loneliness."

"I told you. I'm not lonely. I have friends all over."

"But not the one person you really want. A companion."

"Nobody wants to..."

"Because you convinced yourself they don't. You conditioned yourself to not take life seriously, to laugh at all your problems and pains, rather than trying to find a way to solve them. It's also a convenient way to avoid heartbreak. If you never try, you'll never fail. How many women have you really asked to go to Toledo with you? And not as a joke? I think you're scared, and you mask it with laughter. You live in this self-constructed cocoon where everything is just perfect. Which is fine, so long as you never leave it."

The door to the examination room opened, and both Steve and I jumped to our feet.

"How is she? How is she?" Steve repeated.

The doctor looked down at him, then back over to me.

"He's a little anxious," I told him. "How is she?"

"Her front left leg is badly sprained. But, at least it's not a break. She has bruises to her ribs, and a slight concussion. There does not appear to be any severe trauma to the head. The bleeding was not as bad as it looked. I taped her leg, and gave her something for the pain."

He shook a pill bottle he was holding as evidence.

"I'm going to see her," Steve said, and he walked past the doctor and into the other room.

"How long 'til I can take her?" I asked.

He furrowed his brow and clasped his hands together. "I thought you said she wasn't yours?"

"Well, she is. Now."

"I'm afraid, Mister Gleason, that I cannot release her until I find out who she belongs to. Tomorrow morning, I'll have her transported to the kennel at the hospital."

"Look, I'm paying you for this. That should mean something."

"I'm sorry."

"Walter, tell him, would you?"

But when I spun around looking for Walter's help, he was gone.

"Where the hell did he go?"

"Who?" the doctor asked.

"Walter. He was right there a minute ago."

"There was no one there when I came in."

"Yes there was!" I said, raising my voice. "He's in a wheelchair! How could you miss that?"

"Would you have a seat?" he instructed. "I have to take care of one other matter. Give me a minute."

He disappeared back into the examination room.

Where the hell did Walter go? What's worse, how did the doctor not see him? It didn't give me much comfort to think a guy who couldn't spot a wheelchair in an otherwise empty room just examined my injured dog.

How did I not hear him leaving, though? Going through a door in a wheelchair isn't the quietest activity in the world.

He must have gotten a ride here, because it's too far from the bar for him to have scooted all the way over himself. Maybe whoever drove him was waiting for him outside, and they needed to leave right away.

Would have been nice if he said something, though.

The next thing I knew, something was pulling at my pants leg.

"Dude," Steve was whispering in a panic. "We gotta bolt! Now!"

"Why? What's the matter?"

"That doc is calling the cops. He's saying you hit Valerie, and now you're trying to steal her."

"Let me go talk to him."

"And while you're doing that, the cops come, lock you up, and send Valerie away. Dude, if no one claims her, they kill her. And no one's gonna claim her. She has no human!"

"Well, we can't just leave her here then."

"No shit," Steve slowly pronounced. "What do you think I've been saying? Grab her, and let's get the fuck out of here!"

"What about him?"

"He's on the phone in another room. Come on, let's go!"

I quietly snuck into the exam room. I could hear the doctor, but I don't think he could hear me, so I carefully lifted the ends of the sheet underneath Valerie, and carried her out stork-style.

I laid her on the backseat, and Steve nestled himself as close to her as he could. I shut the roof and looked back.

The front door to the vet's office was just opening.

I shifted into drive, spun my tires, and hauled ass out of there.

36

We drove through the night, stopping only once for gas and a pee break. Valerie slept the entire time, guarded closely by her private, and highly neurotic, nurse.

"How did you feel when your human died?"

"I don't know," Steve mumbled. "Why?"

"I just don't remember you being this upset."

Steve leaned into the front seat and spoke with a gruff whisper. "Valerie's not going to die! Don't say shit like that!"

"I wasn't implying that. I'm just wondering. What did you feel? Were you upset? Scared? What?"

Steve hung his head and thought about it for a minute.

"Honestly, I didn't feel much of anything. It was hearing Ben died that bothered me the most."

"Really? Why?"

"Because he understood me. We talked, and he listened. I never knew how important that was to me. Yeah, sure, my owner fed me, took care of me, but she never understood me. Never knew what I thought or wanted. Up until talking with Ben, I thought that's just the way life always was for us, so why worry about it? But now that I know it's possible with some people, for them to listen and understand you, that's what I want. Isn't that what everybody wants?"

He pushed off from the front seat, and carefully snuggled next to Valerie.

Off to my left, the sun was just coming up, which told me two things: One, I was heading in the right direction, and Two, I needed to take my pills.

I rolled my tongue inside my mouth to create a pool of spit, and swallowed one pill each. Then I stared at my reflection in the side view mirror.

"You will be happy. Always speak your mind. Always tell the truth. Be true to yourself. Don't let others define you. Be the god of your own life. Don't forget her. And, something else that has to do with laughter, and being in the express lane."

That one wasn't quite clear. I knew I'd have to work on it some, but this wasn't the time or place. We had to get back on the road. I couldn't even imagine how much time was lost already.

There was only one small problem. I was so damned tired.

Luckily, there was a Denny's right down the block. Isn't there always?

I parked in a spot halfway between the restaurant and the road. My eyes could barely stay open long enough to lock the doors, but I managed. Within seconds, I was out.

I woke up with Steve on my chest, licking my face.

"Hey, Daryl! Wake up! I remembered!"

"Get off me." My voice sounded like I was talking through a soup can. "What's going on?"

"I remembered!" he repeated.

"Remembered what?"

"I know who that was. The guy that hit Valerie."

"You know him?"

"Yeah. It's the guy from Marcy's restaurant."

"What guy?" I asked. My throat was so dry, it actually hurt to talk above a whisper.

"The guy in the storm, banging at the door. Remember?"

"You're saying that was him? The same one who tried to break into the car with Sinatra?"

"Yes! He's the one who hit Valerie. And the one who tried to hit you."

"Are you sure?"

"Yes. It took me a while, but dude, I'm sure. Sure as shit. Same guy."

"Well, who is he. And why is he following us?"

"I..." He started to speak, but was interrupted.

"Steve?"

His face lit up at the sound of her voice.

"Hi," he softly said, spinning around to look at her.

"Where are we?" she asked.

"We're in my human's car."

I repositioned myself to look.

"Hi," I said. "I'm Daryl."

"Ow. My leg hurts," she quietly moaned. "What happened?"

"You don't remember?" Steve asked.

"No."

"You were hit by a car."

"That's not possible. I'm always so careful."

"It wasn't your fault," I told her. "Steve said the guy hit you on purpose."

"You weren't kidding. He really does know what we're saying!" She looked more shocked at this than in pain from the accident.

"I wouldn't lie to you," Steve said.

I wriggled myself back to normal position and looked out the driver's window. The sun was just coming up. When I fell asleep, the sun was coming up. It couldn't be the same day, because I felt too awake for only a five minute sleep.

"How long was I asleep?" I asked.

"No idea. I didn't look at the clock. It was pretty long, though."

"Why did he hit me on purpose?" Valerie sniffled.

"We don't know," I said. "It doesn't make much sense."

"He didn't say anything?"

"No," Steve explained. "He just drove away, the bastard. I dragged you to the curb and ran for Daryl. He brought you to the vet."

"You guys did all that for me?"

"Of course," Steve proudly announced.

"Why?"

"You don't remember that, either?"

She smiled as the memory returned, and she started to sniff. Steve rubbed his nose against her neck.

"You want a pill for the pain?" I asked her.

"No," she said. "I don't want to be numb right now."

Which reminded me, if this was in fact a new day, I needed to take my pills. I tossed two in my mouth, and tried my damnedest to draw up a little saliva, but it was useless. There just wasn't anything there. So, I gave up and choked them down dry.

"You will be happy," I quietly mumbled to myself. "Always speak your mind. And always tell the truth. Be true to yourself. Define yourself. Don't let others do it for you. Be the god of your own life. Don't forget her. Then whatever he said about laughter and being in the express lane."

I took a quick inventory. Had to pee. Could probably eat, but not starved. Same as always.

I stepped out and did a slow three-sixty of the parking lot. Cars pulling in. Cars pulling out. People getting out of cars. People getting into cars. I wanted to scream. Does anything change? It's always the same stupid things no matter where I go. Everything is so familiar, so goddamn common, yet at the same time, it's all so...

Unfamiliar.

It's like being an alien in your own backyard. And if I feel that removed, that distant, in my own backyard, how the hell is anything going to improve by me driving all the way to Nevada?

Out of nowhere, my hands started to shake. I gripped the wheel as tight as I could to steady them, but it didn't help. The shaking moved into my arms, and quickly spread through the rest of me. Before I knew it, my entire body was convulsing.

My hands stayed firm on the wheel, and I squeezed shut my eyes. It felt like I was in one of those stupid massage chairs at the mall, and the one I picked went haywire.

I think I blacked out for a minute, because the next thing I knew, Steve was leaning on my right shoulder and licking my ear.

"Dude? You okay?"

I took a couple quick breaths and assessed the situation. The shaking was gone, but for some reason, I couldn't pry my fingers from the steering wheel.

"Daryl?"

"What's happening?" Valerie cried.

"We," I stammered. "We should turn back."

Steve jumped into the front seat. "Turn back? Why? What about the pirates? What about your happiness?"

"It's no good."

"What's no good?"

"Any of this. It's not working. I haven't seen any pirates! Everyone I did meet left me, and now I'm all alone, and not any happier!"

"You're not alone, dude. I'm not going anywhere."

"But now there's some guy chasing us. He almost killed you and Valerie. It's not safe."

Her voice came floating softly from behind me. "I thought this was something you needed to do?"

"I thought so, too. But, I'm not so sure if I want to go any further."

"Steve told me this trip is supposed to help make you happy again. Is that true?"

My hands started to quiver again, but before it had a chance to travel, I stretched out my fingers as far as they'd go. The sensation stopped.

"I'm worried that something bad's going to happen," I told them.

"Nothing's gonna happen as long as I'm around," Steve promised. "I know what to expect now."

"You helped me," Valerie started.

"...and me, too!" Steve added.

"You took care of both of us," she continued. "Let us help take care of you."

"Really?" I asked. "You're okay with this?"

"Yes," Valerie excitedly said. "Besides, I want to see what a pirate looks like."

"Come on, buddy!" Steve cheered on. "Let's get back on the road."

"Look out, pirates!" Valerie giggled.

I started the car, and Steve hopped into the back.

"What do you like better, Val? Burger King or McDonalds?"

37

All fed and settled in, we hit the road again, headed for Nevada. Somewhere, in Nevada. Valerie had never been inside a car before, and judging from her behavior, you would have thought being a passenger in the backseat of a Mustang was the most amazing thing ever. We propped her up in the left side corner so she had a better view of the scenery. And just in case Steve or I missed any of it, she made sure to point it out:

"Look at the pretty trees!"

"Wow, that car's going fast!"

"Those are tall mountains!"

"Look at the size of those dogs!"

I gave a quick look to my right to see the big dogs.

"Those aren't dogs." I hollered. "They're cows."

"What are cows?"

Steve, of course, jumped in before I could answer. "Cows are just like big dogs, only stupid."

This was going to be a long ride.

It was probably a good two hundred miles or so before we saw the sign.

I say *good*, because time seemed to pass in the blink of an eye. It felt more like twenty miles than two hundred.

"There it is, Daryl!" Steve announced. "*Welcome To Nevada!*"

Valerie gasped. "We're here?"

"We're in *Nevada*," I explained. "But I have no idea *where* in Nevada the pirates are. It's a pretty big state."

"Turn on the radio," Steve suggested.

"I doubt if they'd have commercials for it."

"Even so, I wouldn't mind hearing some music."

"I like music," Valerie chimed in.

"Oh yeah," Steve grinned. "What kind? We like punk!"

"Who's that?" Valerie asked.

I hope she's kidding.

"You say something?" Steve shouted.

I flicked on the radio and turned up the volume.

"Keep an eye out for signs," I instructed.

"Aye aye, Captain."

I saw him salute me in the rearview mirror. Valerie got a kick out of that.

What a ham.

Like before, the radio was picking up nothing but static. That could be seen as validation that we truly were in the middle of nowhere, or, it could be validation that the radio didn't work. Just in case it was the former and not the latter, I set the tuner at a random spot on the left side of the FM dial. That's generally where college and local stations lurk, so I figured maybe I'd get lucky and catch a signal of a school, or something.

"What was that?" Valerie yelled.

The question was spit out so quickly, it was hard to tell if she sounded worried or excited.

"What was what?" Steve asked.

"I swear I just saw a picture of Daryl," she said.

"Where?"

"Back there," she shouted. "On a pole on the side of the road."

"Why would there be a picture of me on a pole in Nevada?"

"I don't know."

"Are you wanted out here?" Steve asked.

"I don't think so," I told him.

"There's another one!" Valerie shrieked.

"Maybe we should give her a pill," Steve muttered in my ear.

"I'm not crazy!" she insisted. "Just watch. Maybe they'll be more!"

Steve moved over to the right side of the car, and perched his front paws on top of the door. I tried as best as I could to watch, but my main priority was the road in front of me. So I had to rely on Steve to be my eyes for anything off to the side.

About twenty seconds later, I thought I saw something, but wasn't sure until Steve confirmed it.

"What the shit!" he shouted in disbelief.

"Told you!" Valerie smirked.

"It was!" Steve exclaimed. "D, there was a picture of you. On a pole in Nevada."

Damn it.

"I told you," I said. My jaw was so tight I could barely move it. "I said I was worried about something if we went any further."

"Was one of his eyes blacked out?" Valerie asked.

"Hold on," Steve instructed. "There's another one coming up. Slow down."

I took my foot off the gas and tapped the brake.

"It's not blacked out. It's an eye patch! Dude, it's an eye patch! That's it! Your sign! This is the way to the pirates!"

"Yay!" Valerie screamed.

A voice began to break through the static. Faint, but nonetheless existent. I carefully turned the dial millimeter by millimeter until it came in as clear as it could.

"Sorry to interrupt your regularly scheduled static," the voice announced. "But we're taking over your airwaves. Or at least, this portion of them. Welcome to Pirate radio."

"Did you hear that?" Steve spit out.

"Yeah! Shh! Shh!"

The signal was fading in and out. The Voice and The Static were apparently in a cage match to the death, so I cranked up the volume to catch as much as I could.

"Are you part of the pirate crew? If so, it's time to let loose! Be free! Be naughty! Bounce your soul and have some fun! I'm Captain Happy, the leader of this audio ship, and I say, let's set this bastard a-sail!"

Captain Happy? That's what it sounded like he said. If so, it's kind of an odd coincidence.

"And along with me on this voyage," the voice continued. "Is my first mate, uh..."

Another voice tagged in, but was no contest for The Static.

"Peg Leg Pete," the first voice said. "Check that, *No Leg* Pete. Anyway, here's one No Leg picked out for a special friend of ours who's looking for direction. Hope you're listening. And following along!"

"Captain Happy and No Leg Pete?"

"Dude!" Steve shouted. "This is what we've been looking for!"

"Yeah. Sounds like it could be."

A song started to play. It didn't take me long to recognize it.

It only took slightly longer for Steve to get offended by it.

"What the hell is this?" he sniped.

"*Adam and the Ants*."

"What is wrong with you humans? We don't eat each other."

"It's just an expression."

"*Dog Eat Dog* is an *expression*? How so?"

"It means a situation that's really competitive. Or difficult. Like work, or life in general."

"Why *dog*? Why can't it be *Cat Eat Cat*? Or, *Snake Eat Snake*? I think they actually *do* eat each other."

"It's a metaphor."

"Oh, yeah? They why do they say, *brush me, daddy-o*? Everyone knows dogs like to be brushed."

I had a feeling this was going to last a long time, especially when Valerie joined in.

"Oh, Steve. Don't take it so personally."

"How could you not take that personally? It's insulting."

"Who cares what other humans say?" Valerie asked. "Daryl doesn't think you eat dogs. Do you?"

I shrugged. "I wouldn't rule it out. He's got a hell of an appetite."

"Shut up," Steve snarled.

Valerie laughed. And I could tell that he was smiling, but I didn't say anything. I couldn't if I wanted to. Just hearing the happiness in his voice was a reminder of how desperate I was to one day get that feeling back. I couldn't even get myself to muster a sarcastic comment. It's not that I begrudge Steve his happiness. Call me selfish, but I keep wondering when the hell it's finally going to be my turn.

I stepped hard on the accelerator and watched for more photos of myself.

The signal was growing clearer and stronger with every mile. I could make out everything Captain Happy and No Leg Pete had to say. And play. They had very good taste.

Blasting music when you're driving does more than just break up the monotony of never-ending asphalt. It gives you a sense of freedom. Like, *anything's possible, and here's my accompanying soundtrack!* It made me think back to all those road trips to nowhere with Woody, and how much he used to piss me off. Don't ask me to bring the music if you're just going to turn it off. If you don't like it what I chose, then pick something out yourself. Or bring your own goddamn music.

In retrospect, that guy was an asshole. I don't know why I never realized it back then. Not only did he break up a perfectly good band, but he may have ruined Audrey and me, too.

What the hell was I thinking? What made Woody so important? Why did I let him be so important?

"You're a dick, Woody!"

Woody. I don't know why, but I can say that stupid name now without cringing.

Woody.

"A total and complete dick, Woody!"

"You okay?" Steve shouted.

"I don't know. Maybe."

"You better watch your speed. You're doing ninety."

It seemed like we were going a little fast, but I didn't bother to check. I eased up on the pedal until the needle dropped to seventy-five.

I blame it on the Descendents. It hard to go the speed limit when "Can't Go Back" is blaring out the speakers.

I was focused on the road, so Steve was the first to notice, and once he brought it to our attention, both Valerie and I began to spot them ourselves: to the average eye, it might have been nothing more than roadside litter, but we recognized it for what they actually were.

Clues. Signs.

They had to be. It was too coincidental not to be. The closer you looked, the more you could see the pirate theme laid out for our benefit. I didn't say it out loud, because I didn't want to accuse either Steve or Valerie, but, how long were these clues out there and just going unnoticed?

At various points we spotted: a hook, a torn sail blowing in a tree, a broken wicker basket, (a crow's nest - obviously), a large metal block with a chain attached to it, (an anchor), at least a half dozen dead birds, (the captain's parrots. I hope the birds were already dead before it was decided to use them as clues), and quite a few empty bottles of what appeared to be Captain Morgan.

What else could it be?

And if all of this, combined with the radio broadcast, wasn't confirmation enough that we were headed in the right direction, the wooden sign just up ahead certainly was.

Port St. Charles Next 3 Exits

I don't know a lot of pirate history, but I do know that Port St. Charles is in the Bahamas, and that's where all of the pirates hung out. I remember that from movies. This had to be the place.

I slid into the right lane and drove up the exit.

"Why we getting off?" Steve asked.

"Because I think we're here."

"Really?"

"I think so. Which way feels right to you?"

"Shouldn't it feel right to *you*?" Valerie asked.

We coasted to a stop at the intersection, but I wasn't feeling any particular pull in either direction, so I kept my foot on the brake and looked for a sign.

Within seconds, a line of cars formed behind me. Which is weird, because I swear there weren't this many people on the road. The driver of the car directly behind me was hanging out his window and waving like a maniac.

"Come on, already! Do something! What are you waiting for?"

He was signaling to the left, so I cut the wheels in that direction and pressed on the gas.

I drove a couple blocks, but the signs seemed to have vanished. Could we have gone the wrong way?

"Keep looking!" I shouted toward the backseat.

I figured we'd cruise another minute or two in this direction, but if nothing jumped out at us, I'd turn around. Then, a comment Dr. Melvin once made popped into my head. Something about it *all feeling very familiar*.

A strip mall. Just ahead of me to the right.

You can't get any more familiar than one of those!

I rolled up the driveway and found an empty spot by a light post. Steve jumped out of the car, but rather than running ahead like he usually did, he waited for me to scoop Valerie from the backseat.

I didn't mind carrying her, she couldn't weigh more than ten or twenty pounds, so that wasn't the issue. It was more about *how long* I'd have to carry her, considering that she was unable to walk on her own. Just the notion of it seemed rather daunting. Not that I minded so much. I mean, how could you? A guy would have to be a total jerk to feel any other way.

When I saw the abandoned shopping cart, a brief wave of guilt swept over me, but that feeling was quickly suppressed by the cart's pure practicality.

Steve apparently hadn't taken his eyes off of me.

"Everything okay?"

"Yeah. Yeah."

I opened the trunk, removed one of my sport coats, and walked over to the cart, folding and positioning the jacket in the lower basket. Then I lifted Valerie out of the car and carefully placed her on top of the tweed cushioning so she was seated and facing forward.

I chose the tweed for two reasons. One, it was the thickest material, and therefore probably the most comfortable. And Two, *because* it was the thickest, I doubted I'd be wearing it while I was in Nevada.

"What a great idea," Valerie softly said. "Thank you."

I pushed the cart a couple steps, then heard Steve loudly clear his throat.

"Ahem!"

He hadn't moved from the side of the car.

"What?" I asked.

"Aren't you forgetting something?"

I gave myself a quick personal inventory. "Keys. Pills. Sign."

"Me!" he agitatedly exclaimed.

"What about you?"

"Those things are easy to jump out of, but getting into them is a pain in the ass."

"I figured you'd want to be on the outside. You know, like our first line of defense."

"Hmm," he mused. "Good point."

He scampered up to us, and took position on our left flank.

The truth is, I knew he'd never stay inside for any length of time, which meant I'd be spending most of my time lifting him back into the basket. Over and over again. I figured appealing to his ego would cancel the inevitable argument.

He can be so predictable.

We zigzagged through the parking lot, looking for anything that could point us in the proper direction. It wasn't an unusually large strip mall, but it was taking a long time to cover, even with three sets of eyes scanning in all directions. Diligence wasn't to blame for slowing us. If anything, it was the damn sun. I knew Nevada would be hot, but this was downright brutal. And the heat was only magnified by the fact that there was nothing on the ground to provide shade, unless you were some bulimic supermodel who could fit into the shadow of a street light. And judging by the angle of the shadows, I'd say it was about two, maybe two-thirty.

Sweat was streaming down my entire body. I wanted to take my coat off, but that didn't seem fair to the dogs, seeing how they were permanently stuck wearing theirs, so I decided to suffer along with them.

I have to commend Steve. He led our little unit across that burning asphalt without muttering one complaint. Which is quite an accomplishment for him. The little guy was focused and determined. My mind though, started to wander. Even though my eyes saw what was in front of me, my mind, for whatever reason, stopped processing the information. As a result, it shifted my body into auto-pilot. I moved ahead without paying attention to where my legs were taking me. Or why.

All I could think about now was air conditioning and a cold, cold, beer. I didn't even care if it was Old Style or Schlitz. That's how bad it was. I just wanted a tall frosted mug of *something*. Ice cold. Then, for some odd reason, I envisioned myself drinking it inside an igloo. Why the hell I pictured myself in an igloo is a mystery. Never been inside an igloo in my life. Never even seen one close up. But, there I was, sitting in nothing but my underwear no less, gulping down a bottomless glass of beer. And Steve, of course, right next to me, lapping away brew from his endless bowl. He looked the same.

Then Valerie spoke. That in itself was enough to kick my mind back into gear. I was once again back to wandering in the miserable heat of the parking lot, with only one thought regarding my brief visit to the igloo:

Dry heat, my ass.

"Didn't you tell me something about a *cove*?" Valerie asked Steve. The sound of her voice reminded me of listening to a movie through a broken drive-in speaker.

Whenever I went to the drive-in, I'd bring a cooler of ice cold beer with me. And sometimes a girl. But always beer. Damn, I could use a beer.

"Yeah," Steve answered wearily. "What about it?"

"Tell me again."

"A cove is a secluded area of a beach. It's usually where the pirates are headquartered. Why?"

"Look," she wheezed.

Her paw pointed to a small storefront, clandestinely nestled between two larger businesses. The sign read, "The Cove".

"You did it!" Steve exclaimed. "You found it! Bar ho!"

He sprinted full steam ahead toward the building. I, too, picked up my pace, but I didn't want to go so fast that I jostled Valerie all over the cart. At least that would be my excuse if Steve questioned me. But he didn't. He was too busy scratching at the door.

"Open the door! We're here! We finally made it!" His panting and screaming echoed throughout the parking lot.

Since it was doubtful that anyone inside could hear him, or if they did, understand what he was saying, no one had come to open the door. So, when I finally caught up with him, I gave it a strong pull myself.

Air conditioning!

I slid two fingers into my collar and tugged my shirt forward to allow some of that splendidly cool air to flow onto my neck. Then I took a deep breath and pushed the shopping cart over the door sill.

Get Happy

I stood for a moment, and allowed my eyes to adjust from the bright sun to the darkened room.

Initially, my only visions were amorphous blobs, expanding and contracting in a kaleidoscope of bright orange, dark purple and black. Like looking through a microscope with the illuminator dimmed. The room was occupied by other people, I could hear them, even though I couldn't yet pull them into focus. The crowd noise prevalent when I first opened the door had diminished considerably. An uneasy hush fell over the room, as if everyone else was waiting for another person to be the first to speak up.

Then it became clear that the person they were waiting to speak first was me.

"Hello?" I called out.

The response was a bit of a surprise. The entire room felt like it exploded in unison.

"Daryl!"

"Holy shit," Steve gasped. "Look at this."

The figures slowly came into focus.

Aaron.

Russell.

Marcy.

Gavin.

Sinatra.

And Walter.

All of them, grouped together at the bar, smiling and waving at me.

And all of them, too, wearing signs around their necks with a single word spelled on the front: *Happy*.

Once the shock wore off, they came running toward me. In Walter's case, *rolling* toward me. After a string of *hellos*, each of them gave me a good-hearted slap.

And Gavin snapped some photos.

I was stunned. "How did you guys find me?"

Aaron was the first to step forward.

"Shortly after you left, I came looking for you. And in my search, I met him."

He pointed at Russell.

"I was a little skeptical at first, but after answering every one of my questions, it was obvious he was looking out for you. So, we tried to trace your steps and ran into her."

Marcy took over at this point. "It was so weird, right? They showed up the same day you left. Like, right after. I took off as soon as I could and caught up with them. Then we met Gavin."

"I threw a couple things in my van and we hit the road," Gavin added. "Eventually ran into Sinatra."

Sinatra's usually tough veneer disappeared, and in its place crept a smile that seemed to never want to stop growing wider.

"I'll admit," she said. "I got scared when I couldn't find you. Then when they rolled up and told me how you were in trouble, Jordan and I joined in. No questions asked."

"Jordan?" I asked, raising my eyebrows.

She smiled and squeezed the boy standing next to her. "He found me."

"We lost track of you for a while," Aaron announced. "Why did you go north? I said it was a straight shot west."

"Yeah," Russell sarcastically added. "Why didn't you listen to Aaron? Don't you know he's always right?"

"Russell," Aaron dryly stated. "Grow up."

"Maybe...I don't wanna grow up. Ever think of that?"

"Everybody has to sooner or later."

"Not if they're lucky!"

Russell laughed and did a cartwheel.

"Who cares why?" Walter laughed. "If he didn't, I wouldn't have met him. Or any of you. Well, no sooner than I met them, I got in the van with Captain Happy here..."

"Captain Happy?" I repeated. "And No Leg Pete!"

They all smiled. Gavin was especially pleased.

"You did hear us!" he beamed. "Hope you liked it."

"When the signal was clear."

"The convoy headed south to Nevada," Walter explained. "Aaron and Russell in one car. Me and the Captain, Sinatra and Jordan in the van. And Marcy on her Harley."

"And now we found you," Aaron said, with a sigh of relief. "Safe."

Walter used the moment to light up a fat cigar. "But hell, if I knew there was going to be a party, I would have invited some more women!" He then gave a nod to Gavin. "And men, too. Whatever floats your pirate boat."

I turned to Sinatra. "What do you mean, *I'm in trouble*?"

"That guy," she said. "The one that tried to break in the car? He's after you, and he's trying to hurt you."

"How do you know?" I looked over at Steve. "Did you say something to them?"

"And how would I have done that?"

"Is that what he thinks, too?" Sinatra asked.

I nodded.

"A strange man came to my house after you left," Aaron started. "Saying the two of you were traveling together, but he lost you along the way. There was something about his manner I didn't trust. Plus, you hadn't mentioned anything about traveling with anyone other than your dog, so I refused to tell him anything. Good thing, too, because I was right."

"We all discussed it," Walter gravely announced. "He's been following you, probably since Chicago. One step behind you, and one step ahead of us."

"About six-one, six-two," Gavin stated. "Dark hair. Muscular. Like he spends a lot of time working out. Sound like anyone you know?"

"You know who that sounds like?" Steve said.

"Yeah," I told him. "Sounds a lot like Robert."

"Julie's Robert?" Marcy gasped.

"And you all saw him?"

Each of them nodded, completely sure of themselves.

"He came in after you drove off," Marcy said. "Telling me the same story about traveling with you. Daryl, that was the same guy who was banging on the front door during the storm. I'm sure of it."

Russell jumped in. "Same story for me. And comparable to Aaron, I refused to divulge any details. However, I did ask a few questions to those thugs that you encountered in the parking lot. Seems he hired them to rough you up."

"And it occurred to me," Aaron added. "That he could have been the reason your car caught fire."

"And you all came to help me?" I asked.

They seemed rather surprised at my question.

"Well, yeah," Walter sputtered. "You helped all of us, kid. It was the least we could do in return."

"I did?"

"Probably more than you'll ever know."

"Then why did you leave me?"

They stared perplexedly at each other.

"We didn't leave you," Marcy said. "You left us."

"No," I said. "Russell, you left me. You even ran back to the hotel to get your suitcase."

Russell nodded. "I wanted to write down everything you told me before I forgot. It was rather important."

"You said you had a mathematical formula that ensured happiness. Tell me. Please!"

Every head in the group turned toward Russell.

"Actually, what I said was, *What if* I had a mathematical formula. I was trying to make a point about people not doing the work themselves. Sorry to get your hopes up."

"Gavin," I said, motioning to him. "When I woke up, you were gone. Where did you go?"

He smiled. "I went out for coffee and bagels. Didn't you see my note?"

"No. You left a note?"

"Yes, I did," Gavin said with a relieved smile. "I thought you left because of that guy. Robert. When I got back to the house, I caught him trying to climb through my kitchen window. He said he was looking for you. Same description, same lame story. I asked his name, and he took off. You didn't see him?"

"No," I said. "I didn't see anyone."

"Then why did you leave?"

"Because I thought you left. You're sure? That was Robert at your house? Looking for me?"

"Yes," he assured me.

"He's the one who hit almost ran over Hista," Walter added. "And hurt this poor little thing's leg."

"I'm scared, Steve," Valerie panted.

Steve bared his teeth. "I'll kill the motherfucker!"

"Language!" Valerie gasped.

I didn't know what to say. Everyone who I thought left me, had actually never left me at all. In fact, they were all searching for me. To help.

"So, we're all in agreement that it's the same guy," Aaron said. "We're just not in agreement what to do."

"Easy," Gavin seethed. "Find him and kill him."

"Have another cocktail, Gavin," Walter calmly insisted. "The way I look at it, as long as we're all together, we're not in any danger. Let's all just take a deep breath."

"Walter has a good point," Aaron interjected. "Today, let's relax and catch up. I'll come up with a plan for us for tomorrow."

"*You* will?" Russell spit out. "Who made you boss? We're a general assembly, not an autocracy."

"And if you think about it," Walter continued, purposely ignoring Russell and Aaron. "What could be safer than being in a bar full of pirates?"

That's right...

I quickly looked around the room. There was a table at the far end of the room with four middle aged men seated around it. One of them looked familiar, even though I couldn't get a straight on look at him.

"Don?" I called out.

The face shifted from profile and looked at me square in the eyes.

"Daryl?"

I had already started walking over to the table for a closer examination, so by the time he leapt to his feet to greet me, I was close enough for him to step in and hug me. Had I remembered his penchant for reaching out and grabbing what he wanted, I would have kept a safer distance. Whatever. It only lasted a few seconds, then he let go of me.

"You found it!" he exclaimed. "I really did not expect to see you. Welcome!"

One of the other three guys at the table, who never bothered to introduce themselves, by the way, cut into our reception. I assumed they were pirates, just not yet costumed for the upcoming festivities.

"Is this the *Plus One* you were telling us about?" he dryly asked.

"It sure the hell is," Don beamed. "This is..."

He paused for a little too long. I figured maybe it was some custom where you had to introduce yourself.

"Daryl," I said. "I met Don at bar outside Chicago called..."

The three at the table collapsed into convulsions.

"Shhh...!"

"Not so loud!"

"What are you doing?"

"Doesn't he know the rules?"

Don looked slightly embarrassed, and tried to shake it off.

"Remember, I told you," he stated in a harsh whisper. "They don't use real names. Or say where they're from. Total anonymity."

"I forgot. I should probably tell them about that." I turned and pointed to my group, who were busy pulling a couple tables together.

Again, came even more convulsions. If these people were pirates, I half wondered if they caught some disease in a previous port.

"Your *Plus One*," the guy across from me nervously sputtered. "Brought one, two, three, four... *seven more* with him?"

"And two dogs," I added.

"And *two dogs?!*" the guy squealed.

That got the attention of the bartender, who was now suspiciously squinting over at my group.

"To be fair," I asserted. "I didn't bring them with me. They came here looking for me."

"Well, how did they know to even look here?"

"I told them."

The three of them slammed their hands down on the table at the same moment. If they were contestants on a game show, there would have to be a bonus round to break the tie.

"That's just it! You're not supposed to even *tell* other people about this! If a pirate cannot operate under a cover of complete and utter secrecy, he is doomed!"

Don took hold of my elbow and leaned in closer to my ear.

"Do me a favor," he quietly asked. "Tell them I told you all the rules? They're kinda touchy."

I was just about to clear Don of any and all charges of betrayal, but I heard my name being called from across the room.

"Daryl!"

"Are we moving on, or staying?"

"When are those pirates supposed to show up?"

The grunting, sighing, clicking of tongues, and overall vocal disgust coming from Don's table of friends was louder than the screams from my group.

"Inform your friends that they better follow the rules, or they're going to have to leave."

"Rules?" I said. "I thought there weren't supposed to be any rules? Don said..."

"Shh!" one shrieked. "We told you! No names!"

"*Don* said," I boldly continued. "The purpose of this gathering is two whole weeks of doing whatever you wanted. *No rules*."

"Well, there has to be rules!" insisted the guy who now appeared to be the table's spokesman.

I guess even pirates had pushy, loudmouth bosses.

Gavin walked over and put his hand on my shoulder. I'm not sure if he was trying to play peacemaker, or bodyguard.

"Is everything okay? Who are these people?"

"These are the pirates I came to meet," I told him. Then I called out to the rest of them.

"Hey, everyone! The pirates are over here!"

The room suddenly went quiet. So quiet, that the hushed mutterings of "What are you doing?" from the lead pirate echoed through the bar.

"Where are the rest of you?" Gavin asked. "Take me to your leader!"

The pirates exchanged confused looks with each other.

"There is no *rest of us*," the spokesman said. "It's just us."

Gavin was stunned. "These are the people you traveled halfway across the country to meet? These are the ones who are supposed to help you find happiness? Four middle-aged insurance salesmen drinking Appletinis?"

He fell into a fit of laughter.

Over Gavin's snickering, I heard one of the pirates mumble to another.

"I am *not* an insurance salesman. Not anymore. Now I'm a risk assessment manager at an insurance company."

"You're not helping!" another sternly whispered.

Marcy walked toward me at a pace that suggested trouble.

"Daryl," Marcy began, only to be interrupted by the Head Pirate.

"My god," he panted. "No names!"

"This is really stupid." I sighed, then cupped my hands around my mouth and shouted toward the ceiling. "My name is Daryl!"

"I'm Gavin!"

"I'm Russell!"

"Sinatra!"

"Jordan!"

"And I be Walter!"

"I'm Steve! And this is the beautiful Valerie!"

Valerie giggled. "You're pretty cute yourself."

The pirates covered their ears. Three *Hear-No-Evils* not at all interested in locating their other partners.

"This is a little counterproductive," Don remarked. "I finally get recognized by other people, and then I'm supposed to not admit who I am?"

I shrugged, then looked back at Marcy.

"This is it?" she asked. "These are your pirates?"

"That's what they say."

"And this is all of them."

"Yeah."

"I can't believe you traveled across the country looking for answers, and this is what you found. *This* is the wild, deviant, gathering that's supposed to get you to find happiness again?" She turned and addressed the pirates directly. "Do you have any idea how much trouble he went through to get here? Just to find you? Huh? So tell me, how are you going to make him happy?"

Their eyes darted from one frightened face another, each hoping someone else would have the courage to answer.

"Don't be mad at me," Don finally spoke up. "That's what they told me. This is my first time here."

"You should be ashamed of yourselves," Marcy scolded.

The spasms of displeasure coming from the main pirate caught Marcy's attention, and she concentrated deeply on his face.

"I know you, don't I?" It was less of a question, and more of an acknowledgement of personal discovery.

"Yes!" she announced with an emphatic snap of her fingers. "Neal! You're Neal Cosgrove! You came to my restaurant! Remember? I was just telling Daryl about you! How wild!"

Neal the Pirate collapsed in his seat and folded like a broken accordion.

"No. No," he muttered to himself. "Not supposed to happen."

The other two pirates took a small step backwards and turned away their faces.

Don stepped forward and smiled.

"Oh," Marcy remembered. "And this is yours."

She handed me a small backpack that had something or other stuffed inside.

"What's this?" I asked.

"Your money and your cell phone. You left them at my place. You were getting a lot of calls, all the same number. Julie. Sorry, I looked. Then the charge ran out."

"Thanks."

"I just thought I should tell you before I left."

"Leaving? Why are you leaving?"

A commotion broke out at the table where the rest of our party were seated. Aaron was standing with one hand on his hip, and one finger from the other hand confrontationally pointed at the bartender's face.

"There are many other taverns in the area that I am sure will be more than happy to take our money, sir."

"I highly doubt that, mister," the bartender shouted back. He was a tiny man with rather unruly gray hair. He looked like a character from an old movie who came to Nevada in search for a fortune in gold, but only found enough to come down from the hills and buy himself a saloon.

Russell, for whatever reason, decided it was a good idea to jump on top of a table. Gavin applauded his feat, then began to bang away at his acoustic guitar. Which of course caused Russell to join along by clapping his hands and stomping his right foot. I'm not sure if playing a hoe-down was Gavin's original intention, but he didn't seem to mind.

The bartender was not moved to join in.

"Don't go anywhere," I told Marcy. "Please? I should probably go take care of that."

Gavin wandered past me and over to Don's table, strumming his guitar like some wandering restaurant minstrel. He leaned over and addressed the table's occupants.

"Pirates suck!" he sang.

When I approached the bartender, he seemed more frazzled than upset.

"What's the problem," I asked.

"I been trying ta explain," he carefully started. I could tell it was all he could do from losing it. "Those two don't have proper I.D., and as fer the dogs, well, I don't know if there's a law or not, but it's probably best ta not test it. This here is a public establishment. If someone comes in 'n complains ta the Board a Health, I could get fined."

"*Public* establishment?" I asked. "You mean, you're open for business to anyone who walks in?"

"What kind a question is that? Look here, I know we're not full up like some bar inna city, but..."

"No. What I mean is, didn't they rent out this place for a private party?"

Now the bartender looked stunned. There was an awful lot of that going around in here lately.

"Who?" he shot.

"The pirates."

"*Pirates?* Ya know, that's another thing I been meanin' ta ask; what's all this I keep hearin' bout pirates?"

I pointed back over to Don's group, which probably wasn't necessary, since there was nobody else in the bar besides us and them.

"Those guys over there."

He looked at them, and then back to me.

"Them are pirates?" He squinted and leaned forward. "Don't that beat all. Anyway ya look at it, I didn't rent this place out ta nobody. Pirates, er otherwise."

Gavin overheard and started going off on them again.

"What a bunch of cheap-ass posers! You convince a guy to drive across country to find you, and you don't even have the decency to rent a room when you fuck him over?"

Steve jumped out of the cart and stopped a few feet short of their table.

"Bastards! Let me bite them!"

The pirates shuffled back a couple inches in the opposite direction.

"See," the bartender said. "Yer dog's already scaring my customers. And then these two," he pointed a crooked finger at Sinatra and Jordan.

"We're both over twenty-one," Sinatra snapped. "I told you. We lost our wallets."

"You did?" I asked.

She turned to me and gave me the nastiest look.

Then an idea came to me.

"Hey," I called to the bartender. "If this place *was* rented for a private party, could the kids and the dogs stay?"

"But I already said," he insisted. "Nobody rented it out."

"I know. I know. I mean, hypothetically speaking. Could they stay?"

He gave his head a scratch and shrugged. "Yeah. I s'pose."

"How much?" I asked.

His face scrunched up. "For what? Renting it?"

"Yeah. Full staff. All you could eat, all you could drink. Is the owner around?"

"Listen mister, I'm the owner!"

"Okay. So, how much, then?"

"Don't know. Never done it before."

"Well, how much do you make in a day?"

He stared at me with that same suspicious look he had when he first heard the word "dog", so I unzipped the backpack and emptied it on the table.

"Just tell me how long this would rent it out for."

His eyes popped open wide, and beads of sweat quickly accumulated on his forehead.

"How much is that there?"

"About fourteen thousand, give or take. There's more if you need it."

He thought for a second, then stepped back. "Hold on. *Pirates?*"

There was that look again. This time though, I at least understood why it was there.

"It's legitimate," I said. "I swear. It's part of an inheritance."

"Okay. Well, we don't get much business around here this time a year. I s'pose that could get you a few weeks."

"I only need two weeks. You can keep what's left."

I handed him the bag, and he audibly gulped.

"In advance? You serious? Holy cripes! The name's Clem!" He grabbed and hand and gave it a furious shake.

"Is it really?" I only asked because the name seemed so damn appropriate.

"Sure is. Clement J. Blue the Third. Glad ta be a service. Now, what a you folks want?"

Everyone at my table started whooping, and barraging Clem with their orders.

"An Old Fashioned," Aaron called out.

"A Miller Lite," Walter announced. "In a bottle."

"I'll take a Heineken!" Steve shouted.

"You're drinking," Valerie asked. "I thought you were on guard duty?"

"Two margaritas," Sinatra said.

"How about two roast beef sandwiches," Russell shouted. "And a bottle of Riesling."

"You don't pair wine with a roast beef sandwich!" Aaron declared. "You drink beer with roast beef. The darker, the better. Clem, give him a Guinness."

"I don't want beer," Russell insisted. "I want wine."

"At least have a red. White wine with red meat is a travesty. And that's another thing. You eat far too much red meat. Add some vegetables to your diet."

"Clem," Russell added. "Can you cover the sandwich in chocolate sauce?"

Aaron's jaw dropped. "Chocolate is not a vegetable! By the way: Daryl, he has one of your suits. My suits, actually. Did you give approval, or did he steal it?"

"I told you, he lent it to me!"

"These two are like Boog and Hista," Walter laughed.

"Hold up guys," Gavin raised his hands to silence the crowd. "Just one small concern must be attended to first."

He whispered something in Clem's ear. Clem took it in, then motor-boated his lips and headed to Don's table, stopping halfway to double-check with Gavin. Gavin motioned authorization for Clem to proceed with whatever was agreed upon. Clem nodded begrudgingly, took a few steps forward, and slammed his hand on the other table.

"Closed!" he announced.

The so-called pirates were mystified.

"What do you mean?" Neal the Pirate shrieked.

"Private party," he declared. Then he pointed a finger at Don. "You can stay, but you three..."

He paused, and again glanced tentatively over his shoulder to Gavin. Gavin smiled, and waved at Clem to continue.

"...you three *douche bags* gotta leave," Clem reluctantly proclaimed. "Now!"

"Yes!" Gavin laughed, pumping his fist in the air.

The three pirates who weren't Don rose from their chairs and hightailed it out the front door as fast as they could. Don smiled and joined the rest of our group.

"I'm staying," he beamed. "It'll be nice not having to lean over and grab my own beers for a while."

Gavin raised his glass in the air. "To Daryl! The man who finally got me to realize that you must be the person you are, whoever that is, and without apology to anyone else! And that art, like life, is whatever you decide it is!"

"Here, here!" Walter sounded off.

Everyone cheered and drank.

"And to the man," Russell added. "Who caused me to reevaluate the methods of my research. There comes a time when you must utilize all your compiled data to form your own conclusions. There may be millions of answers to every question, but there's only one that works best for you!"

Again, everyone cheered.

Sinatra loudly cleared her throat, and when all eyes turned to her, she giggled nervously.

"I ran away, and didn't think anyone was interested in ever finding me," she stopped, took a big gulp of air, and then continued. "But then I met Daryl. If he hadn't found me, chances are, Jordan wouldn't have found me, either. But even if he did, I probably wouldn't have wanted to get back together with him if it wasn't for Daryl's help."

Sinatra smiled, and everyone released a long *Awww!*

Jordan gave Sinatra a playful nudge.

"Aren't you going to tell them?" he asked.

Sinatra blushed and bobbed her head. "Oh yeah. Jordan asked me to marry him."

The group erupted into applause and shouts of approval.

"Not right away," Sinatra spoke up. "In a year or so, but we are engaged."

"Now this is what I call a party!" Walter exclaimed. "Bartender! Bring out your best champagne!"

"We only have the one brand," Clem confessed. "And it's not very good."

"Uncork it anyway, Clem! I have a feeling it will be the best tasting champagne any of us ever drank!"

"In the spirit of goodwill," Aaron started. "We should invite the pirates back in. There was no need to humiliate them like that."

"Why?" Russell quickly asked. "Do you know them?"

"No," Aaron gruffly replied. "I just know it's right."

"Are you afraid there might be consequences? Do you think they'll come back and beat you up? Maybe you think they have little swords hidden in their pocket protectors?"

"The fact is, Daryl came all the way out here to meet them and..."

"He did meet them," Russell interrupted. "And they were pathetic!"

"As a measure of full disclosure, I will admit that I, at first, was not pleased with the idea of Daryl meeting pirates," Aaron calmly continued. "However, it's possible that if we gave them time, he might learn something."

"Do you agree then," Russell asked. "That's it's also equally as possible that Daryl might *not* learn anything, and that those pirates are utterly and entirely useless?

"Had they been given a chance," Aaron smugly announced. "Perhaps we'd know for sure. Anyhow, you like to ask questions so much. Ask Daryl if they should have been kicked out."

They looked at me for an answer.

"I don't know," I said. "They did seem lame. But you can't really fault someone for that. They weren't hurting anybody."

"Alright," Gavin muttered. "I'll invite them back."

He trudged to the door and called outside. "Hey! Hey you! Get back here!"

Aaron pulled back his shoulders and produced a self-satisfied grin meant entirely for Russell's viewing.

"You're just mad that you're not the one who made the decision to kick them out," Russell shot. "You need to be that guy."

"What guy?"

"The one who decides what's right and wrong for everyone else, or you get all pouty."

"I can see that teaching you manners is going to be tougher than I thought."

"Who made it your job to teach me manners?"

"You did. When you revealed yourself as my next project."

"When are you going to untighten your ass and allow yourself to learn from other people?" Russell laughed. "Ask a few question, instead of always spouting answers and demands."

"That's ridiculous," Aaron insisted.

"I forgot. You're also a know-it-all. Tell me, what's the difference between love and hate? Is it a thin line, or a baseball bat?"

I just shook my head. I swear, it was like I wasn't even in the same room.

Sinatra, leading Jordan by the hand, walked over and introduced him to me. He was skinny, maybe five-nine, short hair, couple earrings, dirty white Converse. Just to look at him, there was really nothing remarkable about the kid. He kind of reminded me of myself at that age. Only, I wouldn't have been caught dead in a Barry Manilow t-shirt.

"You like Barry Manilow?" I asked.

"It's a joke," Sinatra said. "He's being ironic."

"Oh."

I didn't even know they made Barry Manilow t-shirts.

"When I told everyone we were getting married, they all cheered. But you didn't." She pushed up her glasses and gave a quick sniff. "Are you against it? Is that why? You know, it's not like I really give a big goddamn. We're going to get married, whether you like it or not."

I took a deep breath, and quietly asked myself the same questions.

"Do you love each other?"

Without having to appeal for confirmation, they both nodded. The only difference between the two reactions was Jordan's nod was accompanied by a brilliant smile, while Sinatra delivered hers with a scowl.

"Yes," they said together.

"And this is what you want?"

Again, they responded in harmony.

"Then how could I be against that?"

Sinatra didn't seem entirely convinced.

"Really?" she asked. "Or are you just saying that to shut us up?"

"Tell you what," I said. "I'll even pay for it."

Jordan's face stretched in every direction.

"Serious?"

"Serious," I told them. "Whenever you're ready, let me know. It's the least I could do."

Sinatra's mouth formed the words *thank you*, but the sounds were unable to escape. This was not a problem for Jordan, however. He grabbed my hand and shook it with authority.

"I didn't know what to expect meeting you, but everything Sinatra said about you is true. You're all right."

"For an adult," I said, finishing what I felt was the unspoken remainder of his thought.

"Not just for an adult," he said. "For anyone."

Gavin called out for the happy couple to rejoin the celebration, lifting two freshly poured glasses of champagne in the air as bait.

Marcy was not among them. She was still off to the side waiting for me, so I strolled over to meet her.

She smiled, but was unable to maintain eye contact for more than a couple seconds at a time. We stood in silence for a moment before she began nodding her head, seemingly in agreement to a voice only she could hear.

"Okay," she muttered. "I should go."

"Please don't."

She loudly sighed. "Well, I feel foolish staying."

"Why? Did something happen?"

Her face melted into a very familiar expression. I'd seen a similar look of incredulity from Julie any number of times, and almost always in response to the same issue: my inability to know what's going on without being told. Something I always wanted to get better at, but never really knew where to go for the proper lessons.

She paused, waiting for me to figure it out on my own, but when that proved hopeless, she relinquished and explained.

"Because of that night at my place, Daryl. What else would I mean?"

"But, nothing happened," I said.

She gave me the look again. "No kidding. You think maybe that's why I feel stupid?"

"Because I didn't sleep with you?"

She took a moment to organize her words. The look quickly dropped away, and she resumed.

"Because I've had dozens of men that I didn't care all that much about hop in bed with me without thinking twice, but when I finally met someone I did care about, he refused. It made me think."

"I only refused because I'm married. So, even if I did sleep with you, it really wouldn't have changed much."

"Maybe not, but something sure changed for me."

She stopped short when Walter wheeled over within hearing range.

"Here you go, buddy-boy!"

He handed me a cold bottle of beer. Only a few minutes ago, this was all I could think about, and now, I had all but forgotten all about it.

"We never had the chance to really get to know each other," he said to Marcy. "With you riding behind us on your bike."

"I know who you are," she smirked.

"True. And I know who you are," he said.

"Well, what more do you want?"

Walter slowly rotated his head toward me, and grinned ear-to-ear.

"My whole life, I've been waiting for a woman to ask me that."

Marcy seemed to surprise herself by unloading a short burst of laughter.

"What more do I want?" He poetically mused, extending his hand toward hers. I thought for a moment that his intention was to take hold of her hand and kiss it. Or even worse – caress it. But all he did was softly squeeze it. Which was good, because I hate hand kissers. And caressers.

"How about you tell me what're you drinking?" he said. "And don't say *wine*, because a beautiful woman like yourself can't really get anymore cliché than that."

"And a man can't be anymore cliché than calling a woman he just met *beautiful*."

Her sarcasm, oddly enough, seemed to make him even more interested. If he could understand Steve, they'd make a dangerous pair.

"*Touché*," Walter said. "But I'm just callin' 'em like I sees 'em."

She snuck a peek at me and raised her eyebrows. I wasn't sure if it was suppose be an attempt to silently ask about Walter, or for me to suggest a something for her to drink, so I just shrugged. It seemed a suitable answer to either question.

He lifted his beer bottle and gave it a little wave.

"Okay," she said. "I'll have whatever you're having."

"If you insist. Bartender! Two big glasses of impure thoughts!"

She cleared her throat of the laugh that was trying to escape as Walter wheeled himself toward the bar.

It felt awkward just standing there, so I drifted over to the nearest table and pulled out two chairs. Marcy sat down and continued talking like she had never stopped.

"Interesting fellow. Anyway, I told you how I feel about relationships, right? There's something I didn't tell you. That I'm a hypocrite. I was married. Twice." She started rubbing the fingertips of both hands in quick, two inch strokes along the tabletop. "I was crazy in love with both of them. They were my entire world, you know? They were each my first thought of the day, and the last of the night. I got so obsessed with them that I'd wake up depressed if I realized I didn't dream about them, too."

"What happened?" I asked.

She opened her mouth to speak, but stopped, collected herself, then began again. "Chris, my first, died. He was so smart, so funny, and had such a wonderful heart. Not a very strong one, though. Weak valves. Some genetic defect that he didn't know about. I couldn't get over the idea that one day, everything's perfect, and then the next day, out of nowhere, it's all shot to hell. I still can't."

"Sorry."

Her fingers stopped rubbing the table and curled into fists.

"The second was Greg. I knew him through Chris. After Chris died, I fell apart. Obviously, right? Who wouldn't? Anyway, Greg started dropping by. To check on me. Make sure I was okay. But the whole thing was a setup, and I, ha-ha, I stupidly fell for it. He was just after my money. See, Chris left me some money, kind of a lot. His parents were rich, they owned, well, that's not important. What is, is this one knew it. This *Greg*. I can't even stand saying his name. He knew how vulnerable I was and he exploited it. Six months later, I still wasn't over Chris, but *Greg* convinced me to marry him. Three months after that, on Christmas Eve no less, he vanished. He had it planned perfectly. He drained my bank account late enough in the day knowing the bank would be closed for the holidays, so chances were, I wouldn't find out for a while. He took everything: savings, checking, certificates. My *car*. All I had left was the house, and Chris' motorcycle. I made a promise that I'd never allow myself to be put in that position again."

"What position?"

"To be helpless and stupid because of love! When I fall, I tell you, I fall hard, and all the way. There's no gray area with me. I'm in there deep. And because of that, I become vulnerable. And...I get a little over-sensitive. So, if there's even the slightest hint that a guy's doing something stupid, I lose it. I hate that feeling. It's like you fell for some elaborate prank. That's why I tried to bypass the love part of my relationships. I mean, what's love anyway? Stuck in a rut with one person until one of you dies? Or disappears? What is a person left with after that? Nothing. Just loneliness and misery."

"Not every guy's like that."

"But I've been through a lot of guys, Daryl…hey, how weird was it that I knew that pirate, huh?"

She broke eye contact for like the hundredth time, but instead of looking down at the floor as she usually did, she stared off into the empty end of the room and continued.

"I found out there's a big difference between loneliness and being alone. Up until meeting you, I was in denial about how miserable it was making me."

"Here you go."

Somehow, Walter snuck up on us, but only Marcy physically illustrated our surprise by springing about six inches off her seat. Walter thought this was very funny.

"Didn't know I was a ninja, did you?" he laughed.

Gavin, who was carting in speakers and other audio equipment from his van, heard Walter as he passed us.

"Ninjas!" he shouted, like he'd just finally solved some puzzle. "Of course! That's what we are! And that's what we shall be! Fuck the pirates! Long live the ninjas!"

The rest of them laughed and toasted to their new name.

"Long live the ninjas!" they chanted.

Walter smiled. "You have interesting friends, Daryl. Now, what was this I heard about you being miserable? Or was that not meant for my ears?"

"I was just thanking Daryl."

"Thanking him for making you miserable? You cad!"

Marcy stared straight at me. "For opening my eyes."

"I didn't know I did that," I told her.

"Yes," Walter laughed. "Seems a lot of that's been going around lately. Well, I'm glad to hear you're not miserable, because misery serves no practical function. You never know when you're going to go, so why waste the time you have feeling negative? No matter how bad you think life is, you can always improve it. I told Daryl, after I had my legs crushed by that jeep, there were times when I thought, *I can't take it anymore. What's the use?* Then I realized, damn it, I'm still alive! Sure, I might not ever be able to run a marathon, but I could still have fun!"

"You ran marathons?" I asked.

"No, Daryl, that's not what I'm saying. The guy is so literal." He threw Marcy a glance and she smiled. "But I could have. That's what's so incredible about life. Anything is possible. Think about it. We breathe, and think, and laugh, and well, other things I won't mention due to present company. There's just so much to do. The opportunities are endless. Every moment should be savored and celebrated. Shit, I love living. Especially when you consider the alternative."

Marcy sighed and threw her head back. "You know what, Walter? You're right. Absolutely right. We can mourn the dead for a while, but eventually we have to accept reality. And the reality is, we are the ones alive, so we might as well live."

"That a girl," Walter cheered on.

She straightened herself in the chair. "Girl?"

"*That a woman?* That a no sound right."

Marcy let out a long groan, but couldn't contain the smile that accompanied it. "Are all your jokes that bad?"

"Oh, don't you worry about that. Some are even worse. I've got a million of them."

"I bet I've got more," she giggled.

Walter's face lit up. "Is this a challenge?"

She shook her hair and threw down a swallow of beer.

"So, are you staying?" I asked her.

Her hand squeezed mine and she smiled.

"Ready?" Walter asked. "Guy walks into a bar..."

Clem crept up to the table, stepping sideways and bent slightly over his right hip, like he was backing away from some imaginary knife-wielding assailant.

"Daryl, I know yer paying me a lot of money for use a the place, but you gotta do sompin' bout yer dogs."

I looked over at Steve and Valerie. She was still situated in the shopping cart, and he was sitting on his hind legs on top of a table, singing along with a Sammi Smith song that was blasting from the jukebox.

How the hell does he know all these lyrics?

"Is he being too loud?" I asked.

Clem turned to me full face. Sweat was pouring down his forehead.

"Okay," he confided. "You wanna know the truth? I'm a scared a dogs."

"They're not going to do anything to you, Clem. Take my word. Steve talks a big game, but he's harmless."

"Don't matter what you tell me. Don't at all. It's enough that it's in the back a my mind. I can't shake the feelin' jes 'cause you tell me it's alright. It's my right ta be like that. No law says I have ta like 'em. Just the way I am, is all. Ever since I was a kid, okay?"

"Okay. Okay. What do you want me to do? I'm not putting them outside. It's too damn hot."

He scratched his chin looking for a solution. "How 'bout puttin' 'em on a leash? That might gimme peace a mind."

"I don't have a leash."

"There's a pet store down the parking lot. I'd be much obliged to 'ya if 'ya did."

"Fine. I should probably get a room for the night, anyway. There any hotels nearby?"

"Motel's right across the street," Walter chimed in.

I looked out the window to where he was pointing.

"Isn't there some place a little nicer?" I asked.

"Not anywhere nearby," he said. "Besides, that's where we're all staying, my boy."

"Whoo-hoo!" Russell shouted. "I just won fifty bucks playing video poker!"

"With money you bummed from me," Aaron firmly stated.

"*Bummed?*" Russell shot back. "I asked you for five dollars, and you gave it to me. How is that *bumming*?"

"Then give me my five dollars back."

"As soon as I cash this in, Cheapskate!"

"I am *not* a cheapskate!"

Steve raised his head and yelled in frustration, "What's a dog gotta do to get a beer in this joint?"

Clem's jaw clenched.

"I'll go get the leash," I told him. "If you get him a beer."

"Who?" he asked.

"Steve," I replied.

"The *dog?*"

"Yeah. We've been pouring it in that chip bowl. He has trouble picking up a mug."

38

Picking out a leash was a little more complicated than I assumed. You walk into one of those places with only two thoughts in your head: *"Leashes"* and *"Where are they?"* But when you locate them, it takes forever because there are literally dozens of varieties to choose from. At least it was different from map shopping, there were actual distinctions between these. In the end, I decided on a black, two-inch thick belted collar imbedded with a row of rhinestones, and a ten foot chain with a black leather hand strap. Considering I never had any previous experience at making a purchase like this, I think I did all right.

The other bright spot is that I didn't have to travel far. That's what's good about strip malls – if you need something, they probably have it.

The motel required no decisions at all. I said, "I need a room." They said "Fifty dollars," and I gave them a piece of plastic.

Why can't everything in life be that effortless?

That out of the way, I headed back to the bar. Except, I got turned around and started in the wrong direction. The damn place was right across the street from the motel, but my mind, well, my mind was somewhere else. I blame all this sunshine. You can't open your eyes wide enough to see.

After walking about a half mile maze that should have been something like a quarter block of a straight line, I found myself at the back door of *The Cove*.

"I'm back," I announced, fully expecting the party to still be in full swing and no one to even hear me. Instead, it was weirdly silent. Everyone was staring out the front windows, and when they heard me, they all spun around and sighed. Sinatra ran over and hugged me.

"You're okay!" she cried.

"Of course I'm okay," I said. "I just went out to get a leash."

This didn't sit well with Steve. "And who's gonna wear that?"

"You," I told him.

"Like hell I am."

"Long story. Just deal with it. Now, what's going on?"

"He's here," Aaron said, not bothering to turn around.

"Who?" I asked.

"Robert," Marcy reported. "That is him, right?"

I went to the window and looked. It was him. Sure as shit.

"He's been circling," Jordan added.

"He's knows you're around here somewhere," Aaron calmly stated. "Just not exactly sure where."

"What should we do?" Sinatra asked.

Russell laughed to himself, then bent his legs and propelled himself straight up and back, landing in a seated position on top of the bar.

"That's Aaron's department," Russell smirked. "What's your plan, big guy? How you gonna save us from the evildoer?"

Aaron folded his arms across his chest. "There's no need for sarcasm."

"Yes there is," Russell laughed. "Especially when it's in regard to you."

"There's really not much we can do," Aaron began. "So far, he hasn't committed any crimes."

"When did hit-and-run stop being considered a crime?" Russell asked. "Actual or attempted?"

"Hista's not here to testify, and no one saw him hit the dog."

"He has a point," Walter admitted. "As a person who can speak firsthand about being run over by a psychopath, witnesses are important."

"Steve saw Robert hit Valerie," I said.

"Is Steve willing to file a report?" Walter asked.

I looked over at Steve, who was shaking his head in disgust. "Oh, yeah."

"We know he's dangerous," Aaron continued. "But's it's nothing the police would get involved with."

"If you ask me," Gavin grinned. "I say we ninja his ass. Strike a blow for the bullied and downtrodden of the world. And for good taste. The man was wearing a tracksuit, for fuck's sake."

"For the last time Gavin," Walter sighed. "We're not going to kill him. You know, you're a fun kid, but you've got some real anger management issues."

It was my turn to speak up. "How about if I just go out there and..."

They wouldn't let me finish the thought. If this scene were a panel in a comic strip, an enormous word balloon with the word "No!" would be squeezed into the space.

"You crazy?" Sinatra gasped. "What if he runs you over? Or grabs you and hurts you? Then what?"

"He's seen all of us," Aaron pointed out. "Sinatra's right. If he knows we're here, he knows Daryl's here, and what's to stop him from hurting any of us?"

"I request it be entered into the record," Russell sang. "That on this date, Aaron publicly admitted that someone else was right."

Aaron refused to look at him. "You're not helping."

"Well, we can't just sit here prisoner," Gavin fumed.

"I'll go," Marcy declared.

"Oh, no you don't," Walter protested. "If you think he's above hitting women, you're mistaken."

"The only time he saw me, I was in uniform. It's called *The Waitress Principle*. You can see the same waitress every day for years, but when you run into her away from the restaurant and out of uniform, you're unable to recognize her. Trust me."

"What are you going to do?" I asked her.

"I don't know exactly, but I have an idea. I'm gonna wing it and hope for the best. Oh, and charge up your phone. Just in case."

Walter rolled up alongside of her.

"Be careful, *woman,*" he quietly said.

She smiled, then pinched his shoulder and headed for the door.

We all headed for the windows. Yeah, we wanted to be sure nothing happened to her, but we were all just as curious to see what she was going to do.

Initially, it didn't look to be much. She walked slowly across the parking lot toward the street where his car was stationed. She stopped twice, once to remove her jacket, and another to shake out her hair and stretch her neck from side to side. The woman we were watching slowly transformed from the Marcy that was just with us in the bar into someone completely different. But that appeared to be the intention.

Even from our distance, we could see his eyes following her as she strolled in front of his car. She gave him a sideways glance before completely passing by, and although it couldn't have been seen from our angle, it was unanimously agreed that she tossed him some rather enticing bait. What that bait was though, was up for discussion.

Russell said a curious wink.

Walter said it was merely eye contact, because that alone was enough.

Sinatra suggested it was a seductive smile.

Jordan agreed with Sinatra, and was rewarded with a kiss.

All Aaron would say was that she "delivered a come-hither look".

"A *come-hither look?*" Russell cackled. "Ha ha! I must not have been paying attention, because I completely missed the part where she got in her Time Machine, went back to nineteen-twenty-eight, and stole a come-hither look from an unsuspecting dance-hall girl!"

"Why must you turn everything so ugly," Aaron asked.

"Look!"

Other than Gavin, all eyes had been turned on the bickering between Aaron and Russell, but at his command, we refocused our attention to Marcy as she was making her way into the front doors of the motel.

A moment later, Robert stepped out of his car, looked around the area to make sure he wasn't being watched, then followed her path.

Again, everyone seemed to agree on what was happening, but this time, there wasn't much discussion about it.

In short time, Gavin constructed a rather elaborate audio/video set-up. He shaped a U out of three tables in the back corner and arranged his equipment on top. I couldn't believe everything this guy brought with him. He had with him a mixing board, two mp3 players, a laptop, and a couple microphones, along with two guitars and a small drum kit. It was nothing short of incredible. And I'm not sure how, but he rigged all of the TVs so he could show videos while the music played. They were a hodge-podge of various images that didn't appear to connect in any way with the music. Or each other, for that matter. It was about as non-linear as you could get. There were still shots of all of us, individually and together in different pairings, and what I recognized to be some of his artwork. Then he'd have completely random shit, like snippets from James Bond movies, and really old and obscure cartoons. What he really seemed to be obsessed with were these old photos, and segments of home movies. All of some little boy. The kind of photos that everyone has stashed away in their attic or closet – grainy and orangey from time, with most of the true colors long faded away. In fact, they're so common to people like me who grew up in the pre-digital age that they all looked vaguely familiar, whether you were in them or not. Based on the cars and wardrobes, they were from sometime in the mid 70's. The weird thing was, in every picture, the kid looked either pissed off, or sad. I felt like I knew that kid from somewhere. I can't say I understood what the message was that Gavin was trying to get across, but it was rather compelling.

The song requests were flying in faster than Gavin could play them. Many of them were only familiar to the person who asked for them, but every once in a while, there'd be a song that each of them knew the lyrics to, and it would create some sort of magnetic force. Everyone, Clem included, would huddle together and belt it out in unison.

"I'm free fallin'!"

Everyone, I should say, but Gavin and me. Gavin stayed busy behind his tables, working the controls, while I sat at another table by myself, watching that pitiful little kid on the TV monitors. In a splash pool, by himself. In a sand box, by himself. On a swing set, by himself. And on, and on. Didn't this kid have friends? And where in the holy hell were his parents? It was pathetic.

"Free fallin'!"

I needed some air. The rest of them were so involved in the song that I figured no one would try to stop me from slipping out for a minute. I almost tripped over Steve, but he was in his own world. Clem said a leash on its own wasn't enough and insisted that I attach it to something, so I tied it to the front of the shopping cart. Steve was now getting a kick out of pulling Valerie all around the bar, announcing out loud that he was the humble servant, transporting his Queen among the peasants. I thought it best not to translate that to the rest of them. They might not find it so humorous.

Luckily, it was already dark, so when I opened the door, it didn't give me away by filling the room with unwanted sunlight. I crossed the parking lot and wandered over to Robert's car. It was still parked in the same spot, but he was nowhere around.

In fact, no one was around. I couldn't believe how quiet it was. Not that I'm complaining. It was nice to be alone for a moment and clear my head. I took a deep breath and looked up at the sky. The damn thing was so big. One of those nights that dares you to find an empty space in the sky, and just when you think you have won the challenge, a tiny star magically appears in the previous void.

It felt like I had a time jump, because it suddenly seemed like I had been standing there for hours, when it reality, it could very well have been only a matter of minutes. I spun around to head back toward the bar, and smacked into some guy walking in the other direction.

"Excuse me?" he puffed. Maybe he sounded out of breath because he had been walking fast. I didn't want to just blame it on him being fat, which would have been understandable to anyone who saw him. But I happened to see the look on his face when he said *excuse me.* It was the expression of a guy who's fed up with being picked on, even though he's come to terms with the fact that it will continue to haunt him for the rest of his life.

"Sorry," I said, and continued walking.

"What d'ya say?" he called back to me.

I turned back towards him. He removed his baseball cap and was now gaping at me with the most curious of looks.

"I said I was sorry," I clarified. "For bumping into you. My mistake."

"Oh," he mumbled. "It's okay. No problem. Thank you. You have a nice evening."

If it were only that easy.

I doubled my pace back to the bar, but stopped when Marcy called out to me.

"Daryl!" She sprinted over and hugged me. "That is my last time with that. I'm done."

"With what?" I asked.

"You haven't checked your phone?"

"No. It's still charging. Why?"

We walked back into the bar and were greeted loudly, and immediately, by the rest of our group.

"There he is!"

"Oh, he went out to get Marcy."

"You should have had one of us come with you."

"Let's just be glad he's safe."

"Quit telling everybody what to do!"

Marcy smiled. “I see nothing’s changed since I left. Where’s your phone?”

“Plugged in behind the bar.”

As I retrieved it, Walter came rolling up to Marcy.

“What happened? Are you all right?”

“I’m fine,” she replied. “And from now on, hopefully so is Daryl.”

The phone was completely charged, and there was a new notification on screen. A text from Marcy:

Send these to Julie. Love, Marcy.

It was a file. I opened it to find a photo of Marcy in her underwear, lying in bed with Robert, who was stark naked. Unfortunately, I looked at it too long, and saw much more than I wanted to see.

“What did you do?” I was mortified. “I didn’t ask you to do anything like this.”

Walter grabbed the phone out of my hand and had a look himself. He sighed, and handed it off to Gavin.

“I had a feeling he wasn’t such a big shot,” he laughed.

Marcy acted very calm and cool, like there was nothing wrong. So much so, that she was grinning from ear to ear.

“Hey,” she asserted. “It’s okay. I didn’t do anything but strip down to my underwear. You’d see more of me in the summer down at the lake. Clem, can I have a whisky sour? And another Heineken for my cute friend here.” She reached down and scratched Steve on the neck.

“Damn, I love this woman!” he said. Then he quickly spun around and explained to Valerie. “As a friend, I mean!”

“Why?” I asked her.

“Something you told me. Remember when you said he couldn’t handle his liquor? I figured, if I could get him sloshed, real quick, maybe I could get enough compromising pictures of us before he passed out. You send those to Julie. She may have cheated on you, but trust me, the minute she finds out he cheated on her, he’s history.”

“So, nothing happened?” Walter asked.

“No! Yuck!” Marcy spat. “The guy’s gross. I couldn’t wait to get out of there. I only did it for Daryl.” She gave me a quick peck on the cheek. “Hope it works.”

“Who took them?” Russell asked. “There’s always someone behind the camera.”

“I happen to know a friend who’s in town for a visit. Snuck him in the closet when Robert went to the bathroom.”

“Neal the Pirate?” I whispered.

She smiled. “I figured he owed me one.”

Gavin grabbed a microphone and pointed at Marcy. “I nominate Marcy as *Ninja of the Month!* Who seconds?”

"Seconded! Heartily!" Walter shouted, as he threw his arms around her waist and pulled her into his lap. She let out a raucous laugh, and didn't fight it.

"And now, back to the music," Gavin spoke into the microphone. "We have a request. Walter wants Utopia."

I was squeezing the phone so hard I thought it might break apart. Something about it seemed wrong. All I could think of was the look on Julie's face when she opened these pictures, and how much it would hurt her. I hated upsetting her. In fact, I'd deliberately go out of my way just not to upset her. Then another thought snuck into my head. *But why?* Why did I care so much about her happiness? Did I love her so much that I didn't want to see her hurt? Was it because I was looking out for her? The questions wouldn't stop, and grew louder and louder. Why?

"Trapped in a world that he never made."

The truth was, I knew the answer. I just didn't want to admit it. I did what I could to keep her happy because, if she wasn't, sooner or later I'd pay the price for it. It wasn't out of love. It was out of survival. That's no way to live your life, but regardless of the right or wrong of it, that was the perpetual result. So, the question now became, is this worth it? Will the feeling of vengeance that sending these pictures to Julie provide be worth the inevitable consequences?

Across the room, they all seemed so happy. Virtual strangers to each other acting like the oldest of friends. Marcy laughing and flirting with Walter. Her smile so pure and genuine. Aaron and Russell, seemingly bugging the hell out of each other, but unable, or unwilling, to separate. Sinatra and Jordan, young and in love, with an entire lifetime of dreams and possibilities ahead of them. And Gavin, by himself off to the side, but never truly alone, as long as he's creating.

"To happiness!" Walter shouted. "Every year, every month, every week, every day, every hour, every second! Should you never miss a moment of it! And if you ever do, may you produce twice as many new moments as the one you missed!"

The silence that followed only lasted as long as it took to swallow their drinks.

"Daryl?" Marcy called out. "Where's Daryl?"

"It is a little dark, wouldn't you say, Clem," Walter noted.

"I'm over here," I said.

"Did you send it?" she asked me.

"Not yet."

"Well, hurry up and do it," she told me. "It's time to have some fun!"

Ahh, screw it. I pushed the goddamn button and sent them off to Julie.

The lights turned up as brightly as they could go and everyone cheered. Don stretched one arm around my shoulders, and patted the *Happy* sign on my chest.

"It might not be exactly what I said it would be," he smiled. "But it's still pretty damn good, huh?"

I started toward the group, but something near Gavin caught my eye: a Fender Stratocaster. Natural finish ash body.

"Is that a seventy-six?" I asked him.

"Sure is," he said. "She's a beauty."

"That's my guitar! That's exactly what I played when I was in the band."

"No kidding?"

"Bought it for a hundred dollars at a garage sale."

"I got mine from a garage sale, too!"

"My grandfather's the one who actually bought it."

"That was nice of him. Why did he do that? Did you ask him to?"

"No. He knew how much I liked music, and thought I'd like to learn how to play."

"How old were you?"

"Eleven."

"I wish I had a grandfather like that. Mine just yelled about finding a job."

"Yeah, well, mine had his moments, too." I ran my fingers down the neck. Smooth. It was in mint condition, not even the slightest scratch.

"Damn, I loved this guitar. It came with a seventy-six Fender twin-reverb amp. The sound was amazing."

"Okay, that's just spooky. Look."

I don't know how I could have missed it, but there it was, sitting only a few feet away. A Fender TR, just like I had.

"You wanna play it? Go ahead."

It's hard to explain the feeling of having this in my hands again. The mere sensation of the strap gently pressing down on my shoulders as it suspended the weight of the guitar melted away twenty-five years. It transformed me into a wide-eyed teenager, playing in a dive bar for a small crowd of people who were only there to see me.

I twisted the dial to five and strummed a G chord. To my surprise, the sound played through the house speakers. Gavin had turned off the music and plugged the amp into the board. That simple chord aroused everyone's attention, and they all came over for a better view.

"You're going to play?" Sinatra excitedly asked.

"It's been a while," I mumbled. "Besides, I don't know how it would sound. No singer. No rhythm section."

Before I could even finish my damn sentence, Gavin set up a mic stand in front of me, then ran behind the drum kit to play.

"But," I pointed out. "We don't have a bass."

"We'll just have to make do until we find one."

He started banging on the snare, and I recognized the beat immediately. Without putting any thought into it, I leaned into the mic.

"Lobotomy!"

Instinctively, my fingers attacked the strings, and thankfully, all the *correct* strings, like this was just another ordinary occurrence in my life. I couldn't believe how easily this was all coming back to me. It really is amazing all the shit we keep hidden away in our brains.

Sinatra and Jordan jumped to their feet and started dancing. Don, who was standing near them, slammed his beer on a table and began pumping his arms up and down, like he was desperately trying to force the last drops of ketchup from their bottles. Russell was quick to join them, although his moves looked more like he was in a jujutsu competition than on a dance floor.

"Why do you always have to be so foolish?" Aaron chided.

"What's the matter, Grandpa?" Russell laughed, in between performing a series of leaps and kicks. "Too creaky to trip the light fantastic with us young 'uns?"

Aaron's mouth moved in response, but the music obscured the sounds. You didn't have to hear the words to understand the meaning, though. He aggressively stomped to the center of the floor, and began twisting and jerking his body in one of the worst examples of middle-aged-white-man dancing I'd ever encountered.

But hey, at least he was trying.

The only ones who weren't up were Marcy and Walter. Even Steve was on his back legs, and rocking the cart in time. Valerie was having the time of her life.

Marcy sat at a table next to Walter, mouthing the lyrics and tapping out the rhythm on his arm. He caught her longingly eyeing the dancers and took hold of her hand.

"Help me up," he said.

Marcy raised her eyebrows and snapped back her head.

"What? How? I thought you were paralyzed."

"Not completely. It just hurts like bloody hell if I ever try to use it."

"Then why in the world would you want to get up?"

"Because right now," he beamed. "I want to dance with you more than anything else I've ever wanted in my life."

Marcy eagerly smiled. "But, isn't it going to hurt?"

"Not any more than it would hurt sitting here and not dancing with you."

He clicked the lock on his wheels, and planted his left foot on the floor. They grabbed tightly onto each other's forearms, and Marcy slowly pulled toward her. She was actually much stronger than I would have guessed. Keeping all his weight on the good leg, he extended himself to full height, a good six inches or so taller than Marcy, and grabbed on to her waist with both hands.

As soon as it was apparent that he was not going to topple over, everyone applauded this seemingly impossible accomplishment.

"You seemed much taller in the chair," Marcy smiled.

"You're a real funny lady, aren't you" Walter remarked, catching his breath. "Someone move that damn thing outta the way, would you?"

Don scooted the chair back a few feet, then resumed his stationary position on the floor.

"Hit it, boys!" Walter shouted.

I looked back at Gavin, and without saying a word, we knew what to play. Then again, it was pretty obvious. We stuck with the Ramones – *"Let's Dance"*.

As good as our bass-less version was, all eyes were on Walter and Marcy. So, when he used her as support to do a one-legged pogo, nobody could stop laughing long enough to pay attention to us anyway. Not that it bothered either of us.

By the time the song ended, Walter looked spent. Don repositioned the chair directly behind Walter, and Marcy helped lower him back down.

"You're a pretty amazing guy," Marcy remarked.

"My ears are still buzzing," Walter replied. "Did you say *pretty amazing?* Or pretty *and* amazing?"

Marcy hummed a laugh. "Both."

Walter took a deep breath and started picking imaginary lint from the arms on his chair.

"Can I ask you a serious question?" he asked.

"Of course." She didn't appear worried about what it could be, but she was squeezing the hell out of her *Happy* sign.

"Would you like to go to Toledo with me?"

The expression on his face told anyone watching that he was prepared to hear a similar answer to the one he'd always been given.

Marcy furrowed her brow. "What's in Toledo?"

"Nothing," he said with a shrug. "Other than just you and me."

She paused for the briefest of moments, then snatched Walter's hand. "That sounds wonderful. When do we leave?"

Walter was speechless. Which really didn't matter, because his eyes said more than his mouth ever could. Marcy leaned over and gave him a kiss.

After a minute, he snapped out of it, and frowned.

"What?" Marcy worriedly asked.

"Does this mean we really have to go to Toledo?"

She laughed, and playfully slapped his forehead.

"Hey, check it out! He's leaving!"

Jordan was pointing out the front window at Robert, who was storming back to his car. We moved in for a closer look, just in time to watch him angrily peel away.

"Good riddance," Sinatra yelled.

Russell motioned toward the window. "What do you think that means?"

"Isn't it obvious?" Aaron smugly replied.

"Is it?" Russell chided. "How so? Please, elucidate us, oh Wise One."

Aaron cleared his throat. "Julie saw the photos, and called Robert. Now Robert is driving back to Chicago to settle the matter with her."

"Hey, yer phone's ringin'!" Clem called out from the bar.

Aaron cleared his throat again, only this time, a little louder, and with a vicious smirk.

I lifted my hands in front of my face, preparing for a catch. It was still ringing when Clem's underhanded toss landed perfectly in its target. The now room fell silent as I sat down and spoke over the speakerphone.

"Hello?"

"Daryl?" a tinny voice squealed back.

"Julie?" I asked.

A murmur of dissent rumbled through the group, but not loud enough for her to notice.

"Told you," Aaron whispered.

"Thank god I finally got you," Julie continued. "I've been trying to call for the longest time, but you never answer."

"Bad reception, I guess."

Half of my audience giggled, while the other half *shushed* them. That too, neglected to get Julie's attention.

"Where are you?" she asked. "Where have you been?"

"You don't know?"

"No," she, a little too-innocently responded. "How would I know?"

"Did you get the pictures?"

She did not immediately answer, and the momentary lull was filled by the impatient panting of everyone who was now crowded around me.

"Yes," she finally whispered. "Were they real?"

"You recognized Robert, didn't you?"

"Why did you send them to me?"

"I thought you'd want to know. He's been following me."

"That's why I was trying to call you."

"And trying to hurt me."

Again, she paused. The intake of oxygen from the people behind me grew proportionately larger with each passing second. I took a big swallow of my beer so it didn't seem like I was as anxious as they were.

"I had nothing to do with that," she insisted. "I told him to stop, but he wouldn't listen."

"He just took off a minute ago. You know what that's about?"

"I called him about the pictures. He wasn't very happy."

"Join the club."

"I also told him not to come back. It's over, Daryl."

"What is?" I asked.

"Me and Robert. I'm sorry. I made a mistake. Please come home."

The request made sense. This was what I wanted, after all. Wasn't it?

But then I heard the whispers.

"No."

"Careful Daryl."

"Don't fall for it."

"You don't need her."

"Talk about cliché."

"Ask yourself *why*, Daryl."

I looked at Steve.

"What do *you* want to do?" he asked.

"I don't know."

"Then don't give her an answer now."

"Daryl," Julie called out. "Are you still there?"

"Yeah," I told her. "I'll have to call you back."

The simple act of disconnecting the phone call was met with great fanfare. Literally. Russell played *"Hail to the Chief"*.

Who the hell has that on their iPod?

Marcy stepped over and straightened my sign. "How you doing?" she asked.

I shrugged, causing the sign she just fixed to slip out of alignment, but that didn't seem to bother her much.

Walter playfully slapped his hand on my head and mussed my hair. "He's going to be just fine. Who wants another drink? It's on me!"

That elicited a couple giggles, but even more drink orders.

"Is the kitchen still open?" Russell asked.

Aaron clicked his tongue. "Is that all you ever do? Eat?"

"I get hungry because I have a high metabolism," Russell replied. "Sue me."

Gavin thought about it for a moment. "I could eat."

"Me, too," Jordan quickly squeezed in.

Clem frowned. "I thought you all were done eatin', so I sent the cook home. I could make some popcorn."

I don't know what the hell came over me, but I jumped out of my chair like my name was called on a game show.

"I'll cook!"

You'd think me managing the restaurant for so long would automatically make me an expert chef, but the truth is, I haven't worked a grill in years. Before becoming manager, Chuck had me learn every job by working it for a couple months, so I had a better handle on what the other employees were doing. Host, cashier, waiter, busboy, line cook, prep, dishwasher, inventory, I did it all. Host and cashier were easiest, but by far the most tedious. A busboy's job was simple, clean up the messes, but that was without a doubt the toughest. The rest sat somewhere in the middle, each with their individual pluses and minuses.

What I forgot about over time was how smoothly I fell into the art of cooking. And I say *art*, because it can be that, if you take the right approach. I considered telling Chuck that I'd rather be a chef than a manager, but when I mentioned it to Julie, she immediately nixed the idea. She told me she was thinking of my future benefit. She explained that as employees, cooks are on the lower rungs of the business ladder, and do not receive the same level of respect that owners do. If she was here now, she might see differently. When everyone bit into the food I prepared for them, their praise wasn't directed at the owner. Hell, even Clem had trouble containing his enthusiasm.

"Thisis da tasi-est chicken I ever et," he mumbled in between bites. Actually, more like *during* bites.

"I used an avocado-lime paste," I confided. "With a panko and cilantro crust."

"You should cook all the time!" Marcy squealed.

"I agree," Russell proclaimed. "But only cook for us!"

Overall, I think I did a pretty good job. I will admit though, alcohol might have had a little to do with the more intense reactions. But, I'll take it nonetheless.

The unfortunate side effect of eating so much food so late at night is that it brings on sleepiness. Rapidly. Within minutes, we went from boisterous to barely awake. Aaron actually dozed off in his chair, and it was all we could do to stop Russell from drawing a moustache on his face.

"You're right," Russell conceded. "He's probably looking for a reason to back out on our book deal as it is."

"Book deal?" I said. "What book deal?"

"A collaboration. We're going to merge all of the information I've compiled over the years with all of the so-called advice that he's determined to be important."

"I don't believe it."

"It was actually his idea. Since he's fronting the cash, how could I say *no*? Besides, I'm adding footnotes to everything he writes. Hahaha!"

Russell's laughter woke up Aaron. He seemed more embarrassed than groggy.

"What happened?" he asked. Then he touched his face, and gave Russell a look. "You did something, didn't you?"

"Nope," Russell replied. "Wanted to, but they wouldn't let me."

"I'm having second thoughts about this book."

Russell pointed his thumb at Aaron. "Told you."

"We're all knocked out," Walter stated. "Whadda 'ya say we go back to our rooms and get a good night's sleep. We can start again fresh tomorrow."

"Do we have to go back to our own rooms?" Marcy whispered to Walter.

He smiled back. “You’re a dirty old broad.”

“I’m not *that* old,” she smiled back.

“Hey Clem,” Gavin called out. “Mind if I keep everything the way it is? It would be a pain in the ass to break it all down every night.”

“Suits me fine,” Clem said. “Place is yers fer a week, anyway.”

Don plodded over to me and slapped my back.

“Thanks for this,” he smiled.

“Why you thanking me?” I asked. “You told me about it.”

“No. I didn’t tell you about *this*. This was all you. There was nothing until you showed up. I wanted to let you know that now, in case I don’t see you in the morning.”

“Why wouldn’t I see you?”

“Ahh,” he sighed. “I have to head back. My time’s up. But listen, I don’t care if we’re pirates, ninjas, or just Don and Daryl – I want to do this again. Okay?”

“Okay.”

We shook hands, then joined the cleanup. We were slow, but effective. Finally, Clem hit the lights and we dragged ourselves across the street to the hotel.

The room was nothing to write home about. A bed, a chair, a lamp, and a TV set. To say it was sparse would be a gross understatement, but for fifty dollars, you couldn’t expect much more.

Valerie was fast asleep, so I carefully picked her out of the basket and laid her on the right side of the bed. Steve, on the other hand, was not at all showing signs of drowsiness. The guy was bouncing off the walls with energy.

“What a fan-tabulous night!” he shouted. “Man, I had such a great time!”

“Shh,” I instructed. “Don’t wake her up.”

“Oh!” he replied, shifting down to a loud whisper. “Sorry. What a frigging blast! And we get to do that for a whole nother week?”

“Yep.”

“Every day?”

“Yeah,” I said. “And keep it down.”

“Right, right, right.”

I fished my toothbrush out of the suitcase then stepped into the bathroom.

“She’s great, isn’t she?” Steve muttered.

“Who?”

“Who?” he shot. “Valerie! Who else?”

“There’s two other *she’s* with us, don’t forget.”

“Oh, yeah.”

I ran the brush under the cold water and squeezed out a strip of toothpaste. Seeing my reflection in the mirror, a thought came to me.

“What time is it?” I asked Steve.

“I don’t know. Late. Real late.”

“It’s also early, though. Right?”

Steve gave it some thought. "Yeah. I guess it would be. That's pretty cool."

"I'm thinking, maybe I should take my pills now. In case I sleep late."

"Makes sense."

I rinsed out my mouth, and swallowed down two pills with some more water. I looked at my reflection again, and began to recite my morning mantra.

"You will be happy. Always speak your mind. Don't settle for less. Go for ALL! That's one of them, right? Or did I just make that up? Let's see, ah, cook more often. Be a god. That's not right? What the hell else was there? Oh. Ask questions. Goddamn it. I shoulda wrote these down."

"I don't know why the hell you even do them anyway."

"What do you mean? I have to."

"Okay. I've been thinkin' about this for a while. After watching all of you, I've come to the conclusion that life for humans is pretty goddamn amazing! The problem is, too few of you ever realize it! You look at a dog. Your whole life, a dog's whole life, you have to pretty much do what the man says. But you humans don't! Yeah, yeah, I know. Every once in a great fucking while, like with your boss and shit. The only things you *really* don't have control over in life are being born, and dying. In between those two, it's pretty much all up to you. Right?"

"Your point?"

He sighed and shook his head. "Look, if one of these people, Aaron, let's say, if Aaron told you to think for yourself, would you say that to yourself in the mirror every morning?"

"Probably."

"Okay. You see the irony in that, right?"

That, I didn't even have to think about.

"Just because someone else suggested it doesn't mean it's wrong."

"You're a smart guy. You know what to do already, but you just don't trust yourself to do it. As a rule, you've spent your whole life, your whole life, only doing what other people told you to do. And humans are victims of the rules they live by."

"Wow. That's pretty deep."

"I'm no dummy. Look, you gotta stop doin' shit just because other people are tellin' 'ya to do it. If you're gonna do it, do it because *you* want to do it. Do what works best for *you.* Acting this way isn't how Ben raised you."

"Ben did raise me *at all*!"

"Yes, he did! You're so much like him it's scary."

"I am not! Do not say that."

"You are to! You both keep to yourself. Both have trouble relating to other people because you think they're stupid. But you want so desperately to be liked that when it doesn't happen, you get bitter and angry. But you're both nice guys who are just trying to do right. The problem is, you just don't know the right way to do it. Look, I'm not tryin' to tell you want to do, 'cuz that's what I'm tryin' to tell you what not to do. Does that make sense? It's just, you gotta start makin' your own decisions and stop acting like you're a dog. You know what I mean?"

I looked deep into the eyes that stared back at me in the mirror. "I think so."

"You can do anything you want to do, Daryl!"

"Shh," I reminded him. "And no, I really can't."

"Yes you can. *Yes*, you can! You can leave your house. Anytime you want. We can't. You can eat whatever you want, whenever you want. We can't. You can play instruments. Create real art. Follow your dreams. Fall in love and get married. We can't do *any* of that! Do you have any idea how lucky you are?"

He sighed and dropped his belly to the ground. It wasn't a long drop, given how short his legs are, but it was still enough to make his point.

"Gavin said he was going to show you how to draw."

"I was talking about the other stuff."

"Getting married? Why couldn't you?"

"Yeah, right," he grumbled, his jaw barely lifting off the floor.

"Seriously. I've heard it happen before. Don't know how legally binding it is, but it's been done."

He popped back up on his feet and cocked his head to the right. "That can really happen? Dogs getting married? I always thought it was a joke."

"Yeah, really. Why is *that* so important to you?"

He clumsily shuffled back to the bed, and pulled himself up on his back legs.

"Because I love her, Daryl," he said, sniffing gently at her hair. "And I want to marry her."

"Wow."

He spun his head around and growled. "Whadda 'ya mean, *wow*? You think it's impossible for me to love someone?"

"No. I meant *wow* like, *that's great*. I had no idea."

"So, you're happy for me?"

I thought about it for a minute. "I'm not against it."

Steve shook his head. "I swear dude, one of these days I'm gonna see you smile."

"So, have you two talked about it?"

He absently dug his claw into the filthy carpeting. "No. I haven't said anything. I was afraid she'd say no."

"You were just telling me how bad it is that dogs can't do whatever they want. Well, now's your chance. You fell in love, now get married. Follow your dream, Steve."

His energy level spiked, and he was bouncing all over the room like a madman. Or, mad dag, as the case may be.

"I'm gonna do it! I'm gonna do it! But, I want it to be perfect!" He came to a complete stop. "How do you make it perfect? What do you humans do?"

"Generally, the guy would buy a ring. Maybe flowers. Take her out to a nice restaurant..."

"A ring," he mumbled. "I don't know how we'd do that. They don't sell dog rings, do they? Oh! I got it! What about my collar? Could I give her my collar to wear?"

"Sure. Why not? Let me take it off."

"No! Not now. When I propose. It'll be more dramatic that way. Maybe you could take us somewhere nice tomorrow. To a park, or something? I like parks."

"Okay."

He started pacing between the bed and the bathroom door. "No, no. I won't be able to wait that long. I want to ask her as soon as she wakes up. I should get some flowers now. So when she wakes up, she'll see them, and I can pop the question right away. Hey, let me out, will 'ya? And I'll go pick some nice flowers."

"How long is that going to take," I yawned. "I'm exhausted."

"Just keep the window open. I'll hop back in when I'm done. You can go to sleep, buddy. No worries."

"All right."

I pushed open the window and pulled back the curtain.

"Thanks," he said, and sprinted for the window, but stopped short of leaping out. "Any idea what kind of flowers girl dogs like?"

"Can't say that I do. But, ahh, how are you planning on picking them and bringing them back here?"

"My mouth. Why?"

"Then I'd stay away from roses."

"Good point. Hey, one more thing. Would you be my best man?"

"Really?"

"Whadda you mean, *really?* Of course! Who else but you, bro? No matter what, it's you and me, right? Right?"

"Right?"

"Cool. And, hey. I mean it. Thanks for everything. I wouldn't have any of this if it wasn't for you. Tomorrow, I'm takin' care of you."

He jumped to the window ledge and vanished.

I finished up in the bathroom, then clicked off the lamp before getting into bed, only because I didn't think I'd be awake long enough to reach over and turn it off once I plopped onto the mattress.

Just as I was dozing off, I heard whimpering, but not from outside the window. It was from Valerie.

I forced my eyes open and stroked the back of her head. "You okay? Does your leg hurt?"

"No," she wept.

"What then?"

"I heard."

"Oh. How much?"

"Everything. I'm...I'm so happy." She broke down into an all-out crying jag. "Don't tell him I know, okay? He was so excited about making it a surprise."

"I won't."

I wanted to say more, but nothing would come out.

40

When I woke up, I had that nagging sensation that I had never fallen asleep – I felt wiped out, and Valerie was still crying. Except now, it was daylight, and people were pounding on the door and calling for me. So, I guess I did sleep. Sure didn't feel like it, though.

I stared at the ceiling for a moment, attempting to do my routine inventory check, but couldn't get it started due to all the noise.

What the hell. Can't they just go to the bar without me and I'll meet them later?

I rolled over to check on Valerie, but she was gone. When I sat up to look, I found her lying on the floor by the door, sobbing her eyes out. If she fell out of bed, that would explain the tears. Poor thing.

"Steve? Steve?" I hoarsely called out.

That only made her moan even louder. Aw, damn it, I hope he didn't do something stupid.

"Daryl?" a voice called out. I'm pretty sure it was Gavin's, but I was still too groggy to tell. "You awake?"

"Yeah," I scratched. "What's the matter?"

"Oh, my god," Marcy's voice trembled.

"What should we do?" Russell whispered.

"I don't know."

"Somebody needs to do something!"

"Don't touch anything."

"Daryl, my boy," Walter carefully started. "Be ready."

I now heard Sinatra's cries, overlapped by Jordan's soothing hushes. Their sounds melded so perfectly with Valerie's that they were difficult to separate.

I slid the chain from the latch and pulled open the door. It was heavier than usual. I thought maybe someone was holding the knob. They were all there, standing on the concrete walkway outside the door, gaping at me with a mixture of fear and pity. I didn't understand it.

The door swung back and banged into my right shoulder. As I reflexively reached over my left hand to give the area a quick rub, I heard a muffled thump from behind, and a strange shape slowly emerged in my peripheral vision. Whatever it was, I sensed that was the reason they were there. The cause for their sadness. When I turned to view the image in full, I felt someone touching my left arm, as if they were delivering a warning for me not to look.

But I knew I could no longer look in the other direction. This had to be addressed.

I wasn't sure at first what to make of it. A screwdriver was jammed into the center of my door, just below the peephole, and Steve was hanging from the screwdriver by his collar. His head was cocked to the side, similar to the way both he and Melvin would look at me when they were in doubt. Only this angle was more extreme, like his head wasn't even connected to his body. I wasn't sure how he was able to do it.

A sheet of paper was stuffed between his limp body and the collar. On the paper was written:

Now we're even

Sinatra broke free of Jordan's grasp and squeezed past me to scoop up Valerie. The rest of them watched her cradle the dog and kiss the back of her head as she slowly collapsed to the floor.

Since nobody offered any explanation, it was all a mystery to me. What does "*Now we're even*" mean? Why was Steve doing this? Wait. He said he wanted to surprise her. Was this his idea of an elaborate proposal? Did he want to make everyone think he was dead, just so he could "spring back to life", and ask her to marry him? As morbidly grotesque as that may be, I wondered if that's what was really happening. People do stupid things in the name of love, but this was taking it too far.

I couldn't take my eyes off of him. I felt that if I kept watching, I'd maybe catch him sneaking a breath, then I could point it out to everyone and we'd have a good laugh. But, I couldn't wait any longer for him to choose the moment. I needed to find out now. On my own.

I readied myself for the shock, and cautiously stretched my fingers out to his body. I knew it was going to happen. I knew he was going to try and scare me. I'd touch him and he'd scream *gotcha!* It was so like him to do that. I lightly stroked his leg, and quickly pulled back my hand. He didn't move. So, I went in again, lightly pinching his ear. Once again, he didn't move a muscle. Sooner or later he'd have to sneak some air. I poked his belly, hard, over and over again. His skin was so cold.

How the hell long was he going to keep this charade up?

"Why isn't he saying anything?" I whispered.

"Oh, Daryl..."

How could anyone do this to another person? *Why* would anyone do it? It made no sense.

"Somebody take him down. Please!"

Russell cupped his tiny body from the bottom and raised him, while Aaron pulled the collar off the screwdriver. He was held like that for a moment, until Russell finally extended his arms toward me, suggesting perhaps that I should take him. I couldn't. Even if I wanted to, I was unable to move any part of my body. Lips, head, arms. All unresponsive to any neural requests.

"What should I do?"

"Set him down."

"Not by Valerie."

Russell lowered him to the floor and stepped away.

"This had to be that Robert."

"But, we saw him leave."

"Streets go both ways."

My phone began to ring, but it was on the nightstand, and I was still frozen in place, staring helplessly at Steve. Gavin picked it up and answered instead.

"Hello," he spoke into the phone, then he turned to me "Julie."

He tried to place the phone in my hand, but my muscles refused to oblige, and it dropped to the floor.

Marcy wrapped herself around me. "Daryl," she softly breathed in my ear. "I'm so sorry. We're all..." She struggled for the right words, but the right words didn't exist. So she kissed my neck, and quickly moved back to Walter's side.

Someone pushed the button for the speakerphone.

"Hello? Daryl? Hello?" Julie loudly called out from the other end.

"Yeah," I said, clearing my throat afterward.

"Oh, my god! Daryl! Are you okay?"

I couldn't take my eyes off Steve.

"Do you know what he did?" I mumbled.

"Oh, Daryl."

"Do you know what Robert did?"

"Come home. Please? This is where you belong."

"He killed it."

"Please come home. We'll fix everything."

I started crying. Uncontrollably. Like I'd never done in my life.

That's the last thing I remember before I passed out.

We buried him in a nearby park.

Russell offered to do the location scouting, saying he knew a thing or two about parks, and found a place nearby. I felt guilty agreeing to bury him so far away from home, but driving him cross country wasn't an option. Not just from the physical ramifications that Aaron mentioned, either. Marcy reminded everyone that it would have been even more difficult emotionally.

I didn't do much talking after that. It was common knowledge how I felt. How we all felt. They all spoke the words that filled my head, anyway. The words I could not allow myself to utter. Yet when vocalized by them, the pain wasn't nearly as severe as it would have been had they come from my mouth.

The only disagreements came when a few of them voiced their opinions about me going back to Julie. My silence immediately crushed the dissent, and that more or less ended all future discussions on that topic.

Valerie could not allow herself to witness the burial, so I sat with her in the van and watched from the window as the others attended to the ceremony. He was wrapped in my heavy tweed sport coat, and buried with a six pack of Heineken and a bag of Burger King hamburgers and fries. Gavin played a small selection of songs on his acoustic guitar, but I couldn't hear them too clearly over Valerie's wailing. I gave her a couple pills, and she eventually fell asleep in my lap.

After a few minutes, the service was finished, and everyone converged around the open doors of the van.

"I'll drive the Mustang back," Aaron announced.

"Mind if I ride with you?" Russell asked.

"Of course not."

"Who's taking Daryl?" Sinatra insisted on knowing.

Gavin spoke up. "I will."

"Then we're going with you," she told Gavin.

Jordan nodded, and clasped Sinatra's hand.

Marcy looked sadly at Walter. "I got my bike. I guess I could leave it here..."

"Why?" Walter added. "Don't you have room for me on the back?"

Marcy smiled. "What about your leg? And, your wheelchair?"

"I can take the wheelchair," Gavin said. "There's room."

"And I'll take my leg," Walter declared.

Marcy swatted him on the arm, then kissed his cheek.

Once the wheelchair was secured inside the van, our convoy headed back east to Chicago.

41

Since we only stopped for necessities - gas, food, and bathroom breaks – the trip back took about a day. I did nothing but take care of Valerie, which wasn't as easy as it sounded. Not that she was high maintenance, or anything. Her eerie resemblance to Steve was too difficult to bear. Looking at her was a constant reminder of the best friend I lost.

But, she was in pain, physical and emotional, and needed my help, so as difficult as it was to face the constant memory, I couldn't disregard her. In fact, when it hurt me the most, I found comfort in holding her even tighter. It hurt me *the most* so often though, I feared I might accidentally squeeze her to death. Every damn thing was a memory, and every damn memory hurt like hell. Songs, food, driving, the road itself. All of it. The only tangible part of him I had was his collar. I tried to put it on Valerie, like Steve had wanted to do himself, but she violently shook me off. I understood, and didn't lecture. Instead, I clutched it tightly in my free hand, planning to never let it go.

In all her thrashing over the collar, she somehow ripped the tape off her leg. I gave a brief examination, and everything looked fine, no swelling or bruising. I wondered if there was ever any real damage to begin with. I'm not saying she wasn't hurt, but doctors misdiagnose every day. Stupid people.

I threw the pills out the window.

We drove to Ben's house first. There were a couple details that had to be dealt with before I saw Julie. Since I'd been gone for a while, there wasn't much to offer in the way of food, so Marcy and Sinatra took the van and made a quick run to the store while everyone else washed up and settled in. Valerie was out of it, so I carried her upstairs to the room I was using, and laid her on the bed.

The place felt different since the last time I was there. Smaller maybe, but it was also something else. It was that feeling you get after being gone for so long. The result of reconnecting with familiar surroundings after existing in the unknown. That personal sense of home that fastens itself to one place in your life. No matter where you go, or what you do, it patiently waits for your return, with no judgments or criticisms.

If every facet of life could be like this.

Then again, what's stopping it?

I found my journal on the nightstand, and scribbled in a couple entries before I noticed a stack of papers lying on the floor by my feet. More than likely, they were blown astray by a gust through the open window. I picked them up and tapped the bottoms on the table until they were even, then grabbed an empty suitcase from the closet and headed back downstairs.

The room was now deserted. The bathroom door, as well as the door to the first floor bedroom, were both closed, but I could still hear their voices. I thought about making a general announcement, letting everyone know where I was headed, but after the long trip, I figured they could all benefit from some quiet time. Steve's collar and the keys to the Mustang were on the table, so I snatched them both and slipped out the front door without any notice.

Halfway to the car, I realized that I had forgotten one last thing. I snuck back inside the house and removed the baseball bat from the kitchen.

Julie was sitting by the front window when I drove up. By the time I pulled the suitcase out of the car, she was already standing on the front porch.

"Daryl!"

She stretched out her arms, waiting for me to walk up and greet her. My hands were full, so I didn't return the hug she threw on me.

"What's with the sign?" she asked.

I looked down at my chest. It was bent at the corners, and scuffed up a bit, but overall, it was still in good shape.

"It's a reminder."

"Of what?"

"To get happy. To be happy."

"Have you been wearing that a lot?"

"Yeah."

"You can take it off now. People are going to think something's wrong with you."

"Who?" I turned to face the street, but saw not one neighbor.

"And what's with the leash? Come inside. Quick."

I followed her in.

"By the way, where did you get the car?" she asked.

"It was given to me."

"Oh," she knowingly nodded.

I stopped at the mouth of the living room and looked around. The changes were subtle, but still noticeable. To me, at least. The walls and bookshelves displayed more pictures of the two of us than at any time in the past. Each one in a shiny, brand new frame. The TV was gone, and in its place was my stereo from the basement. The loveseat was moved from the wall and placed in the center of the room facing the couch, to create, what I could only assume, some sort of conversation area.

A six foot tall potted plant sat off to the side.

"This isn't right," I remarked.

"I rearranged a few things," she said, straightening her blouse.

"It feels different."

"It's really not. It's basically the same as before, just shifted around a bit."

"What about that?" I asked, motioning to the plant.

"Oh, you," she self-assuredly smiled. "In a couple days, you'll be used to it. You won't even notice it."

I shook my head and walked into the bedroom. She followed me in, but lingered a few feet back as I made my way to the bed.

"So," she teasingly whispered. "What do you want to do to celebrate?"

"Celebrate?" I asked.

"Yes, *celebrate*. We should do something fun! Something *big*, that we couldn't do before! Just the two of us."

"Like a trip, you mean?"

"Exactly! You could always read my mind, my love. Where should we go? Some place romantic."

I looked her square in the eyes. "Will you run away to Toledo with me?"

She stared in silence for a moment, then without any warning or transition, her face expanded like an overblown balloon.

"In *Spain!*," she gasped. "You mean Toledo, Spain! You had me worried."

She broke into an impromptu dance, twisting her hips and pretending to shake fake maracas. The dance looked anything other than Spanish.

"No," I carefully explained. "I mean the one in Ohio."

She halted the dancing, thankfully, and glared in my direction. "What the hell is in Toledo, Ohio?"

"Nothing. Nothing but you and me."

Without breaking eye contact, she smirked and stepped in closer. "You're kidding, right? Daryl, we can go anywhere in the world. Greece, Italy, the Caribbean. *Anywhere!* We finally have the money to whatever we want. Why in the hell would we waste our time going to fucking Toledo? Don't mock me, darling. You know I hate that."

"I tell you what. Why don't you take a few minutes and figure out the perfect vacation for you. Anywhere in the world, for any length of time. Spare no expense, cut no corners."

She ran to me threw her arms around my neck. "So you *were* just joking," she smirked. "For a minute, I thought you were serious."

"Go in the front room and think about it while I pack."

"Okay, but before we go anywhere, I hope you're going to shower and change clothes. No offense, but you really stink. And really, don't wear that stupid sign. Oh, I knew this was all going to work out!"

She breathed a heavy sigh of relief, and disappeared into the other room.

I went about the business at hand and pulled open one of my dresser drawers. The meticulously folded clothes inside were not mine, so I took care as them I redeposited them inside the suitcase. I did the same to all the drawers until every empty space in the suitcase was filled.

"I think I have it!" Julie excitedly called out.

I forced the case closed and snapped it.

"Where?" I asked, walking back into the other room.

She pushed away from the computer desk and spun her chair to face me.

"Okay," she grinned. "It's between two weeks in Paris, or two weeks in Athens. Sartre or Socrates? They're both so tempting. I can't decide. It's too difficult."

I shrugged. "Why not both?"

"What? Really? Are you playing with me again? This isn't another stupid joke of yours like Toledo, is it?"

"No. Both. Two weeks each."

She dropped her head back and groaned orgasmically.

"Oh my god, Daryl, that would be *heaven*!"

"How much?"

She straightened up and wiped the joy from her face. "I knew there'd be a catch."

"No catch. I said spare no expense. I just need to know."

"I'm not sure. Depends on a lot of things. The hotel, meals..."

"Top class hotels," I told her. "Three meals a day. First class airfare. The works. What do you think? Overestimate a little cushion."

"Wow, um..." She stared off into space, mumbling to herself, and doing math in the air with her index finger. A couple times, she had to get online to check a price, but then it was straight back to the air math. When she finally finished, she looked at me with a hopeful wince.

"Well?"

"With shopping, and tours…maybe fifty thousand? Give or take?"

I nodded, and walked back into the bedroom, motioning for her to stay where she was. Within a moment, I was back by her side with the overstuffed suitcase.

She smiled, but then sternly looked me up and down.

"You are going to shower first, right?"

"I think I realized why I haven't been happy," I told her.

She looked back at the computer screen. "Oh?"

"Because I won't let me," I continued. "My whole life, I've listened to everyone else, but never listened to myself."

"You're making very little sense, Daryl. As usual."

It wasn't meant to be in response to that comment, but I reached over and handed her a check.

"What's this?" she asked.

"Fifty-five thousand dollars," I replied. "For your vacation. I gave you five thousand extra. Just in case."

And with that, I set down the suitcase and headed for the door.

"*My* vacation?" she stammered. "What do you mean?"

"All the time we've been together, you never once truly considered anything I wanted."

She paused for a moment before speaking. "Are you kidding me? This about *Toledo?*"

"All you had to do was say *yes*."

"There's nothing in Toledo, Daryl!"

"We didn't have to go to Toledo. We could have gone anywhere. All you had to do was say you *wanted* to go there with me."

"I don't understand you."

"Yeah. I'm just now figuring that out. I'm going home."

I put my hand on the doorknob and twisted.

"But, *this* is your home," she commanded.

I took a brief survey of the room, trying my best to avoid eyeing that completely senseless plant. "No, it's not. And it never really was. Have fun with Robert."

"I told you that's over!"

"Okay. And I'm telling you, so are we." I reached into my pocket and produced two receipts, one from a notary, and the other from UPS. "I had a feeling how you'd answer me. So, I signed the divorce papers. Your lawyer should get them tomorrow. Don't worry, I don't plan on asking for any support."

"Goddamn you, Daryl! Don't you do this!"

"Too late. It's already done." I pulled open the door, but thought of something before stepping out. "If it's true what you say, you might want to take his clothes out of the suitcase before you leave."

"You miserable bastard!" she screamed. "I never loved you! Never! This isn't the end!"

"I really think it is," I informed her. "I'm going home now to sleep for a couple days. Don't bother me."

A picture frame whizzed past my head and crashed into the wall. It was a photo of us from our honeymoon. Before I got soaked.

"I hate you!"

"If that's what you want," I said. "I'm not going to stop you."

I closed the door behind me, and made my way back to the car. The baseball bat was sitting on the floor of the passenger's side. I gripped it with my left hand, and walked slowly up driveway. When I reached the garbage can, I dropped the bat inside.

Something tells me she'll be needing this more than I will.

The drive back was smooth and fast, which was good, because I wasn't kidding when I told her I was going to sleep for a couple days. I was so tired, that I literally thought I could.

The house was silent upon my return. Once I made it up to my room, I removed the sign and peeled off my clothes. She was right, I did stink, but the idea of taking a shower though was quickly disregarded – I honestly thought I might doze off and drown myself.

Valerie was in the same position as she was when I set her down. Just for my own peace of mind, I gently placed my hand on her stomach. Still breathing. Poor thing was through quite an ordeal. I slid under the covers and sank deep into the pillow. Just for the hell of it, I started to count in my head, curious to see how far I'd get.

One.

42

When I woke up, I stared at the ceiling and went through my usual morning inventory:

Who am I? Daryl Gleason.

Where am I? In bed. At home.

What time is it? Sunlight was filling the room, so obviously, it was sometime during the day, but for some reason, I didn't particularly care about knowing the exact time.

Do you have to pee? Wow. Did I ever. How the hell that question didn't appear any sooner in the list was quite a surprise.

I spun myself around to the side of the bed and speed-walked to the bathroom.

So far, I did nothing outside of my normal everyday routine, nevertheless, something about it felt different. Then it hit me: the inventory list wasn't finished. An additional question had somehow snuck into my head.

What now?

While the question itself wasn't entirely new, the fact that I now had a valid response to it was something new.

I don't know.

This was the first time in memory that *I don't know* wasn't meant as a dismissal or a concession, or delivered out of frustration, or a sense of pity. For once, this *I don't know* provided me with a profound sense of possibility. *I don't know*, because now, my options are unlimited. I felt free. And in that instant, I knew.

I knew that I've always been happy. Not every second of every day, but a hell of a lot more than I allowed myself to remember. I just never realized or accepted it because the only times when I thought about it, the only times when I bothered to question it, were the times when I was unhappy.

I was happy when I wasn't looking! Who knew happiness could be such a ninja?

The memories came flooding back into my mind.

I was happy when I was a kid, and I was happy as an adult.

I was happy when I was learning.

I was happy when I was in love.

I was happy when I was playing guitar.

I was happy about sharing what I knew with other people.

I was happy about the prospect of correcting mistakes, and finally getting it right.

I was happy about what the future held.

Happiness could be derived from anything anywhere at any time. I just had to keep my eyes open and be ready for it whenever it decided to appear, and not drive myself crazy worrying that it might not show up at all. I was too obsessed that it might not happen *in time.* I spent so much time concerned about time that I neglected the time I was actually experiencing.

I needed to stop torturing myself about the things I couldn't control, and start enjoying the life as it unfolded in front of me. Be happy just *being!*

It was so damn simple!

That's why I smiled every morning when I woke up, because my mind was clear of all conscious worry. I woke up feeling fresh, with the hope that even within the strictest of preplanned schedules, something unpredictable could happen and make my time even better.

I can do this! I can be happy all on my own, without *guidance* from anybody else!

I turned to the mirror for confirmation, but as I looked deep into that face, the one I thought to be my singular guide to future happiness, I realized that notion was incorrect. I studied the lines, the contours, all its components, and realized for the first time that it's not *my* face. Not exclusively. For good or bad, that face represented a part of each and every person I've made a connection with in my life. It's as if their molecules somehow merged with mine. Which also meant that just as I will always have memories of the past stored away in my mind, I'll always be able to see everyone I loved and missed whenever I look in the mirror. I wouldn't be doing this alone. I'll be free to make my own decisions, but I'll be getting help from everyone I've ever known!

I raised my eyebrows to see if that face understood.

The face looked back and smiled. It was a nice smile, a damn nice smile, and I missed seeing it. That was all the confirmation I needed.

An entire world of possibilities was waiting for me. All I have to do is step outside.

Correction. All *we* have to do is step outside. I felt a wet nose rubbing against my ankle, requesting my attention.

"Good morning," I sang, and bent down to give the little ball of fuzz a pat on the head. "Go get the leash. I bet you're hungry, too." The poor thing. Who knows how long I've been out?

Before walking away, I looked back and told that face what it was waiting to hear.

"You are going to be happy. Very happy. I'm going to make sure of it. Life is going to be good, and it all starts today!"

I would like to say thank you to all of the people who have supported my creative ventures throughout the years: My sisters Kelly and Michelle, my Aunt Pat and Uncle Emmett, my cousins Terri and Donna (the latter who suggested I write this book in the first place), my sister-in-law Lori, and all my nieces and nephews. My friends Brian, and Gina, teachers like Sheldon Patinkin and Don DePollo, and the numerous other family members and friends who have always been there for me.

There are three people though, who must receive a bigger and more heartfelt thank you than anyone else ~ my two kids, Max and Reilly, and my wife Lisa. I would not have been able to any of this without you guys. Thank you.

If you would like to discuss this book, or have any comments, I invite you to visit the Facebook page "Get Happy – The Novel" http://www.facebook.com/groups/191108577687008/

www.ingramcontent.com/pod-product-compliance
Lightning Source LLC
LaVergne TN
LVHW020519100826
845148LV00010B/1287

* 9 7 8 0 6 1 5 7 7 5 7 9 1 *